# The
# *Prayer*
# JARS
## *Trilogy*

# The Prayer JARS Trilogy

3 Amish Romances from a *New York Times* Bestselling Author

## Wanda & Brunstetter

BARBOUR
PUBLISHING

*The Hope Jar* © 2018 by Wanda E. Brunstetter
*The Forgiving Jar* © 2019 by Wanda E. Brunstetter
*The Healing Jar* © 2019 by Wanda E. Brunstetter

Print ISBN 978-1-64352-902-8

eBook Editions:
Adobe Digital Edition (.epub) 978-1-64352-904-2
Kindle and MobiPocket Edition (.prc) 978-1-64352-903-5

All scripture quotations, unless otherwise noted, are taken from the King James Version of the Bible.

Scripture quotations marked NIV are taken from the HOLY BIBLE, NEW INTERNATIONAL VERSION®. NIV®. Copyright © 1973, 1978, 1984, 2011 by Biblica, Inc.™ Used by permission. All rights reserved worldwide.

All German-Dutch words are taken from the *Revised Pennsylvania German Dictionary* found in Lancaster County, Pennsylvania.

This book is a work of fiction. Names, characters, places, and incidents are either products of the author's imagination or used fictitiously. Any similarity to actual people, organizations, and/or events is purely coincidental.

For more information about Wanda E. Brunstetter, please visit the author's website at: www.wandabrunstetter.com

Cover Photograph © Michael Nelson / Trevillion Images

Published by Barbour Publishing, Inc., 1810 Barbour Drive, Uhrichsville, OH 44683, www.barbourbooks.com

*Our mission is to inspire the world with the life-changing message of the Bible.*

Member of the
Evangelical Christian
Publishers Association

Printed in the United States of America.

The
*Hope*
JAR

# Dedication

To Dr. Wilkinson and Dr. Spates, who, through their wisdom
and caring attitudes, offer their patients hope.

*Behold, the eye of the* LORD *is upon them that fear him,
upon them that hope in his mercy.*
PSALM 33:18

# Prologue

*Newark, New Jersey*

Tears streamed down Sara Murray's face as she sat on the living-room floor, going through another box of her mother's things. Mama had passed away two weeks ago after a short three-month battle with colon cancer. By the time she'd been diagnosed and treatment had begun, things were more advanced than anyone had suspected. It shook Sara to the core how quickly it all happened. Her mother never complained of any pain she might have had. When she started feeling under the weather, she made an appointment with the doctor, figuring it was only a virus.

The agony of losing her mother was raw, and the hurt so deep Sara felt as if she were drowning in a sea of tears. She couldn't help feeling bitter. At forty-three, Mama was too young to die. And Sara, who had just turned twenty-four, was too young to lose her mother.

The task of sorting through everything in the boxes was difficult to endure, but many of the items brought back happy memories. Sara felt grateful her stepfather had let her go through Mama's personal things, saying she could take whatever she wanted.

Among the items Sara found first was a pretty scarf she had given Mama on her birthday last year. Sara had no idea then that it would be her mother's final birthday celebration.

She lifted the silky blue scarf, with little designs of black scattered throughout, and stretched the material out, remembering how pretty her mother looked wearing it around her neck. Even though Mama had several other scarves, for some reason she loved this one the most and seldom wore the other ones. She found so many different ways to wear the scarf and matched it with many of the outfits she wore, sometimes adding a pretty pin to hold the lovely item in place.

Inhaling deeply and pressing the silkiness against her face, Sara breathed in the fragrance of her mother's lily-scented perfume. If she closed her eyes, it almost seemed as if Mama was sitting right there beside her. Did her mother suspect when Sara gave her the scarf that it would be her last birthday? There were so many unanswered questions. *Was Mama partial to the blue-and-black scarf because I gave it to her?*

Gulping in air and swallowing past the lump in her throat, Sara couldn't hold back her tears any more than she could all the others she had shed since her mother's death. Watching Mama slip away so fast had been hard, but the absence of her presence was like nothing she'd ever dealt with before.

"Oh Mama," Sara whispered, feeling more alone than ever. "I miss you so much. Why did you have to die?" She looked upward. "If there is a God, why did You take my mother?"

Making it through the viewing and funeral service had seemed almost surreal—she felt nothing. Going through her mother's things, however, brought back the agony of her loss tenfold.

After several minutes, Sara's sobbing lessened, and she pulled herself together, hiccupping a few times. Then she tied the scarf loosely around her neck.

"Score one for Dean Murray," Sara muttered, blowing her nose into a tissue she pulled from her shirt pocket. At least Dean realized Sara could never part with some of her mother's belongings, like this simple but lovely scarf.

For the first six years of Sara's life, it had been just her and Mama. Then Dean entered the picture, and everything changed. He and Mama got married, and two years later Sara ended up with a little brother. She'd never felt close to Dean, and when a baby came along, things got worse. Kenny was the apple of his daddy's eye and could do no wrong. Even now, Dean gave in to his son's every whim.

Sara bit her lip, drawing blood, as she reflected on the many times she'd questioned Mama about her biological father. *Who was he, where did he live, and how come Mama refused to talk about him?* Instead of providing answers to Sara's questions, her mother would be evasive and change the subject. Now that Mama was dead, it was doubtful that Sara would ever know the truth of her heritage or find out who her real father was.

Sara pulled another box across the room and took a seat on the couch. She still hadn't found the Bible Mama told her about before she died and didn't know if it was in any of the boxes Dean had filled with his wife's personal items. For all Sara knew, the Bible Mama spoke of had been thrown out. If Sara understood her mother's dying words right, there was a letter inside the Bible that she'd written to Sara.

*But it doesn't make sense. If Mama wanted me to know something, why didn't she tell me in person, instead of writing a letter?*

Sara reached into the box and pulled out two photo albums, filled with pictures of her when she was a baby. Some of the photos had Mama in them too. She looked so pretty with her long auburn hair.

*Not like mine.* Sara touched her long wavy hair. *I wonder if my father's hair was also blond.*

After flipping through the albums, she noticed an envelope with more photos inside. These were several recent pictures, some from last year. Shuffling through a few of them, Sara stopped at one in particular that had been taken on her mother's birthday. It was funny how a single photo could take you back to the exact moment it had been snapped.

Sara smiled, looking at her mother, posing like a model with the new blue-and-black scarf around her neck. She remembered her own words exactly, asking Mama to *"pose pretty for the camera,"* right after she opened the gift bag with the scarf tucked neatly inside.

Sara wiped her nose as she continued to look at other photos.

Most of the pictures had the date they were taken, embedded right into the photo. On some of the others, her mother had written the dates on the back. "I'll have to buy more albums, so I can arrange these other pictures in order." Sara swiped at a few more tears trickling down her cheeks. Then she returned to the box and took out a small, velvet-lined container. Nothing but costume jewelry in there, so she set it aside. Underneath that were the scarves Mama used to wear regularly before receiving the one from Sara.

Sara had hoped Dean would have given her Mama's wedding ring. What was he planning to do with it anyway? Perhaps he was saving it to give to his son's future wife someday.

She swallowed against the thickening in her throat. If she weren't in the middle of taking business classes at her local community college, she'd consider leaving town. With Mama gone, why should she stay?

Sara thought about her part-time job at a local dentist's office. She enjoyed working there when she wasn't in school, but being a receptionist wasn't something she wanted to do for the rest of her life.

Sara pulled the other miscellaneous scarves out of the box and gasped. Hiding underneath was a Bible. With trembling fingers, she lifted it out and held it against her chest. Why had she never seen this before?

Sara began thumbing through the pages, until she spotted an envelope tucked between the books of Matthew and Mark. She tore it open and read her mother's letter out loud.

> "Dear Sara,
>     If you are reading this letter, it's because I am gone. There aren't enough words to say how much you mean to me. And with what you are about to read, please know I was never ashamed of you. The actions I chose to take when I was old enough to know better are where my guilt lies. You, my sweet daughter, are

*special. Don't ever forget that.*

*After all the years you have asked about your heritage and I've refused to reveal anything, I now want you to know the truth. My maiden name was Lapp. I changed it after I left home when I was eighteen.*

*My parents, Willis and Mary Ruth, live in Strasburg, Pennsylvania, and here is their address. Hopefully, someday you'll get the chance to meet them. If you do, please tell my mom and dad that I love them and always have. Tell them I'm sorry for all the things I said and did to hurt my family before I ran away from home all those years ago.*

*Please let your grandparents know I was too ashamed to tell them about you. I didn't know what they would think of me, being unmarried and pregnant.*

*I am telling you this now because you have the right to get to know them, and they you. I hope and pray someday you will make peace with Dean and your brother. While my husband may not have been the perfect father figure for you, he has been a good provider, and did the best he could.*

*All my love,*
*Mama"*

Sara nearly choked on the sob rising in her throat. *Oh Mama, why couldn't you have told me all this sooner? If you really wanted me to know my grandparents, then why'd you wait till now? We could have visited them together.*

She read her mother's letter several more times before setting it aside. While Mama had written her parents' address on the back of the letter, there was no phone number included. Surely they must have a phone.

As Sara held the letter close to her heart, she made a decision.

She would write to Willis and Mary Ruth Lapp, saying she'd like to come in June, but it might not be until July 5th or after because she had summer classes to finish. If they wanted to see her, she would pay them a visit, and maybe make the trip by bus as far as Philadelphia. Perhaps then she would learn the identity of her real father.

# Chapter 1

Michelle Taylor stared at the contents of her wallet and groaned. She barely had enough money to buy groceries this week, much less pay the rent that was due five days ago. She'd lost her job at a local coffee shop a month ago and hadn't been able to find another position. What little money she had saved went to pay last month's rent. Soon Mr. Henson would be hounding her for June's rent, and if she didn't come through, he'd probably throw her out in the street, like he had the last tenant.

Michelle looked around her shabby studio apartment. It came fully furnished but didn't include more than the basics—a few dishes and cooking utensils, a small kitchen table with two chairs, a well-used sofa, and a bed that pulled down from the wall. In the cramped kitchen area, peeling linoleum held little appeal, nor did the water-stained ceiling. The vinyl on the wall near the kitchen table had been ripped, and the chipped cabinet doors where she kept her canned goods hung askew. The rust-stained sink and crooked blinds on the window completed the gloomy picture in this room, not to mention the hum of the old refrigerator that just about drove her batty.

Then there was the pathetic bathroom. The toilet ran unless she shook the handle a couple of times. Chipped grout, blackened in places with sickening mold, made the faded tile behind the tub/shower combination anything but pleasing. Hard water stains covered the shower door, and some of the tiles on the floor had begun to buckle. The sink faucet dripped constantly, even though

Michelle had tried several times to fix it—a job her landlord should have taken care of. There was nothing high class about this dwelling, but at least it gave Michelle a roof over her head—same as it did for the rest of the building's occupants. No one in this building was high class, most certainly not Michelle.

Emotionally and physically exhausted, she moved from the kitchen area and sank to the outdated, black, imitation-leather sofa. Leaning her head back, and using her fingertips, she massaged her throbbing forehead. *What I should do is get out of Philly and make a new start somewhere else. Guess I could go back to Ohio and see if Al and Sandy will take me in again. Course, it's been so long they might have moved, or at the very least, taken in more foster kids, so they wouldn't have room for an unwanted guest.*

Michelle hadn't seen her foster parents since she graduated from high school and went out on her own six years ago. She hadn't called or even sent a postcard to let them know where she was or how she was doing. "They probably wouldn't care anyhow," she muttered. "Truth be told, Sandy and Al were probably glad to get rid of me."

Michelle squeezed her eyes shut, wincing as her headache worsened. *Shoulda kept my grades up in school. I may have had a chance at a college scholarship and might be workin' at a decent job by now. Guess this is what I get for being a know-it-all and running off the minute I got out of high school.*

When Michelle left Columbus, she'd gone from town to town, taking whatever menial jobs she could find. When things went bad, or she ran low on money, she moved on, always searching—always hoping—wishing she could put down permanent roots. All Michelle had ever wanted was to feel loved and accepted—to feel like she truly belonged. Of course, it was only wishful thinking. At the rate things were going, she'd never have a place she could call "home" and mean it. It was doubtful Michelle would ever know what the love of a caring family was all about.

Her head jerked when someone pounded on the door. *Oh great. I bet that's Mr. Henson, coming for the rent I don't have. If I don't answer, he'll think I'm not here and go away.* She sat perfectly still and didn't make a sound.

The pounding continued. "Michelle! Come on, sweetie, I know you're in there, so open this door."

Relieved that it wasn't Mr. Henson after all, she called, "Coming, Jerry."

Michelle jumped up and hurried across the room. Jerry had been kind of edgy when he came to see her last night, and she didn't want him to make a scene outside her door. A few times before when she'd refused to let him in because he'd been drinking too much, he'd become loud and boisterous. After some of the other tenants complained about the noise, the grumpy landlord warned her that she would have to leave if it happened again.

Another loud knock on the door, and Michelle jerked it open. "Said I was coming. Didn't you hear me through the paper-thin door?"

Jerry's eyelids lowered as he stepped inside and slammed the door shut. "Yeah, I heard ya." He reached out and pulled her close.

Michelle smelled the rotten-egg scent of beer on his breath as soon as he kissed her, and she nearly gagged. Michelle had never acquired a taste for alcohol or appreciated the smell of it. The same thing held true for cigarette smoke. It wasn't that she thought she was too good for those things. They just made her feel sick.

"How'd your day go?" Jerry held Michelle so close she could barely breathe. "Did ya find another job yet?"

"No, I did not. Nobody seems to be hiring right now." Michelle pulled on her shirt collar. "And if I don't find something soon, I'll be kicked out of this apartment building for not paying the rent." She didn't let on that Jerry's yelling outside her door could also get her kicked out. He wouldn't think twice about threatening the landlord.

Jerry released his hold on her and sauntered across the room to the nearly empty refrigerator. "Ya got any beer?"

"No, and I hardly have any food either. If my luck doesn't change soon, I could end up living on the streets with all the other homeless people in this town."

Jerry raked his fingers through the ends of his curly brown hair. It looked like he hadn't washed it in several days. "You ain't gonna end up on the streets, sweetie, 'cause I want ya to move in with me. I told you that last night, remember?"

Michelle did remember. How could she forget? After she'd declined his offer, they'd had a big argument that ended with Jerry grabbing her so tight, she'd been left with bruises on both of her wrists.

"Michelle, did ya hear what I said?" Eyes narrowing, he got right in her face.

She nodded. "I'm just thinking, is all."

"Well, don't think too long. Just pack up your things and let's go. You'll be glad to say goodbye to this place."

"I told you last night that I'm thinking about leaving town— at least for a while. I may go back to Columbus to see my foster parents."

Jerry's brown eyes darkened as his nostrils flared. "And I said I don't want you to go anywhere but with me." His features softened a bit. "I'd miss you, baby. And you'd miss me too. Ya know you would."

Michelle twisted a strand of her long auburn hair around one finger. If she stayed in Philly and moved in with Jerry, he'd want more than she was ready to give him. They'd known each other less than a month, and even though Michelle was attracted to Jerry's good looks, his possessive nature worried her. Almost from the first night they'd met in a pool hall across town, he'd acted as if he owned Michelle. What worried her the most about Jerry, however, was his temper. In her early childhood years, she been the brunt of her parents' anger, until child services intervened and put Michelle and her brothers, Ernie and Jack, in foster care. Unfortunately, they had not all gone to the same home.

If a person could choose their parents, Michelle would certainly not have picked Herb and Ginny Taylor. Dad abused Mom physically and emotionally, and they both abused their kids. Michelle could still see her father standing over her with his belt raised, an angry scowl on his face over something he'd accused her of doing. He hadn't aimed for any particular spot. The belt connected wherever it landed, on her legs, arms, and back. He'd treated the boys just as harshly, often smacking them around until bruises or angry welts appeared.

Their mother was no better. She often pulled Michelle's hair and lashed out in anger. It was usually not because of anything Michelle had done wrong, but rather because Mom was mad at her husband.

One time, when Michelle had defended Ernie for something he'd been unjustly accused of, Mom screamed at Michelle, "Shut your big mouth!" Then she'd grabbed Michelle around the neck and tried to choke her. Fortunately, little Jack started bawling really loud, and Mom came to her senses. She'd never apologized though—just made a few threats and sent Michelle to her room.

Michelle blinked when Jerry waved his hand in front of her face. "Hey, snap out of it. You're spacing out on me, babe. Now go pack up your things and let's get outa here before that money-hungry landlord of yours comes to pay you a visit."

Looking him steadily in the eyes, Michelle thrust out her chin, then vigorously shook her head. "I am not moving in with you, Jerry. So please stop asking."

He drew closer so that they were nose to nose. "You're my girl, and you'd better do as I say."

Michelle couldn't mistake his tone of agitation, and a familiar fear bubbled in her soul. She took a step back, biting the inside of her cheek. "I—I appreciate the offer, Jerry, but as I said before, I'm not ready to move in with you." She spoke slowly and kept her voice low, hoping it would calm him.

"Well, ya wanna know what I think, sugar? I think you don't know what ya want."

"Yes I do, Jerry, and it. . .it's not you." Michelle didn't know where her courage came from, but she felt a little braver.

"What do you mean, it's not me? We've been together almost

every night since we first met." His words slurred as he grabbed Michelle's shoulders and gave her a cruel shake.

"Stop it! You're hurting me." She pushed him back.

He sneered at her. "Ya think this hurts? If you leave me, Michelle, you'll hurt even more. You know you love me, babe."

Michelle swallowed against the bile rising in her throat. She wanted Jerry to leave but feared his reaction if she ordered him to go.

"Come here and give me some love." Jerry grabbed her again, and before she could react, he kissed her neck roughly, while holding her arms tightly behind her back. His lips moved from Michelle's neck to her mouth, and then he pushed her down on the couch. "You're mine. And don't you ever forget it."

Michelle fought against Jerry's brute strength, and when he wouldn't let her up, she bit his arm.

"Why, you little—" He cursed and slapped Michelle's face so hard her head jerked back.

She cried out and somehow managed to wiggle out from under him and off the couch. "If you don't leave right now, I'll scream at the top of my lungs for someone to call the cops. And they will too. You can count on it."

Jerry leapt off the couch and, panting heavily, gave her another hard slap, right where he'd hit her before. Whirling around, he stomped across the room and out the door, slamming it behind him.

Gasping for breath, Michelle ran to the door and bolted it shut. She had to get out of here—not just because she had no money to pay the rent, but to escape the man she'd foolishly gotten involved with.

She dashed to the bathroom and looked in the mirror. Her hand immediately went to the red mark quite visible on her face. "Ouch. I do not deserve this kind of treatment—not from Jerry or anyone."

Wincing, Michelle ran some cool water on a washcloth and dabbed it on the red, stinging skin.

Today was not the first time Jerry had physically abused her, and if she stayed in Philadelphia and kept seeing him, Michelle knew it wouldn't be the last.

⟅⟆

Michelle awoke with a pounding headache. After Jerry left last night she'd had a hard time getting to sleep. Was he right? Should she stay and move in with him? Would that be the sensible thing to do? It would certainly take care of her financial problems.

Michelle shook her head. *What am I thinking? He's a jerk. I need to get away from him now. If I don't, I could end up in an abusive relationship for the rest of my life.*

She pulled herself out of bed and plodded across the room. Staring out the window at the depressing scene, Michelle weighed her options. She was tired of the unexciting view that greeted her every day. Seeing all the buildings surrounding her apartment made her feel closed in. And what little bit of sky she could actually see was dismal, just like her mood. She could either stay here in Philly and keep searching for another job, or get out of town and start over someplace else. One thing was sure: she had to break things off with Jerry. He was a loser and, short of a miracle, he would never treat her with love and respect.

While brushing her teeth, Michelle glanced in the cracked mirror. At least there weren't any marks left where she'd been slapped, and Jerry hadn't loosened any of her teeth. Dad had done that once to Mom, and they'd been too poor to go to the dentist.

Shaking her negative thoughts aside, Michelle got dressed and went to the kitchen to fix breakfast. She'd no more than taken out a bowl for cold cereal when a knock sounded on the door.

"Hey babe, let me in. I have somethin' for you."

Michelle groaned inwardly. Jerry was back. She figured if she didn't open the door, he'd keep knocking and wake the whole apartment complex, including her landlord.

She opened the door a crack, but kept the chain bolted. "What do you want, Jerry?"

"Came to say I'm sorry for last night." He held a pink carnation in his hand. "I wanna start over, darlin'. I promise never to hit you again."

*Yeah, right.* Michelle did not have to think about his offer very long. She didn't trust him not to hit her again. She'd had enough abuse when she was growing up. After hearing the same old assurances from her parents that they were sorry and it wouldn't happen again, Michelle knew good and well that Jerry would never keep the promise he'd just made.

"Sorry, Jerry, I'm not interested in starting over." Michelle shut the door in his face.

"You'll change your mind when you've had a chance to think things over," he called through the door. "I'll be back tomorrow, and we can talk about this again."

"You can come back if you want, but I won't be here," Michelle mumbled under her breath, as she heard his footsteps fading away. She lifted a hand to her still-tender cheek. "You'll never do this to me again. Don't know where I'm headed, but I'm gettin' out of here tomorrow, one way or the other."

# Chapter 2

*Strasburg, Pennsylvania*

Mary Ruth Lapp ambled down the driveway to get the mail. She'd meant to go to the mailbox earlier, but it had rained hard most of the day, and she hadn't felt like going outside. As some of the clouds parted, a glorious sunset appeared with pink, gold, and orange hues. Mary Ruth took in its beauty, while breathing in the fresh after-rain scent.

Some days it was hard to feel positive, with all the terrible things going on in the world, but today wasn't one of them. Mary Ruth's spirits soared as she looked toward the trees and listened to the birds singing overhead as they found places to roost for the night. Of course she had always liked the month of June with the fragrance of flowers bursting open all around and mild temperatures that went well with tilling the garden.

Sighing contentedly, Mary Ruth reached the end of the driveway and pulled the mail out of their mailbox. She sorted through several advertising flyers, along with a few bills. There was also a letter addressed to Mr. and Mrs. Willis Lapp, but the return address was missing. In the place where it should have been was a sticky, rough spot, as though the address label had been pulled off.

She bit her lower lip. "Now I wonder who this came from." Not only was the postmark smudged, so she couldn't tell where the letter had originated, but parts of their address were unreadable. She was impressed that the post office had managed to deliver it.

Mary Ruth decided to open it right there on the spot, but as she struggled to open the envelope flap, it slipped from her hands, landing on the soggy, wet ground.

"*Ach!* Now look what I've done." She bent down and scooped up the letter. Unfortunately, the envelope acted like a sponge, turning it somewhat soggy. Wiping it quickly on her dress, Mary Ruth fussed, "Hopefully I saved the inside, and nothing got smudged."

Despite her curiosity, she decided to wait until she got back to the house to open the envelope. Besides, she was losing daylight, and it would soon be too dark to read.

Back at the house, Mary Ruth placed the bills and junk mail on the kitchen table. Then she sat in a chair and tore the envelope open. Squinting as she read the somewhat blurred words on the page, her heart began to pound. *Oh my! This cannot be. After all these years of hoping we would see or hear from our daughter, and now we find out she has died?*

Unable to read further, Mary Ruth covered her mouth with the palm of her hand, in an attempt to stifle the sobs. But her shoulders shook, and tears rose to the surface anyway.

Once she'd gained some semblance of composure, Mary Ruth rushed into the living room, where she found her husband asleep in his recliner. "Wake up, Willis! We've received some unsettling news."

He sputtered and snorted with eyes half-closed and reading glasses perched on the end of his nose. "Please don't bother me right now, *fraa*; I'm restin' my eyes."

She shook his arm, and when he became fully awake, Mary Ruth waved the letter in his face. "Rhoda's daughter wrote this letter. She wanted us to know that her *mudder*—our *dochder*—passed away two weeks ago from colon cancer."

Willis snapped to attention, his bushy gray brows lifting high as his eyes opened wide. "What are you talking about?"

"It's right here in this letter from Sara Murray. If I'm reading it right, she found a letter from Rhoda in an old Bible. The note said Rhoda left home when she was eighteen, and she told Sara about us. Rhoda asked her daughter to tell us how sorry she was for the things she said and did before she ran away from home. She'd been too ashamed to tell us she was expecting a baby." Mary

Ruth paused and dabbed her eyes with a tissue, before taking a seat on the couch. "Oh Willis, how could we not know or even suspect that Rhoda was expecting a *boppli*? I wonder who the baby's father was. Do you have any idea, Willis?"

He shook his head. "You know how Rhoda could be. She was very private and kept things to herself. Most young women her age would have brought their boyfriends home to meet her parents. But there was no hint of our daughter being courted by anyone. I'm guessing it may not have been any of the young fellows from our church district. Could have been an English man for all I know. They could have run off together and got married."

Willis rose from his chair and sat beside Mary Ruth. "It's hard to accept the fact that we will never see our daughter again in this world, but maybe there's a chance we can meet our granddaughter." He reached over and clasped her hand. "Did she include an address or phone number so we can make contact with her?"

Mary Ruth shook her head, then pointed to the soiled letter. "Not that I could see, but she did say she's coming to meet us and should arrive in the afternoon at the bus station in Philadelphia on the fifth of June. At least, I think that's the date it says. With all the smudges, plus the missing address label, I have no idea how we can contact Sara." She leaned closer to Willis, clutching his arm. "Despite the sadness of learning Rhoda has passed away, the letter from Sara does give my spirits a tiny lift. Doesn't it do that for you, Willis?"

He nodded. "It pains me to realize that our dochder will never walk through our front door again, but it's good to know the granddaughter we never knew existed wants to meet us. Maybe she can shed some light on who her father is. If Rhoda did marry her baby's father and he's still living, then Sara will be able to tell us what we want to know. We might even get the opportunity to meet him sometime."

Mary Ruth dabbed at some fresh-fallen tears. "I can barely take it all in." Her chin trembled as she squinted at the blurry words toward the bottom of the damp paper. The ink had run in several places, making the rest of the letter difficult to read. "Do you think Sara is aware that we are Amish?"

"I don't know, though I would think Rhoda would have told her. May I see the letter?" Willis held out his hand.

She handed it to him. "Some of the words are blurred because I dropped the letter on the wet grass, but June 5th is tomorrow. We need to be at the bus station in Philadelphia to pick Sara up when she arrives." Tears stung Mary Ruth's eyes as she squeezed the folds in her dress. "Oh Willis, how could Rhoda have stayed away all those years without telling us she had a child?"

Before he could respond, she hurried on. "My heart aches to realize we will never see our daughter again, but at least we're being given the chance to meet our granddaughter. It's like a miracle, don't you agree?"

*"Jah."* Willis's eyes also glistened with tears. "I'll need to call one of our drivers right away and see if he can take us to Philadelphia tomorrow." He looked at the envelope he still held in his hand. "Sure wish she had included a picture so we'll know who to look for."

Mary Ruth shook her head. "I don't need a picture. If she is our Rhoda's daughter, I'm sure I will know it the minute I see her."

⁓

*Philadelphia*

As the Lapps' driver, Stan Eaton, parked his van in the bus station parking lot, Mary Ruth's stomach tightened. She turned to Willis and gripped his arm. "What if Sara doesn't know we are Amish? She made no reference to it in her letter—at least the part I was able read clearly. It may come as a shock to her."

"Now, Mary Ruth, we spoke of this yesterday, and you're fretting too much. If Sara doesn't know about her mother's heritage, she will soon enough." Willis reached into his pants' pocket and pulled out the pocket watch he'd had since they got married forty-eight years ago. "According to the afternoon schedule Stan pulled up on his computer for us, the bus should be here soon, if it hasn't already arrived."

"That's right," Stan called over his shoulder. "But schedules are always subject to change. Your granddaughter's bus could get here early or it might pull in late."

Mary Ruth smoothed some imaginary wrinkles from her plain blue dress and made sure there were no stray hairs sneaking out from under her head covering. "Do you think Sara will like us, Willis? Will she be comfortable staying in our plain, simple home? Oh, I hope she can be with us for several weeks. It will take at least that long for us to get acquainted, and we'll want to find out more about Rhoda."

He patted her hand gently. "Try not to worry, Mary Ruth. I'm sure everything will work out. She probably has as many questions to ask us as we do her." Willis pushed the button to open the van door. "Now let's get out and go wait for the bus. I don't see any sign of one at the moment, so I'm sure it hasn't gotten here yet. Either that, or it came in early and has already headed out on its next route."

Mary Ruth opened her door and stepped down. She paused long enough to say a quick prayer, then followed her husband toward the station. When they entered the building, where several people with suitcases milled around, Mary Ruth saw a young woman with long auburn hair standing near the ticket booth.

With excitement coursing through her veins, she caught hold of her husband's arm. "Oh look! That's Sara over there." She pointed. "See, that pretty young woman? Why, she has the same color hair as our Rhoda." She reached up and patted the sides of her head. "And before gray hairs started creeping in, my hair was a golden red too."

Willis squinted as he stared at the young woman. "You're right, Mary Ruth. It's almost like we're seeing our dochder back before she ran away from our home."

Mary Ruth could hardly contain herself. Tears of joy filled her eyes as she and Willis headed in their granddaughter's direction.

As Michelle approached the booth to purchase her bus ticket to anywhere but Philly, she noticed an Amish couple staring at her. They seemed to be sizing her up.

Michelle's scalp prickled, and she rolled her eyes. *What's wrong with those two? Surely this isn't the first time they've seen an English woman. Maybe it is the first time they'd been in a bus station though. Could be they aren't sure what to do.*

While she didn't know a whole lot about the Amish, Michelle had seen a few episodes of a reality show on TV. It was about six young Amish people who hadn't yet joined the Amish church and had been touring the country on motorcycles. Of course, she wasn't sure how accurate the show had been, but it gave her an inkling of what Amish life was all about when the people were interviewed and they offered an account of what it was like growing up in homes with lots of rules and no electricity.

When the elderly couple began walking toward her, Michelle stiffened. *I hope they're not going to talk to me. I wouldn't have any idea what to say to people like them. They look so prim and proper. I probably seem like a hick to them.*

She took a few steps to the right and turned her back on the couple. *They could be here just to purchase a bus ticket, same as me. That show on TV did mention that some Amish people like to travel. Although, at their age, these two would not likely go anywhere on the back of a motorcycle.* It did seem odd, though, that neither the man nor the woman had a suitcase. If they planned to make a trip, surely there would be at least one piece of luggage between them.

"Excuse me, miss, but is your name Sara Murray?"

Michelle winced when the Amish man tapped her on the shoulder. *Oh great, I shoulda figured by the way they were looking at me that one of 'em would end up saying something.*

She turned back around and opened her mouth, but before she could respond to the man's question, the woman spoke. "I'm Mary Ruth Lapp, and this is my husband, Willis. We're your grandparents, Sara, and we're so happy you wrote and asked if you could meet us."

When the lady paused to swallow, Michelle was going to say that they had mistaken her for someone else. But she never got the chance, because the Amish woman quickly continued.

"Since we knew nothing about you until your letter arrived, you can imagine how surprised we were when you stated that you would be coming in on the bus here today." Mary Ruth gave an embarrassed laugh. She was clearly as nervous as Michelle felt. "Of course, when I dropped your letter in the wet grass, it made it difficult to be sure if this was the actual day you said you needed us to pick you up."

Willis nodded. "We were hoping it was, and since you're here, it can only mean that we read the letter right."

Dumbfounded, Michelle wasn't sure what to say. She looked all around and didn't see any other young women in the bus station, so she could understand why the Amish couple may have mistaken her for their granddaughter. *Would it be wrong if I played along with it?* Michelle asked herself. *If I go with them to wherever they live, I'll have a safe place to stay for a while, and I won't have to worry about finding a job or looking for another town to start over in. This could be the answer to the predicament I'm in financially too—not to mention getting far from Jerry.*

Michelle hardly knew what to think about this turn of events, except that a stroke of luck must have finally come her way. Her conscience pricked her just a bit though. *What's going to happen when the real Sara Murray shows up at the bus station and no one is here to pick her up? Does she know where her grandparents live? What if she visits and finds me impersonating her?* Michelle's fingers clenched around her suitcase handle so tightly she feared it would break. Then, throwing caution and all sensible reason aside, she let go of the handle and gave Mary Ruth a hug. "It's good to meet you, Grandma." She smiled at Willis. "You too, Grandpa Lapp."

Willis nodded, and Mary Ruth flashed Michelle a wide smile. "We hired a driver to bring us here to pick you up, and it'll take an hour or so to get to our home in Strasburg. But that's fine with me, because as we travel, it'll give us a chance to get to know a bit about each other."

*Oh boy,* Michelle thought, as the three of them began walking toward a silver-gray van. *I'll need to remember to respond to the name Sara and try not to say or do anything that would give away my true identity. This is my chance to get out of Philly and away from my abusive so-called boyfriend, so I can't do anything to mess it up.*

# Chapter 3

*Strasburg*

As the Lapps' driver pulled onto a graveled driveway, a tall, white farmhouse with a wide front porch stood before them. Several feet to the left was an enormous red barn. No horses or buggies were in sight, but several chickens ran around the front yard, pecking at the neatly trimmed grass. *Probably looking for worms.* Michelle pressed a fist to her lips to cover her smile. *I can do this. After all, how hard can it be to live on a farm for a few days or a week? I'll just have to make sure I answer when they call me Sara.*

"You two ladies can go on inside while I pay Stan and get Sara's luggage from the back." Willis opened the van door and stepped down.

Michelle got out on her side, and Mary Ruth followed. As they began walking toward the house, Mary Ruth slipped her arm around Michelle's waist. "I'm so happy you contacted us, Sara. You have no idea how much having you here means to me and your grandfather."

Michelle made sure to put on her best smile. "I'm glad for the opportunity to get to know you both." Her statement wasn't really a lie. She was glad to be with the Amish couple right now. It was far better than dealing with Jerry and his outbursts of anger and abuse. Depending on how things worked out, she would have free room and board for a few days, or maybe longer. Michelle actually believed, for the first time in a long time, that she had found a safe, comfortable place to stay.

They were almost to the house when a beautiful brown-and-white collie with a big belly waddled up to greet them.

Michelle jumped back. She wasn't used to being around dogs—especially one this large. Ever since she'd been bitten by a snarling dog on the way home from grade school, she'd shied away from them—big or small. Those little ones might look cute and innocent enough, but they had sharp teeth too.

"It's okay," Mary Ruth assured her. "Sadie won't bite. She's just eager to meet you." She reached down and patted the dog's head. "She'll soon have puppies, so I bet she was taking a nap when the van pulled in."

Michelle wasn't convinced that the collie wouldn't bite, but she hesitantly reached out her hand so Sadie could sniff it.

Sadie did more than sniff Michelle's hand however. She licked it with her slurpy wet tongue.

"Eww..."

Mary Ruth snickered. "She likes you, Sara. Sadie saves her kisses for those she accepts."

Feeling a little less intimidated, Michelle bent down and rubbed the dog's ears. They were soft as silk. "Guess I should feel honored then."

"Yes, indeed." Mary Ruth motioned to the house. "Shall we go inside now?"

Michelle nodded, eager to get away from the dog. While Sadie might appear friendly right now, she wasn't sure she could trust the animal. For that matter, Michelle wasn't sure she could trust herself either. Thanks to her impetuous decision, she was now in a precarious position, pretending to be someone else.

Stepping onto the porch, she noticed a few wicker chairs, as well as a finely crafted wooden bench near the front door. Hanging from the porch eaves were two hummingbird feeders, as well as three pots of pink-and-white petunias. The picturesque setting was so appealing, Michelle wanted to take a seat on the porch and forget about going inside for the moment. But she followed Mary Ruth's lead and entered the house.

When they got inside, Michele felt as if she'd taken a step back in time. The first thing she noticed was a refreshing lemon scent.

It reminded her of the furniture polish her foster mother had used whenever she cleaned house. The living room, where Mary Ruth had taken her first, had a comfy-looking upholstered couch with two end tables on either side, as well as a coffee table in front of the sofa. The wooden pieces appeared to be as expertly made as the bench on the front porch.

Matching recliners were positioned on the left side of the room, and on the right side sat a wooden rocking chair with quilted padding on the seat and backrest. With the exception of a braided throw rug placed near the fireplace, there were no carpets on the hardwood floors, yet the room seemed cozy and rather quaint.

An antique-looking clock sat on the fireplace mantel with two large candles on either side. Two gas lamps positioned at opposite ends of the room were the only apparent source of light, other than the windows facing the front yard.

Several balls of yarn peeked out of a wicker basket on the floor next to the rocker. There were no pictures on the walls, but the grandfather clock standing majestically against one wall made up for the lack of photos or paintings. Despite the quaintness of this room, it had a comfortable feel—like wearing a pair of old bedroom slippers.

As if on cue, the stately grandfather clock bonged, its huge pendulum swinging back and forth in perfect motion. Michelle would have to get used to the loud *tick-tock*s and *bong*s, but it was better than the city noises she'd heard out her apartment window in Philadelphia every night when she tried to fall asleep.

"How do you like our grandfather clock?" Mary Ruth questioned. Without waiting for Michelle to answer, she rushed on. "It's been in our family a long time. As a matter of fact, it used to belong to Willis's grandparents."

"It's beautiful, but big, and kinda loud," Michelle answered, hoping she didn't sound rude.

"You'll get used to it." Mary Ruth giggled. "When we first got the clock, it kept me awake at night. But now we hardly notice when it chimes every half hour."

*Every half hour? Oh boy. It will take some getting used to.* Michelle plastered on a fake smile, while nodding her head. *During the day shouldn't be too bad, and hopefully my room will be at the far end of the house, so maybe I won't hear the clock at night.*

One thing she noticed was clearly missing in this Amish room was a TV. But then she remembered from the reality show she'd watched that the Amish did not allow televisions, computers, or other modern equipment in their homes. She thought the narrator said the Amish were taught to be separated from the desires and goals of the modern world. They also believed the use of modern things in their home would tear their family unit apart and take their focus away from God. *Well, maybe they are better off without all the things we, who live in the modern world, have in our homes.* Of course, Michelle didn't have a lot of fancy gadgets. How could she when she kept moving from place to place with only her clothes and a few personal things? If she had a TV available to watch, it was fine, but Michelle felt sure she could get by without it. Actually she didn't care that much about a lot of modern things.

"Here's your suitcase, Sara," Willis announced when he entered the room. He looked over at Mary Ruth. "Would you want to show our granddaughter her room?"

Mary Ruth nodded. "Jah, but if you don't mind carrying her suitcase up the stairs, I would appreciate it. With all the cleaning I did yesterday after we got Sara's letter, my back's hurting a bit."

"That's okay. I can carry my own suitcase," Michelle was quick to say. These people were too old to be lugging heavy things up the stairs. And her oversized suitcase was weighty, because everything she owned was in it. Not that Michelle had an abundance of things, but clothes, makeup, and personal items did take up a lot of space when crammed into one piece of luggage.

"Well then, if you don't mind, I'll head back outside and get a few chores done before it's time for supper."

Michelle took the suitcase from Willis. "It's not a problem. I've been lugging this old thing around for the last six. . ." She clamped her mouth closed so hard her teeth clicked. *Watch what you say,*

*Michelle, or you're gonna blow it.*

"What were you going to say, Sara?" Mary Ruth put her hand on Michelle's arm.

"Oh, nothing. I just meant that I've had the suitcase a long time, and it's seen better days."

"Maybe it's time to buy a new one," Willis suggested.

"I'm short on money right now, so new luggage is not a priority."

"If you'd like a new one, we'd be happy to help."

Michelle looked at Mary Ruth and shook her head. "That's okay. I'm fine with this one. Sometimes it's hard to part with old stuff." It was bad enough she was posing to be the Lapps' granddaughter; she didn't want to take their money or any gifts. Just a comfortable place to stay for a while, and then she'd be on her way. Hopefully, by the time the real Sara showed up, Michelle would be long gone and wouldn't have to offer any explanations.

While Michelle sat with Mary Ruth and Willis at the kitchen table that evening, preparing to eat supper, she studied her surroundings. The kitchen was cozy, but no less plain than the living room or the bedroom Michelle had been assigned. Several pots and pans dangled from a rack above the stove. A set of metal canisters graced one counter, next to a ceramic cookie jar. On another counter sat a large bowl filled with bananas and oranges. There was no toaster, blender, microwave, or electric coffee pot, nor an electric dishwasher. Michelle knew what that meant—washing dishes by hand. She didn't see it as a problem, because none of the apartments she'd rented over the years had been equipped with a dishwasher. So washing dishes had become a part of her daily routine.

The stove and refrigerator were both run off propane gas, which Mary Ruth had earlier explained. Michelle couldn't imagine how these people got by without the benefit of electrical appliances in their home, but they appeared to be content. It would take some getting used to on her part, though, for however long she ended up staying with the Lapps.

Michelle noticed a few herb pots soaking up natural light on the windowsill by the kitchen sink. But the brightest spot in the room was the glass vase in the center of the table, filled with pretty red-and-yellow tulips. Their aroma was overshadowed, however, by the tantalizing smell of freshly baked ham.

Michelle's stomach growled. She could hardly wait to dig in.

Willis cleared his throat, directing her attention to his place at the head of the table. "We always pray silently before our meals."

Michelle gave a nod and bowed her head. Praying was something else she was not used to doing. They'd sure never prayed before meals—or any other time—when she lived with her parents. Her foster parents weren't religious either. Even so, they'd sent Michelle and the other foster kids off to Bible school at a church close by for a few weeks every summer.

Michelle hated it. Most of the kids who attended looked down on her, like she was poor white trash. And when one snooty girl found out Michelle and the others lived with a couple who weren't their real parents, she made an issue of it—asking if they were orphans, or had they run away from home and been placed in foster care as punishment? If there was one thing Michelle couldn't stand it was someone who thought they were better than her.

Then there was the teacher, telling goody-goody stories from the Bible, and making it sound like God loved everyone. Well, He didn't love Michelle, or she wouldn't have had so many troubles since she was born.

Michelle's eyes snapped open when Willis rattled his silverware and spoke. "I hope you have a hearty appetite this evening, Sara, because it looks like my wife outdid herself with this meal." Grinning, he picked up the plate of ham and handed it to Michelle.

"No, that's okay. You go first."

He hesitated a moment, then forked a juicy-looking piece of meat onto his plate. "Here you go, Sara." Willis handed the platter to her, then dished up a few spoonfuls of mashed potatoes, which he then gave to Michelle.

She quickly took a piece of ham and added a blob of potatoes to her plate. Next came a small bowl of cut-up veggies, followed by a larger bowl filled with steaming hot peas. Michelle's mouth watered as she took her first bite of meat. "Yum. This is delicious. You're a great cook, Mary Ruth."

The woman made a clicking sound with her tongue. "Now, remember, I want you to call me Grandma. Referring to me as Mary Ruth makes it seem like we're not related."

*That's because we're not.* Michelle managed a brief nod and mumbled, "I'll try to remember."

"Same goes for me," Willis spoke up. "I'd be real pleased if you call me Grandpa."

"Okay." Michelle picked up her glass of water and took a drink. It didn't seem right to call these people Grandma and Grandpa when they weren't related to her. But if she was going to keep up the charade, she'd have to remember so they wouldn't be offended or catch on to the fact that she wasn't Sara Murray.

As soon as all the food had been passed around, Michelle's hosts began plying her with questions, which was the last thing she needed.

"How old are you, and when is your birthday?" Willis asked.

Michelle rolled the peas around on her plate a few seconds, then decided to tell them the truth. "My birthday is June 15th, and I'll be twenty-four years old." At least that much hadn't been a lie. She hadn't even thought about her upcoming birthday until now.

Mary Ruth smiled and clapped her hands. "Why, that's just ten days away. We'll plan something special to celebrate."

Michelle shook her head. "Oh no, please don't go to any trouble on my account. I'm not used to anyone making a big deal about my birthday."

The tiny wrinkles running across Mary Ruth's forehead deepened. "Not even your mother when she was alive?"

Michelle was on the verge of saying no, but caught herself in time. "I meant to say, since Mom died."

Willis ran a finger down the side of his nose. "But according to your letter, our daughter's only been gone a few weeks."

Michelle's cheeks warmed and she nearly choked on the piece of ham she'd put in her mouth a second ago. "You're right of course. I'm just feeling a little rattled right now. It all happened so quickly, and I'm still trying to deal with her death." Michelle couldn't help thinking: *This is only the beginning of many more lies. How am I going to know what to say or not to say without messing up? It might be best if I don't stick around here too long.*

"It's perfectly understandable that you're a bit muddled, given the fact that you're still mourning your loss." Mary Ruth reached over and gently patted Michelle's arm. "And now here you are sitting with grandparents you didn't even know you had."

Michelle blotted her lips with a napkin. "Yeah, I am pretty overwhelmed right now."

Willis handed her the bowl of mashed potatoes again. "Bet you'll feel better after you've eaten a bit more and have had a good night's sleep."

All Michelle could manage was a slow nod. She only hoped that would be the case, because at the moment, she felt like she might cave in.

❧

When Mary Ruth and Willis retired to their room on the main floor that night, she began to fret. "I hope we didn't bombard Sara with too many questions. She seemed so edgy during supper—especially when we brought up her birthday." She turned to face Willis, who was already situated under the bedcovers. "Do you think Rhoda wasn't a good mudder to Sara? Is that why she said no one made a fuss over her birthday?"

"If you'll remember, she corrected herself." Willis yawned and fluffed up his pillow. "I can't imagine our dochder treating her own flesh-and-blood child poorly." He removed his glasses and placed them on the nightstand. "No reading for me tonight. I'm bushed."

"It's been a long, busy day."

"I hate to bring this up, but I'm sure you must realize that, according to Sara's age, our daughter was definitely with child when she ran away from home."

"Jah, I know. It was mentioned in Sara's letter to us, remember?"

"I do remember, but since some of the words in the letter were unreadable, I thought—even hoped—we may have read that part wrong."

Mary Ruth drew in a breath, but couldn't seem to fill her lungs completely. It was difficult reliving this past event—especially when she'd always felt as if they might be responsible for Rhoda leaving. Perhaps she and Willis had been too hard on her—trying to enforce rules that their daughter was good at breaking. There may have been a better way of dealing with Rhoda than chastising her all the time. Maybe she thought her parents didn't love her and wouldn't have understood if she'd told them the predicament she was in.

*Would we have been understanding or driven her further away by our disapproval?* Tears sprang to Mary Ruth's eyes, and she whisked them away with the back of her hand. "You're right, Willis, and I wish she had told us so we could have helped her deal with the situation."

"According to what our granddaughter wrote in the letter, Rhoda was too ashamed to tell us." Willis's eyebrows gathered in. "Maybe she felt with me being one of the church ministers, it would have been an embarrassment to us. She might have believed that if word got out that a preacher's unmarried daughter was expecting a boppli, it could have affected our standing in this community."

Mary Ruth sank to the edge of the bed and undid her hair from its bun. "I wanted to ask Sara this evening about her father but thought it could wait. She seemed overwhelmed enough with all our other questions."

"True, and that was good thinking on your part. We can talk to Sara about her father some other time." He scrubbed a hand over his face. "We need to be careful what we say about Rhoda to her daughter. Wouldn't want Sara to think her mom was a bad person." Willis heaved a sigh. "That girl was a handful. There's no doubt about it. Always close-lipped about what she was doing with her friends and staying out later than she should have, which caused us both to worry. But we still loved her, although I could always tell she was dissatisfied with the Amish ways. If we could go back and do it over, I'd try to approach the situation with our daughter differently."

"Jah." Mary Ruth sighed as she started brushing out her long hair. "Sara made no mention of her father during our supper conversation either. Is it possible that Rhoda raised her alone?"

Willis shrugged. "I don't know, but I think it's a question that does need to be asked. Maybe after breakfast tomorrow morning, when we're showing her around the farm, I'll bring up the subject."

Mary Ruth moved her head slowly up and down. "Just be careful how you approach it, Husband. Sara just got here, and we don't want to say or do anything that might scare her off. We've lived with the pain of losing our *dochder* all these years, and I certainly don't want to take the chance of losing our *grossdochder* too."

Alone in her room, a strange feeling came over Michelle. Mary Ruth had said when she'd first brought Michelle upstairs that this used to be her daughter's bedroom before she left home. She felt weird knowing this was where her pretend mother used to sleep. *The real Sara should be sleeping here, not me.* It was too late to back away from this. She was here, and the Lapps seemed pretty pleased. If Michelle could fake it for a while longer, until she figured out what she needed to do, everyone would be happy. At least until the real granddaughter showed up. Then a bomb would drop right over Michelle's head.

Turning her thoughts in another direction, Michelle gazed with anticipation at the four-poster double bed. Instead of using shabby covers over a skinny single bed coming down from the wall, she would sleep under the beautiful quilt that covered this bed. The two windows in the room both faced the backyard. Only a dark green shade covered them, but Michelle didn't mind the lack of a curtain. At least there would be no noisy vehicles outside, with blaring horns and screeching brakes moving down the street throughout the night. Except for the clock downstairs, she probably wouldn't hear much noise at all.

Studying the rest of the room, she noticed a wooden nightstand positioned on the right side of the bed and a tall dresser against the opposite wall. At the foot of the bed sat an old cedar chest. Michelle had placed her suitcase on top of the chest, but had only opened it to take out her cotton pajamas and personal items. She was too tired to hang up her clothes tonight. It could wait till morning.

Even though scantily furnished, the bedroom was as spotless as the rest of the house she'd seen so far. The only source of light, other than the windows, was a battery-operated lamp on the nightstand, which Michelle had turned on as soon as she came into the room.

*I shouldn't be here,* she thought. *This room did not belong to my mother, although I wish it had. And I would give almost anything to have caring grandparents like Willis and Mary Ruth.*

Michelle had never known her mother's parents, or her dad's either. The only thing she'd been told about them was that they lived somewhere in Idaho. She had never even seen any pictures of them. Michelle often wondered if her grandparents were bad parents, and that's why her mom and dad had turned out the way they had. Maybe both sets of grandparents were abusers or heavy drinkers. She and her brothers were probably better off not knowing them. There had been enough anxiety in their young lives just dealing with explosive parents.

*Sure wish I knew where Ernie and Jack are right now.* She had tried several times to locate them but always came up empty-handed. Hopefully they'd gone to good homes and had made something of themselves. "Not like me," Michelle muttered. "I'm going down a one-way street that leads to nowhere."

Michelle reflected on all the questions that had been thrown at her since arriving at the Lapps—especially during the evening meal. She'd been so nervous about saying the wrong thing, it had diminished her appetite for what should have been a delicious supper. Maybe it was a good thing she hadn't eaten too much. If Michelle ate like that on a regular basis, all those carbs could pack on the weight.

Thinking back on the conversation they'd had about her birthday and Sara's mother, Rhoda, Michelle hoped she'd been able to cover her tracks well enough by saying she felt a bit rattled. It was certainly no lie, for by the time she helped Mary Ruth do the dishes, she was exhausted from the stress of trying not to say the wrong thing. She suspected there would probably be more questions tomorrow, and she'd be riding an emotional rollercoaster again.

*Guess I'll wait and deal with all that in the morning. Right now I need to go down the hall to take a shower and brush my teeth. After a good night's sleep, maybe I'll wake up with a clearer head and a better idea how to proceed.*

How thankful she was that the Lapps had indoor plumbing and not an outhouse, like that reality TV show had mentioned. Michelle didn't think she could last a day without indoor bathroom conveniences.

When she pulled back the covers a short time later and climbed into the comfortable bed, Michelle's breathing became consistent and the need to sleep took over. Even the grandfather clock down in the living room, bonging out the hour, didn't disturb her rest.

# Chapter 4

Michelle sat up in her bed with a start. What was that irritating sound? She climbed out and padded over to the window.

Lifting the shade, she grimaced. An enormous rooster stood on top of the woodshed, crowing for all he was worth.

She looked at the clock on her nightstand and groaned. It was five thirty in the morning, and dawn had slowly cast a glow on the yard. She sniffed the air. Was that the hearty aroma of coffee she smelled? It wasn't a mocha latte, like they'd served at the coffee shop in Philly, but it smelled almost as good. Someone was obviously up and in the kitchen downstairs.

Michelle glanced around her room again. It still looked the same, only this morning, with the bedcovers in disarray, it appeared lived-in at least.

*I can't believe I'm actually here.* What a stark difference, waking up this morning on a farm, when less than twenty-four hours ago she was still in her stale, dinky apartment in Philly.

Gazing out the window again, she became aware that the loudmouthed rooster had suddenly gone quiet. *Thank goodness. Why couldn't you have done that sooner so I could've slept in?*

Michelle observed how the clouds took on amazing hues of pinks and purple, then faded into orange as the sun made its full appearance. How long had it been since she noticed the sky's beauty and how pretty a sunrise could be?

Watching the clouds change to a puffy white as the sun rose higher, Michelle relived yesterday, meeting the Lapps at the bus station, and then the trip here to Strasburg. It was so different driving out of the city, once they got past King of Prussia, and observing how the landscape changed. No more skyscrapers and huge business offices blocking the view as they drove farther from the Philadelphia region. Instead, she'd seen several small businesses along the road they traveled. But even they became sparser as farms, silos, and fields dotted more of the landscape. Once in the country, she could see into the distance for many miles. A day later, here she was, the guest of an Amish couple who owned a farm. Michelle never would have believed this situation possible when she closed the door in Jerry's face.

*I wonder what he had to say if he went back to my apartment last night and found me gone. Sure am glad he has no idea where I went, so there's no way he can track me down.* Her fingers clenched. *I hope I never meet up with another guy like Jerry. He was a loser.*

Eager for a cup of coffee, Michelle got dressed, went to the bathroom to freshen up, and hurried downstairs. She found Mary Ruth and Willis at the kitchen table with mugs of coffee in their hands.

"Well, good morning, Sara." Mary Ruth was all smiles. "Did we wake you with our chatter down here? We thought you might sleep in this morning."

"No, you didn't wake me. The crowing rooster did."

"That's Hector." Willis chuckled and shook his head. "No need to set an alarm clock, thanks to our predictable and feisty old bird. He's been with us longer than any of our chickens."

Michelle wondered if Willis's reference to the rooster being feisty meant the chicken was mean. If so, she'd have to remember to give him a wide berth.

"Would you care for a cup of coffee, dear?" Mary Ruth rose from her chair.

Michelle held out her hand. "No, that's okay. I'll get it myself." After helping Mary Ruth do the dishes last night, she remembered where the mugs were kept, and the coffee pot was clearly visible on the stove. So she helped herself and joined them at the table.

"What would you like for breakfast, Sara?" Mary Ruth gestured to the refrigerator. "Thanks to our hens, who are laying well right now, we have plenty of eggs There's also a slab of bacon. Did we tell you that Willis raises hogs?"

"No, I don't believe you mentioned it." *Most likely because you were too busy asking me questions.*

The thought of eating bacon and eggs this early in the morning made Michelle's stomach feel queasy. She usually didn't eat much for breakfast anyway. "No thanks. I'll just have a bowl of cold cereal. If you have any, that is," she amended.

"Why, yes we do. In fact, Willis eats a bowl of bran flakes almost every morning, in addition to eggs, pancakes, or whatever else I serve for breakfast. He and I both had bran cereal for our breakfast this morning. We wanted to eat before Willis did his chores."

Willis bobbed his head before adding a spoonful of sugar to his cup.

*Bran flakes?* Michelle took a sip of the darkly brewed coffee and tried to keep her composure. The last thing she wanted was a bowl of bran flakes. "Think maybe I'll stick with coffee."

"Oh my. . . That's not enough for breakfast." Mary Ruth shook her head. "If you don't want bacon and eggs, or cereal, then how about a banana muffin? Ezekiel King brought some fresh honey over the other day. You might enjoy having some of that on your muffin."

"Okay." Michelle mustered up a smile. "A muffin sounds good."

While Mary Ruth went to get the muffin and honey for Michelle, Willis finished his coffee, then set the mug in the sink. "As soon as you're done eating, Sara, why don't you come outside and I'll show you around the place? I'd like to introduce you to our buggy horses and some of the other animals we have—including the hogs."

*Pigs? I bet they smell bad. Oh goody. I can't wait for that.* Michelle offered Willis a phony smile. Maybe life here on the farm wasn't better than living in the city after all. "That'd be nice," she said to Willis. "I'd love to see your animals." If she was going to keep up this masquerade, she'd have to at least act interested in her pretend grandparents, as well as in their critters and anything else that pertained to them.

When Michelle walked with Willis and Mary Ruth through the double doors and entered the well-built, oversized barn, the odor of straw mixed with horse flesh and manure caused her to sneeze. She reached into her shirt pocket for a tissue and blew her nose as a fluffy gray cat darted between her legs. "Yikes!"

"Do you have allergies?" Mary Ruth's brows wrinkled a bit.

"Maybe. I don't know. I've never been around animals that much—especially horses."

"Your mother was allergic to cats. The minute she got around them her nose would start running and then came a sneeze." Mary Ruth patted Michelle's back. "I bet you take after her."

Michelle noticed the sadness in the woman's brown eyes. No doubt she missed her daughter and wished she could have her back.

"Speaking of Rhoda. . ." Willis leaned against one of the horse's stalls. "When we were talking yesterday, you never made mention of your father." He reached under his straw hat and scratched his head. "Did your mother raise you alone?"

Michelle's gaze dropped to the ground. She felt her body heat rising. *What am I supposed to say? I can't very well tell them about my own lousy father. Or my horrible mother, for that matter.*

Michelle blew her nose again, stalling for time. She'd need to think fast on her feet and come up with some decent answers if she was going to make the Lapps keep believing she was their granddaughter.

"Um. . . Actually, my dad and mom are divorced." *Wrong answer, Michelle.* She knew right away from Mary Ruth and Willis's slumped posture and stony expression that this was something they did not want to hear. As Michelle recalled the reality TV show, she remembered someone saying that the Amish didn't believe in divorce. She hadn't thought much about it at the time, but apparently it was true.

"I am deeply sorry to hear that," Mary Ruth said. "Does your father live near you, and do you see him often?"

*Oh boy.* Michelle rubbed her forehead. "No, after the divorce, my dad split. I haven't seen or heard from him since."

"That's a shame." Mary Ruth's tone was soothing. "Do you know if your father used to be Amish?"

*Yikes! Now how am I supposed to know that?* Michelle squirmed, feeling like she was on the hot seat. She moistened her lips with the tip of her tongue. "I'm not sure. My folks never talked much about their past to me." *At least that was the truth.* Michelle's hole of deception seemed to grow deeper with most everything that came out of her mouth.

To avoid telling more lies, Michelle changed the subject. "So whose horse is that, and what's its name?" She pointed to the horse in the stall closest to them.

"That's my mare, Bashful." Willis reached over the gate and stroked the horse's brown ears, which were tipped with white.

The horse nickered in response, then lifted her head over the wooden slat and nudged Willis's chest. "Bashful does well with me but tends to be kinda shy around people she doesn't know." After rubbing her soft muzzle a few seconds, Willis opened his hand to reveal a sugar cube. "You didn't think I'd forget your treat, now did ya?" He spoke tenderly to the horse.

It was cute to see how gently Bashful scooped up the cube. *Maybe someday, if I'm here long enough, she'll eat out of my hand too.*

Michelle looked at Mary Ruth. "Does the horse across from Bashful belong to you, Mary Ruth?"

"Yes. Her name is Peanuts, but once again, I really wish you would call me Grandma."

"Sorry. I keep forgetting." While Michelle was far from perfect, she didn't make a habit of telling lies. But her decision at the bus station in Philly had entrapped her in this huge web of lies.

"Yes, and I do want you to call me Grandpa," Willis echoed.

"Okay," she murmured, barely able to look at either of them.

Why did these two have to be so nice and easy to like? It made it that much harder for Michelle to pretend she was Sara.

Michelle went over to Peanuts's stall with Mary Ruth. She had to get her mind on something else.

"We do tend to spoil our animals." Mary Ruth cradled her horse's head and greeted her with affectionate words. Then she handed Michelle a sugar cube. "Would you like to feed her?"

"I guess."

"Just hold your hand out flat," Willis instructed. "That way she won't pinch your skin."

Michelle giggled when Peanuts used her soft upper and lower lips to gently take the sweet she offered. "I think she likes me."

"Well, sure she does." Willis took a piece of straw out of Peanuts's long mane, and the mare nuzzled his hands as if to say *thanks*.

"Do you have any brothers or sisters?" Mary Ruth asked, leaning against the horse's stall.

Without giving it much thought, Michelle shook her head. "I'm pretty much alone now that my mom is gone."

Willis gave her a soft pat on the shoulder, and Mary Ruth slipped an arm around Michelle's waist. "You're not alone anymore. We're here for you, Sara, and you're welcome to stay with us for as long as you like."

She swallowed hard, her throat swelling from holding back tears. *If you knew who I really am, you wouldn't be so gracious.*

❧

After they left the barn, and Michelle had met the hogs, Willis went to town to run some errands, using his horse and open buggy.

As Michelle started walking toward the house, Mary Ruth paused near her vegetable garden. "Would you be willing to help me in the garden for a few hours?" she asked. "The weeds will take over if I don't keep at it."

Michelle moistened her lips. "Well, I. . ."

"If you'd rather not help, perhaps you can pull up a lawn chair and keep me company. It will give us more time to get better acquainted."

"The things is, I haven't had much experience pulling weeds 'cause my mom never had a garden. But sure, I'll do what I can to help."

"No garden?" Mary Ruth's lips compressed. "I'm surprised to hear this. Why, when Rhoda was a girl, and even into her teen years, she spent a lot of time working in our garden." Mary Ruth's face relaxed and she snickered. "It seemed like that girl always had dirt under her fingernails, and I was often reminding her to clean her hands thoroughly."

Michelle rubbed her sweaty palms down the sides of her jeans. Was she ever going to say the right things? "You see, the truth is, my mom kept so busy with her job, she didn't have time for gardening."

"Oh? What kind of work did she do?"

Michelle pinched the bridge of her nose. *Now what do I say? What kind of job should I give this pretend mother?* "Mom was a hair stylist," she blurted. "She had her own shop and was so busy she hardly had any time for herself." *There we go—another untruth on top of all the others.* Michelle wondered how many more lies she'd have to tell before she gave up the Lapps' hospitality.

⁓

As Mary Ruth knelt on the ground next to her garden, she glanced at Sara. She'd pulled her beautiful auburn hair into a ponytail, and every once in a while, between pulling a few weeds, she would swat at the annoying gnats swarming around their heads.

"What's with all these bugs?" Sara scrunched up her face. "I'm afraid if I open my mouth too wide, I might swallow one of 'em."

"They're gnats, and they always seem to be worse when it's warm and humid—especially after it rains." Mary Ruth flapped her hand at a few of the bugs near her nose. "But don't worry; if you stay here long enough, you'll get used to them. It's a small price to pay for living in the country."

"Yeah, I suppose."

"Your mom didn't care much for the pesky bugs either. She loved nature but couldn't understand why God created gnats and wondered what possible purpose they could have here on this beautiful earth."

Sara frowned as she stuck her shovel into the ground next to a weed. "I think the earth would be a lot more beautiful if there were no irritating bugs."

Mary Ruth rubbed a hand against her heart. She could almost hear Rhoda saying those exact same words one muggy day when they were working in the garden. *Like mother, like daughter,* she thought. *If only Rhoda could be here now, working alongside me and Sara.*

Tears welled in Mary Ruth's eyes, and she blinked them away. So many times she had looked down the driveway and prayed their daughter would return. Rhoda was the second child she and Willis had lost, only at least they'd had her for the first eighteen years. After she'd left home, it felt as if she were dead—oh, the emptiness in Mary Ruth's heart was awful. So many wasted years when they could have been with their daughter, and now, with Rhoda's passing, there was no chance for that.

Before their other son, Ivan, came along, they'd had a baby boy named Jake, who had died two weeks after he was born. Their sweet little boy had a heart condition that ended his life all too soon. Ivan was born two years later, and he grew up to be a fine young man. He was married now, and living in Paradise, not far away. He and his wife, Yvonne, had a daughter, Lenore, as well as two sons, Peter and Benjamin.

Ivan and Rhoda had been close during their childhood and enjoyed swimming, fishing, and doing many other fun things together. He too was devastated when she left with only a note to say goodbye. When Mary Ruth had called to tell him about receiving Sara's letter and shared the sad news of Rhoda's death, Ivan had cried. Mary Ruth sobbed along with him, as the truth set in that the hope of seeing her daughter come home would never be fulfilled.

"You okay?"

Sara's question pulled Mary Ruth out of her musings. "I'm fine. Just thinking about the past, is all."

Sara gave a nod. "Yeah, I do that myself sometimes."

"Well, as our church bishop said in a sermon a few weeks ago, we shouldn't dwell so much on the past. What we are doing today and hope to do in the future are what count in the long run."

Sara kept swatting at the bugs and pulling weeds. Mary Ruth wished she knew what her granddaughter was thinking. Then, thinking of church meetings, she wondered if, were she to sew a few plain-style dresses, Sara would be willing to wear them. She studied the young woman, releasing a sigh. *If Sara remains with us, could she adjust to the Amish way of life? Maybe she would even decide to join our church, get married, and settle down here in our community. That would make me so happy.*

Mary Ruth reminded herself not to expect too much from their granddaughter, but she couldn't help being a wee bit hopeful.

# Chapter 5

When Michelle woke up Sunday morning, every bone in her body ached. Yesterday, she'd helped Mary Ruth clean the house and bake two shoofly pies. When that was done, she'd stupidly let Willis talk her into helping him clean the barn. Big mistake. It was a smelly, dirty job. At least he hadn't asked her to do anything with those horrible hogs she'd seen in the pen outside. But the whole time they'd worked, Willis kept asking her questions about Rhoda. That part was more painful than all the cleaning they'd done.

Mary Ruth had done the same thing while she and Michelle cleaned house and baked. Some of the questions the Lapps asked were the same. Michelle hoped she had given good answers to both of them.

More difficult than helping with chores was being asked so many questions about someone she knew nothing about. Maybe after she'd been here a few more days Willis and Mary Ruth would let up on the questions and talk about other things. It was understandable though, the Lapps wanting to know about their daughter, whose presence they'd been deprived of all these years. Truth was, Michelle had some questions of her own. She was eager to find out how much of what she'd seen and heard on TV about the Amish was true.

Michelle pulled herself out of bed and lifted the shade at the window to look out. No clouds in the sky at the moment—just a bright, sunny day. *I hope the Lapps don't expect me to go to church with them today.* Since the Amish were a religious sort of people, she figured they probably were faithful about attending church on Sunday mornings. Michelle had no desire to sit in church and listen to some preacher talk about how God answers prayer. She'd heard that before when she'd been forced to attend Bible school.

Michelle had actually tried praying a few times when she was a girl but never felt like her prayers reached heaven. If there even was a God. Because if God was real, why did He allow people to treat each other so cruelly? Of course, the Lapps did not seem harsh, but then, Michelle didn't know them that well either.

Michelle's gaze went to the wooden chest at the foot of her bed. Curious to know what was inside, she lifted the lid, revealing a dark blue, Amish-style dress. She took it out, and saw a few more dresses under it, as well as some black shoes and a white, heart-shaped covering like the one Mary Ruth wore on her head.

*I bet these belonged to their daughter.* She was tempted to try on one of the dresses, but thought better of it, thinking Mary Ruth might not approve. *But then, how would she know, if I don't mention what I did? After I see how I look in the bathroom mirror, I'll take the dress off and put it back in the chest.*

Michelle took off her pajamas and slipped the dress on over her head. She didn't wear a dress very often, and the ones she had worn never looked so plain. *I wonder why Amish women wear dresses like this. Another question I should ask Mary Ruth.*

She reached in, picked up the *kapp*, and placed it on her head. *Oh boy. I can only imagine what I must look like.*

Michelle left the room and trekked down the hall to the bathroom. While the mirror over the sink wasn't full-length, at least she could see her upper body.

She giggled at her reflection. If her long hair had been pulled back in a bun, she would almost look Amish.

Michelle took off the head covering, and opened one of the cabinet drawers, where she found several hair pins. After securing her hair in a bun, she put the covering back in place. Silently staring at herself, Michelle wondered what it would be like if she were Amish. Could she handle dressing plain all the time, not to mention all the daily chores and doing without modern conveniences? It would be quite a change from the things she'd become accustomed to.

Michelle shook her head. *Probably couldn't do it, although, except for the bugs, I would enjoy feeling one with nature, like I did when Mary Ruth and I were pulling weeds in her garden.*

Michelle left the bathroom and walked back toward her bedroom. She'd only gone a short ways when she heard footsteps on the stairs. A few seconds later, Mary Ruth appeared in the hallway.

Michelle jumped, and Mary Ruth gasped. "Oh, my word, Sara, you look so much like your mother in that dress."

Embarrassed, Michelle dropped her gaze. "Sorry, Mary Ruth—I mean, Grandma. I should have asked first before trying on the dress."

"No, it's okay. It was your mother's, and you have every right to wear it." Mary Ruth stepped up to Michelle. "In fact, I'd like you to have all her clothes that I've put away. You can take them whenever you decide to return to your home." She placed her hand on Michelle's arm. "Of course you're welcome to stay here indefinitely if you like. We don't expect you to join the Amish church, unless you should choose to do so. But maybe in time you could find a job locally and live here with us. And if you don't want to get a job, that's okay too. Would you at least give it some thought?"

Michelle nodded. She felt like a mouse caught in a trap. When the time came for her to leave, she would go, but not without telling them first who she was.

She glanced down at Rhoda's dress, touching the bodice. "Is there a specific reason Amish women wear dresses like this?"

"We choose to wear plain clothes and do not care to be changing styles designed to achieve glamour and not modesty."

Michelle pointed to the covering on Mary Ruth's head. "And the kapp? Why do you wear that?"

"We wear our coverings in obedience to the Bible. It says in 1 Corinthians 11:5, 'Every woman that prayeth or prophesieth with her head uncovered dishonoureth her head.'"

Michelle gave another nod, although she didn't really

understand it all. The Amish way of life seemed quaint to her, but it held a certain appeal.

"I came up to tell you that breakfast is ready," Mary Ruth said. "Oh, and I also wanted you to know that we'll be having company later on."

"Really? I figured you and Grandpa might be going to church today."

"It's our off-Sunday."

Michelle tipped her head. "What's an off-Sunday?"

"We Amish gather for worship every other Sunday. On the off weeks we will sometimes visit another church district, or we may go visiting. Today, our son, Ivan, and his family will be coming over. They are anxious to meet you."

"I see." Michelle leaned against the wall for support. *I suppose my so-called uncle will also have questions to ask. I just hope I'm able to give him all the right answers.*

❧

"Sara, this is your uncle Ivan. He owns a general store in the area." Willis grinned as he motioned to the two women standing beside Ivan. "And this is his wife, Yvonne, and daughter, Lenore, who is a teacher at one of our one-room schoolhouses in the area. His sons, Benjamin and Peter, couldn't be here today, because they are visiting some friends in Kentucky."

Michelle forced a smile and shook their hands. She felt like a bug under a microscope when tall, blond-haired Ivan studied her face. Did he think she looked anything like his sister, Rhoda, or had Ivan figured out that Michelle was a fraud?

Michelle turned her attention to Ivan's wife and daughter. Yvonne, a tall, slender woman, had brown hair and matching eyes. Lenore looked similar, only her eyes were hazel-colored. She was a few inches shorter than her mother, and was also quite slender. Lenore appeared to be in her early or mid-twenties—it was hard to tell. It wouldn't be right to just ask. Besides, what did it matter? It wasn't as if they were really cousins.

"Welcome, Cousin Sara." Lenore stepped forward and gave Michelle a warm hug.

Lenore's mother hugged Michelle too, but Uncle Ivan remained where he was.

Michelle shifted uneasily. *I don't think he likes me. Can Ivan see into the depths of my soul and know that I'm a phony?*

Ivan cleared his throat a couple of times. "Sorry for staring, Sara. It's just hard to believe my sister's daughter is here in this house."

*No, she isn't.* Michelle bit the inside of her cheek. It was wrong to lie to these nice people, but she couldn't bring herself to own up to the truth.

"Does Sara remind you of your sister, *Daadi?*" Lenore looked at her father.

Michelle didn't know any Pennsylvania Dutch, but she assumed *Daadi* meant Daddy.

Ivan nodded. "In some ways she does. I suppose it's the color of Sara's hair that reminds me of Rhoda. Her facial features are different though, but then I guess she probably looks like both of her parents."

*You got that right, only they're not the parents you're thinking of.* When Michelle was a girl, she'd often been told that she had her father's red hair and blue-green eyes, but her mother's facial features. Truthfully, she didn't care if she resembled either of them. Her biological parents meant nothing to her. The day that social worker came and took Michelle and her brothers away was the day she'd emotionally divorced her parents.

"Why don't we all go outside and sit at the picnic table?" Mary Ruth suggested. "While Willis fires up the grill, we can visit."

Michelle fought the urge to roll her eyes. *Oh great. I bet this will be a time for more questions fired at me.*

～⌒～

As they sat at the picnic table, eating hamburgers and hot dogs, Michelle felt as if all eyes were upon her. At least the smoke from the grill kept the gnats at bay. That was one positive.

She'd already answered dozens of questions—about her mother, where she'd grown up, siblings. Michelle hoped she'd remembered to give the same answers to their guests as she had when Mary Ruth and Willis asked these questions this past week. Michelle concentrated so hard on trying to give right answers, she could barely eat. Despite the gnawing in her stomach, she was glad when the meal was over.

While Michelle, Yvonne, and Lenore helped Mary Ruth clear the table and carry things inside, Willis and Ivan went out to barn to check on Sadie, who was supposed to have her pups any time.

The women had started washing the dishes when Ivan burst into the kitchen. "Hey Mom, Dad wanted me to tell you that Sadie's about to deliver. He thought maybe everyone would like to come out and watch as her babies come into the world."

Mary Ruth looked at Michelle. "How about it, Sara? Have you ever witnessed puppies being born?"

Michelle shook her head. *And I don't think I want to either.*

"Well good, let's go." Mary Ruth gestured to Lenore and Yvonne. "You two are welcome to come with us."

Yvonne shook her head. "I've seen plenty of pups born in my day. I'll remain here and finish washing the dishes."

"Same here. Mom can wash, and I'll dry." Lenore picked up a dish towel and moved toward the sink.

*"Danki."* Mary Ruth opened the back door and stepped outside.

Michelle reluctantly followed. "Does *danki* mean thanks?" she asked as they headed for the barn.

Grinning, Mary Ruth bobbed her head. "If you stay here long enough, I'll bet you'll be speaking Pennsylvania Dutch in no time. Jah, I do."

*Jah* meant "yes," and *danki* was the word for "thanks." Michelle didn't know how many other Amish words she could learn while she was here, but she was off to a good start. Well, maybe not a good start, but a few words learned anyway.

Michelle wasn't certain she cared to watch the birth of Sadie's puppies, but at least it would take the attention off her. And she sure wasn't going to stay in the house with her pretend aunt and cousin, who would no doubt ply her with more questions.

Michelle must have missed seeing it when she was in the barn the other day, but Sadie had a large wooden box to stretch out in, with plenty of room for the pups to move around in once they became active. The bottom of the box had been lined with newspapers, making for easy disposal. Mary Ruth called it "Sadie's whelping bed."

Michelle stood between Ivan and Willis, watching as Sadie panted, stood up, and then lay down again.

"It won't be long now." Willis's eyes sparkled. He was no doubt excited, even though this was probably old hat for him.

*Wish I could be that enthused.* Michelle watched curiously as the first puppy arrived. Once Sadie removed the pup's sac, she began pushing again.

Mary Ruth took over and cleaned the first puppy's nostrils, then gently blew on its tiny face to stimulate breathing.

Michelle's throat constricted when the newborn pup gave a little yelp. No wonder they wanted her to witness this. A mere description would not have been good enough.

"Have you ever seen anything like this before?" Ivan asked.

Michelle shook her head. "I've seen a cat give birth, but never a dog."

"Your mom and I used to play a lot in this barn when we were kids." Ivan made a sweeping gesture of the area around them with his hand. "Being here with you now takes me back to those days." His eyes darkened a bit. "We didn't know how fortunate we were back then, to have loving parents and a wonderful place to grow up."

Michelle almost said she wished she could have known Ivan's sister, but caught herself in time. "Growing up in those days sounds nice. Wish I could have known you and Mom back then." *And I wish I'd had your parents,* she secretly added.

# Chapter 6

When Willis entered the kitchen Friday morning, he found Mary Ruth stirring batter in a large mixing bowl. "Whatcha up to? Are you making *pannekuche*?"

"Sorry, no pancakes this morning. I'm mixing batter for a birthday cake. But I suppose I could whip a batch of pannekuche just for you." She turned and gave his belly a little poke.

He quirked an eyebrow.

"Today is our granddaughter's birthday." Mary Ruth paused to switch hands stirring. "Remember when she told us soon after she arrived that she was born on June 15th? She will be twenty-four years old."

"Oh yes, that's right." Willis put his hand lovingly under Mary Ruth's chin. "Look here a minute. Whatcha got on your *kinn*?"

After being married all these years, her husband's gentle touch still made her heart do a flip-flop, even when he was teasing her. "I must look a mess." Mary Ruth giggled as he wiped some flour off her cheek and it landed on the front of her apron.

"Not to me. You've never looked more beautiful." Willis's gaze remained on her for several seconds. "All that flour on your face and apron shows how hard you've been working." He kissed her cheek on the spot where the flour had been. "So besides the cake, what else are we gonna do to help Sara celebrate her special day?"

"I invited Ivan and his family over again, but he and Yvonne had already made plans to get together with her folks this evening, so they won't be coming. Lenore said she's free though, so I guess it'll be just the four of us."

"That should work out okay then. It'll give Sara a chance to get better acquainted with her cousin."

Mary Ruth nodded. "I was thinking that too. Since the girls are about the same age and both single, they have that much in common. If Sara and Lenore become friends, it'll give Sara another reason to come here often. And who knows, if our granddaughter likes it here, she may even decide to stay in the area or live at our house permanently. We certainly have the room, and it would be nice to see Sara using our daughter's bedroom, instead of it looking so empty." Mary Ruth swallowed. "Maybe sleeping in the same room and in the same bed will give Sara a sense of being closer to her mudder."

"Jah, it might, at that." Willis's eyes twinkled as he tipped his head and grinned at Mary Ruth. "After all this time, it's nice to see such a look of pure joy on your face. It's been a good many years since you've been so enthused about something."

"A long time, I agree." She sighed deeply. "When Rhoda ran away, it wounded my soul. And every year that went by without us hearing from her hurt all the more. I thought we had done something that drove her away, and she wanted to forget us. Now that I know our dochder left a note for Sara, telling her about us, it's given me a sense of peace." Mary Ruth touched her chest. "The realization that Rhoda cared about us enough to want Sara to get to know us is like a healing balm to my hurting soul."

He kissed her cheek. "I understand. Having Sara here has been good for both of us."

"Are you two talking about me?" Sara asked, stepping into the kitchen.

Mary Ruth's face warmed. "Jah, but in a good way. We were just saying how nice it is to have you here. And I'm also happy we can be with you to help celebrate your special day." Mary Ruth moved away from the counter and gave Sara a hug. "Happy birthday, Granddaughter."

"Yes, happy birthday, Sara," Willis put in.

Sara's cheeks turned a light shade of pink. "Danki."

"You're welcome." It tickled Mary Ruth to no end, hearing her granddaughter use a Pennsylvania Dutch word.

"Have you been out to check on the puppies yet this morning?" Sara asked, looking at Willis.

"Not yet, but I will right after breakfast."

"You can go now if you want to." Mary Ruth gestured to the cake batter. "I want to put this cake in the oven before I start breakfast, so there's still a little time if you want to go to the barn."

"All right then. I'll head out there now." Willis looked at Sara. "Would you like to come along?"

"Sure, unless Mary Ruth. . .I mean, Grandma, needs my help with breakfast."

Mary Ruth shook her head. "You go along with your grandpa to the barn. When you get back, I'll have the cake in the oven and a skillet of scrambled eggs with ham ready to eat."

"Okay, thanks." As Sara followed Willis out of the room, Mary Ruth heard her say, "If you don't mind, from now on, I'd like to help by taking care of Sadie and the pups' bedding. That's one less thing you would have to do."

"Danki, Granddaughter. That'd be just fine." Willis quickly came back to grab his hat off the hook. "I forgot this." His face fairly beamed as he glanced at Mary Ruth and winked.

When Mary Ruth heard the sound of the back door open and then close, she went to the window and watched her husband and granddaughter walk to the barn together. With gratitude, she closed her eyes and said a quick prayer. *Thank You, Lord. There is so much happiness in our house again.*

After taking two round cake pans out of the cupboard, she began humming a song they frequently sang at their ice-cream socials. Mary Ruth's motherly instincts seemed to be kicking in. Having her granddaughter here to fuss over was like having Rhoda home again. Willis was right—she truly was happier and felt ten years younger too.

*Those puppies are sure adorable.* Michelle took time to cuddle each one after changing the bedding, freshening up the water, and making sure Sadie's bowl was filled with food. Taking care of Sadie and her babies didn't feel like a chore at all. It was something she could look forward to every day. Even if they were only animals, it made Michelle feel like she was needed.

When she left the barn, Michelle walked down to the mailbox, at Willis's request. It was another simple chore, and she didn't mind doing it. In fact, after being in the smelly, stuffy barn for a while, it felt good to breathe in some fresh air. Even the bugs weren't bad yet, since it was still early in the day.

Michelle's stomach growled as the aroma of pancakes wafted from the house. She'd almost forgotten how much she loved homemade pancakes. Sometimes, her foster mother would make them on Saturday mornings, but she hadn't had any, other than the frozen kind you put in a toaster, since she'd left their home and struck out on her own.

As Michelle approached the mailbox, she wondered if she would find anything inside. It was still early, and she couldn't believe the Lapps' mail would be delivered this soon in the day. But since Willis had asked her to go get it, he must know what he was talking about. It could be that a rural mail carrier had to start early, and Willis and Mary Ruth's house might be on the first part of the route.

Michelle opened the box and was not disappointed. A handful of mail had been left inside. Curious, she thumbed through the stack—lots of advertising catalogs and flyers, a few bills, and one letter. She squinted at the name on the return address. It said: *"Sara Murray."*

Her heart pounded. *Oh no. . . . It's the real granddaughter, and she lives in Newark, New Jersey. I wonder what she has to say. Maybe she wrote to tell her grandparents that they missed her at the bus station. Or she could be letting them know that she plans to come here soon—maybe even today.*

Gulping in several deep breaths, Michelle leaned against the mailbox as she deliberated what to do. If she took this letter inside and gave it to Mary Ruth or Willis, her cover would definitely be blown.

With her free hand, Michelle reached up to rub her forehead. She needed to find out what the letter said. Only then would she know what to do.

Michelle slipped the rest of the mail back inside the box. Clasping Sara's letter, she walked down the road a ways, until she came to a clump of trees. Stepping behind them with fingers shaking, she awkwardly tore open the letter to silently read.

> *Dear Grandpa and Grandma Lapp,*
>
> *I wrote to you a few weeks ago, but since you didn't respond, I am wondering if you even got the letter. I wanted to let you know that it could be toward the end of summer, or even early fall before I'm able to come there to meet you. I had thought maybe July 5$^{th}$, but it doesn't look like that's going to happen. This business class I'm taking requires a lot of homework, so it'll be difficult for me to get away anytime soon. Not only that, but my car is giving me problems, so when I do come, I still may have to take the bus. If I'm not able to drive, I'll let you know so you can decide if you're able to pick me up at the bus station in Philadelphia.*
>
> *I hope you will write back soon so I know that you received this letter. I am looking forward to meeting you both.*
>
> *All the best,*
> *Sara*

*What a stroke of luck.* Michelle drew a breath and blew it out slowly. It was a relief to know the Lapps' granddaughter wouldn't be coming until at least the end of summer. That meant Michelle could continue posing as Sara and reaping the benefits of staying with Willis and Mary Ruth. All she had to do was dispose of this letter. And from now on, she would volunteer to walk out every day to get the mail. It was the only guarantee that the Lapps would never find a letter from their rightful granddaughter.

Michelle sat at the breakfast table, barely listening to Willis and Mary Ruth's conversation. All she could think about was the letter she'd thrown in the burn barrel before bringing the rest of the mail to the house. She'd gone back to the barn, found a box of matches and lit a fire, destroying all evidence of Sara Murray's letter. Fortunately, Willis had already returned to the house by then and hadn't seen what she'd done.

*How much longer can I keep up this charade?* Michelle clenched her napkin into a tight ball. *What if Mary Ruth or Willis should decide to go out and get the mail before I have a chance to get there each morning? And what if another letter shows up from Sara? Boy, have I gotten myself into a mess.*

Mary Ruth tapped Michelle's arm. "Did you hear what I said, Sara?"

Michelle jerked her head. "Uh, no. Sorry, I didn't."

"I asked if there's anything special you'd like me to fix for your birthday supper tonight."

Unable to look at Mary Ruth's face, Michelle kept her gaze fixed on her plate. Her appetite for pancakes had diminished. Although they looked and smelled delicious, she could barely get the first one down. "Don't go to any trouble on my account," she mumbled.

"It's no trouble. There's nothing more I'd rather be doing." Mary Ruth nudged Michelle's arm, and when she looked up, she was rewarded with a pleasant smile. "So, what's your favorite supper meal?"

Michelle's guilt nearly made her confess her deception, seeing how genuine Mary Ruth was toward her. But she felt like a little girl—giddy that someone actually cared. "You might think this is strange, but I really like spaghetti and meatballs."

"That's not strange at all," Willis spoke up. "I like spaghetti and meatballs too."

Michelle looked at Willis, where he sat at the head of the table. "You do?" *I bet he only said that for my benefit.*

Grinning, he bobbed his head.

Mary Ruth clapped her hands. "All right then, it's settled. Tonight, in honor of Sara's twenty-fourth birthday, I will fix her favorite supper."

Michelle finished her glass of milk and dipped the last bite of pancake in the leftover syrup on her plate. She wished the Lapps weren't being so nice to her. It made it all the more difficult to lie to them. But if she told the truth, she'd have to leave. Besides, to coin a phrase, what they didn't know wouldn't hurt them. The truth would hurt them—and her too. So for now at least, she'd keep silent.

⤳

As Ezekiel King approached his horse and buggy, his mother called out to him. "Don't forget the jar of *hunnich.*" She stood on the back porch, holding a tall jar of honey.

Ezekiel walked across the yard, meeting her halfway. *"Ich bin allfatt am eppes vergesse."*

"You're not always forgetting something; only when your mind is somewhere else." Lifting her chin to look up at him, Mom handed him the jar. "So what were you thinking about this time, Son?"

He smacked his forehead. "Beats me. Guess I had my head in the clouds." Ezekiel wasn't about to tell his mother he'd been thinking about buying a car or a truck. Unlike some Amish parents in their area, his folks did not look the other way or knowingly allow their children to take part in questionable things, like some English young people did. Ezekiel thought his mom and dad were too strict. He was twenty-three years old and ought to have the right to do as he pleased. Dad was always on him about joining the church, but Ezekiel hadn't made up his mind about that yet. If he did buy a car, he'd have to keep it hidden, somewhere other than here on his folk's property. Dad would never stand for any son of his owning a motorized vehicle, much less parking it here, where others could see.

Mom poked Ezekiel's arm. "Are you spacing off again?"

He blinked a couple of times. "Sorry. I was thinkin', is all."

Mom's brown eyes darkened. "You can do your thinking while you're heading over to the Lapps' to deliver the honey they ordered."

"Don't see why they want more honey. It wasn't long ago that I delivered a jar to their place."

"Maybe they used it up already. Anyway, it shouldn't matter the reason. They asked, and you have plenty of honey, so you'd best be on your way."

"Jah, okay, but I'm gonna run a short errand when I leave there, so I'll probably be gone a few hours."

She gave a nod. "That's fine. Things are kind of slow at the greenhouse today, so I'm sure your *daed* and I can manage without you for a while this afternoon."

"Good to know." Ezekiel glanced toward the back of their property, where the greenhouse was built. That was another thing frustrating him. He didn't enjoy working there so much. However, Dad insisted that Ezekiel, being the oldest son, should take over the business someday, whether he wanted it or not.

Ezekiel was glad he'd become a part-time beekeeper, because it gave him something else to do besides fool with plants and flowers all day. Not that he had anything against the greenhouse business—it just wasn't what he wanted to do for the rest of his life. Truthfully, Ezekiel wasn't sure what he wanted, but right now it didn't include joining the Amish church. What he wanted more than anything was to know more about the English world and enjoy some of the things his parents had forbidden him to do.

He said goodbye to Mom and put the jar of honey in a cardboard box inside his buggy. Then he released his horse, Big Red, from the hitching rail, hopped into the buggy, and headed down the driveway. There was no doubt in his mind. As soon as he left Willis and Mary Ruth's place, he was going to look at a used truck one of his friends had for sale. And if Ezekiel thought it was the right one for him, he might end up buying it either today or sometime soon.

# Chapter 7

"Would ya mind helping me feed the hogs this morning?" Willis asked Michelle when they finished breakfast.

Mary Ruth squinted at him. "For goodness' sakes, Husband, today is Sara's birthday. You should not have asked her to do a *garschdich* chore like that."

"Feeding the hogs isn't a nasty chore," he responded. "It's a *eefach* task. You just take the food out and dump it over the fence."

"If it's so simple, then why don't you do it yourself?"

"Because I have some other chores to do, and—"

"It's okay," Michelle interjected. "My birthday's no big deal, and as long as I don't have to get in the pen with the hogs, I don't mind feeding 'em."

Willis grinned. "See, I figured as much. This little gal is a chip off the ole block."

Mary Ruth rolled her eyes, and Michelle merely nodded. She'd done plenty of unpleasant chores over the years—at her birth parents' request and again for her foster parents. Then when she'd struck out on her own, more chores waited at the various jobs she'd done, not to mention trying to keep on top of things at the apartments she'd lived in.

Michelle felt safe here at the Lapps' and didn't mind whatever chores they asked her to do. It was kind of like payment for her room and board.

While Michelle took the dishes over to the sink, she listened to Mary Ruth and Willis talk, but she couldn't understand what they were saying because they spoke in their native Pennsylvania Dutch.

"I'll take the food out to the hogs now," she said, turning to Willis. "When I come back inside, I'll help Mary Ruth get the dishes done."

Mary Ruth flapped her hand. "Don't bother about that. I'll take care of those this morning. After you feed the hogs, feel free to do something you'd enjoy for the rest of the day. Your cousin Lenore will be here around six o'clock, and we'll eat shortly after, so that gives you plenty of time to do whatever you want today."

Michelle shrugged and headed out the back door with a large bowl of table scraps that had been sitting on the end of the counter. *What is it I'm supposed to do today? I'm not used to having time on my hands. I've kept busy doing something ever since I got here.*

Michelle had been staying with Mary Ruth and Willis for ten days, but already she was in somewhat of a routine. She liked keeping busy and helping the Lapps. And every night when she retired to bed, sleep came easy after a day of activities from living and working on a farm.

Outside, Michelle paused to look up at the clear blue sky. Today had started out to be a beautiful morning. Yesterday's rain had taken away the humidity.

Michelle drew a deep breath, enjoying the fresh air that reached her nostrils. How nice to no longer deal with smog or the smell of vehicle fumes, like she'd been accustomed to in Philadelphia.

She glanced toward the country road. *Maybe after I feed the hogs, I'll take a walk to see the nearby area. Or I could spread a blanket on the grass and lay out in the sun and relax with a book. I haven't done that in a long while.*

Still undecided, Michelle moved across the yard. She'd only made it halfway to the hog pen when the whinny of a horse startled her. At that moment, she felt something brush against her leg. Taking another step forward, Michelle stumbled over a rock and fell facedown in a mud puddle.

❧

Ezekiel arrived at the Lapps' in time to see a young woman with long auburn hair fall flat on her face in the mud. The bowl she'd been holding, along with all its contents, went flying. He pulled his horse up to the hitching rail and hopped out of the buggy. "Are you okay, miss?" he hollered. Running over to the young lady, he held his hand out to help her up, but she refused to take it.

"Yeah, I'm fine. Never better." Groaning, she clambered to her feet, wiping off the mud that stuck to her clothes. "Bet it was a stupid cat that brushed my leg."

Ezekiel looked around. He didn't see any sign of a cat. "Are ya hurt?"

"No, I'm not hurt." She swiped a hand across her dirty face. "Who are you?"

"My name's Ezekiel King. What's your name? Don't believe I've met you before." He suppressed a chuckle when she squinted at him and a hunk of mud fell off her eyelid. Looking beyond the smudges of dirt, Ezekiel couldn't help noticing her beautiful blue-green eyes, which seemed to grow deeper in color as her fair skin turned a blushing red.

"My name is Mich—I mean, I'm Sara Murray, Willis and Mary Ruth's granddaughter."

He narrowed his eyes. "Lenore's the only granddaughter I've ever known about."

"Well, it just goes to show you don't know everything." She bent down, grabbed the empty bowl, and dashed toward the house.

Ezekiel started after her, but then remembered he needed to secure his horse and get the honey he'd brought along. He hurried back to his buggy, eager to get to know about this English woman who claimed to be the Lapps' granddaughter. Despite her obvious irritation with him, Ezekiel thought she was kind of cute.

Michelle raced into the house, hurried up the stairs, and made a beeline for the bathroom to get cleaned up. It was bad enough she'd fallen on her face in the mud, but to have done it in front of someone she didn't even know was humiliating. The long-legged Amish man with thick brown hair probably thought she was a klutz. He seemed to want to carry on a conversation with her. But Michelle had no intention of remaining in the yard, looking like such a mess. She glanced down at herself and grimaced. *What a way to meet a friend of the Lapps, especially a guy who wanted to help me up.* And to make matters worse, she'd almost given him her real name.

"I'll end up getting myself thrown out of the Lapps' home if I'm not careful," Michelle mumbled as she turned on the shower and threw her dirty clothes in a heap. At least she had a robe in the bathroom to put on till she went to her bedroom for clean clothes. Right now she just wanted to get cleaned up. Hopefully, by the time she went downstairs, the nice-looking Amish fellow would be gone.

❧

Ezekiel stood on the Lapps' back porch, wondering why no one had answered his knock. Could the granddaughter be the only one here today? If so, maybe she was too embarrassed to let him in. He lifted his hand to knock again when Mary Ruth came up from the outside cellar entrance.

*"Wie geht's?"* she said, smiling at him. "Did you bring the hunnich I ordered?"

He nodded and gestured to the small box he held in one hand. "How are you today, Mary Ruth?"

"I couldn't be better. Danki for asking." Her smile widened. "The weather's beautiful today, jah?"

He nodded again.

"Don't you just love how clean everything looks and smells, after a soaking rain like we had yesterday?"

Mary Ruth was right. Ezekiel thought everything looked refreshed—except for the young woman who'd run into the house, all embarrassed a few minutes ago. "I agree. Tonight when it's dark, I may get my flashlight and catch some night crawlers out in the yard. The rain and now this warmth we're having should make it easy to search for worms for fishing."

When Mary Ruth gave no response, Ezekiel cleared his throat. "By the way, I met a red-haired woman when I pulled my rig in a few minutes ago. Said she was your grossdochder, Sara."

"That's right. She was taking some scraps to the hogs." Mary Ruth set the basket of laundry on the ground underneath the clothesline and joined him on the porch.

He bit back a chuckle, still remembering how the poor girl had looked when she fell in the mud. "Umm. . . Your granddaughter never made it to the pigpen."

Mary Ruth tipped her head. "Oh? Did something happen?"

"Sure did." Ezekiel explained about Sara falling in the mud, and the table scraps flying every which way on the grass. "I introduced myself, and after Sara said she was your granddaughter, she took off for the house like a bee was in hot pursuit."

Mary Ruth put both hands on her cheeks. "Oh dear. Not a good thing to happen on her birthday."

Ezekiel's forehead wrinkled. "I'm *verhuddelt* though. I didn't even know you had another granddaughter, much less anything about her being here on her birthday."

"No need to be confused." Mary Ruth grasped the door handle. "Come inside with the honey and I'll explain."

As Ezekiel sat at the kitchen table, listening to Mary Ruth tell him about how they'd received a letter from Rhoda's daughter saying her mother had died, his interest was piqued. "I'm sorry for your loss, Mary Ruth. Please tell Willis I extend my condolences to him too."

"Danki, I will."

"How long will your granddaughter be staying with you?"

"We don't know for sure. Sara said she's currently out of a job, so we told her she can remain here for as long as she wants." Mary Ruth's tone sounded hopeful. "Willis and I would be happy if she stayed indefinitely. She's such a nice young woman, and having her around makes it feel almost like we have our daughter back."

Ezekiel didn't know a lot about the Lapps' daughter, Rhoda, but he had heard his folks talk about her a couple of times over the years. Mom mentioned once how bad she felt for Mary Ruth and Willis, having their only daughter run off and never hearing from her again. To find out Rhoda had recently died and that the Lapps had a granddaughter they'd known nothing about was quite a shock. "So today's her birthday?"

"Jah. She's twenty-four years old." Mary Ruth's eyes brightened. "We're having a little birthday supper for Sara this evening, and her cousin Lenore will be joining us. I think it's good for Sara to spend some time with other people her age and not just us old folks."

Ezekiel shook his head. "You're not old. Leastways, neither you nor Willis seems old to me."

She chuckled, fanning her face with her hand. "It's very kind of you to say that."

"I meant it. You and Willis are young at heart, and it shows by the things you say and do."

"Well, we both try to keep a positive attitude and enjoy doing things outdoors and keeping active. Maybe that's why we seem young at heart." She picked up the jar of honey and tapped the lid. "Look at this beautiful golden color. I bet this'll be as good as all the other honey you've brought us."

"Did you finish the last jar already? It wasn't long ago that I brought one by."

"No, we still have some, but now, with Sara here, I thought she might enjoy the honey as much as we do, and I didn't want to run out." Mary Ruth went to the cupboard and took out an old coffee can. "How much do I owe you?"

"Same as usual." Ezekiel heard footsteps, and he glanced toward the door leading to the living room, expecting the red-haired woman to join them in the kitchen. But she never did. It could have been Willis he'd heard, or if it was Sara, she'd gone into a different room.

"I suppose I'd better go." After Mary Ruth paid him, Ezekiel rose from his chair. "I have an errand to run before I head for home." He started for the door, but stopped and turned around when she called out to him.

"Say, I have an idea. If you're not busy tonight, why don't you join us for supper? I'd like you to get to know Sara, and it'll give you a chance to visit with Lenore."

*I wonder if Mary Ruth and my* mamm *are in cahoots.* He held his hands behind his back, rubbing a tight spot on the left side. Ezekiel's mother had been trying for a couple of years to get him and Lenore together. She kept saying Lenore and Ezekiel had a lot in common, but he didn't think so.

If Mary Ruth was trying to play matchmaker, it wouldn't work. Ezekiel and Lenore had little or nothing in common. Besides, she'd joined the Amish church soon after turning eighteen. Ezekiel, on the other hand, had no idea if he'd ever join. As far as Ezekiel was concerned, he and Lenore would not make a good match. Despite all that, it might be nice to come for supper this evening. Not only could he get to know Sara, but it would give him an opportunity to ask her some questions about the English world.

Smiling at Mary Ruth, Ezekiel said, "I'd be happy to join you for supper. What time would ya like me to come?"

"Six o'clock is when I told Lenore to be here."

"Sounds good. I'll see you then." Ezekiel turned and went out the door. *Wonder if I should bring Sara a gift for her birthday. If I can find something she likes, it might make her more willing to answer my questions and forget what happened outside when she fell.*

# Chapter 8

*Newark*

Sara walked into her living room and kicked off her shoes. Today's class at the local college had been mind-boggling. Business Law was not going to be one of her easier courses. That fact had been obvious on the first day of class, and today had been another confirmation. But it was required for getting her degree in business. Sara had finished another semester in May, but she signed up for Business Law over the summer months. It was a six-week course. Fortunately, the class was small, and it would be easier to concentrate on this one course.

Sara had to wonder if it would have been better to take an online course so she could work at her own speed instead of the allotted time in the classroom. It was too late to change her mind though, so she would have to buckle down and do her best to get a good grade and complete all her assignments on time.

There was also the issue of finances. Sara had refused any help from her stepfather when he'd offered to pay the tuition. Her situation would have to be much worse before she'd accept financial aid from him. It was a matter of pride that came from the need to prove she could succeed on her own.

Sara looked around the cozy room. The beige couch was strewn with colorful throw pillows, and on either side of it sat two wooden end tables. A recliner was positioned at one end of the living room, and the wooden rocker her mother had picked up in an antique store was situated close by. The hardwood floor was covered by a large area rug. A flat-screen TV had been mounted to the wall directly across from the couch, but Sara didn't spend much time watching television. Between her part-time job and studies, she had little free time and preferred to read a book or make some beaded jewelry.

When Sara turned eighteen, it was decided that she could move into the other half of the duplex her mother and Dean had bought shortly after they were married. The rent was reasonable, since they only charged her half of what any other tenant would normally pay. Even though her mom was right next door, Sara liked having a sense of independence. This was the first time she'd lived alone, not to mention it got her away from having to watch Mama and Dean spoil her brother, Kenny. Now that her mother was gone, it was hard for Sara to admit, but she appreciated the cheap rent Dean still let her pay. Otherwise, she wouldn't be able to take this college course.

A picture of Mama on the end table to the right of the couch caught Sara's attention. It had been taken at Christmas two years ago. Mama wore a Santa hat on her head and a silly grin to match. Sara couldn't remember her mother ever being anything but pleasant. She was a kindhearted person with a positive attitude. Sara enjoyed the humorous side of her too. She remembered how one day when Mama had done her pretty auburn hair in a new style, she'd gone to bed that night with a silk nightcap over her curls. Kenny made fun of the way she looked, but Mama just laughed and said, *"I'm sure this must be how all the glamorous movie stars keep their hair looking so perfect all the time. And if it's good enough for them, it's just what I need."*

Chuckling at the memory, Sara flopped onto the couch and jammed the blue-and-white, quilted throw pillow her mother had given her several years ago between her knees. *"It's for your hope chest,"* Mama had said. *"Someday after you're married or living on your own, you can put it on your own bed or couch."*

"Seeing as I've never had a serious boyfriend, I doubt I'll be getting married anytime soon," Sara muttered. "But at least I'm living on my own and have a nice couch to curl up on."

Sara hadn't been the social type during high school or even

after starting college. She was a nose-to-the-grindstone kind of person, always making her schoolwork and part-time jobs her priority.

The pillow slipped, and she grabbed it, holding the soft cushion against her chest as more memories of her mother flooded her mind. Sara wondered if she would ever adjust to not having Mama around. Tears sprang to her eyes as she untied the scarf she wore and pulled it from around her neck. It was the same one she'd given to her mother, and she wore it often, just to feel closer to Mama. Sometimes Sara tied it through the side loop of her jeans, and occasionally she carried it in her purse. Having the scarf close made it seem as if a part of her mom was always with her.

At this stage of her grief, Sara needed all the reinforcement she could get, even if only from a blue-and-black scarf. Oh, how she missed the times she and Mama would sit and enjoy a cup of coffee or tea together while they engaged in conversation. It had become a fun routine for Sara to walk next door and catch up with Mama for a while each day. But now, all she had left were the memories.

Years ago when Mama married Dean, Sara had resented him—especially when he began telling her what to do. He wasn't her father, after all, and clear into her teen years, Sara's bitterness toward him grew.

*But who is my father?* she asked herself for the umpteenth time. *Why did Mama refuse to tell me his name or say anything about him?* Not knowing was a hard pill to swallow.

Closing her eyes, Sara squeezed the pillow tighter. A bigger grudge seemed to be seeping around every corner of her heart. *My mother is dead, and I'll probably never get to meet my real dad unless my grandparents can provide me with that information.*

She opened her eyes. *I don't understand why they haven't responded to either of my letters. Maybe they don't live at that address anymore. For all I know, they could have moved or even died.* Sara wished she was free to go to Strasburg immediately and find out for herself. But in addition to needing to be here for class, her car had started sputtering on the way home, insurance was due, and she also needed new tires. So even a short trip out of town was out of the question at the moment. Hopefully by the time she was able to make the trip, things would improve.

⤙⤚

*Strasburg*

"Where are you going?" Ezekiel's twenty-year-old sister, Amy, asked when he shoved on his straw hat and headed for the back door. "Don't you know supper's almost ready?"

He turned to look at her. "I realize that, but I'm going to the Lapps' house for supper tonight."

She squinted her blue eyes at him. "Willis and Mary Ruth Lapp?"

He nodded. "I took them a big jar of hunnich earlier today, and Mary Ruth invited me to come back for the evening meal." Ezekiel made no mention of meeting their granddaughter or the fact that it was Sara's birthday. Amy, curious as she was, might try to make something of it.

His sister's petite hands went straight to her hips. "As I'm sure you must know, Mom and Dad went away for supper this evening, leaving me to cook for you, Abe, and Henry." She gestured to the stove. "And in case your sniffer isn't working well right now, I'm making your favorite fried chicken. In fact, it'll be done shortly."

Ezekiel felt bad, running out on his sister's good meal, but he was curious about the Lapps' newly found granddaughter and looked forward to getting to know her better, so he wasn't about to stay home.

"Sorry, Sis, but I told Mary Ruth I'd be there. I had no idea you were making fried chicken." He moved back across the room and gave her shoulder a light tap. "I'm sure our brothers will enjoy the tasty meat, and whatever else you're making to go with it. I'll have to settle for leftovers tomorrow—if there are any, that is. You know I like fried chicken cold, just as well as when it's hot."

Nodding, Amy lifted her shoulders. "Okay, but don't blame me if Abe eats all the *hinkel*. Fried chicken's his favorite meal too."

Ezekiel snickered. "That eight-year-old brother of ours is a growing boy, and he likes a good many foods. Bet he could eat a whole cow in one sitting."

Amy lifted her gaze to the ceiling, then waved her hand at him. "Go on with you now, and tell Mary Ruth and Willis I said hello."

"Will do." Ezekiel went out the door, calling, "See you later, Sister." First, he needed to stop at the greenhouse to pick out a plant for Sara, and then he'd hitch up Big Red and be on his way.

~⊃∾~

"Happy birthday, Sara." Lenore smiled when she entered the house and handed Michelle a small box wrapped in pink tissue paper.

Embarrassed, Michelle felt warmth flood her face. She hardly knew what to say. It had been a long time since anyone cared enough to give her a birthday present. But of course, the gift Lenore brought really wasn't meant for her. This pretend cousin thought she was giving Sara Murray a birthday present.

Michelle took the gift and managed to murmur her thanks. "You didn't need to bring me anything though."

"I wanted to. Besides, it's a privilege for me to help celebrate my new cousin's birthday." Lenore's sincerity showed in her pretty hazel eyes.

Michelle gazed at the package. "Should I open it now or wait till after we've eaten supper?"

"Why don't you wait?" Mary Ruth suggested, joining the girls in the living room. "Supper's almost ready, and we'll eat as soon as Ezekiel gets here."

Ezekiel?" Michelle tipped her head.

"Yes, dear one." Mary Ruth looked at Michelle affectionately. "He's the young man who brought the honey today." She glanced at Lenore. "Since you and Ezekiel are friends, I thought it would be nice if he joined us. Oh, and I wanted him to get to know Sara too," she quickly added.

Michelle didn't know who was more surprised at this—she or

Lenore, whose forehead had wrinkled. *I wonder if my pretend cousin doesn't care much for Ezekiel.* Truthfully, Michelle's brief encounter with him today hadn't impressed her. Of course with him seeing her face-down in the mud, he probably didn't think much of her either.

Mary Ruth gestured to the sofa. "While we're waiting for Willis to get out of the shower and Ezekiel to arrive, why don't you two take a seat so you can visit?" She turned toward the kitchen door.

"Aren't you going to join us?" Michelle asked. She didn't feel comfortable being left alone with someone she barely knew. What was there for them to talk about?

"I still have a few things left to do in the kitchen," Mary Ruth replied.

"Is there anything I can do to help?" Lenore was quick to offer.

Mary Ruth shook her head. "Just relax and enjoy yourselves. I'll let you know if I need help with anything." Smiling cheerfully, she ambled out of the room.

Michelle took a seat on the couch, and Lenore did the same. "Aren't you afraid to drive a horse and buggy all by yourself?" Michelle asked, for lack of anything better to say.

"No, I'm used to it and have driven one for a good many years now. When I'm not teaching, I like to help out by running errands for my mother and sometimes my dad. It's a help, especially to Mom if she's busy with something at home," Lenore added.

"So how far is it from your home in Paradise to here? That's where Mary Ruth—I mean Grandma—said you live, right?" Michelle's fingers, toes, and every part of her body tingled. She'd been so afraid she would trip up and say something wrong, and sure enough, she'd done it. *I have got to remember to call the Lapps Grandma and Grandpa. If I'm not careful, sooner or later, someone will catch on that I'm an imposter.* She twirled the ends of her hair around her fingers and tried to relax. *Of course, my calling Mary Ruth by her first name might not seem so strange to Lenore. After all, she thinks I've just recently learned that the Lapps are my grandparents. So it's only natural that I wouldn't think of them as my relatives yet.*

Lenore nodded. "Our home is only about nine miles from here."

"Oh, I see." Michelle wasn't sure what else to talk about, but Lenore had some questions of her own. "How do you like it here in Lancaster County? Are you getting used to life on the farm?"

"Well, I haven't been here long enough to decide. But so far it seems to be going well." Michelle gave her tingling earlobe a tug. "I am curious about one thing though."

"What's that?"

"My only encounter with any Amish has been the few I have met since coming here. I was wondering if other Amish communities in different parts of the country were the same as in Lancaster County."

Lenore shook her head. "Various areas are definitely different, although many of the differences are subtle."

"Such as?" Michelle kept her focus on Lenore, eager to hear her response.

"There are different styles for the men's hats and prayer coverings for the women. Also, the length and color choices of Amish women's dresses can vary. Even the types of suspenders the men wear can be different."

"Interesting." Michelle shifted her position on the couch. "Is that all?"

"No. In Lancaster County we ride scooters, but in other places—like certain Amish communities in Indiana, Illinois, and Ohio—they are allowed to ride bicycles."

"Why is that?"

Lenore shrugged. "It's whatever the church leaders decide. You see, some groups of Amish are allowed to use cell phones, especially if they are business owners, but others can't have a phone at all. Of if they do, it must be kept in a phone shed or inside the barn, but it must be outside the home."

"Lots of rules then, huh?"

"Yes, but they all serve a purpose. In some areas the farmers are allowed to have a tractor, but some cannot. Oh, and some Amish can have rubber tires, while others can only have iron wheels."

"What about indoor plumbing? Do most Amish homes have hot and cold running water in the house like my grandparents do here?" The more Michelle learned, the more interested she became. The Amish were truly a fascinating group of people.

"Most Amish do have indoor plumbing these days," Lenore replied, "but there are still some in the plainer, more conservative districts that use outhouses."

Michelle wrinkled her nose. "Eww. . . Don't think I could ever get used to that."

As quickly as the subject of church rules and differences in communities had been brought up, Lenore changed the subject. "I never got to meet your mother, but my dad talked about her all the time. He really misses his sister and has talked about their childhood a lot."

All Michelle could do was smile. She was at a loss for words.

Lenore giggled. "I have two brothers, and I'm close to both of them, so I can only imagine how hard it would be if one of them ran off and we never saw him again."

Michelle frowned. This conversation had turned too negative. But before she could think of anything else to say, Lenore spoke again.

"From the things Dad has said, it seems as though he and Aunt Rhoda had a fun childhood."

Michelle held her breath. She thought sure Lenore would say more about the Lapps' daughter, and how she left home without a trace, but fortunately, the conversation changed again.

"How long do you plan on staying here with our grandparents?"

Michelle released her breath and answered carefully. "I'm not sure. I'd like to stay through the summer, but it all depends."

"Grandpa and Grandma would like that." Lenore smiled. "They'd probably be happy if you stayed with them indefinitely."

Michelle squirmed, feeling more uncomfortable by the minute. *If they knew who I was they'd be glad to see me go.* She cleared her throat and asked a question, hoping to calm herself.

"What's it like teaching Amish children?" she asked, changing the subject. "Did you have to go to college and get a degree in order to teach?"

"Oh no." Lenore shook her head. "I graduated eighth grade, like all other Amish scholars, but I didn't get any other schooling, except learning how to work at my dad's general store. You see, when an Amish child graduates eighth grade, they most always learn a trade. Or at the very least, they'll end up working in a relative's place of business."

"Really? How come?" Michelle didn't see how anyone could be a schoolteacher without getting a degree. And the thought of only going through the eighth grade instead of graduating from high school seemed strange to her.

"We Amish have always believed that too much education can make a person proud. To us, an eighth-grade education is sufficient." Lenore shifted her position. "However, once a student graduates, they further their education by training as apprentices for their future jobs. In my case, I had excelled when I was attending school, and it pleased me when the members of our Amish community approved me as a teacher." Lenore's upturned face radiated the joy she obviously felt because of being a schoolteacher.

"One thing you might find interesting about our Amish schools is that we have a special Christmas program every year, where the scholars get to share poems, recitations, and songs for their families. The children will often exchange gifts with others in their class." Lenore's face brightened even more. "It's a joyous occasion, and one that both teacher and students look forward to during the Christmas season."

Michelle picked at a hangnail that had made an appearance this morning shortly after she'd helped Mary Ruth do the dishes. "That's all very interesting, Lenore. Thanks for explaining."

Her pretend cousin gave a nod. "If you have any other questions, let me know. I'd be happy to answer them for you."

"Okay, I will." In some ways, Michelle wished she'd been able to end her education after the eighth grade. But if she had, it would have been a lot harder to get a job—even one waiting tables or taking orders at a coffee shop. A lot of employers wanted their employees to have at least a high school degree. Of course with the Amish, it was different, since most places of business where Amish people worked hired them based on their ability to do the job well. This was something else Michelle had learned by watching the reality show. It was one of few things they'd mentioned that actually made sense. And since Lenore had just said Amish young people learned some kind of a trade after they finished their formal education, Michelle figured that part of the segment she'd seen on TV must be true.

At the sound of a horse and buggy, Michelle turned her head. *Oh great, that must be Ezekiel. I can't believe Mary Ruth invited him to join us for supper.*

⁓

When Ezekiel knocked on the door, he was greeted by Willis, whose damp hair gave evidence that he'd recently taken a shower.

"Evening, Son. Glad ya could join us tonight." Willis swiped at a drip of water rolling down his forehead.

Ezekiel grinned and sniffed the air. "Me too. Something smells mighty good in here."

"That would be my fraa's special pasta sauce. Spaghetti's one of Sara's favorite meals, so that's what Mary Ruth is fixin' tonight." Willis gestured to the first room off the hall. "Lenore's here. Let's join her and Sara in the living room while we wait for Mary Ruth to call us for supper."

When Ezekiel entered the living room, he found Sara and Lenore sitting on the sofa beside each other. Feeling a bit awkward, he stepped forward and handed Sara a purple African violet. "Happy birthday."

Her eyes widened a bit, and her fingers trembled slightly as she reached out to accept his gift. "It's beautiful, thank you. I certainly wasn't expecting a gift from you." Sara looked at Lenore. "Or you either."

Lenore smiled. "Everyone should get a present on their birthday."

Mary Ruth entered the room, and seeing Ezekiel, she said, "I'm glad you're here. We can eat our supper now."

"Look what Ezekiel brought for Sara." Willis pointed to the plant Sara held.

Mary Ruth leaned in closer and gave an approving nod.

Ezekiel handed Sara something else. "Here is a small saucer you can put under the African violet. There are holes in the bottom of the pot it's planted in, and instead of waterin' it from the top, like you'd do for most other potted plants, you'll need to water this one from the bottom."

"Okay." Sara's uncertain tone let him know she was a bit confused. "How does that help the plant?"

"After you put the water in the saucer, it will get drawn up into the dirt through the holes at the bottom, and the roots will grow downward, toward the moisture."

She nodded. "Thanks, I didn't know that."

"Once your plant gets established and it grows a little bigger, you can even take one of the leaves and put it in water."

Her nose twitched as she stared at the plant. "How come?"

"After some time passes, you'll eventually see tiny little roots coming out of the bottom of the violet's leaf," Mary Ruth said before Ezekiel could respond. "Once the roots grow more, you can plant the leaf, and it will start a new African violet."

Ezekiel bobbed his head. "We do that in the greenhouse to get new plants started."

Sara smiled. "That's amazing."

"Years ago, when the African violet my mother gave me got too big, I used to take leaves from it to start new plants," Mary Ruth continued. "Once they began to grow, the smaller plants made for nice gifts."

"She still has her mother's African violet. It's in our room, sitting by the window," Willis added.

"Since Sara has already received one gift, would it be all right if she opened mine now? It shouldn't take long." Lenore gestured to the present sitting on the coffee table.

"Go right ahead, Sara. Supper can wait a few more minutes."

Sara set the African violet on the table and picked up Lenore's gift. Her fingers trembled once more as she tore the paper off and opened the lid on the box.

Ezekiel wondered why she seemed so nervous. Surely she was used to receiving gifts on her birthday. But maybe not from people she barely knew. He watched with interest as she removed three rubber stamps, two ink pads, and some cardstock. Sara stared at the items like she'd never anything like them before.

"Have you ever done any stamping and card making?" Lenore asked.

Sara shook her head.

"Well, that's okay. I'll teach you. It'll give us something fun to do as we get to know each other better."

"Thank you." Sara pressed her fingers against her smiling lips. "This has been the best birthday ever."

"Well, it's not over yet." Mary Ruth moved toward the dining room. "We have our meal to eat, and then Willis and I have a gift for you too."

Willis nodded. "After that, there will be *kuche* and *eis raaham*."

"What is that?" Sara rose to her feet.

"It means, 'cake and ice cream,'" Ezekiel announced.

"Oh, okay." She looked up at him with a hopeful expression. "In addition to learning more things about the Amish way of life, I hope I can learn a few Pennsylvania Dutch words while I'm here visiting."

"Don't worry. We'll teach you whatever you want to know." Mary Ruth put one arm around Sara's waist and the other arm around Lenore's. It didn't take a genius to see how happy she was to have both of her granddaughters visiting.

Since he wasn't part of their family, Ezekiel almost felt like a fifth wheel on a buggy. But he'd always felt welcome in this home. Willis and Mary Ruth treated him kindly—almost like he was part of their family. Sometimes, he felt more comfortable here than he did at home, where his folks—especially Dad—were often critical of him.

Well tonight he wasn't going to think about that. He planned to enjoy a good meal, relax, and have a nice time. He was curious though about what gift the Lapps would give Sara after supper. From the gleam in Mary Ruth and Willis's eyes, he had a feeling it was something special.

# Chapter 9

This spaghetti is scrumptious, Mary—I mean Grandma." Michelle blotted her lips with a cloth napkin. Mary Ruth had set a lovely table tonight, using her best china dishes and fancy glassware. Apparently some things this Amish family owned weren't so plain. "My only complaint about the food is that I ate too much."

Mary Ruth smiled. "I'm glad you like it. While pasta dishes aren't traditional Pennsylvania Dutch meals, in this house we do enjoy spaghetti, pizza, and lasagna sometimes."

Willis bobbed his head. "Anything my fraa cooks is *appeditlich*." He winked at Michelle. "That means 'delicious.'"

"Appeditlich," Michelle repeated. "Jah, the meal is appeditlich."

Everyone nodded, even Mary Ruth. Michelle was certain the woman wasn't bragging. She simply enjoyed eating the spaghetti.

Michelle patted her stomach. "If I keep eating all this good home-cooked food, I'll get fat."

Willis looked at her over the top of his glasses. "A slender girl like you could probably eat twice as much as you did this evening and never gain a pound. I doubt you'll ever be *fett*." He winked. "That word means 'fat.'"

Michelle smiled. It had been a long time since she'd eaten food this good or with such nice people. Most of her meals since she'd been out on her own either came out of a can or a box that needed to be heated in the microwave.

Michelle glanced across the table, where Ezekiel sat next to Lenore. Had he been seated there because they were a couple? *Not that it's any of my business.* She looked away. *While I'm staying here, maybe I should ask Mary Ruth to teach me how to make some of her tasty recipes. I need to have something positive to take away with me when I leave—something besides the memories.*

"Would you like another piece of sourdough bread?" Mary Ruth asked, breaking into Michelle's thoughts.

"No thanks, I'd better not." She thumped her stomach.

"Oh, that's right." Willis grinned mischievously. "You need to save room for dessert."

"Oh my." Lenore held her stomach. "I don't know if I'll be able to eat any dessert."

"Me neither." Michelle shook her head. "I ate way more than I should have."

Mary Ruth looked at Ezekiel. "How about you? Have you got room for cake and ice cream?"

He nodded. "But I might need to let my supper settle awhile first."

"Not a problem. We'll wait an hour or so to eat our dessert." Mary Ruth got up from the table. "I'll put the dirty dishes in the sink to soak, and we can all go out to the barn."

Michelle's forehead wrinkled as she glanced at Lenore, who'd gotten up and quickly begun clearing away the dishes. Michelle did the same. She couldn't figure out why Mary Ruth wanted them to go out to the barn. *Maybe she wants to show Ezekiel Sadie's puppies.* If so, it was fine with Michelle. She looked forward to seeing them again.

⁓

"The puppies have grown since I saw them last." Lenore knelt beside the box and reached inside to pet one of the pups. "I was helping my mamm do the dishes while they were being born, but I'm glad she and I took the time to go out to the barn once we were done in the kitchen."

"Does *mamm* mean 'mom'?" Michelle asked.

"Yes." Lenore grinned at Michelle. "See, that's one more Pennsylvania Dutch word you have learned this evening."

Willis chuckled. "Pretty soon you'll be speaking the Dutch like you've lived here in Amish country all your life."

*I wish I could stay here for the rest of my life.* Michelle's chest grew heavy, knowing a happy life here with Willis and Mary Ruth was out of her reach.

"It's amazing how quickly puppies grow." Ezekiel's comment redirected Michelle's thoughts.

Mary Ruth gave Michelle's arm a little tap. "Do you have a favorite pup?"

"Yes, I do." Michelle leaned over and picked up the runt. "This little one has to struggle to get what he wants, so he's the one I'm rooting for." *Kind of like me. I've been struggling all my life and still don't have what I really want.*

Willis put his hand on Michelle's shoulder. "Well, he's yours. Happy birthday."

Michelle shook her head. "Oh no, I can't take the puppy with me when I leave. I don't even know where I'll be going."

Mary Ruth's forehead creased. "What do you mean, Sara? Won't you return to your home?"

"Um. . .yeah. . . I just meant. . ." Michelle wiped the dampness from her forehead. "I may not stay there. I might move someplace else."

"Where would you move?" Lenore asked.

Michelle put the pup back in the box and stood, massaging her temples. Her head felt like it was going to explode. "I. . . I'm not sure. The lease on my apartment will run out soon, and then I'll have to decide whether to renew it or move. Besides, I don't think my landlord would allow me to have a pet." Michelle was getting in deeper with added lies, but what other choice did she have? She had to make the Lapps keep thinking she was their granddaughter—at least until she was ready to leave.

"If you stayed here with us, you wouldn't have to worry about paying rent for an apartment or whether you could have a dog." Mary Ruth looked directly at Michelle. "You will think about it, won't you?"

Michelle nodded slowly. The thought of staying here held appeal, but it wasn't possible. It was only a matter of time before she would have to leave. While she was here though, she planned to enjoy all of Mary Ruth's and Willis's attention, as well as the sense of responsibility she was learning from them.

Willis gave Michelle's arm a tender squeeze. "We want you to have the pick of the litter. And if you're not able to take it, should you decide to leave, we'll keep the pup here and you can see it whenever you come to visit."

Michelle clasped her hands loosely behind her back as she gazed down at Sadie and her brood. "Thank you. It was a thoughtful gift, and I'm definitely going to claim the littlest pup."

"What are you gonna call it?" Ezekiel questioned.

Michelle directed her gaze to him. "I don't know. Any suggestions?"

He shrugged. "Guess you could just call it Runt."

"Or how about Tiny?" Lenore interjected.

Michelle sucked in her lower lip. "I suppose either of those names could work, but I'd like it to be something unique."

"Well, I think I'll leave you three young people here to figure it out while I go inside and get things ready for dessert." Mary Ruth tapped her husband's arm. "Are you coming, Willis?"

He hesitated a moment, then nodded. "I'll put a pot of coffee on, while you get out the plates and whatnot."

She smiled and gave his full beard a little tug. "I'll wait to cut the cake and take out the ice cream until our granddaughters and Ezekiel come in."

Michelle watched as Willis and Mary Ruth ambled out of the barn, holding hands. While she'd never asked how old they were, she figured they were both probably in their late sixties. They hadn't given into old age by any stretch of the imagination though. Despite their slower gaits, they kept moving and doing chores. Truth be told, some people their age would have a hard time keeping up with Mr. and Mrs. Lapp. Michelle hoped by the time she became as old as they were, she'd have even half their determination and energy. Was it wishful thinking that one day she too might have somebody special to grow old with?

Leaning his full weight against a wooden post, Ezekiel watched Sara sitting on a bale of straw, holding her puppy. The light from the battery-operated lantern overhead shone down on her head. He noticed that she wore very little makeup. She didn't need it. Sara was a natural beauty. Her creamy complexion, slender features, and pretty auburn hair were enough to turn any man's head. Ezekiel figured Sara probably had a boyfriend, or at least dated a lot of men. In fact, he was surprised she wasn't married by now. Of course, Ezekiel was close to her age, and he wasn't married. For that matter, Lenore was still single, and to his knowledge, she'd never had a serious boyfriend.

Lenore stood up. "Most of the puppies are either sleeping or eating now, so I think I'll head back to the house and see if Grandma needs help with anything." She turned toward Sara. "Feel free to stay out here for a while longer with your furry little birthday present. It'll probably be another fifteen minutes or so before our dessert is ready to eat. I'll ring the bell on the back porch to let you both know when it's time."

Ezekiel nodded, and Sara smiled. "Okay."

After Lenore left the barn, Sara stood up and put the puppy back in the box. "I don't want this little rascal to miss out on a meal, and I'm thinkin' maybe we should go back to the house. I wouldn't want to miss out on the cake and ice cream."

Ezekiel stepped up next to her. This was the first time he'd had the chance to speak to Sara alone, and he didn't want to miss it. "Lenore said she'd ring the bell when it's ready. Besides, the cake and ice cream are in honor of your birthday, so I'm sure they won't eat without you."

She dipped her head slightly and giggled. "I guess you're right." Sara kept her attention focused on the box. "Would it be dumb if I called the pup Rascal?"

He shook his head. "If ya ask me that sounds like a good dog's name."

"Glad you like it." Sara started moving toward the barn door.

"Before we go in, could I ask ya a question?"

She stopped walking and turned to face him. "What do you want to know?"

He came alongside her. "I was wonderin' if you like being English."

She tipped her head. "In what way?"

"In all ways. Do you enjoy everything the English life has to offer?"

Sara's long hair swished back and forth as she shook her head. "Not even."

"Not even what?"

"It's a figure of speech. I don't begin to like everything about the English way of life." She pursed her lips. "But I was born into it, so I really have no choice."

"Your mother was Amish, and she left her family to become English, so she must have seen something good in it."

Sara crossed her arms, staring blankly across the room as though she could look into her past. "I can't say what it was. She never talked to me about her reason for leaving the Amish faith or what she thought was good about being English." She looked back at him. "Does that answer your question?"

"Sort of, but it doesn't tell me what it's like to live in the English world."

"Let's just say, it's not all it's cracked up to be." Sara turned and started walking toward the door again. "I'm going back to the house now. Are you coming?"

"Yeah." As Ezekiel shuffled his feet across the yard, while she practically ran toward the house, his thoughts turned inward. He was past the age most young people got baptized and joined the Amish church, and his parents had been hounding him to do it. But Ezekiel wasn't ready to commit, and he wished he knew what road he was meant to travel. Would he be happier if he were English, or would his life be more satisfying if he remained here and joined the Amish church?

# Chapter 10

When Michelle came downstairs Sunday morning, a knot formed in her stomach. Mary Ruth and Willis would be leaving for church after breakfast, and they had invited her to go with them.

She'd never been to an Amish church service and didn't know what to expect. Mary Ruth had explained a few things, like the fact that the service would take around three hours and a light meal would follow. Willis mentioned the sermons and songs would all be in German. Michelle wondered how she would make it, sitting for so long while listening to a language she didn't understand. Short of pretending to be sick, she saw no way out of going.

"Shoulda taken German instead of Spanish in high school," Michelle mumbled before entering the kitchen.

Mary Ruth set a platter of sticky buns on the table and smiled at Michelle. "What was that, Sara?"

Michelle shook her head. "It was nothing. I was thinking out loud."

"I do that sometimes myself." Mary Ruth gestured to Michelle's dark green, ankle-length skirt. "Is the skirt I made last week comfortable enough for you?"

Michelle looked down at the plain material and nodded. While it was nowhere near her normal attire, the elastic waist and lightweight material felt comfortable. She'd chosen a simple white blouse to wear with it, along with a pair of black flats. At Mary Ruth's request, Michelle had worn no jewelry or makeup today. In fact, since coming to live here, she'd pretty much given up wearing makeup and jewelry. Comfortable or not, this was Michelle's new image, and these days, no one from her past would likely recognize her.

"Since we will be leaving soon, I'm keeping breakfast simple this morning." Mary Ruth pointed to the sticky buns on the table. "There are also some hard-boiled eggs in the refrigerator, if you would like one."

"Thanks." Michelle opened the refrigerator and removed a brown egg. After cracking and peeling it on a paper towel, she took a seat at the table.

A few seconds later, Willis entered the room. "The horse and buggy are ready to go, so as soon as we're finished eating, we can be on our way to the Kings' place."

"Why are we going there?" Michelle asked. "It was my understanding that we'd be heading to church after breakfast."

"We will. Our church service will be held in Vernon's barn today." Willis peered at Michelle over the top of his glasses. "I thought we explained that we Amish don't worship in a church building. We take turns holding our bi-weekly services in one another's homes."

"If you mentioned it, I must have forgot." She couldn't imagine what it would be like to have church in a barn.

"That's right," Mary Ruth agreed. "If the house isn't big enough, we meet in a barn or shop on that person's property. Any building that's big enough to hold all the families in our church district."

"Oh, I see." Michelle realized she had a lot more to learn about the Amish way of life. She had a hunch she'd only scratched the surface. But with each thing revealed to her, she found herself becoming more fascinated.

Michelle sat next to Lenore on one end of a backless wooden bench, feeling out of place and hoping her presence didn't stick out like a sore thumb. She pursed her lips. *I wonder where that old saying came from. It doesn't make much sense, if you think about it.*

With her back hurting from sitting this way for the past hour and a half, it was difficult to stay awake. The slow monotonous hymns sung in a language she didn't understand seemed so repetitive. Although it was amazing to listen to this crowd of people singing in unison. As they sang one stanza after another, their a cappella music seemed to fill every corner of the barn, and drift to the rafters. Surely anyone within a five mile radius could hear the melancholy tones coming from the Kings' farm. And perhaps the music, sung with such sincerity, was heard all the way up to heaven.

Michelle shifted to the left a bit, trying to find a comfortable position and not bump into Lenore. *Wish Mary Ruth would have mentioned that we women would be facing the men during the church service.* She had noticed Ezekiel watching her a few times when he should have been looking at his songbook. *The* Ausbund. *I think that's what Lenore called it when the books were handed out.* To be polite, Michelle had taken one, but the only purpose it served was to have something in her hand to hold onto.

Some of the other young men in the service today had also glanced her way. No doubt they were curious about the young woman wearing her hair up in a bun, but with no covering. She wondered what everyone thought of her long skirt and blouse, instead of a plain colored dress with a white apron, like all the other women wore today. *They probably wonder who I am.*

Michelle clasped her fingers together and twiddled her thumbs, wishing the time would go faster. If she was going to stay with the Lapps through the summer months, they would expect her to accompany them to church. So she would have to get used to sitting here like this every other Sunday. It was either that or come up with some excuse to stay home.

The congregation stood, and Michelle resisted the temptation to sigh with relief as she joined them. A tall, bearded man began reading from the Bible. At least she thought it was a Bible. The book was black and looked like some of the Bibles she'd seen.

Michelle remembered Mary Ruth telling her that when a person needed to go out to stretch their legs or use the restroom, it was usually during the reading of the scriptures. She glanced around and saw several young mothers with babies in their arms leave the barn. A few men left with young boys too, and some of the older women as well. Mary Ruth remained in place, however, and so did Lenore.

Michelle fidgeted. *Do I stay or go?* With a need to give her back a rest, she scurried out the barn door behind a young pregnant woman.

Once outside, Michelle drew in a few deep breaths, although the air wasn't as fresh as she'd hoped it would be. The sun was out in full force, and the air felt humid and sticky.

Michelle walked around for a bit, to stretch her legs, until a swarm of gnats congregated around her head. *Great. My back is sore, and now I have to deal with these irritating bugs.*

Given the opportunity, she followed a couple of women into the house. Michelle needed a drink of water and the chance to use the restroom. She paused in the living room to ask one of the women holding a baby where the bathroom was. After being told it was down the hall, Michelle headed in that direction. There was a line outside the door, so she leaned against the wall and waited, hoping she wouldn't have to make conversation with anyone.

No such luck. The elderly woman in front of Michelle turned and offered her a friendly smile. "My name is Esther Fisher, and you must be Mary Ruth's granddaughter Sara."

Michelle nodded. *I wonder how she knew that. Guess news travels fast around here.*

"Mary Ruth and I have been friends for a good many years, and after Rhoda left home, I was deeply concerned." Esther's expression sobered. "Mary Ruth and Willis have suffered a great deal over the years, but having you come into their lives has brought them both joy and peace." She clasped Michelle's hand. "We are all glad you're here."

"Thank you." Michelle could barely get the words out. Not only had she deceived the Lapps, but she was basically lying to every person she met in their Amish community. Michelle felt a twinge of guilt, but not enough to end her charade. She was in a safe place—far from Jerry—and didn't need to worry about looking for work or wondering where her next meal would come from. She couldn't give this up—not yet anyway.

Ezekiel had been watching Sara when he should have paid attention to the songs they were singing. There was something about the Lapps' granddaughter that made him want to know her better. And it wasn't simply the fact that she was English.

As he stood during the reading of scriptures, he grew antsy. He'd seen Sara go out and wished he could follow. He would like the chance to talk to her again. But that wouldn't be acceptable behavior here at church. The men stayed together, and the women did the same. They even ate at separate tables during the noon meal. Although the service was here at his folks' place, it would still look bad if he went out and was seen talking to her.

Ezekiel popped his knuckles as he thought about Sara's birthday supper. It brought a smile to his lips, remembering how peaceful she'd looked holding the pup she named Rascal. He'd have to make another trip to the Lapps' home soon and see how the puppies were doing. It would also give him a chance to visit more with Sara.

"This is not the time or place to be popping your knuckles," whispered Ezekiel's cousin, Raymond, as he bumped his arm.

Ezekiel let his hands fall to his sides and glanced toward the barn door. Still no sign of Sara, and she'd been gone quite a while. *I wonder if she got distracted talking to someone in the house. Or maybe she's not coming back at all. Sitting in the stuffy barn all that time may have been too much for her.*

Ezekiel had seen that happen with a few other people—especially visitors who weren't used to sitting for so long and with no air-conditioning. Some young fellows who hadn't joined the church yet would go out during scriptures and not come back in till church was almost over.

Once when Ezekiel was in his early teens, a friend of his brother Abe walked out during scriptures and didn't come back. Ezekiel's dad later said that if any of his boys ever pulled a shenanigan like that, they'd be doing extra chores for at least a month. More chores held no appeal for Ezekiel, so if he left the building for any reason, he'd always made sure to return in a timely manner. Ezekiel's father held a tight rein on his children, but he'd never been physically abusive. For that much, he was thankful.

Ezekiel snapped to attention when Raymond bumped his arm again and pointed to the wooden bench they'd been sitting on. Scripture reading was over now, and everyone had taken their seats, in readiness for the first sermon.

Ezekiel glanced at the women's section. Lenore sat on the bench where she'd been before, but Sara's place was empty. He couldn't help but wonder what Mary Ruth and Willis thought about that. Surely they'd seen her go out, and they must realize she hadn't come in.

A few minutes later, with her head down and cheeks pink, Sara entered the barn and took her seat. Many heads turned in her direction, including Ezekiel's.

Sara clasped her hands and folded them in her lap. No doubt she was embarrassed, but at least she had come back.

# Chapter 11

"Where do you think you're going, Son? I was talkin' to you."

Ezekiel's skin tingled as his face warmed. "I'm going out to check my bee boxes," he mumbled, turning to face his father.

"You can do that later—when you're done working in the greenhouse."

Ezekiel drew a quick breath and released it with a huff. "Why can't Henry help in the greenhouse today? He's out of school for the summer and doesn't have much else to do."

"Not true," Mom spoke up from the other side of the greenhouse. "I've been keeping your little *brieder* busy with lots of chores around the yard and even some inside the house."

Ezekiel grunted. "Okay, okay. What do you need me to do, Dad?"

"For starters, all the plants in here need watering. And then..."

Dad's words faded as Ezekiel pulled his thoughts inward. He would do whatever needed to be done here, but during his lunch break, he planned to check his bee boxes, because that was important, even if Dad didn't think so. Afterward, he'd head over to the Lapps' place. If he could talk to Sara awhile, it might put him in a better mood. Since she wasn't Amish, maybe she'd understand the way he felt about certain things. No one here did, that was for sure.

As Michelle headed for the barn to check on the pups, she kicked a small stone with the toe of her sneaker, sending it flying across the yard. Yesterday at church had been horrible. Well, maybe not horrible, but certainly not what she'd hoped it would be. "Boy, I'm still sore."

Michelle rubbed the small of her back. Sitting for three hours on hard, backless benches had been difficult enough, but seeing so many people staring at her when she returned to the barn was embarrassing. Michelle hadn't planned to be gone so long, but after she came out of the Kings' bathroom, a pretty young woman named Amy had introduced herself as Ezekiel's sister. They'd ended up talking for a while, which made them both late returning to the church service. No one seemed to notice Amy when she slipped into the barn and took her seat. *Probably because they were all looking at me—the newcomer who didn't fit in.*

When church was over and the noon meal had been served, the only young people who spoke to her were Amy and her pretend cousin Lenore. Michelle had definitely been an outsider, but at least Mary Ruth, as well as a few of the older women, had engaged her in conversation. With the exception of Mary Ruth though, they were probably all merely trying to be polite to the newcomer.

Ever since Michelle was a child, she'd never really felt like she fit in anywhere. Even though she'd made a few friends since being out on her own, they'd mostly been poor choices. When people like Jerry, who had abused her physically and mentally, came into her life, she was duped into thinking they cared about her. Michelle had never received much nurturing and craved even the smallest kindness anyone might have offered her. But then, whenever her so-called friends' true colors showed, reality set in, and Michelle realized they'd only been using her.

*I've gotta quit thinking about this and focus on something positive,* Michelle told herself as she entered the barn. And what could be more uplifting than holding little Rascal? The puppies were innocent little creatures. They knew nothing more than being fed, finding a comfortable place to sleep, and having a little love showered on them. *If only life could be that simple.*

Michelle made her way over to the box and stood staring down at the litter. The pups were all nursing, and she didn't want to disturb them or Sadie, who napped while her babies fed.

*Maybe I'll sit over there awhile and wait till they finish eating.* She took a seat on a bale of straw and took a piece of gum from her shirt pocket. Michelle was about to unwrap it when a movement out of the corner of her eye caught her attention. "Why, it's a mouse," she whispered, not wanting to scare the little thing. The rodent scampered across a shelf, then darted behind a couple of old jars. Michelle watched as it went into a hole and disappeared.

While some people might have run screaming out of the barn upon seeing a rodent, Michelle had never been afraid of mice. She'd seen plenty of them during the years she'd lived at home with her parents. Her mom didn't keep the place clean, and her dad never fixed much of anything. The place was always a mess, so it was no surprise to see a few mice scurrying through it. Even some of the apartments Michelle had rented were occupied with the plump, long-tailed creatures.

Since the mouse was gone, Michelle focused on the glass canning jars. They looked old. Curious, she decided to take a closer look.

Michelle put the gum back in her pocket and went to get the stepladder that had been leaning against the wall near the barn doors. After hauling it across the room, she positioned the ladder in front of the shelf. Once she'd climbed it and taken a closer look, she knew for sure they were antique jars.

Michelle picked the first one up to inspect the bubbles in the glass, and spotted another jar behind it, only this one was a pale blue. But the pretty color wasn't what interested Michelle the most.

"Looks like there's a bunch of folded papers inside." Michelle turned the jar every which way and shook it, before pulling the wire back and removing the glass lid.

Holding the jar with both hands, Michelle returned to her seat on the bale of straw. She reached inside, retrieved a piece of paper, and silently read the message written there. *"Dear Lord, I know I'm not worthy, but please answer my prayers."*

Michelle pursed her lips. *I wonder who wrote this, and why did they put their prayer in this jar?* Eager to know what some of the other papers said, she pulled out another one.

*"Lord, I need Your direction. Show me the right path."*

Michelle's brows furrowed. *Whoever wrote these must be a religious person. Was it Mary Ruth? But why would she put her prayer requests in an old jar and leave it here in the barn, hidden behind other jars? Could it have been Mary Ruth's way of journaling her thoughts? Should I ask her about it?*

Michelle rolled the question around in her head, studying the other pieces of paper still inside the jar. *I better not. If she did write those prayers, they were personal. She might not want anyone to know about it. For some folks, some things aren't meant to talk about.*

Michelle heard whimpering coming from Sadie's box, so she put the two papers back in the jar, secured the lid, and returned it to the shelf. Some other time when she came out to the barn to look at the pups or do a chore for Willis, she would take the jar down again and read more.

Returning to Sadie's brood, Michelle reached into the box and picked up Rascal, careful not to disturb the other pups who lay close to their sleeping mother. The pup cried in protest as a little milk dribbled down his chin. According to Willis, the puppies' eyes should be opening soon—usually around two weeks after they were born. Michelle looked forward to watching the pups grow—especially Rascal. She hoped he would catch up to his brothers and sisters, but even if he remained the smallest, he'd always be her favorite.

"You're okay. I've got ya, boy." Michelle spoke soothingly as she carried Rascal to the bale of straw she'd been sitting on previously. She held the pup up to her face and giggled when the little fellow licked the end of her nose. Michelle inhaled the aroma of Rascal's sweet puppy breath. It felt comforting to sit here holding the pup and stroking its soft head. "Wish I could take you with me," she murmured, while Rascal curled up in her arms.

"Are you goin' somewhere?"

Michelle jumped at the sound of a booming male voice. A few

seconds later, Ezekiel made his way deeper into the barn and came to a halt next to her.

"You startled me." She shifted on the bale of straw. "I didn't hear a horse and buggy come into the yard."

"That's 'cause I came on foot." Ezekiel took a seat beside her, gently bumping her shoulder as he did so.

"You live quite a distance away. How come you walked over?"

"My horse threw a shoe this morning and the farrier can't come out till tomorrow morning. So it was either walk or ride my scooter." He gave a forced laugh. "It's kinda hard to ride one of those on a gravel road like what's out in front of the Lapps' place."

"I guess it would be." Michelle scooted over a bit. "Would you like to hold my pup?"

"Sure." Ezekiel held out his hands, and when she handed him Rascal, he nuzzled the puppy with his nose. "The little guy sure is cute."

"I'm one hundred percent in agreement." Michelle's posture relaxed. She felt contentment sitting here beside Ezekiel. He was easy to talk to, and he liked her dog. "So what brings you by today? Did you come to see Willis?"

"Nope. Came to see you."

"Oh?" Michelle couldn't imagine why he would want to see her.

"I wanted to talk to someone who doesn't complain about everything I do."

"Who's complaining about what you do?"

"My dad. I can never do anything right it seems. And to top it off, he wants me to take over the greenhouse someday." Ezekiel placed the sleeping pup in his lap. "But I have other plans."

Michelle wasn't sure if he wanted her to ask what his plans were or just listen. She would listen, but she wasn't concerned with his problem, because she had enough of her own to worry about.

"Want a piece of gum?" Michelle asked.

"Sure, why not."

Michelle took out the piece she'd previously put in her pocket and tore it in half. "I only have this one, but I'm willing to share it."

"Thanks." Ezekiel sat silently a few moments, chewing the gum, then lightly bumped her arm. "You never did answer my question."

"What question was that?"

"When I first came in I heard you say something about wishing you could take—I'm guessing, Rascal with you. Then I asked if you were going somewhere, but you didn't respond."

"Oh, I. . .uh. . .was just talking to the pup—saying I wish I could take him with. . ." Michelle stopped talking and cracked her gum.

Tipping his head, Ezekiel pursued his questioning. "You mean, take him when you leave your grandparents' house and go back to your own place?"

"Yeah, only I don't really have a place." Michelle bounced a curled knuckle against her mouth. "I mean I do have a place, but I may not stay there."

"How come?"

"Well, I might want to move. Besides, my landlord doesn't allow pets, so I wouldn't be able to take Rascal."

"Yeah, I remember you mentioning that on Friday. But you'll be comin' back here for visits, right?"

*No. When I go, I can't come back.* Michelle wished she could be honest with Ezekiel but instead added more to her lies. "Yeah, I hope to, anyhow."

"Willis and Mary Ruth would sure be disappointed if you didn't come back to see them."

All Michelle could manage was a brief nod as she heard a van pull into the yard. "I bet that's Grandpa and Grandma returning from their shopping trip. They hired one of their drivers to take 'em to some stores in Lancaster today."

"Makes sense. Especially if they had a lot of things to get. There isn't much room in the back of our carriages—even the market buggies." Ezekiel massaged his forehead. "That's why I want a car or truck of my own."

Michelle studied the curves of his face and along his jawline. "Are you serious?"

"Yep. I've wanted one for a long time, but my dad would pitch a fit if I bought one, much less drove it home."

"Guess that makes sense, since you're Amish and aren't supposed to drive cars. Right?"

"It would be true if I'd joined the church already, but I haven't, so. . ."

"You mean you're allowed to own a car?"

"Well, I would be if my dad was okay with it." Ezekiel grunted. "Some of my friends have a car. But Dad's made it clear he doesn't want me to buy one. Even said if I did, he'd never let me have it anywhere on his property."

It didn't take a genius to see how frustrated Ezekiel was over his dad's refusal to let him buy a car. *But there are worse parents out there, that's for sure. Just ask me. If only I could tell you, Ezekiel. . . I have the world's worst parents.*

"Mind if I ask you another questions about the Amish way of life?" Michelle asked after a lengthy pause.

"Sure. Ask away."

"Can anyone join the Amish church?"

His eyebrows shot up. "Why are you askin' me that question? Do you think you might want to join?"

Michelle leaned against the post behind her back. "No, of course not. I was only curious, that's all."

"Well, I guess anyone could join if they were willing to give up their modern way of life and abide by all the rules of the Amish church." He reached up and scratched a spot behind his left ear. "I think it'd be a difficult transition, though, 'cause there'd be many changes that would have to be made."

"Like what?"

"For one thing, they'd have to learn our Pennsylvania Dutch language. And of course change to the simple way of dressing." He pointed to Michelle's denim jeans. "An Amish woman would never be allow to run around in those."

She snickered. "No, I suppose not."

"Yep, in order to become Amish, an English person would need to give up most of the modern conveniences they'd become used to having." Ezekiel shook his head. "I suppose it could be done, but I doubt many could do it."

"You're probably right." Michelle stood. "Guess I should put Rascal back with his mother and go outside to see if Grandma and Grandpa need my help carrying in groceries."

"Yeah, sure. I'll help with that too." Ezekiel followed Michelle across the room and stood watching as she placed the puppy in the box.

"I hope things work out for you with your dad," Michelle said as they walked out of the barn.

"Me too, but it's kinda doubtful." Ezekiel's shoulders slumped. "But I'm gonna get what I want someday, regardless of how my dad thinks I should live my life."

Michelle wasn't sure how to respond, so she hurried her steps. Apparently, she wasn't the only person here with problems. Well at least Ezekiel wasn't lying to his dad. For Michelle, however, every day she was here brought more dishonesty. If she wasn't careful, pretty soon she might actually believe the lie she'd been telling Willis and Mary Ruth. Truthfully, she wished it wasn't a lie, for she'd begun to wish she were the real Sara.

# Chapter 12

"Oh, there you are, Sara. And it's nice to see you too, Ezekiel." Mary Ruth smiled when Michelle and Ezekiel joined her and Willis at the back of their driver's beige van. It was different than the one that had picked them up at the bus station in Philadelphia earlier that month.

"We were in the barn, looking at the puppies." Michelle reached in and picked up a paper bag. "I'll help you carry the groceries inside."

"I can help with that too." Ezekiel grabbed two grocery sacks. "It'll give me something constructive to do before I head back home."

"All right, but first I'd like you both to meet Brad Fuller. Our other driver, Stan, introduced Brad to us, and he will be driving part-time this summer whenever Stan's not available." Mary Ruth motioned for them to follow her to the front of the van, where a young man with medium brown hair stood talking to Willis.

Mary Ruth stepped up to him. "Sara, this is Brad Fuller. He's attending college in Lancaster and is planning to become a minister someday." She motioned to Sara. "This is our granddaughter Sara Murray. She's here visiting us for the first time, and since she doesn't have a car, she may call on you for a ride sometime."

Brad held out his hand. "It's great to meet you, Sara."

"Nice to meet you too." Michelle struggled not to stare at his eyes. They were the most vivid blue—almost mesmerizing. He gave a brief smile, while Michelle pulled her gaze aside.

Mary Ruth introduced Ezekiel, and the men shook hands.

"In addition to driving for some of the Amish in the area, I'm also available to do odd jobs," Brad explained. "I'm open to do just about anything during the summer months, but in the fall I will go to a university in Clarks Summit, Pennsylvania, to earn my master of divinity degree. It's just north of Scranton—about 146 miles from here." He pointed upward. "I'm following a call God placed on my life when I was a teenager."

Michelle couldn't imagine anyone being so devoted to God that they'd want to become a minister, much less spend all that money on college. But then Willis was a minister in his Amish church, and he seemed like a pretty normal man. And from what Mary Ruth had told her, Willis didn't attend college or even take a home-study course to achieve that position. He'd acquired the unpaid job during the drawing of lots. She'd explained that only married men who were members of the local Amish church were eligible for a ministerial position.

The ordination was usually held at the end of a communion service. Men and women who were church members would go to a designated room in the house and whisper the name of a candidate to a deacon, who would then pass the name on to the church bishop. The names of those men who'd received three or more votes were placed in the lot. Those in the lot were asked if they were in harmony with the ordinances of the church and articles of faith. If they answered affirmatively, they were to kneel in prayer, asking God to show which man He had chosen.

Next, a slip of paper with a Bible verse on it would be placed in a songbook, randomly arranged with other songbooks, the same number as equal to the candidates considered. Seated around the table, the men who were candidates were supposed to select a songbook. When they opened the books, the lot fell on the man who had the slip of paper with the Bible verse inside.

Mary Ruth also mentioned that the term of office for a minister was usually for life. She had told Michelle that each Amish church district had a bishop, two ministers, and one deacon, who were called from within the congregation via the drawing of lots.

"Well, I need to get going. There's someone else I need to pick up." Brad broke into Michelle's thoughts when he spoke and handed her a card. "Here's my number. Feel free to give me a call whenever you need a ride."

"Thanks, I will." She grabbed another grocery bag from the back of the van and followed Mary Ruth, Willis, and Ezekiel to the house. Maybe when it was time to leave the Lapps' house for good, she would call on Brad for a ride to the bus station.

As Brad pulled his van out of the Lapps' driveway, he thought about his meeting with their granddaughter. He was surprised Sara wasn't wearing Amish clothes. Could she or her parents have been Amish at one time and left the faith? Brad wasn't an expert on the Amish way of life, but he'd heard from Stan that some Amish young people chose the English way of life rather than joining the Amish church. Maybe that was the case with Sara.

When a groundhog ran across the road in front of him, Brad slammed on the brakes. Some people might not have cared that it was only a groundhog, but Brad wasn't one of them, even if he didn't have a fondness for this type of animal. No matter what, they were all God's creatures, and he wasn't about to hit one on purpose.

"I need to keep my attention on my driving," Brad scolded himself as he sat back, letting the car idle. He removed a small notepad from his shirt pocket to look at the address again where he needed to pick up a young Amish mother who was taking her baby to a doctor's appointment. "There should be crossroads right up ahead, and then I need to turn left."

Looking into the rearview mirror, he saw a vehicle slowly coming up behind him. "Guess I better get moving." Putting pressure on the gas pedal, Brad glanced over into the field and saw the groundhog, standing on its hind legs. Shaking his finger in the critter's direction, he rolled down the window and hollered, "Good thing I saw you." Grinning at his reflection in the side mirror, Brad mumbled, "at least my eyesight didn't let me down."

Farther up the road, he saw the crossroad where he needed to turn. Approaching it, Brad put his signal on and turned left. The farm was only a few miles down the road.

Once more, the Lapps' granddaughter came to mind. *I wonder how long she'll be staying with the Lapps.*

Brad hoped Sara would call on him for a ride sometime. It would give him a chance to get to know her and ask a few questions. Sara was a beautiful young woman, but during their brief meeting, he had sensed something might be troubling her.

Brad had the gift of discernment, and his intuitions about people were usually correct. His mother often said he would make a good minister because he understood people and could almost see into the windows of their souls. Brad saw his intuitions as a gift from God—one that would help him counsel and minister to people.

⁂

"Thank you for helping me put the groceries away." Mary Ruth smiled as she and Sara put the canned goods on a shelf in the pantry.

Sara nodded. "No problem. I'm happy to do it."

"Brad seems like a nice young man, don't you think?"

"I guess so." Sara reached for a can of black olives and placed it on the shelf. "I didn't really talk to him long enough to form an opinion."

"Stan knows Brad's dad, and he gave him a good recommendation. He said Brad is dependable and a hard worker."

"I see."

"So we'll probably be calling on him for help with several things here at the farm this summer."

Sara grabbed a few more items and placed them on the shelf. "I hope he works out well for you."

It was probably wrong to be thinking such things, but Mary Ruth hoped if Sara and Brad got along well, it might give her a reason to stay. Not that spending time with her grandparents wasn't reason enough. But it would be good for Sara to spend time with a young person who had dedicated his life to serving God. While it was nice to see Sara and Ezekiel getting along well, Mary Ruth hoped he and her other granddaughter might get together. Of course, Lenore had become a church member and was settled into the Amish ways, but Ezekiel hadn't yet joined and seemed a bit unsettled. It was a concern to his parents and everyone else in their community.

Mary Ruth's brows furrowed. *I shouldn't even be thinking about any of this. It's none of my business who Sara, Lenore, or even Ezekiel ends up with. I just want the best for both of my granddaughters.*

"Did you and Grandpa stop by somewhere for lunch?" Sara's question pulled Mary Ruth out of her musings.

"Yes. We ate at the Bird-in-Hand Family Restaurant. How about you? Did you fix some lunch?"

"Not unless you count chewing a piece of gum."

Mary Ruth's brows furrowed. "How come you didn't eat the leftover chicken I told you was in the refrigerator?"

Sara shrugged. "I wasn't really hungry. It wasn't the first time I've gone without eating a meal."

Mary Ruth wondered what her granddaughter meant by that. Surely when she was a child Rhoda would have fed her regularly. She was about to ask when Willis sauntered into the kitchen.

"Looks like you two have all the groceries put away." He glanced at the fully stocked pantry. "I was plannin' to help with that, but after Ezekiel helped bring in the sacks, the two of us got to talkin' and time got away from me."

"It's not a problem. Our granddaughter was a big help." Mary Ruth gave Sara's shoulder a squeeze. "Makes me wonder how we got along without her."

"Thanks, I just like to help out." Sara dropped her gaze to the floor. "I appreciate being here, more than you know."

Mary Ruth looked over at Willis and noticed his wide grin. She felt sure he was equally happy to have Sara staying with them.

As Michelle lay in bed that night, she reflected on the jars she had found in the barn that afternoon. While she and Mary Ruth put the groceries away today, she'd been on the verge of asking her about those jars—especially the blue one full of folded papers. Michelle's curiosity had been piqued when she found the jar, and even more so after she'd read the two prayers. Would writing a prayer down on paper and then putting it in a jar, be better than saying a prayer out loud? Of course, from what she'd observed so far from living here, the Amish only prayed silently. But they might be inclined to write a prayer down if there was some special meaning behind it or they didn't want anyone else to know their thoughts.

Pushing her head deeper into the pillow, Michelle closed her eyes. The sound of crickets chirping through her open window each night was soothing. *Think I'll have another look at that blue jar the next time I'm alone in the barn. Maybe I'll find a clue as to who wrote those prayers.*

# Chapter 13

When Michelle finished breakfast and looked at the simple calendar on the kitchen wall, she was reminded that it was the last Friday in June. It didn't seem possible she'd been with Mary Ruth and Willis close to a month already.

Since coming here, Michelle had established a normal routine, and one of the first things she did every day after breakfast was get the mail. Fortunately, her pretend grandparents were okay with it, and even said they appreciated her willingness to help with so many things.

*If they only knew why I offered to get the mail, they might not be so appreciative,* Michelle thought as she stepped out the back door.

It was another warm day, already high with humidity. Michelle could only imagine how oppressive it would be by the end of the day. She hoped to get all her chores done before it got too hot, and then maybe she could go for a walk over to the nearby pond. It would feel mighty good to take off her shoes and wade in the shallow part of the cool, inviting water.

Michelle approached the mailbox and pulled down on the handle to open the flap. There were only two envelopes inside. She reached in to retrieve them, but as she was shutting the metal flap, both letters slipped from her hand.

"Oh great." She picked up the first one, but as a gust of wind came along, it carried the second letter out of reach.

As Michelle ran to retrieve it, the wind had its way with her again. To make matters worse, Sadie, who had followed her down the driveway, dropped the stick in her mouth and ran after the envelope like it was a game. Before Michelle could reach the letter, the dog snatched it and ran around Michelle in circles.

Michelle groaned. "Come on now. This is ridiculous. Sit, Sadie! Sit!"

To her surprise, the collie stopped running and dropped the envelope at Michelle's feet. "Whew!" Michelle leaned down, and gasped when she picked it up. Even though the envelope was soiled, there was no mistaking the return address. The letter was from Sara Murray.

She jammed it in her jean's pocket, then hurried up to the house. First stop was the kitchen, which she was relieved to see was empty. Mary Ruth was probably in the basement doing laundry.

Michelle dropped the other letter on the kitchen table and ran up the stairs to her room. After rolling her shoulders to get the kinks out, she flopped on the bed and tore the letter open.

> *Dear Grandma and Grandpa,*
>
> *I am concerned because I still haven't heard from you in response to my first two letters. I would still like to come see you when my business class is done. Since neither of my letters were returned to me, I have to assume you received them. Please write soon. I am eager to hear from you.*
>
> 

*Your granddaughter,*
*Sara*
> 

*Maybe I should write her a letter, pretending to be Mary Ruth. If I can get Sara to give up on the idea of coming here, or at least postpone it for as long as possible, I can relax and enjoy my time in Strasburg.*

Michelle took some paper and a pen from her nightstand and wrote Sara a letter, signing it, "Mary Ruth." The message stated that they had received her letters, but since summer was a busy time for them, they would prefer she wait until sometime in October to come for a visit.

It was devious, but Michelle had too much at stake to let Mary Ruth and Willis see Sara's letter, which of course would let them know Michelle was not who she'd been pretending to be. With barely a thought concerning her actions, she ripped up Sara's letter, and took the evidence outside to the burn barrel.

Once all traces of the evidence was gone, Michelle started back toward the house. Halfway there, she noticed Willis's horse and buggy at the hitching rail. She wasn't sure if he'd gotten back from someplace or was preparing to leave.

Michelle moved over to the rail and reached out to touch Bashful's long neck. The mare seemed gentle enough, nuzzling Michelle's hand, while slowly shaking her head.

"I wonder what it'd be like to drive a horse and buggy," she murmured, continuing to stroke the horse. "If Lenore can do it, why can't I?"

"Would ya like to find out?"

Michelle jumped at the sound of Willis's voice. She whirled around, surprised to see him standing a few feet away. "Oh, I didn't know you were there."

"That's 'cause I was in the barn." He grinned. "Just came out and saw you over here petting my horse."

"Are you going somewhere?"

"Nope. Just got back. Went over to talk with our bishop about a person in our community who told a lie that could hurt someone."

Michelle's heart pounded as her breathing accelerated. *Is it me? Have they figured out that I'm an imposter?*

His posture relaxed. "It's okay now though. The person in question admitted what they did was wrong and apologized to the one they had lied about."

Michelle sagged against the horse's flanks with relief. Quickly changing the subject, she gestured to Bashful. "She seems pretty gentle."

"Wanna try driving her?"

"You mean now?"

He bobbed his head. "Now's as good a time as any, don't ya think?"

"I guess so." Michelle's palms grew sweaty. She hadn't expected Willis to be so quick to jump on the idea. While Michelle did want to learn how to drive the horse and buggy, she wasn't sure she was ready.

"All right then, hop in the driver's side and take up the reins. I'll release the horse from the hitching post and get in the passenger's side." Apparently Willis thought she was ready.

Michelle's anxiety escalated, and she rubbed her damp palms along the sides of her jeans. "We're not going out on the road, are we?"

"Not yet. It's best if you work up to that. For today, we'll just drive around the place." Willis gestured to the open area on the other side of the barn. "It will help you get a feel for it. Sound good?"

Michelle hesitated a minute, before nodding. "Okay. Guess it shouldn't be too hard."

"Go ahead and get in." Willis opened the door on the right side of the buggy and instructed Michelle to take up the reins. Then he went around front to release Bashful from the rail.

It felt strange, sitting in what would be the passenger's side in a car, and even weirder not to have a steering wheel to control where the vehicle went.

Michelle's throat felt so dry she could barely swallow as she gripped the reins hard enough to turn her knuckles white.

Bashful's head bobbed up and down in a quick motion, and she snorted and pawed at the ground.

"Whoa girl, easy does it. I'm new at this, so give me a chance."

Michelle moistened her parched lips and cleared her throat, hoping to prepare herself for what was to come. *I can do this. Willis will explain everything, and it's gonna be fine.*

After Willis released the horse, he came over to the passenger's side and opened the door. He put one leg in the buggy, but before he could get all the way in, the horse backed up, and the buggy gave a lurch. The next thing Michelle knew, Willis was on the ground, and she was at Bashful's mercy.

# Chapter 14

W hoa! Whoa!" Michelle's hands shook so badly that she could hardly hold onto the reins. Poor Willis lay on the ground, while Bashful's hooves practically flew over the gravel as she jerked the carriage and headed in the direction of the driveway. No matter how many times she said, "Whoa!" or pulled back on the reins, Willis's stubborn horse ignored her commands.

A few seconds later, Michelle caught sight of Mary Ruth running out the back door. Waving her arms, she shouted, "Whoa, Bashful. Whoa now, girl."

To Michelle's amazement, the horse slowed to a stop. Mary Ruth caught hold of Bashful's bridle and led her back to the hitching rail.

As soon as the horse was secured, Michelle jumped down from the buggy and raced over to Willis, who'd managed to get to his feet. "Are you okay?" she panted, taking in several ragged breaths.

"Don't think anything's broken, but I fell on my arm, and it hurts like the dickens." Willis held it protectively against his chest.

Before Michelle could respond, Mary Ruth rushed over to them. "Ach, Willis, what happened?"

"I was gonna give Sara a driving lesson," Willis explained, "but before I could get in the buggy, Bashful backed up, and I fell."

Mary Ruth took a few deep breaths, as though trying to calm herself. "Better let me take a look at your *aarem*. It could very well be *verbroche*."

"I'm sure my arm is fine." He shook his head forcefully. "I don't have time for a broken arm. I've gotta take care of the hogs, not to mention all the other chores around here that need doin'."

Mary Ruth's hands went straight to her hips. "I'm going to the phone shed and call one of our drivers. You need to be looked at, just in case."

Willis held out his arm, wincing when he moved it around. "Don't think I could do this if it was broken."

Her forehead wrinkled as she turned to face Michelle. "Would you help me talk some sense into this stubborn man?"

Michelle wasn't sure if anything she said would make a difference, but at least she could try. "Grandpa, I think maybe Grandma is right. It would be a good idea to at least go to the clinic and have your arm checked out."

His face relaxed a bit as he slowly nodded. "I can see I'm outnumbered here, so okay, I'll go."

After Brad Fuller came to pick up Willis and Mary Ruth, Michelle headed for the barn. As she entered the building, she glanced at Bashful's stall, where Mary Ruth had put her before Brad arrived.

"Stupid horse," she mumbled. "You shouldn't have backed up unless I told you to. And you shoulda stopped when I said 'whoa.'"

Bashful whinnied, as though in response, and swished her long tail.

"Bad horse. Bad." Michelle shook her finger at the mare. "Shame on you for causing your owner to fall."

Bashful turned around and walked to the corner of her stall with her head hung low.

"Good, you need to stand in the corner and think about what you did." Michelle reprimanded the horse again, then paused and shook her head. "Look at me, talking to this horse as if she understands what I'm saying." As much as Michelle would like to learn how to drive a horse and buggy, it wouldn't be with this high-spirited horse.

Since the Lapps would be gone for a while, Michelle remembered the jars, but first she checked on the puppies and transferred them to the cardboard box, kept nearby. After she put fresh paper in the whelping bed, Sadie got in and looked up at Michelle as if waiting for her to bring the puppies.

Michelle snickered and, one by one, placed the pups inside the box with their mother. Sadie sniffed each one, and when they'd all been returned, the collie laid on her side, so the puppies could nurse.

Michelle watched them feed a few minutes, then glanced over at the shelves where the antique jars were kept. After hauling the stepladder over, she climbed up and took down the blue jar. With the Lapps gone, this was a good opportunity to read more of the papers inside.

She took a seat on the same bale of straw she'd sat on before, shook the jar to distribute the papers, and then removed the glass lid. After taking the paper nearest the top out, and unfolding it, she read out loud the words that had been written.

" 'Let us therefore come boldly unto the throne of grace, that we may obtain mercy, and find grace to help in time of need' Hebrews 4:16."

She sat quietly, rereading the Bible verse. Underneath it, in smaller print, a prayer had been written. *Lord, I am overwhelmed by my guilt. Please, have mercy on me.*

Michelle looked up, gazing at the rafters above her head as she attempted to gather her thoughts. *If Mary Ruth is the one who wrote these notes, then what did she have to feel guilty about? Could she have told a lie to someone? Broken some church rule? I wish I could come right out and ask her.*

Michelle lowered her head, focusing on the piece of paper again. *Why do I keep thinking Mary Ruth wrote the notes? It could have been Willis, or someone else. For all I know, these messages could have even been written by more than one person.* She wasn't sure why, but Michelle felt a compelling need to know.

She slipped the piece of paper back in the jar and took out another one. It read: *"Last Sunday during church, the bishop said we should ask God to reveal His will and show us what He wants* us to do. *That's what I'm asking now, Lord. Please show me what I should do.*"

One thing for sure, Michelle was certain whoever had written the notes must be Amish. Why else would they have mentioned what the bishop said during church?

Michelle looked up again. *Does God really show people what they should do? Did He show the person who wrote this note what he or she was supposed to do?* She bit the inside of her cheek. *Would God give me direction if I asked?*

She shook her head. *I'm not a religious person, and I've never been good at praying. He probably wouldn't listen to me.*

Michelle put the piece of paper back in the jar and secured the lid. Then she climbed up the ladder and placed it back on the shelf, behind the others. She couldn't rely on prayers to get her through life. She'd made it this far on her own and would continue to do so. No jar full of prayers or wishful thinking could change the course of her life. Michelle was on her own, and always would be.

As Brad approached the Lapps' home, he glanced in his rearview mirror. He was glad to be available to help them out, and pleased that Willis hadn't been seriously hurt when he fell. A bad sprain would heal, but he'd still have a hard time doing his chores with one arm in a sling.

When Brad pulled into the Amish couple's yard, he turned in his seat to face them. "I'm free to stay and help with any chores you might need to have done today, Mr. Lapp. No charge," he quickly added.

Willis shook his head. "I appreciate the offer, but I'm sure I can manage."

Mary Ruth scowled at her husband. "There isn't much you can do with only one hand, Willis." Before he could respond, she looked at Brad and said, "We'd be happy to have your help, but I insist on paying you something for your trouble. You have to earn a living, and from what Stan told us about your schooling to become a minister, I'm guessing you can use some extra cash."

Brad couldn't argue with that. Between the loans he'd taken out, plus money he'd borrowed from family members, he had quite a debt to repay. In some ways, he envied Amish ministers because they weren't required to get any formal training in order to preach God's Word. Even so, it was worth the financial sacrifice to answer God's call on his life.

"How about this," Brad said. "I'll do whatever chores you need to have done today for free, and if you have more things for me to do in the future, you can pay me. How's that sound?"

"It's more than fair." Mary Ruth smiled and nudged her husband's good arm. "Don't you agree?"

Willis nodded. "My wife can at least pay you for the ride you gave us to the clinic, and then I'll show you what all needs to be done yet today."

⁓

When Michelle heard a vehicle outside, she looked out the kitchen window and saw Brad's van pull up near the house. She hurried out the back door, eager to find out how Willis was doing.

Michelle watched as Mary Ruth and Willis got out of the van, and she rushed forward when she saw that Willis had his arm in a sling. "Is it broken?"

"Just a bad sprain." He looked over at Brad, who'd also gotten out of the van. "This nice young man volunteered to do some of my chores today, no charge."

Michelle glanced at Brad, noticing his dimpled smile. He was not only good looking, but charming as well. The fact that he'd volunteered to help Willis without pay made him almost too good to be true. Nothing like Jerry, that was for sure. Of course Michelle didn't know Brad well enough to make that call, but he seemed respectful—a rare quality, compared to a creep like Jerry. Maybe while she was here, they could get better acquainted. Michelle would have to think about it, but after Brad was done working, she might ask for a ride to the post office so she could mail her letter to Sara Murray.

# Chapter 15

It had been three days since Willis sprained his arm, and the doctor said it might take about three weeks to heal completely. He did a fair job doing a few of the simple chores with his good arm, but Mary Ruth, Michelle, and Brad did most of the heavier work.

The job of feeding the chickens, cleaning the coop, and gathering eggs had been assigned to Michelle. While they weren't her favorite things to do, her chores beat feeding the hogs. Brad took care of that chore whenever he had time to come over, and at other times, Willis and Mary Ruth managed the task together. This morning however, when Ezekiel stopped by, he'd volunteered for the job.

Michelle stood outside the chicken coop, watching as Ezekiel finished feeding the hogs and stepped away from their pen.

She moved across the yard to talk to him. "I see you got roped into helping today."

He shook his head. "I didn't get roped into anything. Came over here because I wanted to see you. After I arrived and found out about Willis's arm, I figured the least I could do was offer to help out."

"I'm sure my grandpa appreciates it." The longer Michelle was here, the easier it became to refer to Willis as her grandfather. Truthfully, she wished he was. She'd give anything to have grandparents like Willis and Mary Ruth. They were kind, caring, gentle people, with hearts as big as the sky. It was wrong to lead them on, but Michelle couldn't help herself. The longer she stayed, the more she wanted to remain here and be their real granddaughter.

Ezekiel snapped his fingers in front of Michelle's face. "What are you thinking about, Sara? You looked like you're a thousand miles away."

She blinked. "Uh. . .just thinking about the chickens, is all. So why'd you come here to see me?"

"Wondered if you were planning to go to the Fourth of July festival that's comin' up in two days."

She shrugged. "I hadn't heard about it, but I suppose it might be fun. Guess it'll depend on what my grandparents have planned."

"Yeah, that makes sense."

Michelle gestured to the barn. "Want to come with me to see the puppies?"

"Sure. Bet they've grown quite a bit since I last saw them."

"Yes, they have."

When they entered the barn, Sadie got up, stretched lazily, and ambled toward the door. Michelle figured the dog might be glad they were here. The pups would be occupied, giving Sadie a chance to go outside and be by herself for a while.

Michelle and Ezekiel knelt outside the new enclosure Willis had built for the pups before his accident. The height was just enough to keep them in, but low enough for Sadie to jump out whenever she needed to.

"Boy, they really have grown." Ezekiel reached in and lifted the largest one out, while Michelle took Rascal in her arms.

"I know. It's hard to believe they are three weeks old already." Michelle rubbed her chin against Rascal's soft head. "They opened their eyes last week."

"They're sure cute. And look how active they are." Ezekiel chuckled when one of the pups nipped at another one's leg. That puppy, in turn, pounced on a different pup, and soon they were all running around, yipping and chasing each other.

"Let's take the puppies we're holding and go sit over there." Michelle pointed to a couple of folding chairs.

After they sat down, each with a pup in their lap, Michelle was at a loss for words. Meanwhile the other puppies carried on even more, no doubt wanting some attention too.

"Now that you've been here awhile, how do you like it?" Ezekiel asked.

"My grandparents are wonderful, and I'm slowly getting used to living on the farm." Michelle scrunched up her nose. "There's one thing I can do without though."

"What's that?"

"The bugs. Especially those tiny little gnats. I hate it when they get in my hair or try to fly into my eyes." The skin around her eyes tightened. "It seems the more I swat at them, the more they like aggravating me. Truth be told, feeding the pigs is better than puttin' up with those pesky bugs."

Ezekiel chuckled. "Don't think anyone likes 'em, but it's something we all have to deal with."

"The next time I help Grandma in the garden, maybe I'll spray some bug repellent all over my clothes."

His forehead wrinkled. "That might not be the healthiest thing to do, Sara. Some of that bug spray is pretty powerful. Maybe you could try wearing a hat so they don't get in your hair."

"Guess I could try your suggestion, but will a hat keep them out of my eyes?"

"I think so."

Michelle shrugged her shoulders. "Anyway, at the very least, a hat might keep 'em from driving me so buggy." She snickered. "No pun intended."

He gave a wide grin. "Speaking of buggies, I heard Willis sprained his arm while trying to teach you how to drive his horse and buggy."

Michelle shook her head. "It never got that far. The poor man was knocked to the ground when he was trying to get in the buggy and his horse decided to act up. I tried to get Bashful to stop, but she wouldn't listen or cooperate with me. It was only when Grandma came out and hollered at the horse that she finally settled down." She lifted her shoulders with a sigh. "So I'll probably never learn how to drive a horse and buggy, and I was looking forward to it."

Ezekiel rolled his eyes. "Believe me, it's not that exciting. But if you really want to learn, I'll be happy to teach you."

"Really?"

"Sure thing. It'll have to be on a day I'm not working at the greenhouse though. Or maybe we could try early some evening."

"How come you're not working at the greenhouse right now?"

"We were caught up on things, and Dad said I could take off the rest of the day." He touched the tip of the puppy's nose and smiled. "Of course, I didn't mention that I'd been planning to come over to see you."

"Would your folks object to you seeing me?"

"I don't know. Maybe. Mom and Dad are worried that I might decide not to join the Amish church and end up going English."

Michelle pushed a wayward strand of hair out of her face. "Oh, and you think they believe being around me might lure you in the wrong direction?"

"Yeah, something like that."

"Don't you have other English friends?"

"A few."

"Then I don't see why my being your friend would make any difference to your folks."

"Maybe it wouldn't, but they might worry that we could end up seeing each other as more than friends." He glanced at her, then averted his gaze to the sleeping pup on his lap.

"Well, we wouldn't want them to get the wrong idea, so maybe it would be best if you don't teach me how to drive the horse and buggy."

Ezekiel shook his head with a determined expression. "No, it's okay. I'm old enough to do what I want, and I'd really like to teach you. As a matter of fact, I taught my sister Amy how to drive our buggy when she was in her early teens."

"I met your sister at church, the first time I went there with my grandparents. She seemed nice and was easy to talk to."

"Yeah, she's a good *schweschder*."

Michelle tipped her head to one side. "What's a schweschder?"

"The word means 'sister.'"

"Oh, I see. What other Pennsylvania Dutch words can you teach me?"

He rubbed his chin. "Well, let's see. . . Can you guess what *hundli* means?"

"I have no idea."

Ezekiel pointed to Rascal, sleeping contently in Michelle's arms.

"Does it mean 'puppy'?"

"Jah. And the word for dog is *hund*."

"Okay, I think I can remember that. *Hund* means 'dog' and *hundli* means 'puppy.'" Michelle smiled, feeling kind of proud of herself for learning a couple of new Amish words.

"Okay now, so what do you think about me teaching you how to drive a horse and buggy?"

"Sounds like a plan, only not with Bashful. After what she did to Willis, I don't trust her."

"We can use my horse then. Big Red's a large animal, but he's gentle as a kitten and listens well. I'll bet using him, I could teach you pretty fast."

"All right." Michelle bobbed her head. "Whenever you're free to begin, just let me know." She lifted Rascal into her arms and stood. "In the meantime though, I promised Grandma I'd help her pick peas." Michelle didn't mention it, but she had something else she needed to do first. Then she added, "Tomorrow, she's gonna teach me how to can them, which should be an adventure in itself, because I've never been all that handy in the kitchen." She wrinkled her nose. "My idea of cooking is sticking a frozen dinner in the microwave and turning on the power."

He laughed, and they made their way back to the puppies' enclosure, where the rest of Sadie's brood had all settled down and lay sleeping in various places—some practically on top of each other.

In all Michelle's twenty-four years, she'd never expected to become friends with some good-looking Amish guy in Lancaster County, Pennsylvania. But after meeting Ezekiel and Brad, she was coming to realize there were actually some nice guys in this world. Jerry could use a few lessons from both of them on how to treat a lady.

❧

"All right, boy, let's go!" Ezekiel snapped the reins, and Big Red took off toward home. He'd enjoyed his time with Sara today and hoped he would see her at the Fourth of July festival. The more time he spent with Sara, the more he liked her. If she stuck around long enough, he might even ask if he could take her out on a date.

*It's funny that Amy never said anything to me about talking with Sara. It was probably just girl-talk anyway. I wonder what my folks would say if they knew I wanted to court an English woman.* He reached under his straw hat and rubbed the side of his head. *Is that what I want to do, or am I only interested in the Lapps' granddaughter because she's English?*

Ezekiel thought about the truck he'd gone to look at, wondering yet again, if he dared buy it. The older model truck had been fixed up and looked as good on the inside as it did outside, which made it even harder to turn down. It was in mint condition, and according to his friend, "ready for the open road."

Ezekiel probably wouldn't be taking the truck on any long trips, but it would be great to have it to run errands and whatever else he decided to do. *Sure would be better than a horse and buggy or my scooter—especially in bad weather. And it would be safer too.*

Ezekiel was old enough to make his own decisions, so there was nothing his dad could do if he did buy the vehicle. *But then what if he doesn't let me park on his property?* That would make it difficult whenever Ezekiel wanted to go anywhere with the vehicle. And if he parked it at one of his relative's place, Dad would probably find out and start lecturing him again. The negatives seemed to outweigh the positives. It was a no-win situation. Unless Ezekiel decided to leave home and step out on his own, he might never be able to do all the things he longed to try.

"Decisions, decisions," Ezekiel mumbled. "Sure wish I knew what to do about that truck."

～⌒～

Remembering the letter she'd written and still hadn't mailed, Michelle stepped into the house. "Grandma," she called. "Are you in here?"

"Yes, Sara. I'm in the kitchen."

Michelle entered the room. "I know I promised to help you in the garden this afternoon, but would you mind if I went for a walk first?" She placed her hand protectively over her pocket, where the letter was safely hidden.

Mary Ruth looked at Michelle with a curious expression. "Is everything all right?

"Of course. Why wouldn't it be?" Michelle shifted uneasily. Did Mary Ruth find out she'd written a letter to the real Sara? Michelle had hidden the letter inside her suitcase, waiting for an opportunity to mail it. Unfortunately, she'd forgotten about it until now. It was important to get it in the mail today.

Mary Ruth put her hand on Michelle's shoulder. "You look a bit distressed. Did Ezekiel say something while he was here to upset you?"

"No, I just need some air and feel like going for a walk to clear my head. Do you mind? I won't be gone long, and when I get back I'll help you with whatever needs to be done."

"Of course you can go for a walk. I'll manage fine on my own till you get back." Mary Ruth smiled.

"Okay, thanks. See you in a bit."

As Michelle walked out of the house and headed toward the road, she felt like a traitor, leaving Mary Ruth alone to do the work by herself. But she needed to mail that letter. Once the deed was done, she could help with the peas and then enjoy the rest of her day.

# Chapter 16

Perspiration beaded on Michelle's forehead as she made the tre[k] from the post office back to the Lapps' place. She had know[n] where it was, having seen it a week ago when she went shoppin[g] with Mary Ruth, but hadn't realized the two-mile walk would tak[e] its toll on her in this heat. The hot weather wouldn't have bee[n] so bad, but the humidity was stifling. Michelle's clothes stuck t[o] her as she reached into her jean's pocket for a rubber band to ti[e] her long hair up in a ponytail. The creek she'd recently walked b[y] looked inviting, even just to soak her feet in the shallow end fo[r] a while. But there was no time to pause and cool off. Michell[e] wanted to get back so she could help Mary Ruth with the peas.

She could have called Brad or the Lapps' other driver, Stan, t[o] take her to the post office but had decided she didn't want to pa[rt] with what little money she had for such a short ride. And Michell[e] certainly couldn't expect Willis or Mary Ruth to pay for her rid[e] to the post office, especially if they'd known her reason for goin[g] there.

Well, the deed was done, and with any luck, it would guarante[e] her a few more months of living with the Lapps.

Michelle wiped her sweaty forehead and kept walking deter[-] minedly, her ponytail swinging back and forth across her sweat[y] back. In one respect, she felt guilty for her deception, becaus[e] Willis and Mary Ruth were nice people. On the other han[d,] what they didn't know wouldn't hurt them. Of course, they woul[d] find out sooner or later when the real Sara made an appearanc[e.] But Michelle wouldn't be around to see their displeasure wit[h] er act of deceit. Hopefully once she left, she would stop feeling ʊ guilty.

Michelle was about halfway back to the Lapps' when a horn onked, and a convertible pulled up alongside of her. Three young ɛllows sat inside, in addition to the driver, who looked to be round eighteen or nineteen years old.

"Hey babe. Where ya headed?" The guy in the front passenɛr's seat leaned forward and gave a shrill whistle.

Michelle looked straight ahead and picked up her pace.

The car cruised alongside of her, and a couple of the young ıen made some crude remarks.

Michelle wasn't sure whether she should run or keep walking t her current speed. Even if she ran, she couldn't get ahead of the onvertible. She didn't want these guys to know it, but she was ɛared. The best thing to do was try to ignore them, in the hope ıat they would drive on.

The last time Michelle had felt this frightened was when Jerry macked her face and then refused to leave her apartment. She was ɔrtunate that he went without a fuss, because the situation could ave gotten much worse.

When the driver pulled up ahead and onto the shoulder of ıe road, it blocked Michelle's path. The hair on the back of her ɛck and arms lifted as she froze in place. She wanted to flee or ıde, but there was no place to go. *Please God. Send someone to help ʋe.* It was the first prayer Michelle had said in a long time, but in ɛr desperation she couldn't think of anything else to do. Who new when another car would come by? Out here on these counɪy roads, the traffic was often light, and sometimes hardly any ɛhicles at all sped by.

A redheaded guy with a face full of freckles got out of the ackseat and moved toward Michelle. "Come on, babe. Hop on in, ıd we'll take ya for a ride. It's a mighty hot day, and cruisin' in a ɔnvertible's a good way to cool off."

When Michelle didn't answer, he added, "What's wrong, darn'? Ain't we good enough for you?"

The other fellows laughed, which only encouraged the red head. "Maybe you're just playin' hard to get."

Hoping he wouldn't know how truly frightened she was, Michelle forced herself to look at him. "I am not playing hard to get, and I don't need a ride. I'm almost home, but thank you just the same." Maybe showing some courage while also being polite would make them leave her alone. Unfortunately, this only seemed to aggravate the freckle-faced fellow.

"Oh really? And where's home?" He grabbed her arm roughly.

Michelle pressed both elbows against her sides, wishing she could make herself invisible. "It's up the road, and if you don't let go of me, I'll scream."

"Oh yeah? And who's gonna hear ya, except me and my buddies? I don't see nobody else around."

"You're wrong, Buddy." The driver of the car pointed to the farm across the road. "See those cows over there in the field? I'll bet they're gonna come over here and rescue the pretty gal."

The others in the car whooped and hollered, calling Michelle a few names she'd never repeat, while the one holding her arm pulled her against his chest.

Michelle's legs felt weak, like she might fall at any moment, but the firm grip he had on her right now kept her upright. This guy was so forward, he even reached back and took the rubber band out of her hair. Running his fingers through her long tresses, his face was so close, she could smell his stale breath.

"Nice." He picked up a thick strand of her hair and brought it up to his nostrils, inhaling a long slow intake of air. "Real nice."

Michelle choked back a whimper as he continued teasing her. *Please God, help me.*

She opened her mouth and was about to scream when a van that seemed to come out of nowhere pulled up behind the convertible. It gave her the opportunity and extra time to stomp on the pushy guy's foot.

"Ouch! Why you little—" He swung back his hand as if to slap her but backed off when the van door opened.

Michelle almost fainted with relief when Brad got out. What were the odds that he would come along just when she needed him? *Could it have been my prayers for help?*

<hr />

"What's going on here?" As soon as Brad stepped out of his vehicle, the freckle-faced guy limped closer to the convertible.

"Uh, nothin'. We were just seein' if she needed a ride."

"Well, she doesn't. So please get back in your car and move on down the road." Brad spoke calmly but with authority.

With a grunt and brief shrug, the red-haired fellow got back in the car, told the driver to go, and they headed on down the road.

As they sped off, Brad heard the driver shout at the guy who sat slumped in the backseat, "Way to go, stupid."

When Sara looked up at Brad, he couldn't help noticing her trembling lips, or the tears in her eyes. "Th—thank you so much. I can't believe you came along when you did."

"Did they hurt you?" His brows wrinkled as he studied her flushed face, feeling concern.

She shook her head. "I'm fine. Just a bit shaky inside."

"I'm glad you're okay." Brad gestured to his van. "Why don't you hop in? I'll give you a lift home. I assume that's where you were heading?"

"Yeah. I went out for a walk and had started back when those guys showed up." She opened the passenger's door and climbed in, while Brad went around to the other side. He shuddered to think of what might have happened if he hadn't come along when he did. *I need to get Sara's mind off what might have happened.*

"Can I ask you a question?" Brad asked, after he'd pulled onto the road and noticed out of the corner of his eye how Michelle twisted her pretty, long hair, holding it up off the back of her neck.

"Sure, go ahead."

"Stan mentioned that when you came to visit your grandparents, it was the first time you'd been there. I'm wondering why you'd never gone to see them before."

She stared down at her hands, clutched tightly in her lap, and drew a quivering breath. "Until a month ago, I didn't even know I had grandparents living in Strasburg."

"Didn't your parents tell you?"

"Umm... I didn't know till after my mom passed away."

"I see." Brad didn't push any further, since Sara was still clearly upset about her encounter with the guys in the convertible. But Brad had more questions he wanted to ask. And maybe he would once they got better acquainted.

"So tell me more about you." Brushing his arm with her hand, Sara glanced over at him. "I know you're studying to become a minister, but that's about all."

"What else do you want to know?"

"Just wondered where you are from. Is your home here in Lancaster?"

"Nope. I was born and raised in Harrisburg. Moved down here and rented a small apartment near the college I've been attending in Lancaster. But that was after I'd worked for my dad a few years."

"I see. So what does your father do in the capital of Pennsylvania?"

"He's a chiropractor. He and my mom hoped I'd follow in his footsteps and someday take over the business." Brad shook his head. "But that's not God's call on my life." He glanced over at Sara to see her reaction, but she sat staring straight ahead.

"I've known for some time that God called me to be a preacher," he added.

"Are your folks okay with it?"

"They are now but they weren't at first." Brad put on his blinker and turned into the Lapps' driveway.

When he pulled up near the house, Sara looked over at him and smiled. "Thanks for the ride and for coming to my rescue. You're my hero."

"No problem. I'm glad I came along when I did." Brad's ears tingled with the warmth spreading through them. He didn't want to be seen as a hero, but it was nice to be appreciated.

Sara opened the van door, but hesitated. Then she turned back to face him. "Do you have any plans for the Fourth of July?"

"Nothing special. I may drive over to the festival everyone's been talking about. How about you? Are you doing anything with your grandparents that evening?"

"I mentioned the festival to Mary Ruth—I mean Grandma. She said I should go if I want to, but I don't think either her or Grandpa plans to attend the festivities."

"I'd be happy to take you if you need a ride." Brad saw this as another chance to get to know Sara better.

"Actually, if I did decide to go, I'd planned on calling you to see if you'd mind driving me there. I would pay you of course."

He lifted a hand. "No payment is needed. Since I'd be going myself, I would be more than happy to give you a ride."

"Okay then, it's a date." Her cheeks colored. "I—I mean, I'll see you around seven o'clock on the Fourth."

He grinned. "I'm looking forward to it."

As Brad drove away, he smiled. He could usually figure people out after one or two meetings, but he had a feeling there was more to Sara that met the eye. The visible tension on her face and the way she kept looking away when they were talking told Brad there was a bit of uncertainty about her.

*Maybe I can draw her out.* He tapped the steering wheel with his knuckles. *With God's help, I might be able to help Sara deal with whatever is bothering her.*

❧

After Michelle said goodbye to Brad, she found Mary Ruth in the garden, picking peas.

Mary Ruth looked up and smiled. "I'm almost done—just one more row to go."

"I'll help you with it." Michelle hurried to the potting shed and got a container, a pair of cotton gloves, and a canvas hat she'd found on the shelf in her closet that morning. She'd taken it out to the shed after breakfast and placed it beside the gardening gloves. When she'd secured the hat on her head, she joined Mary Ruth in the garden.

"Where'd you get that?" Mary Ruth pointed to the hat when Michelle knelt on the ground. "I don't believe you've worn it before At least not since you came here anyway."

"Oh, I didn't bring it with me, Grandma. I found it on the closet shelf in the guest room this morning. Thought it might help keep the gnats out of my hair and eyes."

"Good idea. So how was your walk?" Mary Ruth asked as they picked the last of the peas.

"It was okay. Brad picked me up on the way home and gave me a ride back here." Michelle was not about to tell Mary Ruth about the encounter she'd had with the bullies in the convertible. She'd be upset and wouldn't want Michelle to go anywhere by herself Besides, other than shaking her up a bit, no harm had actually been done—thanks to Brad coming to her rescue.

"That was certainly nice of him. He seems like such a caring young man."

Michelle gave a nod. *I know that more than anything now.*

"I'm surprised he's still single."

"Maybe he doesn't have time for dating, with his school schedule and summer jobs."

"That could be. Or maybe he hasn't found the right woman." Mary Ruth gave Michelle a sidelong glance.

Michelle hoped Mary Ruth wasn't insinuating she might be that woman. After all, she hardly knew Brad. Although if she were being honest, she did find him attractive. But could Brad be interested in someone like her? She couldn't even imagine what it would be like to be married to a pastor. *Now where did that thought come from?*

Michelle pulled several more peapods from the vine and dropped them into her bucket. *I shouldn't even be thinking about this. Brad Fuller and I are worlds apart. When summer is over, he will resume his studies, and I'll go back to my old life—living from day to day, while trying to find something meaningful to do with the rest of my life.*

"I was wondering if you and Grandpa made a definite decision about attending the Fourth of July festival."

Mary Ruth shook her head. "I think not. But as I said before, you should go if you want to. We could call one of our drivers to take you there."

"Actually, I would like to go, and Brad offered to drive me."

"Oh? What did you tell him?"

"I said yes."

Mary Ruth gave Michelle's arm a light tap. "I'm glad, and I am sure you will both have a good time."

"I hope so." Michelle paused to push the brim of her hat back a bit.

# Chapter 17

Didn't Sara look nice this evening when Brad picked her up? Mary Ruth glanced over at her husband, who sat on the couch beside her, reading the latest edition of *The Budget*.

"Huh? What was that?" He placed the newspaper on his lap and turned to face her.

Mary Ruth repeated her question about Sara.

He squinted over the top of his glasses. "To tell you the truth, I didn't really notice. What was she wearing?"

"She had on a pretty skirt and top, but it wasn't her clothes that made her look so nice. It was the cheerful smile she wore as she went out the door." Mary Ruth's brows wrinkled. "I think maybe we've been holding her back."

"What do you mean?"

"It seems like all Sara's done since she got here is help us with chores. Especially after you sprained your arm."

"She hasn't complained."

"True, but a young woman her age needs to have some *schpass*."

"Sara seemed to be having fun on her birthday."

"Jah, but she didn't have that bubbly expression, like she did tonight." Mary Ruth released a puff of air. "Our granddaughter is not Amish, Willis. She may not enjoy spending all her time with us Plain old folks. Brad is English, like Sara, and she might rather be with her own kind."

"Puh!" Willis picked up the newspaper and gave it a flap. "If Sara didn't enjoy our company, do you think she would still be staying here with us?"

"I don't know. She might not want to hurt our feelings." Mary Ruth nudged his arm with her elbow. "Did you ever think of that?"

Willis shrugged. "I suppose you could be right. Maybe our granddaughter wants to go home and is afraid to say anything because she doesn't want to hurt our feelings."

Tears welled in Mary Ruth's eyes as she clasped her hands together. "I hope that is not the case. I want Sara to stay with us for as long as possible. Her being here is almost like having Rhoda back. And since she has no job or family to go home to, I see no reason for her not to remain here permanently. Only if she wants to, that is."

He slowly nodded. "But if she wants to go, we can't force her to stay for our sakes. We need to give Sara the freedom to go whenever she wants."

"I'll talk to her about it soon. See if she's happy here or would rather leave." Mary Ruth stood. "I'm going to the kitchen for a glass of cold buttermilk. Would you like one too?"

"That'd be nice. And I wouldn't mind a bowl of popcorn to go with it."

She lifted a hand. "Sure, no problem."

When Mary Ruth entered the kitchen, she reflected once more on Sara's happy expression as she went out the door this evening. If there was even a chance that their granddaughter and Brad might become a couple, it could guarantee that she would stay awhile— maybe even permanently. Especially if Brad took a church in the area once he became a minister. Mary Ruth's lips formed a smile, and she began humming a tune from her youth. *Now wouldn't that be something?*

*Lititz, Pennsylvania*

"Here we are." Brad pulled his van into a nearly full parking lot and turned off the engine. "Wish we could have come earlier today, to take in the parade and some of the other afternoon festivities. But at least we'll be able to see the fireworks display and get involved in some of the other fun activities."

Michelle smiled, feeling a bit self-conscious all of a sudden. She and Brad weren't here as a couple, and she didn't expect him to hang around with her all evening, but how could she bring up the subject without embarrassing Brad or making him feel obligated to spend the evening with her?

"Looks like there's quite a few people here," Brad commented after they'd left the van and made their way toward the festivities.

"You're right. We'll probably get lost in the crowd."

"I hope not, but let's plan to meet back here at the van by ten o'clock in case we do."

"Okay." Michelle assumed from Brad's comment that he planned to go off on his own. That made it easy, because now she wouldn't have to bring up the subject.

They had no more than entered the park when she caught sight of Ezekiel and Lenore walking side by side. They were some distance away and didn't appear to see them. Michelle wondered if they had come here together. Maybe the two of them had begun courting and were on a date.

As they walked farther away, the sound of familiar music caught Michelle's attention.

"Oh look, there's a carousel over there." She pointed in that direction.

Brad smiled. "Sure enough. It looks small compared to the ones I rode on as a child at the carnivals in Harrisburg every summer." He chuckled. "At least I thought they were big back then."

Michelle nodded as a memory from the past came to mind. On one of the rare occasions when her dad was sober and things were halfway normal at home, her folks had taken Michelle and her brothers to a state fair. Dad had bought tickets so she, Ernie and Jack could ride the merry-go-round. Michelle chose a horse that had been painted all white, except for a black tail. She'd sat up there so happy, feeling like she was on top of the world. When they'd gone home later that day, Dad had started drinking. He and Mom ended up in a huge fight, and before long, the police showed up at their door.

Her throat constricted. *Why couldn't I have grown up in a normal household, with good parents who got along with each other and didn't abuse their kids?*

"Hey, are you okay?" Brad placed his hand on her shoulder. "You look upset."

The comforting act caused the dam to break, and despite her resolve, tears coursed down Michelle's cheeks.

"What's wrong?"

She sniffed deeply and reached into her skirt pocket for a tissue. "Seeing the carousel reminded me of something from my childhood. Guess I'm just too sentimental." Michelle wasn't about to tell Brad the whole story. If he should repeat it to Willis and Mary Ruth, they'd think their daughter, whom Michelle had never even met, was a terrible mother.

Brad put his hand on Michelle's back and gave her a gentle pat. "Nothing wrong with being sentimental. We all get nostalgic at times."

"Yeah, I guess."

"Would you like to get something to eat or drink before the fireworks start?" he asked.

"Well, umm... I didn't bring any money with me."

"No problem. It's my treat."

"Thanks. I am kinda hungry." Michelle felt herself relax.

He grinned. "All right then, let's see what we can find."

As they headed toward the food booths, Michelle noticed Ezekiel again. This time he was looking in her direction. She waved, and he nodded in response. Lenore had her back to Michelle and seemed to be looking at something in one of the booths. Maybe she would have the chance to say hello to both of them later.

Ezekiel stood in line at the cotton candy booth. After Lenore went off to join some of her friends, he'd decided to get something to eat. Not that cotton candy was the best choice, since it was full of sugar, but it reminded him of when he was boy. Back then Ezekiel's life had been carefree, and he hadn't thought much about whether he would join the Amish church someday or become part of the English world. Now the prospect of leaving his Amish heritage consumed his thoughts. He didn't want to disappoint his parents, but he ought to have the right to make his own decisions about the rest of his life.

Ezekiel paid for his treat and moved on toward the area where the fireworks would be displayed. He'd seen Sara walking in the same direction with that English fellow, Brad. Before that, he had also witnessed Brad with his hand against Sara's back.

*I bet they came here together. He probably asked her on a date.* Ezekiel licked some sticky cotton candy from his lips and kept walking. When he'd mentioned the festival to Sara she had said she wasn't sure if she'd be coming or not. He'd hoped she might come here with him. *Guess it's my fault. I should've followed up with her.*

Ezekiel didn't understand why he felt envious. He barely knew Sara and certainly had no claim on her. *Maybe I'll have the opportunity to get to know her better when I start teaching her how to drive a horse and buggy.* In addition to giving Sara her first lesson tomorrow, it would give him the chance to find out if something was going on with her and Brad.

# Chapter 18

*Newark*

When Sara returned home from her class on Thursday, she was pleased to discover a letter in her mailbox postmarked, *"Strasburg, Pennsylvania."* It had to be from her grandparents. *I am so glad they finally responded.*

Almost breathless, she hurried into the house, tossed the rest of the mail on the kitchen table, and pulled out a chair. Her fingers trembled a bit as she tore open the letter:

> *Dear Sara,*
>     *We were pleased to receive your letters and look forward to meeting you. But since summer is a very busy time for us, we would prefer you wait until sometime in October to come here for a visit.*
>                         *Most sincerely,*
>                         *Willis and Mary Ruth Lapp*

In one sense, Sara felt relieved that her grandparents wouldn't be available to visit with her until October. It would give her plenty of time to finish her summer class and prepare for meeting them. In another sense, she was disappointed that she couldn't meet them sooner. At least between now and then they could communicate via letters. The next time Sara wrote to her grandparents, she would ask for their phone number. If they had one, it was obviously unlisted since she'd had no luck finding it via the internet.

Sara's forehead wrinkled as she reread the letter. As the words sank in, she became somewhat baffled. *Was I wrong in hoping they'd be a little more excited about finding out they had a granddaughter?* She sighed, glancing at the return address on the envelope. *But again, what did I expect to happen?*

Her lips formed a grim line as she continued to discuss the issue with herself, only this time out loud. "It would have been nice to put me ahead of their busy summer. After all, they just learned their daughter died, and I'm their daughter's offspring."

The more Sara went over this, the more she became unsure about her grandparents. The fact was, they'd taken their time getting back to her. That spoke volumes.

Sara continued to study the letter. Her grandparents sounded polite enough, but the more she read over the letter and got to the part about their busy summer, the more disappointed she became. This wasn't anything like she'd expected. Sara had daydreamed about her new grandparents' response and expected they would show more emotion than this. She had conjured up a wonderful emotional reunion once they finally met. It would be the type of reunion she'd watched on certain TV shows that brought together people who had been separated for a long time. One show brought people who had been adopted together with their biological parents. Sara cried along with them as they met for the first time.

*What kind of people are the Lapps anyway?* she fumed. *Was this letter their way of saying I'm no big deal?*

Sara's stomach growled, so she set the letter aside and went to the refrigerator to see what she could grab to eat. An idea had just occurred to her, and she needed something to nibble on while she pursued her search. "I don't know why I didn't think to do this before."

Sara went to the living room and brought her laptop out to the kitchen table. After signing on, she dug out a box of crackers and a jar of peanut butter from the cupboard. That would be easy to eat while she googled some information.

After making a few cracker sandwiches and pouring herself a glass of iced tea, Sara returned to the kitchen table. Using Google

Maps, she took the return envelope and typed in her grandparents' address. After hitting ENTER, the site pinpointed exactly where Willis and Mary Ruth Lapp lived.

She changed the screen to the Satellite view and zoomed in. "Well here's something I didn't realize. They live on a farm." Sara studied the rooftop of the farmhouse and a barn. Surrounding the property were fields and a lot of open space. *Maybe this is what they meant by being busy this summer. Depending on what they grow, it could take up a lot of their time to farm the place. I wonder if anyone lives there with them, or if they have to hire help with the place.*

Sara continued to stare at the screen. *So this is where my mother grew up.* Seeing the map of her grandparents' place made Sara even more determined to go there and meet them. No matter how the Lapps felt about her, she needed to see for herself what they were like and give them a chance to get to know her. If anything good came of meeting them, maybe she would find out who her real father was.

When a knock sounded on the back door, Sara shut her laptop, put the letter back in the envelope, and tucked it inside her purse. No doubt it was Dean. The last thing she needed was for him to see the letter and ask a bunch of questions. *Learning about Mama's parents is none of his business. If Mom had wanted Dean to know, she would have told him.*

<hr />

### Strasburg

"Before we begin your first lesson, I have a question for you," Ezekiel said as he and Sara stood beside his horse and buggy.

"What's that?" With an anxious expression, she glanced at Big Red.

"Since you won't be staying here permanently and will be returning to your English world at some point, how come you want to learn to drive a horse and buggy?"

She turned her head to look at him. "I think it'll be fun, and it will give me a better understanding of my grandparents' way of life.

Of course," she added, "after seeing my grandpa get hurt when he tried to teach me, I'll admit I am a bit nervous."

"The accident really wasn't your fault. You weren't used to Bashful, and she wasn't used to you." Ezekiel shrugged. "Besides, your grandpa wasn't seriously hurt, and he's doing better now."

"Yes but not well enough to do all the chores on his own." Sara pointed across the yard. "Which is why Brad will be coming over later today to mow the lawn."

"Speaking of Brad, I saw you with him last night at the festival in Lititz. Were you two on a date?"

Sara's ponytail swished as she shook her head. "He drove me there, and we walked around together for a bit, but it wasn't a date." She pointed at Ezekiel. "I saw you and Lenore there too. Were you on a date?"

He pulled his fingers along his cheek bone, realizing he'd neglected to shave this morning. "Course not. I've known Lenore since we were kids, and there are no romantic feelings between us. Least not on my part anyway."

"Then why were you with her last night?"

"We shared a ride in her driver's vehicle. We were together for a few minutes when we first got there, but then we went our separate ways." Ezekiel opened the door on the right side of the buggy. "I don't know why we're standin' here talking about this anyway. I've got a lesson to teach, and you have some learning to do about driving a horse." He paused, sliding his tongue over his lips. "Say before we begin, I have a favor to ask."

"What's that?"

"If I teach you how to drive a horse and buggy, would you be willing to teach me to drive a car?"

Sara's auburn eyebrows lifted high on her forehead. "You said before that you don't own a car."

"Not yet, but I've been eyeballing a truck that's for sale in the area. I wasn't sure if I wanted it, but I'm actually thinkin' about buying the truck now."

"Are you allowed to do that? I thought Amish people didn't

drive cars. Isn't that why you hire English drivers to take you some places?"

Ezekiel struggled not to roll his eyes. Wasn't Sara listening when they'd had this conversation before? Or maybe she'd just forgot. "You're right." He tried not to sound perturbed. "Once a person has joined the Amish church, they are not allowed to own or drive a car. My folks hire a driver if they need to go outside the area or if a trip takes more than ten or fifteen miles by horse and buggy."

"What do they have against cars?"

"It's not the vehicle itself. The Amish believe owning a car could lead to a tearing apart of family, church, and community. And people who have cars tend to be away from home more, which can make the community more scattered." He frowned. "My dad says owning a fancy car could easily become a symbol of pride." Ezekiel pushed his straw hat farther back on his head. "Since I haven't joined the church, I would be allowed to buy a car. Only thing is, my folks—especially Dad—are against it. So if I get the truck, I'll need to park it someplace else 'cause I'd never be allowed to keep it on my parents' property. That's something Dad's made very clear to all his children."

Sara shook her head. "I didn't realize Amish parents were so strict. I heard some of them looked the other way when their young adult children went through their running-around years. *Rumspringa*. Isn't that what it's called?"

"Yeah. The Pennsylvania Dutch word for it is *rumschpringe*. It's a time that allows Amish young people who have not joined the Amish church yet to experience the modern world. Of course, some get this privilege and some don't. It varies from church district to district."

"Do you get to wear English clothes during that time of running around?"

He nodded. "Course not all Amish teens and young people do. Some are content to wear Amish clothes, and they just enjoy the freedom of going to movies, dances, or taking long trips with their friends. A couple of my friends went to Disney World during their running-around time, and my cousin Raymond spent some time in Sarasota, Florida."

"I see." Sara shook her head several times. "Boy, there are so many things I still don't know about the Amish."

"Such as?"

"I'm curious to hear how the Amish religion began."

"Well, the Amish people are direct descendants of the Anabaptists of sixteenth-century Europe. The Anabaptist religion came about during the Reformation."

Sara tilted her head to one side. "*Anabaptist* is a word I've not heard before. What exactly does it mean?"

"The term first started out as a nickname that meant 're-baptizer' because this group rejected the idea of infant baptism."

"How come?"

"An infant doesn't have a knowledge of good and bad."

She stood quietly, gazing at the ground. She slowly lifted her head. "Is that it? Or is there anything else about the Anabaptists you'd like to share?"

"I can tell you more if you like."

"Sure, go ahead."

Ezekiel wasn't sure why Sara would be so curious about the Amish, but he was willing to share what he knew. Maybe her curiosity had to do with the fact that her grandparents were Amish and she wanted to know and understand them better.

"Before they came here to America, the Anabaptists were seen as a threat to Europe's religious and social institutions, so they were often persecuted."

Her eyes widened. "Seriously?"

"It's true. And some of the things that were done to them were so horrible it's hard to talk about."

Her eyes darkened. "That is so sad."

"Yeah. No one should be persecuted for their religious beliefs." Ezekiel folded his arms while shifting his weight. "Another thing you might find interesting is that the Amish religion is a branch of the Swiss Mennonites. The group got its name from its founder, Jacob Amman. Another leader was named Menno Simons, and the people who followed him were called, 'Mennonites,' " he explained. "Eventually, those who followed Jacob Amman formed a new group known as the Amish."

Sara stared at Ezekiel with widened eyes. "Wow, you sure do know a lot about the Amish religion."

"Well I should, seeing as to how I was raised in an Amish home. And actually, most Amish don't like to think of it as their religion, since they confess to be Christians, just as several other denominations do. They prefer to say that being Amish is a way of life rather than a religion." He waved away a bee trying to land on Sara's arm. "I'd be the first to admit that I don't have all the answers concerning Amish life, but having attended church with my folks ever since I was a baby, I've learned a lot."

"Yet you still haven't made a commitment to join your family's church?"

"That's right." Ezekiel rubbed the back of his hot, sweaty neck. "So changing the subject, how about it, Sara? If I decide to buy that truck or some other vehicle, will you teach me how to drive? I'll get a learner's permit first of course."

Her forehead wrinkled slightly before giving a hesitant nod. "Sure, I guess so."

Grinning, he clapped his hands. "Great! So hop up in the buggy and let's be off."

❧

As Michelle crawled into bed that night, she inhaled deeply. The sheets smelled so good—like fresh air. It was one of the benefits of hanging laundry outside. While it might be more work than tossing clothes in a dryer, it hadn't taken her long to get used to pinning freshly washed laundry on the line in the Lapps' backyard. In fact, she rather enjoyed the task.

Michelle snuggled beneath the cool linens and closed her eyes. Today had been a good one, and she'd enjoyed Ezekiel's company as much as she had Brad's the night before. It made no sense that she could get along well with two men from opposite backgrounds, but she felt equally comfortable with both of them. Michelle had enjoyed the pleasant conversation she'd shared with Brad during the Fourth of July festival, but she'd also liked being with Ezekiel today. He'd been patient and kind as he taught her how to hitch and unhitch Big Red. And Ezekiel made it seem easy when he took Michelle through the steps of driving the horse and talked about safety measures.

She'd been nervous at first, but by the time they returned to the house, Michelle felt more confident. Of course, having Ezekiel by her side, ready to take charge if needed, had bolstered her confidence. Though she still couldn't believe that he wanted her to teach him how to drive a car. While Michelle didn't have her own vehicle, she'd gotten her driver's license when she was seventeen years old and had driven her foster parents' car a good many times—running errands and picking up the younger kids in their family from school activities. She had renewed her license and driven Jerry's car a few times when he was too drunk to drive himself home. She hoped if and when Ezekiel asked her to teach him that she'd feel up to the task.

She also appreciated Ezekiel taking the time to answer some of her questions about Amish life. She had lots more of course, but those could wait for another time.

It pleased Michelle that Brad and Ezekiel were polite and respectful toward her. Nothing like Jerry had been during the time they'd been a couple. Michelle couldn't believe she had put up with his verbal abuse. When it became physical abuse, she'd had the good sense to get away from him.

Her throat constricted, and she swallowed hard. *Guess maybe at first, I thought I deserved no better. I wonder what it would be like to have a boyfriend like Ezekiel or Brad, who I'm sure would treat me like I was special—not someone to control, push around, or yell at.*

Michelle rolled onto her side. There was no point thinking about this. She couldn't have a relationship with Brad or Ezekiel, even if she wanted one. They didn't know the real her, and if either man learned the truth about her false identity, she felt certain they would never speak to her again.

"I should leave now, before someone gets hurts," Michelle murmured into her pillow. "If I had a lick of sense, I'd pack my bags and head out of here early tomorrow morning, before Mary Ruth and Willis are out of bed."

# Chapter 19

Michelle couldn't believe how quickly the time had gone since she'd first arrived at the Lapps'. But it was the middle of July, and she'd been here over a month already. She wished she could make time stand still so she would never have to leave this special place.

When Michelle entered the barn in search of her gardening gloves, she paused to look up at the antique jars on the shelf overhead. It would only take a few minutes to get the jar full of prayers down and read one or two. She'd been so busy helping Mary Ruth keep up with all the garden produce lately that she hadn't taken the time to get the jar down for several days.

*Think I'll take a few minutes to do that now. Maybe something written on one of those pieces of paper will give me a clue as to who wrote the messages.*

Michelle placed her garden gloves and shovel on Willis's workbench and dragged the ladder over to the shelf where the jars sat. Since Willis was at a doctor's appointment and Mary Ruth had accompanied him, Michelle had plenty of time to look at the notes without interruption. The produce she planned to pick in the garden could wait for a while longer.

Once she had the prayer jar down, she took a seat on the now-familiar bale of straw and leaned against the wooden post behind it. Since Michelle had pushed the notes she'd previously read to the bottom of the jar, she pulled one out near the top and read it out loud.

" 'Watch and pray, that ye enter not into temptation: the spirit indeed is willing, but the flesh is weak' Matthew 26:41."

Michelle shifted on the straw poking into her backside. *The person who wrote this must have been faced with some kind of temptation. Did they give in to it or hold fast?*

Michelle couldn't count all the times she'd been tempted—to steal, to cheat, to get even, to lie. And at some point or another, she had succumbed to each one. There was no doubt about it—her flesh was weak.

She folded the paper in half and pushed it to the bottom of the jar. *One more. I'll just read one more note and then head out to the garden. It wouldn't be good if I didn't get something done while Willis and Mary Ruth are gone.*

On the next paper Michelle withdrew, a prayer had been written. *"Dear Lord, You forgive my sins and give me hope."*

She contemplated it a few minutes before putting the folded paper back in the jar. Holding the antique container between her knees, Michelle folded her hands beneath her chin in a prayer-like gesture and looked up. "God, if You're listening, is there any hope for me?"

Except for the soft nicker of Mary Ruth's buggy horse, the barn was silent.

*Well, what did I expect? Did I really think God would open the windows of heaven and shout something down at me? I'm just a foolish young woman whose life isn't going anywhere. Why would He care about someone like me?*

Michelle's cheeks burned hot, and it wasn't from the outside heat creeping in. *I should have followed through with my plan to leave this place soon after I got here. The longer I stay, the harder it gets to go.*

Michelle leaned her head against the wooden post and covered her mouth with her hand to stifle a sob. *If I tell Mary Ruth and Willis the truth, they'll be upset, and I'll have to go knowing how much I hurt them. But how can I tell the truth without wounding the ones I've come to care about?*

The rumble of a vehicle approaching drew Michelle's thoughts aside. She stood and took a peek out the barn door. The Lapps were back, and she needed to get a grip on herself and decide what to do. *Do I tell them the truth and pack my bag, or keep pretending for a while longer?*

❧

After Mary Ruth climbed out of Brad's van, she turned to Willis and said, "If you'll take care of paying our driver, I'll go see how Sara is doing in the garden."

Willis gave a nod. "That's fine, but Brad plans to do some work for me today, so I probably won't pay him till he's done for the day."

"That's fine." Mary Ruth patted her husband's arm. It was good he no longer had to wear the sling, but it might be another week or so before he could proclaim that his arm was completely healed. Even though Willis was able to do several chores by himself now, he still needed help with some things on the farm. Since Sara kept busy helping Mary Ruth so much of the time, she appreciated having Brad available to help Willis like he had. Their son Ivan helped on occasions too, but between all the responsibilities he had at his general store and his chores at home, he didn't come by to help as often as Mary Ruth would like.

She stood silently a few seconds, watching as Willis spoke to Brad. Turning away, she headed across the yard.

As Mary Ruth approached the garden, she saw Sara down on her knees, pulling weeds. The young woman looked up and smiled. "How'd Grandpa's appointment go?"

"It went well. He doesn't have to wear the sling anymore, but Dr. Kent cautioned him not to overuse it." Mary Ruth glanced over her shoulder, looking toward the van parked in their driveway. "So Brad will be here a few hours this afternoon to help with some of the heavier chores."

"That's good, and I'm glad Grandpa's arm is better."

"We are too." Mary Ruth smiled. "I'm going in the house now to change into my work dress. I'll be back soon to help you finish the weeding."

"Okay. No hurry though."

Michelle swatted at several gnats buzzing her head. *Oh great. Not this again.* They'd had some rain early that morning, and it seemed the pesky bugs were bent on revenge. Mary Ruth had said this was typical after a rain. *Guess I shoulda worn that old canvas hat, but I stupidly misplaced it.* She sighed. *Oh well, this chore will be over soon enough, and then I'll be out of the bugs' path.*

"The gnats are nasty today aren't they, Sara?" Mary Ruth knelt beside Michelle.

"That's for sure. They've been buzzing my ears and trying to get in my eyes and up my nose." Michelle drew in a breath and sucked in a bug. "Eww..." She coughed and almost choked.

Mary Ruth wrinkled her nose. "I've had that happen to me before, and it's not fun to know you've swallowed a bug."

"I think one of 'em may have bit me." Michelle rubbed her forehead. "How come they don't seem to be bothering you?"

"Well, for one thing, I don't wear any hairspray or perfume. Some bugs are attracted to certain smells."

Michelle shifted her position. *So much for thoughts about telling Mary Ruth the truth. The minute I saw her get out of Brad's van my resolve went out the barn door.* Truth was, even though she'd been here less than two months, Michelle had begun to think of Mary Ruth and Willis as her adoptive grandparents. She wished she could stay with them permanently.

"Sara, did you hear what I said?"

Michelle jerked her head. "Uh, sorry, I was deep in thought. Was it something about hairspray?"

Mary Ruth bobbed her head. "Some bugs are attracted to certain smells."

"I'll try to remember that the next time I do any work in the yard."

"The other thing you might do is wear a scarf, or what about that old canvas hat you said you'd found in your mother's closet? You still have it, don't you?"

"No, I haven't seen it for a while. Would it be okay if I wear one of Grandpa's old straw hats? I think there's one hanging on a peg in the barn."

Mary Ruth's eyes widened a bit. "Well, I guess it would be all right, but wouldn't you rather wear one of my scarves?"

Michelle shook her head. "The straw hat might work better, and it will serve a dual purpose by helping to keep the sun out of my eyes."

"Very well. Feel free to help yourself."

"Danki, I will." Michelle tipped her head to one side. "Did I say that right?"

"Yes, you certainly did." Mary Ruth winked. "I bet if you stay here long enough, you'll pick up a lot more of our Pennsylvania Dutch words."

Michelle clambered to her feet and headed to the barn. The mere thought of leaving here put a lump in her throat.

❧

"I forgot to check for eggs this morning," Mary Ruth said when they finished weeding. "Would you mind doing that, Sara, while I start supper?"

"Sure, I'd be happy to do it." Michelle rose and brushed a clump of dirt off her jeans.

"Oh, and if you see Brad, please tell him he's invited to stay and eat with us."

"All right, I will." Michelle returned Willis's old hat to the barn, then hurried off to the chicken coop. As she opened the door of the small wooden structure, the hinge on the door gave an irritating creak.

When Michelle stepped inside, her nose twitched from the smell of dusty feed, fragments of straw, and chicken feces. This was not a place she cared to linger in very long. She hoped she wouldn't end up with a sneezing fit.

Michelle located the egg-collecting basket on a wooden shelf inside the door. She also discovered the chickens in an uproar—squawking, kicking up pieces of straw that had been spread on the floor, and running about as though they'd been traumatized by something.

"Simmer down. I'm not here to hurt you." Michelle shooed two overzealous hens away. If she hadn't put Willis's straw hat back in the barn when she left the garden, she would have used it to flap at the chickens right now. "Come on, ladies. I just came out here to get a few eggs. And if you don't behave, you may end up going without supper this evening."

Feeding the chickens and gathering eggs was not one of Michelle's favorite things to do. But it was better than throwing food into the hog trough. Those fat pigs could make such a racket, snorting and trying to push each other away, like their last meal had been served and they might miss out. They were all greedy. How was it any wonder those hogs were so fat?

Michelle reached into the first nest she came to, and pulled out two nice-sized, perfectly shaped brown eggs. Placing them carefully into the basket, she moved on. Meanwhile, the hens kept making a racket, the pitch of their screeching rising higher and higher. It was unnerving. Michelle was tempted to set the basket down and cover both ears.

When Michelle approached the next nest, she froze. Not far from where she stood lay a huge black snake staring back at her, with its tongue darting in and out. The reptile looked strange with a big bulge in its body. It was also creepy.

With her breath caught in her throat, she felt paralyzed, unable to move. The chickens' continued ruckus only added to Michelle's crippling fear. She took short steps and slowly backed away, never taking her eyes off the shiny, scaled serpent, and hoping she wouldn't knock any of the water feeders over. Michelle wanted to be sure the snake stayed where it was, and that it wouldn't follow her. Even after a hasty exit out the squeaky door, once she was outside the coop, she kept looking back, hoping the snake would remain where it was until she got help.

Except for one time at the zoo, Michelle had never seen a

snake up close. And the previous time, there had been a wall of glass between her and the reptile.

Beads of sweat erupted on her forehead as she continued her retreat, whimpering and needing to put a safe distance between herself and the coop where the snake had taken up residence.

*Oomph!* She backed into Brad.

He took hold of Michelle's shoulders and turned her around. "What's wrong, Sara? Your face is just as white as snow."

"There's a snake in there." She pointed toward the coop.

Brad gave her arm a light pat. "Don't worry; it's not unusual to find a snake in a chicken coop. It's probably just a common black rat snake. I'll take care of it for you."

By "take care of it," Michelle assumed Brad meant he would kill the snake. But since he had no weapon, she didn't see how he could manage it. Surely he wasn't foolish enough to try and kill the snake with his bare hands. Well, she wasn't going in with him to find out.

Michelle waited outside the coop door while Brad went inside. The thought of what he might encounter sent shivers up her spine.

She cringed when a short time later Brad came out with the ugly black snake wrapped around his arm.

"Look here." He pointed to the bulge inside the snake. "This reptile swallowed an egg. See how big it is right behind its head?"

"Eww. . ." Michelle could barely look at the snake.

Brad started walking toward the adjacent field.

"Wait! Aren't you gonna kill that horrible thing?"

He stopped walking and turned to look at her. "Nope. Snakes like this are good at keeping the mice population down around farms."

Michelle glanced at the now-quiet chicken coop, wondering if she could ever muster up the nerve to go in there again. As much as she enjoyed being with the Lapps, maybe she wasn't cut out for country life.

# Chapter 20

"Do you think Sara's been acting strange lately?" Mary Ruth asked Willis as they got ready for bed one evening in late July.

He took his glasses off and rubbed the bridge of his nose. "In what way?"

"Well, some days she seems happy and content, and other days her mood is so sullen." Mary Ruth placed her head covering on the dresser and picked up her hairbrush. "There are times when we're talking and she doesn't seem to even hear what I'm saying. And when Sara does respond, she won't always make eye contact with me." She moved over to the bed and sat down. "I'm concerned about her, Willis. Yesterday I offered to give her all the clothes Rhoda left behind when she ran away from home, but Sara said she would prefer that I keep them. Don't you think that's strange?"

"Maybe she's had enough of us and wants to go back to her own life. We can't force our granddaughter to stay here, you know." Willis leaned over and fluffed up the pillows on their bed. "And as far as her not wanting Rhoda's clothes—what would she do with them, Mary Ruth? Sara's not Amish, so she wouldn't be likely to wear them."

"True. And I would never try to keep her from leaving when she decides to return to her home. As you know, we've both told her that while we would like her to stay with us permanently, she's free to go whenever she likes." Mary Ruth heaved a sigh. "I just want our precious Sara to be happy—even if it means not staying here with us."

Willis took a seat beside Mary Ruth, placing his hand gently against her back. "I heard her talking about us to Ezekiel the other day when he came by to see if we were running low on honey."

Mary Ruth's ears perked up. "What did she say?"

"Said she dreaded the day she'd have to leave, and that she enjoyed being here very much." He gave Mary Ruth's back a few comforting pats. "So you see, there's nothing to worry about. If Sara truly likes it here, maybe when she does return to her home, she'll pack up all her things and come back to stay. Would ya like that, Mary Ruth?"

"Of course I would. And I'm sure you would too. Having Rhoda's daughter living here permanently would give me nothing but pleasure." She leaned her head on his shoulder. "Even though it's wrong to selfishly ask God for things, I'm praying that's exactly what will happen."

"I'm going out to get the mail now," Michelle announced after breakfast the following morning. She still couldn't believe how early the mail came on this rural road. Back in Philadelphia, she sometimes wouldn't get her mail until close to supper time. Of course, it was mostly junk mail, which was why she hadn't even bothered to put in a notice with the post office when she left Philadelphia in a hurry. By not forwarding her mail, there was no way Jerry could contact her either. For sure, he was the last person she wanted to see or hear from again.

"If you have something else to do, I can get the mail on the way to or from my reflexology appointment." Mary Ruth began clearing the table.

"No, that's okay. I'll get the mail now and bring it in before you go." Michelle sprang to her feet. It was important that she be the one to get the mail, in case another letter came from the Lapps' true granddaughter.

"All right then, I'll start the dishes while you're doing that."

Willis looked up from the newspaper he had just unfolded to read. "Sara, would you like to say goodbye to the puppies who'll be going home with their new owners today?" he asked.

Michelle nodded. While she hated to see the pups leave, it was nice to know they'd be going to good homes. It was hard to believe the rambunctious little critters were over six weeks old already. Willis had asked around to see who might want one, and with the exception of Rascal, all the puppies had been spoken for.

Michelle thought about how Willis and Mary Ruth had given her the puppy as a birthday gift. She'd become attached to the little fellow and wished she could take him along when she left the Lapps' home for good. But it wasn't a wise idea, since Michelle had no idea where she was going for sure or what kind of a place she might end up renting.

"Your cousin Lenore should be here around ten o'clock, so you have plenty of time between now and then to spend with the pups," Willis commented.

"Okay. I'm going out to get the mail now, and then I'll head to the barn as soon as I've done the dishes for Grandma." She looked at Mary Ruth. "I don't want you to be late for your appointment. I've heard that reflexology can help with a good many things."

"Yes, and my friend, who treats people for a donation only, says massaging the feet and its pressure points can bring relief when my neck, back, or head starts to hurt." The older woman's face radiated with joy. "I thank you for your thoughtfulness, Sara. You're such a sweet granddaughter."

Michelle cringed inwardly. *If Mary Ruth knew the real me, she wouldn't think I was so sweet.*

As Michelle made her way out to the mailbox, her shoulders slumped. How much longer could she keep doing this? If Mary Ruth or Willis ever went out and got the mail before she did and found a letter from the real Sara, Michelle would be caught in her trap full of lies. She tried not to think about it and simply concentrate on enjoying being here for as long as she could, but it became harder every day.

When Michelle approached the mailbox, a car sped by, going much too fast, and leaving a trail of dust following it. She could still hear the gravel crunching under the tires as the vehicle raced farther up the road. Didn't people have better sense than to travel at a high rate of speed on these back country roads? Anyone who lived in the area had to know horse and buggies traveled up and down this road. Even the tourists, who came to observe the Amish people living in the area, should know better than to exceed the speed limit.

Michelle looked up and down the road. Fortunately, there were no children out with pony carts this morning. In fact, she didn't see any horses and buggies.

Michelle remembered Ezekiel saying during her driving lesson last week that buggy accidents could occur from many causes: human error, horse error, runaway horses, barking dogs, certain road conditions, loud noises from motorcycles or trucks, and of course speeding cars. In his opinion, most accidents happened because non-Amish drivers were either inconsiderate or in too big of a hurry.

Michelle had to agree. She'd witnessed some Amish buggies being cut off by vehicles trying to pass. As long as she was given an opportunity to drive an Amish buggy, she would use caution.

Directing her thoughts back to the mailbox, she pulled on the handle and reached inside for the stack of mail. Thumbing through the ads and bills, she discovered another letter from Sara Murray.

*Oh no.* Her fingers trembled as she stuck the letter in her pocket. *I wish she'd stop sending letters. It freaks me out every time another one comes.*

Michelle ran up the driveway and into the house, nearly colliding with Willis, who stood near the back door.

"Whoa! Where are ya going in such a hurry?" he asked, stepping aside.

"I just wanted to put the mail on the table so I could get started on the dishes."

"No hurry about the mail." Willis raised his thick brows. "The postman usually brings bills and advertising catalogs, and an occasional letter from someone we know. So I doubt we got anything that can't wait to be looked at till later." He gestured to the stack of mail as Michelle placed it on the table. "Right now, I have chores to do, so I'd better get outside before the day warms too much. Heard it's going to be another hot one." Willis made a hasty exit out the back door.

Michelle figured Mary Ruth was in her room getting ready for her appointment, so she would wait until after she left to open Sara's letter. In the meantime, there were dishes to do.

As soon as the dishes were done, and Mary Ruth had left the house, Michelle raced upstairs to her room. She couldn't take the chance of Willis coming back inside and finding her reading Sara's letter. Since the dishes were done and no one had shown up yet to pick up their puppy, this was the perfect time to see what Sara had written.

Michelle took a seat on the bed and tore open the envelope. Reading it silently, she frowned.

> *Dear Grandpa and Grandma,*
> *I received your letter and wanted to reassure you that I won't come to visit until sometime in October. I am wondering, however, if you have a telephone. If so, could you please write back and give me the number? That way I can keep in better contact and let you know exactly when I might be coming to Strasburg.*
> *Your granddaughter,*
> *Sara*

Michelle placed the letter in her lap and groaned. *How am I going to answer that? Maybe I'll just ignore it. I do have to destroy this letter though, and I'd better do it now.*

Rising from the bed, she ripped the letter into small pieces, then hurried downstairs. She would throw the remnants in the burn barrel, like she'd done before. It was the only way to keep the Lapps from finding out that she wasn't Sara Murray.

# Chapter 21

Michelle sat on the back porch, holding Rascal in her lap. The puppy's soft, fleecy fur was nothing like his mother's yet, and it would be awhile before he lost his sharp puppy teeth. Since he was the only pup left from the litter, Michelle hoped to pay more attention to Rascal and maybe teach him some tricks. Rascal needed to get more social too. In a way, Michelle wished he would stay in this smaller stage, so adorable and cute. Unfortunately, she wouldn't get the chance to see the dog when he was all grown up. The poor little guy seemed lonely without his brothers and sisters to play with. They'd all gone home with their happy new owners yesterday.

Michelle sighed. *I hope all the puppies adjust to their new surroundings.* She understood how the pups may have felt last night, without the comfort of their mother, brothers, and sisters. Even though Michelle had been taken from an abusive home and put in a better, more stable one, she had always felt out of place in the foster home and lonely for her younger brothers.

Even Sadie, lying listlessly on the porch beside Michelle, wasn't herself today. It almost appeared as if the dog's eyes were weeping. One would think after caring for a batch of pups all these weeks, the dog would be somewhat relieved to see them go. But apparently Sadie's maternal instinct was stronger than her need to have time to herself. Although Michelle wasn't a mother, she figured any good parent would feel the same way—putting the needs of their offspring ahead of their own. It hurt to think that her own flesh-and-blood parents had never cared much about nurturing their children or meeting their needs. Michelle's mom and dad had so many problems they could barely function at times, much less provide a stable environment for their family.

Lest she give in to self-pity, Michelle put her focus on Rascal again. "You're sure a cute little thing." The puppy's floppy ears perked up when she stroked his head. "Maybe what we all need is a little exercise. It might help us not feel so gloomy."

Michelle lifted the pup and set him on the porch beside his mother. Then she hopped up, ran into the yard, and picked up a small stick. "Come on Sadie—fetch!" Michelle tossed the stick across the yard.

Perking right up, the collie lifted her head, leaped off the porch, and chased after the stick. Then she brought it back to Michelle and dropped it at her feet.

"Good girl, Sadie." Michelle picked it up and threw it again.

*Woof! Woof!* Sadie took off like a streak. Apparently this play-time was just what she needed.

As if not to be outdone, Rascal practically flew off the porch and chased after his mother, yipping all the way.

Michelle figured Sadie wouldn't give up her stick, so she found a smaller one and tossed it for Rascal. It didn't take the little fellow long to get the hang of playing fetch, for soon he was romping back and forth, grabbing the stick in his mouth. Of course, getting him to bring it to Michelle was another matter. Once he got hold of the stick and claimed it for his own, Rascal raced off to the other side of the yard. In order to regain the twig, Michelle had to chase after the pup. Sadie, however, kept bringing her stick back to Michelle, and the game continued.

Michelle worked with Rascal a bit more, now that Sadie laid down to watch. "I'm sure you are too young yet, but for fun, I'll give it a try."

She sat the pup down and put the stick in front of him. When Rascal picked it up, Michelle gave a command. "No Rascal." She took the stick from his mouth, and placed it back on the grass. Michelle did this a few times, until Rascal finally sat there staring at the stick when she said no.

Then Michelle commanded Rascal to bring the stick to her. "Come Rascal. Bring me the stick." Michelle giggled when Rascal stayed sitting and cocked his head to one side. In hopes that the pup would understand, she took the stick and put it in Rascal's mouth, telling him to "Stay." Then, patting the side of her leg, she gave the command again. "Come, Rascal."

Rascal took off with the stick in his mouth, but instead of bringing it to her, he headed in the opposite direction.

Michelle chased after him but was soon out of breath and laughing so hard her sides ached. "Whew! Your pup is wearing me out, Sadie. But Rascal did pretty well for his first time chasing a stick." She plopped down next to Sadie and rubbed a spot between the collie's ears. It felt good to be so carefree and able to find enjoyment in the simple things. If she truly was the Lapps' granddaughter, she would stay here permanently and perhaps, if she ever felt ready, even join the Amish church someday. Right now though, she didn't know enough about their way of life or religious beliefs to determine if she could become a church member. Of course, under the circumstances, becoming Amish was nothing but a foolish notion. Once her true identity had been revealed, no Amish member would want her to be a part of their church.

Sadie barked when a horse and buggy pulled into the yard, and Rascal dropped his stick and joined in, making smaller *Arf! Arf!* noises.

Michelle shielded her eyes against the glare of the sun, watching as Ezekiel pulled up to the hitching rail. She wondered if he'd come to give her another driving lesson.

Ezekiel hopped out of his buggy and quickly secured his horse. "Hey, how's it going?" He waved at Sara.

"It's going good." She motioned to the yapping dogs. "I was entertaining Sadie and Rascal. Thought I'd try to teach the little fellow how to fetch."

"How'd he do?"

"Not too bad for as young as he is." Michelle offered a thumbs-up and grinned. "I'm sure he'll get the hang of it in time."

Ezekiel squatted down and greeted the animals. "I take it Willis must have found homes for the rest of Sadie's pups?"

"Yes. Only my little Rascal is left to pester his mother."

Ezekiel wiped his chin when Sadie became a little too exuberant and gave him a few slurps with her tongue.

Meanwhile, Rascal kept busy tugging on Sara's shoelaces. Laughing, she bent down and picked the puppy up, rubbing her cheek against his soft fur.

"Where are Willis and Mary Ruth today?" Ezekiel asked. "Are they in the house?"

Sara shook her head. "Grandpa went to meet with the other ministers in their district about something pertaining to one of the church members who is having some physical problems. And Grandma is helping her Amish neighbor Caroline, who just got out of the hospital."

"Oh? What's wrong with Caroline?"

"She had her gall bladder removed."

"That's too bad. I hear gall bladder issues can be quite painful."

Sara nodded. "What brings you by today, Ezekiel? Did you come to give me another driving lesson?"

"Not exactly, but if you agree to come with me, you can drive on the way back, because I plan on going after my own vehicle."

Her eyes widened. "I'm not sure what vehicle you're talking about, but there is no way I'm driving a horse and buggy by myself." Sara shook her head vigorously. "I am nowhere near ready for that."

"I figured if I followed along slowly behind, you'd be okay." Ezekiel couldn't hide his excitement. "I bought that truck I told ya about, and I wanna park it on my cousin's property. From there, we'll head back here to your grandparents' place."

Sara's forehead creased. "Wait a minute now. Didn't you ask if I'd be willing to teach you how to drive a car?"

"Well, yes, but. . ."

"So if you don't know how to drive, how are you going to follow me anywhere?"

Ezekiel's ears burned like someone had set them on fire. "Sorry if I misled you. The fact is, I've been practicing some in my friend Abe's car. And even though I don't have my license yet, I'm able to drive fairly well. I just need a little more practice. And I did get my learner's permit the other day," he quickly added.

Sara glared at him. "But you shouldn't drive by yourself with only a learner's permit—not to mention still needing more practice. If you were to get stopped by a cop, it wouldn't be good. And your folks would probably find out about it too."

Ezekiel folded his arms. "I'm well aware of all that. But it's only a short distance from where I'll be picking up the truck to my cousin's house, and I'll be very careful."

"I have a better idea. Why don't you let me drive the truck to your cousin's and you can drive your horse and buggy? That would be much safer, don't you think?"

"How 'bout we discuss this on the way to get the truck?" He moved closer to Sara, giving fluttery hand movements as he talked. "Will you please go with me? I'll make it up to you somehow."

"You don't need to make anything up to me." Sara tugged her ponytail. "I'll go because you're my friend, but let me first put the puppy away. I also need to leave a note for my grandparents, so they won't worry if they get back while I'm gone."

He drew a deep breath through his nose. "Thanks, Sara. I really appreciate this."

Michelle's fingers gripped the reins so tightly her knuckles whitened. She had to be crazy to let Ezekiel talk her into driving his horse and buggy without him along to tell her what to do. "But how could I refuse him when he sounded so excited to drive the truck?" Michelle's breath came out in nervous spurts of air. "Steady, boy. Easy does it." Why hadn't Ezekiel asked his cousin or one of his friends to go along with him, instead of relying on her?

They would have handled Big Red much better than she ever could. Every bump she encountered and every passing of a car put Michelle's nerves on edge. But so far the horse was behaving himself. He just plodded along at a steady pace.

Michelle glanced in the side mirror and saw Ezekiel's truck behind her. She wondered if he was worried about driving it by himself, with so little experience.

As a convertible passed on the opposite side of the road, Michelle's fear escalated. It was the same group of guys who had taunted her the day she'd walked back to the Lapps' from the post office. If Brad hadn't shown up when he did, Michelle didn't know what she would have done, or how far the young men might have gone in their quest to torment her.

*I hope they didn't recognize me. Don't know what I would do if they turned around and came back to give me trouble.*

She glanced in her mirror again and relaxed a bit when their vehicle kept going. If they had come alongside the buggy and given her any problems, Michelle hoped Ezekiel would have come to her rescue the way Brad had that day.

Michelle jumped when Ezekiel tooted his horn behind. Luckily, Big Red didn't seem to be affected by the noise.

She glanced in the mirror again, and seeing the truck's right blinker come on, she guided the horse up the next driveway. This must be where Ezekiel's cousin lived. What a relief to know she would soon be turning the horse and buggy over to Ezekiel.

His cousin's farm was neat as a pin, just like the Lapps' place. Instead of pigs in the barnyard, however, Michelle saw a small herd of floppy-eared goats. Some were white, and others were black. It was cute how they all came up to the fence and noisily bleated, curious to see who had arrived.

Michelle had just pulled Big Red up to the hitching rail near the barn when she heard the shrill sound of a siren. She stepped down from the buggy in time to see a police car pull in behind Ezekiel's truck. *Oh no. I wonder what he did wrong. Or could it have been me?*

# Chapter 22

Ezekiel's mouth felt so dry he could barely swallow. He couldn't imagine what he'd done wrong, other than maybe following the buggy too close. He got out of his new truck and stood by the door, waiting for the officer to approach. He was glad when Sara joined him, because he needed the moral support.

"Did you know the right blinker on your buggy isn't working?" The deputy sheriff looked at Sara.

She shook her head slowly, then glanced at Ezekiel.

"Sorry, sir. We didn't know." Ezekiel exhaled through his nose. When he'd heard the siren and seen the patrol car pull onto the driveway, he was sure he would be in trouble for driving alone, with only a learner's permit. "I'll make sure to get the blinker working again. Thanks for letting us know."

"So whose buggy is it—yours or hers?" The deputy motioned to Sara.

"It's mine."

"Oh. I assumed it was hers, since you were driving the truck."

Ezekiel explained that the truck and buggy were both his. Sweat beaded on his forehead, and he reached up to wiped it off. He sure hoped the officer wouldn't ask to see his license.

The deputy nodded his head. "Yeah, I get it. Some of you Amish young people like to have the best of both worlds. I guess you'll have to sell the truck when you join the church though, right?"

All Ezekiel did was offer a brief nod. He wasn't about to tell the officer that he probably wouldn't be joining the church.

"Okay then, I'll be on my way. Just don't forget to get that blinker fixed." The deputy gave a wave and got back in his car.

Ezekiel turned to Sara. "Guess we'd better go. I need to get back home, and you do as well. I'll park the truck around back of my cousin's house, and we can be on our way."

～ಌ～

Michelle waited by the buggy until Ezekiel came back. She still couldn't believe he had bought a truck or that he'd lied to her about not knowing how to drive. Of course, who was she to talk? She'd been lying to Mary Ruth, Willis, and everyone else she had met since her arrival in Lancaster County.

She moved up to Big Red and patted his side. *I'm sure there are a lot of people in this world—and maybe even this community—who have lied about something or are keeping some deep dark secret to themselves.* Her gaze dropped to the ground. *So why do I feel guilty for letting the Lapps think I'm their granddaughter?*

Michelle lifted her head when she heard Ezekiel approach. "Are you ready to go? he asked.

She nodded. "What about the blinker? Do you think we'll get stopped again because it doesn't work?"

He bopped the side of his head. "Oh, yeah. I forgot about that. I'll go in my uncle's workshop and see if he has any spare batteries lying around."

"Is he in there working?"

"Nope. The whole family is gone right now. They're on a camping trip with some of their friends. They won't be back till sometime toward the end of next week."

Michelle's face tightened. "So you're just gonna walk into your uncle's shop and take something without asking?"

"Yep. I'm sure he wouldn't mind. Besides, I'll replace it with a new one before they get home."

"What about your truck? Is that something they don't know about either? Did you park it here without asking, and because they're not home, you don't think they are any the wiser?"

A splotch of color erupted on Ezekiel's cheeks. "That's not how it is at all."

"How is it then?"

"I told you before that my cousin said I could park the truck here. His folks aren't as strict as mine."

"But aren't they likely to tell your parents?"

Ezekiel shook his head. "I don't think so. I'll come over to see them as soon as they get home and explain the situation."

Michelle fiddled with the top button on her blouse, to avoid eye contact with him. "Okay, suit yourself. I'll wait in the buggy until you get the blinker working."

⌒

## Paradise, Pennsylvania

Brad had spent the entire morning taking an Amish family to and from the Walmart store in Lancaster. He'd just dropped them off at their home and decided he would head down to Strasburg and see if the Lapps needed any work done. It would give him a chance to say hi to Sara too. He'd enjoyed her company at the Fourth of July festival a few weeks ago and thought he might see if she would like to go out for supper with him tomorrow evening. Secretly, he hoped to get better acquainted in an environment where so many people weren't milling around.

Brad thought about the night he'd joined the Lapps for supper. It would have been an opportunity to get to know Sara better, but unfortunately, Willis monopolized most of his time. Throughout the meal he'd talked, almost nonstop, about everything from the weather to the benefits of raising hogs. Mary Ruth had managed to get in a few words, asking Brad more about the call on his life to be a minister. Sara, on the other hand, had been quiet during the meal, barely looking in Brad's direction. He wanted to ask if something was bothering her but didn't get the chance. After the meal was over, Willis invited Brad into the dining room and challenged him to some Amish card game he'd never played before. By the time they were done, Sara had gone to her room, saying she'd developed a headache.

"I wonder if she was trying to avoid me," Brad mumbled. "Though I can't see why she would. Don't think I've said or done anything to offend her." He shrugged. "But then, who knows? I could have said something she didn't like without even realizing it."

Brad worried sometimes about his relationships with people. As a minister, he couldn't be putting people off or making them uncomfortable. He would need to have a good rapport with the people in his church and be sensitive to their needs.

### Strasburg

When Brad turned his van up the Lapps' driveway, he saw Sara getting out of a buggy. Then he caught sight of Ezekiel stepping out of the other side of the buggy and realized they must have been somewhere together. Brad wondered if Ezekiel was interested in the Lapps' granddaughter. If so, did Sara like him?

"Hi, Sara. Is Willis at home?" he asked, stepping up to her. "I came by to see if he has any chores for me to do today or even sometime in the near future."

"My grandpa's not here," she replied. "Or at least he wasn't when Ezekiel picked me up to. . ." She paused, glancing over at Ezekiel. "Uh. . .he took me out for a horse and buggy driving lesson."

"I see." Brad glanced at the tall Amish man and smiled. "It's nice to see you again."

Ezekiel gave a nod. "Good to see you too."

"I'll, um, go check the buggy shed and see if either Grandma or Grandpa's carriages are there." Sara twisted a strand of long hair around her fingers.

"Okay, thanks." Brad thought she seemed a little nervous today. Did it bother Sara that he was here and had seen her and Ezekiel together?

As she headed toward the buggy shed, Brad decided to ask Ezekiel a question. "I'm curious as to the reason you're teaching Sara to drive a horse and buggy. She's not planning to become Amish, is she?"

Ezekiel rubbed a hand across his chin. "I don't think so. Sara just said she wanted to learn, and I volunteered to teach her. Guess she thought it would be fun and a way to get to know her grandparents' way of life a little better."

"I see. Well, before he sprained his arm, wasn't Willis going to teach her?"

"Yeah, but that didn't work out, so I was glad to pitch in and take over for her grandpa. We've been using my horse, which has worked out better too, since Big Red's easy to drive and doesn't spook easily."

"Guess that makes sense." Brad really wanted to ask Ezekiel what his intentions toward Sara were, but it would be too bold, and probably not appreciated. Besides, it was really none of his business.

Brad waited quietly, staring at Ezekiel's horse. The animal stood patiently at the hitching rail, flipping his tail against the flies invading his space. He did appear gentle enough, at least here, where he didn't have to pull a buggy.

A few minutes later, Sara returned, shaking her head. "There are no buggies in the shed, and I don't know when either of my grandparents will be home. You're welcome to wait for them if you like."

"Okay, thanks, I will." Brad glanced at Ezekiel again, wondering if he too planned to stick around. He was pleased when Ezekiel told Sara he needed to go and climbed into his buggy.

Sara went around front and released the horse from the rail. "See you soon, Ezekiel," she called as he backed up his horse.

"Sure thing." Ezekiel looked at Brad. "See you around."

Brad nodded and waved. Then he turned to Sara and smiled. *Guess I'll get right to the point.* "Say, if you're not doing anything tomorrow night, I was wondering if you'd like to go out for supper with me."

Sara pushed a wayward strand of hair away from her face. "Sure, that sounds nice."

He smiled. "Great. I'll pick you up around six o'clock."

# Chapter 23

That evening it started to rain, and just as Michelle was getting ready for bed, Mary Ruth knocked on her door and asked if she'd like to come out to the barn. "One of the sows is about to give birth. Your grandpa and I thought you might enjoy seeing the process."

Michelle's eyebrows lowered and pinched together. For the first time since coming here, she wished she was someplace else. Watching pigs being born was not her idea of fun. Not to mention going outside in the drenching rain. But she didn't want to hurt Mary Ruth's feelings or act disinterested.

"Okay, sure," Michelle called through the closed door. "I'll be out there pretty quick."

"All right. I'm heading out to the barn now. We'll see you soon. Oh, and Sara, make sure you wear a jacket. It's pouring outside."

"Okay, Grandma." Michelle smiled, despite the interruption. It felt nice to have someone care for her the way Mary Ruth and Willis did. They were truly the grandparents she'd never had. How different her life would be if she had known these good people since she was a young girl.

*Guess I should enjoy their company while I can, 'cause it won't last forever.* Michelle slipped into her jean jacket and left the room. Downstairs, she grabbed an umbrella in the metal stand near the back door.

Outside, the rain came down in torrents, and thunder sounded in the distance. Michelle cringed when a flash of lightning lit up the yard. Looking to the west, she saw several bright, zig-zaggy streaks where the fury of the storm seemed to be much worse. She hated thunderstorms—she had ever since she was a child. The noise and bright flashes had scared her the most, especially when she had been all alone in the unfinished, upstairs bedroom. The rain sounded louder, pounding on the roof like a herd of elephants. The thunder and lightning seemed to be right outside her bedroom window, which had only added to Michelle's fear. When the wind howled, it made the windows sing eerily. And hiding under the covers, like she'd often done, didn't help. Giving in to her anxiety, Michelle would end up flying down the stairs with her blanket to sleep on the couch for the remainder of the night. Of course, Dad made fun of her the following morning, saying there was nothing to be afraid of and she ought to grow up and quit being such a baby. Michelle's fear of storms was being passed on to her brothers, who he'd found huddled together and asleep under their bed that morning.

Pushing her negative childhood memories to the back of her mind, Michelle dashed across the wet grass, flung open the barn doors, and stepped inside. Willis and Mary Ruth's voices could be heard coming from the back of the building. Michelle headed in that direction. She found them both sitting on folding chairs near the pregnant sow's pen.

Willis looked up at her and smiled. "Glad you could join us, Sara. Your grandma and I feel it's necessary to be on hand during the birth of Penny's piglets, and we figured you might like to witness it too.

Laughter bubbled in Michelle's throat, but she held it back. She couldn't believe Willis had actually named the mother pig.

"There's another folding chair if you'd like to sit on it." Mary Ruth gestured with her head.

"No, that's okay. I'll sit here." Michelle took a seat on a bale of straw.

Outside, the storm grew closer. She heard the wind howling as pelting rain hit the metal barn roof, while booms of thunder continued to sound. The storm didn't frighten her so much now. In fact, it felt kind of cozy inside the barn with all the familiar sounds and smells.

*I might feel differently if I was alone in my room right now. Would I end up sleeping on the Lapps' couch?*

Michelle yawned, pulling her knees up and wrapping her arms around her legs. She figured it might be a long night, waiting to see the piglets being born, but she didn't mind. It was nice being with Willis and Mary Ruth and listening to them chat. Even when they spoke in their native language, it didn't bother her. And since this would be the first time she'd seen a sow give birth, she'd be learning something new about farm life.

"Well, would you look at that?" Mary Ruth gestured to Sara. But her granddaughter had drifted off to sleep with her head on her bent knees.

Willis snickered. "Guess the excitement of watching Penny give birth wasn't enough to keep her awake."

"It is almost midnight, and I'm about ready to fall asleep myself." Mary Ruth kept her voice down. "Hopefully the rest of the piglets will be born soon."

"Should be." Willis yawned and reached for the thermos of coffee Mary Ruth had brought out to the barn a short time ago. He opened the lid and poured himself a cup. "Want some?"

She shook her head. "If I drink anymore *kaffi*, I'll be wide awake by the time we go to bed."

"Not me. I've always been able to drink coffee right up till I hit the hay, and it never bothers me."

She poked his arm playfully. "Jah, well, you're an exception."

He grinned. "Guess so."

Mary Ruth sat quietly with Willis, watching as three more piglets came into the world. A short time later, the sow laid on her side so all fifteen of her babies could nurse. It was a precious sight, and Mary Ruth never got tired of seeing the miracle of birth.

She glanced at Sara, who was still asleep, and her thoughts

went to Rhoda. Mary Ruth remembered well how their daughter used to react when any of the farm animals had babies. Rhoda would get all excited and sit there watching all day if she didn't have chores to do.

Mary Ruth hadn't expected their daughter to run off like she did—not in a million years. She had spent many years blaming herself for Rhoda's departure. Was there something she had said or done to cause their daughter to run off? Had they been too hard on her? Or not hard enough? But that was all behind her now. Blaming oneself did no good, and she had determined that she wasn't going to do it anymore. Thanks to Sara's letter, telling them who she was, Mary Ruth knew that Rhoda had left home by her own choice. She'd been embarrassed to tell them she was expecting a baby.

Mary Ruth's eyes watered, and she sniffed, hoping they wouldn't spill over. *How wonderful it would have been if we could have offered Rhoda support and been a part of the birth of our granddaughter. We would have done all we could to help our daughter during that difficult time. I wish she would have been brave enough to come to us with her problem.*

Despite her best effort, a few tears trickled down Mary Ruth's cheeks. *Oh Rhoda, how I wish we could have seen you one last time before you died. If only you had contacted us, we could have talked things through and assured you of our love and concern.*

Mary Ruth's only comfort was having Rhoda's daughter here with them. It was as though God had seen her and Willis's grief and brought Sara to them as a healing balm. And that's exactly what she was. The joy Sara brought to Mary Ruth and Willis was beyond words. She hoped they never lost touch with her and could see each other often, even if Sara chose to return to her home.

Michelle woke up feeling groggy and disoriented. It took her a few minutes to realize where she was. But after seeing Mary Ruth and Willis standing against the sow's stall, it didn't take her long to realize she was in the barn.

After sleeping on the bale of straw all that time, Michelle's body ached. She stood and stretched her sore muscles. Once she'd gotten some of the kinks out, she glanced toward the pen, blinking and rubbing her eyes. "Wow, look at all those piglets! I can't believe I slept through the whole thing. Why didn't you wake me?"

"Your grandpa wanted to, but I said no, you needed your rest more than seeing Penny give birth." Mary Ruth pointed to the baby pigs lying beside their mother. "She had fifteen little ones. Isn't that something?"

"I'll say. Bet the poor sow's more tired than I am." Michelle moved in for a closer look. "That's a lot of babies, but they're cute little things."

"Yes, indeed." Willis gave a loud yawn as he stood. "Well, everything seems to be okay here, so we should go into the house and try to get a few hours' sleep before it's time to get up and do our chores."

Mary Ruth nodded. "Guess that would be good, but not for too long, because soon it'll be time to fix breakfast."

"Oh, don't worry about that," Michelle said. "I'll take care of fixing breakfast this morning."

"Why, thank you, Sara." Mary Ruth slipped her arm around Michelle's waist. "You're always willing to help out. I just don't know what we would do without you."

Michelle smiled, although her insides quivered. *What would they think if they knew the real me?*

After Mary Ruth and Willis headed to their room, Michelle went back out to the barn. She wasn't sleepy anymore and thought it was a good chance to read a few more notes in the prayer jar. Each time she held the glass container, like she was doing now, her curiosity was piqued. As she shined the flashlight she'd brought along onto the paper, Michelle wished once more that she knew who had written the notes and why they'd chosen certain Bible verses, like the one she'd just read.

*"Wherefore come out from among them, and be ye separate, saith the Lord, and touch not the unclean thing; and I will receive you. And will be a Father unto you, and ye shall be my sons and daughters, saith the Lord Almighty" 2 Corinthians 6:17–18.*

With hands clasped under her chin, Michelle pondered the words, hoping to figure out their meaning. *How does one come out and be separate? Is this what Amish people are trying to do—be separate from the rest of the world by their Plain lifestyle and strict religious views?*

Her forehead wrinkled. *And what about the part of the second verse that says the Lord will be our Father and we shall be His sons and daughters? Maybe I should ask Brad about this verse when I go out to dinner with him tomorrow night.*

Michelle glanced at her watch. *It will actually be tonight, since it's now two o'clock in the morning.* She yawned and put the folded paper back in the jar. *Guess I need to try and get a few hours of sleep before it's time to start breakfast.*

She put the old jar back on the shelf behind the others and picked up her flashlight, prepared to leave the barn. *Maybe before I go back in, I'll take a quick look at the piglets and see how they're doing.*

Michelle walked back to the sow's stall and, shining the light, she looked in. Penny was sleeping, and so were fourteen of her babies. One of the brood, a little smaller than the others, had wandered off by itself and couldn't seem to find the way back to its mama. Its high-pitched squealing didn't seem to bother Penny. *Poor mama. She must be exhausted.*

Michelle opened the stall door and slipped quietly in. When she bent down to pick up the wailing piglet, her throat clogged up, and tears sprang to her eyes. These pigs had a mother as well as brothers and sisters. Michelle had no one except a pretend grandma and grandpa. And all the crying she'd ever done over the years hadn't brought anyone to comfort her.

Her thoughts went to her brothers, Ernie and Jack. How old would they be this year? "Let's see." Michelle counted on her fingers. "I can't believe my baby brother, Jack, will be twenty, and Ernie, twenty-two years old." Oh, how she wished she knew what had happened to them after they were taken from their parents. Had they gone to the same foster family, or had they been separated from each other, like she had been?

The last time Michelle saw them would be etched in her mind forever. She was only ten years old at the time, but it was like yesterday. As the car drove away, taking her brothers from her, a scream lodged in her throat. Their eyes locked with hers for the very last time, as they watched from the back window of the car. Michelle saw the desperation in Ernie's and Jack's faces but was helpless to do anything about it. Her heart felt like it had been broken into a million pieces. The vehicle got farther and farther away, and her brothers faded along with it—the last of her family being stripped away. Then it was Michelle's turn to be taken away, leaving her parents and getting into a car with strangers who would take her to a new place. Fourteen years ago, Michelle and her brothers had become wards of the state, and there was nothing she could do about it.

A sense of longing welled in her soul. Did Jack and Ernie ever think about her, or were the boys too young back then to even remember her now? Surely at six and eight years old, they would have recalled something about their sister. But maybe it was best if they didn't. Michelle had nothing to offer her brothers, and she hadn't done anything to make Ernie and Jack proud.

Blinking back tears as she refocused her thoughts, Michelle put the tiny pig next to its mother and left the stall. Turning back for one last look, she saw that all was quiet now, as the little runt squirmed in between the others.

*Who knows, maybe someday our paths will cross. If I ever get my life stable, I hope the day will come when I can find my brothers, and we'll never be parted again.*

# Chapter 24

"Thank you for fixing our breakfast." Mary Ruth smiled at Michelle from across the kitchen table.

"No problem. It was the least I could do, considering all you've done for me." Michelle paused to drink some of her apple juice. "You two have become like the family I never had."

Willis's brows lifted. "But your mother and father were your family."

Michelle's face warmed. "Yes, of course. What I meant was, you're the grandparents I never knew."

"So you never met your father's parents?" Mary Ruth asked.

Michelle shook her head. "Guess they didn't want anything to do with my dad." She had spoken the truth in that regard. Of course, Michelle had no idea what the real Sara's situation might be. For all she knew, Sara Murray might have a great relationship with her other grandparents.

Relief spread through Michelle when the Lapps changed the subject. Anything she would say to them about the family they thought she had would be a lie anyway.

While Willis and Mary Ruth talked about the baby pigs, Michelle wondered about the real Sara Murray. Michelle wished in some ways that she could meet and get to know the Lapps' granddaughter. It would be interesting to get acquainted with the young woman they believed her to be. What did Sara look like? What kinds of things did she enjoy doing? Did she have a job or a boyfriend? Were Michelle and Sara anything alike? She doubted it.

Michelle didn't even know what the Lapps' daughter looked

like, because they had no pictures of her. All she knew was that her own hair, ironically, was the same color as Rhoda's. That fact made it easier for Michelle to pass herself off as their granddaughter.

As Michelle stared at her plate of scrambled eggs and ham, her appetite diminished. *If Sara knew I was here, pretending to be her, I bet she'd hate me.*

❧

### Newark

Sara took a seat at the kitchen table and opened her plastic box full of beads. Since today was Saturday and she had no college classes or work schedule, it was a good time to make a few pieces of jewelry. Sara enjoyed this hobby—something she'd begun doing when she was in high school. She planned to make something for herself today, and perhaps another time she would make something to take to Strasburg when she went to meet her grandparents in October.

Sara hummed as she picked out certain colors. "Think I'll make a scarf ring to wear with the blue scarf Mama loved so much." She continued to hum while separating out the various shades of blue beads. When Sara was a little girl, her mother used to hum to her when she was sick or had a hard time falling asleep. She recalled how the roles reversed when Mama became so ill. In fact, Sara had been humming to her mother when she passed away.

Pushing the painful memory aside, she picked up several more glass beads and turned her thoughts toward the Lapps. *Maybe when I do this again, I'll make Grandma a bracelet or necklace. And Grandpa might like a keychain.*

Sara could hardly wait to meet them and learn about her mother's childhood. She tried not to think of the short letter she'd received that seemed so impersonal. Sara wanted to believe she had misinterpreted her grandparents being too busy to meet her just yet. Even more so though, she had high hopes of finding out everything about her father. *I'm sure they must know who he is.*

When Brad arrived at the Lapps' place to pick up Sara, he found her kneeling outside the barn door, petting the Lapps' collie.

"Last night one of my grandpa's sows gave birth to fifteen piglets. Would you like to see them?" She stood up and motioned him over, while Sadie darted across the yard, chasing after a black-and-white cat.

"Sure." Brad joined Sara, and when they entered the barn, she led the way to the sow's stall.

"Just look at them. Aren't they cute?" Sara leaned over the gate, pointing to one of the smaller baby pigs. "That's the runt. Early this morning, I had to help the poor little thing find its way to the mama."

Brad smiled at the enthusiasm he saw on her face. "Pigs are sure cute when they're babies. But then I guess most animals are."

Nodding, Sara pulled back from the gate. "We can go now if you're ready. I just wanted you to see the piglets." A lock of her long auburn hair fell against her cheek as she stood up straight.

Instinctively, Brad reached out to brush it back in place. He was surprised when she flinched and drew her head back. "What's wrong? I only wanted to push that hair away from your eyes. Sorry if it seemed I was being too forward."

"Y–you startled me." Her chin trembled a bit.

Brad looked at her, feeling concern. "I'm sorry, Sara. I reacted on instinct."

A tiny crease formed just above her nose. "Do you always fix women's hair when it gets out of place?"

"No, no, that's not what I meant." Brad felt like a bumbling idiot all of a sudden. "Uh, I think maybe we should go before I say or do anything else stupid."

She gave a quick nod and practically ran out the barn door.

They hadn't gotten off to a good start this evening. Brad could only hope the rest of their time together would go smoothly.

"Oh my word. I've never seen so much food in all my life." Michelle stared at all the stations loaded with a variety of food. There was something for everyone here at the Shady Maple Smorgasbord.

Brad chuckled. "I'm guessing it's the first time you've been here then."

She nodded. "If I tried a little of everything, you'd have to carry me out of here in a wheelbarrow."

His chuckle went deeper. "You're not only beautiful, but you have a sense of humor too."

A warm flush crept across Michelle's cheeks. Was Brad flirting with her? Had his touching her hair in the barn earlier meant something more than concern she might end up with it in her eyes? *Don't be ridiculous. You're reading more into it than there actually is. I'm sure Brad has no interest in me.*

"Well, let's dish up and get on back to our table." Brad gestured to the stack of plates on the end of one of the buffet stations. "You go first, Sara."

"Okay." Michelle chose all the things she liked best, and when she was satisfied with the amount on her plate, she filled her glass with iced tea and returned to their table. Brad wasn't far behind her.

When they sat down, he reached over and took her hand. "Do you mind if I pray before we eat?"

"No, that's fine." Thinking he would offer a silent prayer, the way Mary Ruth and Willis did, she bowed her head and closed her eyes. However, Michelle was surprised when Brad prayed out loud.

"Heavenly Father, we thank You for the food we're about to eat. Please bless it to the needs of our bodies, and thank You for the many hands who prepared it. And thanks for the opportunity to spend more time with Sara so we can get to know each other better. Amen."

Michelle opened her eyes and looked around. It made her uncomfortable when Brad began praying out loud, and she hoped no one else had heard him. She relaxed a bit when she saw that nobody seemed to be looking at them.

As they ate their meal, Michelle thought about her reaction when Brad pushed the hair out of her face in the barn. She had tried to act nonchalant, but inside she'd been shaking. She would never have admitted it to Brad, but his unexpected gesture brought back the memory of when Jerry slapped her face so hard that it left an imprint on her cheek.

Michelle set her fork down and drank some iced tea. *I should have known Brad would never do anything like that. He seems kind and gentle—an all-around nice guy. Maybe too nice for me.*

"I see your plate's almost empty." Brad broke into her thoughts. "Are you ready to check out all the pies, cakes, and other treats?"

Michelle held her stomach. "Oh boy. I'm not sure I have room for any dessert."

He flapped his hand. "Sure you do. No one leaves Shady Maple's without sampling at least one piece of pie or some cake and ice cream." He wiggled his eyebrows and stood. "You gonna join me?"

She groaned. "Okay. Why not?" Michelle followed Brad to the dessert stations. After perusing all the pies, she chose cherry.

"What? No shoofly pie?" Brad pointed to his plate. He'd taken a slice of shoofly, plus a couple of other kinds of pie.

"I don't know where you're going to put all that," she said when they returned to the table.

He patted his stomach. "I think there's still enough room in there."

Michelle shrugged. "Whatever you say. You must know your limits."

As they ate their pie, she decided to bring up the verse of scripture she'd found in the old jar that morning. "Since you're planning to become a preacher, I bet you know the Bible pretty well."

"Well, I'm certainly no expert, but I have studied the scriptures."

She folded her hands and placed them under her chin. "So could you tell me what a certain verse means?"

"I'll give it a shot. What verse is it?"

" 'Wherefore come out from among them, and be ye separate, saith the Lord, and touch not the unclean thing; and I will receive you. And will be a Father unto you, and ye shall be my sons and daughters, saith the Lord Almighty.' " Her forehead wrinkled. "I think I understand the first part, because that's what my Amish grandparents are doing. What I don't understand is how God can be anyone's father."

"God created everything and everyone," Brad explained. "So by creating us, He became our father. And when we accept Jesus Christ as God's Son, we also become God's son or daughter. Does that make sense?"

"I guess so." Michelle wasn't about to admit that not much about the Bible seemed logical to her. If not for the verses she'd found in the glass jar, she wouldn't even be acquainted with the scriptures. Although she'd been going to church with Willis and Mary Ruth every other Sunday, everything was spoken in a language she couldn't understand, so it all seemed quite confusing. And anything she'd learned when attending Bible school a few times as a girl had gone in one ear and out the other.

"Do you own a Bible, Sara?" Brad questioned.

She shook her head "I read the verse on a slip of paper I found at the Lapps'—I mean, my grandparents'."

"Maybe what you need is a study Bible. It would help explain many of the verses found in the Bible."

"Why would I need a special Bible to study? All I was asking about was just one verse."

He touched the back of his neck. "I figured if you had a question about one verse, there might be others."

"Maybe." Feeling the need for a change of subject, Michelle finished the rest of her pie and asked if he was ready to go.

Brad looked down at his empty plate and nodded. "I couldn't eat another bite."

"I can imagine."

He smiled and gave her a wink.

As they left the restaurant and began walking toward his van, Michelle struggled with her emotions. *As much as I enjoy Brad's company, I feel guilty when I'm in his presence. Does he know I am hiding a secret?*

# Chapter 25

*Strasburg*

Monday morning while Mary Ruth gathered eggs, Michelle went down to the basement to get some empty jars to use for canning tomatoes. After the snake incident, she'd been relieved when Mary Ruth said she would resume her previous job of getting the eggs every day. Just the thought of seeing that ugly black snake in the nest sent shivers up Michelle's spine. She hoped she wouldn't find anything frightening in the unfinished basement.

The cement floor had numerous cracks zig-zagging across it, and the rusty drain near the antiquated wringer washing machine looked nasty. The air smelled of mildew mixed with the milder scent of laundry detergent drifting out of an open box on a shelf near the washer. The natural light coming from two small windows positioned high on the wall helped the basement seem not quite so dreary.

To provide more light in the room, Michelle had taken a battery-operated lantern. The gas lamps hanging throughout most of the Lapps' home were good sources of light, as well as heat, but Michelle always felt a bit nervous whenever she had to ignite one. The last thing she needed was to cause an explosion or set the room on fire, for lack of paying close enough attention.

A spray of dust sifted into Michelle's face when she pulled a cardboard box marked CANNING JARS off one of the shelves. She managed to place it on a metal table a few seconds before a sneeze overtook her. She needed a tissue, but there were none in her pocket. *Oh great. Just what I don't need right now.* Michelle didn't want to go clear back upstairs for something to blow her nose on, but she needed to take care of this matter now.

She looked around, hoping there might be something down here she could use. An old towel or even a clean rag would do. Michelle felt relief when she spotted a roll of paper towels standing beside the box of laundry detergent. Quickly tearing one off before another sneeze came, she blew her nose and threw the soiled paper towel in the garbage next to the washing machine. *Now back to business.*

Lifting the light so she had a better look at all the shelves lining the walls, Michelle spotted a box marked, Rhoda's Toys. Curious to see what was inside, she took the box down, set it on the floor, and opened the flaps. Inside, she found a cloth doll with no face, several children's books, a coloring book, two small boxes of crayons, and a variety of miniature kitchen utensils. Apparently Mary Ruth hadn't been able to part with these things her daughter used to play with.

Michelle's heart clenched, thinking how devastating it must have been for the Lapps when their only daughter ran off and never contacted them again. Although Michelle hadn't run off from her own parents, she often wondered if they ever thought about her or wished things had been different. Had Mom and Dad sought help for their problems—particularly Dad's drinking, which had been a major cause for most of his abuse?

As she stood to return the box to the shelf, Michelle noticed an old jar toward the back. Looking closer she saw it was full of folded papers. The glass container appeared to be similar to the one she'd found in the barn, only this one was light green instead of pale blue.

Michelle climbed up on a stepstool she'd discovered and took the jar down. Then she used the top step of the stool as a seat and sat down. Michelle wasn't about to go back to the kitchen until she'd seen what kind of messages this antique vessel contained.

With anticipation, she reached into the jar and removed the paper closest to the top. Unfolding it, she saw a Bible verse: *"When thou passest through the waters, I will be with thee; and through the rivers, they shall not overflow thee: when thou walketh through the fire, thou shall not be burned; neither shall the flame kindle upon thee."* Isaiah 43:2.

Following the verse, a prayer had been written: *"Dear Lord, please walk beside me during this distressing time in my life. Guide me, direct me, and lead the way."*

Michelle's pulse raced. *Whoever wrote that must have been dealing with a challenge or going through something awful. I wonder what the problem was and how it all turned out. If only these walls could talk.*

She glanced around the dingy basement, inspecting each of the metal and wooden shelves. *Could there be more jars full of messages hidden here or someplace else?* This whole jar thing seemed like an unsolved mystery—one Michelle might never know the answer to.

"Where have you been, Son?" Ezekiel's mother pressed her thin lips together. "Our supper guest is here, and it's time to eat." She gestured to Lenore, standing near the kitchen table.

"Hello, Ezekiel. It's nice to see you again." Lenore offered him a fleeting smile, then took out four plates and began setting the table.

"Nice to see you too." Until this moment, it had slipped Ezekiel's mind that Lenore would be coming over. He'd thought her visit was going to be earlier in the day and was surprised to find out she'd be staying for supper. If Mom had told him the specifics, he must have forgotten. As far as Ezekiel knew, Lenore's reason for coming by was to pick out a plant from the greenhouse for her mother's upcoming birthday.

He pulled his fingers through the back of his thick hair. *I wonder if Lenore came over while I was gone this afternoon, and then Mom decided to invite her to join us for supper. Or could my matchmaking mother have set the whole thing up earlier so I'd have no choice but to spend time with Ivan Lapp's daughter?*

Ezekiel's mother would never admit it—especially to him—but

she had been trying to get them together as a couple for the last two years. Well, it wouldn't work. It wasn't that Ezekiel had anything against Lenore. She was kind of pretty, in a plain sort of way, and also quite intelligent. But they didn't have much in common. Besides, she had already joined the church and was committed to being Amish. Not a good fit for him, since he still had visions of being part of the English world once he figured out how to tell his mom and dad.

Ezekiel could only imagine the tongue lashing he'd receive if either of his folks knew he'd bought a truck and had parked it behind the home of Raymond's parents. Dad didn't like that his brother Arnold was more lenient with his children and looked the other way when they went through their running-around years. He thought Arnold should make his young people toe the line, the way he'd always tried to do.

"Well, don't just stand there, boy." Dad stepped up to Ezekiel and tapped his shoulder. "Let's get washed up so we can eat our meal."

"Jah." Ezekiel followed his dad down the hall to the bathroom. He groaned inwardly. After working most of the day at the greenhouse and then taking care of his bees this afternoon, all he wanted to do was relax. Company for dinner was not what he'd planned on at all.

❧

As Michelle sat with Willis and Mary Ruth, eating supper that evening, she thought about the jar she'd found in the basement. *I wonder how many more there might be hidden around the Lapps' farm.* Who had authored the notes she'd found was also a puzzle.

Michelle glanced over at Mary Ruth, who was sitting straight up in her chair while eating a spoonful of scalloped potatoes. *Was it her? Could she have placed those secret notes in the jars when she was going through some difficult times? Does Willis know anything about them?* To ask might open up old wounds for either one of them. No, it was better to say nothing. Michelle had already created a problem for the Lapps when she'd come here under false pretenses. Once she left Strasburg, she would leave the old prayer jars and the notes in them behind.

"Your scalloped potatoes and pork chops are appeditlich, and so is my favorite sauerkraut salad." Willis looked over at his wife with a tender expression. "You spoil me so good."

Mary Ruth chuckled. "You always say that, Husband."

"Course I do, 'cause it's the truth."

Michelle nodded in agreement. "Your food is real tasty, Grandma. I wouldn't be surprised if I haven't put on some weight since I've been here."

"I'm glad you two are enjoying the meal, but with all these nice things you've said, I'm having a hard time not letting it go to my head." Mary Ruth fanned her face with her paper napkin. "And you know what they say about *hocmut*."

"What does that word mean?" Michelle asked.

"It means 'pride,'" Willis explained. "Although not in these exact words, the Bible says, *'Der hochmut kummt vor dem fall.'*" He looked at Michelle, while tapping his knuckles on the table. "The translation is: 'Pride comes before the fall.'"

"I see." From all that Michelle had observed about this couple, neither of them had a prideful bone in their body. In addition to their kindness, both were the most humble, genuine people she'd ever known.

Willis and Mary Ruth bantered back and forth about several topics for a bit, before Mary Ruth turned to face Michelle, placing her hand gently on Michelle's arm. "You looked tired this evening. Did I work you too hard canning tomatoes?"

Michelle shook her head. "I am kinda tired though. I think the heat and humidity is getting to me."

"That makes sense, since you're probably used to having air-conditioning," Willis interjected. "Here, in order to cool off, we have to hope a cool breeze comes up when we have the windows open. Or if it gets too hot, we'll find shade underneath one of the tall, leafy trees in our yard and sit a spell with a glass of cold tea or lemonade."

"Actually, I've never lived in a place with air-conditioning."

Mary Ruth tipped her head. "Really? Not even when you were growing up?"

Michelle opened then closed her mouth, as she struggled to find the right words. "Um. . .no, not even when I was a young girl. My folks didn't spend their hard-earned money on things they didn't really need."

"Makes sense to me." Willis reached over and gave Mary Ruth's hand a few taps. "Guess we did something right when we raised our son and daughter. Ivan learned how to be frugal, and it's nice to know that Rhoda did too."

Thinking it would be a good time to raise a question she'd been pondering, Michelle asked, "Were Ivan and Rhoda—I mean my mom—the only children you had?"

Mary Ruth dropped her gaze to the table. "We had a son, but he had a heart condition and died when he was two months old. We were thankful for the time we had with him though, as well as the chance to raise our other two children."

Tears came quickly to Mary Ruth's eyes, and she excused herself from the table. As soon as she left the room, Willis slowly shook his head, looking sadly at Michelle. "Your grandmother is pretty sensitive when it comes to the baby we lost. Even though it's been a good many years ago, I don't think she's ever completely gotten over it."

Michelle wasn't sure what to say in response. She was sorry she'd asked the question. This poor couple had been through a lot and they deserved to be happy.

Lacking the right words, she reached over and patted Willis's arm. *I'll bet Mary Ruth wrote all those notes after Rhoda left home. That must be why many of the messages seem so sullen. She was grieving for the loss of not one, but two of her children.*

Ezekiel could hardly get a bite of food in his mouth because Lenore kept asking him questions. When she wasn't talking, his little brother Henry babbled on about a bunch of unimportant things.

"What did you do today?" Lenore's focus remained on Ezekiel.

"Worked in the greenhouse for a while, then took some honey from my beehives." He picked up his fork, but before he could put a piece of roast beef in his mouth, another question came.

"Will you be attending the young people's singing this Sunday evening?"

Ezekiel shrugged his shoulders. "Probably, but I'm not sure."

She smiled. "I am planning to go. I always enjoy our time of singing and the games we play beforehand."

"The food that's served is always good too," Ezekiel's brother Abe interjected.

Amy snickered and nudged him with her elbow. "You would say something like that. You always have food on your mind."

"Not so." Abe shook his head. "I think about my job workin' for the buggy maker, and also playing volleyball with my friends, which I'll be doin' Sunday night at the singing."

"Sounds like all you young people are planning to go to Sunday's gathering, and that's a good thing." Dad passed the potatoes to Ezekiel for a second helping. "Your mamm and I used to look forward to the singings when we were courting." Wiggling his brows, he gave her a quick glance. "Gave us a chance to spend more time together—especially on the drive to and from the event."

Mom nodded with an enthusiastic grin. "I remember those days well." She cast a sidelong glance in Ezekiel's direction. "Half the fun of attending young people's gatherings is the chance to visit with your date as you travel to and from."

Ezekiel clenched his fork so hard he thought it might bend. He hoped Lenore wasn't expecting him to take her to the singing or offer a ride home from the event. He didn't really want to go, but his folks would be disappointed if he didn't. So since he'd most likely attend, he wanted to go with Sara. He planned to ask her when they got together for another driving lesson later this week. He hoped she would say yes.

"Say, Mom, what's for dessert?" Henry looked at their mother with an expectant expression.

"I made a lemon shoofly pie this morning." She looked at Dad and smiled. "Because it's your daed's favorite."

Tilting his chin, Henry frowned. "Is that all we're havin'? You know I don't like lemon so much."

Mom gestured to the refrigerator. "There's a chocolate-and-peanut-butter pie in there too. Think you might be able to eat a piece of that?"

Henry lifted his chin, and his blue eyes brightened. "Jah, sure. I could probably eat more'n one."

Mom chuckled, and Dad ruffled Henry's hair. "Bet you could eat the whole pie."

Ezekiel was glad someone else had been able to get in a few words, squelching Lenore's constant prattle. But just when he thought he was in the clear, she turned in his direction again. It appeared that Lenore was about to say something when Amy spoke up.

"What have you been doing this summer, Lenore, now that you're not teaching school?"

Lenore blotted her lips with a napkin and smiled. "I've been working part-time at my folk's general store. I've also done a lot of gardening, and even had some time to do a bit of bird watching. Why, the other day when I was outside pulling some weeds, I spotted a. . ."

Lenore's words were muted as Ezekiel's thoughts pulled inward again. He was pleased that someone else was conversing with the schoolteacher, and he would be even happier when this evening was over.

# Chapter 26

During breakfast the following morning, Ezekiel's mother kept looking at him as though she wanted to say something. But every time she opened her mouth, Dad cut in. It almost seemed as if he was doing it on purpose. Normally, he wasn't this talkative. Especially if he was in a hurry to eat and get outside to prepare the greenhouse for the day's business.

When everyone finished breakfast, Dad grabbed his straw hat and started for the back door. "You coming, Ezekiel?"

"Jah, I'll be right behind you."

"You too, Henry." Dad looked over his shoulder at Ezekiel's younger brother. "Your help is also needed in the greenhouse today."

"Okay, Daadi." Henry practically jumped out of his seat and raced across the room. The boy always seemed eager to do whatever Dad said. No doubt there would be no question about whether Henry joined the church when he grew up. He'd apply for membership, if for no other reason than to please their parents. Ezekiel, on the other hand, wasn't that compliant. He just needed more courage to speak up and say what was on his mind.

Soon after Dad and Henry went out, Ezekiel picked up his straw hat and started across the room. He'd no more than put it on his head and grabbed hold of the doorknob when Mom hollered, "Wait a minute, Son. I want to ask you a question."

He let go of the knob and turned to face her, glancing briefly at his sister, who had begun to clear the dishes and put them in the sink. "What's up, Mom?"

She left her place at the table and stepped up to him. "I was wondering if you've decided yet whether you'll be going to the singing this Sunday."

Ezekiel's toes curled inside his boots. *I shoulda known this was coming.* "Jah, Mom, I'll most likely go."

"Good to hear." A slow smile spread across her face. "Have you considered inviting Lenore to go with you? She's not being courted by anyone, you know."

He cringed. *Should have expected that too.* "No, Mom, I won't be inviting Lenore. Thought I'd see if Sara might like to go."

Her dark eyebrows lifted, and she swiped a finger down her suntanned face. "The Lapps' other granddaughter?"

He nodded.

Before Mom could respond, Amy turned from the sink and pointed at him. "I knew it, Brother. You're sweet on Sara, aren't you?" Her chin jutted out as she smirked at him.

Feeling the heat of embarrassment cover his face, Ezekiel tugged at his shirt collar. It felt like it was choking his neck. "I'm not sweet on anyone. Sara and I are just friends."

"I hope that's true, Son." Tapping one bare foot and then the other, Mom jumped back into the conversation. "Sara's not Amish and she won't be staying with her grandparents forever. So don't get too attached to her. Lenore's a better choice for you, and she's already joined the church."

Ezekiel's jaw tensed. He was on the verge of telling his mother that he had no plans to court Lenore, much less join the Amish church, but something held him back. He would never admit it to anyone, but there were times when the thought of going English sent shivers of apprehension up his spine. Ezekiel had been blessed with the support of his family for so long, he wasn't sure he could make it in the English world without them. Even so, his curiosity with modern things and desire to try some of them out kept him unable to give up his dream. It was stupid to be on the fence about this. He wished someone he trusted would tell him which way to go. For now though, there was only one place for Ezekiel to go nd that was out to the greenhouse.

"I need to go help Dad." He glanced at his sister, then back at is mother. "I'll talk to you later, Mom."

"Okay. Tell your daed I'll join you all in the greenhouse once Amy and I get the dishes done."

"Sure, I'll tell him." Ezekiel went out the door. Even though t was obvious that Mom wasn't fond of the idea of him asking a oung woman who wasn't Amish to the singing, he looked forward to seeing Sara this Friday afternoon. Not only did he enjoy ner company, but being in her presence strengthened his desire to eave the Amish world behind.

The morning had started out humid, and as Michelle made her vay to the barn, she paused to wipe her sweaty forehead. She'd seen Brad briefly when he came to pick up Willis for a dental appointment. She wished she could have talked to him longer, but maybe here would be an opportunity when he and Willis returned. She nadn't seen Brad since they went to the Shady Maple, and she had a few more questions about the Bible she wanted to ask.

When Michelle entered the barn, she was greeted by her frisky pup and his mother, both wanting to play.

She bent to pet each of their heads, then shooed them away. Not now, you two. I want to check on the piglets, and I volunteered to help Mary Ruth bake some bread this morning."

The dogs tipped their heads and looked up at her as if they understood every word she'd said. Then Sadie gave a deep bark, nd Rascal followed with a weak imitation, before both dogs raced out of the barn.

Michelle snickered. In the beginning, she was unsure about iving around so many animals, but she felt differently now and vas thankful for the opportunity to spend time with most of the ritters here on the Lapps' farm.

*It seems I really could be a farm girl,* Michelle mused. She smiled, emembering how when she'd first arrived at the Lapps' farm, she had to convince herself that she could do this. Everything seemed so foreign and quaint. Michelle wasn't sure back then that she could even last a day, much less all these weeks.

Hearing the distinctive squeal of pigs, Michelle made her way over to Penny's stall. She stood for a while, watching the piglets nurse, and a peaceful feeling encompassed her. It was fun to watch the little babies wiggling around and crawling over each other, as they competed to get to their mother's milk.

Michelle couldn't believe in the nearly two months she'd been here how much she had come to love this place. She'd learned to bake, cook, tend the animals, and even drive a horse and buggy. She felt comfortable wearing less makeup and plainer clothes too. Even the emotional pain she had endured in the past seemed to be slowly receding. She had begun to feel as if living here with the Lapps was where she belonged.

*Wish there was something I could do to keep the real Sara from coming here to meet her grandparents—or at least prolong it further.*

She tapped her chin. *Maybe there is. I can write her another letter, pretending to be Mary Ruth, and say October's not a good time either. Or I could even say they've changed their minds about meeting her at all.*

Michelle heaved a sigh. But that would be heaping one lie on top of another. Mary Ruth and Willis did want to get to know their granddaughter. Trouble was, they believed they already were. Well, she had all of August and September to decide what to do. Meanwhile, Michelle would enjoy every minute possible with Mary Ruth, Willis, Ezekiel, and Brad. They had all become like family to her.

Michelle sucked in her bottom lip. *If they knew what I did, they'd probably turn their backs on me, and any trust they once had would evaporate like ice on a hot summer day.*

Michelle took one last look at the baby pigs and went back across the barn. If she had time to look at some of the notes in the prayer jar again, it might help her decide what to do. But Mary Ruth was waiting for her, so it would be better to get the jar down some other day when no one else was around. Right now, Michelle had no choice but to keep up her charade.

❧

Brad and Willis pulled into the drive at the same moment as Sara stepped out of the house to shake a tablecloth. Before Brad even got out of the truck, the wonderful aroma of fresh bread wafted from the home's open windows.

"Smells like the women have been doin' some baking in there." Willis grinned. "I know what I'll be having for lunch today."

Brad smiled. "I'm heading to the barn to start on the chores you asked me to do."

"I'll be out to help just as soon as I tell Mary Ruth I'm home and see if I can snitch a piece of bread. Ya want one too?"

"Sure, if she can spare it I'd enjoy a piece." Brad watched as Willis headed for the house just as Sara stepped back inside. Brad was disappointed that she hadn't waved, but apparently Sara hadn't seen him. Hopefully he could catch her sometime later.

❧

When Willis and Mary Ruth went to the living room to chat, Michelle began washing up the utensils and bread pans. Earlier, she and Mary Ruth had put on a pot of chicken-corn soup that still simmered. They'd also made two pies, several batches of cookies, and four loaves of bread.

Michelle was tired and wondered where Mary Ruth got her stamina to do all this baking in one morning. The kitchen felt stifling, with no air coming through the windows on this muggy day.

She paused from her chores to wipe the sweat on her brow as she looked out the window. The tree branches were still, suggesting there wasn't a hint of air moving out there. As Michelle washed the next bread pan, she spotted Brad working in the corral on a fence board that had come loose.

Her hands remained in the soapy water, but she couldn't take her eyes off him. He had removed his shirt as he worked out under the blazing sun. Even from here, Michelle could see the sweat gleaming on his back. *I'll bet he could use a break and something cold to drink.*

Michelle dried her hands and took a tall mug from the cupboard, then filled it with iced tea. When she walked by the table, she grabbed a few cookies and wrapped them in a napkin, which she put in her apron pocket. She also draped a hand towel over her arm, in case Brad wanted to wash up, and then headed out the door.

"Sorry to interrupt, but I brought you something," Michelle called as she approached the corral.

"No problem, I was done with this project anyway and am ready to move on to the next one Willis wants done." He stopped his work and leaned against the fence post. "Is it a piece of bread? Willis said he might bring me one."

She shook her head and held out the cookies and mug of cold tea. "Willis—I mean Grandpa—popped into the kitchen for a minute, but then he and Grandma went to the living room to talk. Guess he must have forgotten about the bread."

Brad gave her a dimpled grin. "Well, I'm grateful for the break and appreciate the cookies and cold drink. This tea sure looks inviting." Brad gulped down the icy cold drink.

Michelle watched his Adams apple move each time he took a swallow. When some of the tea dribbled down his chin and over his throat, she resisted the temptation to wipe it off for him.

Brad emptied the glass and used the back of his hand to wipe the moisture from his mouth. He drank the rest of the tea so quickly, Michelle wished she'd brought two mugs instead of one.

"I brought you a towel so you can clean up when you're finished with the fence."

"Thanks. That was thoughtful of you. I'll wash my face and hands before I eat the cookies." Brad took the towel, went over to the hose, and turned it on.

Michelle watched as he rinsed off. She couldn't help noticing the water trickle down his broad shoulders and corded stomach muscles just below his chest. For a fleeting moment, she wondered how it would feel to have his strong arms holding her close.

She looked away, the heat of embarrassment flooding her face. *I hope he didn't notice me staring at him.* The hard work Brad had been doing this summer had obviously given him this healthy physique.

"Would you like some more ice tea?" Michelle asked, hoping her voice didn't sound as shaky as she felt at the moment. "I can go in and bring out more."

"Maybe, before I start work on the next project, but let's sit and visit a few minutes first."

Michelle took a seat at the picnic table while Brad grabbed his T-shirt from the fence post where he'd hung it earlier and pulled it on down over his head.

"Okay." Michelle sat quietly as Brad seated himself across from her and then she handed him the napkin and cookies.

"Thanks."

"You're welcome."

Brad had the prettiest blue eyes, and today they looked even bluer because his face had a healthy tan. For the moment, Michelle was at a loss for words.

"What's wrong? Do I have cookie crumbs on my face?"

"Uh, no. I just can't think of anything to say right now." All thoughts of asking Brad more about the Bible vanished, like a thief in the night. There was no question about it—Brad was different than any man she'd ever known. And it wasn't only his good looks.

❧

Brad was surprised at how quiet Sara had become. All the times he'd been with her before, she'd been quite talkative. "Maybe I will have some more iced tea," he said to break the silence.

"Sure, no problem." Sara got up and made a dash for the house, leaving Brad's empty mug on the picnic table. He watched her ponytail bounce as she approached the back porch.

Brad had a hard time understanding Sara sometimes. One minute she seemed happy and chatty, and the next minute her mood turned sullen. He wondered if he'd said something to offend her; although he couldn't think of what it could be.

When she didn't return right away, Brad went to the toolshed to get out what he needed to repair the corral gate, which was close to falling off. Poor Willis couldn't keep up with all the work around this place. It was a shame some of his family didn't live here on the farm with him and Mary Ruth. An elderly couple shouldn't be by themselves with so many responsibilities. *But then, maybe they enjoy the challenge of taking care of their home and property,* he told himself. *That's what probably keeps them going.*

Brad's concern for others was almost his downfall. He often worked too hard and didn't spend enough time having fun, but he'd always been the compassionate sort—often putting other's needs ahead of his own.

He'd just gotten into position to begin working on the gate when Sara returned with another mug full of tea. "Sorry for taking so long." She pushed a wayward piece of hair back in place. "I was helping Mary Ruth get lunch on the table, and they wanted me to extend an invitation for you to join them."

"That sounds good. Guess Willis doesn't plan on helping me do any work till after he eats." Brad rubbed the back of his neck where a mosquito had bit. *Or is the elderly man getting forgetful?*

Sara flapped both hands in front of her face. "Whew! I believe the humidity has become even thicker. What I wouldn't give to be in an air-conditioned room right now."

"I know what you mean. Say, before we go inside to eat, I'd like to ask you something."

"What's that?"

"If you're not busy Friday night, would you like to go out with me for an ice-cream cone or some other sweet treat?"

"Sure, I'd love to." Michelle gathered up the empty mug and headed back toward the house. Halfway there, she turned and called, "Are you coming, Brad?"

"Yep. I'm right behind you." He might not get the chance to see Sara too many more times before he left for seminary in a few weeks, so he was glad she'd accepted his invitation to go out Friday night. He thumped his forehead. *What am I doing? I need to stop thinking about that young woman all the time. Even though I enjoy being with Sara, she may not be the right girl for me.*

# Chapter 27

Friday afternoon, as Mary Ruth took clothes off the line, she reflected on the enjoyable time she and Willis had with Sara last evening. It had been another warm day, so they'd eaten supper outside on the picnic table. Willis cooked steaks on the barbecue grill, and Mary Ruth served potato salad, dilled green beans, coleslaw, and corn on the cob. For dessert, they'd enjoyed refreshing raspberry sherbet.

After the meal, the three of them had sat on the porch and visited as they waited for the fireflies to make an appearance. The only downside was that Sara seemed quieter than usual. They'd be talking about something, and then Sara would stare off into space, as though her thoughts were someplace else. Mary Ruth wondered if their granddaughter might have grown tired of them by now and felt ready to return to her home. She debated about bringing up the topic, but decided it might be best to wait and see if Sara brought it up herself.

Bringing her thoughts back in line, Mary Ruth looked to her right, watching as Sara stood on the porch, shaking the braided throw rugs that went inside the front and back doors. She was a hard worker and never complained when asked to do a task. With the exception of not wanting to gather eggs since she'd seen the snake, Sara seemed to have adapted well to farm life.

Mary Ruth removed a kitchen towel from the line and dropped it into the wicker basket. *Would Sara ever consider giving up her English life to become Amish? Is it too much to hope that she might want to stay here permanently?* This topic had crossed Mary Ruth's mind multiple times, and she'd also discussed it with Willis. Like her, Willis wanted their granddaughter to stay, but he'd reminded Mary Ruth often that it was Sara's choice.

*If only Rhoda hadn't run off, we could have known our granddaughter since she was a boppli.* Mary Ruth shook her head. But if she'd stayed here, would she have married an Amish man, and if so, who would she have chosen? The man she had married was obviously English, since she hadn't run off with any young Amish men in the area—at least no one they knew about. Who knew what secrets their daughter had kept from them during her time of running around?

*Life is full of choices.* Mary Ruth stared up at the billowy clouds overhead. *By choosing one direction, it takes us down a certain path, but a different direction would lead to another.* She supposed it did no good to ponder the outcome of either.

"Can I help you finish taking the laundry off the line?" Sara asked, stepping into the yard.

Mary Ruth smiled. "I appreciate the offer, but I'm almost done." She gestured to the few remaining clothes on the line.

"Is there something else you would like me to do before we start supper?"

"I can't think of anything at the moment." Mary Ruth turned at the sound of a horse and buggy approaching. She wasn't surprised to see Ezekiel's rig pulling in. He'd been coming around a lot lately. Mary Ruth was pleased that he'd been teaching Sara how to handle a horse and buggy. Although neither had admitted it—at least not to her—she had a feeling something more than friendship was developing between Ezekiel and Sara. This in itself might be enough to keep Sara in Lancaster County. Of course, Brad seemed to have taken an interest in her too, but he had no plans to stay in the area permanently. Once Brad got his minister's license, he could be called to preach at a church in a different state.

*One more thing I shouldn't worry about,* Mary Ruth reprimanded herself. *The man our granddaughter chooses will be up to her, and the same holds true about where she will live.*

Michelle went up to Ezekiel's buggy as soon as he stepped down. He grinned at her. "Hey, I haven't seen you for several days. How are you doing?"

"Okay. How about you?"

"I'm fine too. Came over to see if you have time to go for another buggy-driving lesson?"

"You mean today?"

He nodded. "Thought maybe we could take a ride in my truck too."

"I can't today because it'll be time to help my grandma with supper soon."

Ezekiel's shoulders slumped. "I didn't realize it was getting so late. Could we go after supper?"

"Sorry, but I have plans this evening."

"Oh, I see." Tilting his chin down, Ezekiel cleared his throat. "There's something else I wanted to ask."

"What's that?"

"This Sunday evening there's gonna be a young people's singing. I was wondering if you'd like to go with me."

Michelle smiled. "Sure. I haven't been to one before, and I think it would be fun."

He rubbed his hands together. "Sounds good. I don't always go to the singings, but since you'll be with me, I'll look forward to going to this one."

*Lancaster*

Friday night came, and the humidity had not lifted one bit. They drove with the windows down, and Brad couldn't help noticing Sara's auburn hair lifting off her shoulders as the breeze from the open windows cooled them. He could have turned on the air-conditioning, but sometimes, a breeze—even a warm one—felt nice when driving.

"At least we are getting some air." Sara pulled her hair back and wrapped a rubber band around it, making a long ponytail. Brad wished she had left it down.

They pulled into the ice-cream store's parking lot. "Well, here we are." He grinned at her. "Should we order at the window instead of going inside?"

"Sure, that's fine with me."

They got out of Brad's van, walked up to the window, and ordered two strawberry ice-cream cones. Then they sat at an outside table, away from the others, to enjoy the refreshing, cool treat.

If Brad didn't know any better, he'd swear this was couple's night as he glanced at the other patrons who'd also chosen to sit outside. For an ice-cream store, it was kind of odd not to see any children with their families milling around. But all the tables were occupied by couples. Most of them looked to be about the same age as he and Sara, but Brad also noticed another couple—an elderly man and woman, both with silver hair. While eating their dishes of ice cream, the older couple laughed and enjoyed a conversation together as if they were the only two people in the world. *I hope someday I'll find my soul mate—someone I'm madly in love with—and we can spend the rest of our lives growing old together.*

Brad took a long look at Sara. Could she be that person? He certainly enjoyed Sara's company, but he needed to know more about her.

"This is a nice way to spend the evening. I'm glad you invited me." Sara wiped a dribble of ice cream off her chin.

Brad nodded. "There's nothing like a frozen treat to help cool down in this heat."

"True."

When Sara finished her cone, he asked if she would like another.

She shook her head. "That was good, but one's enough for me. You go ahead and get another cone if you want to though."

"No, I'm good too. If you're not in a hurry to go, let's stay here and talk for a while."

"Okay." Sara settled against her chair. "Tell me more about your schooling."

"What would you like to know?"

"How long will it be before you start preaching at a church?"

"It'll be a few years yet." Brad leaned his elbows on the table, looking at her intently. "I'll be leaving for seminary on September 2nd, and then it will be an intense couple of years as I train for the ministry."

"Won't you miss Lancaster County after you're gone?"

"I'll admit, I've enjoyed driving for some of the Amish in the area and working on the local farms during the summer, so yeah, I most likely will miss it. The jobs I've done gave me a chance to do something physical, not to mention clear my head after all my studies, which can be mentally exhausting." Brad smiled. "But my goal is to be a minister, and it's what I need to do." He pointed at Sara. "What about you? What goals have you set for yourself?"

Sara dropped her gaze. "I have no goals."

"Nothing at all?"

"Nope."

His brows furrowed. "What about your grandparents? Surely you have some goals that involve spending time with them in the future."

She pulled in her bottom lip. "Well, I don't know. You see, the truth is. . ." Sara's voice trailed off. "Oh, never mind. I just live from moment to moment, that's all."

Brad had the feeling there was something she wasn't telling him. Should he press to find out what is was, or let it drop? He didn't want Sara to think he was being pushy.

A knot formed in Michelle's stomach. She had been caught off guard when Brad asked about her future goals, and she'd almost blurted out the truth of her deception. Thankfully, she had caught herself in time. Brad was a good person—maybe even righteous. He would look down on her and probably insist she come clean with the Lapps. Any good feelings he may have had for Michelle, who he believed was Sara, would be tossed out like yesterday's garbage. She wouldn't blame him either. These last few months, as much as Michelle had enjoyed having Mary Ruth and Willis as her pretend grandparents, she'd begun to loath herself for lying to them. It was wrong to take advantage of those good people, and the only way to resolve the situation was for her to go. *Maybe I could ask Brad to drop me off somewhere when it's time for him to leave for seminary.*

She shifted in her chair, wondering how she would explain her reason for going at that particular time. *It might be best if I don't involve Brad. My problem is not his, and when he goes off to finish his schooling, I'll never see him again.*

Brad reached across the small table and placed his hand on hers. "Is something bothering you, Sara? I'm a pretty good listener, so if you'd like to talk about it, I'm willing to listen."

She shook her head. "No, I'm fine. I was thinking about how after you leave for seminary, we'll probably never see each other again."

"Well, you never know. Our paths might cross again someday. Maybe some time when you're visiting your grandparents, I'll make a trip to Strasburg, and we'll reconnect."

Michelle's voice lowered to a near whisper. "That would be nice."

❧

As Ezekiel approached the ice-cream store in Lancaster, he decided to stop for a treat. He'd had a busy week helping his parents in the greenhouse and delivering honey to his loyal customers. So this evening, he figured he deserved a break, and it was a good chance to take his truck out for a spin.

Ezekiel let go of the steering wheel with one hand and swiped his arm across his sweaty forehead. He couldn't wait for this humidity to break. While he had been talking to one of his customers today, they'd mentioned the news said the hot, sticky weather would finally end on Saturday when storms were expected to come through, leaving a swath of cool, comfortable temperatures for the next several days. Ezekiel sure hoped it was true. He looked forward to taking Sara to the singing Sunday evening and would appreciate good weather.

When Ezekiel pulled his vehicle into the parking lot, he was surprised to see Brad and Sara there, getting up from a table and heading to Brad's van. They hugged before stepping up and into the vehicle.

Ezekiel drew back, feeling like someone had punched him in the stomach. Was this a date they were on? Is this what Sara meant when she said she had plans for the evening?

He sat hunched over the steering wheel, watching as Brad's van pulled out of the parking lot. He'd suddenly lost his appetite for ice cream or anything else.

Ezekiel's scalp prickled. *Of course Sara would rather spend time with Brad. She's English and so is he. I'll bet she only accepted my invitation to go to Sunday's singing so she wouldn't hurt my feelings. If I were English or she was Amish, maybe something more could develop between Sara and me.*

Even though Ezekiel had often wondered about being English, his feelings weren't as complicated or as confusing before Sara came along. Spending time with her had caused him to think about being English even more.

# Chapter 28

*Strasburg*

On the way home from church Sunday afternoon, Mary Ruth turned in her seat to look at Sara. "I know we ate after church was dismissed, but it wasn't a big meal. How would you like to go on a picnic with your grandpa and me?"

Sara's pretty blue-green eyes sparkled. "Sounds like fun. Would we have it in your backyard?"

"Nope," Willis spoke up. "We'll go to the pond out beyond our place. Unless you got adventuresome and ventured there on your own, I don't think you've seen it yet." He glanced back at her and grinned. "The ole' pond is one of my favorite fishing holes."

"I have seen a few ponds in the area, but I don't believe I've been to the one you're talking about. Are we gonna do some fishing today?" Sara asked.

He shook his head. "I never fish on Sundays. Besides, you'll be going to the singing with Ezekiel later today, and we wouldn't want to hold you up for that."

"Okay, but can we go fishing some other time?"

"Sure thing. We'll try to make time for that."

Mary Ruth smiled. "Your mother enjoyed fishing. But then I guess you knew that, right?"

Silence.

Mary Ruth turned to look at Sara again. "Did you hear what I asked?"

Sara blinked rapidly. "Umm. . . What was it?"

"I mentioned that your mother liked to fish and asked if you knew it."

Forehead wrinkling, Sara slowly nodded.

*Sara seems kind of off today. I wonder if something's bothering her.* Mary Ruth glanced at Willis to see if he'd also noticed, but his concentration appeared to be on the road.

"I miss your mother so much," Mary Ruth murmured, "but I'm thankful to God for bringing you here."

Once more, Sara was silent. Perhaps she was also missing her mother. It probably wasn't a good idea to talk about Rhoda so much, but Mary Ruth couldn't help it.

As Michelle rode in Ezekiel's open buggy on the way to the singing that evening, all she could think about were Mary Ruth's questions this afternoon—first on the way home from church and again during their picnic lunch. Previously, Michelle had managed to make things up when either Mary Ruth or Willis asked about their daughter. At first she'd been quiet and unresponsive when Mary Ruth began questioning her today, but as time went on and more questions were asked, she'd given the best answers she could. Apparently, whatever she'd said must have been satisfactory, because Mary Ruth finally quit asking and talked about other things. In fact, by the time they'd arrived back at the Lapps', Michelle's pretend grandma wore a peaceful expression.

*Too bad I didn't feel a sense of peace,* Michelle thought with regret. *I don't know if I'll ever feel any tranquility or sense of harmony in my life.* She shifted on her seat. *Is it wrong to want happiness? The Lapps have said many times that having me here has brought them joy. So is my lie really such a horrible thing?*

Michelle knew the answer, but it was hard to acknowledge, even to herself. If she'd never come here in the first place—never pretended to be Sara Murray—she wouldn't be in this predicament. She would be living on her own, who knew where, and the Lapps would have been reunited with their rightful granddaughter.

*When they finally do meet the real Sara, they'll probably like her better than me anyway. I bet she's a decent person who would never take advantage of two sweet old people the way I have.*

"We're here." Ezekiel startled Michelle out of her gloomy introspections. "Welcome to Emmanuel Fisher's home."

Michelle rubbed her forehead, trying to collect her thoughts.

"You okay, Sara?" Ezekiel touched her arm. "You were quiet most of the way here."

"I'm fine. Just doing a lot of thinking, that's all."

When Michelle stepped down from Ezekiel's buggy, she was greeted by Lenore.

"Hello, Cousin." Lenore clasped Michelle's hand. "You just missed a rousing game of volleyball, but I'm glad you could join us for the meal and our time of singing."

Michelle smiled. "Thank you. I have never attended a singing before, so I'm anxious to find out what it's like."

Lenore linked arms with Michelle. "Let's go inside. I'm sure they're getting the food set out by now."

Michelle looked back at Ezekiel. "Aren't you coming?"

"I'll be in as soon as I get my horse put away."

"Oh, yeah, of course." Michelle hesitated a moment, but at Lenore's prompting, she followed her into their host's enormous barn. One would never know any animals had ever been housed here. The entire building looked as clean as Mary Ruth's kitchen, and it smelled good too, with none of the usual barn odors. Someone had done a good job cleaning.

Inside, several long tables with backless wooden benches had been set up. Another table held platters with plenty of sandwiches, chips, and other snack foods. On one side of the room a group of young men had gathered, and the women seemed to be staying by themselves. Michelle assumed once the festivities got started, the men and women would integrate. She was disappointed, however, when Ezekiel entered the building and headed straight for the men. Since he had brought her to this function, she figured it was sort of a date and that he would spend the evening with her. Was it normal for the men and women to segregate at a singing, or only when they first got here?

Michelle didn't have to wait long for her answer. After everyone gathered for silent prayer, the men dished up their plates and took seats at one long table together. When it was time for the women to get their food, they sat at an opposite table.

Michelle looked at Ezekiel, but engrossed in eating, he seemed not to notice. She went through the line with the other young women, then took a seat at the table with them, making sure to sit next to Lenore. Most everyone made Michelle feel welcome, but a few kept their distance, eyeing her with questioning looks. Michelle couldn't blame them. She didn't feel like she belonged here either.

She looked down at the simple blue dress she wore. It was one Mary Ruth had made for her. Although not as plain as what the Amish women dressed in, it made her feel more a part of this community.

Michelle leaned closer to Lenore and whispered, "When will we start singing?

"As soon as we finish eating."

"I have one more question."

"What's that?"

"Will we sit with the guys during the singing?"

Lenore shook her head. "They sit on one side of the room, and we sit on the other. It's pretty similar to the way it is during our church services."

"You mean there'll be preaching and Bible reading?"

"No, just singing, but we sit separate from the men."

"I see." Michelle sipped some lemonade. *I wish Ezekiel had explained all this to me ahead of time. When he invited me to attend the singing, I might have said no.*

"How'd you like the singing? Did you enjoy yourself this evening?" Ezekiel asked as they headed for the Lapps'.

"It was okay, I guess, but I would have enjoyed it more if you hadn't been on the opposite side of the room." Sara gave an undignified huff. "What was the point in asking me to go with you if we weren't gonna be together?"

He swallowed hard. "I thought you knew how it would be."

"How could I? I've never been to a singing till this one."

"I'm sorry, Sara. You're right. I should have explained things before we got there."

She shrugged. "It's okay. Guess it's no big deal, since I won't be here much longer anyway."

Ezekiel jerked his head. "What do you mean?"

"Come on, Ezekiel. You must realize I can't stay here forever. I need to get back to my own life soon."

"But you'll come back for visits, right?"

"I don't know."

He glanced at her, then back at the road again. "Your grandparents would be awful disappointed if you didn't come back to see them." *And so would I.*

"Them and me both."

"Then what's the problem?"

Sara stared down at the small black purse she clutched in her lap. "I guess there is none. Can we please talk about something else?"

"Sure. Actually there is another thing I'd like to ask you."

"What is it?"

"It's about Brad." Ezekiel pulled back on the reins a bit, to slow Big Red. He didn't want to get to the Lapps' before he had a chance to find out what he wanted to know.

"What about Brad?" she asked.

"I saw the two of you together at the ice-cream store in Lancaster Friday evening."

Her eyes widened a bit. "You did?"

"Yeah. I went there in my truck to get some ice cream and saw you and Brad hug each other before you got in his van."

She nodded. "I was thanking him for the ice cream he treated me to."

"So you were on a date." Ezekiel phrased it as a statement, not a question. It was fairly obvious Brad had taken Sara there on a date.

"I wouldn't call it a date exactly."

"Then what would you call it?"

Sara reached into her purse and withdrew a pair of nail clippers. "Just two friends getting together for what could be the last time." She opened the clippers and snipped a jagged nail. "Brad will be leaving for seminary in a month, and if he keeps busy driving some of the Amish in the area, plus odd jobs, there might not be another opportunity for us to see each other again before he goes."

"I see." Ezekiel rolled his tongue around in his mouth. He wanted to say more on the subject, but didn't want Sara to think he was being pushy. And if he wasn't careful, he might say something stupid and blurt out that he'd come to care for her and wished she felt the same way.

As Mary Ruth and Willis got ready for bed that night, she brought up the subject of Sara. "Do you think our granddaughter had a good time with us today?"

"Jah, I believe so." Willis rubbed the back of his neck. "Why do you ask?"

"Didn't you notice how quiet she was during the picnic, and also on the buggy ride there and back home?"

The wrinkles in his forehead deepened. "Now that you mentioned it, she was quieter than usual. But I don't think it's anything to worry about. Maybe she was tired."

"You're probably right. Sara seems kind of moody at times. It's hard not to be concerned." Mary Ruth took a seat on the end of bed and pulled the pins from her thinning hair. "Talking about Rhoda today made me miss her all the more."

"Maybe you shouldn't talk about her so much then."

She narrowed her eyes at him. "You're kidding, right? There's no way I could ever forget about Rhoda or our precious little Jake either."

Willis put both hands on his hips as he moved closer to the

bed. "I am not suggesting we should forget about our deceased *kinner*. But talking about them all the time is a constant reminder of the pain we endured losing them." He sat beside Mary Ruth and took hold of her hand. "I say we focus on our son, Ivan, his family, and the newest member of our family—sweet Sara."

Mary Ruth sniffed, leaning her head on his shoulder. "You're right, Willis. I am grateful for your good advice. Just knowing we've been given the chance to meet and get to know Rhoda's daughter gives me a sense of joy and peace."

Willis puts his arm around Mary Ruth and gave her a tender squeeze. "My heart feels at peace too."

# Chapter 29

*Newark*

Sara woke up with a headache, but she wouldn't skip work this morning or her afternoon class. Both were important to her future. She hurried to get dressed, then went to the kitchen to make herself a cup of coffee.

Sara picked up her planner and took it with her to the table. In two months she would be going to Strasburg to see her grandparents. Sara had hoped to receive another letter from them, but she'd heard nothing since the last one, asking her to wait until October.

"Maybe they don't want to meet me after all," she murmured. "I'll write them again in a few weeks to be sure. As much as it will hurt, I don't want to go barging in there if I'm not wanted."

Sara had already determined that if she wasn't welcome, she would accept their wishes and not go, but oh how she hoped the Lapps wouldn't say no. She so desperately wanted to meet them and learn about her mother's life before she'd left home. *A link to my mother's past will be a connection to my future.*

A knock sounded on the back door, interrupting Sara's musings. She rose from her seat to see who it was.

"I saw your car in the driveway and figured you hadn't left for work yet." Her stepfather's dark brows lifted. "Or are you having car problems again? Because if you are, and you need a lift..."

Sara shook her head. "For the moment, the little beast is running, but who knows for how long." She gestured for him to come inside. "I got paid last Friday for the few hours I worked at the dental clinic that week, and the week before, so I can pay this month's rent now."

"Are you sure? Don't want you to cut yourself short."

"No, it's okay." Sara couldn't help wondering why Dean was being so nice. Normally, he wanted the rent money on the first of every month, without question. Why the sudden change? He must have some sort of agenda.

She opened her purse and handed him the cash. "Here you go. Don't spend it all in one place." Sara gave a small laugh, hoping to diffuse any tension she may have created by repeating a line he used to say when she was a girl. She'd never really known how to take anything Dean said back then. Sometimes when he said something and she thought he was kidding, she would say something back and then be accused of having a smart mouth. There were other times when Sara thought her mother's husband was being serious, and it turned out he was only teasing. Or at least, that's what he said. Dean was a hard person to figure out, and she'd given up trying.

Sara often wondered what it was about Dean Murray that had appealed to her mother. Did Mama think he was good looking, witty, smart, or would make a good provider? He'd done a fair job of providing for them over the years, but Sara didn't care much for the man. And the fact that Dean favored his biological son, Kenny, had done nothing to put him in Sara's good graces.

"Well, I need to get to work myself," Dean announced. "Is there anything you need before I go?"

She shook her head. "But thanks for asking."

"No problem." Dean stuck the rent money in his shirt pocket and went out the door.

Inhaling a deep breath, Sara returned to her chair and the now-lukewarm coffee. *I wonder what my real father is like. Is he nice looking? Kind? Caring? Does he even know about me? If so, has he tried looking for me all these years? Hopefully, all my many other questions will be answered once I meet the Lapps.*

"What on earth happened in here?" Ezekiel frowned as he and his parents entered the greenhouse. Someone, or something, had knocked over several potted plants, spilling dirt and containers onto the floor.

Dad's forehead wrinkled as he surveyed the situation. "Maybe Henry left the door open when I asked him to close up Saturday evening. Shoulda followed behind him I guess."

"Well, nothing seems to be broken, at least," Mom said. "If Henry did leave the door open, I'm sure he didn't do it on purpose."

Ezekiel rolled his eyes. His twelve-year-old brother could do no wrong in their mother's eyes. *I never got away with something like that when I was Henry's age.*

"We'd better get busy cleaning up the greenhouse and trying to repot the fallen plants before any customers show up." Dad went to get the broom.

"How'd things go at the singing last night, Ezekiel?" Mom asked as she knelt to pick up two potted plants. "We were already in bed when you got home, and I forgot to ask this morning during breakfast."

Ezekiel gave a forced laugh. "Let's just say, it didn't go as well as I'd hoped."

She tipped her head, looking up at him. "What do you mean?"

"Sara didn't have that good of a time."

"How come?"

"She expected we would sit with each other."

"Well, that's what you get for takin' an English girl to an Amish function." Dad entered the greenhouse and started sweeping up the dirt on the floor. "You should have invited Lenore or one of the other available Amish women."

Ezekiel knew if he responded he and Dad would end up arguing. So instead of offering a comeback, he went down on his knees to pick up a couple of clay pots. As soon as things slowed down in the greenhouse today, he planned to check on his bees.

Ezekiel headed out to the far edge of their property to tend his bees. As he approached, he was surprised to see one of the boxes had been knocked over. Several bees hovered around the fallen hive, trying to get back inside.

Staring at the box on the ground, Ezekiel figured some animal must have knocked over the hive. He didn't think it was a bear, although it was not uncommon to have bear sightings around Lancaster County. A recent newspaper article stated that a captured bear had been released in the game lands north of Harrisburg, but he doubted one would travel this far.

Ezekiel tapped his foot. *Course, I guess it could have been a bear. They do love honey, as well as feasting on the bees. They like to eat the bee's larvae as well.*

But after looking at the damage a little more closely, Ezekiel figured maybe a raccoon or even a skunk got into the hive. Probably the same critter that had gotten into the greenhouse and made a mess.

In a hurry to get the hive set back up, Ezekiel didn't take the time to put on a head net. Big mistake! Buzzing bees swarmed all around his face. The next thing he knew, he'd been stung in several places. Already, he could feel his cheeks beginning to swell.

Ezekiel groaned. "That's just great. I was going over to see Sara later today for another buggy-driving lesson. How can I go there looking like this? I'll be lucky if I can even see to drive the horse and buggy."

❧

Michelle went into the barn to look at more of the notes she'd found in the prayer jar. Each time she did this, she came away with something new to ponder. One of the messages she'd found today was in the form of a prayer and dealt with bitterness.

*"Dear Lord,"* Michelle read silently, *"I don't mean to feel bitter, but the hurt in my heart has festered like an embedded splinter. I heard it said once that hurt fertilizes bitterness, making it grow like a weed.*

*That's exactly what has happened to me."*

"I can relate to that," Michelle mumbled. "I've lived through a series of hurts in my life. Mom and Dad hurt me. My foster parents hurt me, and so did Jerry."

She shifted on the bale of straw, wondering how to go about freeing herself from bitterness caused by deep-seated hurt. She couldn't simply wave a magic wand over her head and ask it to go away. If it were possible to dispel the hurts life brought, there had to be something more.

Hearing a horse and buggy pull into the yard, Michelle hurried to put the jar away. The note, however, she slipped into her jean's pocket. If Willis and Mary Ruth had returned home, she didn't want them to see what she had discovered. The two prayer jars she'd found had become Michelle's little secret.

Outside in the yard, she discovered Ezekiel's buggy, not the Lapps'. Michelle smiled and waved, but when he stepped down and moved closer to her, she looked at him with concern. "What happened, Ezekiel? Your cheeks are red and swollen."

"I know. I stupidly didn't bother to put on my protection mask when I went to take care of the bees this morning, and believe me, I paid the price for it." He grunted. "Found one of the hives had been knocked over—probably by a raccoon or some other critter. And when I went to pick it up, the bees came after me."

"That's a shame. Are you okay?"

He nodded. "Mom had some stuff to put on the stings, and she gave me a homeopathic remedy called Apis mellifica. It helped quite a bit with the pain and kept the swelling from getting worse."

"That's good about the remedy, but I'm sorry about your beehive."

Ezekiel scrunched up his nose. "That's not all of the trouble we faced this morning. When we went into the greenhouse, we discovered that some animal had been in there and knocked over several plants, making a mess to clean up on the floor."

"Sounds like it wasn't a good start to your day."

"That's for sure."

"Well, I'm glad it wasn't any worse." Michelle reached out to rub Big Red's ears. "So what brings you by today, Ezekiel? Shouldn't you still be at the greenhouse working?"

"Nope. My dad said I could have the rest of the day off. Think he felt sorry for me when he saw what the bees did." He secured his horse to the hitching rail. "I came by for two reasons. First, to see if you'd like another buggy-driving lesson, and second, to invite you to my birthday supper tomorrow evening."

"That sounds nice, but are your parents okay with me being there? I'm not part of the family or anything."

Ezekiel waved his hand. "Don't worry about that. It's my birthday, and they said I could invite whoever I want. I'll come over and pick you up around five. Is that okay?"

Despite Michelle's apprehension over what his parents would think, the idea of helping Ezekiel celebrate his birthday gave her a sense of joy. "I look forward to it, and will be ready by five."

# Chapter 30

"*Hallich gebottsdaag*, Son." Ezekiel's mother gave him a hug as soon as he entered the kitchen.

"Danki, Mom."

Ezekiel's father, sister, and two brothers echoed Mom's happy birthday greeting as they all took seats around the breakfast table.

He grinned. "Thanks, everyone."

"I made your favorite johnnycake to go with fried eggs and ham." Mom placed a platter on the table, along with a basket filled with the tasty cornmeal biscuits that had been baked in a square pan and cut into several thick pieces.

Ezekiel smacked his lips. "Yum. You're spoiling me today, Mom."

She smiled and gave his shoulder a pat before taking her seat at the table. Then all heads bowed for silent prayer. When the prayer was over, Mom passed the food around, starting with Ezekiel.

As he looked around at his family, Ezekiel felt a true sense of belonging. If he decided to go English and move away, he would miss the closeness they had. But a few others he knew who had jumped the fence kept in touch with their families, so maybe it wouldn't be so bad. Ezekiel certainly wouldn't want to be completely cut off from his folks or siblings. So if he decided to go English, he would make sure to visit as often as possible. Hopefully, they would visit him too.

"Are you looking forward to your birthday supper this evening?" Amy asked. "Our big sister and her husband are expected to be here, so the whole *familye* will be together."

Ezekiel nodded before biting into one of the johnnycakes. "I invited Sara to join us too."

Mom's brows furrowed, and Dad cleared his throat real loud. "We were planning to keep this more of a family get-together."

"I'm sorry about that, but I thought it'd be a good chance for you all to get to know Sara better." Ezekiel took a deep breath, trying to keep his composure. It didn't take a genius to see that his parents didn't approve of Sara. Which was why they needed to get to know her.

Mom wiped a speck of egg yolk from her chin before looking at him. "I suppose having Sara here will be all right, since I also invited Lenore and a couple of your other friends."

Dad cast her a sidelong glance, but said nothing.

"It's a good thing the swelling in your cheeks has gone down." Abe bumped Ezekiel's arm. "With all that company we'll be having this evening, you wouldn't want to show up looking like a squirrel with his cheeks full of nuts."

Ezekiel bumped his brother back. "Very funny."

"So what are ya hopin' to get for your birthday this year?" young Henry chimed in.

"Maybe some new bee supplies, or a cover for—" Ezekiel stopped short of finishing his sentence. He'd almost said he would like a cover for the seat of his truck. He'd done a good job so far hiding his purchase from Mom and Dad and didn't want to blow it. If they found out the truth, it would put an end to any kind of birthday celebration.

"A cover for what, Ezekiel?" Mom asked.

"Um. . . I was thinking a throw cover or blanket would be nice to have in my buggy for when the weather gets colder." Internally, Ezekiel justified what he'd said, because it wasn't really a lie. It would be nice to have a new blanket to drape over his or any passenger's legs when it felt chilly while riding in the buggy.

At five o'clock on the dot, Ezekiel showed up to take Michelle to his house for his birthday supper. Looking out the kitchen window, she watched him pull his horse and buggy up to the hitching rail. She was certain he wouldn't have picked her up in his truck. Especially since he'd be taking her to his parents' house to spend the evening. He no doubt had said nothing to them about his recent purchase.

"Ezekiel's here, Grandma. So I'm gonna head out now." It was strange, but Michelle had actually gotten used to calling the Lapps Grandma and Grandpa.

Mary Ruth turned from where she stood at the stove, preparing supper for her and Willis. "Have a good time, and please tell Ezekiel we said happy birthday."

"I sure will." Michelle grabbed the gift bag she had for Ezekiel, along with a sweater in case the air turned chilly, and went out the back door. She found him waiting near his buggy.

"You look really nice tonight, Sara." He touched the sleeve of her dress—another simple one Mary Ruth had made, only this one was green. "I'm glad you were free to come to my house for supper."

"I wouldn't have missed it. Happy birthday, Ezekiel." She handed him the present. "I hope you like what I got."

He smiled down at her. "You didn't have to get me anything. Just spending the evening with you is gift enough for me."

Michelle felt an ache at the back of her throat. Ezekiel was so sweet and kind. She enjoyed being with him more than any man she'd ever met. *Even more than Brad,* she realized for the first time. "Would you like to open your gift now? Or would you rather wait till we get to your house?"

"Think I'll open it now." Ezekiel reached inside the gift bag and smiled when he withdrew a pair of binoculars. "Well, what do ya know? I lost my old pair about a year ago and haven't gotten around to replacing them." He leaned close to Michelle and gave her a kiss on the cheek. "Thank you very much."

Michelle's pulse quickened. While uncertain of Ezekiel's intentions, she'd never received such a gentle, heartfelt kiss before. It was nothing like Jerry's smothering, forceful kisses, showing no tenderness at all. Being with Ezekiel was like a breath of fresh air. If she could stay here in Lancaster County permanently, Michelle felt that she could most certainly fall in love with this man. But she couldn't allow herself to give in to those feelings—not with her leaving this place soon. It wouldn't be fair to Ezekiel—assuming he felt the same way about her, which she suspected he might.

"Well, shall we get going?" Ezekiel opened the passenger's door for Michelle. "Sure don't wanna hold up my birthday meal. Mom wouldn't like that at all."

"And I couldn't blame her." Still unsure and a bit nervous about how his family would react to her being there, Michelle hoped everything would turn out all right.

Ezekiel guided his horse and buggy into a long driveway, which had a sign at the entrance that read: Kings' A-Bloom Green-house. Several large, majestic oak trees lined the driveway heading to the house. It surprised Michelle to see the lovely home Ezekiel's parents had. It was a large farmhouse done in stunning limestone. The cooper roof appeared to have developed a beautiful patina, no doubt after years of exposure to the weather. Beautiful flowers adorned window boxes on the entire main level, and colorful flowerbeds throughout the property made the lush green yard even more attractive.

They passed the house and drove toward the back, where a huge barn sat. The lower half was done in limestone, to match the house, while the upper half was wood and had been painted white. The barn also had a metal roof, but it was hunter green. Beyond the barn stood a greenhouse that seemed to stretch for miles. Michelle looked forward to visiting it someday, as she felt certain there'd be an overwhelming amount of pretty flowers and plenty of shrubs to check out.

Ezekiel glanced at Sara from across the table. Mom had somehow made sure to seat her opposite of him and put Lenore in the seat to his left. She was up to her old tricks again, and it irked Ezekiel to no end. His siblings were all polite and friendly to Sara, but his parents were another matter. Mom and Dad were obviously uncomfortable with Ezekiel's English guest, although she kept trying to make conversation with them. Did she sense his parents' disapproval?

Ezekiel figured their main complaint was Sara being English. Did they think she would sway him to leave home and not join the Amish church? Were they worried she might try to turn him against his family? Ezekiel thought he knew Sara pretty well, and there was no way she would do any of those things.

Ezekiel's cousin Raymond, who sat on the other side of him, leaned closer and said quietly, "My daed wants you to move your truck. It's in the way, and he needs it to be gone by noon tomorrow."

The whole room got deathly quiet. Apparently they'd all heard every word Raymond had said. Ezekiel's face heated, and Raymond covered his mouth with the palm of his hand. "Oops! Sorry, Cousin. I didn't mean to spill the beans or for anyone to hear me."

Ezekiel's father's lips pressed into a white slash. "What's this about a truck?" He leveled an icy stare at Ezekiel.

Ezekiel felt like a bird that was about to be devoured by a hungry hawk. He was caught and had no choice but to fess up. "I bought a truck, Dad. And I parked it at Raymond's place because I knew you'd never allow me to have it here."

Dad's face reddened as he swatted at thin air. "Ya got that right!"

Mom sat beside Dad, tapping all five fingers of her right hand against the tabletop, but she never said a word. She didn't have to. Her clenched jaw and deep frown said it all.

Ezekiel looked at his brothers and sisters, hoping one of them might take his side, but they all remained quiet with their eyes averted. Sara also sat quietly, looking down at her half-eaten plate of fried chicken, mashed potatoes, and pickled beets.

*I shoulda told my folks the truth sooner,* Ezekiel berated himself. *And I should have never trusted Raymond to keep quiet about the truck.*

Dad leaned forward, his elbows on the table. "You are either going to sell the truck or find another place to live. Is that clear?"

"But Dad, I just turned twenty-four and shouldn't be treated like a child."

His father glared at him. "Then you oughta stop acting like one. And need I remind you that you're way past the normal age of someone joining the church?" He shook his finger, the way he used to when Ezekiel was a young boy. "You'd better make up your mind soon, before it's too late."

*Too late for what?* Ezekiel felt tempted to pound his fists against the table, but he held himself in check. Gritting his teeth, he pushed back the chair he sat upon and stood. "You'd better get your purse and sweater, Sara. It's time for me to take you home."

Without a word, she rose to her feet and followed him out the door. So much for a happy birthday. Ezekiel had only two choices now—sell the truck or move out and find a place of his own. Neither seemed like a good choice, but he'd have to make a decision, and soon.

# Chapter 31

Saturday morning, after looking at and pondering more of the writings inside the prayer jar she'd found in the basement, Michelle decided to take a walk down the road. For a day this late in the summer, it was beautiful—warm, but comfortable, with low humidity. The mugginess in the country was a bit easier to take than in the city. She remembered the nights in her apartment back in Philadelphia when it was almost too hard to breathe. At least here in the wide-open spaces, she didn't feel so constricted and closed in.

*Poor pup.* Michelle looked toward the barn when she heard Rascal whimpering. She felt kind of bad for leaving Rascal at home but didn't want the puppy to get used to walking along the road, where he could get hit by a car or even a horse and buggy. Besides, she was miffed at him this morning. She'd found the little dickens out behind the barn, chewing on the canvas hat that had gone missing. Apparently Rascal had found it, and now the hat was practically shredded. Definitely not good enough to wear any longer. So after scolding the puppy and taking what was left of the hat away, Michelle decided to work off her frustration by taking a walk. Some time alone would also be good for reflecting on how things had gone at Ezekiel's birthday supper.

Michelle had been getting to know the people in the community and felt close to the Lapps. But if Ezekiel's parents found out who she really was, they'd have a good cause to dislike her. While they hadn't actually said the words to her face, Michelle felt sure from their coolness toward her that Vernon and Belinda King didn't think she was the right girl for their son. No doubt they would prefer someone like Lenore for Ezekiel.

*Ezekiel has a lot to deal with right now,* Michelle thought as she made her way down the path along the side of the road. *Now that the truth is out, he's been forced to choose between his truck and living at home with his family. How could his parents make their son face such a thing?*

She kicked at a twig with the toe of her sneaker. *Ezekiel and I are two of a kind. Life hasn't been fair to either of us, and we've both become liars. I wonder if he feels as guilty as I do for keeping a secret.* While it hadn't gone well for Ezekiel when the truth came out, Michelle could only imagine how bad it would be for her once the Lapps found out about her deceit.

Her thoughts went to Willis and Mary Ruth. *How can I keep deceiving those good people? They think I'm one person, when I'm really another.* Tears blurred her vision, and she blinked to clear it. *I don't deserve all the kindness they've shown me. If only there was some way I could make it up to them.*

Michelle had to be gone by October, but unless her deception was discovered before then, she planned to stay until a few days before the real Sara arrived. The mere thought of leaving this place and the special people she'd come to know and love caused her heart to feel as though it would break and send her world spinning into a sea of depression and gloom.

When a car pulled up alongside Michelle, she stopped in mid-stride. In the front seat sat a rugged-looking, dark-haired man. He reminded her of Jerry. Not necessarily his appearance, but the way he looked at her with such a smug expression.

Michelle's mouth went dry as she had a flashback, remembering how a few weeks ago she'd been stopped by those obnoxious young men on her way back to the Lapps' house from the post office. Fortunately, Brad had come along and offered her a ride home. She gulped. *But today I'm on my own.*

"You look lost. Do you need a ride somewhere?" The driver's voice was smooth, and his expression overly confident.

She shook her head.

He rode slowly beside her as she kept walking and looking straight ahead.

"You sure about that?"

She gave a quick nod and picked up her speed. Michelle's hands turned clammy, as her adrenaline spiked. *Here I am in the same predicament.* She bit her lip, hoping to see Brad pull up once again, or even Ezekiel, and come to her rescue. *What should I do? I can never outrun his vehicle, any more than those threatening teenagers' convertible.* She sent up a quick prayer. *Please help me, God. Make this guy move on and leave me alone.*

"Okay. Sorry I bothered you. You looked lonely, and I figured you might need some company."

"I don't."

He shrugged, then waved. "Okay, pretty lady. Have a nice walk."

When the car moved on, Michelle pressed a palm against her beating heart and blew out a breath of relief. Wiping the sweat from her brow, she kept her eyes focused up ahead. *I pray that guy doesn't turn around and come back.* This would be the last time she would take a walk out here by herself. In the big city, she realized she had to be careful and keep eyes in the back of her head, but Michelle didn't expect the threat to be here. Next time she wanted to go for a walk, she would bring Sadie or even Rascal along. Some people were intimidated by a dog. Plus, she was sure Sadie, at least, would try to protect her.

Michelle turned and headed back toward the Lapps'. She hadn't gone far when she spotted Ezekiel's truck coming in the opposite direction. *Where was he when I needed him?*

The truck slowed, then stopped. Ezekiel opened the passenger's door. "Hop in, Sara, I'll give you a ride home."

With no hesitation, Michelle climbed in and buckled her seatbelt. "Where are you headed? Did your dad kick you out? Are you leaving your family and striking out on your own?"

"Nope. Not yet anyway. Just picked up the truck from my cousin's house, and now I'm takin' it to a friend's home in Smoketown."

Her brows lifted. "Smoketown? That's a ways from here, isn't it? How are you planning to get home from there?"

"Sam will give me a ride with his horse and buggy. I'll head there as soon as I've dropped you off home." Ezekiel pulled out onto the road.

Michelle drew in her lower lip. "The Lapps' house is not really my home."

He rubbed his chin. "Yeah, but it is while you're visiting them, right?"

Michelle's mind raced with the possibility of telling Ezekiel the truth. Would it ruin their friendship if he knew? Would he be as understanding about her situation as she was with his?

"I'm sorry about the other night." Ezekiel broke into her thoughts. "I wanted to talk to you about it when I took you home, but I was too upset to make any sense. Besides, I was embarrassed."

"You mean because your folks insisted you get rid of your truck?"

"Partly, but mostly because of the way they treated you during supper." He groaned. "They're afraid I'm getting serious about you. Mom came right out and accused me of that this morning. She thinks you're the reason I've decided not to join the church."

"Am I?" she dared to ask. "And have you decided for sure not to join?"

"You're not the reason I won't join, but I do have deep feelings for you."

Michelle sat beside Ezekiel, too stunned to speak. *So my suspicions are true.*

"You're awfully quiet. Are you upset because of what I said?"

"No, I'm just surprised, is all."

Ezekiel pulled his truck onto the Lapps' driveway, then stopped the vehicle and took hold of her hand. "You had to know."

"Well, I. . ." Michelle moistened her parched lips.

"I was hoping you might care about me too, Sara."

"I—I do, but. . ." She paused, searching for the right words. "I'm not the person you think I am. You deserve someone better than me."

Ezekiel slipped his arms around Michelle and pulled her close. "You're everything I need. As soon as I get a little more money saved up, I may decide to get a place of my own, and then. . ."

Michelle put her finger against his lips. "I can't talk about this right now. Go ahead and take the truck to your friend's place. We can discuss this in a few days."

Ezekiel kissed her cheek. "Okay, sounds good."

~❧~

Mary Ruth glanced at the grandfather clock on the far living-room wall. "I wonder what's taking Sara so long"

Willis set his newspaper aside and looked at Mary Ruth. "As usual, you worry too much. She said she was going for a *geloffe*, and some walks take longer than others."

She grunted. "I realize that, but Sara said she wouldn't be gone long."

"Well, maybe she's already back and just hasn't come inside yet. She could be out in the barn or doing something with one of the *hund*."

"I suppose, but still. . ." Her stomach quivered as she reflected on the day they realized Rhoda had left home. *Surely our grand-daughter would not leave without saying goodbye. Oh, I hope that is not the case.*

Mary Ruth stood. "I'm going outside to look for her."

"Suit yourself, but I still think you're worried for nothing."

Ignoring her husband's comment, Mary Ruth went out the front door. She'd no more than stepped onto the porch when she spotted a truck sitting at the end of their driveway. *Now that's strange. I wonder who the vehicle belongs to.*

Mary Ruth remained on the porch, watching. She was surprised when a few minutes later, Sara stepped out of the truck. As she began walking toward the house, the truck backed out of the driveway and pulled onto the road.

"I'm glad you're back. I was concerned about you," Mary Ruth admitted when Sara joined her on the porch.

Sara tipped her head. "Really? Was I gone that long?"

Mary Ruth nodded. "Almost two hours."

"Well, I'm sorry for causing you to worry. Ezekiel picked me as I was walking back, and he gave me a ride the rest of the way."

Mary Ruth frowned. "Does he own that truck?"

"Yes, but. . ."

"Oh dear. I bet his parents are upset. They're quite strict, and I don't think either of them would approve of any of their children owning a motorized vehicle."

"But Grandma, Ezekiel is twenty-four years old, and he's not a member of the Amish church. Shouldn't he have the right to do whatever he pleases?"

"Not as long as he's still living under his parents' roof." Mary Ruth folded her arms. "He needs to respect and abide by their rules. Our children were taught that as well. Although. . ." Her voice trailed off. "Never mind, Sara. Since you weren't brought up Amish, I can't expect you to understand our ways. Let's go inside. It's time to start lunch."

Sara went silently into the house. As Mary Ruth stepped in behind her, she was hit with the realization that no matter how much she may want it, Sara was not Amish and could never comprehend what an Amish parent went through when one of their children went astray. She could only hope, for Vernon and Belinda King's sake, that their son Ezekiel didn't make the same mistake Rhoda had made. She also hoped that the Kings didn't say or do anything to drive him away.

# Chapter 32

*Lancaster*

Brad sat at the kitchen table in the small apartment he shared with his friend, Ned, contemplating whether he should go over to the Lapps to see Sara before he left town. She had seemed so troubled the last time they talked. Brad wanted to help her in some way. He'd dialed the Lapps' phone number so many times, but always hung up before leaving a message.

Once school started, Brad knew any free time he'd have would be minimal. His conscience told him to wait and not be pushy—let Sara get in touch with him if she wanted to connect before he left. Another part of him wanted to forge ahead and try to counsel her if needed. Brad didn't know why he'd been vacillating so much. He just needed clear direction.

He opened his Bible to James 1, verse 5, and read it aloud. " 'If any of you lack wisdom, let him ask of God, that giveth to all men liberally, and upbraideth not; and it shall be given him.'"

Brad bowed his head. *Why am I still struggling over this, Lord? I know You have placed a call on my life, and it does not include a relationship with a woman who is not a believer. Yet I can't get Sara out of my thoughts. Please give me wisdom and the strength to say no to my fleshly desires. Remind me daily to keep my eyes upon You. Amen.*

Brad wasn't sure if his attraction to Sara was purely physical or if it went deeper, but he could not allow himself to get caught up in a relationship with a woman who didn't share his devotion to God. Besides, he was almost certain Sara was hiding something—perhaps from her past—that could also stand in the way of a relationship with her.

*Maybe this is why I'm attracted to Sara. Is my sense that she needs help in some way the reason I'm drawn to her?* Brad ran his hand down the side of his face. Never had he felt so confused. For a fleeting moment, he wondered if he had what it took for the ministry. Shouldn't he be able to discern things better if he was a servant of the Lord?

Brad left the kitchen and looked around his apartment at all the things he still needed to pack. He was glad he'd be leaving for seminary in a week. Getting into his studies and putting his focus on the goal before him should take his mind off Sara, although he would remember to pray for her and hopefully keep in touch.

❧

### Strasburg

Michelle sat in the back of the Lapps' buggy, trying to relax while Willis drove the three of them to town for lunch. It was the last Friday of August, and things were happening too fast. Brad would be leaving for seminary next week, and she hadn't had a chance to say goodbye to him yet. Between all the garden produce Michelle had been helping Mary Ruth pick and process, plus housekeeping, laundry, and taking care of her dog, there was little time for socializing. She figured Brad must be busy too, since he hadn't come by the house for several weeks. Willis had called Brad for a ride one day last week, but Brad said he was busy packing and doing a few runs for other people, so he'd have to pass. Michelle wondered if he might be avoiding her. It was probably for the best that he'd be leaving soon. Brad deserved someone better than her—a woman who shared his faith and didn't tell lies to get what she wanted. Besides, she'd already decided that she and Ezekiel were better suited.

*Not that I can be with either man.* She leaned her head against the back of her seat and closed her eyes. Between the steady *clip-clop* of the horse's feet, and the gentle sway of the buggy, it was difficult to stay awake.

Yawning, Michelle thought about how upset Mary Ruth

had seemed last week when she found out about Ezekiel's truck. Michelle couldn't blame her. The idea that Ezekiel might leave his Amish roots was probably a reminder to Mary Ruth of what her daughter had done when she left without a good explanation or telling them goodbye in person.

Michelle drew a breath, unable to fill her lungs completely. *Here I am, supposed to be the Lapps' granddaughter, and I'll be leaving soon. Just like Rhoda, I'll be yanking the rug out from under them. Of course,* she reminded herself, *soon after I'm gone, the real Sara will show up, and then things will be better—at least for Mary Ruth and Willis.*

She pressed a fist against her chest. Michelle could hardly stand to think about the day she would need to go and wondered how best to let her pretend grandparents know she was leaving. If it wasn't for their real granddaughter coming in October, Michelle could have stayed here forever.

She was living a dream right now, but it shattered every time she faced the truth: *This isn't real. It's only a sham—one I created myself the moment I left the bus station in Philly with two of the greatest people I've ever known.*

A desire to escape the sadness filling her being was so intense, Michelle almost asked Willis to stop the horse so she could get out of the buggy. But that was ridiculous. Where would she go with so little money and only the clothes on her back? And what reason would she offer for getting out of the buggy and running off down the street?

Michelle tugged her earlobe. *This is ridiculous. I need to get a hold of myself and quit thinking such dumb thoughts. Jumping out of a buggy in the middle of the road is no way to make a sensible exit.*

"We're almost at the Hershey Farm Restaurant," Willis announced, halting Michelle's contemplations. "Just a few more blocks to go."

Michelle sat up straight. She'd never eaten at this restaurant before and hoped the food was good. Her appetite had diminished since Ezekiel's birthday supper, and thinking about the mess she'd made of her life, it was hard to get in the mood for a noon meal.

Willis pulled Bashful to a stop at a red light. He'd taken his closed-in buggy today, since showers were predicted for this afternoon.

As they waited at the light, Michelle glanced at the car that had pulled up beside them in the left-turn lane. Her eyes widened, and she stifled a gasp when she realized it was none other than Jerry's car. She'd recognize it anywhere, with rust forming around the spot that had been damaged, and the big dent in the passenger rear door that never got fixed after Jerry had been involved in a fender-bender. He had used the insurance money he'd received for something else.

Michelle scooched as far back in her seat as possible, but leaned forward briefly to peek out the window, to be sure she hadn't imagined it was Jerry. No, it was him all right. She cringed and ducked her head when she saw him looking at their buggy with a smirk on his face.

Remembering a derogatory comment he'd made once about the Amish while they watched that reality show together, Michelle could almost guess what he must be thinking. Jerry thought the Amish were living in the dark ages and shouldn't be allowed to drive their horse and buggies on the roads. He'd commented on the women's long dresses, saying they looked like pioneers.

Michelle's heartbeat picked up speed. *What is he doing here in this area? Oh, I hope he didn't see me here in the backseat. Wish I was dressed in Amish clothes right now. It would be a good disguise.*

The fear Jerry had instilled in her life came back to Michelle in a flash. Being with the Lapps all this time, she'd been able to put him and those feelings of fear behind her. But now, seeing Jerry again had dredged up the past—a past she'd rather forget. Sitting here at the red light, a few feet from Jerry's vehicle, caused Michelle to break out in a sweat. *Now I won't be able to go anywhere without looking in every direction and wondering if Jerry is close by.*

She drew a deep breath through her nose and gave a noisy exhale when the light changed and Jerry turned left. *Even if he did catch a glimpse of me, I'm sure he didn't realize who I was. I know Jerry well, and he would never expect me to be in an Amish buggy.*

"Is everything all right back there, Sara?" Mary Ruth turned in her seat to look at Michelle. "You've been awfully quiet since we left home, and then a few seconds ago, you made a strange sort of gasping noise."

"I'm fine," Michelle assured her. "I'm tired and sorta dozed off for a few minutes." Michelle wasn't about to mention seeing Jerry. She glanced out the window again. No sign of Jerry's car, so that was a relief. If he had recognized her, he would have turned around and come back to check things out. Michelle could only imagine how things would play out if Jerry met Willis and Mary Ruth and found out that Michelle had been posing as their granddaughter. Everything would blow up in her face.

*I'll need to be more cautious from now on,* she told herself. *I'll have to watch out everywhere I go and be on the lookout for Jerry. This is one more reason I can't go out walking alone anymore.*

# Chapter 33

As Michelle sat on the unyielding wooden bench during church the first Sunday of September, her thoughts went to Brad. He would be leaving the area tomorrow, and she might never see him again. She should have tried to get in touch with him this past week. But she kept talking herself out of it. What would be the point? From what he had told her, his studies would keep him busy, and he'd have little time for much else. Besides, she'd also be leaving soon. So the friendship she had developed with Brad would be a thing of the past.

She glanced across the room and found Ezekiel staring in her direction. At least she thought he was looking at her. He could have been watching a fly on the wall opposite him, for all she knew. One thing was certain: Michelle was not the only person in the room ignoring the sermon being preached.

*Of course, I have a good reason*, she told herself. *I don't understand German.*

Michelle had made up her mind that when the time came for her to go, she wouldn't look back or focus on all she'd lost. But it would be a challenge. Living here all these months and getting to know the Lapps had made her feel as if she had a real family. For the first time in Michelle's life it seemed as if she could be truly happy.

She bit her lip to keep from crying. *But I guess happiness for me is not in the cards. I'll always be a loser, longing for something just out of my reach.*

❧

Ezekiel glanced at Sara, who was fanning herself with the back of her hand. He couldn't blame her for that. The heat inside Roman

Beiler's barn, where church was being held this morning, was stifling. Ezekiel would be glad when summer came to an end and the cooler temperatures of fall took over. Only three more weeks to go, and it would truly be autumn.

He swiped at the sweat running down the back of his neck and onto his shirt. *Sure hope the weather realizes it too and that autumn is not just a word on the calendar.*

Ezekiel had been so busy helping his parents in the greenhouse lately and delivering jars of honey to his customers, it was hard to believe summer was waning—especially in the face of this relentless heat. And after last night's downpour, the air was so muggy it was hard to breathe—particularly in close quarters such as this.

Ezekiel's attention was drawn to Sara again. He hadn't had the chance to see her since he dropped her off at the Lapps' in his truck before taking it to his friend's place.

Ezekiel felt guilty for keeping the vehicle when Dad thought he had sold it. But at the same time, he just couldn't let go of the truck, nor could he muster up the courage to move out of his parents' home. Ezekiel felt like a teenager—wanting a certain thing so badly on one day that he could taste it, and desiring something else just as much on the following day. He needed to grow up and stop changing his mind, because he couldn't have it both ways.

*Maybe when Sara goes back to her hometown, I'll go with her.* Ezekiel tugged on his shirtsleeve. *It would be a lot easier to strike out on my own if I settled in a town where I knew someone.*

Now that it was nearing the end of the season for harvesting honey, Ezekiel hoped to have a little free time so he could see Sara more often. He would like to talk about his plan and see if she'd be okay with him tagging along. *And when Sara leaves, she'll have transportation, because I'll have my driver's license by then and can give her a ride in my truck.*

Ezekiel swiped a hand across his forehead, where more sweat had collected. But the greenhouse work would be picking up, since they raised poinsettias for the Christmas season. That might make it difficult to leave if Sara decided to go before Christmas. Some major businesses in the Lancaster area had quantities of poinsettias pre-ordered to give out to their employees for the holiday. Many of their regular customers bought plants for Christmas gifts too. So the months coming up would be a super busy time for the greenhouse, and Mom and Dad would need Ezekiel's help.

Ezekiel reached around and rubbed a spot on his back, where it had begun to kink. *Here I go again. . . Changing my mind about leaving. If I did venture out on my own soon, I'm sure Dad could hire someone to take my place in the greenhouse.*

He shifted on his bench, trying to find a comfortable position. *Not sure what I'd do with the bees though. Maybe I could talk Abe or even Henry into taking over my honey business. It wouldn't take much to train them. Think I'll talk to Abe about it in the morning.*

⁓

The following morning, Mary Ruth and Michelle made a trip to the Kings' greenhouse. Mary Ruth said she wanted to buy some basil, mint, and parsley. She also mentioned purchasing tulip and crocus bulbs, which she would plant in the next few weeks.

When Michelle followed Mary Ruth into the greenhouse, she felt the increase in temperature. *Too warm to be working here all day,* she thought. *I'm surprised Ezekiel hasn't found another job where he can make enough money to support himself.*

She spotted Ezekiel's mother waiting on a customer. Ezekiel was nearby, watering some plants. Apparently he hadn't seen them yet, but when Belinda finished with her customer and welcomed Mary Ruth, Ezekiel set his work aside and hurried over to Michelle.

While Belinda helped Mary Ruth find what she was looking for, Ezekiel suggested he and Michelle step outside.

Michelle looked past Ezekiel and noticed the wrinkles in his mother's forehead as she glanced her way, but Mary Ruth seemed oblivious to all of it, as she perused the pots of herbs. *Does Belinda really think I'm a bad influence on her son? Doesn't she realize he's not happy being Amish, and it has nothing to do with me? He felt that way before I came into the picture. Ezekiel told me so.*

"There's something I want to ask you," Ezekiel said when they stepped outside and away from the greenhouse.

She tipped her head back to look up at him. "What is it?"

"Whenever you decide it's time for you to return to your hometown, I'd like to go along. In fact, I'll drive you there in my truck."

Her eyes widened. "You want to go to my house?"

"No, I'm not asking to move in with you, Sara. I just thought if I could start over someplace where I know someone, it would be easier. I'm planning to talk to my brother Abe about taking over my bee business, and Mom and Dad can hire someone to take my place here in the greenhouse." Ezekiel leaned against the retaining wall that had been built near the greenhouse. "I have some money saved up, and if I can't find a job right away, I'll sleep in my truck."

Michelle shook her head. "Not a good idea, Ezekiel. No one should ever have to live in their vehicle. It's not safe, and the conditions would be anything but ideal." Her voice lowered. "Besides, I'm not sure yet when I'll be going back to my home, so I can't make any promises about you going with me." Truth was, Michelle didn't want Ezekiel to take her to wherever she was going. It would give his parents one more reason to dislike her. And of course, she'd be blamed for his leaving. Not that it would really matter once she was gone, but Michelle didn't want to live with any more blame. She'd already done enough to feel guilty for.

Seeing Ezekiel's desperate expression, she clasped his arm. "Let me think about it, okay?"

He nodded slowly. "I'll talk to you again soon."

Michelle fingered the neckline of her blouse, which was sticking to her like glue. She needed to make a decision soon as to what day she should leave and whether to include Ezekiel in her plans. *I wonder what he'd say if he knew I don't even have a home to return to. When I leave Strasburg, I'll have to decide which direction to go. One thing is certain: it'll be as far away from here as possible. I don't want to be reminded of all I've left behind.*

# Chapter 34

On Monday morning, the last full week of September, it was all Michelle could do to roll out of bed. During the night, a terrible windstorm had struck with lots of heavy rain pelting the roof. All the noise kept her awake for several hours. At one point, she almost grabbed her blanket and went down to the living room to sleep on the couch. It was okay doing that when she was a little girl, but being a grown woman, she shouldn't be acting so childish. It didn't stop her though from pulling the covers up over her head, no matter how hard it was to breathe.

Groaning, she lifted the window shade and peeked out. The yard below was littered with leaves, branches, limbs, sticks. *Oh boy. That mess is gonna take awhile to pick up. Guess I'd better get dressed and head downstairs to breakfast. I'll need all the strength I can muster in order to get through this day.*

Downstairs in the kitchen, Michelle found Mary Ruth in front of the counter, stirring pancake batter. She looked at Michelle through squinted eyes. "You look tired. Did last night's storm keep you awake?"

"Yeah. Did you and Grandpa get any sleep?"

"A little." Mary Ruth pointed to the back door. "Your grandpa's already outside picking up some of the debris in the yard. He said I should call him when breakfast is ready."

"I'll help him as soon as I've had something to eat." Michelle patted her midsection. "I don't work well on an empty stomach."

Mary Ruth smiled. "I understand. I'm the same way." She gestured to the kitchen table. "Oh, there's a letter for you."

"Y–you went out and got the mail?" Michelle's heart pounded. What if another letter had come from the real Sara?

"No, dear. The letter is from Brad, and it didn't come in the mail. He dropped it by fifteen minutes ago and said it was for you."

Michelle's fingers trembled as she reached for the envelope. Although thankful Mary Ruth had not gotten the mail, Michelle's feelings about the letter from Brad were conflicted. Why hadn't he asked to speak to her in person? Did he think it was easier to say goodbye this way?

"If you'd like some privacy, you can read his letter in the living room." Mary Ruth pushed a wisp of hair back under her dark colored head scarf. "I'll let you know when it's time to eat."

"Okay, thanks." Clasping the letter to her chest, Michelle ducked out of the kitchen and went straight to the living room. Taking a seat on the couch, she read Brad's letter silently.

> *Dear Sara,*
>
> *As I'm sure you know, I'm leaving town today— heading to the seminary up in Clarks Summit, where I'll be until I'm through with my ministerial studies. I thought about coming by to see you last week but decided it would be better to say goodbye this way. I can express myself easier with written words than if I spoke to you in person.*
>
> *First, I want to say that I've enjoyed spending time with you these past few months. I wish, however, that we could have become better acquainted. In talking to you, I've always felt you were dealing with some sort of problem but might be afraid to talk about it. I feel I may have failed you, because as a future clergyman, it will be my job to help people deal with their problems. Perhaps I am lacking in that area, because in all the times we've talked, you have never truly opened up to me.*
>
> *When we first met, I felt an immediate attraction,*

*and I don't think it was just physical. We enjoyed each other's company, and I wanted to get to know you better. It didn't take long for me to realize though that you don't share my passion for Christ and the ministry to which I feel called.*

*You seem happy when you're with your grandparents, and it's obvious they are very fond of you. Have you thought of moving to Strasburg permanently? Who knows—you might even decide to join the Amish church someday.*

*Well, I've said more than I planned to in this letter, so I'll end it by saying, I'll be praying for you. And if you ever need to talk, I'm only a phone call away.*

*May God bless you in the days ahead, and draw you close to Him.*

*All the best,*
*Brad*

Tears welled in Michelle's eyes and dribbled down her cheeks. *Brad knows there's something not right about me. Maybe I should have told him the truth. Being the decent man he is, Brad probably could have given me some good direction.*

She rocked back and forth, holding his letter against her chest. *But if I had told Brad who I really am, I'm sure he would have insisted that I admit it to Willis and Mary Ruth. I cannot tell those good people what I did to their face. I just can't.*

⁂

"Did ya ever see such a mess?" Willis called to Michelle as the two of them worked on cleaning up the yard.

She shook her head. "That was some storm we had last night."

"I'll say." He hoisted a few broken branches into the wheelbarrow. "And now, thanks to all that rain, we have more humid weather. I, for one, will be glad when the cooler temperatures get here."

Nodding, Michelle kept working on the pile she'd started. After Willis unloaded the wheelbarrow by the woodpile near the garden shed, she would haul her stack of wood out there.

While Michelle worked, she reflected once again on the letter she'd received from Brad this morning. It probably was for the best that they hadn't said their goodbyes face-to-face. It would have been difficult for her to look at him and not break down. It wasn't just knowing she'd never see him again, although that was certainly a portion of it. The hardest part for Michelle would have been to face Brad, knowing all this time she'd been living a lie. She longed to tell him the truth, but she feared his reaction. Now he was gone. She would never have to know what his response to her deception would have been had she told him.

Michelle was on the verge of bending down to pick up a strip of bark when she heard a snap. Before she had time to react, a limb that had broken off from the tree overhead clunked her on the head, bringing Michelle to her knees. "Yeow!"

Willis was immediately at her side, and Mary Ruth, who had stepped outside, joined him there. "Ach! Sara, are you all right?" Mary Ruth's fear was evident in her quavering voice.

Michelle tried to stand as she brought a shaky hand to the top of her head. "I–I've got a mighty big lump, and I feel kinda woozy." Her vision blurred as she weaved back and forth, and dropped back down to her knees.

Mary Ruth fingered the lump and gasped. "I don't see any blood but that lump is huge. Willis, you'd better call one of our drivers. I think we need to take Sara to see a doctor—she could have a concussion."

Willis nodded. "I will help you get Sara on her feet and into the house. Then I'll run out to the phone shed and make the call."

❧

As Mary Ruth sat beside Sara on the couch, her concern for the young woman escalated. Sara had begun saying some strange things—mentioning people's names Mary Ruth had never heard of and talking about events that made no sense at all. And she didn't recognize Mary Ruth at first. The poor girl was clearly disoriented.

"Why can't Al or Sandy take me to the doctor? They took me there once before."

Mary Ruth placed her hand gently on Sara's shoulder. "Who are Al and Sandy?"

No response. Sara closed her eyes.

"Don't go to sleep, dear. If you have a concussion, you need to stay awake."

"I'm tired. Think I might throw up."

Mary Ruth dashed into the utility room and grabbed a bucket. She returned to the living room barely in time for Sara to empty her stomach into the bucket. "Wh–where's Mom and Dad? Why aren't they here? Don't they care that I'm sick?"

Mary Ruth looked up at Willis when he entered the house. "She's not doing well. Did you get a driver to take us to the hospital emergency room?"

"Jah. Stan Eaton should be here soon."

Mary Ruth released her breath. "Thank the Lord."

# Chapter 35

It had been seven days since Michelle got hit on the head, and she still didn't feel quite right. While the nausea and dizziness were gone, the bump continued to hurt, and it was hard to concentrate or think clearly. The doctor said she had a moderate concussion, and it could take a few weeks to heal. Michelle was kept at the hospital overnight for observation and sent home the following day with instructions to rest. The doctor also reminded her not to engage in any strenuous activity that might lead to another injury.

Mary Ruth had told Michelle that right after the accident she'd been disoriented and didn't seem to know where she was for a time. Michelle had also talked about some people Mary Ruth didn't know, whom Michelle had never mentioned before. Michelle hoped she hadn't said anything that revealed her true identity, but if she had, surely Mary Ruth would have mentioned it by now.

It was hard to sit around and do nothing, but what other choice did she have? Mary Ruth hovered around, making sure Michelle followed the doctor's orders and didn't do anything she wasn't supposed to do. Willis took care of all the outside chores, including clearing away the rest of the mess that had been left from the storm. Some of his neighbors, as well as Ivan, offered to help out, but he insisted on doing it by himself. No wonder Mary Ruth sometimes called him stubborn.

Ezekiel had come by twice to see how Michelle was doing, and also to offer his help if needed. Lenore dropped by once, on her way home from teaching at the schoolhouse. It felt good to know people cared about her, even though they didn't realize she was someone else.

Michelle's biggest concern was not being allowed to walk out and get the mail the first few days after her injury. Fear that another letter from Sara Murray would come left her feeling anxious. But fortunately, no letters had been delivered, and now that Michelle was able to walk without feeling woozy, Mary Ruth had given in and let her resume getting the mail each morning. It was about the only thing she was allowed to do however. Mary Ruth made sure of that.

This afternoon, as Michelle sat in a wicker chair on the front porch with Rascal snuggled in her lap, she thought about the quote she'd read this morning: *"Every day is a second chance."* While Mary Ruth had been busy fixing breakfast and wasn't aware of what Michelle was doing, she had gone down to the basement to look around and read some of the notes in the prayer jar again.

On one of the slips of paper she'd also read Psalm 33:18: *"Behold, the eye of the LORD is upon them that fear him, upon them that hope in his mercy."*

Michelle wasn't sure what it meant, but she'd put both pieces of paper in her pocket, as she had done with a few others she'd found in the prayer jar inside the barn. She planned to take them with her when she left this place, as a reminder of her time in Strasburg.

"Mind if I join you?" Mary Ruth broke into Michelle's contemplations.

"Of course not. Please do." Michelle gestured to the chair beside her.

Mary Ruth took a seat and reached over to stroke Rascal's head. "This little guy sure seems to like you, Sara."

Michelle nodded. "I like Rascal too, and I'm gonna miss him when I go back home, which should be soon. I've been here several months and have probably worn out my welcome by now."

Mary Ruth pressed a hand to her abdomen. "No, you haven't, and I wish you would reconsider and stay for a while longer. Why, you're still recovering from a head injury. Besides, it would be so nice if you could be here for the holidays this year. Thanksgiving will be here before we know it, and then Christmas."

"I'm curious—how do the Amish celebrate the holidays?" Michelle asked.

"Well, Thanksgiving is celebrated in our district in much the same way as many English people celebrate it. In the morning we gather our family for devotions, and everyone often shares something they feel grateful for." Mary Ruth folded her arms and leaned her head against the back of her chair. "Then the adults and older children have a time of prayer and fasting during the morning hours. But around noon we gather with our family members for a delicious, traditional Thanksgiving dinner."

"So you have turkey, gravy, mashed potatoes, and all the trimmings."

"That's correct. We might also have a variety of vegetables and salads, as well as fresh bread or rolls." Mary Ruth licked her lips. "And of course after the meal, we eat dessert and spend the rest of the day visiting while the children play games."

"Sounds like a relaxing day and a lot of fun too." Just hearing about it caused Michelle to wish she could be here for Thanksgiving and take part in helping to cook, as well as eat, the meal. "What about Christmas? Do you celebrate the same we English people do?"

"To a certain extent we do, but there are no decorated trees or blinking lights inside our homes," Mary Ruth clarified.

Rascal woke up and began to squirm, so Michelle set him on the porch floor. A short time later, he ambled down the steps and into the yard. "So you don't do any Christmas decorating at all?"

"Some Amish string the Christmas cards they receive around a room in their home. And a few people might set out some candles or greenery, but nothing fancy."

"What about gifts? Do you give each other Christmas presents?" Michelle found all this information about Amish traditions to be so interesting.

"Yes. On Christmas morning after we've had devotions, the children will open their gifts." Mary Ruth's voice was light and bubbly. "In the afternoon, we share a big meal, and if Christmas Day falls near the end of the week, some church districts hold their service on Christmas morning instead of the usual Sunday service."

Michelle clasped her hands behind her neck. "It all sounds wonderful. I'm sure you must have a good time."

"Yes, we certainly do, and we'd really like you to stay through the holidays, Sara."

Seeing Mary Ruth's pleading expression, Michelle nodded. "Okay, I'll stay until after Christmas."

Mary Ruth placed her hand on Michelle's arm and gave it a tender squeeze. "That's *wunderbaar*. I know Willis will also be pleased."

Michelle swallowed around the lump in her throat. There was no way she could keep the promise she'd made. The real Sara would be arriving sometime this month, and she had to be gone by then. As soon as she felt strong enough, she would leave the Lapps a note explaining the truth and head out on her own.

"Thanksgiving will be a wonderful occasion." Mary Ruth's face radiated with pleasure. "We'll invite Ivan, along with his wife and children, and there will be so much good food we won't know what to do with it all."

When Mary Ruth began to reminisce about what the holidays were like when Rhoda was a girl, Michelle concentrated on Rascal and tuned her out. It was too painful to hear about this, knowing she would not have the opportunity to be a part of their holiday celebrations. No doubt, Michelle would probably be sitting in some dreary old apartment, feeling sorry for herself on Thanksgiving, as well as Christmas.

Michelle wished she had some good recollections of the holidays, but her upbringing hadn't left any pleasant memories. As a child, Thanksgiving always ended up with her parents fighting. On one Christmas, a neighbor called the cops, and Dad was hauled off to jail. Not much good about those holidays to remember.

The time Michelle had spent with her foster parents was a little better, but nothing like she'd hoped it would be. Al and Sandy Newman were nice enough, but they had three kids of their own, plus Michelle and two other foster children, so they couldn't afford to do much for the holidays.

When asked by her friends in school about what she got for Christmas, Michelle couldn't admit how things really were, so she would pretend everything was great and make things up about all the gifts she'd supposedly received. Maybe the reason pretending came so easy to her was because she'd had a lot of practice. But if it was the only way she had to get a sense of truly belonging, however temporary, Michelle would keep pretending for as long as she could.

Compared to living with her birth parents, being with the foster family hadn't been nearly so bad. But here, with Mary Ruth and Willis, it was like having a real family—grandparents who cared about her and took care of her needs. Too bad it couldn't last.

Ezekiel urged Big Red on. He was eager to see Sara and find out how she was doing today. A hit on the head could be serious, and if she didn't take it easy, there might be repercussions. The last time he'd gone to see Sara, she'd looked tired and appeared to be distracted. Hopefully after more than a week of recovery, she was doing better.

Approaching the Lapps' driveway, Ezekiel guided his horse and buggy off the road. When he pulled up to the hitching rail, he spotted Mary Ruth sitting on the porch, snapping green beans.

"I came by to see Sara," he said, stepping onto the porch. "How's she doing today?"

Mary Ruth barely looked up from her task as she mumbled, "She's better but still needs to rest." Eyebrows squeezing together, she added, "I don't think it's a good idea for her to go anywhere with you today."

"I didn't come to ask her to go anyplace with me." Ezekiel tapped his heel against the wooden porch slats. "Just wanted to see how she's doing." He glanced at the back door. "Is she inside?"

Mary Ruth shook her head. "She took a walk out to the barn with Rascal a short time ago."

"Oh, okay. I'll head out there and say hello."

When Mary Ruth gave no response, Ezekiel turned, trotted down the steps, and ran to the barn. He found Sara inside, sitting in a pile of straw. Her puppy was curled up beside her with his head in Sara's lap.

"I talked to your grandma and she said you were in here. Didn't see any sign of your grandpa though."

"He went to the bank."

"Oh, I see. So how are you feeling today?" Ezekiel squatted down beside her. "Is that bump you got still pretty sore?"

She reached up and touched the top of her head. "A little. The swelling's gone down quite a bit though."

"Good to hear." He lowered himself to his knees and moved closer to her. "I think Mary Ruth is still *umgerennt* with me."

"Why would she be upset?"

His eyes widened. "Oh, you knew what that meant?"

Sara nodded. "Willis says it sometimes when he's upset with the hogs. When I questioned him about the word, he explained its Pennsylvania Dutch meaning." She touched Ezekiel's arm. "Why do you think Mary Ruth is upset with you?"

"She's been less than friendly ever since she found out I own a truck. I can't understand why it would bother her so much. I'm not their son or any other relation of theirs." He lowered his voice. "Don't think she's said anything to my folks about it though. If she had, Dad would be all over me for not selling the truck and parking it at my friend's place." Feeling a headache coming on, Ezekiel massaged his forehead. "My daed says if there's one thing he can't tolerate, it's a liar."

Sara sat quietly, staring straight ahead.

He snapped his fingers in front of her face. "Did ya hear what I said?"

"Yeah. I was just wondering how you feel about people who don't tell the truth."

He shrugged. "Well, it all depends on who's lyin' and what they're lying about."

"So do you believe it's all right to lie to your folks?"

"I'm not really lying. I told Dad I would move the truck off my cousin's property, and I did." Ezekiel didn't understand why Sara was questioning him like this. "Do you think I should sell my truck and join the Amish church? Is that what you're getting at?"

"I don't know what you should do, Ezekiel. It's a decision you'll need to make. Guess what I'm wondering is how you feel about not telling your parents the truth. Doesn't it make you feel guilty?"

He nodded. "Yeah, it does. But if I tell 'em I still own the truck, Dad may kick me out of his house."

"Guess there's always a consequence for not telling the truth." Sara glanced toward the barn door, then looked back at Ezekiel. "There's something I need to talk to you about, but you have to promise not to tell anybody—just like I never told anyone about your truck. At least not till you drove me home in it that day."

Nodding, he shooed a pesky fly away from his face. "I care about you, Sara, and you can tell me anything."

She heaved a sigh. "I'm not the person you think I am."

He placed his hand on her shoulder and gave it a squeeze. "I think I have a pretty good idea what kind of person you are."

"No, you don't. In fact, you don't know me at all."

"Yes, I do. I know you're kind, sweet, and—"

She held up her hand. "I'm none of those things. I'm an imposter."

He tipped his head to one side. "What are you talking about?"

"My name is not Sara Murray. I'm Michelle Taylor, and the Lapps are not my grandparents."

Ezekiel's thoughts scrambled, as he tried to digest what she'd said. "Are you making all this up just to tease me, or has that whack you took on the head messed with your brain?"

Sara's lips trembled, and her eyes glistened with tears. "I am not making this up, and it has nothing to do with getting hit on the head. When Willis and Mary Ruth went to the Philadelphia bus station back in June to pick up their granddaughter Sara, they thought I was her." She paused and drew in a shaky breath. "I needed a place to go real bad, so I went along with it and let them believe I was Sara."

Ezekiel sat quietly with his hands folded in his lap, as Michelle went on to explain things. When she got to the part about intercepting the real Sara's letters, he'd heard enough. "I thought we were friends, Sara—I mean, Michelle. A true friend would never deceive someone like that, especially not to this extent." He glanced toward the door. "And what about Willis and Mary Ruth? How could you have lied to those good people?"

It was all Ezekiel could do to keep from shouting. All these months he thought he and this pretend Sara were drawing closer—that they might even have a future together some day, if he decided to go English. Now he realized she'd been playing him for a fool. Worse yet, she'd conned two of the nicest people in the world into believing she was their granddaughter. How despicable was that?

Ezekiel leaped to his feet. Feeling a tightness around his eyes, he said through clenched teeth: "I wish you'd never come to Lancaster County." With that, he whirled around, jerked open the double barn doors, and made a beeline for his horse and buggy. He'd never felt so betrayed in all his life. Sara—Michelle—was not the woman for him.

# Chapter 36

*Newark*

Sara's thoughts raced as she began packing her bags and getting ready for the trip to her grandparents' house this morning. It had been difficult to wait until October, but here it was October 3rd, and she would soon be greeting the Lapps for the first time. She was excited, yet nervous.

There was so much she wanted to share with them. Sara was eager to tell her grandparents about the business classes she'd taken at the local community college this summer, and how she'd been working part-time at a dental office. She also thought they might want to know what her childhood was like. And of course there were personal things about her mother to share with Willis and Mary Ruth.

She took a seat on her bed, holding the blue-and-black beaded bracelet and matching necklace she'd made for her grandmother along with the keychain for her grandfather. In addition to the silver ring for his keys, there was a small leather patch connected to it that she had etched with the letter *L* for Lapp.

Sara planned to drive to their home in Strasburg, instead of taking the bus as she'd originally planned. Since some repairs had been done to her vehicle, it only made sense to go there by car. If Sara had figured it right, the trip would take a little over two hours. She could travel at her leisure and make stops along the way, as needed.

She hoped to stay several days, or even a few weeks with her grandparents, if Mary Ruth and Willis had a spare room and wanted her to stay that long. Since she hadn't heard from them since that last letter, she wasn't even sure if she'd be welcomed much less invited to stay in their home. The Lapps might be satisfied with just a short visit.

Her lips pressed together. *Well, I won't know till I get there, so I may as well stop worrying about it.*

Sara was about to close the suitcase when she looked toward the nightstand and saw her mother's Bible. *Oops, I cannot forget that.*

Sara took the Bible and opened it, making sure her mother's note was tucked safely inside before she put it under her neatly packed clothes and zippered shut the suitcase. She felt it necessary to show her grandparents the letter their daughter had written.

Then Sara remembered her birth certificate that she wanted to take along. She had gone to the local office supply store and made a copy of it to give her grandparents. Although they hadn't asked in their letter to see a birth certificate as proof of who she was, Sara wanted to make sure she could prove she was Rhoda's daughter. The Bible, the note her mother wrote, and the certificate should be enough to verify who she was.

Sara rose from the bed and stood in front of the full-length mirror to check her appearance. She'd chosen a pair of crisp linen slacks in navy blue, and a white tank top with a short-sleeved navy blue jacket for her traveling attire. Around her neck she wore her mother's favorite scarf, and the scarf ring she had recently made held it in place.

Her long blond hair had been freshly washed, and as always, she'd let it air dry. One advantage of having naturally wavy hair was the ease of styling it.

Satisfied that she looked all right, Sara picked up her suitcase and handbag. Taking one last glance in the mirror, she left her room. *Well, Mama, here I go.* It was time for her adventure to begin.

### Strasburg

Michelle felt grateful that Mary Ruth and Willis were out running errands and wouldn't be back until sometime this afternoon. It gave her the time she needed to get ready for her departure and be gone before they returned.

Knowing the real Sara could be here any day, Michelle couldn't wait any longer. Besides, she worried that Ezekiel might say something to the Lapps about what she'd confided in him before she had the chance to leave.

Michelle couldn't deal with her deceit anymore, but there was no way she could face Mary Ruth and Willis with the truth. She'd taken the coward's way out and left them a note on the kitchen table. As soon as the Lapps had left this morning, Michelle called their driver, Stan, to pick her up. Then she'd packed her bags and now sat on the front porch, waiting for his arrival.

She wished she could see Ezekiel before she left and apologize to him for ruining their relationship, but he'd left in such a huff yesterday, she felt sure he wouldn't want to talk to her. Anything that may have been between them had been destroyed once Ezekiel learned the truth about her deceit. *If I were Amish and joined the church, I'd most likely be shunned for the lie I've told.*

Michelle shifted on the bench she sat upon. *Who is he to cast judgment on me, anyhow? Ezekiel's been lying to his parents all these months about his truck, and he won't make a commitment to join the Amish church or decide to officially become a part of the English world. He's just stringing his family along, all because he's too afraid to make a decision he might later regret.*

Under the circumstances, Michelle believed a clean break was for the best. Once the Lapps found her note, they would tell Ezekiel and others in their church district why she had left. Then undoubtedly Ezekiel would tell them he already knew. Michelle would never have to see any of them again, so hopefully, she could move past all of this and find her way through life on her own. Although she couldn't imagine that she would ever amount to anything.

As Michelle continued to wait for Stan, Rascal and Sadie plodded onto the porch with wagging tails. A sense of sadness washed over her, as she leaned down and let the dogs take turns licking her hands. She was not only saying goodbye to the people she'd come to think of as her family, but also to the loving animals she'd grown so fond of here on this farm. She would miss taking care of them, especially Rascal, who had come to depend on her.

"Sure wish I could take you with me," Michelle murmured, stroking Rascal's silky soft head. "But it's just not possible, since I'm not sure where I'll end up or if and when I'll find a job."

Michelle had no money of her own. What little she'd had when she first came here, she'd spent on necessities, not to mention Ezekiel's birthday gift. Since she knew where the Lapps kept some extra cash, she'd opened the cupboard this morning and taken down the old coffee can. She'd removed all the money she thought she'd need to get by on until she found a job. Not only was she a liar, but she was a thief as well.

*But I'm gonna pay it back as soon as I can,* she told herself, hoping to justify why she'd taken it. *I'll get a money order and mail it to them, as I promised I would do in the note I wrote.*

Tears pooled in Michelle's eyes when Stan pulled his van into the yard. It was time to go. Time to leave this place that had been her home for the nearly four months she had lived here. "Goodbye, Rascal. Bye, Sadie. Take care of each other, okay?" She gave both dogs one last pat.

❧

*Bird-in-Hand, Pennsylvania*

"I'm glad we decided to stop for lunch before doing the rest of our errands." Mary Ruth smiled at Willis from across the table at the Bird-in-Hand Family Restaurant. "The salad bar is so good here, and it's just the pick-me-up I needed right now."

He nodded in agreement.

"Too bad Sara didn't want to come along. It would have been nice to have her with us today."

"Jah, but Sara still needs to take it easy, so maybe it's best that she stayed home where she can rest."

"You're right, as usual." Mary Ruth smiled before taking a drink of iced tea. "I'm so glad she decided to stay through the holidays. Having her here to help us celebrate Thanksgiving and Christmas will be wunderbaar. We'll have to come up with something special to give her."

"Well, one thing's for sure. She doesn't need another hund. Maybe I should make Sara a cedar chest to put her cherished items in or use as a hope chest. I'll have to work on it in the early mornings, or maybe after she's gone to bed. Wouldn't want the surprise ruined ahead of time." Willis winked at Mary Ruth. "The way she and Ezekiel have been hanging around together so often, I wouldn't be one bit surprised if they didn't end up getting married someday."

"Since Sara wasn't raised in the simple life, it's doubtful she'd want to become Amish." Mary Ruth pursed her lips, as they finished their lunch. "If she and Ezekiel should develop deep feelings for each other, he'd likely go English. Which is what I suspect he wants anyway." She lowered her gaze to the table for a few seconds, then lifted her head. "Just like our Rhoda, he's not satisfied with the Plain way of living. Otherwise, he wouldn't have bought a motorized vehicle."

"Some young people can't see what's right before them." Willis motioned for the waitress to bring their receipt. "Guess they don't realize how much it hurts their family when they run off and do their own thing."

As they went up to the front desk to pay for their lunch, a young, blond-haired woman stood by the register, asking the cashier for directions.

"How far is it from here to Strasburg?" Mary Ruth heard her inquire.

"You're only about fifteen minutes from there," the cashier explained. "There's a road right here past the restaurant—North Ronks Road. Stay on that until you hit Route 741, which will take you right into Strasburg."

"Thanks. That sounds easy enough." The blond-haired woman smiled politely, then went into the restroom.

"How was your meal?" the cashier asked when Willis stepped up to pay.

"It was very good, thank you." He handed her cash and waited for the change.

After the young man counted back his change, Willis turned to Mary Ruth. "I'll be right back. I need to put a tip on our table for the waitress."

"Okay." Mary Ruth looked toward the restroom and saw the blond woman come out. She stopped to look at a rack of books for sale by the entrance door.

Willis returned a few seconds later. "Have a nice day," he told the cashier as he and Mary Ruth headed for the door. At the same time, the woman asking for directions went for the door handle too.

"Here, I'll get it for you." She held the door open until Mary Ruth and Willis went out.

"Why, thank you." Mary Ruth smiled.

"You're welcome." The blond walked swiftly through the parking lot.

As Mary Ruth and Willis headed to the area where they'd secured their horse and buggy, Mary Ruth paused and glanced over her shoulder in time to see the young woman get into a small blue car.

"Did you hear that young lady ask for directions to Strasburg?" she asked Willis.

"Jah. It's too bad we couldn't ask her to follow us. But then if we had, she'd have to drive pretty slow." Willis took Mary Ruth's arm and helped her into the buggy before untying the reins. "The cashier gave good directions, so I'm sure she'll find her way."

"Jah." As Mary Ruth settled herself on the seat, she thought about the conversation she and Willis had during lunch. How would Ezekiel's parents feel if he and Sara did end up getting married? Would they accept her into the family, despite her not being Amish? If Ezekiel did end up going English, would Belinda and Vernon blame Sara for it?

Remembering once again the sinking feeling she'd had when their daughter left them a note, saying she was leaving home, caused Mary Ruth to tear up. *Oh, I wish I could quit thinking about this.* She wondered sometimes if the pain of it would ever completely go away. Well, at least their life was filled with happiness now that they'd met Rhoda's daughter. This was where Mary Ruth needed to keep her focus.

*Strasburg*

Michelle was about to step off the porch when a light blue compact car pulled into the yard. Going past the van, the vehicle pulled up close to the house. An attractive young woman with long blond hair got out and stepped onto the porch. "Excuse me, but is this where Willis and Mary Ruth Lapp live?"

All Michelle could do was nod her head. Her intuition told her this young lady was here for a purpose.

The woman smiled. "I'm their granddaughter, Sara Murray. I've written them several letters, and their response was that I should come here to meet them in October. So, here I am. Are they home?"

Heart pounding and barely able to speak, Michelle squeaked, "They're out running errands, but the front door is open, so feel free to go inside and wait for them." Without explaining who she was or where she was going, Michelle grabbed her things and headed for Stan's rig.

*Yip! Yip!* Rascal followed.

Tears clouding her vision, Michelle shook her head and signaled for the pup to go back. "Sorry, buddy, but you can't come with me. Go back on the porch with your mama."

The dog whimpered, and with his tail between his legs, he ambled slowly toward the house. Rascal stopped once and turned toward Michelle, but when she clapped her hands and shouted, "Go back!" he made a hasty retreat.

Michelle opened the back door of the van, tossed her things

inside, and took a seat. "Let's go, Stan. There's no time to waste." She quickly buckled her seatbelt.

Stan's eyes narrowed slightly, as though confused, but then he backed the van out of the driveway. Just before he pulled onto the road, Michelle looked back toward the house and saw Sara crouched on the porch, petting Rascal. *I hope she's good to my puppy.*

Michelle gripped the end of her seatbelt, pulling it so tight she could barely breathe. *She's the one my pup belongs with, not me. She's Mary Ruth and Willis's rightful granddaughter.*

"So where are you headed?" Stan asked, glancing over his shoulder.

"I don't know. How far will a hundred dollars take me?"

# Chapter 37

## Harrisburg, Pennsylvania

Michelle could barely see through the film of tears in her eyes. Leaving Willis and Mary Ruth's home had been harder than she imagined. It was the only place she had ever felt secure and as if she truly belonged. Most importantly, while living with the Lapps, Michelle had felt, for the first time in her twenty-four years, what it was like to be loved unconditionally.

Thinking about her deceitfulness to the grandparents Michelle wished she had made her almost nauseated. How could she have treated those good people that way? But what would Mary Ruth and Willis have done had she told them who she was? Would they have accepted her or asked her to leave? Would they have understood Michelle's situation and forgiven her once they knew the truth?

She squeezed her eyes shut, hoping the tears wouldn't flow. *And what do they think of me now that they've no doubt read my note? I bet they couldn't wait to tell Ivan and his family. Lenore, who I'd begun to think of as a good friend, will probably think I'm a terrible person.*

With her eyes remaining closed, Michelle thought about how one evening, a few months ago, she and Lenore had gotten together to do some stamping and card making with the birthday gift Lenore had given her. Lenore had been so patient, teaching her how to emboss the cards she'd stamped by holding them carefully and not too close over one of the gas burners on Mary Ruth's cooking stove. There would be no more fun times like that for Michelle—relaxing, while talking and learning something new with a special Amish friend. *Only, Lenore believed I was Sara. My pretend cousin had no idea she was teaching a fraud how to make such lovely homemade cards.*

Michelle nearly choked on the sob rising in her throat. The thought of never seeing any of the things or people she'd left behind in Strasburg was almost too much to bear.

"Are you sure this is where you want to be dropped off?" Stan asked when he pulled up to a rundown hotel.

Her eyes snapped open, and she blotted the few escaping tears. "Yeah. The hotel sign says they rent rooms by the day, week, or month. So until I get a job, it's probably about all I can afford right now. If this place doesn't work out, I'll have to look for something else." Michelle leaned over the seat and handed him two fifty-dollar bills. "Thanks for the ride. I appreciate it."

He gave her back one of the bills. "I appreciate your generosity, but fifty dollars more than covers my gas to and from Harrisburg."

Michelle felt grateful for Stan's kindness. Right now, she could use the extra money—even if it wasn't rightfully hers.

"You sure you're feeling okay? It hasn't been very long ago that you suffered a concussion."

"I'm fine now." She opened the back door, grabbed her things, and hopped down. "Thanks again, Stan. Have a safe trip back."

He opened his mouth like he might say more, but merely nodded instead. "Take care, Sara. I hope to see you again sometime."

She didn't bother to correct him or say that seeing him again was doubtful. He'd find out soon enough from the Lapps that she wasn't their granddaughter. For that matter, most of the Amish community in Strasburg would likely know the truth before the week was out. It was one more reason she could never show her face there again.

Michelle wasn't sure why she'd chosen Harrisburg to start over. Maybe it was because the city was fairly large, so she shouldn't have too much trouble finding a job. She would stay here for a while, at least—until she decided it was time to move on.

Michelle felt thankful Stan hadn't asked her a bunch of

questions on the ride up here from Strasburg. The only thing she'd told him was that she'd overstayed her welcome at the Lapps' and needed a fresh start in another location.

Fingers gripping her suitcase handle while she fought back tears, Michelle entered the dreary-looking hotel.

*Strasburg*

Sara opened the door hesitantly and stepped inside. It didn't feel right to enter a house uninvited when no one was at home. She wished she could have asked a few more questions of the young woman who left here in such a hurry. For the first hour after arriving, Sara had remained on the porch with the whining dogs. When she couldn't stand the noise any longer, she decided to go inside, as the auburn-haired woman had suggested.

Standing in the living room, looking around, she had second thoughts about being here. It felt as if she were invading someone's space. A very simple, plain space at that.

Her grandparent's house was neat as a pin, but there were no frilly curtains on the windows, just dark green window shades. A braided throw-rug lay on the nicely polished hardwood floor in front of the stone fireplace. She also noticed a Bible on the coffee table, and next to it was a stack of magazines.

The room was devoid of knickknacks except for the small clock on the mantel with two candles on either side. Across the room stood a large grandfather clock, which had begun bonging when Sara came into the room.

She looked for a switch to turn on the light, but found none on any of the walls. Then Sara spotted two lamps setting next to a couple of recliners. She was looking for a knob to turn one on when she heard gravel crunching outside. Someone must have pulled into the driveway.

Sara hurried to open the door and was surprised to see an elderly couple dressed in plain clothes, getting out of a horse-drawn carriage. They were Amish.

*Well no wonder the house looks so plain, and there are no light switches on the walls.* Sara's stomach tightened as her body heat rose. *Why didn't Mama mention this in the letter she'd written and tucked in her Bible?* Throughout her childhood, Sara had never heard anything about her mother being born into an Amish family. Whenever Sara asked about her heritage, Mama was always vague and changed the subject.

Now Sara realized the jewelry she had made her grandma would not be appropriate to give. But the key ring for Grandpa could be used for house keys at least, since they didn't have a vehicle to drive.

Sara's palms grew sweaty as she stood on the porch and waited for them to join her. The couple looked kind of familiar to Sara. Had she met them somewhere before?

Sara smiled, even though her nerves were on edge. If the last letter she'd sent to the Lapps had gotten here, they should have known she was coming today. But if that was the case, why hadn't they been at home waiting for her?

"I wonder who the blond-haired woman is on our porch." Mary Ruth stood beside Willis as he unhitched his horse. "Wait. Isn't that the young woman we saw at the restaurant, asking for directions, and then she was kind enough to hold the door open for us?"

He shrugged. "Kinda looks like her, doesn't it? Maybe she's a friend of Sara's, or she could have come to the Strasburg area trying to sell something."

"True. Should I go talk to her or wait till you've put the horse and buggy away and we can go up to the house together?"

"It's up to you. I may be awhile when I take Bashful to the barn. She's worked up a pretty good sweat, so I'll need to rub her down."

"I'll go then. If she is selling something, I'll just politely tell her we're not interested."

Willis nodded and led his horse away.

As soon as Mary Ruth stepped onto the porch, the young woman stretched out her hand. "Didn't I see you a short time ago, back at the Bird-in-Hand restaurant?"

"Yes, we just had lunch there." Mary Ruth smiled and shook her hand. "I overheard you asking the cashier for directions to Strasburg."

"Yes. Yes, that was me." The woman looked at Mary Ruth with the oddest expression. "This might seem hard to believe, but I'm Sara Murray, and you must be my grandmother, Mary Ruth Lapp."

Blinking rapidly, Mary Ruth took a step back. "I don't know what kind of game you're playing, but our granddaughter is here at our home..." She pointed. "She's inside our house."

The young woman tipped her head. "Are you talking about the woman with long auburn hair?"

"Yes. Her name is Sara Murray, and—"

"No, it's not—unless there are two Sara Murrays. I've written to you several times about coming to visit, and you responded, saying I should wait until October. In fact I sent a letter a few days ago, letting you know I would be here today." Her forehead wrinkled a bit. "But I'm guessing the letter hasn't gotten to you yet."

"I don't know. Our granddaughter usually goes out to get the mail." More confused than ever, Mary Ruth leaned against the porch railing for support. Her mind raced, trying to process all this and frantically searching for answers that made sense. Surely there had been some mistake. This young woman on her porch could only be an imposter. "Where is Sara—the auburn-haired woman now? I need to ask her a few questions so we can get this all straightened out." Mary Ruth couldn't imagine why this person had showed up claiming to be Sara when their real granddaughter was inside, no doubt resting as she should be.

"She's gone. When I arrived here a few hours ago, she was sitting on the porch with her suitcase, and there was a van parked in the driveway." The woman paused and drew a quick breath. "As soon as I introduced myself, she said you were out running errands and that the front door was open, and I should go in." She gestured toward the partially open door.

"I set my luggage and purse in the living room, but I did not go in any other rooms because it didn't feel right to be in your house when you weren't home. I felt relieved when you got here and hoped you might be as eager to meet me as I was to meet you and my grandpa."

Unable to think or speak clearly after all that had just been explained, Mary Ruth stood staring at the woman in utter disbelief.

"Was your daughter's name Rhoda?"

"Yes."

"My mother's name was Rhoda, and I wrote a letter to let you know she had died." She folded her arms. "I have no reason to lie about this. I'm telling the truth. That other woman, whoever she is, got in the van with her suitcase and left."

"What you've said makes no sense." Mary Ruth shook her head. "My husband and I picked our granddaughter up at the bus station in Philadelphia four months ago, and she's been living here with us ever since."

"Well, she's not here now, and I'm sorry, but she's not your granddaughter. Trust me, I am Rhoda's daughter."

Gathering her wits, the best she could, Mary Ruth turned in the direction of the barn. Cupping her hands around her mouth, she hollered, "Willis! You'd better come to the house right away!"

Moments later, Willis, holding his straw hat in one hand, showed up. "What's all the shouting about? Didn't I tell you I was gonna rub the horse down?" He glanced briefly at the young woman, then back at Mary Ruth. "Is there a problem?"

She gave a decisive nod. "Jah, I believe there is, and I think we should all go inside and get to the bottom of this."

Willis faced the young woman. "If you're selling something, sorry, but we're not interested."

"No, I'm not a salesperson. I'm your granddaughter, Sara Murray."

The wrinkles across Willis's forehead deepened as he looked at Mary Ruth through squinted eyes. "Didn't you tell her that our grossdochder is in the house?"

"I did, but she insists that she's Sara and said the auburn-haired woman told her to wait for us in the house, and that she"—Mary Ruth paused to wipe a tear from her eye, barely able to swallow—"She said Sara—or whoever she is—got in a van and left."

"Whoever she is?" Head flinching back slightly, Willis tugged his beard. "Let's all go in the house and talk about this. There has to be some explanation."

Back inside the living room, Sara took a seat on the couch, while the Lapps sat in the matching pair of recliners. Feeling a desperate need to prove to them who she was, she went to her suitcase and took out her mother's Bible. Then she reached inside her purse and pulled out a manila envelope. "Inside this envelope is my birth certificate, and here is my mother's Bible. If you open the Bible, you'll find the note my mother left, telling me about you. I brought both along in case you had any questions or doubts about my mother being your daughter." She got up and handed the envelope and Bible to the woman whom she felt sure was her grandmother.

Mary Ruth stared at the Bible, running her hands over the worn cover. Slowly and tenderly, she opened it as if afraid to see what was inside. "Why, this was my own mother's Bible. She gave it to me a few months before she died, and then in turn, I gave the Bible to Rhoda, thinking it might help her decide to settle down and join the Amish church." She looked up at Sara with the raw sentiment she must be feeling and gingerly took out the note.

Sara watched with pity when her grandmother's hand went to her mouth. "It's Rhoda's handwriting all right." Her voice shook with emotion as she handed the note to her husband. Clutching the Bible close to her chest, Mary Ruth's chin trembled. "And this is indeed the Bible we gave her shortly before she turned eighteen."

Next Mary Ruth pulled out the piece of paper from the manila envelope. After reading it over, she got up and showed it to her husband. "What do you make of this, Willis?"

"I don't know." Rubbing his forehead as though in extreme pain, he left his chair, ambled into the hallway, and disappeared into another room.

Sara returned to the couch and waited nervously for him to come back.

A few minutes later, Willis shuffled into the living room, holding a piece of paper and slowly shaking his head. "She's gone, Mary Ruth, and her name is not Sara."

Mary Ruth looked up at him with furrowed brows. "Who is she then?"

"I found this note from her on the kitchen table. Her name is Michelle Taylor." Willis pressed one hand to his temple. "And if that's not bad enough, her message said she'd taken money from the coffee can in our cupboard."

Mary Ruth's mouth hung slightly open. "Oh my! I never in a million years expected she would do something like that."

"Yeah, well supposedly she plans to pay us back when she finds a job." Willis waved the piece of paper he held and grunted. "I doubt we'll ever see Michelle again, much less any of the money she took."

Sara shifted uneasily in her seat. It was difficult seeing her grandparents having to deal with all this. She wished there was a way to make them feel better, but she couldn't think of anything beneficial to say.

"But—but why would she deceive us like this all these months?" With slumped shoulders, Mary Ruth dropped her gaze to the floor. "I thought she cared about us."

"In the letter, she apologized for lying and said she'd wanted to confess but couldn't find the nerve to do it. She felt leaving this way was better." Willis's face contorted. "Maybe it was best for her, but certainly not us."

Mary Ruth's cheeks appeared hollow as she stared vacantly across the room. "If only she had come to us sooner and told the truth."

Willis moved closer to Mary Ruth and handed her the note.

"Here. You can read it. There's more."

Her eyebrows lifted. "Seriously?"

"Jah. While Michelle was here, she intercepted the real Sara's letters and kept them from us. Oh, and she also wrote Sara back, pretending to be you."

Mary Ruth held the piece of paper her husband had found, and as she read it, tears coursed down her wrinkled cheeks. "Oh dear. Oh dear. . . I thought she cared about us as much as we did her."

Sara inhaled sharply as she sagged against the couch. *I know they are both suffering, but I'm their real granddaughter. Don't they even care about me?*

# Chapter 38

W e weren't very cordial earlier to our rightful granddaughter," Mary Ruth said as she helped Willis rub down his horse. "The poor girl looked so verhuddelt when we showed her to the other guest room upstairs and said we were going out to the barn to take care of a chore."

"She did look confused, and we sure couldn't give her the room Sara—I mean Michelle—stayed in. Under the circumstances, it wouldn't seem right."

"That's true, especially when the bed would need clean sheets and everything." Mary Ruth sighed. "This is all such a shock, Willis. I can't get over the fact that we were lied to all these months and had no idea Michelle wasn't our granddaughter. It certainly seemed as if she was."

"It is hard to comprehend," he agreed, "but some things are beginning to make sense to me now."

"Like what?"

Willis set the curry comb aside and moved closer to Mary Ruth. "There were times when she acted sort of *naerfich* and like she might be hiding something."

"Jah, and after she got hit on the head, she was mentioning people's names that we'd never heard before. At first she didn't seem to know who I was." Grimacing, Mary Ruth shook her head. "But I assumed all that was because she was disoriented due to her concussion."

"Look how hard it was for her to call us Grandpa and Grandma at first and how vague she was when we asked certain questions."

Willis massaged the bridge of his nose.

"I still can't believe that young lady helped herself to the money we had in the cupboard." Mary Ruth's face tightened as she slowly shook her head. "I wonder if we'll ever hear from her again, or if she will pay us back."

Willis shook his head. "No. As I said earlier, I doubt we'll ever see the money or Michelle, for that matter." Bashful nickered, and he reached out to pet the horse's flank. "We have to accept the fact that we may never hear from her again. Although, from what I read in her note, it did seem that she was genuinely sorry for pretending to be our granddaughter, as well as for taking the money."

"Since she had no cash of her own, she was most likely desperate. Without funds, how would she be able to start over?"

Willis bobbed his head. "The part that really got to me in Michelle's note is where she told about the letters our real granddaughter had written and she'd intercepted. What kind of a person could do something like that, Mary Ruth?"

"I don't know. And to think that she went so far as to write Sara back and pretend it was me who'd sent the letter." Mary Ruth's hands dropped to her sides. "I haven't felt this deflated since Rhoda ran away from home."

Willis slipped his arm around Mary Ruth's waist and pulled her gently to his side. "There is really nothing we can do for Michelle except pray for her. What we need to do now is focus on our true granddaughter, who is waiting for us in the house, and make sure she feels welcomed."

Sara stood at the foot of the bed in the guest room she was taken to before her grandparents went outside. This was not the kind of greeting she'd hoped for, and the disappointment she felt caused her to wonder if she should spend just one night and return to her duplex in the morning. What this Michelle person had done was deplorable, yet Willis and Mary Ruth seemed more focused on the imposter than they were on Sara.

As much as she hated to admit it, Sara felt envious of her imper-sonator. All those months Michelle had been here, pretending to be her and taking advantage of two elderly people who apparently wanted to meet their granddaughter so badly that they'd fallen right into the play-actor's trap.

Sara's jaw clenched. *It should have been me getting to know my grandparents, not the redhead. And now I have to wonder if I'll ever get a chance to bond with them.*

Sara turned away from the bed and stared out the window, watching as her grandparents crossed the yard and headed for the house. *I wish there was something I could say or do to worm my way into their hearts.*

She thought about the blue dress and black apron her grand-mother wore. It reminded her of the special scarf she'd given to her mother. *Is that why Mama liked the scarf so much? Did it make her think of her mother's blue dress and black apron?*

Sara jumped when a knock sounded on the bedroom door. "Come in," she called.

The door opened, and her grandmother stepped inside. "I'll be starting supper in a few hours. Is there anything special you would like, or would you care for a little snack to tide you over?"

Sara shook her head. "I'm not a fussy eater, so don't go to any bother on my account. I made a sandwich this morning to eat during my trip, and I ate that when I got outside of Newark. But I am a little hungry, now that you mention it." She moved toward the door. "If you'll show me what you'd prefer that I eat, I'd be happy to fix my own snack. And later, I'll be more than willing to help you with the evening meal."

At first Mary Ruth shook her head, but then she nodded. "All right. Working in the kitchen together will give us a chance to get acquainted. I have many questions I would like to ask, and I'm sure you do too. So how about if I peel an apple, and you can cut some cheese to go with it?"

"That sounds perfect."

They left the room together and descended the stairs. As they started down the hall toward the kitchen, Mary Ruth stopped walking and slipped her arm around Sara's waist. "I hope you will be patient with me and your grandfather. Learning that the young woman we thought was Rhoda's daughter was only pretending to be her has been quite a shock to us both. We grew to love the young woman very much. It's going to take a bit of time for Willis and me to adjust to this, but we are pleased to finally meet our real granddaughter."

Sara's throat constricted, and she could barely swallow. "Thank you, Grandmother. I have so been looking forward to meeting you both, but if my presence here is too painful, I don't have to stay. I can return to my home in Newark in the morning."

The older woman shook her head so hard the ties on her kapp swished across her face. "No, we want you to stay with us for as long as you can."

In a voice choked with tears, Sara said, "I can stay a couple of weeks, but then I'll have to get back to my part-time job."

Her grandma's face fairly beamed as she nodded her head. "I understand, and we'd be pleased to have you here for two weeks. It will give us all a chance to get to know each other."

Ezekiel had calmed down some since Michelle's confession yesterday, but he still didn't understand why she had done it. After supper, he'd decided to make a trip over to the Lapps to see if she had told Willis and Mary Ruth the truth yet. He hoped she had, and if so, he was eager to hear what their response had been. All of this had gotten him to thinking about his own dishonesty with his parents. He had to reach from within and admit to Dad that he hadn't sold the truck but had moved it to his friend's place in Smoketown. Even if telling the truth meant having to move out of his parents' house, it was the right thing to do.

When Ezekiel pulled his horse into the Lapps' yard, he saw a blond-haired woman sitting on the porch next to Mary Ruth. He'd never seen this person before and wondered if she might be new to Strasburg, or maybe a friend of the Lapps from out of the area.

After securing Big Red to the hitching post, Ezekiel hurried across the yard. "Where's Sara, and how is she doing this evening?" he asked, looking at Mary Ruth.

Before Mary Ruth could respond, the young woman spoke. "My name is Sara Murray, and if you're referring to the auburn-haired woman whose real name is Michelle, she's gone."

Ezekiel reached under his straw hat and scratched the side of his head. "Huh?" He looked back at Mary Ruth. "Where did she go?"

Mary Ruth gestured to the empty chair beside her. "Have a seat and I'll explain everything."

Ezekiel sat and listened as she told about Michelle's letter, and how when the real Sara showed up, Michelle had gotten in a driver's van and driven off. She touched the young woman's arm. "This is our real granddaughter. Michelle was only pretending, and as you can imagine, Willis and I are deeply hurt by her deception."

He nodded. "I understand. I was too."

Mary Ruth's brows drew inward. "What are you saying, Ezekiel? Did you know Michelle was an imposter?"

"Not until yesterday when I came to see how she was doing. That's when I found out the truth." He looked at Mary Ruth. "Remember, you told me she was in the barn?"

Mary Ruth slowly nodded.

"Well, when I went out there to talk to her, she confessed the whole thing to me." He shifted his weight on the chair. "I was so upset that I rushed out of there and went straight home to think things through." Ezekiel sighed. "I never expected she would just up and leave without saying anything to you. Especially since she was still recovering from her head injury."

Mary Ruth leaned her head back and groaned. "Oh that's right. She's not out of the woods yet. I really wish she would have told us the truth. I realize now that basically none of the things Michelle said to us were true."

"Would you have understood if she had told you to your face

that she'd been deceiving you and Willis all along?"

"Jah, I believe so. Well, maybe not at first."

"It's hard to forgive when someone you've come to care about hurts you," Willis said joining them on the porch.

Ezekiel jumped up. "Here, Willis, you can have my seat."

Willis held up one hand. "Stay seated, young man. I'll get one of the folding chairs inside the house." He stepped inside and returned a few minutes later with a metal chair. "Now where were we?" he asked, sitting down.

"You were saying it's hard to forgive someone who has hurt you," the real Sara spoke up.

Willis nodded. "Ah yes. Even though it is difficult, the Bible tells us in the book of Matthew, chapter 6, verse 14: 'For if ye forgive men their trespasses, your heavenly Father will also forgive you.'"

Mary Ruth pinched the skin at her throat. "I only wish we knew where Sara—I mean, Michelle—went when she left here. Someone needs to be in contact with her to make sure she's all right."

"Who was her driver?" Ezekiel asked.

Mary Ruth shrugged, then looked over at Sara. "Do you remember what color the vehicle was that she got into?"

"It was a gray minivan. I didn't see the license plate though."

Willis snapped his fingers. "Our only driver with a gray van is Stan. Jah, I'll bet he picked Michelle up. So if it was Stan, then he'd know where she is."

Ezekiel stood. "Should I go call him now and see what I can find out?"

Mary Ruth shook her head. "Stan usually goes to bed early. It's best that we wait till morning to make the call." She looked at Ezekiel. "We'll let you know what we find out."

❧

*Harrisburg*

Michelle lay on the lumpy mattress in her stuffy motel room, staring at the ceiling. She had originally thought she might ask the

Lapps' driver to take her to the train station, and then she would head for Columbus, Ohio, where her foster parents lived. But she'd decided not to go there after all. She had been gone six years with no contact whatsoever and might not be welcome. Now she was in Harrisburg, a city she'd never visited before and where she knew no one. Such a lonely existence. She missed Mary Ruth, Willis, Ezekiel, and even little Rascal. *Too bad I couldn't have brought him along to keep me company.* It might seem weird to someone else, but Michelle even missed the bonging of the Lapps' grandfather clock. She pretty much missed everything about being on Willis and Mary Ruth's farm.

Michelle had to figure out what to do next. It hurt too much to think about what she'd left behind in Strasburg. It was best to concentrate on the future. Could she find a job and a decent place to live? She sure didn't want to stay here any longer than necessary. The price of the room might be cheap, but the place was a dump. Not nearly as comfortable as her cozy room at the Lapps' with clean sheets and a colorful quilt on the bed. As soon as she found a job, she would look for an apartment she could afford.

Maybe it was best she didn't know any people in Harrisburg. She was so ashamed of what she'd done to Willis and Mary Ruth she couldn't face anyone right now—not even strangers.

She sat up, reached into her purse, and pulled out a slip of paper she'd found in one of the prayer jars. Her chin trembled as she whispered the words, "Dear God, help me to trust You with the present, as well as the future."

The question was: Could she do it? Did she even have a future?

# Chapter 39

It had been nearly two weeks since Michelle arrived in Harrisburg, and here she was, still living at the bug-ridden hotel. The place was crawling with ants, and she'd seen a roach in the bathroom. She'd been able to find a job waiting tables at a local diner, but it would take time before she had enough money saved up to look for a decent place to live—not to mention the need to return what she took from the Lapps.

Michelle felt closed in. She opened the window to let in some air. Even though it was early October, the weather remained warm and humid. The air-conditioning unit inside her hotel room was old and didn't work well enough to keep the room cooled. It was so rickety and noisy there was no point in turning it on. To make things worse, the room smelled like stale cigarette smoke—no doubt from whomever had stayed here before. The walls were paper thin, and she could hear the TV and conversations going on in the rooms on either side of her.

At least she had a microwave, so she could heat up any leftovers she brought home from her break at work. But oh how Michelle missed the delicious home-cooked meals Mary Ruth made.

She'd gotten off work a short time ago, and her hair reeked of grease from working in the restaurant all day. The schedule Michelle had been given was crazy. Sometimes she worked the day shift and other times the evening hours. Her boss was a big burly guy. Not real friendly, but okay. She was just glad to have found a job. Michelle also felt relieved that the lump on her head had receded and she no longer suffered from headaches. It would have been difficult to work anywhere if she was still in pain.

Susan, one of the single waitresses who was close to Michelle's age, was friendly and easy to work with, and they usually had the same shift. Right now, it seemed Susan was her only friend. The desk clerk at the hotel where she was staying seemed pretty nice too.

The restaurant was small, and the tables and chairs were set too close together, making it difficult to get around. Despite the fact that it sat on the corner of a secondary street and farther up from the office district in Harrisburg, a nice flow of customers came in. From what Michelle could tell, they were mostly regulars who either lived or worked in the city. A few of them, she'd learned, worked at the state capitol, some at the courthouse, and others in offices around the Capitol District. They were decent people, for the most part, and tipped well, but some who stopped in for a bite to eat were questionable.

Unfortunately, later in the evening people disappeared off the sidewalks, except at the corner where she worked. It became a hangout, drawing some of the local young men, who stood around smoking and looking for trouble. Quitting time was unnerving when Michelle left to walk back to her hotel after the evening shift. Cat whistles from the guys became a normal thing, and sometimes a not-so-nice comment reached her ears.

But for the most part, that was the extent of them bothering her. As long as they left Michelle alone, she could put up with their jeers. Of course, that was minimal compared to what she'd gone through when she lived with her parents or had dealt with Jerry.

Michelle got by on as little as possible and felt grateful for the food she was offered as part of her compensation for working at the restaurant. Since she planned to put money in an envelope to pay back the Lapps, there wouldn't be much left for food and personal items.

Moving down the narrow hall and into the bathroom, Michelle gazed at her reflection in the bathroom mirror. Her throat tightened as tears sprang to her eyes. She'd been miserable ever since she left Willis and Mary Ruth's and hadn't really been able to relax.

Ever since she'd arrived in Harrisburg, her nerves had been on edge. Michelle felt like she did when her brothers were taken away. She was downright depressed. *Wish I'd never pretended to be Sara Murray. I've really made a mess of my life.*

Michelle had gotten used to wearing little or no makeup while living with the Lapps, but since she was working again, she'd begun wearing makeup. But the makeup felt heavy on her face, and her eyes itched from the mascara and eye liner. She couldn't wait to get back to her room each night when her shift was over so she could wash the makeup off. Next came the shower with lukewarm water, and finally, she collapsed on the bed.

Each night before going to sleep, Michelle would read the few prayer-jar notes she had brought with her. They gave her a sense of peace and, most importantly, hope. Tonight, the paper she took out was Isaiah 41:10: *"Fear thou not; for I am with thee: be not dismayed; for I am thy God: I will strengthen thee; yea, I will help thee; yea, I will uphold thee with the right hand of my righteousness."*

*Oh Lord, I do need Your help. I'm just not deserving.* Michelle sniffed and reached for a tissue. Her thoughts turned to Ezekiel and the special friendship that had developed between them. She had kept her growing feelings for him to herself, knowing she would someday leave, but now she could freely acknowledge that she had fallen in love with Ezekiel, not Brad.

But it was too late for any kind of relationship between them. She had ruined things with her lies. Ruined her chances with the Lapps, and with Ezekiel, and with Brad. Michelle was well aware of Ezekiel's interest in the English life, but deep down she didn't want to be the reason he might leave the Amish faith. His parents were already uncomfortable with her, and if he left, they'd probably blame her. Well, there was no cause for them to be concerned about that now.

Michelle rolled over and punched her pillow, trying to find a comfortable position. She still couldn't believe how upset Ezekiel had gotten with her when she'd admitted the truth. Didn't his conscience let him realize that he too was a liar?

*If I were really Sara Murray and could have stayed in Strasburg permanently, I may have joined the Amish church and maybe Ezekiel would have too.* After getting a taste of how the Amish lived, and the decency, kindness, and honesty she saw in the Lapps, how could she ever measure up or be good enough considering everything that had happened in her life?

A song popped into her head. She'd learned it in Bible school when she was living with her foster family. She began to sing the words, surprised that she remembered them at all. "Jesus loves me! This I know, for the Bible tells me so; Little ones to Him belong; They are weak, but He is strong. Yes, Jesus loves me! Yes, Jesus loves me! Yes, Jesus loves me! The Bible tells me so."

Feeling as though the song had been meant for her, Michelle closed her eyes. *If Jesus loves me, I hope He hears this.*

Michelle whispered a prayer asking God's forgiveness, before closing her eyes and drifting off to sleep.

### Strasburg

Sara was about to head upstairs to bed when Mary Ruth called out to her. "I almost forgot—when your grandpa went out to check for mail this evening after supper, there was a letter for you."

Sara paused. "Are you sure? No one knows I'm here except my stepfather, and I would think if he wanted to get a hold of me, he would have called my cell phone."

"It's addressed to you." Mary Ruth held out the letter.

"Okay, thanks. I'll take it up to my room and read it there." Sara took the letter. "Goodnight, Mary Ruth—I mean, Grandma."

Mary Ruth smiled. "I hope you sleep well, Sara."

"You too." Sara nodded and hurried from the room. She'd been here nearly two weeks now and still hadn't gotten used to the idea that this pleasant Amish couple were actually her grandparents. It seemed like she was living a dream. A very simple, plain one at that.

Michelle Taylor's name had only been brought up a couple of

times since Sara's first day here, but Willis and Mary Ruth had asked her dozens of questions about their daughter, wanting to know anything she could tell them about her mother. What was Sara's life like growing up? Where did they live? Did she have any siblings? What did Rhoda do for a living? How did she die? So many of their questions had brought back a flood of memories for Sara—some happy, others sad.

Sara had asked them plenty of questions too—including if they knew who her biological father was. She was greatly disappointed when they said they had no idea. In fact, her grandparents said they'd been wondering about that too. With frowns, they did comment that Sara's mother had always kept pretty quiet about who she saw or what she did during her running-around days.

It was a surprise to learn that Willis and Mary Ruth had no idea their daughter was expecting a baby when she left home. That bit of information Sara had learned when she'd read the letter Mama left for her in the Bible. It had been a shock to her as well, although she'd suspected it because of growing up without a father until Mama had married Dean. The part Sara hadn't known until reading the letter was that her mother had run away from home. It was hard to understand how Mama could have left such loving parents.

*Mama must have been a bit of rebel during her younger years,* Sara thought as she climbed the creaking stairs. *I can only imagine the agony of what her parents went through when she ran away from home and never contacted them again.*

Her heart ached as she clutched the doorknob and stepped into the guest room. *And then they had to deal with that auburn-haired woman's deceit.* Sara wished there was something she could do to alleviate their pain. *Would it help if they knew who my father was, or is it only important to me?*

Sara had determined in her heart, even before she arrived here, that she would leave no stone unturned in trying to locate her father. Surely there had to be someone in this community who knew who he was. Unfortunately, on this visit she'd spent most of her time just getting to know her grandparents. The next time she came to Strasburg to visit her grandparents, she would do some asking around and see if anyone the Lapps knew might be able to shed some light on things.

Taking a seat at the small desk in the room, she turned on the battery-operated lamp and tore open the letter that had no return address. Silently, she read it:

> *Dear Sara,*
>
> *I am settled in at the seminary and decided to take a few a minutes from my studies to write and see how you're doing.*
>
> *I trust you got the note I dropped off the day I left Strasburg. Wish we could have said goodbye in person, but maybe it was better this way.*
>
> *I've enclosed a card with a Bible verse on it, along with my mailing address here. I hope you will write when you have the time. As soon as I have a free weekend, I'd like to come there for a visit.*
>
> *Give my love to Willis and Mary Ruth, and remember, Sara, I am praying for you.*
>
> 

*All God's best,*
*Brad*
> 

Sara set the letter aside. It was obviously not meant for her. The man clearly knew Michelle, whom he believed to be Sara. He sounded like a nice guy and was apparently religious. But he had no idea Michelle had deceived him.

Her scalp prickled. *Oh boy. This poor man will be coming here to see the woman he knows as Sara, and my grandparents will be the ones to tell him the truth. Sure hope I'm not here when it happens.*

# *Chapter 40*

When Ezekiel woke up the last Saturday of October, he made a decision. He'd finally connected with Stan Eaton yesterday and found out where he'd taken Michelle. Stan had been gone for three-and-a-half weeks, visiting his sick mother who lived in Iowa. Now that he was back in the area, Ezekiel learned that Stan had driven Michelle to Harrisburg the day she'd left the Lapps'. Apparently she had asked him to drop her off at a hotel that was not in the best part of town.

Thinking more about it, Ezekiel shook his head. *I bet she's low on money by now. I'll take some extra cash with me, just in case.*

He had taken some time to process what he'd learned from Stan, and even though he was still upset with Michelle for the way she'd left, not to mention the reason for it, Ezekiel felt compelled to see her. Since he hadn't sold his truck, and now had his driver's license, he could get to Harrisburg without hiring a driver.

Two days ago, Ezekiel had told his parents the truth about not selling the truck, but so far Dad hadn't asked him to leave. It would probably come sooner or later. But it didn't matter, because Ezekiel had made up his mind about what he was going to do.

*Harrisburg*

Since Michelle didn't have to work until evening, it would be good to take some time for herself and get acquainted with more of her surroundings. It seemed that all she had done since arriving in Harrisburg was work and sit around feeling sorry for herself.

So recently, she'd asked her coworker Susan if there was anything close by to see or do that wouldn't cost any money.

Susan had given Michelle a few suggestions, and she decided to walk up Front Street to see the view of the Susquehanna River. Michelle grabbed her keys and her jacket and left the hotel for her small venture.

After walking the few blocks and crossing the street, Michelle found herself in a grassy area. Beyond that, the flowing river came into view. Huge trees grew on this stretch of public land with massive branches donning leaves of autumn's brilliance. Today was Saturday, and traffic on Front Street was light, unlike Monday through Friday when people traveled to the city for their jobs.

That was one thing Michelle had noticed right away. Not only was the traffic heavy in Harrisburg during the work week, but the view out her hotel room window was boring—kind of like it had been in Philadelphia. Boy, how she missed looking out into the Lapps' backyard from her upstairs bedroom window in Strasburg, where she could look as far as her eyes would let her, and see the big open sky. From her hotel room and the restaurant, Michelle saw mostly brick and mortar, which she had hoped to never see again.

"Wow, this view is amazing," Michelle murmured as she took a seat on one of the park benches. Activity surrounded her everywhere. It seemed to be a popular place to come for those wanting to get away for a spell. Michelle watched people jogging, riding bicycles, and walking their dogs along the macadamized pathway. There were also some folks sitting on benches, reading a newspaper or book. But most, like herself, sat quietly staring out, no doubt, enjoying the spacious view.

Michelle took a deep breath and let it out slowly. She hadn't felt this relaxed since leaving Strasburg. She would have to try and come to the riverfront more often, for it wasn't confining here, like in her room back at the hotel.

As Michelle looked across the river, she could see clear to the other side. *That must be what I hear people referring to as the West*

*Shore.* She had heard that term used at the restaurant quite often too. This side of the river, she'd learned, was called the East Shore.

Michelle turned her head when she heard some honking, and watched a small flock of geese land in the grass a short distance away. An older man and woman, sitting closer to the birds, took out a bag of cracked corn and threw it toward the geese.

Michelle smiled when the geese hungrily snatched up the food then took off in flight toward the river. She watched them land on one of the islands, which jutted out toward the middle of the river. Other birds mingled along the island's shoreline. One bird stood out among the rest: pure white with extremely long legs. From where she sat, several bridges were in view, crossing over the water to the West Shore. When Michelle looked in the other direction, a mountain range could be seen. *I wonder how long it takes to get up there.*

Michelle thought it was truly a breath of fresh air, seeing the river and beyond, as far as the eyes could see. It was exactly the outlet she needed after being cooped up at work and inside her dinky hotel room, and it was a good way to get her mind off her troubles. She was thankful she had taken Susan's suggestion and come here today.

As Michelle looked up the river, something caught her attention, and as it got closer, she realized it was a tree branch. The limb moved slowly along with the water's flow, bobbing up and down in the ripples like a giant cork. *I wonder where that branch will end up. It's kind of like me, not knowing where I'll wind up.*

Just as she was about to get up, her friend Susan plopped down beside her. "Hey girl, I was hoping you would make it out to view the mighty Susquehanna River. What do you think of our beautiful waterway?"

"You were right. It's a nice place to come, and just across the street from all of that." Michelle pointed to the buildings behind her.

"That's one perk for working in Harrisburg. We have river frontage to escape to." Susan grinned. "Not all of Harrisburg looks old and rundown, like the neighborhood where Dan's restaurant is located. There are a lot of fun things to see and do in the city."

"Like what?"

"There's a state museum, and farther up the river is Fort Hunter, where they have several events throughout the year. There's also a sportsmen's show, the Pennsylvania auto show, and a big horse show."

"I would enjoy the horse show. When I lived in Strasburg, I was around horses a lot." Michelle's thoughts took her back to a day when she'd hosed off Mary Ruth's horse, Peanuts. As warm as it was that afternoon, it had felt good for both the mare and Michelle to have cool water spraying on their bodies. Michelle almost chuckled out loud, remembering how the leaky nozzle on the hose had caused a spray of water to be aimed in her direction.

Then Michelle reflected on another day when one of the Lapps' chickens had followed her around the yard, cackling and flapping her wings. The silly chicken didn't quit carrying on until Michelle stopped walking and bent down to stroke the hen's soft feathers. After that, Michelle was fairly sure she'd made a new barnyard friend. Then there was Willis's horse, Bashful. Michelle had been a bit leery of her at first, but after she was around the mare longer, they too became friends. In fact, it didn't take long before Michelle had Bashful eating out of her hand.

Susan tapped Michelle's arm. "Well, you need to go to the horse show then, and maybe I'll even go with you. And you know what else, Michelle?"

"What's that?"

"If you stick around Harrisburg, in January there's the annual farm show at the Farm Show complex. Think you might enjoy that too?"

"Yeah, I would. But I'm not sure how long I'll be living in Harrisburg."

"How come? Do you have someplace else to go?"

Michelle shook her head. "No, not really. It all depends on how well things go with my job, and whether I'm able to find an apartment I can afford." Michelle pushed a strand of unruly hair behind her ear that seemed determined to blow across her face. A nice breeze coming off the river rattled the leaves overhead. A variety of birds flew close to the water's surface.

Michelle felt a little better about her current situation, knowing she could at least attend some interesting events and also come to the riverfront to unwind a bit. She looked over at Susan. "I can't believe all the birds I've seen since I got here."

"Many of them are migrating south right now, and they stop over here at our river."

"We should come here on our lunch break some time. There is so much to observe by the river. And I didn't realize this was so close to where we work either. It really is a pretty place."

"Yes, Harrisburg has a lot to offer. I live not far out of the city, but I come here a lot when I have free time." Susan stared out at the river too. "I like your suggestion about coming here on our lunch break sometime."

Michelle smiled. She felt thankful she had made a new friend in Susan. She'd never realized how important friendships were until she lived in Strasburg and had become friends with Ezekiel, Brad, and even Lenore. Those days were gone though, and it was time to move on.

"You know, my grandma said that when my daddy was a little boy, he had a hard time pronouncing the word *Susquehanna*." Susan's voice broke into Michelle's thoughts. "Guess he used to call this body of water, 'the second-handed river.'"

"That's really cute." Michelle chuckled, then she pointed. "What's that over there?"

"It's called City Island. They have baseball games there, and a little park where kids can play. A lot of the people who work in Harrisburg park their cars on City Island too." Susan pointed in that direction. "They park their cars over there and just walk back across the bridge. By the way, that's the Market Street Bridge."

"That's interesting. I might wanna walk across that bridge sometime."

"Hey, do you want to take a walk now? It's Saturday, and we

have most of the day to do something." Susan stood up. "This is a great place to get some exercise."

"Not only that, it looks like a wonderful area to come and clear your mind. Almost like the country, where I used to live," Michelle said. "Maybe we can get lunch somewhere after we walk awhile, since we still have a lot of time before we have to work the evening shift tonight."

"I know just the place. It's a nice little sub shop where we can have a leisurely lunch. Then you can tell me all about where you used to live."

"Okay, let's go, and we'll work up an appetite."

*Strasburg*

"I wish you didn't have to go so soon, Sara." Mary Ruth placed her arm across Sara's shoulders after they had finished eating an early lunch. "We've barely had a chance to get to know you."

"Your grandma's right," Willis put in. "Can't ya stay another week or so?"

"I would love to, but I can't afford to be gone from my part-time job any longer. I've already stayed longer than I planned. My boss is great, but if don't get back to work by Monday, he might decide to hire someone else permanently—maybe even the young woman who's been taking my place these past couple of weeks." Sara gave Mary Ruth a tender squeeze. "I promise to come back for Thanksgiving and again at Christmas. That is, if I'm still invited."

"Course you are." Mary Ruth nodded. "It will give you the opportunity to get to know your Uncle Ivan and his family better too. Even though you were able to meet them while you were here, you didn't get to spend much time together."

"I look forward to knowing them all better—especially my cousin Lenore." Sara smiled. "Never knew I had a cousin until I came here."

Mary Ruth thought about Lenore's reaction when she'd found out Michelle had been posing as Sara. She, as well as the rest of her family, had been quite upset about the situation. Mary Ruth didn't have the nerve to tell them Michelle had taken all the cash they'd been putting away inside their coffee can for incidentals and a small vacation fund. Truth be told, she and Willis would probably never see that money again.

But maybe Michelle needed it more than they did. And it wasn't as if she'd taken everything they owned, for they still had money in their bank account. They were getting along okay and didn't really miss the amount that had been stashed away in their cupboard. Despite all that, what Michelle had done was wrong, and some folks might not be so quick to forgive. Mary Ruth was sure, however, that Ivan and his family would eventually find it in their hearts to forgive Michelle's misdeed.

After all, there were plenty of verses in the Bible to remind people of the importance of forgiveness. Jesus was a prime example, for when He hung on the cross, close to death, Jesus asked God to forgive those who had crucified Him, for they knew not what they were doing. Of course Michelle did know what she was doing, but that didn't mean her deeds shouldn't be forgiven. *Hate the sin, but not the sinner.* She'd heard Willis quote that phrase in several of the sermons he'd preached over the years.

Turning back to Sara, Mary Ruth smiled and said, "I believe you and Lenore can be good friends."

"I hope so." Sara reached for her suitcase. "And now, I'd best be on my way."

"Here, let me get that for you." Willis stepped forward.

"It's okay. I can manage, Grandpa."

He hesitated but finally nodded.

Mary Ruth held back a chuckle. Their granddaughter was independent, just like her mother had been, and dear Willis had a hard time not taking charge of things. Sooner or later, he would learn that some folks liked to be self-sufficient.

They followed Sara out the door and walked her to the car. Mary Ruth was pleased when Sara allowed Willis to put her suitcase in the trunk of the car. Hugs were given all the way around, and then Sara said a tearful goodbye and got in her car.

Mary Ruth, swallowing against the lump in her throat, stood beside Willis and watched as their granddaughter drove away. *I hope Sara keeps her promise and comes back for Thanksgiving.*

### Harrisburg

Ezekiel arrived in Harrisburg shortly before supper. It didn't take him long to locate the hotel Stan had told him about. It wasn't in the best part of town, but he figured Michelle had chosen it for the cheaper rate advertised on the lighted reader board outside the building. Unable to find a spot to park his truck in the hotel lot, he realized he'd have to look for something on the street. He finally located an empty spot, put money in the parking meter, and went inside the rundown building.

After making some inquiries at the front desk, Ezekiel felt relief hearing that Michelle was still staying here. The female clerk said she wasn't supposed to give out room numbers to just anyone asking. But since Ezekiel looked like an honest sort and said he was Michelle's friend, she told him that his friend's room was on the fourth floor. The desk clerk also mentioned the room number.

Ezekiel thanked the young woman and headed for the elevator. Looking around after he got on, Ezekiel knew without a doubt that he was nowhere close to home. One of the first things he noticed were the smudges and fingerprints on the walls, not to mention crumpled gum wrappers, dirt, and even a few flattened plastic water bottles. Metal rubbed against metal, and there were squeals and squeaks as the doors shut. It was too late now, but Ezekiel wished he'd taken the stairs. As the elevator began its ascent, Ezekiel wondered what would happen if there was a power outage or even an elevator malfunction. Being trapped in a confined space like this would be frightening enough if there were other people inside with him. But the thought of being stuck here by himself sent shivers of apprehension up Ezekiel's spine.

*Just breathe and try not to think about it,* he told himself.

The elevator shuddered and made a sudden jerk, and then the door came open. *Fourth floor. What a relief.*

Ezekiel wasted no time stepping out. A few minutes later, he found the room Michelle had rented and knocked on her door. Unfortunately, she didn't answer, so he assumed she wasn't there.

Heading back to the lobby, he took the stairs. Then, checking with the desk clerk again, Ezekiel asked if she knew where Michelle might have gone.

"If she's not in her room, then she's probably at work," the tall, dark-haired woman said.

"Can you tell me where that is?"

She leaned over the counter, as if sizing Ezekiel up and down. "Yeah, I do know, but I'm really not supposed to give out that information either."

His patience waning, Ezekiel tapped his foot, then leaned against the counter. "You told me her room number a few minutes ago, so what would it hurt to give me the name of the place my girlfriend works?"

The woman's scrunched up face relaxed slightly. "Well, why didn't you say she was your girlfriend in the first place? You just said she was a friend before. Course I'll tell ya where Michelle works."

On the one hand, Ezekiel was relieved that the desk clerk would give him the information he needed. But on the other hand, he couldn't believe he'd blurted out that Michelle was his girlfriend. At no point had he ever asked her, nor had she ever said she wanted him to court her. Even so, there had been a spark between them. Ezekiel had even admitted to Michelle, when he'd thought she was Sara, the feelings he had developed toward her. He felt sure she had developed the same feelings for him during her stay in Strasburg.

*Of course, Michelle had lied about her name, so maybe she'd only pretended to be interested in me,* Ezekiel thought.

He stood straight when the brunette woman handed him a slip of paper. "Here's the name and address of the restaurant where

Michelle works. It's just about three blocks from here."

"Thanks." In his eagerness to leave the hotel, Ezekiel almost tripped over his own big feet. Righting himself before he toppled over, he stuck the paper in his pocket and made his way out the door. He figured since the place where Michelle worked wasn't far, he would go to the restaurant on foot. A walk in the evening air might be just what he needed to clear his head.

Walking down the street, Ezekiel couldn't get over all the big buildings he saw. Some looked like offices, and others were stores. He'd never seen so many places to eat either, tucked in and around everything else.

As he continued to walk, large homelike structures appeared, some three stories high with huge porches. The buildings looked old, and some were rundown, but most appeared to be well cared-for. Surprisingly, huge trees seemed to grow right out of the sidewalks.

Ezekiel glanced toward one of the porches where several people sat. They stared at him as if they'd never seen an Amish man before. *This is making me uncomfortable.*

Ezekiel picked up his pace and nearly fell on his face when he tripped over a section of concrete that a tree root had lifted up. As he moved on, he could still hear the porch-sitters talking and chortling. He hoped they weren't laughing at him.

When Ezekiel approached the eatery a short time later, he noticed a group of young men, hanging around outside, smoking and drinking. When he walked up to the front door, one of the men hollered, "Say, buddy, what's with the straw hat? You ain't one of them Amish guys, are ya?"

Ezekiel ignored the man's question and reached for the door handle. But before he could get it open, another fellow grabbed his arm and turned him around. With one quick swipe, he knocked Ezekiel's hat off his head.

Then, someone else gave Ezekiel's other arm a hefty punch and snorted. "I think he's a yellow chicken. That's what I think."

The rest of them joined in and kicked his hat around as if

it were a ball. One guy remained close to Ezekiel, as if ready to pounce on him, in case Ezekiel tried to fight back.

As he looked from this guy, to the others who were playing with his hat, Ezekiel wasn't sure how to deal with the situation. One thing was sure. He didn't want any trouble. *Should I stand up for myself? Run? Or try to reason with them?*

# Chapter 41

"L isten now, fellows, I don't want any trouble. I just want to go inside so I can see my girlfriend." Ezekiel held his ground, staying close to the restaurant's front door. He couldn't believe the predicament he was in. It had been hard enough waiting for Stan to return home so he could locate Michelle. Then Ezekiel had dealt with the flighty desk clerk. And now that he was in front of the place where Michelle worked, he faced an even bigger challenge.

The guy who'd begun the taunting, leaned so close to Ezekiel that he could smell his raunchy breath. "Oh yeah? Who'd go out with a big oaf like you?"

Before Ezekiel had the chance to respond, the second young man hauled off and hit him in the stomach.

*Umpf.* Ezekiel doubled over and dropped to his knees. He'd been taught from an early age not to fight. The Amish were pacifists and should not retaliate. The Bible said in Matthew 5:39: *"But whosoever shall smite thee on thy right cheek, turn to him the other also."* Ezekiel also remembered another verse in that chapter that said: *"Love your enemies, bless them that curse you, do good to them that hate you, and pray for them which despitefully use you, and persecute you."* This was a tall order, and Ezekiel wasn't sure he could abide by it right now. Every fiber of his being wanted to defend himself.

His muscles quivered as he struggled to get up, heat coursing through his body. He fought the urge to vomit. What he wanted more than anything was to punch the guy who'd hit him, but he was clearly outnumbered here. And if he did fight back, what kind of message would it send? Certainly not a good Christian witness.

Besides, he'd likely end up in worse shape than he already was.

Glancing at her watch, Michelle realized she hadn't been at work an hour, and already her feet were killing her. *I can't even think about how many hours I still have to work.* She ground her teeth together so hard her jaw ached. Not only did her feet hurt from walking along the riverfront earlier today, but for the last ten minutes, one of the customers had been giving her a hard time. Frank was a guy who came in at least once a week and reminded her of Jerry.

She knew his type and tried to stay clear, but it was difficult in this small restaurant with its confined eating area. Frank constantly asked her out and showed no respect when she said no. This time, however, Frank had become more insistent. When Michelle walked by his table, he grabbed her arm. "I'm tired of you always saying no to me. What's the matter, babe? Ain't I good enough for you?"

Before Michelle could respond, someone in the restaurant hollered, "Hey, there's a fight goin' on outside!"

Frank let go of Michelle's arm, and she almost lost her balance. She recovered the plates on her tray in time to keep them from falling onto the floor. Fights outside weren't unusual, so she didn't follow Frank or any of the other patrons over to the window. But when she heard someone shout that there was an Amish guy outside getting roughed up, Michelle dashed across the room to see what was happening. As far as she knew, no Amish lived in Harrisburg. *Maybe it's an Amish man just passing through, and he stopped for a bite to eat. But why here, in this crummy part of town?*

Michelle slipped between two customers so she could peek out the window. She was stunned to discover Ezekiel lying on the ground. Two big guys with raised fists stood over him. With no thought at all for her safety, she jerked open the door and hollered at the guys to stop.

They sneered at her, and one of them let loose with a couple of cuss words. "Now don't tell me *she's* your girlfriend," the biggest guy taunted.

To her relief, Dan, the owner of the restaurant came out. "Okay you scumbags. . . Break it up, or I'll call the police."

Looking none too happy, one of the guys mumbled something to Ezekiel, and then he and his buddies all slunk away.

Michelle dropped to her knees beside Ezekiel, cradling his head in her hands. "Are you badly hurt? Do we need to call for help?"

"No, I'll be okay." He took her hand and clambered to his feet.

"What are you doing here anyway?" she asked, leading him inside and over to a seat.

"Came to see you."

Michelle's friend, Susan, came over and handed him a wet washcloth, which he held against a place on his face that appeared to be scraped.

"But how did you know where to find me?" Michelle took the chair beside him.

"I found out Stan drove you away from the Lapps'. Took me awhile to talk to him about it because he was out of town. But when I did make connections, he said he drove you to a hotel here in Harrisburg, and he gave me the name of it." Ezekiel paused and took a drink of water another waitress had brought him. "I went there, but you weren't in your room, so I talked the desk clerk into telling me where you worked. Then I came over here so I could talk to you. But thanks to those bullies I encountered, I never made it through the front door."

It was all Michelle could do to keep from hugging Ezekiel, but she didn't want to give those in the restaurant anything more to talk about. Besides, she wasn't sure how Ezekiel would respond. The last time they'd seen each other, he'd been pretty upset with her.

"How'd you get here?" she questioned. "Did Stan drive you up from Strasburg?"

Ezekiel shook his head. "Came in my truck."

"So you still haven't sold it, huh?"

"Nope, but I did come clean and tell my folks where I'd taken it." Ezekiel rubbed his stomach. "Boy, that guy could sure hit. Feels like I've been head-butted by one of my uncle's goats."

"I'm sorry you were subjected to that. Maybe you should have stayed home today."

"No way! I wanted to see you. We need to talk."

Michelle wasn't sure what they had to talk about, but she excused herself and went to speak with her boss. "Would you mind if I left a little early today? I know my shift started less than an hour ago, but this is kind of important, and I need to leave."

He nodded. "Sure, go ahead. I'm guessin' you want to spend some time with your friend."

"Yes, I do. I need to make sure he's really okay."

"Well, go on then." Dan flapped his hand. "Looks like it's gonna be a slow night anyway, so I'll see you tomorrow, late afternoon, for the evening shift."

"Okay, thanks."

As Michelle headed back to the table where Ezekiel waited, she caught sight of Frank stealing tip money off several of the tables. "Hey, what do you think you are doing?"

Quicker than she could blink, her boss ran past and wrestled the guy to the floor. "I can either call the police, or you can hand over the money you took—now!"

"I'll give up the money," Frank mumbled. He handed over all the bills, and when Dan let him go, Frank turned and glared at Michelle. "You think you're so smart, don't you?"

She shook her head. "No, I just know the price people must pay for their dishonesty."

With a loud snort, the troublemaker ambled out of the restaurant.

Michelle returned to the table where Ezekiel waited with a wide-eyed expression. "Unless you have somewhere else to go, let's head over to my hotel so we can talk and you can get cleaned up."

"I have no place else to go. I came here to see you, remember?" Ezekiel clasped Michelle's hand. "By the way, how are you doing?

You look good, so I assume that bump you took on the head is much better."

She nodded. "I haven't had any problems since I came here. At least not with my head."

"I'm glad." He gave her fingers a tender squeeze.

Michelle felt a mixture of hopefulness and humiliation. If Ezekiel hadn't come here, he wouldn't have gotten beat up. But if he'd stayed down in Lancaster County today, she wouldn't have this opportunity to apologize to him or find out how Willis and Mary Ruth were doing.

# Chapter 42

*Strasburg*

The rocking chair creaked beneath Mary Ruth's feet, as she sat rocking, staring at the note Michelle had left on their kitchen table. How many times had she read the young woman's message revealing her true identity? *Probably as many times as I've read Rhoda's note.* While parts of Rhoda's note gave Mary Ruth peace of mind, Michelle's note still confused her.

She couldn't help wondering where the young woman was and how she was doing. During the months Michelle had spent with Willis and Mary Ruth, a bond had been created between them. At least for Mary Ruth it had. She had no idea how Michelle truly felt about them. Since everything the young woman had told the Lapps had been a lie, Mary Ruth wondered what Michelle's life was really like. Who were her parents? Where did she come from? Why had she pretended to be Sara? Despite Michelle's deception, Mary Ruth couldn't help missing her.

Slowing the rocker, she released a heavy sigh. *I suppose we will never know anything about her past. But at least I can keep praying for her, asking God to keep Michelle safe and on the right path.*

"Whatcha doin' in here? I thought we were gonna have lunch."

Mary Ruth jumped at the sound of her husband's voice. "Ach, you scared me, Willis!"

"Sorry about that." He ambled across the room and stopped in front of her chair. "So how come you're here and not in the kitchen? It's past lunchtime already, and you said you would call me when the meal was ready."

"I apologize, Willis. I got busy doing some cleaning and lost track of time. Then, feeling kind of tired and depressed, I came in here to rock and think for a bit."

He placed his hands on her shoulders. "You're missing our grossdochder, right?"

"Jah. It is lonely without her."

"Don't forget. Sara will be back next month, for Thanksgiving."

Mary Ruth nodded. "I'm also missing the young woman who pretended to be Sara."

He cocked his head. "Figured as much. Those four months she was with us created a connection. It's just a shame she wasn't honest with us from the beginning."

"I'm partly to blame as well."

"How so?"

"I was so excited to meet our granddaughter at the bus station that day, I never even thought to question whether the young woman we thought was Sara truly was." Mary Ruth lifted her hands and let them fall back in her lap. "She went with us so willingly, I just assumed. . ." Her voice trailed off. "Oh well, what does it matter now anyway? We've finally met Rhoda's rightful daughter, and Michelle ran off, unable to face us. We'll probably never know where she is or how she's doing."

"Jah, and I have to say once again that I seriously doubt we'll ever see the money she took from us." Willis shuffled his feet. "So let's put it in the past and try not to think about it, okay?"

"It is in the past, but I can't guarantee I won't think about it." Mary Ruth stood. "Let's go to the kitchen, and I'll fix us something to eat."

❧

*Harrisburg*

Michelle sat in a chair across from Ezekiel inside her stuffy hotel room. Even with the window open, it seemed too warm. Of course, it didn't help that the hotel's furnace didn't work any better than the air-conditioning. Her room was always too warm or too cold.

Michelle was glad Ezekiel hadn't been seriously injured by

those guys outside the restaurant, but the question he'd just posed had slammed into her like a horse running at full speed into the barn.

"I can't believe you want me to go back to Strasburg with you." Michelle stuck a fingernail between her teeth and bit off the jagged end. "I don't have all the money I took from the Lapps to return to them, and just thinking about facing Mary Ruth and Willis again makes my heart palpitate."

"It won't be as bad as you think, Michelle. The Lapps are good people. I'm sure they've already forgiven you by now."

She sniffed. "Don't see how they could. What I did was awful. I've asked God to forgive me, but I can't seem to forgive myself."

Ezekiel nodded. "Believe me, I understand. I've had trouble forgiving myself for lying to my folks all this time. It was a huge burden off my shoulders when I finally admitted to Dad that I still owned the truck."

"So what are you saying—that I should admit what I did to Mary Ruth and Willis face-to-face?" Michelle shifted on the hard-backed chair she sat upon. "I already told them I was sorry in the note I left on their kitchen table."

Ezekiel glanced around the room. "You don't belong here, Michelle. Your place is with the people you love in Strasburg, and who also love you."

She shook her head vigorously. "The Lapps would never invite me to stay at their house again. And even if they did, I wouldn't feel right about it. Besides, they have their rightful granddaughter now, so I doubt they're even thinking of me. I can't imagine how the real Sara feels about me either."

"Not true. I can't speak for Sara, but Willis and Mary Ruth have both mentioned you to me several times." Stretching his arms over his head, Ezekiel gave her a playful grin. "Rascal misses you too. I've seen the sadness in his puppy dog eyes."

Michelle pressed a palm against her chest. Merely thinking about the dog she'd left behind put an ache in her heart. "Do the Lapps know you're here?" She leaned slightly forward.

"No. I told no one I was coming to see you. Stan probably suspects, since I asked him to tell me where he'd brought you."

She drew in a deep breath and sighed. "Even if I did go back, it would only be to apologize again and give them back the money I took." Frowning, she rubbed the bridge of her nose. "Only problem is, I don't have all of it yet. The restaurant doesn't pay much, and most of what I earn I have to use for the weekly rate on this crummy room. It could take months till I have enough saved up to pay the Lapps back."

"I'll loan you the money, and you can pay me back when you're able." The sincerity she saw in Ezekiel's eyes was almost enough to make her agree to go back to Strasburg with him.

He got up from his chair and moved across the room. Clasping her hands, he pulled Michelle to her feet. "I care about you, and I'd like the chance to court you."

She tipped her head back and gazed into his brown eyes. "That's the sweetest thing anyone has ever said to me, Ezekiel."

"Does that mean you'd be willing?"

"Willing to let you court me, or willing to return to Strasburg and face Willis and Mary Ruth?"

"Both." He placed a gentle kiss on her forehead.

Michelle's heart pounded. "Have you decided whether you want to remain Amish or go English?"

"I haven't made up my mind for sure yet, but after getting a little taste of the English world, I'm not sure I would fit in." He touched his stomach. "I am a bit baffled and dissatisfied with what I've seen so far. Truth is, I'm probably not cut out to be English."

"Ezekiel, what you experienced outside the restaurant doesn't paint a picture of the entire English world." Michelle lifted her hands and let them fall against her sides. "It's true, there are some bad ones, like I'm sure there are in the Amish world. But there are a lot of good English people too, same as the Amish."

"What you've said makes sense." He slipped his arms around her waist. "To tell you the truth, my decision about whether to go English or join the Amish church might depend on you."

"What does that mean?" She reached up and pushed a lock of hair out of his eyes.

"It means, if the only way I can be with you is to live in the English world, then I'll do it. But if you'd be willing to. . ."

"Willing to what? Join the Amish faith?"

"Yes."

Michelle gave Ezekiel a playful tap on the arm and snickered. "Yeah, right. Can't you just see the Amish church allowing someone like me into their flock? That's never gonna happen, Ezekiel, and you know it."

"I'm no better than you. But if I were to take the necessary classes and showed that I'm sincere in my desire to serve the Lord and follow the rules of the Amish church, I'd be allowed to join."

"But I'm an outsider," Michelle argued. "And even on the off-chance that they did allow me to join, it would be a difficult transition."

"Oh, I don't know about that. I saw what you did when you lived with Willis and Mary Ruth. You enjoyed the simple things and even wanted to learn how to drive a horse and buggy." He pointed to her. "That was the real you, not the pretend Sara."

Michelle couldn't deny it. She had enjoyed her time at the Lapps' and had even daydreamed on several occasions what it might be like if she were Amish. Even so, she felt sure it was just a foolish dream, so why get her hopes up?

"Do you care about me?" Ezekiel asked.

"Yes, I do." Her words came out in a whisper.

"Do you trust me?"

She slowly nodded.

"Then go back to Lancaster County with me, face the Lapps, and let's see where things go from there." He gestured to the line of ants crawling across the floor. "Anything you might face in Strasburg can't be as bad as the way you're being forced to live here."

"I'd have to go by the restaurant and tell my boss that I'm quitting."

"No problem. We can do that."

"And I'd also need to let the desk clerk here know I'm checking out for good."

"Yep." Ezekiel leaned a bit closer. "So how about it, Michelle? Are you willing to go back with me now?"

Michelle's thoughts raced as her heart beat a staccato. "I may be crazy, but jah, I'll go."

He grinned and gave her a kiss—this time full on the lips.

Michelle melted into his embrace. *How could I have ever thought I might be falling for Brad? Ezekiel is the man I love.* While Michelle felt apprehensive about going back to face Willis and Mary Ruth, she was ready to accept whatever they decided. She didn't know what the future held for her or Ezekiel, but having him by her side would make it easier. They would need to put their faith and trust in God, and with His help, Michelle and Ezekiel could face any obstacles that may lay ahead.

"I don't want you to worry about anything either," Ezekiel said as they pulled slowly apart. "I'll help you pack up your things, and soon we'll be heading for home."

*Home.* Michelle liked the sound of that. For the first time in many months, she felt a sense of hope and peace. She couldn't be sure yet, but perhaps returning to the Amish community in Strasburg was God's will for her life—and Ezekiel's. Maybe one of the prayers Michelle had found in the old blue jar inside the barn would become her prayer for life.

# Ezekiel's Favorite Johnnycake

Ingredients:

1 cup cornmeal
1 cup flour
¼ cup sugar
4 teaspoons baking powder
½ teaspoon salt

1 cup milk
1 egg, beaten
¼ cup vegetable oil or
   melted shortening

Grease 8-inch square baking pan. In bowl, mix cornmeal, flour, sugar, baking powder, and salt. Add milk, egg, and oil to dry ingredients, stirring only enough to blend. Spread in baking pan and bake at 400 degrees for 20 to 25 minutes. Serve warm or cold with butter.

# Mary Ruth's Tasty Scalloped Potatoes and Pork Chops

Ingredients:

5 cups peeled and thinly
  sliced raw potatoes
1 cup chopped onions
Salt and pepper to taste
1 (16 ounce) can cream of
  mushroom soup
½ cup sour cream
6 pork loin chops (1 inch
  thick)
Chopped fresh parsley

In greased 9x13-inch baking pan, layer half the potatoes and onion. Sprinkle with salt and pepper. Repeat layer. Combine soup and sour cream and pour over potato mixture. Cover and bake at 375 degrees for 30 minutes. Meanwhile in skillet, brown pork chops on both sides. Place pork chops on top of casserole. Cover and return to oven for 45 minutes or until pork chops are tender. Uncover during last 15 minutes of baking. Sprinkle with parsley and serve. Yields 6 servings.

# Discussion Questions

1. Have you ever wondered what it would be like to set your modern, worldly things aside and live on an Amish farm for several months with no electricity or modern conveniences? What would be the one thing you'd have the hardest time giving up?

2. If you had been Michelle, would you have been honest with the Lapps right from the start? If you had decided to pretend you were their granddaughter, would you have been able to deceive them for as long as Michelle did without breaking down?

3. Mary Ruth and Willis Lapp were deeply grieved when their only daughter, Rhoda, left home when she was eighteen and never made contact with them again. If you had an adult child old enough to make their own decisions, and he or she left home without word of their whereabouts, how would you cope with the situation? Would you try your best to find them?

4. Have you ever lost a loved one quickly, as Sara did, and barely had time to deal with their illness before they were gone? How did you get through the ordeal? Were there any verses of scripture that helped you along the way?

5. Do you think Willis and Mary Ruth Lapp wanted so badly for their granddaughter to truly be coming home to them that they threw caution to the wind and approached the first person at the bus station who they thought was their granddaughter? Should they have asked more specific questions to make sure it really was Sara?

6. Michelle deceived everyone she met while living in Strasburg. If you had been any of them (the Lapps, Brad, Ezekiel, Ivan, Lenore) would you have been able to forgive her when you found out what she did?

7. Michelle's interest was piqued when she discovered some old jars that contained prayers, sayings, and Bible quotes. It was because of these notes that she began thinking about someone other than herself. Have you ever found a note in an unusual place and didn't know who had written it or why? Did it make any kind of an impact on your life?

8. If you were the real Sara, how would you have felt after discovering that someone had been pretending to be you?

9. At one point Michelle convinced herself it was okay to deceive the Lapps because she had grown fond of them and didn't want to hurt them. Is there ever a time when it's all right to keep the truth from someone, for fear of them getting hurt?

10. Ezekiel had also been living a lie, keeping the truth from his parents about the truck he'd bought. Why do you think some Amish young people want to have modern things or take part in some activities that English young people might do?

11. How do you think Amish parents should deal with their young people who try out worldly things? Should they look the other way, hoping their children will become dissatisfied with what the world has to offer? Or should Amish parents forbid their children to experience what English young people do?

12. When Ezekiel was attacked by a group of bullies outside a restaurant, he chose not to fight back. He had been taught from an early age that Matthew 5:39 says if someone hits us on the right cheek, we are supposed to turn our left cheek to him as well. How do you interpret this verse? How would most people react if they were picked on by bullies, the way Ezekiel was?

13. Would the unkind greeting Ezekiel got in Harrisburg outside the restaurant where Michelle worked give you the impression that's how the English world really is? Does it make sense that, following the incident, Ezekiel became a bit more hesitant in his decision to become English?

14. Did you learn anything new while reading this story in regards to the Lancaster County Amish? In what way is their life different from any other Amish community in America?

15. Were there any verses of scripture, prayers, or sayings that Michelle found on the slips of paper inside the old jars that spoke to you or touched your heart in some way? What was your favorite quote?

# The *Forgiving* Jar

# Dedication

To my special Amish friends who live by the scriptures
and know the meaning of forgiveness.


*And be ye kind one to another, tenderhearted, forgiving one another,
even as God for Christ's sake hath forgiven you.*
EPHESIANS 4:32

# Prologue

### Strasburg, Pennsylvania

It was a beautiful clear night, but even as the stars twinkled above, they shone in stark contrast to the mood inside Ezekiel King's truck. As they approached the home of Willis and Mary Ruth Lapp, Michelle Taylor's apprehension grew. She clutched her purse straps so tight the lack of circulation tingled her fingers. Michelle was no stranger to being cast away, but right now she felt more nervous and fearful of rejection than at any other time in her life.

Ezekiel must have sensed Michelle's anxiety, for he let go of the steering wheel with one hand and reached over to touch her arm. "It's gonna be all right. You have nothin' to worry about."

"That's easy for you to say. You're not the one who has to face the Lapps." She released her purse straps and pushed a lock of shoulder-length hair away from her face. "I'd rather have a tooth pulled without anything to deaden the pain than speak to the Lapps in person. I don't know if I can forgive myself, let alone expect them to."

"Don't say that." Ezekiel's tone was reassuring. "I've known the Lapps a long time. You'll soon find out that your worries are for nothing."

As they passed more familiar places, Michelle's fretfulness intensified, even though Ezekiel tried to help her cope. "I really blew it when I didn't come clean with them before. What if they don't want to see me? They might slam the door in my face."

Taking hold of the wheel with both hands again, Ezekiel shook his head. "The Lapps aren't like that. They'll let you in and listen to whatever you have to say."

"I don't expect them to invite me to live with them again. I just want the chance to tell Mary Ruth and Willis how sorry I am for impersonating their granddaughter." Michelle blew out a puff of air. "I've never been more ashamed of myself than doing that to people who have made me feel loved like no one else ever did."

"I'm sure they will forgive you."

"I hope you're right, because if they won't speak to me, I can't return to Harrisburg. I quit my job, remember? Maybe I'll have to catch a bus and head for Ohio after all. If I beg my foster parents in Columbus, they might take me in." Michelle bit the inside of her cheek and winced. "I deserve whatever I get."

Ezekiel turned up the Lapps' driveway. "I don't think it'll come to that, but even if things don't go well, I am not letting you leave." He turned off the engine and reached for her hand. "We'll figure out something—together."

Michelle nodded. She didn't know what she would do without Ezekiel. If he hadn't come to Harrisburg to get her, she wouldn't be here right now. She'd have probably spent the rest of her life moving from town to town, trying to hide from the past. Well, however things ended up, it was time for her to face the music.

# Chapter 1

*One month later*

Glancing in her rearview mirror as she slowed for a stop sign, Sara Murray smiled when she noticed a horse and buggy coming up behind her car. She rolled down her window to listen to the steady rhythm of the hooves engaging the pavement. Sara breathed in the crisp, fresh air. It was good to be back in Amish country, and even better to be heading to her grandparents' house to celebrate Thanksgiving a few days from now.

She still couldn't get over the fact that her mother had been raised in an Amish home, or that she hadn't known anything about it until she'd arrived in Lancaster County earlier this fall. A letter Sara found after Mama's death had revealed her grandparents' names and stated that they lived in Strasburg. Sara had wanted to meet them right away, but due to her part-time job at a dentist's office, plus taking some business classes, she was unable to go to Strasburg until fall.

Another shock had awaited Sara: a young woman had been living with the Lapps for several months, pretending to be her. It was hard not to be bitter about that, but Michelle Taylor had left the first day Sara arrived, so it was behind her now. Sara had spent several weeks getting to know Willis and Mary Ruth Lapp and was glad for this opportunity to spend more time with them.

Last week, the dentist Sara worked for had decided to retire, so she was currently out of a job. She hoped to move out of the duplex she rented from her stepfather in Newark, New Jersey, and move to Strasburg permanently. Perhaps, if her grandparents were willing, she could live with them—at least until she found another job and could rent a place of her own.

When Sara came upon another horse and buggy, in front of her this time, she waved at the cute little girl peeking out the back of the buggy, then pulled into the oncoming lane to pass. There was something about being in these surroundings that filled her with a sense of tranquility. It almost felt as if she belonged in Strasburg.

*I probably would be living here now if Mama had remained Amish and not run off when she was a teenager.* It grieved Sara to know her mother had given birth to her out of wedlock, and never explained who her biological father was. *If he knew Mama was expecting a baby, why didn't he marry her? Was my father Amish, or could Mama have gotten involved with an English man?* These questions had plagued Sara ever since she'd learned of her heritage. As much as she hated to acknowledge it, the truth was, she might never learn all the facts. In any case, it wouldn't stop her from asking questions in the hope of uncovering the truth. Deep in her heart, Sara believed she had the right to know.

When Sara pulled onto the Lapps' driveway, she felt a sense of lightness in her chest. After staying with her grandparents and enjoying their warm hospitality previously, this seemed like coming home. Of course, things had been a bit strained between them at first—especially before they'd accepted the fact that Sara was truly their granddaughter and the other woman, Michelle, had only pretended to be her.

"What a dirty trick to play on someone as kind and trustworthy as my grandpa and grandma," Sara muttered. "I don't understand how that young woman could live with herself for taking advantage of two sweet people. I hope she's miserable and is paying for her misdeed." She tapped the steering wheel with her knuckles. "I'm glad I won't have to deal with Michelle. Who knows what I might say?"

It wasn't like Sara to be vindictive or wish something bad would happen to someone, but reflecting on what her grandparents had gone through filled her with irrational thoughts.

*Just relax and enjoy spending the holiday with Grandpa and Grandma,* she told herself. *I will not allow anything or anyone to spoil our first Thanksgiving together.*

Sara pulled her car up near the barn, turned off the engine, and got out. After removing her suitcase from the trunk, she headed for the house.

Sara knocked on the front door and waited. When no one answered, she knocked again, a little harder this time. She'd called and left a message last night, letting them know she would arrive this afternoon. Sara expected they'd be waiting for her arrival, since Grandma had said during their phone conversation a week ago last week that she and Grandpa were looking forward to Sara's visit.

She knocked a third time. When there was still no answer, Sara stepped off the porch and walked around back. Maybe they were doing something outside, despite the chilly day. Seeing no sign of anyone in the backyard, she rapped on the back door. When that failed too, Sara glanced toward the barn. *I wonder if they could be in there.*

Sara entered the barn and was greeted by two collies—one slightly larger than the other. "Hey, Sadie. Hey, Rascal. How are you doing? Are you glad to see me?"

The dogs responded with barking and wagging tails.

Sara giggled and went down on her knees to pet them. She glanced over at the pen where the pigs were kept. Some slept next to the snoring sow, while others rooted through the straw. "My how those piglets have grown." Sara turned and gave the two excited collies her full attention. "Where are your owners?" She stroked one dog's ears, while gently patting the other dog's head. The question was silly, since the dogs couldn't talk, but the words came out before Sara thought about what she was saying.

Rascal nuzzled her hand with his nose. Then his pink tongue came out and slurped Sara's arm. "You two are quite the welcoming committee. Just wish I knew where my grandparents are."

"They went to the grocery store to get some things for our Thanksgiving meal."

Sara jumped at the sound of a woman's voice, and a sudden coldness flooded her soul when she saw who had spoken. "Wh–what are you doing here?" she asked as Michelle stepped out of the shadows. "I—I thought you were gone. Have you been hiding here in my grandparents' barn?"

Michelle shook her head. "Course not. I've been living with them for the past month."

Sara's mouth gaped open. "What?"

"I came back to apologize for making them believe I was you. And they graciously forgave me. Even invited me to stay until I found a job."

"Is that so? Well then why were you hiding in the shadows where I couldn't see you?"

"I didn't know anyone was here till I heard you talking to the dogs. At first I didn't realize who you were." Michelle's voice lowered. "These days you can't be too careful."

"Don't I know it?" Sara wanted to say more to this person who could not be trusted, but she held her tongue. Her body temperature had gone from chilly to hot. *What were Grandpa and Grandma thinking, inviting this imposter to stay with them? And why didn't they tell me Michelle was living here?* Sara felt betrayed. She was tempted to return to Newark. But she would stay put until they got home, for she needed some answers. In the meantime, she wouldn't say another word to the deceitful young woman in the barn. Sara would wait in the car until her grandparents returned.

Sara's hands shook as she sat in her vehicle, fuming. *How could Grandpa and Grandma have let that devious young woman back into their lives?*

Glancing at the barn, where Michelle had remained, Sara shifted on her seat. *How am I supposed to spend Thanksgiving with them now?* She couldn't imagine staying in the same house with Michelle for even one day. This put a damper on her asking Grandpa and Grandma if she could live with them until she found a job. *Maybe if I explain how I feel about Michelle, they'll ask her to leave. After all, she's not part of the family.*

The more Sara stewed about this, the angrier she became. If she had a job to return to and her stepfather, Dean, hadn't found a renter for the duplex, she'd turn around right now and head back to Newark. *Maybe I should go anyway. The duplex won't be rented out until next week, so I'd have a place to say until then. But if I leave, the little conniver will have the upper hand.*

Sara didn't have long to contemplate things, because the *clip-clop* of a horse's hooves drew her attention to Grandpa and Grandma's arrival. When their horse and buggy pulled up to the hitching rail, she got out of the car.

Her grandparents stepped down from the buggy, and while Grandma headed toward Sara's car, Grandpa waved at Sara before securing the horse. Forcing a smile, Sara gave her grandmother a hug.

"It's so good to see you again," Grandma said with feeling. "We've been looking forward to your visit and hope you can stay with us a bit longer this time."

Sara bit her lip, pondering how best to say what was on her mind.

"Is everything all right, Sara? You look upset."

Sara pointed to the barn. "When I first got here, I went in there, looking for you and Grandpa. I found Michelle Taylor instead."

Grandma nodded. "Why, yes. She's been with us for almost a month now. Didn't I tell you in one of our phone calls?"

"No. I would have remembered if you had." *And I would not be here right now.* Sara shifted from one foot to the other. "Michelle was the last person I expected to see this afternoon."

"She came back with Ezekiel, to apologize in person for what she had done," Grandma explained. "So your grandpa and I decided Michelle could stay here until she's able to find a job."

"You could forgive her, just like that?" Sara snapped her fingers.

Grandma nodded. "The Bible teaches us to forgive."

Before Sara could comment, Grandpa joined them and gave her a hug. "It's mighty nice to see you again, Granddaughter. How have you been?"

"Other than losing my job last week, I was okay until I got here and found Michelle in the barn. I had planned to ask if I could stay with you until I find a job and am able to get my own place. But since she's here, that won't work out. I should just go back to Newark." Sara figured she may as well be honest.

Grandma slipped her arm around Sara's waist. "Now don't be silly. We'd love to have you stay with us. Since we have more than one guest room, it won't be a problem to have both you and Michelle living in our home. We've been looking forward to having you, and would be very disappointed if you left."

Sara made a feeble attempt at smiling. "Oh, okay." While she didn't want to be in the same house with the imposter, at least she would be here to keep an eye on things and make sure Michelle didn't do anything else to hurt Grandpa and Grandma Lapp.

# Chapter 2

Michelle fluffed up her pillow and rolled onto her side, trying to find a comfortable position. Lying there, she put a finger to her mouth and bit the end of a rough cuticle. *After I help out with the morning chores with Willis, I'll make some time to cut and file my nails.*

Tucking her hand back under the covers, she smiled. *I've grown to enjoy helping out here at the Lapps' place, even if the work is hard on my hands.*

When she first went to bed, Michelle had looked through a magazine she'd gotten a few days ago, reading some of the articles and smelling the sample perfumes it had inside. She still couldn't shut off the thoughts that crept in and ended up setting the publication on the floor.

She released a long sigh, one of many given since she'd been in the privacy of her room. *I'm the last person Sara wanted to see, but I can't let her negative attitude get to me.*

Normally, Michelle would have no trouble getting to sleep, but tonight was different. All thoughts were on the young woman in the room across the hall—the person she'd pretended to be.

*Sara would barely even look at me during supper this evening. Guess I can't blame her. Seeing me here is a constant reminder of how I led her grandparents on. I'd probably feel the same way if the situation was reversed.*

Michelle turned onto her back. *But if the Lapps can forgive me, why can't Sara? Maybe she's not the forgiving kind. Sara might not even be a Christian.*

Michelle's lips pressed together as she heaved another weighted sigh. *Of course, until I had read some scriptures and felt God's love for the first time, I wasn't a believer either. But if Sara knew the kind of life I've had, maybe she would be more understanding and realize that during the time of my deception, I needed the Lapps really bad.*

A little voice in the back of Michelle's head reminded her that Sara had lost out too, not knowing for so many years that she had grandparents as wonderful as Willis and Mary Ruth.

One thing was sure, Michelle wanted Sara to know how sorry she felt for all the wrong she had done.

*I don't feel right about being in her mother's room either.* Michelle punched her pillow as she made a decision. *Tomorrow I'll suggest that we switch rooms. But if things don't improve between us soon, I'll have no choice but to move out, with or without a job. Maybe Ezekiel knows someone who would take me in. It won't be his folks though; of that much I am certain.*

⁓

Sara sat on the end of the bed in the guest room across the hall from Michelle. As she brushed her long hair, she heard the "pretender" across the way, snoring. *Oh great.* Sara frowned. *Tack on one more thing to keep me awake tonight.*

It wasn't right that the imposter had been given the bedroom that used to belong to Sara's mother. She should be sleeping there, not Michelle. Didn't Grandma and Grandpa care anything about her feelings? Surely they had to realize how uncomfortable it was for her to be staying in their house with a person who had no right to be here.

Sara got up and went over to the window. It was chilly outside, but she needed fresh air, so she opened it a crack. She drew several deep breaths to clear her head. Outside, Sara heard dried leaves rustling in the breeze as they blew across the yard below. *I wonder if I'll be able to sleep tonight, with the queen of sawing logs close by.* She grimaced. *I'd like to go over there right now, knock on her door, and holler at her to stop.*

Standing rigidly, she continued to look out at the night sky. *Hopefully this awful noise won't occur every night.*

It wasn't good to let stress control her like this, but Sara couldn't move past it. *Do Grandma and Grandpa care more about Michelle than they do their own flesh-and-blood granddaughter? Is that why they gave her Mama's room?* It was foolish to have such thoughts, but it was hard to think differently.

Rubbing her hands up and down her arms to ward off the shivers, she turned away from the window. Grandma had said during supper this evening that she hoped Sara and Michelle could get to know each other and become friends.

*Fat chance! I'm not interested in getting to know the great pretender. But I'll keep my feelings to myself so I don't upset Grandpa and Grandma. If I complain, it might give them a reason to choose Michelle over me.*

She flopped back onto the bed. *They can forgive her if they want to, but I'm not that forgiving.* Sara hadn't admitted it to her grandparents or anyone else, but she still struggled with mixed feelings about her own mother's deception. It didn't make sense that Mama had kept her Amish heritage a secret. While she may have been embarrassed about having a baby out of wedlock, it didn't excuse her for not telling Sara about her grandparents. Sara had been cheated out of knowing them all those years. What fun she could have had with Grandma and Grandpa, coming to visit and staying on the farm.

As a child, Sara had envied other kids whose grandparents doted on them. Her stepfather's parents had lived in Canada and traveled a lot before they died. Sara had only met them once, when Dean and Mama first got married. Unfortunately, on one of their trips, they'd been killed when their plane crashed. So she had grown up with no grandparents at all.

Sara couldn't understand why some people weren't honest. She'd never liked being lied to or kept in the dark. Sara had always tried to be honest. "If everyone were honest, the world would be a better place," she muttered.

As her thoughts wandered, something else came to mind. *What did I do with that letter from Brad Fuller?* In October, when Sara first visited her grandparents, a letter had come for her. Sara's muscles tensed. *It wasn't really meant for me, but for the person pretending to be me, whom he thought was Sara.*

From the things Brad said in his letter, he sounded nice. He'd mentioned being settled in at a seminary. As Sara recalled, he'd also included a Bible verse with the letter. So she assumed he was religious.

The scent of country air lingered in her room as Sara got up to close the window. *Brad mentioned his studies, and stated that he would pray for me. Was he going to school to be a preacher?* She sat back down on the bed and plopped backward, staring at the ceiling. *Oh yeah, now I remember. . . . I threw the letter out. It's a good thing too, or else I'd feel obligated to give it to Michelle. But I can't fret about this stuff all night. I need to try and get some sleep.* Sara pulled back the covers and climbed into bed, as she breathed in the scent of clean sheets. She would deal with everything in the morning.

❧

"You're tossing and turning quite a bit. Are you having trouble getting to sleep?" Willis asked Mary Ruth.

"*Jah.*" She sat up in bed, pushing the pillow up to support her back.

He sat up too, and reached for her hand. *"Was is letz do?"*

"I'll tell you what's wrong here." Mary Ruth used her other hand to massage her pounding forehead. "The two young women we care about are not getting along well. Couldn't you feel the tension between them before, during, and after our evening meal? Why, they barely said more than two words to each other."

"True. And I have to admit it was a little awkward just you and me doin' most of the talking while we ate supper."

"*Jah.* We'd toss questions out to the girls, but hardly got responses from either of them."

"You're right," Willis agreed. "But maybe things will go better in a few days or so. Sara and Michelle need a little more time to get to know each other. It's only the first day."

Mary Ruth shook her head. "I don't believe a few days of getting to know each other will solve the problem. Truthfully, I think Michelle feels uncomfortable around Sara because of how she pretended to be her. And if I'm not mistaken, Sara is upset with

Michelle and has not forgiven her for letting us believe all those months that she was our granddaughter."

"Bet you've hit the nail right on the head." Willis gave Mary Ruth's fingers a gentle squeeze. "I keep forgetting what a *schmaert* woman I married."

"I'm not that smart—just perceptive."

"So besides faithfully praying, what are we gonna do about the situation between Sara and Michelle?"

Mary Ruth tilted her head. "I think we should talk with them."

"Together or individually?" He shifted under the covers.

"It might be best to speak to each of them alone. Maybe you could talk to Michelle, and I'll speak with Sara. What do you think, Willis?"

"It's worth a try. Michelle likes to help me with the animals. So tomorrow morning while we're feeding the horses, I'll bring up the subject of Sara."

"Okay. While you're doing that, I'll ask Sara to help me with something in the kitchen. Then, while we are working, I'll speak with her about Michelle."

"Sounds like a plan." Willis released Mary Ruth's hand. "Ready to go to sleep now?"

"I—I hope so."

"Lie down, close your eyes, and give the situation to God." Willis's gentle tone was soothing.

"I'll try." It wasn't always easy to give up control and turn things over to God, but Willis was right—that's what she needed to do.

Mary Ruth flattened her pillow. She appreciated the discussion they'd had and felt thankful for her dear, caring husband. She couldn't imagine trying to deal with this situation on her own.

Yawning, she closed her eyes and prayed, asking the heavenly Father to give her the right words when she spoke to Sara. *And please soften her heart toward Michelle so she's willing to listen,* she added before falling asleep.

# Chapter 3

The hickory-smoked aroma of frying bacon drew Sara into the kitchen. Grandma turned from where she stood at the stove and offered a wide smile. "Good morning, Sara. Did you sleep well?"

Sara slowly nodded. She wasn't about to admit that she'd barely slept. Grandma would likely ask why, and then Sara would either have to make something up or admit that her stress over Michelle's presence was the reason she'd tossed and turned most of the night. That had been coupled with the nerve-racking snoring filtering across the hall.

"What can I do to help with breakfast?" Sara asked, hoping her grandmother hadn't noticed her unhappy mood.

Grandma gestured to the refrigerator. "You can get out some eggs and scramble them up while I finish frying the bacon."

"Okay." Sara got out the items and closed the refrigerator door. How nice it was to have some quality time with Grandma this morning. "Is Grandpa outside doing chores?" She grabbed a bowl from the cupboard and started cracking the eggs into it.

"Yes." Grandma placed the cooked bacon aside on a paper towel. "He took a mug of freshly brewed coffee with him before heading out the door."

Sara shook some salt and pepper into the bowl. "There seems to be plenty of things to do around a farm like this." She picked up the wire whisk and mixed in the seasonings. *Why didn't my mother appreciate the simple life? I'd like some answers, but I need to be patient.*

Sara had finished mixing the eggs with a small amount of milk, when Michelle entered the room.

"Good morning. Did you get a good night's sleep?" Grandma gave Michelle the same friendly smile she'd shared with Sara.

"Sure did." Michelle glanced at Sara. "Good morning."

"Morning," Sara mumbled, barely looking at Michelle. *Sure wish I could come right out and say what's on my mind.*

Michelle moved over to stand beside Grandma and kissed her cheek. "What do you need me to do this morning?"

Sara's jaw clenched. *Michelle acts like she's the granddaughter, not me. Is she still pretending, or it is just wishful thinking?*

"Since Sara is mixing the eggs, why don't you set the table?" Grandma suggested.

"I can do that. Should I get out some milk or juice too?"

Grandma nodded. "We have orange and apple juice in the refrigerator, so you can set out both, if you like. That way, we'll have beverage choices."

"Okay."

While Michelle set the table and took out the juices, Sara put the egg mixture in a frying pan with a little vegetable oil and placed it on the propane stove. She was reminded once again that she'd been looking forward to spending time with Grandpa and Grandma, and now she had to share them with Michelle. To make matters worse, Michelle had given Grandma a kiss on the cheek. *I should have done that instead of dwelling on my negative feelings.*

"I'm going to start looking for a job today." Sara glanced over at Grandma.

"Can't it wait till after Thanksgiving?" Grandma placed the bacon on a plate and covered it with foil. "I was hoping you'd be free to help me do some baking after breakfast, and it would be nice to sit and visit with you this afternoon."

"I suppose I could wait until Monday." Sara stirred the solidifying eggs in the skillet.

Grandma smiled. "That'll be fine."

"What about me?" Michelle asked. "Won't you need my help with the baking, Grandma?"

Sara nearly had to bite her tongue to keep from saying anything. *Who does Michelle think she is, anyway? She shouldn't be calling my grandmother* Grandma. *Michelle had some practice when she'd lived here before, pretending to be me, but that doesn't make it right.*

"If you want to help, that's certainly fine, but I assumed you would help Willis take care of the animals after breakfast," Grandma replied.

Sara pressed her lips together to keep from blurting out her thoughts. She had a feeling Michelle only wanted to help bake so she could horn in on her time with Grandma.

The more Sara thought about it, the more upset she became. *Why does my life have to be so complicated?*

By the time Grandpa came in for breakfast, Sara had no appetite for food. Even the scrambled eggs didn't appeal to her. She forced herself to sit at the table for the prayer so she wouldn't appear impolite.

"I checked phone messages before coming into the house." Grandpa looked over at Michelle, who sat to the left of him. "There was a message for you from Ezekiel."

Michelle's blue-green eyes lit up. "What did he have to say? He's still joining us for Thanksgiving, I hope."

"Ezekiel's still coming, but he wanted you to know that he may only be here for dessert."

Michelle's brows furrowed. "How come? He said he would eat dinner with us."

Sara drank her glass of juice as she listened to Grandpa's explanation. She too was curious about why Ezekiel wouldn't be joining them until after dinner tomorrow.

"Ezekiel said in his message that his family wanted him to join them for their Thanksgiving meal." Grandpa took two slices of bacon and passed the platter to Michelle. "Guess now that he's gettin' along better with his folks, he wants to keep the peace."

From her seat next to Michelle, Grandma reached over and patted the imposter's arm. "At least he'll be joining us for pie and coffee."

Michelle nodded slowly.

Sara toyed with her fork. It was too bad Ezekiel wasn't coming for dinner, because it would keep Michelle busy with him instead of gushing over Grandma and Grandpa and hanging on their every word. This would've given Sara an opportunity to spend more time with her grandparents.

Sara had to wonder, though, how things could work out between Michelle and Ezekiel, since he was Amish and Michelle was not. Of course, if it did work out, she'd be married and out the door. *Goodbye to her, and all the troubles she's caused,* Sara mused. *But the odds are he'll see through her phony bologna and drop Michelle like a bare hand holding a hot skillet.*

Sara forced herself to eat the last bite of egg on her plate. *It's none of my business how Ezekiel and Michelle work things out. I have enough of my own problems to muddle through. And it's good I'm not involved in a relationship with a man right now. It would complicate my life even more.*

⤙⤚

"You're kinda quiet this morning," Willis said as Michelle helped him groom his horse Bashful. "Are you still upset because Ezekiel won't be eating dinner with us tomorrow?"

She shook her head. "As long as he can come for part of the day, I'm okay with it."

Willis set the curry comb aside and gestured to a bale of straw outside his horse's stall. "Let's have a seat over there. I'd like to talk to you about something."

"Okay." Michelle set the brush down that she'd been using on Bashful's mane, opened the stall gate, and took a seat on one end of the straw bale. She sat quietly until Willis joined her. "What did you want to talk to me about?"

"Sara."

"What about her?"

He pulled a piece of straw from the bale and stuck it between his teeth. "Mary Ruth and I have noticed the tension between you and Sara."

"Yeah, it's there, but I think it's mostly because she resents me being here." Michelle bent down to pet Rascal when he bounded up to her, wagging his tail. "I was planning to talk to her after breakfast, but she went into the bathroom before I had the chance. And since I wanted to help you with the animals, I came out here."

"It would be a good idea for the two of you to talk things out." Willis stroked the top of Sadie's head, for it appeared she wanted some attention too.

"I'm gonna ask if she'd like to trade bedrooms with me. I figured Sara might like to have the room her mother slept in when she was a girl."

Willis nodded. "She slept there during her brief visit with us, when you were living in Harrisburg."

"I should have guessed as much and insisted on taking the other guest room when Ezekiel brought me back here."

"I think Mary Ruth suggested you sleep in there because it's the room you had during your first stay with us."

"Right. Before you knew I wasn't your granddaughter." Michelle stopped fussing with Rascal and placed her hand on Willis's am. "I still feel terrible about all the lies I told you and Mary Ruth whenever you asked questions about my past. It's hard to understand how you could both be so forgiving."

"Forgiveness doesn't come easy when a person has been wronged, but according to scripture, it's the right thing to do."

"Maybe you should tell Sara that. I'm sure she hasn't forgiven me for impersonating her."

"Give her some time and try to be patient and kind. I believe in due time, she'll come around."

"What kind of pies will we be making this morning?" Sara asked after she'd finished her cup of tea.

"Pumpkin is your grandpa's favorite, so we'll need to make a few of those. Since your mother's brother and his family will be joining us, I'll make sure there are a few apple pies too because apple is Lenore's favorite. If some of the pies aren't eaten, then they can take one or two home with them." From across the table, Grandma smiled at Sara. "What kind of pie do you like best?"

Sara shrugged. "I like most pies—except for mincemeat. I've never acquired a taste for it."

"I understand, and don't worry, there won't be any mincemeat pies for our Thanksgiving dessert." Grandma rose from the table and placed her empty cup into the sink. Then she sat down again. "Before we get started, there's something I want to talk to you about."

Sara squirmed in her chair. *I bet it's about the pretender.* "What is it, Grandma?"

"I can't help noticing how cool you've been toward Michelle. Are you upset because she's staying here with us?"

Sara slid her finger around the edge of her cup as she weighed her options. *I can either pretend I have no problem with Michelle or blurt out the truth.* She went with the second choice.

"To be honest, Michelle being here does upset me. What she did to you and Grandpa was deplorable, and now she's living here—even sleeping in my mother's old room—like she's one of the family."

"I'm sure she'd be willing to switch rooms with you." Grandma lifted her glasses and rubbed a spot on the bridge of her nose. "When she returned from Harrisburg, I wasn't thinking when I offered her that room. She'd occupied it before, when we thought she was you, so—"

The back door opened, and Michelle stepped into the room, interrupting Grandma's sentence. Michelle glanced at the stove, then looked at them. "I thought you two were baking."

Grandma shook her head. "Not yet. We decided to drink some tea and talk awhile." She gestured for Michelle to take a seat at the table. "Would you like me to fix you a cup?"

"No thanks. I just came in to speak with Sara about something. Then I'm going back outside to help Grandpa—I mean, Willis, feed the hogs."

"Okay. I'll leave you two alone while I go down to the basement to get some apples." Grandma left the table, picked up a large plastic bowl, and hurried from the room.

When Michelle took a seat across from her, Sara tipped her head to one side. *I feel a bit railroaded into this talk. I wanted to spend some downtime with Grandma, not engage with the imposter this morning.* She offered Michelle full eye contact. "What did you want to talk to me about?"

"Well, for starters, I'd like to switch rooms with you. The bedroom I've been sleeping in was your mother's, and I think you should have it."

Sara slowly nodded. "Thank you. I feel the same too."

Michelle leaned forward, her elbows on the table. "I'm not asking you to be my best friend or anything, but as long as we are both living here, I hope we can be civil to each other and try to get along."

"Okay." Sara's words came out in a near whisper. Earlier, she had been ready to let Michelle have it, but now that she had the opportunity to unleash her feelings, the words wouldn't come. It wouldn't be easy to act cordially toward the imposter, but for Grandma and Grandpa's sake, she would try.

# Chapter 4

*Clarks Summit, Pennsylvania*

On a day meant for families, Brad looked at the piece of turkey on his plate and wrinkled his nose. Neither it nor the mashed potatoes and gravy held any appeal. Looking around, it seemed a few others had also ended up at this restaurant. A man trying to calm a fussy little boy looked as miserable as Brad felt. Eating by himself at a local all-you-can-eat buffet was not the way he'd hoped to spend Thanksgiving. He had planned to spend this holiday in Harrisburg with his folks, but Mom had come down with the flu last night, so Dad called and asked Brad not to come. Not only was Mom not well enough to cook, but she also didn't want to expose Brad to what she had. Brad would keep his mother in his prayers and later today check in on her and Dad to see how they were doing.

Since most of the other seminary students Brad knew had gone home to be with their families, he was left alone to eat by himself. He'd thought about driving down to Strasburg to spend the day with the Lapps but changed his mind. It wouldn't be fair to drop in on them without an invitation, and even if he'd called yesterday and left a message, he wouldn't have felt right about inviting himself to share their Thanksgiving meal. Maybe during his Christmas break he would go down to see his old friends. He was especially eager to see how Sara was doing and find out if she'd received his letter. Brad had hoped she might write back to him, but maybe it was for the best that she hadn't. A long-distance relationship wasn't a good idea—especially with a young woman who was not a believer. It had been a difficult decision for Brad, because he enjoyed Sara's company, but his faith in God and calling to be a minister came before anything else.

He forked a piece of meat into his mouth. While it was nowhere near as tasty as the turkey his mom always made, at least he wouldn't go hungry. The families dining together around him appeared to be happy. Even the fussy little boy had calmed down and was eating the mashed potatoes on his plate.

Brad lifted his glass and sipped some ice water. When classes started up again next week, his mind would be on his studies.

*Strasburg*

"You outdid yourself with this meal today, *Mamm*," Grinning at his mother, Sara's uncle Ivan made a sweeping gesture of the array of food on the table. "I bet you got up at the crack of dawn to fix all this for us. And look at the size of that turkey. It must be at least a twenty-four pounder."

Grandma gestured to Sara and Michelle sitting beside each other at the table. "I can't take credit for all the work. These two did their share and then some."

Michelle's cheeks turned pink, and Sara's face warmed too. "I was more than happy to help," she said.

Michelle bobbed her head. "Same here."

"Mary Ruth, you should have let us furnish some of the food," Ivan's wife, Yvonne, spoke up. "After all, with us being here, there are five extra people at your table. And you know how our boys like to eat." Yvonne glanced over at her two grown boys, who were eyeing the big bowl of mashed potatoes.

Sara looked at Grandma to see her response. She wasn't surprised when Grandma smiled and said, "Not a problem. I enjoy the opportunity to cook a nice meal for my *familye*."

Sara had heard her grandmother say that word before, and knew it meant "family." The Pennsylvania Dutch language intrigued Sara, and she hoped she would eventually learn to speak it too—or least understand more of the words so she would know what was being said when Grandma and Grandpa spoke it to one another or other family members. Even Michelle had one up on her, sometimes using Pennsylvania Dutch words Sara's grandparents had taught her.

"The food looks good, Grandma." Ivan's twenty-year-old son Benjamin spoke up. "I was invited to eat at my girlfriend's home today, but I'm glad I came here to be with our family. I'll see Marilyn tomorrow instead."

As everyone bowed their heads to say a silent prayer before partaking of the meal, Sara's thoughts went to her mother and how she'd taught Sara to pray silently when she was a girl. Back then, Sara hadn't realized praying this way was a tradition Mama had grown up with. She'd always thought it was her mother's way of praying without offending Sara's stepfather, who was not a religious man.

*But now that I look back,* Sara thought, instead of praying, *if Mama thought Dean would disapprove of her praying out loud, then why did she send my brother and me to Sunday school? Wasn't she worried that Dean would be upset about that too?* Some things about Mama still made no sense to Sara, although she still missed her mother and wished she could have her back.

Sara heard Grandpa's napkin rustle, so she opened her eyes and looked up. Everyone else did the same. She had to admit all the food on the table looked mighty tempting, not to mention the delicious aromas enveloping her senses.

Grandpa rose from his seat and cleared his throat. "This year something different will occur. I'd like to pass the tradition of carving the Thanksgiving bird on to Ivan."

"I'd be honored, *Daed.*" Ivan stood and waited for his father to pass him the plump turkey.

All eyes were on Grandpa as he picked up the platter and held it out to his son. Sara licked her lips, but nearly jumped out of her seat when Grandpa lost his grip. The platter tilted, and the turkey slid onto the floor. Following a huge *splat,* the stuffing shot out of the bird's cavity like a bullet, and smeared all over the floor.

It looked like Ivan had made a valiant effort to save the catastrophe from happening, but in so doing, he banged his knee against one of the table legs, knocking over the two burning candles adorning the Thanksgiving feast.

"Fire!" Ivan's oldest son, Peter, yelled as everyone jumped back from the table.

Sara gasped, watching as the beautiful white tablecloth caught fire.

All the guests scurried, trying to help. Grandma scooped up one of the fallen candles, and Michelle retrieved the other one. Yvonne grabbed the pitcher of water that was on a side table and threw it on the smoking cloth. Ivan picked up the turkey, put it back on the platter, and took it out to the kitchen, while Lenore went to get a grocery bag to spoon up the steaming filling all over the floor.

Sara couldn't do anything but stand with her mouth gaping open. *This reminds me of a movie I once saw.* She had to bite her lip to keep from giggling.

"I'm sorry, Mary Ruth." Grandpa's regret could be heard in his voice. "You worked so hard to make dinner perfect." He grabbed several napkins and dabbed up the water on the table where the tablecloth now smoldered.

"It was an accident." Grandma chuckled as if she was used to this sort of thing happening. "What would a family gathering be without a bit of chaos? And just think about the memory we can all talk about in years to come."

"What can I do to help?" Sara asked.

"How about pulling the skin off the turkey?" Grandma suggested. "There's nothing wrong with the meat under the skin, since it landed upright on the floor."

Grandpa snorted. "Guess if the turkey was gonna take off like that, it couldn't have landed any better."

By now everyone was laughing and making jokes about the flying turkey that tried to get away from the table. What was even funnier was watching Benjamin and Peter scooping mashed potatoes onto their plates, and eating as if nothing was amiss.

Sara couldn't recall having this much fun on any Thanksgiving she and her family had ever celebrated. All this laughter had taken her mind temporarily off Michelle crowding her space.

"I think we have everything under control now." Grandma hiccupped from laughing so hard. "We'll give the stuffing from the floor to the pigs. That way they'll have a Thanksgiving treat too. Peter and Benjamin, would you two mind taking it out after we eat?"

"Sure, Grandma," they said in unison.

"It's a good thing we made an extra pan of filling," Michelle said.

"That's what I usually go for first," Yvonne chimed in.

Even though there was a hole in the tablecloth, everything else was back in order. "We'll have to get a new covering for our table to use for future Thanksgivings." Grandpa pointed at the blackened material.

"Or maybe we should keep using this one." Grandma winked at him. "Think of the conversations we'll have each year when Ivan carves the turkey."

Again, Sara was amazed at how the family worked together to remedy the situation and could still laugh about it. The people at this table were not only good hearted and deeply rooted in their faith, they found humor in what most folks would be upset about.

The skinless turkey sat near Ivan, who stood over it, swiping two carving knives together. "Okay, let me get this turkey sliced so we can eat. I don't know about the rest of you, but I'm starving." He looked over at his sons. "I hope you two saved us some mashed potatoes."

"There's still plenty, Daed." Peter grinned mischievously.

As the food got passed, conversation around the table began. Sara's cousins, Benjamin and Peter, talked fishing with Uncle Ivan and Grandpa, while the women exchanged information about quilting and baking. It was a different experience, seeing how the Amish celebrated this holiday. Growing up in Sara's home, they may have had harvest-colored decorations in several of the rooms.

And Mama's scented candles burning in the kitchen always permeated the house with pumpkin pie or cinnamon-apple fragrance. But there was no joyful camaraderie, like these good people shared. Oh, there were some good times, Sara had to admit, but for the most part, holidays were quiet and dull by comparison.

Sara listened quietly as she enjoyed the succulent turkey and other tasty food. It was as if the turkey mishap had never happened. Being here with her newly found family felt right. It made her wish once again that she'd grown up knowing her grandparents, aunt, uncle, and cousins. If Sara's mother had remained Amish, then perhaps she too would be a part of the Amish community. She wondered where her mother would have sat at this same table as a young child, and later, as a young lady. Sara could only imagine how Mama would have spent her holidays here in this house. Playing indoors after the meal, enjoying her cousins with a board game, and maybe warming up by the fire singing songs together—were these the things Mama used to do?

Sara poured gravy over her mashed potatoes and held out the bowl to Grandpa. At first he didn't seem to notice, because he sat, looking intently at Grandma. Sara could see he still felt bad, but Grandma winked again, probably to let him know everything was okay.

Glancing across the table at her cousin Lenore, Sara blotted her lips with a napkin. *Could I fit in here if I were to become Amish? Would I be able to give up my modern ways?* She didn't know why she was thinking such thoughts. Turning Amish when she'd grown up English would be a challenge—one Sara didn't feel up to—at least not right now. Maybe someday, after she'd lived here awhile, she might ponder the idea. For now though, she would concentrate on getting to know her Amish relatives better and, of course, finding a job. Hopefully, some business in the area would be in need of a receptionist. If not, then she would consider some other type of work when she went job hunting next week.

Sara forked some creamy mashed potatoes into her mouth. She couldn't help smacking her lips—the potatoes were so smooth and free of lumps. *How in the world did Grandma do it without using an electric mixer? No wonder Ivan's sons made sure they got to the mashed potatoes first.* Yvonne was right—her boys sure liked to eat. Both were already on second helpings.

Sara looked forward to dessert and tasting at least one of the mouth-watering pies she had helped Grandma bake. She hoped she wouldn't put on extra weight while living here, because of her grandma's hearty cooking. While living under her grandparents' roof, Sara looked forward to learning how to fix some Pennsylvania Dutch meals. Her forehead wrinkled. *Too bad Michelle lives here too.*

Sara had to admit she felt a little better toward the pretender since she had switched rooms with her. It felt right to be back in her mother's old bedroom. It made Sara feel closer to Mama to sleep in the same bed she'd had until she left home so unexpectedly.

A knock sounded on the front door, bringing a halt to Sara's contemplations. Grandma excused herself and went to see who it was. She returned to the dining room a few minutes later with Ezekiel at her side.

"Sorry I'm late," he apologized. "My mom insisted I stay there until I'd tasted a little bit of everything on the table." Removing his straw hat, Ezekiel looked at Michelle. "When you're finished eating, and if you're not gonna eat dessert right away, would you like to go for a buggy ride?"

Her gaze went to Grandma.

"You two go ahead. I won't get the pies out till everyone's meal has settled."

"Okay, great." Michelle ate the last piece of turkey on her plate, and then she pushed away from the table. "I'll get a jacket, and then we can go." She sent a smile in Ezekiel's direction.

Sara struggled not to say anything as Michelle hurried from the room. Didn't the young woman have the good manners to stick around long enough to help clear the table and do the dishes? Apparently her desire to spend time with her boyfriend took precedence over anything else.

Sara's face tightened when Michelle returned several minutes later, wearing a jacket. "I'm ready to go, Ezekiel."

Grinning, he nodded. As they headed for the door, Ezekiel stopped and turned around. "We'll be back in plenty of time for dessert."

"Well, if you're not, there won't be any *boi* left to eat, 'cause my *fraa*'s pies are always the best. In fact, everyone just wants to gobble them up."

Grandma smiled in response to her husband's compliment. "Don't worry about that." She poked Grandpa's arm. "There's plenty to go around. Even if someone wants seconds." Grandma glanced at her grandsons, both nodding their heads.

Ezekiel snickered, as he guided Michelle out the door.

Sara's teeth clenched as she fought the temptation to call Michelle out on not clearing her dish before leaving. But she kept her thoughts to herself and let the little pretender waltz happily away.

*I wonder what it'd be like to have a boyfriend who'd look at me the way Ezekiel looks at Michelle. I wonder what Ezekiel sees in Michelle. Apparently, he's forgiven her too, but I don't see how. The truth is she also lied to him when she pretended to be me.*

# Chapter 5

As a chilly breeze blew through Michelle's hair, she looked over at Ezekiel and smiled. The weather was typical for this time of year, but the crispness of the air was invigorating as it blew into the buggy where the flaps were open.

Michelle took a deep breath, enjoying the scents of the season. The fragrance of dried leaves still lingered from autumn, and the tang of wood smoke drifting out of chimneys from nearby homes permeated the air. The whiffs of smoke reminded her of campfires from cookouts her foster parents used to have in the backyard. Ezekiel's horse, Big Red, exuded a pleasant aroma too, and over it all drifted the sweetness of dried hay.

Riding in Ezekiel's buggy was more fun than riding in his truck. Hearing the steady *clip-clop* of his horse's hooves was a soothing sound. Michelle had missed seeing and hearing Amish horse and buggies during the brief time she'd lived in Harrisburg. And of course she'd missed Ezekiel. Every time she was with him, the moments seemed to go by so quickly. Michelle was thrilled to have some time to talk privately with Ezekiel. The Lapps' house was full of company this evening, so she and Ezekiel probably wouldn't even be missed.

Her thoughts transferred to Sara. The only downer wasn't the fire earlier at the table, or the turkey that flew off the platter, but the ongoing cold treatment from the Lapps' granddaughter. *Will she ever warm up to me? Is there something I could do or say to make things better between us?*

"How was your meal today?" Ezekiel asked, halting Michelle's thoughts. "From what I saw on the table, it looked like there was plenty of food to eat."

"There sure was." Michelle patted her stomach. "I ate more than my share too. But we almost didn't have any turkey."

"How come?"

She relayed the story of how the turkey had ended up on the floor. "I thought Mary Ruth would be upset, but she took it all in stride. Once the fire was out and the mess cleaned up, we all had a pretty good laugh."

"What fire?"

"Ivan tried to save the turkey, but in doing so, he hit his knee on a table leg," Michelle further explained. "That, in turn, toppled the candles over, and then the tablecloth caught fire. You almost had to be there to believe what you were seeing; it all happened so fast."

"I bet."

"Then we all jumped in to help. Well, Sara didn't at first. She looked stunned by it all. But eventually she did pitch in. And Benjamin and Peter. . . They both sat there, eating through it all." Michelle laughed. "It was kinda comical now that I think about it. Oh, and poor Ivan. You could tell he felt terrible. And so did Willis."

"I probably would have too if had happened to me." Ezekiel chuckled. "But then, things like that can happen to the best of us."

"Mary Ruth was so good about it. She even joked about keeping the tablecloth with the burned hole in it. Said it would give them something to talk about during future Thanksgivings."

"That's not somethin' they're likely to forget. It'll be some memory, all right." He leaned over and sniffed her hair. "Jah, I believe the whole story now, 'cause your hair smells like smoked turkey."

"Are you kidding?"

"Nope."

She squinted, and then laughed.

He joined in. "A good belly laugh feels good. Jah?"

"Definitely. And *danki*, because I needed that today."

"Glad I could help." He spoke softly, close to her ear, sending shivers up Michelle's spine.

"I'm glad you can take my teasing. Some folks, like my little brother, don't like it when I joke around. And if I pester Henry too much, he really gets upset." Ezekiel paused to flick the reins. "He's always been kinda sensitive."

"I can relate, on both counts, because sometimes I'm sensitive too. And when we were kids, still living with our abusive folks, my youngest brother, Jack, didn't appreciate it whenever I teased him. Ernie never seemed to mind it much though, 'cause he was a jokester himself." Swallowing against the lump that had formed unexpectedly in her throat, Michelle folded her hands tightly in her lap. She still thought about her two brothers, even though she hadn't seen them since they were all separated and put in foster care. She hoped the boys were happy and had made good lives for themselves. But oh, how she wished she could see them again.

Michelle closed her eyes. *But I have no desire to see my biological parents. They messed up royally and don't deserve to have any contact with their children.* Her nails pressed tightly into her palms. *Probably wouldn't be glad to see us, anyhow.* Despite Michelle's unhappy childhood, she still prayed for her parents. She hoped someday they would see the error of their ways and get help for their addiction to alcohol, as well as some anger management assistance.

They rode along quietly for a while, until Ezekiel broke the silence. "I've made a decision."

Her eyes snapped open. "What about?"

"I'm gonna sell my truck and join the church."

"For sure?"

"Jah. Thought I wanted to be English, and it might be all right for some. But I've come to realize it's not for me."

"Was it getting beat up outside the restaurant where I worked in Harrisburg that led you to that decision?"

"That may have been part of it, but the biggest reason is my family. It would be hard on my folks if one of their children went English." He paused, releasing a breath so loud it sounded more like a groan. "I don't want to hurt them like that."

"I understand, but if you join the Amish church, you won't be able to see me anymore. At least not socially or. . ." Her voice trailed off.

"That's the only reason I'm holding back from joining the church."

"What do you mean?"

"I don't want to lose my relationship with you." Ezekiel let go of the reins with his left hand and reached for Michelle's right hand, sending shivers up her arm.

"So what are we going to do?" she asked.

"Would you consider joining the Amish church?"

Stunned, Michelle could only stare ahead into the darkness, as her mind reeled with his sudden question.

"Hey, did you hear what I said?" He squeezed her fingers.

"Yes, I did. I'm just not sure how to respond."

"I don't expect you to give me your answer right away, but would you at least think about it?"

"Of course. In fact, the idea of becoming Amish has crossed my mind more than once since I first came to Lancaster County."

"Really? How come you haven't mentioned it?"

"I figured it wouldn't be possible, so there was no point in saying anything." Michelle shrugged. "Besides, am I good enough?"

"That's not what you should be asking yourself. If you want it bad enough, anything is possible, Michelle. The question is—do you want to join the Amish church?"

"I–I'm not sure. I need to give it more thought. And lots of prayer," she quickly added.

❧

"I wonder why Michelle and Ezekiel aren't back yet." Grandma looked at the grandfather clock in the living room.

"I don't know, but I'm more than ready for dessert. And if I don't move around a bit, there's a good chance I'll fall asleep in my chair." Grandpa got up from his recliner and stretched. Then he walked over in his stocking feet to the front window and gazed out toward the road. "I'm sure they'll be here soon—especially since you have those delicious pies waiting to be sliced."

Grandma stood too. "You're probably right. I suppose we could begin setting things out." She looked around the room. "Is anyone else ready for dessert?"

"I am," Benjamin and Peter said in unison.

Their mother made a clicking noise with her tongue. "You two are always hungry. You could leave the table from eating a big meal and be ready to eat again within an hour."

"Yeah—especially when we are offered some dessert," Peter said, while Benjamin nodded his head.

Sara left her seat on the couch. "Why don't you stay here and relax, Grandma? I'll go to the kitchen, set the desserts out, and get a pot of coffee going."

"And I'll help her." Lenore rose from her seat. "I'll get some water heating for those who want tea."

"Thank you." Grandma smiled. "You girls are so thoughtful."

"Think while you're doin' that, I'll take a walk out to the barn." Grandpa looked at Uncle Ivan, then over at his sons. "Anyone want to join me?"

"Jah, sure." Uncle Ivan, Benjamin, and Peter got up and followed Grandpa to the door.

"Wait a minute, boys," Yvonne called. "Don't forget to take this stuffing out to feed the hogs."

Benjamin turned around and took the bag of filling his mother held.

"Thanks, Mamm." He grinned. "Sure wouldn't want Grandpa's pigs to miss out."

Grandma sat down on the couch, and Aunt Yvonne took a seat beside her. Sara, accompanied by Lenore, went to the kitchen.

"The pies you and Grandma made sure look good." Lenore pointed to the array of desserts sitting on a small table in one corner of the room. "Oh, and I see there's even a loaf of bread. Is it pumpkin?"

Sara nodded. "I made that one myself. It's from a recipe my mother used to make during the fall and winter months."

"I can't wait to try it." Lenore took a stack of dessert plates from the cupboard. "How are things going? Does Michelle living here bother you?"

Leaning against the counter, Sara sighed. "Everything about Michelle irritates me. I may seem judgmental, but I don't condone her actions and can't understand how she could have lied to Grandma and Grandpa all those months, pretending to be me." She lifted her shoulders. "Maybe she had a reason, but no one has ever told me what it was. I hope one of these days I'll find out why. For Grandpa and Grandma's sake though, I've been trying not to say anything negative about Michelle, but it's not easy."

Lenore nodded. "I felt the same way when I learned she had let our grandparents believe she was you."

"How did you get past it?"

"After talking with my folks and praying about it, we all realized we needed to forgive Michelle." Lenore filled the coffee pot with water and set it on the stove.

"I might be able to forgive her for pretending to be me and deceiving our grandparents, but I'm having a hard time with her living here."

Lenore filled the teakettle with water and set it on the burner near the coffee pot. "It would be a challenge, but Michelle doesn't really have any other place to go right now."

Sara nodded. "Neither do I."

"Really? I thought you had a duplex in New Jersey."

"It belongs to my stepfather. I was only renting from him." Sara explained how she'd been hoping to move to Strasburg and live with her grandparents until she found a job and a place of her own.

Lenore smiled. "I'm sure Grandma and Grandpa are happy to have you here, and they'd probably be pleased if you stayed with them indefinitely."

"That may be true, but if Michelle continues to live here, I'm not sure I can stay and watch her trying to win them over. It seems as if she's competing with me for their love and attention."

Lenore moved over and slipped her arm around Sara. "Please try to give it a little more time. I'm sure things will work out."

"I hope so." Sara lifted her chin. "But if they don't, I'll definitely move out. I don't want to be the cause of any more discord in this house."

Sara and Lenore had just taken the desserts into the dining room when Michelle and Ezekiel showed up.

"Sorry for being gone so long," Michelle apologized. "Is there anything I can do to help?"

Sara made an effort to smile as she thanked Michelle for her willingness to help. "I think we have everything set out."

The men came inside a few minutes later, and everyone gathered around the table. As they enjoyed dessert and drank their hot beverages, Sara received several compliments on her pumpkin bread.

She smiled. All in all, with the exception of the turkey incident, it had been a nice Thanksgiving. But the next few days might be very different—especially with Michelle involved.

# Chapter 6

Michelle sat on the back porch, petting Rascal. It had been two days since her buggy ride with Ezekiel, and since then, she'd barely thought of much else. While he hadn't actually proposed marriage, Ezekiel had let Michelle know he wanted to pursue a relationship with her. But in order for him to do that, she'd have to become Amish.

"Could I do it?" she murmured, stroking her dog's ears. "Would it be possible for me to make all the necessary changes in order to become an Amish woman and fit into this community?"

Rascal's ears perked up, and tipping his head to one side, he looked at Michelle as if to say, "I bet you could do it."

She grinned. *If only I could read your mind. Or any other animal's, for that matter.* Her thoughts went to Willis's horse, and how she'd mistrusted him at first. Michelle had done much better when Ezekiel taught her to drive, using his docile horse and comfortable buggy.

*At least that's one thing I could do well if I decided to join the Amish church. And I wouldn't mind dressing plain or doing without electricity or modern things either.*

Michelle stopped petting Rascal and shifted her position on the porch step. While she had picked up a few of the Pennsylvania Dutch words, the hardest part for her would be learning to speak the Amish language fluently. She'd also have to learn German, in order to understand what was being preached during church and other Amish services, such as weddings and funerals. Although Michelle respected the way of the Plain people, and wanted

Ezekiel to court her, taking classes to prepare for church membership was a big decision—one she couldn't make on a whim. She needed to be certain it was the right thing for her before she committed to anything. More prayer was needed—of that much Michelle was certain.

A smile touched Michelle's lips as she remembered how she'd felt when Ezekiel had held her hand. His grip was firm and warm, even reassuring. She could hold onto his hand forever. Michelle didn't think it was possible, but the more time she spent with Ezekiel, the more she loved him.

"Would you mind taking these down to the basement for me, Sara?" Grandma pointed to the freshly washed canning jars on the kitchen counter. They'd used the applesauce the jars had contained this morning, when Sara helped Grandma make several loaves of applesauce bread that they would take to church tomorrow. One of Grandma's good friends was hosting church at her home, so Grandma wanted to take something to help out. The bread would be served with the noon meal.

"No problem. I'll put the jars in one of the empty cardboard boxes I saw on the back porch and take it to the basement. Is there any particular place you want me to put the jars down there?"

"There's a row of shelves on one side of the room for empty jars," Grandma replied. "On the opposite wall are the shelves for glass jars I've filled with the fruits and vegetables I canned this summer and early fall."

"Okay." Sara smiled. "I'll get the box and be back here soon to pick up the jars."

When Sara stepped out the back door, she spotted Michelle sitting on the porch step with Rascal in her lap. She appeared to be deep in thought and didn't seem to notice Sara had come out to the porch. Either that or she chose to ignore her. Without saying a word, Sara picked up the cardboard container.

Back inside, Sara loaded the canning jars into the box.

Turning on the battery-operated light at the top of the stairs, she walked carefully down into the nearly darkened room. Once she reached the bottom, she placed the box on a small wooden table near her grandmother's old-fashioned washing machine. Seeing a battery-operated lantern nearby, she clicked that on for additional light.

Sara spotted the wooden shelves where the empty canning jars were kept. After putting each of the jars from the box in place, she was about to head back upstairs when something caught her attention. It appeared to be a very old canning jar, partially hidden behind some other antique jars. What piqued Sara's interest the most, however, was the fact that the antique jar looked as though it had been filled up with folded pieces of paper.

Thinking perhaps the papers had been inserted to protect the old glass, she looked away. But then, Sara's curiosity got the best of her. She reached up and took it down from the shelf.

Placing it carefully on the wooden table, she removed the old lid and reached inside. Surprised, she discovered the piece of paper she'd taken out had writing on it.

Sara squinted at the words: *"We pray because we need to see God work."*

She pursed her lips. *I've prayed for many things over the years, but I've never seen God work. At least not in the way I wanted things to happen.*

Even though Sara's mother had taken her and Kenny to church a few times when they were children, Sara never understood why there was so much emphasis on prayer. She wondered sometimes if people only prayed because they thought it was the right thing to do—something to prove they were religious—and that praying might get them into heaven.

Sara's thoughts were temporarily halted when, from the exposed ceiling above, she heard water rushing through the pipes that lead to the kitchen. *Grandma must be busy at the sink still. Is she wondering what is taking me so long down here?*

It didn't seem right to go snooping through something that

wasn't hers, but hopefully she wouldn't get caught.

When the water stopped running, and Sara heard footsteps above, she froze in place. She hoped Grandma wouldn't come down to check on her. Sara wanted to see if something had been written on the other papers inside the jar. She couldn't stop at one.

She reached in and took out another slip of paper. Sure enough, something had been written there too. Sara read the words silently to herself: *"And we know that all things work together for good to them that love God, to them who are the called according to his purpose"* Romans 8:28.

She stared at the jar. *Whoever wrote these notes must have been a religious person. But I wonder what their purpose was in putting the slips of paper inside this jar. Should I ask Grandma about it or keep silent? If she's the one who wrote them, she might have done it secretly. If Grandma is the author of these notes, could she be hiding them for some reason? Maybe I shouldn't mention it to her.*

She let out a long breath. If Sara chose to tell about this, it would be obvious that she'd been snooping. *I'll remain silent about those papers in the old glass jar—at least for now.*

Sara refolded the papers and put them back in the jar. She might come down here another time and see what some of the other papers said. Right now, she needed to get back upstairs and see what else Grandma needed help with today.

*At least I am helping out.* Sara frowned, as her muscles tensed. *That's more than I can say for Michelle today. Apparently she thinks more about herself than others.* Sara clenched her fingers around the jar. *But then, that doesn't surprise me. If the imposter could live here with my grandparents all those months, pretending to be me, she's obviously selfish and self-centered. I wish Grandma and Grandpa would see her for what she is instead of expecting me to accept Michelle and even be her friend.* Sara shook her head. *That's never going to happen.*

Ezekiel paused to look around while a customer dug through her purse for a wallet to pay for the purchases she'd placed on the counter. Here it was, the Saturday after Thanksgiving, and shopping season had jumped into full swing. The family's greenhouse buzzed with activity, and the entire King family—even Ezekiel's sister Sylvia, who'd gotten married early last spring—had been helping out today. In addition to being Saturday, when normally they were busy with customers who worked during the week, an air of excitement could be felt. Christmas was less than a month away. Holiday orders needed to be filled, and customers came and went, buying poinsettias and sprigs of holly to decorate their homes. Even a few English clergymen had stopped by to get flowers for their churches.

It was a good thing Ezekiel had prepared the bee boxes for the long winter months ahead. There would be no need to do much more than monitor the boxes from time to time until spring approached. This was a blessing, since the greenhouse needed the whole family's attention.

In November, all the honey had been collected, processed, and jarred, ready for his steady clients. Ezekiel left plenty of honey for the bees, so they would have enough food to survive the cold weather ahead. He made adjustments to the bee boxes, protecting the hives from the snowfalls and bitter air but making sure to allow good ventilation. Ezekiel even weighted down the tops of the hives to guard them against toppling over from the strong winds that often accompanied winter storms.

"Thank you and come again soon." Ezekiel smiled at the lady, who waited patiently for him to box up her poinsettias.

"I will. You have some lovely flowers and plants here in the greenhouse." The customer left, carrying her poinsettias with care.

As another patron got ready to pay, Ezekiel heard a crash and glanced in the direction of the sound.

A child had accidentally knocked over a flower, sending dirt and a shattered clay pot into one of the aisles. The little boy wailed when his mother pointed a finger and scolded him. Ezekiel's mom got on it very quickly and had it cleaned up in no time. The child calmed down right away when she handed him a candy cane.

Ezekiel smiled. His mother had always been good with children. He was sure she and Dad looked forward to the day one of their adult children would make them grandparents.

His sister Amy kept busy helping another customer pick out flowers for a centerpiece she wanted to make. Meanwhile, Ezekiel's brother Abe and their father were busy adding freshly made Christmas wreaths to the wall, as several customers gathered around to look at those too. It was a good thing Abe and Dad had made some extra wreaths this morning, because they were selling quickly. Ezekiel didn't see his younger brother anywhere. Most likely, Henry was still in the barn, cleaning the horses' stalls. Dad had sent him there a while ago, giving him a list of chores to do.

Ezekiel's customer smiled and glanced toward the wreaths before leaving. "There is nothing like the smell of fresh pine. I may have to go look at those before I leave."

When she walked toward the wall of wreaths, Ezekiel waited on the next customer who didn't have any purchases in his hands. "Good afternoon, Mr. Duncan. Are you here to buy some flowers or one of our Christmas plants?"

"You could say that, I guess." The middle-aged man smiled and handed Ezekiel his receipt. "I'm here to pick up my order that I placed two weeks ago. Remember, I purchased fifty poinsettias to give out to my employees, plus a few extra to decorate the office too." Mr. Duncan was the manager of an insurance office in Lancaster. "I believe you waited on me when I stopped by a few weeks ago to put in my request."

"Oh, you're right. Give me a minute, and I'll go in the back and bring them out." Feeling a bit confused, Ezekiel took the customer's order form. He'd had a hard time concentrating on his work today. Unlike other times when the greenhouse was busy and he was at the point of being frazzled, today a warm and light-hearted feeling kept his mood a happy one—although distracted. All he could think about was Michelle and the good time they'd had on Thanksgiving. Especially the ride when they were alone in his buggy.

He would have liked nothing more than for Michelle to have said yes about joining the Amish faith so their courtship could happen sooner and progress at a faster pace.

Ezekiel blew a puff of air through his lips. *I can understand why she was hesitant though. After all, I didn't jump in and become English just because I thought that's what she wanted. Patience is what I need, and the willingness to give her some time.*

Ezekiel came to where the larger orders were waiting and was surprised to find Abe putting poinsettias into a box. "Do you know where Mr. Duncan's order is?"

"I'm filling it now," Abe answered. "I have a few more boxes to fill, and then it will be complete. This is a big order and should have been filled last evening."

Ezekiel pinched the bridge of his nose. "It says on the receipt he'd be picking it up today."

"I guess it was missed," Abe muttered. "Don't want to disappoint Mr. Duncan, so I'm working on it as fast as I can."

"Here, let me help you. We shouldn't keep the man waiting. He's one of our best customers."

Abe looked at Ezekiel with lowered brows. "Exactly."

They worked together quickly to complete the order, and filled five boxes of poinsettias. "I'll go get the cart so we can load these into his car," Abe volunteered.

While Ezekiel waited, his thoughts turned to Michelle once more. He couldn't wait to see her, but with the way things were going and the busy days ahead at the greenhouse, he wasn't sure when it would happen.

# Chapter 7

Monday morning after the breakfast dishes were done, Sara slipped into a jacket, grabbed her purse, and headed for the back door.

"Where are you going?" Grandma called from the kitchen table, where she sat writing a letter.

Sara turned around. "Out to find a job. Remember, I told you I wanted to start looking today?"

"Yes, but I thought you might decide to wait a few more days." Grandma peered at Sara over the top of her reading glasses. "There's no rush in finding a job, is there?"

Without making reference to what she'd previously said about finding another place to live, Sara explained that she'd seen several job openings in this morning's newspaper and wanted to check on them. "With the way the market is these days, it's important that I do this when the opportunity strikes. The positions being advertised may not be available long."

"I suppose you are right."

"One of the jobs is working in a flower shop. I thought that seemed interesting."

"Have you ever worked in a flower shop?"

"No, but I think it might be fun to learn. I've always liked flowers, and I'm a quick learner."

Grandma tapped the end of the pen she held against her chin. "I wonder if the Kings might need someone to work in their greenhouse. They sell poinsettias this time of the year, and with Christmas only a month away, they might need some extra help."

"I'll keep that in mind." Eager to be on her way, Sara smiled and said, "Well, I'd better go." She turned and reached for the doorknob, but before she could open the door, Grandma spoke again.

"Will you be back in time for lunch?"

"I don't think so, Grandma. I might be gone until late afternoon."

"Oh, okay. I'll see you later then." She put her pen to paper again.

Sara gave a backward wave and opened the door. When she stepped outside, she was surprised to see Michelle hitching Grandma's horse to one of Grandpa's closed-in buggies. Sara was even more taken aback when Michelle got into the buggy, picked up the reins, and headed down the driveway toward the road. The pretender sure hadn't taken long to adapt to the new mode of transportation. Sara frowned. *What is that girl up to, and what's she trying to prove?*

It seemed odd that Michelle would be going anywhere with the horse and buggy by herself, not to mention wearing denim jeans and a long-sleeved sweatshirt under her teal blue puffer coat. The only people Sara had seen riding in the typical gray carriages here in the Lancaster County area were dressed plain.

*I bet she's going over to her boyfriend's house.* Sara had noticed the sick-cow looks exchanged between Michelle and Ezekiel when everyone sat down to enjoy their Thanksgiving desserts.

Sara got into her car and started the engine. *Whatever happens between Michelle and Ezekiel is none of my business. I need to concentrate on landing a job. Hopefully, I'll find one today.*

Michelle guided Grandma's horse to the hitching rack outside the Kings' greenhouse, got out, and secured Peanuts to the rail. Peanuts nickered to another horse already at the rail. In fact, several horse and buggies, as well as many vehicles, were parked outside the greenhouse. Due to the number of customers who were probably shopping inside, Michelle assumed most of Ezekiel's family was here working today. She wanted to speak to him about the things she'd thought about last night before going to bed, but didn't want any of his family to hear their conversation. While she wasn't sure yet about joining the Amish church, Michelle needed to know more about taking classes and what all would be expected of her. She was also eager to find out when Ezekiel planned to join the church.

When Michelle entered the greenhouse, she noticed right away that they appeared to be having a good day. A number of customers had come out, despite the cold weather. She found Ezekiel's mother, Belinda, setting some poinsettia plants on a shelf. A heater nearby blew warm air, which helped keep the plants at the correct temperature.

Walking up to Belinda, Michelle smiled. "Hi, Mrs. King. Is Ezekiel here?"

Belinda shook her head. "Not in the greenhouse, at least. I wish he was though, because we could use his help right now."

"Where is he?" Michelle glanced around.

"Out checking the beehives—although I'm not sure why, since he already winterized them." Ezekiel's mother's tone was cool, and she barely made eye contact with Michelle.

*She still doesn't like me—even though I came back to Strasburg to apologize to the Lapps for letting them believe I was Sara.* Michelle fidgeted with her purse straps. *Should I talk to Belinda about what I did—maybe apologize to her too, since she probably thinks I offended the entire Amish community?*

Before Michelle had a chance to say anything, an elderly Amish couple entered the building. Belinda walked away from Michelle and went to see what they wanted.

*It's just as well. I may have said the wrong thing anyway, which would have only made things worse. Truth be told, no matter what I say or do, Belinda will probably never think I'm good enough for her son. Maybe it'd be best if I don't see Ezekiel anymore. He'd be better off with some nice young woman who grew up Amish.*

Michelle hurried from the greenhouse. She was almost to her

buggy, when Ezekiel came around the corner of the building. "Hey, Michelle. I didn't expect to see you here today." He pulled his jacket collar tighter around his neck. "Did you come to buy something?"

"No, I came to see you."

"I'm glad you did." He stood next to her. "I just came from checking on the bee boxes. It's good to monitor them from now until spring. Anyways, I'm heading to the house for something to drink before I help in the greenhouse again. Why don't you come along and we can visit awhile?"

"I was just in the greenhouse with your mom, and it's pretty busy in there. Are you sure you don't want to go in and help them right now?"

"We won't be long." He smiled and gestured toward the house.

Michelle hesitated but finally nodded. *I may as well get this over with. It's best that I let him go now.*

<hr />

After Ezekiel and Michelle entered the kitchen, he pulled out two chairs and motioned for Michelle to take a seat at the table. "Would you like something hot or cold to drink? I can heat up some hot water for tea or cocoa."

She shook her head, watching as he went to the sink to wash his hands. "No thanks."

"How about some of my mamm's banana bread? It's pretty tasty."

"I'm sure it's delicious, but I'm not hungry right now. As I said before, I came over here to talk to you about something."

"Oh? What about?"

Michelle had almost worked up the nerve to say what was on her mind when Ezekiel's sister Amy entered the room. She glanced at Michelle, looked away, then turned to face her again. "I was surprised to see you at church yesterday. I didn't realize you'd come back to Strasburg."

"I've been back a month already. And I attended church two weeks ago."

Amy's brows furrowed. "I didn't realize that. I visited a friend's church district two weeks ago, so I wasn't at the service you attended and had no way of knowing you were there."

"Oh, I see." Michelle couldn't judge by Amy's tone of voice whether she disapproved of her, but the young woman's expression said it all. Apparently, like Ezekiel's mother, his sister thought Michelle wasn't good enough for him. *The truth is, I'm not. He deserves better.*

Ezekiel cleared his throat real loud, looking right at his sister. "Did you come to the kitchen for any particular reason?"

She shrugged. "No, not really. I heard voices and came to see who was here."

"I brought Michelle into the kitchen so we could visit without interruptions."

Amy poked her brother's arm. "Okay. Okay. I can take a hint. I have to get back out to the greenhouse anyway. Business is booming, as you well know. Don't be too long, Ezekiel. Your help is also needed today." She glanced briefly at Michelle, then hurried from the room.

Ezekiel took a seat across from Michelle. "That sister of mine. . . She says things sometimes just to get under my skin." He leaned his elbows on the table. "Now what was it you wanted to talk to me about?"

She drew a deep breath. "It's about joining the Amish church. I've been thinking a lot about it these past few days."

"I hope your answer is yes."

"Not yet. I need to ask you some questions about everything that would be expected of me if I did decide to become Amish." Michelle massaged her forehead. "But now I'm having second thoughts."

"What are your second thoughts?" Ezekiel questioned.

"For one thing, it would be a big change for me to give up the only way of life I've ever known." She held up two fingers. "I'd have to learn, not one, but two languages."

Ezekiel folded the fingers she held up, and encompassed her

hand in his. "Not a big problem. I can help you with that."

Michelle's gaze flitted around the room. "It's obvious that your mother and sister don't approve of me. So I think it would be best if you forgot about me joining your church and found someone else to court—someone who is honest and upright. You ought to choose a young woman who is already Amish."

Ezekiel shook his head vehemently. "It's not up to them, and I don't want anyone else."

"You may think that right now, but if the right girl came along—"

"You are the right girl, Michelle. I thought that when I believed your name was Sara, and I still think it now."

Fearing she might cave in, Michelle pushed her chair away from the table and stood. "I can't talk about this anymore. Please, give me some space. I'm confused and afraid of failing," she confessed, putting a hand to her hip. "Furthermore, please don't try to force me into this."

His cheeks puffed out. "I won't force you to do anything you don't want to do, but I hope you will think about it more. Don't say yes now, and don't say no. Just pray about whether you should join the Amish church." He stood too and placed his hand on her arm. "The first of nine instructional classes in preparation for baptism and joining the church start next Sunday." He paused and moistened his lips. "I've already agreed to take the classes that will be taught about thirty minutes before church service begins. So if you decide to take part in those classes, please let me know before then."

"When would the baptism take place?" Michelle asked.

"In the spring. And if you have some specific questions concerning what all would be expected of you, I'm more than willing to answer them and put your mind at ease." Ezekiel moved his hand from Michelle's arm to her waist. "Don't give up on us, please."

Offering no response to his statement, Michelle looked at her watch. "I've gotta go, Ezekiel. I want to buy something in your parents' greenhouse, and then I'll need to get back to the Lapps'. Willis is expecting my help with some things today." She made a beeline for the door. It had been a mistake coming here to speak with Ezekiel. Being near him made her want to say she would do whatever it took in order to join the Amish church so they could be together. But that would be the wrong motive for making such a drastic change. If Michelle were to become Amish, it had to be for the right reasons.

# Chapter 8

"How did the job hunting go?" Grandma asked when Sara returned home at three o'clock. "Were you successful?"

Sara smiled, quickly hiding a purchase she had made around the corner so Grandma wouldn't see. Fortunately, the surprise was well hidden in a big shopping bag. "I sure was. Starting tomorrow, I'll be working at a flower shop." She hung up her jacket and purse, then took a seat at the kitchen table. "They hired me on the spot."

"Oh, at Kings' Greenhouse?"

"No, it's a florist here in Strasburg."

"That's wonderful, Sara. What will you do there?"

"I'll be doing the books, answering the phone, and waiting on customers. Since I've taken some business classes, the flower shop is a good fit for me."

"So you won't be making the flower arrangements?"

"Nope. Don't know if I'd be good at that, although it might be fun to learn. Think I'm better with beads." Sara snapped her fingers. "Speaking of which. . . I keep forgetting to give you and Grandpa something I made. Is he around? If so, I'll go up to my room and get the gifts right now."

"Yes, he's here." Grandma motioned to the living-room door. "After we ate lunch he said he wanted to catch up on his reading before doing more chores, so he's relaxing in his easy chair." She snickered. "The last time I checked though, your grandfather had dozed off. But he may be awake by now."

"Okay, I'll go up and get the gifts and meet you in the living room."

When Sara entered the living room with gifts behind her back, she found her grandparents sitting on the couch engaged in conversation. They appeared to be quite interested in what the other was saying. Sara hated to interrupt, so she waited a few minutes until they finished talking. *These two truly have a special connection. Someday I hope to have that same kind of relationship with my husband. If I ever fall in love, that is.* Sara wasn't about to settle for second best when it came to choosing a mate for life. Although Dean had treated her mother fairly, to Sara, he and Mama didn't seem like soulmates. Sara's mother had her interests, and Dean had his. Mama had a quiet personality, and Dean was outgoing.

"Your grandma said you have something for us." Grandpa's deep voice pulled Sara's thoughts back to the present.

"Yes, I do. I was going to give them to you when I visited last month but I didn't have Grandma's gift done yet." Sara held out her right hand and handed the beaded keychain she'd made to her grandfather.

His face lit up as he pointed to the initial "L" she had etched into the leather patch. "This is a great gift. Thank you, Sara. I'll keep my house keys on it."

Pleased that he liked the gift, Sara presented Grandma with the black-and-blue coin purse. "I made this from an old scarf my mother used to wear."

"Oh my! Thank you so much." Grandma's eyes teared up as she held the item against her chest. "Knowing you used something of my daughter's makes this even more special to me."

She stood and gave Sara a hug. "And now, how about the three of us sharing a cup of hot tea?"

"And don't forget to bring in some of those pumpkin cookies you made after lunch." Grandpa smacked his lips.

"How would you know what I baked, Husband? You came right in here after lunch and took a snooze." Grandma flapped her hand at him.

He wiggled his bushy brows. "My eyes may have been sleeping, but my sniffer was wide awake."

Sara laughed. "You are so comical, Grandpa."

"Jah, well, I don't set out to be. Funny stuff just comes out of my mouth." He winked at Sara.

"Okay, I'm going to get the goodies now." Grandma turned toward the kitchen.

"I'll help you." Sara hurried along behind her grandmother.

"Where's Michelle?" she asked when they entered the kitchen. "Will she be joining us for tea and cookies?"

Grandma shook her head. "She hasn't been back since she left this morning. Said she was going over to see Ezekiel."

"Oh, I see." Sara wouldn't admit it to Grandma, but she was glad Michelle hadn't returned yet. It was nice to have some time alone with her grandparents. If the pretender was here, she would have monopolized the conversation.

As Sara got the water heating for tea, Grandma took out several cookies and placed them on a tray.

"You know," Grandma said, "dark blue was one of you mother's favorite colors."

"Yes, she wore the scarf I used to make your coin purse a lot. Mama had a couple of blue dresses too."

"She took after me in that way." Grandma sniffed. "I still miss her so much. I am sure you do as well."

Nodding, Sara touched her chest. "The memory of Mama will always be with me." She wished she could express how she felt about her mother's deceit. Grandma didn't need to know Sara hadn't forgiven her mother for keeping her heritage a secret. Sara couldn't imagine the pain Mama had put her folks through by leaving home and never contacting them. Grandma and Grandpa Lapp were kind and loving. Surely they would have welcomed their daughter back with open arms. *How could Mama not have known how much they loved her?* Sara wondered. *Her parents did not deserve to be treated that way.*

Once the tea was ready, Sara carried the cups and teapot to

the living room, while Grandma brought out the tray of cookies and placed it on the coffee table in front of the couch. They all took seats, and after everyone had a cup of tea and a cookie, Sara decided to ask a few questions about the Lancaster Amish.

"When I stopped for lunch at a restaurant in Bird-in-Hand today, I heard someone mention how they looked forward to the mud sale that would take place in the spring of next year." Sara looked at Grandpa. "What is a mud sale anyhow?"

Grandpa leaned slightly forward, with both hands on his knees. "Local volunteer fire companies in Lancaster County raise funds through what they call 'mud sales.' Many of the items available at these auctions are sold outside during the spring when the weather is normally wet."

"Which, of course, makes the ground muddy," Grandma interjected. "That's why the auctions are called mud sales."

"What kind of things do they auction off?" Sara questioned.

Grandpa spoke again. "Everything from furniture, tools, building materials, farming equipment, garden items, livestock, and Amish buggies to a variety of quilts."

Sara reached for another cookie. "I'd like to learn how to make a quilt someday."

Grandma's eyes brightened. "Then I shall teach you. Maybe during the cold winter months, when there isn't so much work to be done outside, we can set up my quilting frame and I'll teach you and Michelle how to make a simple nine-patch quilt for your beds."

Sara smiled, but inside she fumed. *Why does Michelle, who isn't a family member, have to be included in everything?* It seemed as if Grandma—and Grandpa too—thought of her as one of their granddaughters. This irked Sara, but she kept her thoughts to herself. If she said what she truly felt, her grandparents might think she was a terrible person. *They may even choose Michelle over me. I'll bet the pretender would like that. Truth be told, she's probably hoping I'll move back to New Jersey so she can have my grandparents all to herself.* Sara's spine stiffened. *Well, that's not going to happen. Even if*

*I do move out of Grandpa and Grandma's house to a place of my own, I'll be living somewhere in Lancaster County.*

❧

When Michelle arrived home—feeling as if this truly was her home—she put Peanuts in the stall and rubbed her down real good. "You sure have a nice, heavy winter coat already." Michelle patted the mare's neck. "But it's not that surprising, with the cold weather we're having."

Michelle continued grooming Peanuts, while talking to her. She understood the horse's hard work and wanted to reward the animal with some proper care in return.

When Michelle left the mare's stall, she took a few minutes to pet Rascal and Sadie, who had eagerly greeted her.

"You two go play now or take a nap," Michelle instructed the dogs after she'd given them what she felt was enough attention.

Sadie slunk away, but Rascal remained by Michelle, pawing at her leg.

She bent down and patted the dog's head. "All right, pooch, go find something else to do."

Rascal gave a pathetic whine, and Michelle lifted her gaze to the ceiling. "Some dogs would do anything to get attention." She gave Rascal another few pats, then sprinted out of the barn.

When Michelle entered the house a few minutes later, she heard Willis and Mary Ruth talking to Sara. Their voices came from the living room. She stepped partially into the room. "Hi, I'm home."

"Come join us." Mary Ruth pointed to the coffee table. "There are still a few cookies left, and I'd be happy to fix you a cup of tea if you'd like."

"No, that's okay. I don't wanna interrupt," Michelle replied. "Besides I was planning to help Willis with any chores he needed to get done this afternoon. Is there anything I can get started on?"

"You're not interrupting," Willis said with a shake of his head. "And we can get to those chores later. Please, come have a seat."

Feeling like a fifth wheel on a buggy, Michelle came fully into the room and sat on one end of the couch. She glanced over at Sara, seated on the other end, and smiled. "How's your day been going so far?"

"Okay." Sara didn't look at Michelle.

"Sara got a job working at the flower shop in town," Mary Ruth said.

"Have you had any job offers?" Sara asked, barely glancing in Michelle's direction.

"Not yet. But after I left the Kings' place this morning, I stopped by several restaurants in the area to see if they were hiring." She frowned. "So far, nothing. I'll keep trying until I find a job though."

"What kind of work are you looking for?" Sara asked.

"I've done some waitressing in the past." Michelle lifted her shoulders. "But I'll do most anything if it pays well enough. I'd even wash dishes—although it's not my first choice."

Sara made no comment, but Willis and Mary Ruth both encouraged Michelle to be patient. "The right job for you will open soon," Willis said.

Michelle didn't understand why she hadn't found anything yet. She'd been here a whole month without a single interview. *I need to get out there again tomorrow and make an effort to find something, even if I have to look outside of Strasburg. I can't sit around here mooching off the Lapps any longer. There must be some restaurant in Lancaster County that needs help and would be willing to hire me.*

"Look what Sara made for us." Mary Ruth held up a coin purse, and then motioned to the key ring lying on the end table next to Willis's chair.

"How nice." Michelle didn't want Willis to think she wasn't interested, so she picked up the gift and looked it over. "Oh, this reminds me. I'll be right back."

Running outside to the buggy, she felt a pang of jealousy creep in. *Sara has a job, and I don't. The Lapp's are impressed with her little gifts. I hope they'll like what I got them today.*

Michelle retrieved the poinsettia Ezekiel's mother sold her this morning. While it wasn't homemade like Sara's gifts, it was home grown and would add a little pre-Christmas feeling to the inside of the house.

❧

"While Michelle is outside, I have something else I want to give you." Sara got up and brought the bag she'd left in the hall into the living room. "Here you go."

"I can't imagine what else you could be surprising us with." When Grandma peeked inside, her fingers touched her parted lips. "Look here, Willis. Isn't it lovely?" She took the plant out of the bag and held it up.

Grandpa nodded agreeably. "Bet it would look nice on the dining-room table."

Grandma rose to her feet and gave Sara a hug. "Thank you, Sara. I've never seen a poinsettia this big before, and it's such a beautiful deep red."

"You're welcome. I'm glad you like it. After I got the job at the flower shop, I couldn't resist getting a poinsettia for you. The store is filled with them."

"It's sure a beauty." Grandpa offered Sara a wide grin.

At that moment, Michelle burst into the living room. "I have something for—" She stopped talking as she looked at the beautiful poinsettia Sara had given them. It was twice the size as the one Michelle held. "I—I had hoped to surprise you with this," she stammered. "But I see that you already have a much nicer one."

Before Grandpa or Grandma could say anything, Michelle set the poinsettia on the coffee table and dashed out of the room. Her footsteps could be heard bounding up the stairs, followed by the slamming of her bedroom door.

"Oh dear." Grandma looked at Grandpa with eyes widened. "I'd better go see if she's all right."

# Chapter 9

Michelle was glad when Sara left for her job the following morning. This gave her a rare moment to talk to Mary Ruth privately. She needed to apologize for her rude behavior last evening when she'd run out of the room after seeing the poinsettia Sara had given her grandparents. Michelle had even skipped supper last night—partly because she was still upset, and also because she'd developed a headache.

As Michelle approached the sink, where Mary Ruth stood washing the breakfast dishes, her throat felt like it was filled with a wad of cotton. Picking up the dish towel, she tried to swallow. "I owe you an apology, Mary Ruth. I shouldn't have been envious of the poinsettia Sara gave you and Willis. It was childish of me to hide out in my room last night too. Will you forgive me for ignoring you when you knocked and called out to me through the bedroom door?"

Mary Ruth smiled as she turned to look at Michelle. "Of course I accept your apology. I am concerned though about the competition going on between you and Sara. I had hoped the two of you might become friends by now, instead of vying for our attention and trying to one-up each other."

Michelle lowered her gaze. "It's not jealousy of Sara, for she is your granddaughter. I still feel that I owe you and Willis something to make up for my deception. And whenever I try to do anything nice for you, Sara always does something better." She lifted her head. "Besides, I don't see how Sara and I can ever be friends. Simply put—she doesn't like me, and probably never will."

Mary Ruth shook her head. "Never say never. If you show Sara you are friendly and try to be kind, I'm certain in time she will warm up to you."

"How much time?" Michelle's forehead wrinkled.

"I don't know, but Willis and I have been praying for both of you."

"Thanks. Truth is, I need a lot of prayer right now, and it's not just about my situation with Sara."

"What is it?" Mary Ruth questioned. "Or is it something you'd rather not talk about?"

Michelle heaved a sigh. "I think it's something I *need* to talk about."

"I'll dry my hands, and we can sit at the table while you tell me what's troubling you."

"That's all right. I can talk and dry the dishes as you wash."

"Okay then." Mary Ruth resumed her chore. "I'm all ears."

"I am trying to decide whether or not I should join the Amish church."

Mary Ruth dropped her sponge into the soapy water, sending bubbles halfway up to the ceiling, while a few foamy suds landed on her nose. "Goodness." She giggled, using her apron to wipe the soapy blob off.

Michelle joined the carefree moment, laughing and smacking her hands together to pop a few little bubbles floating in front of them.

"Are you truly serious about joining the Amish church?" Mary Ruth asked, once their laughter subsided.

Michelle gave a decisive nod. "Ezekiel plans to join in the spring, and he wants me to take instruction classes with him in preparation for baptism."

"Is becoming Amish something you truly want to do?" Mary Ruth picked up the sponge.

"I—I think so. But I know it'll be a challenge, and I'm not sure if I am up to it."

"You seem to have adapted well to our Plain lifestyle." Mary Ruth pushed up her damp sleeve. "I've never heard you complain about not having electricity or all the modern conveniences that are not found in our home. You've also learned how to drive a horse and buggy."

"True, but that's not the part I am concerned about."

"What then?"

"In addition to learning how to speak Pennsylvania Dutch fluently, I'd be required to learn German so I can understand the sermons that are preached during church."

Mary Ruth sponged off a spatula, rinsed the object well, and placed it on the drying rack. "Willis and I can help you with that."

"Do you think I'm smart enough to learn both languages? I was never at the top of my class in school, and I didn't get good grades. Truth is, compared to most of the other kids, I felt stupid."

"You're not stupid, and that's in the past. You've already learned several words from our everyday language, and I have no doubt of your ability to learn more." Mary Ruth's tone was reassuring.

Michelle pulled the dishcloth across one of the clean plates. She tried to envision herself in Amish clothing and living a wholesome lifestyle, like the woman she wished was her grandmother. *But maybe I'm like my own mother—a liar and a person people don't trust.* Michelle felt as though she were sinking in deep despair, unable to handle this rising challenge. "There's something else, Mary Ruth." She set the dry plate aside.

"What is it, dear one?"

"I don't feel worthy of becoming Amish. My life has been full of imperfections, and everyone in this area knows how I deceived you and Willis when I pretended to be your granddaughter." Michelle's posture slumped. "I still haven't completely forgiven myself, and there may be some in your church district who have not forgiven me either."

"It's in the past, Michelle. You prayed and asked God to pardon your sins, and you've apologized to us too. If you feel led to become Amish, then I think you should pursue it." Mary Ruth offered Michelle a sweet smile and gave her a hug. It felt reassuring. "And thank you for opening up and sharing your feelings with me," she added. "You are on a new path with your life, and Willis and I will be praying for you."

Tears welled in Michelle's eyes. "Danki for listening, and for the good advice. I will pray about the matter a few more days before giving Ezekiel my decision."

Sara had only been working at the flower shop a few hours when she realized how much she was going to like her new job. She inhaled deeply. How pleasant it was to be surrounded by so many beautiful floral arrangements. Even though it was chilly November outside, it smelled like springtime inside the store.

Several people had come in already this morning, and Sara kept busy waiting on customers and answering the phone to take orders. With Christmas less than a month away, business would no doubt be thriving from now through the end of December.

"Have the poinsettias I ordered come in yet?" Sara's boss, Andy Roberts asked, stepping up to the counter where she stood. "The poinsettias we have are selling fast, and the same holds true for the Christmas cacti. Hopefully the plants I ordered will be here soon."

"I haven't seen any sign of a delivery truck yet."

"No, it won't be a truck. The people I order many of my flowers from are Amish. They either deliver them with their horse-and-market buggy, or sometimes will hire a driver who owns a van."

"Oh, I see. It's nice you're able to buy flowers and plants locally."

Dragging his fingers through his thinning gray hair, Andy nodded. "I appreciate the fact that there is a greenhouse in the area that can provide me with flowers pretty much all year. I also like that it's Amish-owned, because they are easy to work with. I've never been dissatisfied with the quality of their flowers and plants." He motioned to the back of the store. "Welp, I'd better get busy and help my wife with making the arrangements. Karen wouldn't appreciate it if she got stuck with all the work while I stayed out here yakking all day. Let me know if you need anything," Andy called as he ambled toward the back room.

Sara looked around the shop again. Since she had been so busy, she hadn't noticed how few poinsettias were actually left in the store until Mr. Roberts mentioned it. She was glad she bought the beautiful one yesterday, because right now only a couple of small ones remained.

A few minutes later, a tall Amish man entered the store. He was slender and had a full beard that was gray, which was in sharp contrast to his mostly light blond hair. With only a few wrinkles on his face, Sara figured he might be in his late forties, but the beard made him appear older.

"May I help you?" she asked when he stepped up to the counter.

He nodded. "Came in to buy a bouquet of flowers for my wife's birthday." His blue eyes twinkled under the lights in the store. "I've been doin' that on her birthday every year since we got married, and sometimes I get Mattie flowers for no occasion at all."

"I'm sure she appreciates your thoughtfulness." Sara opened the cooler to show him what was available. "These are the bouquets that have already been made up. Do you see anything your wife might like?"

His forehead wrinkled as he rubbed one hand down the side of his black trousers. "Don't think so. What else have you got?"

Sara glanced toward the back room. "I'll go get one of the owners and see if they can make something up that would be more to your wife's liking."

"Okay." The man reached under his straw hat and scratched the side of his head. "Are you new here? Don't recall seeing you before."

"Today's my first day on the job," Sara explained. "And I am new to the area. Now, if you don't mind waiting, I'll be right back."

"Don't mind a bit."

Sara hurried to the back room, and was pleased when Karen said she would be right out.

Sara returned to her place behind the counter in time to see Ezekiel King enter the store.

"Sure didn't expect to see you here." Ezekiel gave Sara a wide smile. "I'm guessin' because you're behind the counter that you're not one of the customers."

"You're right. I started working here this morning," she responded. "What brings you into the flower shop, Ezekiel?"

"Came to deliver some poinsettias."

"Oh, so you're the delivery they've been waiting for."

"Yep. This florist and a couple others in Lancaster County buy their Christmas flowers from our greenhouse." Ezekiel glanced at the Amish man who stood waiting in front of the counter. "Hey, Mr. Fisher. How are you?"

The other man shuffled his feet. "Do I know you?"

"Not personally, but I met you once when I stopped by your bulk-food store in Gordonville. My folks have a greenhouse here in Strasburg."

"I see." Mr. Fisher's attention turned to Karen Roberts when she came out of the back room. As he explained to her what he wanted for his wife's bouquet, Ezekiel continued his conversation with Sara.

"I'm glad you were able to find a job so quickly. Michelle's been lookin' for a month now and hasn't found a single waitressing position."

Hearing Michelle's name caused Sara to think about how Michelle responded last evening when they'd both given Sara's grandparents a poinsettia. After seeing the look of disappointment on Michelle's face, and then watching her run out of the room, Sara realized the reason for the young woman's disappointment. *I probably would have felt the same way if I'd given Grandpa and Grandma the smaller plant. But she should have gotten past it, instead of staying in her room all evening and ignoring Grandma when she knocked on her bedroom door, wanting to talk. It just showed Michelle's immaturity.*

"Did you hear what I said?"

Sara jerked her head. "What was that, Ezekiel?"

"I asked if you would hold the door while I bring in the poinsettias."

"Oh yes. Certainly."

Before they reached the door, a thunderous crash sounded outside on the street. Watching through the glass doors, Sara saw that a car had been rear-ended. Both drivers appeared to be okay, as they got out of their vehicles. But soon, a shouting match ensued.

Sara looked at Ezekiel with raised eyebrows and motioned to the angry man. "I wonder why he's so mad. Look at all the dents already on the side of his car. That's worse than the new one he's pointing to on the front fender of the other's man vehicle."

The taller man, dressed in a gray business suit, stood shaking his head as he pointed to the spot on his car that had suffered the damage. It was easy to put two and two together on what had happened. Apparently, the well-tailored man had made a quick stop and the other guy couldn't brake quickly enough.

"I wonder how long this will take." Sara continued to watch.

Ezekiel shrugged his shoulders and pointed to the police car pulling up. Quickly, the officer directed both guys to move their vehicles off the road.

"Guess it's safe to go out now," Ezekiel commented. "A little excitement—the kind we don't need. But at least no horse and buggy was involved. That happens all too often."

As Sara held the door, she watched while Ezekiel unloaded a box full of poinsettias from his driver's van. Most of them were the traditional red, but a few were an off-white, while a couple of others had a pinkish hue. It would be fun to place them around the store among the other displays. Meanwhile, she heard Mr. Fisher say he had some errands to run and would be back later to pick up his wife's bouquet.

Sara didn't know Mattie Fisher, but she couldn't help feeling a bit envious of the woman. *Being married to a man who brought flowers on her birthday every year must make Mrs. Fisher feel very special.* It wasn't only the idea of getting a pretty bouquet Sara envied; it was the thought of having a man care about her so much that he'd go to extra lengths to make her birthday special.

*Not like Dean, who was so into his work and recreational sports that he sometimes forgot Mama's birthday and even their wedding anniversary.* Sara bit her bottom lip until she tasted blood. *I wish I knew what my real father was like. Of course, if he didn't care enough to marry Mama when she was pregnant, then he probably wouldn't have been a good husband either.*

# Chapter 10

*Clarks Summit*

Brad headed down the hall toward the cafeteria. All was quiet except for the rhythmic sound of his footsteps on the polished floor. It was hard to believe today was the last day of November, and also the last day of classes for this week. In just a few short weeks, he would be leaving the seminary for a much-needed Christmas break. It would be good to take some time away from his studies and all the pressures he faced in order to finish his masters of divinity degree. There was so much to learn before he could apply for a church. Sometimes, his head felt like it was spinning. Expository preaching, Christian leadership, and biblical counseling were all classes he was expected to take. Although Brad was eager to shepherd a flock of his own, the idea frightened him a bit. What if he wasn't up to the task? Would the congregation relate to him, and he to them? If it was a small church, how much responsibility would be placed upon him?

Brad remembered one church he and his parents had attended when he was boy. It had been small and without enough willing people to do all the jobs. That meant poor overworked Pastor Jenkins was responsible not only for preaching and shepherding the flock but also directing the music, hauling neighborhood children to Sunday school in his van, and taking care of a good deal of the janitorial duties.

As Brad sat at one of the lunch tables inside the cafeteria and took out the sandwich he'd packed this morning, his thoughts drifted toward home. Except for a lingering cough, Mom's bout with the flu was behind her. Fortunately, Brad's father didn't get sick and was able to take time off work to care for Mom during the worst of her illness. Apparently Dad's immune system was stronger than hers.

Brad looked forward to being with his parents for Christmas, but he was also eager to spend part of his holiday break in Lancaster County. It would be good to see everyone he knew there again. Many of the folks he'd worked for, like Willis and Mary Ruth Lapp, were almost like family and made him feel as if he had a second home.

"Mind if I sit here?" Holding a tray full of food in one hand, Elliot Whittier looked down at Brad.

"Be my guest." Brad motioned to the empty chair across from him.

"I see you brought your own lunch," his friend commented as he took a seat.

"Yeah. It's cheaper than buying a hot meal every day." Brad unwrapped his tuna fish sandwich, then thumped his stomach. "It'll fill the empty hole, I guess."

"Today it looks as if the kitchen staff is working in slow motion." Elliot chuckled. "Guess they're in need of some time off too." He shook some ketchup on his hamburger. "So how are you liking it here?"

"It's okay. Just a lot harder than I thought it would be."

Elliot nodded and licked a blob of ketchup off his finger. "I know what you mean. There's a lot more to becoming a minister than meets the eye."

"That's for sure."

"With all the studying I have to do, it's putting a crimp on my social life." Elliot's brows furrowed as he took a bite of his burger. "I'm worried my girlfriend, Mindy, might break up with me if I don't find the time to take her out pretty soon. At the rate things are going, we may never get married."

Brad reached for his bottle of water. "Didn't realize you were engaged."

"We're not officially. I'm waiting until I complete seminary to propose to her." Elliot tipped his head, looking curiously at Brad. "Think you'll ever get married? I mean, having a wife is not criteria for pastoring a church, but it would sure make it easier to share the burden with a good helpmate at your side."

Brad shrugged his shoulders. "If I found the right woman, I would consider marriage. But that's not a concern for me at this point, since I currently have no girlfriend. And to be honest, I don't know where I'd find the time to date anyone right now." He smiled. "So for now, it's best that I concentrate on my studies and keep my nose in the books."

*Strasburg*

Despite the chill seeping into the buggy, Michelle's face felt like she'd been in the sun too long. She was heading down the road toward the Kings' place, ready to give Ezekiel her answer. After praying about it these last few days, Michelle had made her decision about whether to join the Amish church or not. She hoped it was the right one, because many doubts still swam around her head about the future.

From past experience, it seemed that so far, every decision she'd made in her life turned out to be wrong. Yet through it all, she'd persevered. Giving up was not in her nature. When Michelle left Lancaster County after leaving a note for the Lapps admitting she had pretended to be Sara, she'd been tempted to give up. But after reading some scripture, she had fallen under conviction and felt as if God had given her a sense of purpose. She certainly hadn't expected that part of the purpose would be returning to Strasburg with Ezekiel to face Willis and Mary Ruth. And the last thing Michelle ever expected was to be living in their home again by invitation.

"Your owners are such good people." Michelle spoke out loud as she shook the reins a bit to get Peanuts to go faster. The mare whinnied as though in agreement.

One thing about taking a ride in the buggy, it gave her mind something else to focus on while moving along at a slower pace. Michelle kept rehearsing what she wanted to say to Ezekiel about her decision.

She rolled her shoulders to release some tension. Michelle hoped Ezekiel was at home or in the greenhouse, for if she didn't speak to him today, she might lose her nerve.

Ezekiel was heading to the house to get the ham sandwich Mom had put in the refrigerator for him, when a nickering horse pulling a buggy trotted into the yard. He recognized Mary Ruth's mare, and was pleased when he saw Michelle in the driver's seat of the buggy.

Ezekiel's gaze rested on her, picturing his girl being Amish. Michelle adjusted so naturally to driving a horse and buggy. He felt sure she could become Amish if she chose to. *But I shouldn't get my hopes up,* Ezekiel chided himself. He wondered if she'd come here to give him her answer about taking classes to join the church.

Ezekiel turned away from the house and hurried over to the hitching rail near their barn. After Michelle got the horse stopped, he secured Peanuts to the rail. Then he went around to the driver's side to help Michelle out, but by the time he got there, she'd already stepped down.

"I'm glad to see you." Ezekiel resisted the urge to pull her into his arms. With customers coming and going from the greenhouse and family members taking turns up at the house to eat their lunch, hugging Michelle in broad daylight wouldn't be appropriate.

"I'm glad to see you too." She looked up at him, then glanced off to the left when two fluffy cats darted out of the barn.

"Would you like to come inside and have lunch with me? We can share my ham sandwich."

Michelle shook her head. "I ate at the Lapps' before Willis and Mary Ruth took off with his horse and buggy for town. They had several errands to run."

"Okay, well, at least come inside out of the cold. We can talk while I eat my lunch."

With only a slight hesitation, Michelle began walking toward the house. Once inside, she took off her jacket and hung it over the back of a chair at the kitchen table. "Is anyone else here right now?" she questioned.

"You mean, any of my family?"

"Yeah."

Ezekiel shook his head. "It's my turn for lunch, while everyone else works in the greenhouse. When I get back to work, Mom and Amy will come up and eat."

"Something smells really good in here." Tipping her head back, she sniffed. "There's a hint of cinnamon in the air."

"Mom baked homemade sticky buns this morning. Would you like one with something hot to drink?"

"No thanks. Since you're busy today, I won't take up much of your time." Michelle took a seat at the table. "I'm here to give you my answer about joining the Amish church."

Ezekiel's hands felt clammy, and he resisted the urge to pace. "I'm glad you've reached a decision." He sat down in the chair beside her, rubbing both palms against his pants legs. "Can I just say something before you give me your answer?"

"Of course."

"No matter what you have decided, it won't make any difference in the way I feel about you." Ezekiel swiped his tongue across his parched lips. "Even if we can't be together as boyfriend and girl-friend, I'd like to still be your friend." He leaned back in his chair.

She gave him a dimpled smile. "Is that all you wanted to say?"

"Jah."

"Okay, now it's my turn." Michelle touched her pink cheeks and exhaled. "After much thought and prayer, I've come to the conclusion that I do want to join the Amish church. So if you'll promise to help me through the transition, I'll take the necessary classes with you."

"I'm so glad." Ezekiel glanced around to be sure none of his family had come into the house. Then he leaned closer to Michelle and gave her a quick, but meaningful kiss. "You won't regret it, I promise. We will do this together, and I'll support you in every way."

Michelle gave the side of his face a gentle stroke with her thumb. "Danki."

He felt an unexpected release of tension throughout his body. "You're welcome."

They sat smiling at each other, until Michelle pushed back her chair and stood. "I need to let you eat so you can get back to work. Besides, I promised to do a few chores for Willis and Mary Ruth while they're shopping in town. So I'd better be on my way."

"Okay. I'll see you on Sunday. Oh, and don't forget to get there early. Our first class will begin thirty minutes before the church service starts."

"Don't worry. I'll be there in plenty of time."

After Michelle headed out the door, Ezekiel got up and watched out the window until her horse and buggy were out of sight. Then he closed his eyes and sent up a heartfelt prayer. *Thank You, Lord, for giving Michelle the desire and courage to pursue an Amish way of life. I also want to thank You for giving me hope that I might have a lifelong future with her.*

Ezekiel turned from the window and went to the refrigerator. He felt ever so thankful she had agreed to take classes in readiness for church membership. Once they'd both gotten baptized and became members, Ezekiel would be free to ask Michelle to marry him.

❧

Since no one else was home and Sara didn't have to go to work until the afternoon, she decided to go back to the basement and look at the old jar filled with paper notes again. She was eager to find out what some of the others might say. Maybe something in one of them would give her a clue as to who the author of those notes might be.

Slipping on a sweater and holding the battery-operated lantern, Sara made her way down the creaky wooden steps, holding tightly with the other hand to the shaky handrail. As her feet touched the cement floor, the shelf where the laundry soap, bleach, and stain removers were kept came into view. A pile of old rags lay on another shelf, along with a box of matches and several rolls of paper towels.

The groan of a shifting wooden beam, and an unidentifiable scratching noise, set shivers up her spine. *Sure hope I don't encounter any mice down here.*

Sara held the light in front of her, shining it to the right, to the left, down on the floor, and up toward the ceiling. She didn't like dark, damp places, but her desire to find what other messages were in that old jar took precedence over her fears.

Sara made her way over to the shelves. "Eww. . ." After walking into a clingy web, she wiped her face, then ran her fingers through her hair and down over her clothing. "I hope there was no spider in that web." The idea of it crawling on her somewhere made Sara cringe.

When she reached the shelf where the empty canning jars were located, Sara held the lantern higher until the antique jar came into view. The old, bubbled glass was a light seafoam green. The lid on top of the jar looked like tarnished silver. Funny she hadn't noticed those details when she'd seen the jar before. *Could this be a different one, or am I seeing the jar more clearly today?*

After unscrewing the lid, and laying it on the wooden table near the antiquated washing machine, Sara shook the jar, in an attempt to read a different message than she had the last time.

Sara reached in and took out a piece of paper that had been folded twice. After smoothing out the creases, she read the message out loud. "Life's situations can become an opportunity for transformation."

*Transformation to what?* Sara wondered. *Who wrote this, and what does it mean?*

She pondered the words a few more seconds before taking out and reading another slip of paper. This one had a Bible verse on it: " 'To whom ye forgive any thing, I forgive also: for if I forgave any thing, to whom I forgave it, for your sakes forgave I it in the person of Christ.'"

There it was again—that word "forgiveness." Sara pursed her lips. *I don't see why it's so important for people to forgive. When a person's done wrong, it's only human to feel angry or hold a grudge. I am not doing anything mean, or trying to punish those who have hurt me, so I don't understand why I need to forgive.*

Hearing footsteps from the room above, Sara hastily put the papers back in the jar, closed the lid, and returned the jar to its shelf. She was certain Mary Ruth and Willis couldn't be back from town this soon, so it must be Michelle she'd heard upstairs. *Maybe I'll stay down here with the cobwebs and spiders awhile longer. It would be better than facing her right now.*

# Chapter 11

During supper that evening, Sara toyed with her chicken and dumplings as she listened to Michelle tell Grandpa and Grandma about her visit with Ezekiel and how she'd decided to prepare for joining the Amish church in the spring.

*Why is she doing this?* Sara wondered. *What reason could Michelle possibly have for becoming Amish? She must have some ulterior motive—something that goes beyond wanting to be with her boyfriend.*

Sara picked up her glass of water and took a drink. *By becoming Amish, Michelle might hope she can get even closer to Grandpa and Grandma, and perhaps even gain something from them. But what could it be? Their attention? Love? Support? Or could she be hoping to someday receive an inheritance from their estate?* From what Sara understood, the imposter didn't own anything but the clothes on her back. *Yes, I'll bet she is after something.*

Sara's jaw clenched as she set her glass down a little too hard, and some water splashed out by her plate. She grabbed a napkin and wiped it up before anyone noticed her annoyance. *If Michelle goes through with her plan to join the Amish church, it'll drive an even bigger wedge between us.*

Sara breathed deeply, trying to squelch her agitation as she listened to more of Michelle's plans. *Wish I didn't feel this way. Am I jealous because Michelle got to know my grandparents first and she spent all those weeks with them, as they drew close to her? I have the right to feel this way. It should have been me instead of Michelle they picked up at the bus station in Philly that day. I am the real granddaughter, and yet here she is.*

It perturbed Sara whenever she heard Michelle speak Pennsylvania Dutch, and more so, seeing how much it pleased Grandma and Grandpa. It was obvious that in spite of Michelle's deceitfulness, she had managed to worm her way into their hearts.

Sara's fingers dug into her palms. *I have Mom to blame for this. It's because of her that I feel so defeated and mistrusting. If only she'd been honest with me.*

Feeling a need to get the topic off Michelle and onto something else, Sara mentioned the accident she and Ezekiel had witnessed in front of the flower shop yesterday. "You should have seen how angry one of the men got. I thought for a while he might hit the other guy."

"That isn't the way an Amish man would have acted, is it?" Michelle looked at Sara's grandfather.

He shook his head. "Hopefully not. Getting angry and shouting at someone when an accident occurs is not the way to handle things."

"Nor is it the Christian thing to do," Grandma put in.

"Some people, like my ex-boyfriend, are full of anger, and you never know what might set them off." Michelle's voice cracked. "I never should have gotten involved with Jerry. He was a loser and an abuser. I'm glad to be shed of him."

Grandma placed her hand on Michelle's arm and gave it a few pats. "You've been through a lot, but that's all in the past. You have a new future to look forward to now."

If the pretender was telling the truth, and not making things up in order to prey on Grandma and Grandpa's sympathies, then Sara couldn't help feeling a bit sorry for her, because no one deserved to be abused. But if Michelle made up the story about the angry boyfriend in an attempt to get pity, then shame on her.

It was hard to know what to believe where the auburn-haired woman was concerned. Sara wished she could come right out and question Michelle's motives. But she wouldn't say anything in front of her grandparents. She would, however, keep a close eye on Michelle and make sure she didn't do anything to hurt Grandpa or Grandma ever again.

As they continued with supper, Mary Ruth glanced at her husband, wondering if he had noticed Sara's demeanor at the table this evening. Their granddaughter was clearly uneasy around Michelle and had not been her friendly self since she returned here before Thanksgiving. *No doubt our precious granddaughter feels threatened by Michelle's presence in this house, even though I have tried to reassure Sara that our love for her hasn't changed because Michelle's come back and is here with us.*

Willis didn't appear to notice Sara's pinched expression when Michelle shared her news about joining the Amish church. He seemed pleased with the idea and kept his focus on the chicken dumplings rather than paying attention to Sara's response to the information Michelle had shared with them. Nor had he said much, other than his one comment when Sara changed the subject to the accident that had taken place outside of the florist's.

Mary Ruth forked a piece of tender chicken into her mouth. *Is my husband oblivious to what's still going on between Sara and Michelle? Maybe men don't take note of such things, the way we womenfolk do.*

She glanced at Willis again, but he didn't seem to notice. *Or maybe he's choosing to ignore it, hoping things will work out between the young women without our further interference. I've spoken to Sara once and he talked with Michelle, so it's time for me to take a step back and give the situation to God.* Mary Ruth blotted her lips with a napkin. *If Sara's attitude toward Michelle doesn't improve by Christmas, I will talk to her again, because this can't go on indefinitely.*

### Clarks Summit

Seated at the table in the kitchen of his apartment, Brad reflected on when he was a boy and had visited this area with his folks. Clarks Summit, with its four dams called Cobbs, Fords, Interlaken, and the Summit Lake Dam, was a great vacation spot. He recalled how his family liked to come up on a warm sunny day and visit one of the four reservoirs to cool off. His mom would pack up food for lunch, and Dad brought a portable barbecue along with some folding chairs.

While eating his supper, Brad decided to check in with his parents to see how things were going. He had been praying for them and hoped things had improved.

"Hey, Mom, how are you doing?" Brad put his cell phone on speaker so he could eat his evening meal and talk at the same time.

"Better. My cough's subsiding, and I have more energy."

"Good to hear." Brad twirled some noodles on a fork and slurped up some spaghetti, then washed it down with milk from his glass.

"Are you eating, dear? I don't want to interrupt your supper."

"No, it's okay. My phone's on speaker so I can eat while I'm talking with you, no problem."

"Did you have a nice Thanksgiving?"

"It was all right. I ate at a local restaurant. It wasn't like your good home-cooked meals, but I survived."

"Sorry you had to be alone. It was a bad time for me to get the flu."

"It's okay, Mom. You didn't get sick on purpose."

"That's for sure. So how are things going there with your studies?" she asked.

"The course I'm taking now is tough, but I'll get through it." Brad put another forkful of spaghetti in his mouth and ate it before speaking again. "I'm sure looking forward to Christmas break though. I need some downtime and a chance to rest my tired brain. Also, it'll be nice to spend a little time with you and Dad."

There was a pause. His mother cleared her throat. "Umm. . . About Christmas. . ."

"What about Christmas, Mom?"

"I heard from my sister today, and she's scheduled to have a hysterectomy two days before Christmas."

"So you're going to Seattle to be with her." Brad finished his mother's sentence.

"Yes, I need to be there. As you know, your aunt Marlene has been all alone since her husband died a year ago, and she can't take care of herself when she comes home from the hospital. I will probably need to stay for several weeks past Christmas."

"I understand. Will Dad be going with you?"

"He will, but only for part of the time. He'll stay through the holiday, but when he needs to return to work, he'll fly home." Her voice faltered. "I feel terrible about leaving you alone on Christmas. You'd be welcome to go with us to Seattle, but I'm sure there are other places you'd rather be for the holidays."

Brad took another drink from his glass. "Actually, I had planned on spending some of my Christmas break in Lancaster County. I'm sure if I let them know ahead of time that I'll be in the area, my Amish friends Willis and Mary Ruth Lapp will invite me for Christmas dinner. At least I hope that's the case, because I'd sure like to see them again."

"Are you sure it's not their granddaughter you're eager to see? From what you mentioned in one of our phone calls this past summer, you and Sara were sort of dating."

"We did see each other socially a few times," he admitted, "but she's not the right girl for me."

"How do you know?"

Brad lifted his gaze to the ceiling. *I shouldn't have told Mom anything. Now she'll pester me to death if I don't tell her everything—or at least what I think she wants to know.*

"For one thing, Mom, I don't believe Sara's a Christian."

"Ah, I see. You were wise not to get serious about her then."

"Yes. Besides, I had a hunch she was interested in a young Amish man in Strasburg. Sara hung out with Ezekiel quite a bit." Brad reached for a napkin and wiped his mouth. "Before I left for seminary, I wrote Sara a letter saying goodbye and that I wished her well and would be praying for her."

"Sounds to me like your dad and I raised a smart man. With your plans to become a minister, the last thing you need is to be married to a nonbeliever. But then, I have to ask: Would Ezekiel be interested in her if she doesn't believe in God? And also, if Sara is not a Christian, how is it she would be interested in an Amish man? Aren't most Amish people Christians?"

"The ones I know sure are. But that's something Ezekiel will have to work out with her, if he's interested."

"Oh, sorry, Brad. Your dad just came in the door, so I need to get supper on the table. I fixed his favorite spaghetti with marinara sauce."

Brad chuckled. "That's what I'm eating right now too. Only my meal isn't homemade. It came out of a can."

"Oh my. Those meals in a can aren't that healthy."

"I know, but I have a lot of studying to do yet this evening, so I didn't have time to cook anything from scratch."

"Someday you'll meet the right woman who will not only cook you well-balanced meals, but she'll also be a helpmate in your ministry."

"Yes, if I'm meant to get married, God will send the right woman, and I will know it without a doubt. And now, Mom, I'd better let you go or I'll soon hear Dad grumbling."

She snickered. "Take care, Brad, and safe travels to the Lancaster area when you go. Oh, and please stay in touch."

"I will, and you do the same. Please let me know when you get to Seattle, and I'd appreciate a report on how Aunt Marlene is doing. And remember," he added, "I'll be praying for your sister, as well as for you and Dad, as you travel to Washington state."

When Mom hung up, Brad clicked off his phone. As he grasped his fork to finish his meal, a vision of Sara popped into his head. He had to admit he'd been attracted to her pretty auburn hair, blue-green eyes, and slender figure. But looks weren't everything, and unless she'd come to know the Lord since he last saw her, Brad would not allow himself to get involved with Sara again. He would, however, call and leave a message for the Lapps, letting them know he planned to be in their area over Christmas vacation. He also needed to call his friend, Ned Evans, whom he had shared an apartment with while attending college in Lancaster before coming to seminary. Hopefully, Ned wouldn't mind if he stayed with him for two weeks. It would be like old times.

# Chapter 12

*Strasburg*

Michelle gazed at the plain blue dress lying on the end of her bed. It was hard to believe the frock was hers. For the last two weeks Mary Ruth had been giving Michelle sewing lessons, and last night she'd finished hemming the Amish dress she had made mostly by herself. It would be the first of several, because one plain dress in her closet was not enough.

Michelle was still amazed at the idea of having to sew dresses to be used for different occasions. She would need clothes for church, work, and someday maybe her own wedding attire.

*I shouldn't jump too quickly on that idea,* she told herself. *I've got a lot to overcome first, and Ezekiel hasn't proposed to me yet either.* She giggled and stifled it with her hand. *But it's hard not to get excited, especially at the thought of accomplishing my goal.*

Since Michelle had made up her mind to join the Amish church, she figured it was best if she wore Amish clothes from now on. No more makeup, jewelry, or ponytails for her either. During the day, Michelle's hair would be worn in a bun at the back of her head, with a white, heart-shaped covering on top. For work around the house or chores outside, Michelle would wear a dark-colored scarf on her head. Only at night would her hair be let down.

For some reason, images of Michelle's biological parents, Herb and Ginny Taylor, popped into her mind. *If my real parents could see me now, wouldn't they be surprised? But then, with the kind of life they lived, maybe they're no longer alive.* Her mouth twisted grimly. *I know one thing: they couldn't have cared less when that woman from child services took me and my brothers away. They all but shoved us out the door. And what's even worse, we ended up in different foster homes, never to see each other again.*

It angered Michelle whenever she thought of her so-called parents and how they could have ruined her life if she'd continued living with them. "But you didn't get the chance to mess up my brother's and my lives any more than you did." Michelle spoke as if they were standing right in front of her. Thinking of Ernie and Jack made her feel sad. *I pray they're okay. It's not likely, but maybe someday our paths will cross.*

Switching her thoughts back to the current situation, Michelle didn't mind the idea of wearing Amish dresses, or even using a horse and buggy as her main mode of transportation. What bothered her most was the language barrier. Although Mary Ruth, Willis, and Ezekiel had promised to work with Michelle on learning the Pennsylvania Dutch language, she still doubted her abilities.

*I wonder if Sara will ever decide to join the Amish church,* Michelle thought as she slipped the dress on over her head. *Since her mother grew up in an Amish home, I would think she might be inclined in that direction.* Sara had never mentioned the idea in Michelle's presence, but then Sara said as little as possible to Michelle.

Michelle put the blind up and stood a few feet from the window. Seeing her image reflected in the glass, she used it like a full-length mirror. It wasn't fully daylight yet, so she could see herself pretty well. Michelle turned at different angles to see how she looked in the Amish dress. It might take a little getting used to, but she liked it. *It fits me well, like it was custom made, and it feels comfortable to wear.* Michelle slipped on the apron and tied it in the back.

Mary Ruth had done a wonderful job helping her measure correctly and making sure it all went together as it should. At times it was still difficult for Michelle not to call Mary Ruth "Grandma," because she made her feel like part of the family.

*The fact is Sara has that complete right, not me.* Sighing, Michelle picked up her brush and worked through all the tangles in her hair. Then she pulled her hair back into a bun, making sure the sides were twisted the way Mary Ruth and other Lancaster Amish women wore theirs. *I wonder if others will think I fit in.* She glanced at her reflection in the mirror on her dresser and shook her head. *Why am I filled with so much self-doubt? If only I could be more confident, like Sara. She seems so self-assured.*

Hoping to keep her nervousness from showing, Michelle drew a quick breath, opened her bedroom door, and started down the stairs.

~⁊~

Sara took out a frying pan and put just enough coconut oil in the bottom to keep the eggs she would soon be frying from sticking. She'd come down earlier than usual to help start breakfast, wanting a few moments alone with her grandmother before Michelle showed up. "Since I've only been working at the flower shop two weeks, it's going to be a while before I have enough money saved up to rent an apartment in town," she said, looking at Grandma, who had taken a pan of biscuits from the oven. Her glasses had steamed over from the moist, hot pan of food.

Grandma's nose crinkled as she squinted at Sara over the top of her glasses. "And you know, dear one, we've had this discussion before. You should realize by now that your grandpa and I would be disappointed if you moved out of our house anytime soon. We haven't had a chance to really get to know you." Grandma took out some flour for making gravy.

It hadn't taken Sara long to learn that biscuits and gravy were one of Grandpa's favorite things to have with his scrambled eggs. "I won't be moving anytime soon. I promise."

Grandma's mouth opened like she was about to say more, but Michelle entered the room. Sara's grandmother placed her hands against her cheeks and made a little gasping noise. "*Ach*, Michelle—you look so Amish in that dress." She glanced at Sara, while gesturing to Michelle. "Didn't she do a nice job making it?"

Without speaking, Sara nodded. It was hard to understand why Grandma and Grandpa got so excited over every little thing Michelle did.

She reached for the egg carton near the stove. *I still feel sometimes that they care more about Michelle than they do me. Is it because they've known her longer, or is it her personality they enjoy?*

When Grandpa came in from outside, Sara put her thoughts to rest until he made a comment about Michelle's dress. "Well now, don't you look nice this morning, Michelle. If I was basing it on your appearance only, I'd believe you were already one of us."

"Danki." Michelle's cheeks reddened. "I hope I don't look too *lecherich.*"

Grandma shook her head. "Of course you don't look ridiculous. You look like a pretty young Amish woman."

Sara resisted the urge to give a negative comment and kept her focus on the eggs she'd begun breaking into the pan. This morning, she would scramble them as they cooked. To her way of thinking, Michelle was looking for a compliment—something to make her feel good about herself. *Well, she's not going to get any compliments from me.*

Sara wished she could find something about Michelle that she liked, but the longer they both lived here, the more things the imposter did to irritate her. And the way her grandparents had accepted Michelle without question made it even more difficult for Sara.

Grandpa removed his straw hat and placed it on a wall peg. "Not to change the subject or anything, but I just came from the phone shack, and there was a message from Brad Fuller."

Michelle turned her head in Grandpa's direction. "What did he say?"

"Said he'll be in the area for Christmas and wants to spend some time with us while he's here." He looked over at Grandma. "If Brad doesn't have any other plans, should we invite him to eat with us on Christmas Day?"

"Of course." Grandma bobbed her head. "It will be nice to see him again and find out how things are going with his ministerial studies." She turned toward Michelle. "I imagine Brad will be *verschtaunt* to see that you're back living with us again and have decided to become Amish."

Michelle shook her head. "He won't be surprised that I'm living here, because as far as he knows, I never left."

"Oh, that's right." Grandma gestured to Michelle's dress. "But he won't expect to see you wearing that, and Brad will likely be pleased when he learns of your decision to join the Amish church."

"I hope so." Michelle moved slowly across the kitchen. "I'm looking forward to seeing Brad again, because I have so much to tell him about how I've changed since we last saw each other."

The discussion going on caused Sara to recall the letter she'd gotten from a man named Brad. She assumed it was the same person they were talking about and couldn't help wondering what he was like. Sara had made no mention of the letter to Michelle, since she'd thrown it away when she returned to her duplex back in October. And she saw no reason to bring it up now.

❧

"You're sure in good spirits today, Son," Ezekiel's mother commented as she placed a bowl of oatmeal in front of him and took her seat at the table. "What's that big smile you're wearing about?"

"Jah," Dad put in. "For the last couple of weeks I've heard you whistling a lot. This morning, during chores, it sounded like you were serenading the horses." He chuckled.

A wave of heat rushed to Ezekiel's face. He wished he didn't blush so easily. "One reason I'm happy is because I'll be seeing Michelle this evening. We're going out to supper." He shifted his position on the chair. "But the main thing that has put me in a good mood is the decision Michelle made two weeks ago."

Mom tipped her head. "What was that?"

"To go Amish. She took her first instruction class with me a week ago, Sunday."

"I didn't realize she was part of that class," Ezekiel's sister Amy interjected.

"Neither did I." Mom's fingers moved slowly as she touched

the neckline of her dress. "What is her reason for wanting to join our church?"

"She feels it's the right thing for her—same as me." Ezekiel touched his chest. "After my encounter with those fellows up in Harrisburg who roughed me up, I realized the English world that I'd thought I wanted to be a part of is not for me."

"Are you sayin' that all English people are bad?" Ezekiel's twelve-year-old brother Henry questioned.

"No, not at all. There are many good people among the English." Ezekiel reached for the bowl of brown sugar and added some to his oatmeal. "It was when those guys were calling me names and making fun of me being Amish that my eyes were opened. I'm not ashamed of my heritage, and I don't want to separate myself from the people in my life who are special to me."

"Since you haven't joined the church yet you wouldn't be shunned if you went English," Abe said.

"I know that. I just wanna be Amish. Is that all right with you?" Ezekiel spoke louder, to make sure he had gotten his point across.

Dad held up his hand. "Okay, boys. . . Let's not start a discussion that might end up in an argument this morning." He looked over at Ezekiel. "Before we pray and start eating, I would like to ask you a question."

"Sure, Dad." Ezekiel sat with both hands in his lap.

"Is Michelle hoping you will marry her? Is that why she's so eager to join our church?"

Feeling like a bird trapped in a cage, Ezekiel's gaze traveled from his mother, to his three siblings, and then back to his father. "I—I don't believe that's the reason she wants to become Amish, since I've made no mention of marriage to her." He reached up and rubbed the back of his ever-warming neck. "But the truth is, I do want to marry her. And someday, when the time is right, I will propose marriage."

All eyes widened, and his mother's mouth turned down at the corners. "Oh Son, I hope you'll give that some serious consideration. Michelle was not raised Amish, and she doesn't think the way we all do." Deep wrinkles formed across Mom's forehead. "But my biggest concern with your interest in her goes well beyond that."

Ezekiel leaned slightly forward. "What do you mean?" He was glad none of his siblings had joined the conversation. They all sat quietly in their seats.

"That lie she told to the Lapps about being their grand-daughter. . ." Mom blinked her eyes. "If Michelle is capable of hurting two kind and generous people like Willis and Mary Ruth, then there's no telling what she might say or do to disappoint you or someone else."

"People can change, you know," Ezekiel said. "And I firmly believe that Michelle has had a change of heart. She's apologized to the Lapps, and also confessed her sin to God. So don't you think you oughta give her a chance, just like the Lapps have done?"

Mom took a drink of water and set her glass back on the table. "Whether she's changed or not remains to be seen." She looked over at Dad. "Should we say our prayers?"

"Of course." Dad bowed his head, and everyone else did the same.

Ezekiel's silent prayer was only a few words: *Lord, I pray that you will help my folks—particularly Mom—see Michelle for the wonderful person she truly is.*

# Chapter 13

O h look! It's snowing!" Michelle pointed out the living-room window. "I hope it sticks and we end up with a white Christmas. Isn't this exciting?" She glanced in Sara's direction, but the Lapps' granddaughter didn't look up from the book she was reading as she lay stretched out on the couch. Today was Monday—Sara's day off from working at the flower shop—and she'd acted kind of tired all morning.

Michelle pursed her lips. *Didn't Sara hear what I said, or is she ignoring me on purpose? How much longer will she carry a grudge against me?* In Michelle's eyes, it seemed like nothing she said or did around Sara was right. *Guess I should be used to it, but by now, I'd hoped for a different outcome.*

Michelle pressed her nose against the window's cold glass and blew her breath, watching it steam up. *I won't let Sara bring me down.* Michelle encouraged herself with the pleasure of watching the lightweight feathery snowflakes float slowly to the ground. Then she drew a smiley face before wiping the glass clean.

Ever since Michelle had announced that she wanted to become Amish and had begun wearing plain clothes, Sara's attitude toward her had become even colder. It didn't make sense. *Why should she care that I've decided to join the Amish church?* Michelle asked herself.

Sighing, she moved away from the window. "Think I'll go down to the basement and tell Mary Ruth it's snowing. I also want to see if she needs my help with the laundry."

"I already asked, and she said no." Sara lifted her head from the pillow. "But go ahead if you want to. Maybe she'll accept *your* help."

Ignoring Sara's sarcastic tone, Michelle left the room and headed for the basement. Whether Mary Ruth allowed her to help with the laundry or not, at least her company would be more pleasant than Sara's.

Before going downstairs, Michelle stopped in the kitchen to get a drink of water. Leaning against the counter, she took a deep breath. *Sometimes I wish I could move out and get a place of my own. It's hard being in the same house with Sara.*

Without coming out and actually saying so, Sara had been relentless in reminding Michelle how she felt. Her actions spoke louder than words. Sara's grandparents had accepted Michelle's apology, but it was obvious Sara was not ready to forgive Michelle for what she had done.

*I need to get a job before I can move out. But since I have no car or horse and buggy, I'd have to find a place to live in that's close enough to walk to my job and to wherever church is being held, since I'm now taking classes with Ezekiel. Guess I'll have to stay put awhile longer and quit feeling sorry for myself.*

Michelle's thoughts went to the first Sunday class she'd taken with Ezekiel. The group consisted of ten young people, made up of mostly young women, but there were four men who were no doubt ready for marriage. One fella seemed older than the others. He was there with a younger woman whose resemblance to him was uncanny. Michelle figured she must be his sister or cousin. She liked how the classes and church were held on Sundays. It wasn't as bad as she'd thought it would be either. The instructional lessons were based on what the Amish called the Dordrecht Confession of Faith. It was an important statement of the Amish faith that had been written in the Netherlands in 1632. The ministers who were present during the class encouraged the youth and exhorted them to study the complete articles of faith and the scriptures that supported each one. Two articles per Sunday were used, as well as Bible stories of faithful patriarchs. On that first Sunday, those in the class learned about article 1, "Of Faith in God and the Creation," as well as article 2, "Of the Transgression by Adam of the Divine Command."

The one thing that stood out the most in Michelle's mind was that without faith it was impossible to please God, and that those who came to God must believe there is a God and that He is a rewarder of those who seek Him.

Reflecting on her desire to please God, Michelle decided that she needed to pray for her parents, and perhaps even make an effort to contact them. While she had no desire to go back home, letting them know where she was and what her plans were for the future would be the right thing to do. There was also a chance that if she talked to her mom or dad, they might know what happened to Ernie and Jack.

On the second Sunday of classes, they were taught article 3, "Of the Restoration and Reconciliation of the Human Race with God," and article 4, "Of the Coming of our Redeemer and Savior Jesus Christ."

It was also a comfort knowing Ezekiel was taking the classes. While Michelle understood most of what had been said, it had been more difficult to deal with some of the curious stares from the others in the class.

*I'm not giving up,* she told herself. *People can stare all they want.* Michelle sighed, allowing her thoughts to return to the present. *Guess I feel the same about Sara and won't surrender to her either. Maybe someday she'll understand the situation I was in that made me do that deceitful thing.*

Before heading downstairs, Michelle glanced out the kitchen window and a smile formed on her lips. *I hope it keeps snowing. It's so pretty when everything gets covered in white.*

As Brad entered the town of Strasburg, the sight of several horse and buggies heading in the opposite direction brought a smile to his lips. He was definitely back in Amish country, and happy to be on his way to the Lapps'. While Christmas was still a few days away, he'd decided to stop by their place to say hello and deliver a gift before heading over to Ned's apartment. Willis and Mary

Ruth's home wasn't too far out of the way, and he was eager to see how they were doing. The couple had always treated Brad with genuine warmth. He couldn't help being drawn to their open-hearted kindness.

"I'd say the world would be a better place if there were more people in it like Willis and Mary Ruth Lapp," Brad said out loud, before slowing down to avoid hitting a dog. Fortunately, after he honked his horn, the mutt moved out of the way.

"People should keep their dogs in the yard," he muttered. "It's not safe for them to get out in the road."

After driving several more blocks, Brad turned his vehicle off the main road and headed farther out to the country. Snowflakes had begun to fall, and he turned on his windshield wipers to whisk them away. The roads were still bare, and hopefully would remain that way until later when he headed to Ned's place.

"Snow for Christmas would be kind of nice." Grinning, he sang "Jingle Bells," followed by "White Christmas." By the time Brad reached the Lapps' driveway, he was definitely in the Christmas spirit.

He parked his van near the barn, got out, and started for the house. Then, remembering the Christmas cactus he'd picked up before leaving Clarks Summit, he ran back to the vehicle. Brad had opened the door on the passenger's side when Willis stepped out of the barn.

"Howdy, Brad. Sure good to see you." Willis stepped up to Brad and gave him a hearty handshake. Snowflakes landed on Willis's hat, turning the brim and top white.

"It's great to see you too." Brad looked around. "Are Mary Ruth and Sara inside?"

"Yes, and so is Michelle. I have a few more things to take care of in the barn, but why don't you go ahead to the house? When I come in we can sit down and talk awhile."

"Sounds good." Brad had no idea who Michelle was or why Willis had mentioned her. He assumed she must be a friend or some relative he hadn't met before. "Before I go in though, do you need some assistance with your chores in the barn? I'd be happy to help with anything."

Willis shook his head. "Thank you, but it's nothing I can't handle myself. Besides, you've been driving a few hours and probably should relax awhile. You go on ahead. I'm sure the ladies will be glad to see you."

"All right then. I'll see you in a bit." Carrying the cactus, Brad made his way up to the house. He stepped onto the front porch and knocked on the door. When it opened, a beautiful young woman with long blond hair looked at him with a curious expression. He figured she must be Michelle.

"May I help you?" she asked.

"Yeah, I'm here to see Sara and Mary Ruth. Willis said they were both in the house."

The young woman tilted her head to the right. "I'm Sara, and Mary Ruth is in the basement with her other houseguest. Would you like me to call her?"

Brad scratched the side of his head. "You said your name is Sara?"

"That's right."

"Are there two women named Sara here today?"

"No, just one." She pointed to herself. "I'm Sara Murray—Willis and Mary Ruth's granddaughter."

"Huh?" With a jerk of his head, Brad's mind raced, searching for answers but finding none. This made no sense. Had Willis set this up to play a trick on him? Mary Ruth's husband was full of wit, but how could he have known Brad would be stopping by here today? As far as Willis knew, Brad wasn't coming to their house until Christmas Day.

The pretty blond's blue eyes seemed to bore into him. "The Lapps are my grandparents, but since it appears you don't believe me, I'll get my grandmother. Please, wait here on the porch." She closed the door so quickly, Brad felt a *whoosh* of air.

He shuffled over to the wooden bench on the covered porch, set the plant on the small table next to the bench, and sat down. *Wish I would've brought a pair of gloves with me.*

Pulling his coat collar up closer around his neck, then blowing on his cold hands, Brad felt more confused than ever. *How can that woman's name be Sara Murray? It has to be some kind of a joke.*

After a few minutes, the front door opened. This time, he was greeted by Mary Ruth. "Oh dear. I'm sorry you were left out here in the cold. When Sara said someone was waiting on the porch to see me, I had no idea it was you." She stepped out, and when Brad stood up, Mary Ruth gave him a hug. "We didn't expect you until next week, on Christmas Day."

"Right." Brad bent down and picked up the cactus. "I came into town a few days early, and since I'd bought this for you, I decided to drop by before going to my friend Ned's place."

She looked up, offering him one of her sweet smiles. "I'm glad you did. Now please come inside out of the cold. The way it's snowing right now, the flakes are beginning to blow in on the porch."

"Yeah, you're right." Brad followed Mary Ruth into the house and handed her the plant. The house was pleasantly warm and just as inviting as he remembered. It made him wish the snow would fall a little harder so he could stay.

"Thank you, Brad. This is a lovely cactus, and it was so thoughtful of you." She placed it on the table in the entryway. "Come into the living room now. Sara is waiting there, and I'd like to introduce her to you."

Brad raised his eyebrows but remained silent. *Why would Mary Ruth need to introduce me to Sara? After all the time I spent with her this summer, I should know Sara pretty well by now. Could Mary Ruth be in on the little charade Willis set up?*

When Brad entered the living room, he was surprised to see the blond-haired woman who had claimed to be Sara sitting on the couch.

"Brad, this is our granddaughter Sara." Mary Ruth gestured to the young woman, then motioned to him. "Sara, this is Brad Fuller. As we mentioned before, he will be our guest for Christmas dinner."

"But I thought. . ." He quickly ended his comment. Holding his earlobe between his thumb and index finger, Brad gave it a tug.

He was about to ask if Mary Ruth was teasing him, when a woman with auburn hair, wearing an Amish dress and a white *kapp* on her head, entered the room.

"Oh Brad, you came early." She came slowly toward him.

He stared at her in disbelief. It was Sara—the one he'd gotten to know this past summer.

"I need to confess something. My name isn't Sara Murray— it's Michelle Taylor." Her eyes glistened with tears as she pointed to the blond-haired woman. "She's the real Sara, and I–I'm an imposter. At least, I was when you thought I was her."

Brad's muscles tightened and his head jerked back. He was speechless. Apparently this was no joke. He, however, felt like a fool. How could this woman who'd pretended to be the Lapps' granddaughter have pulled the wool over his eyes? *I'm a smart man,* Brad told himself. *I should have sensed she was lying to me. And what about the Lapps? How did they feel when they found out the truth?*

From the affection Brad saw on Mary Ruth's face as she looked at Michelle, he realized there was no displeasure. If he were being honest with himself, Brad had to admit there had always been this feeling about the young woman named Michelle that hadn't seemed right. It was as though she'd been hiding something, yet he couldn't discern what it was. He'd let his guard down and had foolishly been taken in by her. He should have gone with his gut instinct and asked the right questions or probed deeper into her personal life.

Brad pressed his lips tightly together, lest he say the wrong thing. Now it all made sense. He felt a mixture of betrayal and anger. And on top of his frustration with Michelle, here sat the real Sara Murray, and he had no idea what to say to either of them. The way Sara sat with her arms folded, he doubted she wanted to talk at all. But Brad couldn't leave until he had some answers. Not only about the reason Michelle had lied to him, but he wanted to know why she was dressed in Amish clothes.

# Chapter 14

Sara sat on the couch, too stunned to say a word. *So this is the same man who sent that letter to Michelle, thinking she was my grandparents' granddaughter. Brad was completely in the dark about Michelle's deceit. No wonder he looks so confused and somewhat disturbed. Poor guy.*

"I—I should go," Brad mumbled, shuffling toward the front door. "I need time to think about all of this."

"Wait, Brad. Please let me explain." Michelle's voice shook as she clasped his arm.

He stopped walking. "Think I've heard enough."

Grandma stepped forward. "Brad, I think you ought to at least hear her out before you go."

He sank into the closest chair. "Okay, Michelle, you have my undivided attention."

Sara could tell by the way his knee bounced that he'd rather be anyplace but here. She couldn't help feeling sorry for him. The unsuspecting man had been duped, just like she and her grandparents had. But now it was time for him to hear the full story—or at least, Michelle's version of it. *When the pretender finishes telling her side of things, maybe I'll jump in with my part of the story.* She clasped her hands tightly together. *Or maybe it would be best if I kept quiet and let her do all the talking. No matter what Michelle says, unless Brad is gullible, he will surely see her for what she is.*

Sara still couldn't get over all the drama Michelle had caused by pretending to be her. *Why couldn't she have just told Grandma and*

*Grandpa she wasn't their granddaughter when she met them at the bus station in Philly?*

Turning her attention fully on Michelle, Sara watched as she sniffed, then swiped at the tears on her reddened cheeks. She was either fully embarrassed to be forced into confessing her misdeed to Brad, or Michelle had become an actress.

Sara noticed Michelle's obvious discomfort as she leaned slightly forward with her arms held against her chest. No doubt she was using these few extra minutes to think about what she wanted to say.

"My real name is Michelle Taylor, and I'm no relation to Mary Ruth and Willis. I was at the bus station in Philadelphia, needing a place to go, when I met the Lapps, and they assumed I was their granddaughter." Michelle took a seat in the recliner. It was the one Grandpa usually sat in. Then more explanation spilled forth.

"Desperate to get out of Philly, I went along with it and came here with them, pretending I was the woman they'd been looking for." She paused and drew a shaky breath. "I'm sorry for deceiving you, Brad. What I did was wrong, and I hope, like Mary Ruth and Willis did, that you'll find it in your heart to forgive me."

Sara glanced at Brad, waiting for his reaction. Would he be as forgiving as her grandparents had been, or would this man put Michelle in her place? She hoped it would be the latter.

"I forgive you, Michelle." Brad spoke softly. "But I wish you had told me the truth on your own during the time we spent together this past summer."

"I—I wanted to, and I almost did on one occasion, but I was afraid of your response. I was worried it would ruin our friendship, and I was afraid you would tell the Lapps." Michelle blotted the tears on her cheeks. "Also, I'd gotten in so deep with my trail of lies, I didn't know how to get out without hurting someone." She looked at Sara's grandmother. "Especially Mary Ruth and Willis. During the time I was living here, I came to love them and almost felt as if they were actually my grandparents. In the end, it seems I hurt everyone." Michelle glanced in Sara's direction.

Sara grimaced at the sour taste in her mouth. She pressed her lips together to keep from blurting out what she thought. *Nice performance, Michelle.*

"We felt love for Michelle too—when we believed she was Sara, and yes even now," Grandma put in.

Sara could hardly hold her composure. *I knew it. I bet they love her more than me.*

"When did you tell them the truth?" Brad's question was directed at Michelle.

"A few months ago. I had been intercepting Sara's letters, and when her last one came, saying she'd be coming here soon, I realized it was time to go." Michelle lowered her gaze, fingering the ties on her head covering. "I couldn't face Mary Ruth and Willis with the truth, so I took the coward's way out and left a note on the kitchen table, confessing what I'd done. Then I asked one of their drivers to take me to Harrisburg. And that's where I lived till Ezekiel came and talked me into coming back here."

"After she apologized, we invited her to stay with us again." Mary Ruth smiled as she gestured to Michelle. "Now she is preparing to join the Amish church."

Brad's eyebrows lifted. "So that must be why you're wearing an Amish dress."

Michelle nodded. "Ezekiel and I are both planning to join the church in the spring. We've already started taking classes." Her tone was enthusiastic. "He and the Lapps have been helpful with teaching me how to speak the Pennsylvania Dutch language."

"Michelle is a good learner. I think she'll do just fine becoming Amish like us." Mary Ruth's face seemed to radiate with joy.

Sara sat, biting her tongue through all this "Michelle" time. *Please give me strength. . .Oh, how I want to say what's really on my mind about the pretender. I'd like Brad to know how she has pushed her way into my grandparents' lives.* Sara hoped he wasn't taken in by Michelle's sob story.

Brad rubbed the back of his neck. "Well, this is certainly a surprise. I'm happy for you, Michelle."

"Does that mean I'm forgiven for deceiving you?"

"Of course, but I'll admit, I am disappointed you didn't come and talk to me about this when I was here during the summer."

Michelle dropped her gaze. "I know."

At that moment, Grandpa entered the room. "My chores are done." He grinned at Brad. "Now we can sit and visit awhile. I'd like to know how things have been going for you these last few months." He looked at Grandma. "But before we do that, why don't the two of us go to the kitchen and get some coffee and something sweet to serve?"

Grandma rose from her seat. "That's an excellent idea, Willis."

Sara was on the verge of asking if they wanted her help, when Brad turned to her and said, "Sorry if it seemed as though you were being ignored or left out of the conversation since I got here. I'd like the chance to visit with you too."

"Maybe some other time. I have a few things I need to do in my room." She fled the room and raced up the stairs. She needed time by herself to process things. Apparently Brad was taken in by Michelle, like her grandparents were. Sara wondered if there was anything she could have said to make him see what Michelle was really like.

Upstairs in her room, Sara went to the window and opened it, sucking in some much-needed air. Snowflakes blew in onto the window ledge, while others melted onto the floor. She'd never expected Brad would show up, or that he'd be sucked in by Michelle and her excuses.

Sara stood, immersed in thought, continuing to calm herself as she breathed in the fresh, crisp air the opened window allowed. As the snowflakes continued falling and a squirrel scampered through the backyard, she watched this tranquil moment while using her fingers to rub circular motions around her throbbing temples. *I hope Brad finds out for himself what a fake Michelle is. She can't fool everyone forever. Sooner or later the imposter is bound to trip up and someone will finally see through her.*

As Brad sat in the living room, enjoying coffee and some of Mary Ruth's delicious sticky buns, his thoughts went to Sara. She was a beautiful young woman, with shiny blond hair that reminded him of spun gold. But she had been anything but cordial. In fact, throughout his conversation with Michelle, Sara seemed agitated. Could there be something about him she disliked, or was she upset with Michelle for stealing her identity? If that was the case, he couldn't blame her, but then why would she be living here at the Lapps' with Michelle? For that matter, it seemed strange Mary Ruth and Willis would invite Michelle to live here, knowing she had impersonated their granddaughter. Not to mention that the real Sara was here too.

Licking his fingers, Brad reached for another sticky bun.

Michelle giggled and handed him a napkin. "Here, looks like you need this."

"Thanks." Brad's answer was stiff as he watched Michelle's smile slowly fade and her eyes look downward.

He shifted on his chair. *Wish I had a chance to talk to Sara privately. I'd like to know what her thoughts are about Michelle. If she's holding a grudge against her, I might be able to help—or at least offer some support if she needs it.*

"Say, Brad, didn't you hear what I asked?"

Willis's question pulled Brad's thoughts aside. "Uh no. Sorry, I must have spaced out." He turned his attention to Willis. "What did you ask?"

The older man held out the plate of sticky buns. "Wondered if you'd like another one of these."

"No thanks, I'd better not." Brad thumped his stomach. "I've already had two, and if I eat another I'll be too full to join my friend Ned for lunch."

"You could stay and eat here," Mary Ruth suggested. "We'd be happy to have you share our noon meal."

"I appreciate the offer, but I should get going. Ned will probably be wondering why I haven't shown up yet." Glancing out the window, Brad set his coffee cup down and stood. "The snow hasn't let up, so it's probably good I'm leaving now. I'll be back for Christmas dinner though." He grinned at Mary Ruth. "Wouldn't want to miss out on your holiday meal, which I am sure will be delicious."

"You don't have to wait until Christmas to come over," Michelle interjected.

"That's right," Mary Ruth agreed. "Feel free to come over any day you like."

"How about tomorrow?" Willis poured himself another cup of coffee. "Sara will be working at the flower shop in town, but the rest of us will be around."

"I can't say for sure whether I'll be by tomorrow, but it will be soon, I promise." Brad's face radiated heat as he noticed Michelle watching him intently. It looked as if she might say something, but she sat quietly with one hand on her hip.

Brad said his goodbyes, put on his jacket, and went out the door. When he climbed into his van and waited for the engine to warm, he saw Michelle rush out of the house with a shawl around her shoulders, as she ran toward the barn.

*I hope she's okay.* Brad thought to himself. *I probably should have stayed and talked to her more. She's been through quite an ordeal and had a lot of guilt to deal with before she admitted the truth to Mary Ruth and Willis.*

Brad rubbed his hands in front of the vent, where the heat was now flowing. He waited a few minutes longer to see if Michelle would come out of the barn. *Should I go in and talk to her—see if she's upset?* He thumped the steering wheel. *No, I'd better go. If Michelle went there to be alone, she might not appreciate me barging in.*

Brad put the van in reverse and turned toward the road. *Maybe tomorrow I'll take a ride into Strasburg and see if I can find the flower shop where Sara works. If I go shortly before noon, I might be able catch her before she takes a lunch break. There are a few questions I'd like to ask.*

# Chapter 15

*Lancaster, Pennsylvania*

Where you headed, sleepyhead?" Ned asked when Brad grabbed his jacket and slipped it on.

"I'm going to Strasburg. Thought I mentioned it last night before we went to bed."

"If you did, I don't remember." Ned combed his fingers through his thick brown hair. "But then you didn't have a lot to say after you got here. Figured you were tired from the trip, so I didn't ply you with a bunch of questions about how things were going at the seminary or in your personal life. Oh, and since you slept in so late, you totally missed breakfast, and I was going to make you a good one too." He pointed to the frying pan sitting on a hot pad near the stove. "Before you walked into the kitchen, I was about to come knocking on your door. Didn't think you'd want to sleep all day."

"Yeah, I was kinda out of it."

"Did you sleep okay on that new mattress in the other bedroom?"

"It was fine." Brad managed a weak smile. As tired as he was, he hadn't gotten much sleep last night, thinking about the situation with Michelle and Sara. A ton of questions reeled through his head, none of which he had the answer to. Brad saw no point in telling Ned any of that though. "Since I'll be here till New Year's, we'll have a chance to get caught up with each other's lives." He zipped up his jacket.

"Good point." Ned smiled.

"It's okay. I'll be eating lunch soon. And hey, I'll take a raincheck on that breakfast."

"You got it." Ned headed to his desk. "Welp, I have some bills to pay, and I need to get them done and in the mail before noon. You have a nice day, and I'll catch you later."

Brad waved and went out the door. He was eager to get to Strasburg, although unsure of what he would say when he saw Sara.

### Strasburg

Michelle opened her closet door and looked at the English clothes still hanging there. *I should put these in boxes and give them to a thrift store.*

She pulled a blouse off the hanger and held it up to see what shape it was in. This was one of her favorite tops. She enjoyed wearing it for special occasions.

Michelle placed the blouse on the bed and stood back. *But I need to move on, and the only way to do that is to purge all of these English clothes.*

She went back to the closet and removed the rest of her clothes from their hangers. After folding them into piles, she put the items in plastic bags, ready to be taken to the thrift store.

*Now I need to get busy and make more Amish clothes.* Michelle slid the hangers to one end of her closet. She then headed for Mary Ruth's sewing room and took a seat at the treadle machine. As Michelle worked on another plain dress to add to her wardrobe, it felt as if she might be getting the hang of things. *Maybe I won't need to call on Mary Ruth for help so much anymore.*

She'd never expected to enjoy such a simple pleasure as sewing a dress, much less be able to make it herself. She didn't remember her biological mother sewing. And even though Michelle had seen her foster mom at the sewing machine a few times, she'd never volunteered to teach Michelle how to sew.

When the thread snapped, and Michelle paused to rethread it, her thoughts went to Brad. When he'd stopped by yesterday and she apologized for hiding the truth of her identity, he'd forgiven her. But had he really? Or did Brad only say so to make himself look good in Mary Ruth's eyes? Since his goal was to become a preacher, how would it look if he'd refused to accept her apology?

Then there was Sara. Even though she'd been acting a little more civil lately, Michelle felt sure it was for her grandparents' sake. Who knew what Sara really thought?

Michelle picked up the piece of material again and stitched the first seam. *Why don't things ever work out for me? Every time I'm with Ezekiel, he offers me hope. But when he isn't around to offer reassurance and someone even looks at me with disapproval, my doubts surface.* She suspected she no longer had Brad's approval and felt sure he was disappointed in her.

Yesterday, when Michelle had rushed out to the barn, she'd gone straight to the prayer jar she previously found there, hoping for some reassurance. After reading a few verses of scripture that an unknown person had written and put in the old jar, Michelle found a measure of comfort. In particular, 2 Corinthians 5:17 spoke to her: *"Therefore if any man be in Christ, he is a new creature: old things are passed away; behold, all things are become new."* It reminded her that since she had accepted Christ, she was a new person, forgiven of her sins, and could begin anew. It didn't matter what others thought of her or how they responded. She just had to keep that verse in her heart and hold her head up high. But Michelle needed to take each day as it came and spend much time in prayer.

❧

With Christmas coming next week, customers had flowed in and out of the floral shop all morning. Right now, however, with the noon hour approaching, there seemed to be a letup of shoppers.

Sara's stomach growled, and she glanced at her watch. *This might be a good time to get something to eat.*

With food on her mind, she thought about the promise she'd made this morning to bring supper home from one of the local restaurants in town. Grandma seemed pleased, and Grandpa said it would be good for Grandma to take a night off. Since her grandparents liked chicken potpie, Sara knew the family-style restaurant that Karen Roberts had recommended would be the perfect place.

Sara was glad for the opportunity to do something nice for her grandparents. And bringing home a meal would be something Michelle hadn't done, at least.

About to head into the back room to tell Andy and Karen she was leaving for lunch, Sara paused when the shop door opened and Brad stepped in. *I wonder what he's doing here.*

As Brad approached, Sara offered him what she hoped was a pleasing smile. "I'm surprised to see you. Did you come to buy flowers for someone?"

He shook his head. "Came to see you."

"How did you know where to find me?"

"It was mentioned yesterday that you worked at a flower shop here in Strasburg, and since this is the only one in town, I figured it had to be the right place." He moved closer to Sara. "If you haven't eaten yet, I'd like to take you out for lunch so we can get better acquainted."

"I'm surprised you didn't invite Michelle to join us. I gather the two of you are pretty good friends." Sara hoped her sarcasm wasn't too obvious.

Brad's gaze flicked upward. "As you may already know, I did some work for your grandparents this summer. They also called on me to drive them some places. So Michelle and I became friends while she was living with the Lapps."

"You mean, when you thought she was me?"

He gave a nod. "But if she hadn't been there pretending to be Sara Murray, then it would have been you I'd have gotten to know." His gaze was so steady, she felt as if his blue eyes were holding her captive.

Looking away, Sara mumbled, "Be that as it may, we didn't get to know each other this summer, and I'm not sure there's any point in us going out to lunch today."

"Have you already eaten?"

"No."

"I haven't either, and if you'll let me, I'd like to treat you to lunch. In addition to getting better acquainted, I want to ask a few questions about Michelle."

"I doubt I'll be able to tell you anything you don't already know, but if you'll wait a few minutes, I'll tell my boss I'm taking my lunch break now." Sara didn't know why she'd agreed to go, but at least this would give her a chance to let Brad know what she thought of Michelle. Sara had a feeling he might be interested in Ms. Taylor, and it would be too bad for him if he got caught in her trap, the way Ezekiel had.

Brad's lips parted slightly, as a slow smile spread across his handsome face. "I'm more than happy to wait for you."

"Okay." Curling her trembling fingers against her moist palms, Sara hurried toward the back room. *Sure hope having lunch with him is not a mistake. What if Brad repeats everything I say to Michelle?*

As Brad sat across the table from Sara at Isaac's Famous Grilled Sandwiches, he admired her beauty. Since she'd made no mention of a husband and didn't wear a wedding ring, he assumed the Lapps' granddaughter must be single. *But if Sara is married, then wouldn't her husband have come with her to see Willis and Mary Ruth?* Brad looked at her intently. *She could be in a serious relationship or even engaged.*

*Don't know why I'm even thinking such thoughts,* he reprimanded himself. *I'm here to talk about her situation with Michelle, not concern myself with her relationship status.*

"So tell me a little about yourself." He clasped the mug of hot chocolate he'd ordered to go with his Gooney Bird turkey sandwich on pumpernickel bread. "I'd also like to know how it is that Michelle ended up pretending to be you for so long."

"There's not much to tell about me. I'm single, and I grew up in Newark, New Jersey, with my mother, stepfather, and later a half-brother." Sara pulled a napkin from the holder between them and blotted her lips. "And as far as how Michelle ended up pretending to be me. . . I figured you would have asked her that question."

"I only know the little bit she told me, but nothing from your perspective."

"What exactly do you want to know?" Sara bit into her avocado and roasted red pepper salad.

Brad scratched his head. He thought he'd just told her what he wanted to know. *Maybe I didn't explain it well enough.*

"For starters. . . Is the story Mary Ruth and Willis told true, about not knowing they had a granddaughter named Sara until they received a letter from you in June? Or maybe it was late May," he amended.

"It was June, and yes, the story they told is true. I wrote to them after I found a note in my mother's Bible soon after her death. The letter didn't give me a lot of information—only that I had grandparents living in Strasburg whom she had never told me about. It also gave their name and address." Sara paused to take a sip of hot tea. "Mama also said she hoped I would get the chance to meet them some day."

"Did your mother tell you that your grandparents were Amish?"

She shook her head. "I had no idea until the day I first met them in October."

"After you found your mother's letter, why did it take you so long to meet Willis and Mary Ruth?" Brad's curiosity piqued.

"I wrote to Grandma and Grandpa right away, saying I wanted the chance to get to know them." Sara set her cup down. "I explained that I would like to come sometime after I finished my summer business classes. I also mentioned that I may take the bus to Philadelphia." She pursed her lips. "I waited to hear back from them, and when they didn't respond, I wrote again."

"How did Michelle come into the picture?"

"From what Grandma told me, they thought my first letter said I'd be arriving at the bus station on June fifth, and that I wanted them to pick me up." Sara drummed her fingers on the table. "So they went there, and when they saw Michelle, they mistook her for me."

Brad frowned. "I can't believe she went along with it, knowing she wasn't their granddaughter."

"It was a devious thing to do. And to make things worse, once Michelle was settled in at Grandma and Grandpa's, she intercepted all the other letters I sent them throughout the summer months." Sara's brows lowered. "The imposter even went so far as to write me a letter, pretending to be Grandma."

"What did it say?" Brad felt fully drawn into the story and was eager to hear more.

"She said they were really busy and asked me to postpone my visit until fall." Sara's fingers trembled a bit, as she placed her hands on the table. "I thought it was kind of strange, but of course I waited, and the day I finally arrived, which wasn't by bus after all, Michelle met me at the door. She said the Lapps weren't home and that I should go inside and wait for them. Then, the great pretender made a run for it." She blinked rapidly. "Of course I had no way of knowing at that point who she was or what all had transpired."

"Whew, that's quite a story." Brad shook his head. "It's hard to believe that—"

"Oh, it's the truth all right. I have no reason to lie about it." Sara looked at Brad with a piercing gaze. "Unlike Ms. Michelle, I am not one to make up stories."

He held up his hand. "Never said I didn't believe you. I'm just shocked, hearing how it went and struggling to figure out why Michelle was so deceitful."

"It's not hard to understand, if you think about it."

"What do you mean?"

"She's trying to steal my grandparents from me." Sara grimaced. "And I'm sure she has an ulterior motive."

"Like what?"

She shrugged. "I haven't figured that out yet, but I will. . . You can count on it."

Brad sat quietly, trying to piece everything together. According to Michelle, she was genuinely sorry for what she'd done and had turned over a new leaf. But what if Sara was right and Michelle did have an ulterior motive for worming her way into Willis and Mary Ruth's lives? Even though Brad wouldn't be in the area for more than two weeks, he planned to look into this further and hopefully find out more. Maybe he'd been too quick to forgive and look the other way when Michelle asked his forgiveness. If she was using Willis and Mary Ruth for some underhanded reason, she needed to be stopped, and soon.

# Chapter 16

I don't see why you have to eat dinner at the Lapps' today," Ezekiel's mother said when he slipped on his jacket and started for the back door. "Our family should be together on Christmas Day."

Ezekiel halted and turned to look at her. "I told you a week ago that I wouldn't be here for the afternoon meal today."

"Jah, but I thought. . ."

"What?" Ezekiel's fingers dug into his palms. "Did you think I would change my mind and stay home today?"

Her nose crinkled. "Christmas is a time to be with one's family, and I would think you'd want to spend the holiday with us."

"Figured you wouldn't mind, 'cause I ate the Thanksgiving meal here. Plus, I was here last night with all of you when some of my aunts, uncles, and cousins came over. I realize that I've never missed a Christmas here at home, but today, I wanna be with my *aldi*." Ezekiel paused for a breath. "Since we've been so busy in the greenhouse these past few weeks, I haven't had the chance to see Michelle much lately."

Mom opened her mouth in readiness to say more, but Dad cut her off.

"Let the boy alone," he spoke from across the room, where he sat at the table with a cup of coffee. "Don't you remember how many holiday meals I ate at your folks' house when we were courting?"

Ezekiel's eyes widened, waiting for his mother's response. She remained silent. He couldn't believe his dad had stuck up for him and seemed to understand that he wanted to spend time with his girlfriend. If Dad was okay with him courting Michelle, maybe eventually Mom would be too.

⁓

Brad was eager to get to the Lapps' house, but he kept his speed down since there was snow and ice on the road in many places where it had not been melted by the sun.

Ned left early to be with his family, but under his little three-foot Christmas tree, Brad had found a package for him. Grinning, he reached up and touched the red woolen scarf around his neck. "That Ned—always thinking of others."

Even though he'd dropped off a cactus the day he arrived, Brad didn't want to go to the Lapps' empty handed, since they'd asked him to join their Christmas gathering and meal. So yesterday he'd gone to the local bakery and bought an assortment of cookies to bring for dessert. He looked forward to the meal, not to mention seeing Sara again. He hoped he might also have a few minutes alone with Michelle so he could ask some questions and hopefully find out if she was up to anything, as Sara suspected. He had stopped by the Lapps' two days ago, but Michelle wasn't home. Mary Ruth said she was out, seeking a job at one of the local restaurants.

With a houseful of company today, Brad figured he may not get the chance to speak to Michelle privately, but it wouldn't stop him from making observations.

When Brad pulled his van into the Lapps' yard, he spotted a horse and buggy at the hitching rail. He turned off the engine and got out of his vehicle, then joined Ezekiel by the horse. "Merry Christmas." He reached out to shake his friend's hand. "Nice to see you. How are doing?"

"I'm doin' well, and Merry Christmas to you too." Ezekiel grinned, returning Brad's firm handshake. "It's good to have you back in the area. How long are you planning to stay?"

"Just through the holidays. I'll be returning to the university in Clarks Summit on New Year's Day. I have a long ways to go before my studies are done."

"Well, I'm glad you're here." Ezekiel removed the bit from his horse's mouth. "Since I'll be here awhile, I'm takin' Big Red to the barn. Want to come along, or are you anxious to get up to the house?"

"Can't say I'm not eager to get in out of the cold or enjoy the delicious aroma that's no doubt coming from Mary Ruth's kitchen, but I'll take a walk to the barn with you." Brad was glad for the opportunity to talk to Ezekiel alone. Maybe he could offer some answers concerning Michelle.

When they entered the barn, Brad breathed in the aroma of sweet hay in the air. A couple of horses were already in the stalls, munching away on their supper.

Ezekiel put Big Red in an empty stall, wiped him down, and made sure the horse had something to eat and drink. Brad pet Sadie and Rascal as he waited until Ezekiel finished, then he asked his first question.

"I heard you've decided to join the Amish church, and that Michelle's planning to as well."

"You heard right." Leaning against the horse's stall, Ezekiel smiled. "I had an experience up in Harrisburg when I went there looking for Michelle. It made me realize that living the English life isn't for me." His face sobered. "Not to say all English are bad. I just came to the conclusion that I need to appreciate my heritage and don't have to be embarrassed about the way we Amish choose to live. My family means a lot to me too which also helped in making the decision."

Brad's head moved slowly up and down. "Makes sense to me. I am a little curious though why Michelle, who led us to believe her name was Sara, decided to join the Amish church."

"You know, she's sorry for that." Ezekiel's gaze dropped for a few seconds, before he looked directly at Brad. "Has she explained things to you yet?"

"Some. But I'm not sure I have all the facts."

Ezekiel brushed some stray pieces of hay from his jacket.

"What do you wanna know?"

Brad figured he may as well be direct. "Why would she have let the Lapps believe she was Sara? Has she told you that?"

Ezekiel nodded. "Michelle's had a rough life. When she was a kid, she and her brothers were taken from their abusive parents, and she lived with foster parents until she struck out on her own when she turned eighteen. To this day, she still doesn't know where her two brothers ended up. Can you imagine that?"

"I'm sure it's been tough, but what happened when she left her foster parents?"

"Michelle went from town to town and worked at whatever jobs she could find." Ezekiel licked his lower lip. "Then she got involved with an abusive man and lost her job in Philadelphia about the same time. There was one thing Michelle was sure of—she could not tolerate his abuse. She was desperate and went to the bus station to buy a ticket so she could get away from the boyfriend and start over in some other place."

Brad leaned against the wooden beam near him. "Is there more to the story?"

Ezekiel nodded. "While Michelle was at the station, the Lapps showed up, thinking she was their granddaughter. You have to remember, the Lapps didn't know they had a granddaughter until Sara wrote the first letter. So when they saw a young woman with the same auburn hair as their daughter's, they were convinced she was Sara. Then, because Michelle was desperate to get away, on impulse, she went along with it and let them believe she was Sara."

Brad's head tilted while he mentally weighed this information. "Didn't she realize the truth would eventually come out?"

"Sure, but like I said, she was desperate." Ezekiel reached across the stall gate and gave Big Red's head a few pats. "I'm not condoning what she did, but I wanted you to understand what drove her to making a poor decision."

"Many people make wrong choices because of their circumstances, but lying, and even telling half-truths are never right." Brad joined Ezekiel in petting the horse. "So what is Michelle's reason for joining the Amish church? Is it to please you? I've known for some time that you were interested in her."

Ezekiel's cheeks reddened. "I can't deny it. Ever since the first day I met her—when I saw her fall in the mud—I was attracted. 'Course I didn't let on right away."

"She's interested in you too, I presume." Brad couldn't help smiling.

"Yeah. In fact, we've begun courting."

"I see." The word *courting* seemed a bit old-fashioned to Brad, and he was on the verge of posing another question, when the Lapps' son, Ivan, entered the barn with his sons, Benjamin and Peter. *Well, at least I found out the reason Michelle did what she did, even though it wasn't right. Because of her deceit, the Lapps were hurt, and most of all, Sara.* Brad looked out the barn doors toward the house. *I need to reach out to her in support.*

With the exception of Michelle's presence, Sara couldn't recall a better Christmas. Even though there was no tree, adorning ornaments, twinkling lights, or other decorations in her grandparents' cozy home, it didn't deter the spirit and festivity of the day. Except for Brad's Christmas cactus and the two poinsettias she and Michelle had given to her grandparents, one would think it was a normal family gathering. Nonetheless, Sara felt the overwhelming joy of this holiday celebration. Last week, when she'd brought the chicken potpie home for supper, she'd felt the same joy, seeing the twinkle in Grandma's eyes as she thanked Sara for her thoughtfulness.

This morning had started with a hearty breakfast. Afterward, preparation for the family meal began. Even before that, Grandma had put the ham in the oven for a slow bake. The aroma of the meat as it slowly warmed up made Sara's mouth water in anticipation.

Grandpa and Grandma had insisted Sara and Michelle should not give them any Christmas presents. Grandma said just having them both here was gift enough, and Grandpa agreed. So Sara and

Michelle said they didn't want any gifts either.

Michelle wore another new outfit—a teal green dress with a black apron she had made, while Sara donned a pretty satin red blouse and black skirt. She wore a simple heart-shaped necklace, but decided to leave her earrings out for today.

Now as Sara sat at her grandparents' extended dining-room table, she tried to keep her focus on the playful banter going on between Grandpa and Uncle Ivan. The love and respect they felt for one another was obvious, even with their kidding and poking fun at each other's corny jokes. Every now and then Sara glanced at Brad, and each time she did, she noticed him staring at her. Sara wished she could get in his head and know what he was thinking. Did he find out something more about Michelle? If so, would he share it with her?

Before they'd sat down to her grandmother's delicious ham dinner, Brad had sought Sara out and asked if he could take her to lunch again—tomorrow if she was free. She'd agreed to go—partly because he was good looking and charming, but mostly because she wanted to talk more about Michelle. Sara hadn't mentioned it when she and Brad ate lunch at Isaac's restaurant the other day, but she hoped that Brad might persuade Michelle to move out of their house. Giving the pretender the cold shoulder sure hadn't worked.

Sara looked to her left, where Michelle sat, giving Ezekiel a dose of her cow eyes. Throughout most of the meal, their conversation had been to each other. Michelle was obviously smitten with him. A person would have to be blind not to notice her love-sick actions. Could she be using her relationship with Ezekiel to find favor with Grandma and Grandpa?

*I wouldn't put anything past her,* Sara thought. *Everything about today would be perfect if Michelle weren't here.* Sara forked a piece of succulent ham into her mouth. *She's not even part of the family, and yet here she sits at our table, sharing Christmas dinner as though she too is Grandma and Grandpa's granddaughter.*

Sara wondered how long she would have to endure this ongoing trial with Michelle. And how did this current test benefit her anyway? Sara felt sure she was in the right and Michelle was in the wrong. Sara thought she'd forgiven the imposter, but deep down, she hadn't.

Sara's only hope was for Michelle to either find a job and move out on her own or marry Ezekiel and settle into a home with him. Sara needed a chance to be with her grandparents without Michelle always around. Michelle needed to make a life of her own. The whole idea that the pretender was even living here was ridiculous. As far as Sara was concerned, Grandma and Grandpa's generosity went too far. She didn't want to see them get hurt again. But if Michelle was up to no good, there might not be anything she could do to stop it.

# Chapter 17

"Thanks for agreeing to meet me for lunch today, even though we just saw each other yesterday," Brad said when he and Sara took seats at Strasburg Pizza the day after Christmas.

She nodded. "I'm glad I could. Things are slow at the flower shop today, so there was no problem with me going out for lunch."

"What kind of pizza do you like? Or would you rather have a cold or hot sub sandwich?"

"I only have an hour lunch, so I'd better choose something that can be made up quickly." Sara perused the menu. "Maybe I'll go with a readymade pizza slice topped with veggies."

Looking down at his menu and back at her, he asked, "Is that all you want to eat?"

"Yes." Placing both hands against her stomach, she laughed. "Think I ate enough yesterday to fill me for a week."

He grinned. "Same here. That grandma of yours is some cook. The ham was sure delicious. I can still remember the juiciness of it."

A muscle jumped in Sara's cheek as she flicked her gaze upward. "For your information, Mr. Fuller, Michelle and I helped with the meal."

"I kinda figured you did." He scrubbed a hand over his face. "Sorry about that. It was all great."

"Never mind, it's okay." Sara changed the subject. "It feels sort of funny working the day after Christmas. I used to work at a dentist's office in New Jersey, and my boss always closed the day after Christmas, to give everyone two days off."

"Did you mind going to work today?" Brad asked.

"No, not really. I am a little tired, but I like working here, so it wasn't too hard to come in."

"I understand." He heaved a sigh. "It will be hard for me to get back into the swing of things once I head back to school. I'll have to get my brain into study mode again."

"Do you really plan to become a minister?"

Brad nodded. "It's been a dream of mine for a long time. I'm looking forward to the day I get to pastor a church full-time."

"I see." Sara looked around the pizza shop. "Sure is busy in here for the day after Christmas."

"Yeah. I suspect a lot of the restaurants have plenty of customers today. This is a hectic day for the stores, with customers returning gifts and hitting all the after-holiday bargains."

"I never got into doing that." Sara shook her head. "I don't mind a good sale, but it's the crowds I can't deal with."

"I'm with you on that."

A commotion at a nearby table caused Sara and Brad to look in that direction.

"I didn't order a pizza!" The man yelled when the waitress brought his order. "You were supposed to bring me a steak sub and fries. I have to be back at work in twenty minutes, so now I'll have to take my lunch to go. That is, if you can get it to me in time."

"I'm sorry, sir," the young waitress apologized. The poor thing looked as if she was on the verge of tears. "It's my first day on the job. I'll get the right order for you, and it will be on the house."

"Well, that's more like it." The guy leaned back in his chair.

Sara looked back at Brad and whispered, "That man seems a bit frazzled."

"Bet he works in a store"—Brad winked—"and is dealing with Christmas returns."

Sara giggled. "He must be having a bad day."

A waiter came, interrupting their conversation. Sara ordered a slice of vegetarian pizza, along with a small tossed green salad, and a glass of water.

"I'll have the same as her." Brad smiled up at the waiter. "Only, make that two slices of pizza instead of one."

The young man nodded. "Do you want water too?"

"Nope. Think I'll go with an orange soda."

"Okay. I'll return with your drinks shortly."

When their waiter moved away from the table, Brad leaned closer to Sara and said, "When Ezekiel arrived at your grandparents' yesterday, I went to the barn with him while he put his horse away."

Sara tipped her head with a quizzical expression.

"I asked Ezekiel some questions about Michelle." Brad paused to collect his thoughts. "He explained Michelle's reasons for pretending she was you."

"Oh? And what would those be?"

Brad repeated everything Ezekiel had told him.

Sara's forehead wrinkled. "She's not the only person with problems from the past. And certainly, not everyone goes around lying to get what they want or uses their own misfortune to gain something from someone. At least, I never would. I believe Michelle's reason for impersonating me goes deeper than having an unhappy childhood and needing a place to live." She blew out a quick breath. "I truly believe Michelle is after something."

"What do you think she wants?"

Before Sara could respond, their waiter was back with the water and soda. "Your pizza should be out shortly." He looked at Sara. "Would you like your salad before the pizza comes out?"

She shook her head. "It's fine if you bring them at the same time."

"Okay." He hurried from the table.

"Now, back to my question. . . What do you think Michelle wants?" Brad asked.

"For one thing, she's vying for my grandparents' love and attention. I think she would like them to care more about her than they do me."

Brad was about to refute that statement, when Sara spoke

again. "I also think Michelle may be hoping for something—like an inheritance when they die someday. She probably wants to join the Amish faith to get in their good graces."

With elbows on the table, Brad clasped his fingers together. "For their sake, as well as yours and Ezekiel's, I hope that's not true. Ezekiel is obviously in love with Michelle, and he believes her intentions are good."

"I'd like to think so, but I have a knack for reading people." Sara lifted her chin. "In my opinion, Michelle is not to be trusted, so I'm keeping an eye on her."

Their meal came then, so Brad decided to drop the subject and talk about something else. His intuition told him that Sara had some deep issues of her own to resolve, but he wouldn't bring that up now. Maybe some other time, if he gained her confidence, he could delve into Sara's personal life. One thing was for sure: he'd like to know where she stood spiritually.

❧

"I have a favor to ask," Sara said when she and Brad finished their lunch.

He looked at her intently. "What is it?"

She wiped some crumbs off her slacks and set her napkin aside. "Since you knew Michelle from the time you worked for my grandparents, I was wondering if you could persuade her to move out of their house."

His brows furrowed. "Why would I do that?"

"Because she has no right to be there."

"She might not have the right, but Willis and Mary Ruth must want Michelle there, or they wouldn't have invited her to stay in their home."

Sara poked her tongue along the inside of her cheek. "You're on her side, aren't you?"

He shook his head. "I'm not taking anyone's side. I just think this is something you should discuss with your grandparents, not me, an outsider."

"You're not really an outsider. You're Michelle's friend, and Grandma and Grandpa's too."

"True, but unless they ask for my opinion, I won't voice my thoughts, let alone tell them what to do."

"Okay, no problem. I'll take it up with Michelle myself." With a huff, Sara pushed her chair aside and stood. "I need to get back to the flower shop so Mr. and Mrs. Roberts can take their lunch break."

Brad jumped up. "As soon as I pay the bill I'll give you a lift."

"Don't bother. The shop's not that far. I'll walk." Without giving him a chance to respond, Sara rushed to the front of the restaurant and slipped out the door.

⁂

"Christmas went well, don't you think?" Willis asked when he came into the kitchen for lunch.

Mary Ruth nodded and placed a loaf of bread on the table. "It's sure quiet around here today, with Sara working at the flower shop and Michelle out looking for a job."

Willis chuckled as he took a seat at the table. "You like lots of action around you, jah?"

"Not necessarily action, but it is nice to have someone to talk to."

He pointed to himself. "Don't you enjoy talking to me?"

"Course I do, but you spend a good deal of the day doing chores and taking care of the hogs. And when you're here in the house, you find a newspaper or magazine to read. I feel kind of left out at times."

Willis got up and came around to the side of the table where Mary Ruth stood. "I'll try to do better in that regard." He gave her a hug. "After all, neither of the girls will be livin' here forever, so I may as well start spending more time with you now."

She smiled up at him. "You're such a good husband. What would I ever do without you?"

He tweaked the end of her nose playfully. "I hope when the

good Lord decides to take us, we both leave this earth together."

She flapped her hand. "Go on now, and sit yourself back down. Let's have no talk of death or dying. I'm sure you're *hungerich*, and so am I, so let's eat ourselves full."

When Michelle arrived back at the Lapps', her spirits soared. She'd been hired as a waitress at one of the busiest restaurants in Ronks. Amish and English folks both liked to eat there, and while she was waiting to be interviewed at one of the back tables, she'd noticed how a constant flow of customers kept the other waitresses on their toes. Michelle would be working five days a week, with Mondays and some Saturdays off. It was a good thing she'd kept the comfortable shoes she'd worn while working at the restaurant in Harrisburg.

*I'm not sure Sara will like it with me having Mondays off too, but, oh well. . . She'll just have to get used to it.* Michelle would miss spending her days with Mary Ruth and Willis, but it would be nice to have money she could contribute to their expenses. With a steady paycheck and tip money, she also hoped to open a savings account at the local bank. Of course, her first paycheck would be used to pay back the money she'd taken from their coffee can of emergency cash when she'd run off to Harrisburg in October.

"Sure wish I could undo the past," she murmured as she unhitched Peanuts and led her into the barn.

*Woof! Woof! Woof!*

Michelle looked down at Rascal, pawing at her leg, and shook her finger. "Not now, pup. I need to put Mary Ruth's horse in her stall."

*Woof!* The dog's tail wagged so fast it looked like a blur.

"Go in the yard. I'll play fetch-the-ball when I'm done here."

Rascal let out a pathetic whine, then slunk out of the barn.

Michelle shook her head. *That mutt always wants my attention. Poor thing. I haven't spent much time with Rascal lately. I'll have to pay him more attention on my days off, and Sunday afternoons too.*

Peanuts nickered softly as she led the mare into her stall for a thorough rubdown. When Michelle was done, she left the stall and started for the barn doors. "Okay, now it's Rascal's turn. I'm sure he's ready to play."

Michelle had no more than stepped outside, when Sara's car came up the driveway. The next thing she knew, Rascal, barking wildly, raced toward the vehicle. Normally, he wasn't prone to car chasing, but for some reason, he was today.

"Sara, stop!" Michelle clapped her hands and hollered, "Come here, Rascal. Get away from that car!"

As though seeing it in slow motion, Michelle watched in horror as Sara's car hit Rascal, knocking the poor pooch to the cold, snow-covered ground.

# Chapter 18

Sara's hands shook so badly, she could hardly open her car door. In the six years she'd been driving, she had never been involved in an accident or hit an animal. Sara had seen Rascal running toward her car, but the driveway was slippery, and when she turned the wheel to avoid hitting the dog, he'd gotten in the way.

Her heart pounded, and her legs felt like two sticks of rubber as she made her way to Rascal's lifeless form. She knelt on the snow-packed ground beside him, hoping to see the extent of his injuries.

"You hit my dog! Oh no. . . Oh no. . . Rascal!" A shrill voice seemed to come out of nowhere.

Sara looked up through a film of tears and saw Michelle running toward her. "I—I didn't do it on purpose. The ice. . . The snow. . . The dog. . ."

Michelle dropped down beside Rascal, calling his name over and over while stroking his head. The poor dog did not respond. "No, no. He can't be dead," she wailed. "He's the only dog I've ever owned." Her voice shook with raw emotion. "He's not even a year old yet."

"M—maybe he's not dead. He could just be unconscious." Even as the words came out of her mouth, Sara feared they weren't true. So far, Rascal had not made a sound—not even a whimper—or so much as moved a muscle. Even if the dog was still alive, he'd most likely been seriously injured.

While Michelle remained in the snow, stroking her dog's head, Sara clambered to her feet. "I'll go get Grandpa. He will know what to do."

Michelle didn't even look up.

As she started for the house, Sara glanced back. She almost wished she hadn't. It was a pitiful, heart-wrenching sight to see Michelle bent over her beloved pet. Even worse was when she put her ear to the dog's body to see if there was a heartbeat. "Oh please, God," Sara murmured, looking up toward the sky. "Don't let her dog be dead."

Being in shock herself, and moving on a slippery surface, Sara hurried on. She found her grandmother in the kitchen, putting a meatloaf in the oven.

"Oh Sara, I didn't realize you were home." Grandma closed the oven door and turned from the stove. "How was your day at the flower shop? Was business slower than usual now that Christmas is over?"

With so many questions being thrown at her at once, Sara could hardly speak. Her day at work and how many customers came in didn't matter at all. Sara's only concern was the poor dog lying on the cold ground next to her front tire—not to mention Michelle's reaction to what had happened to her dog.

Grandma tilted her head. "Sara, your face is as pale as goat's milk. Is anything wrong? Please tell me, did something happen outside?"

Tears spilled onto Sara's cheeks. "I—I hit Rascal. Michelle is outside with him, but I think I killed him." Sara swallowed, fearing she might get sick.

Grandma's eyes widened. "Oh no. I'm sure it was an accident, for I know you didn't hit Rascal on purpose." She gave Sara a supportive hug.

She remained in Grandma's embrace, while more tears escaped her eyes. Then, regaining her composure, Sara stepped away, drying her tears. "Thank you."

Sara's gaze darted to the window, then back to her grandmother. "Where's Grandpa? We need him to help us."

"He's in the living room, probably taking a nap. I'll go get him." Grandma moved from the kitchen much faster than usual.

Sara wasn't sure if she should go back outside and wait, or remain in the kitchen until Grandpa came out. She opted for the latter, needing his support and not knowing if Michelle would accept her apology.

As Michelle held Rascal's head in her lap, deep sobs poured forth from the depths of her soul. She knew without anyone telling her that the dog was dead, for there was no sign of life in him at all. While Michelle sat with Rascal, a memory slipped in from when he was a puppy, and why she had chosen the runt. Rascal had been a lot like her, struggling to survive. Besides being the smallest in the litter, he'd had to squirm his way in between the larger puppies in order to get some milk. Michelle could not refuse such a little fighter.

Michelle smiled briefly, but then the next wave of tears began. "Oh Rascal, I truly am sorry," she sobbed, as a sense of guilt overcame her. "All you wanted to do was play when I came into the barn, and I made you wait. Today I refused to play, and it cost you your life."

*If only you hadn't run at Sara's car. If she'd only seen you in time and stopped her vehicle, you wouldn't be slipping away from me now.* Michelle felt horrible and full of regret. Minutes ago, Rascal was full of life and wanting a little attention. *If I'd only taken some time to play ball with my devoted friend, he would still be here now.* All the rehashing and *if onlys* made her feel even worse.

Michelle closed her eyes, holding out hope that her suspicions were wrong. She hadn't felt this helpless and full of despair since she and her little brothers were separated. But at least Ernie and Jack hadn't been killed, only taken away and never seen again. Once Rascal was buried, she would never see him again either.

Rascal's mother approached from the barn and slinked slowly up to Rascal. Michelle could hardly stand watching poor Sadie sniff over her puppy. Then the collie lay down between the pup and Michelle, resting her head on Michelle's leg.

"Oh Sadie." Michelle cried even harder when the collie let out a sad whimper. Reaching out and pulling Sadie closer, Michelle buried her face in the collie's neck and found a slight thread of comfort in the warmth of the dog's fur. Sadie whined again, as if she understood.

Hearing voices, Michelle looked up and saw Willis and Sara come out of the house and plod toward her through the snow.

"Let me see how badly he's been hurt." Willis knelt down and checked Rascal over. Then he put his hand in front of the dog's mouth and listened for breath with his ear. "I'm so sorry, Michelle." His voice sounded flat, almost monotone. "Rascal is gone."

She sniffed deeply. "I—I think I already knew. I listened for a heartbeat, but he hasn't drawn a breath. Even so, I didn't want to give up hope."

"I apologize. As soon as I saw him running at the car, I should have stopped." Sara put her hand on Michelle's trembling shoulder. "I didn't realize how icy the driveway was either. Oh Michelle, I am so sorry."

"I'll go to the house and get a box to put him in." Grandpa rose to his feet. "There's a patch of ground out back by the burn barrel where the ground isn't so frozen. I'll bury him there."

Michelle could only nod as tears coursed down her cheeks. She'd given no response to Sara's apology and couldn't even think to do that right now. All she wanted was to get away from this horrible scene and mounting grief. She needed to be with Ezekiel and seek comfort from him.

"Can I take the horse and buggy out again, Willis?" she asked, hiccuping as she tried holding back more tears. "There's someplace I need to go."

His eyebrows squished together as he tugged on one ear. "Well, yes, but Mary Ruth has supper in the oven."

Michelle stood, brushing snow off her dress. "I couldn't eat anything right now. I need to see Ezekiel."

"I can drive you over," Sara offered. "Please let me do that for you. You're in no condition to take the horse and buggy out right now."

"I'm fine."

Willis eyed Michelle. "If you're determined to go by yourself, then go ahead and take the horse and buggy. I'll ask Mary Ruth to keep some of the meatloaf warm for you."

"Don't bother. I wouldn't be able to eat it." Michelle watched as

Sadie followed Willis to the house. Then, looking Sara straight in the eyes, she said, "In case you didn't know, Rascal was a gift from Mary Ruth and Willis for my birthday last June." Unable to say any more, Michelle took off for the barn to get Mary Ruth's horse. The thrill of finding a job today was long forgotten.

After securing Peanuts to the reins, Michelle pulled the carriage from the buggy shed and wheeled it so she could easily back the horse up to it. Peanuts nickered and stomped with an eagerness to go somewhere. This usually made Michelle happy, but right now her whole body felt numb.

She moved to the front of the horse. The mare's soft eyes, full of life, looked back at her. Warm tears dribbled down Michelle's face. Her heart felt as though it was breaking. Michelle stroked the horse's soft muzzle. *I hope Ezekiel is done for the day at the greenhouse and hasn't gone anywhere. I really need his support.*

Sara walked slowly back to the house. At this moment, she felt as if the weight of the world rested on her shoulders. She'd said she was sorry, but Michelle had not accepted her apology. *Doesn't she realize I didn't do it on purpose? It's not like I set out to run over her dog. If Michelle hadn't been here impersonating me this summer, she wouldn't be going through this right now.*

The more Sara thought about it, the more upset she became. She felt guilty enough without facing Michelle's accusing look and her refusal to acknowledge Sara's apology or her offer to drive Michelle to Ezekiel's. Trying to justify the situation by saying it was Michelle's fault as much as hers didn't give Sara vindication.

She kicked at a clump of snow as she neared the porch. *If I could undo what happened, I surely would.*

She stepped near the threshold of the door and paused, remembering her conversation with Brad at noon. Sara was set then to have it out with Michelle, but how could she now? Hopefully, Michelle would find the comfort she needed in the arms of her Amish boyfriend.

Ezekiel had come out of the greenhouse and was getting ready to head for the house, when a horse and buggy entered the yard. He was surprised when it pulled up to the hitching rail and Michelle got out. Ezekiel hadn't expected to see her this evening.

The minute he saw her tear-stained face, Ezekiel knew something was wrong. "What is it, Michelle? You look *umgerennt*."

Her chin trembled. "I am very upset. My dog just died, and it's Sara's fault."

Ezekiel gasped. "Oh no! What happened?"

Sniffling, and practically choking on sobs, Michelle told him everything that had occurred. "I couldn't stay and watch as Willis buried Rascal. And I can't be around Sara right now. I needed to be with you, Ezekiel."

He pulled Michelle into his arms and gently patted her back. "I don't think Sara did it on purpose. It sounds like an unfortunate accident."

She pressed her face against Ezekiel's chest. "Sara said she was sorry."

"Did you accept her apology?"

"No, I could barely look at her without feeling anger."

"There are many passages in the Bible about forgiveness. Can you think of one?"

"I—I can't remember where it's found, but as I recall, there's a verse that says: 'For if ye forgive men their trespasses, your heavenly Father will. . .' " Michelle's voice trailed off.

" 'Will also forgive you,' " Ezekiel finished the quotation. "It's found in Matthew 6:14. And the verse after that says, 'But if ye forgive not men their trespasses, neither will your Father forgive your trespasses.' "

Although crying so hard her sides ached, Michelle knew what she must do, no matter how difficult it was. For without forgiveness, no healing would come.

# Chapter 19

When supper was over, and the dishes were done, Sara volunteered to take the empty canning jar the green beans had been in down to the basement. Michelle still hadn't returned, and Sara figured she'd probably stayed at Ezekiel's parents' house for supper.

Although Grandma's meatloaf had tasted good, Sara hadn't had much of an appetite. How could the day after Christmas turn so tragically wrong?

When Grandpa came inside after burying Rascal, he'd looked so sad it made Sara feel even worse. She'd never owned a pet, but was learning quickly how much they could be part of one's family. *Maybe I should have helped Grandpa when he buried Michelle's dog.* But Sara couldn't bring herself to do so. How could she, when it was her fault? A few minutes alone in the basement might help, especially if she took down that old jar again and read some of the messages inside. It could even take her mind off the current situation and the guilt she felt.

Holding a flashlight in one hand, and the clean jar in the other, Sara made her way slowly down the basement stairs. When she reached the bottom, she found the battery-operated lantern and clicked it on. After putting the canning jar away, she reached up behind the antique jars and took down the one filled with notes. Taking a seat on a wooden stool, she poked her fingers in, pulled out a slip of paper, and read Matthew 7:1 silently: *"Judge not, that ye be not judged."*

Sara flinched. Ever since she'd arrived at Grandma and

Grandpa's and found Michelle living here, she had been judge and jury. Michelle was guilty of impersonating her. She had openly admitted it and even apologized. But Sara had not forgiven her, and at every turn, she judged Michelle for every little thing she did.

*Maybe I shouldn't judge her. Michelle might not be the horrible person I've made her out to be.* Sara tapped her foot. *Even if she is up to no good, the Bible says I should not judge her.*

Sara drew a deep breath and reached in for another piece of paper that quoted Matthew 5:44: *"But I say unto you, Love your enemies."*

She swallowed hard as tears sprang to her eyes. *I have seen Michelle as an enemy, but the Bible says I'm supposed to love her.*

Sara squeezed her eyes shut. *How am I supposed to do that? How can I love Michelle when she's trying to take my grandparents from me?*

She opened her eyes and was about to put the papers back in the jar, when she heard footsteps coming down the stairs. Hurriedly, she crammed the papers back in, but before she could make a move to return the jar to its shelf, someone spoke.

"Mary Ruth said I would find you down here."

Sara jerked her head. Michelle stood not more than a foot away. Barely able to respond, she murmured, "I—I came down to put the empty bean jar away."

Michelle pointed to the antique jar in Sara's hand. "I see you found one of the mysterious prayer jars."

Sara's mouth opened slightly. "Y–you know about this?"

"Yes, and there's another one on a shelf in the barn." Michelle offered Sara a weak smile. "Some of the notes I found inside those jars helped me a lot. They made me realize what I was doing was wrong."

Sara sat quietly, unsure of what to say. Finally, she asked another question. "Do you know who wrote the notes, or why they are in this jar?"

Michelle shook her head. "I've wondered if Mary Ruth might have written them, but I was hesitant to ask. Thought if she is the author, it might be too personal or she wouldn't want to talk about it."

Sara nodded slowly.

Michelle moved closer and touched Sara's shoulder. "I want you to know that I forgive you. After talking about it with Ezekiel, and thinking things through, I realized it wasn't your fault. I'm also to blame for not paying attention to my dog. Rascal shouldn't have been chasing your car, and the snow and ice only made things worse. Will you forgive me for not accepting your apology before?"

Tears welled in Sara's eyes. She was overwhelmed with relief. "There's nothing to forgive on my end, but I appreciate knowing you don't hold me responsible."

Michelle pulled Sara into a hug, and Sara did not resist. It was the first time since she and Michelle had been living here that Sara had good feelings toward Michelle, and a great load was beginning to lift.

❧

"I got a job today," Michelle announced as she sat in the living room that evening with Willis, Mary Ruth, and Sara. The mood had been somber up until now.

Mary Ruth's eyes brightened as she set her knitting needles aside. "That's *wunderbaar!*"

"Jah, congratulations," Willis said with a twinkle in his eyes.

Sara nodded as well. "Where will you be working, and what will you be doing?"

"It's at Dienners Country Restaurant in Ronks, and I'll be waitressing." Michelle pulled her fingers along the top of the black apron she wore over her plain dress. "From what I hear, it's a favorite restaurant with Amish as well as English people. And the best news of all is that I'll be starting tomorrow." She looked over at Willis. "I can still help you with chores before and after I get off work and also on my days off."

He smiled. "We'll see how it goes."

"What are your days off?" Mary Ruth questioned.

"Sundays, Mondays, and some Saturdays—same as Sara. Of course, I would never work on Sunday, even if the restaurant was open that day." Michelle quickly added.

"How will you get to work each day?" Mary Ruth picked up her knitting needles again. "You could drive the horse and buggy to Ronks, because there's a hitching rail outside the restaurant, but it wouldn't be good to leave the horse there all day."

"You're right," Michelle agreed. "I'll have to hire a driver to take me to work in the mornings. Once the spring weather takes over I can walk home from there. The three-and-a-half-mile jaunt might do me some good." Michelle patted her stomach and giggled. "Your good cooking is catching up with me."

"There's no need for that." Sara shook her head. "I'll drop you off at the restaurant before going to work at the flower shop. Then I can pick you up again when I get off in the afternoon. Ronks isn't that far from the flower shop."

"It's nice of you to offer, but my hours might not coincide with yours."

Sara shrugged. "It doesn't matter. If you end up working a later shift, I can always come back here after I leave work and then go to Dienners and pick you up when your afternoon shift ends." She gave Michelle a reassuring smile. "It's not that far away, and it won't take long by car. Maybe ten minutes, if that. We can work something out, so don't worry about a thing."

Alone in their room that night, Mary Ruth sat down on the bed beside her husband. "Things are looking up, don't you think?"

Closing the book from the page he'd been reading, Willis pushed his glasses back in place. "What'd you say?"

"I said, 'Things are looking up.'"

He squinted at her. "In what way?"

"For one thing, after many weeks of searching, Michelle has finally found a job."

Willis tugged his left ear. "Jah, that's a good thing."

She nudged his arm. "And could you believe how well Sara and Michelle got along this evening? There were no curt remarks on either side, and what a surprise when Sara offered to give Michelle a ride to and from work."

He moved his head slowly up and down. "It was unexpected—that's for sure. I wonder what brought on the change."

Mary Ruth turned her hands palms up. "I have no idea, but it's an answer to prayer. It's sad what happened to poor Rascal today, but maybe this tragedy turned into something positive."

"Jah, even poor Sadie seems lost right now, so she'll need some extra attention for a spell."

"I'm sure she misses her puppy as much as Michelle does." Mary Ruth looked toward the window. "Do you think we should have brought Sadie inside and let her sleep in Michelle's room tonight, or even here in ours?"

"Sadie is in the barn where she's used to being. She might be lonely, but she'll be okay."

"I hope things keep going like they are between the girls. I enjoy their company so much, and to see them getting along better is such a blessing." Mary Ruth placed both hands on her chest.

He patted her arm. "We need to pray that what happened between Sara and Michelle tonight will continue on in the days ahead."

"I wholeheartedly agree." Mary Ruth removed her head covering and prepared for bed. Michelle had gone up to her room early this evening, leaving them alone with Sara in the living room. Mary Ruth had been tempted to ask about her granddaughter's change of heart but had decided it was better to hold back. If either Sara or Michelle wanted to talk with her about it, she felt sure they would. In the meantime, she'd keep praying and showing them love.

After coming upstairs, Sara stood in front of the mirror on her bedroom wall, holding one of her mother's old heart-shaped head coverings by its ribbon-strings. She'd found it, along with several other items in the cedar chest at the foot of her bed.

*I wonder how I would look wearing this.* She pulled her hair back into a bun and pinned it in place, then set the kapp on her head. With the exception of the jeans and rose-colored top she wore, Sara almost looked Amish. *Could I be happy wearing plain clothes all the time?* she wondered. *Michelle seems to be, and she has no Amish heritage.*

Leaving the kapp on, Sara moved away from the mirror and took a seat on the bench near the window. She bent down to remove her shoes and socks. Wiggling her bare toes, she closed her eyes and tried to picture what her mother must have looked like when she lived here as a teenager. *Was Mama unhappy being Amish, or did she run away from home only because she felt guilty and couldn't face her parents with the truth about being pregnant?*

Sara had so many unanswered questions she wished she could ask her mother right now. And of course the biggest question of all was, *Who is my father?*

Her eyes snapped open. *Will I ever find out, and if I were to meet him, would he welcome me as his daughter? How would I react if I did find him? He'd be a stranger to me.* Sara inhaled and blew out a shallow breath. *Maybe it would be best if I never find the answer. I should probably forget about trying to find my father.*

# *Chapter 20*

*Lancaster*

S o what's on your plate this morning?"
Brad grinned at his friend from across the table and pointed to his poached eggs.

Ned groaned. "Very funny. I meant what do you have planned for today?"

"I know. Just kidding." Brad snickered. "Well, let's see. First thing after breakfast I plan to make another trip to Strasburg." He added some salt and pepper to his eggs. "Since Sara will be at work today, it'll give me a chance to talk to the Lapps privately. Of course, if Michelle is there, that might make it more difficult to say what's on my mind."

Ned's eyebrows rose. "How come you don't want Michelle to hear what you're saying?"

"Because it concerns her and Sara and how they've been acting toward each other."

"Oh yeah, that's right. You did mention them being at odds."

"It's worse now than ever." Brad shook his head.

"Did something else happen?"

"Sara still resents Michelle for pretending to be her, and she feels that Michelle has been taking advantage of Willis and Mary Ruth Lapp. She also believes Michelle has an ulterior motive."

"Do you think she does?"

"I don't know." Brad paused to eat a few bites of his eggs. "Sara asked if I would suggest to Michelle that she move out."

"Wow. Did you agree to that?" Ned slathered a blob of peanut butter on his toast.

"No way. Sara got irritated and said I was siding with Michelle." Brad grimaced. "I guess many people often look for someone to blame when something doesn't go their way."

Ned bobbed his head. "You're right. When I was a kid and my little brother fell out of a tree, our sister blamed me because I wasn't watching Dennis. I can remember the incident as though it happened yesterday—probably because I felt so guilty."

Brad nodded with understanding. "The problem with guilt is until we let go, our thoughts can be consumed with it—sometimes to the point of it making us sick or affecting our relationships with others."

"I agree." Ned finished the rest of his toast and swiped a napkin across his face. "I'd better go. Don't wanna be late for my dental appointment." He pushed back his chair and stood. "I hope things go well when you talk to the Lapps."

"Same here." Even though Brad had prayed when he'd first sat down at the table, he closed his eyes and offered another petition to God. "Please fill my mouth with the right words when I speak to Willis and Mary Ruth. And give all three of us wisdom to know how to help Sara and Michelle realize they need to set their differences aside."

*Ronks, Pennsylvania*

"It was nice of you to drive me to work this morning, but don't feel that you have to do it every day if our schedules conflict." Michelle looked over and smiled, as Sara pulled her car into Dienners' parking lot.

"Not a problem. I'll do it whenever I can, especially because we'll be getting into the coldest part of winter soon." Sara turned off the engine. "Since we're here a few minutes early, I'd like to talk to you about something."

"Sure, what is it?"

Sara cleared her throat. "Well, shortly after I came to visit my grandparents for the first time, I received a letter from Brad."

"Oh? I didn't realize you had known him before."

"I didn't. The letter was obviously meant for you, because he knew you as Sara."

"Oh yeah." Michelle's cheeks colored. "What did his letter say?"

Sara tapped her chin. "I can't remember word-for-word, but the gist of it was that he wanted to let you know he had settled in at the seminary in Clarks Summit."

Michelle nodded. "That's right. Brad told me he would be going there in one of our earlier conversations. Did he say anything else I should know about?"

"He said he hoped you had gotten the note he'd brought by the Lapps' before he left. Oh, and there was a Bible verse included with his letter." Sara paused, wondering if she should say more.

"What else?"

"Umm. . . Brad also mentioned that he hoped you would write him sometime and as soon as he had a free weekend he'd like to come here for a visit."

Michelle pursed her lips. "I see."

"Was there more?"

"He asked you to give his love to your grandparents and said he was praying for you."

"You mean, *your* grandparents."

"Yes, but he thought they were yours."

Michelle's head moved up and down. "I really messed up, didn't I? Everyone in this Amish community would have been better off if I hadn't let them think I was you."

"It's in the past and can't be changed." *Then why can't you forget about trying to find out who your father is?* The little voice in Sara's head reminded her that, despite her best intentions, she had not left her past behind, and may never unless she found the answer she sought.

"Do you still have Brad's letter?" Michelle asked.

Sara shook her head. "I didn't think I would ever see you again, so I threw the letter away."

"Oh, I see." Michelle gave one of her head covering strings a tug. "Guess it really doesn't matter, since he didn't say anything I don't already know." She sucked in her bottom lip, and then let her mouth relax. "There was a time when I thought I might be falling for Brad, but I quickly realized we weren't suited and that I had no future with him." She smiled. "Ezekiel and I are meant to be together, even if his mother doesn't think so."

"Maybe Belinda will change her mind."

Michelle shrugged. "I hope so, because I can't imagine what it would be like if Ezekiel and I ended up getting married and there was still tension between his mother and me."

Sara gave Michelle's arm a light tap. "Well, as my mother used to say, 'Remember to take one day at a time.'"

"Good advice." Michelle looked at her watch. "Oh goodness. I better get inside. My boss wanted me here a little early to go over some things I need to know. Don't want to start off on the wrong foot my first day."

"I heard a car pull into the yard," Mary Ruth shouted from the kitchen. "Would you please see who it is, Willis? I would do it, but I'm in the middle of rolling out pie dough."

"Jah, okay," he called back.

Mary Ruth was putting the dough into the pans when Willis entered the kitchen with Brad. "This is a nice surprise." She gestured with her head. "If you'd like to take a seat at the table, I'll make some coffee as soon as I get the pie shells in the oven to lightly brown."

"Sounds good." Brad took a seat, and Willis did the same.

"Too bad the pies aren't baked yet," her husband commented. "I could go for something a little sweet right about now."

"Not a problem," Mary Ruth assured him. "There are plenty of peanut butter *kichlin* in the cookie jar. Feel free to get some out for our guest, as well as yourself."

Willis didn't have to be asked twice. He got right up and walked over to the ceramic jar on the counter. Soon he and Brad, both with smiling faces, were nibbling on cookies.

"Delicious!" Brad smacked his lips. "Did you make them, Mary Ruth?"

She shook her head. "Michelle did."

"Speaking of Michelle, where is she today?" He glanced around as though expecting her to join them.

"She should be in Ronks by now." Mary Ruth smiled as she poured pumpkin filling into the lightly browned pie shells, ready for further baking. "She got hired as a waitress at Dienners, and this was her first day on the job."

"That's good to hear. I imagine Sara's working today too?"

"Sure is." Willis spoke before Mary Ruth had a chance to respond to Brad's question.

"Good to know. I'm glad neither of them is here right now."

Mary Ruth returned the pies to the oven and turned to face Brad. "How come?"

"Because I don't want them to hear what I'm about to say." Brad reached for another cookie.

Mary Ruth placed a pot of coffee on the stove, then took a seat across from Brad. "What is it you wanted to tell us that the girls aren't supposed to hear?"

He rested both arms on the table. "Sara has talked to me about Michelle and how she feels about her pretending to be your grand-daughter all those months. She is clearly upset, not only with that, but about Michelle living here with you." Brad's gaze went from Mary Ruth to Willis. "Has she spoken to either of you about it?"

"We have talked, but not specifically about that." Mary Ruth shook her head. "We have noticed the tension between Sara and Michelle. . .until last night, that is."

"What happened last night?"

"We have no idea," Willis spoke up. "They just acted more civil toward each other."

"You probably don't know this, but something unfortunate happened yesterday," Mary Ruth added.

Brad remained silent as she explained what happened to

Michelle's dog. As Mary Ruth described the outcome, Brad's expression changed from curiosity to a look of disbelief.

"And then last evening, after Michelle told us she found a job, Sara offered to give her a ride to work," Willis interjected.

Brad's eyes widened. "That's really something. Never expected to hear this kind of news when I came over here. Wonder what brought on the change, especially after what happened to Rascal."

Mary Ruth got up to get the coffeepot. "I have no idea, but I am ever so grateful. Sara is our flesh-and-blood granddaughter, and we love her dearly, but we also care about Michelle."

Willis bobbed his head as though in agreement.

"I understand." Brad accepted the cup of coffee Mary Ruth offered him. "It sounds like an answer to prayer."

"Yes, indeed." Mary Ruth poured coffee for herself and Willis and took her seat at the table. "I only hope whatever good has transpired between the girls will last."

⁓

Each time Brad entered the Lapps' house, he appreciated the warm and inviting feeling, and this morning had been no different. He'd enjoyed talking with Willis and Mary Ruth, and was especially happy to hear of the turnabout with Sara and Michelle. He felt sure it couldn't have been anything he'd said to Sara that had influenced her, but it didn't matter. He was just glad things were going better between the two young women.

Driving back to Ned's apartment, Brad thought about Sara. He wasn't happy with the way things had ended the last time he was with her. Here it was Thursday already, and he only had five more days before he had to be back at the university.

"I have to work it in somehow to see Sara before I go back." He spoke out loud. "I wonder what she's doing on New Year's Eve. Think I'll stop by the flower shop sometime tomorrow or the next day and see if she has any plans."

# Chapter 21

*Ronks*

Michelle shivered as she stood outside Dienners, waiting for Sara to pick her up. It had been a busy day at the restaurant, and her feet ached from being on them for the breakfast and lunch shifts. Even her comfortable shoes didn't seem to help her feet today. She had only agreed to work two shifts every day to make more money. The morning shift started at seven, and the afternoon shift ended at three. Since Sara started at eight and left her job in Strasburg at four, it meant Sara went in early and Michelle stayed at Dienners an hour after quitting time, waiting for her ride. While Sara's offer to take Michelle to and from work was generous, this wasn't the ideal situation.

*Sure wish Sara and I worked the same hours.* Michelle blew on her hands, getting colder by the minute. *Maybe Sara's boss would be willing to change her work schedule to match mine. But then I guess he wouldn't need her to come to work that early every day.*

If Michelle had a car of her own, she could drive herself, but that would defeat the purpose of trying to live a Plain life while waiting to join the Amish church.

Michelle thought about all the frustration it caused Ezekiel when his folks found out he'd bought a truck. Things were much better between him and his parents since he'd decided to join the church and sell the vehicle. At least now, and even after Michelle and Ezekiel became members, they would be allowed to ride in other people's cars.

A horn honked, drawing Michelle's thoughts aside. She looked to the left and spotted Sara's car pulling into the parking lot, so she hurried that way.

"How was your first day on the job?" Sara asked after Michelle took a seat on the passenger's side.

"It went fine, and I made some good tips, but boy, am I ever tired." Michelle reached down and rubbed the calf of her right leg. "It's been so long since I waitressed that I forgot what it was like to be on my feet for so many hours." She looked over at Sara and smiled. "I'm glad I don't have to walk home, and I appreciate you going out of your way to pick me up."

"It's no bother. I am happy to do it," Sara replied. *Since I hit your dog, it's the least I can do.*

"How did your day go?" Michelle asked.

"It went well, but things were kind of quiet. Only a few people came into the shop to buy or order flowers."

"Bet it will get hectic again close to Valentine's Day." Michelle slipped off her shoes and wiggled her toes near the heat vent.

Sara nodded as she pulled out of the parking lot. "Andy and Karen Roberts already warned me about that. They said it would be even more demanding than Christmas, with folks flocking into the store to buy flowers. But I think I'll be up to the challenge. And it will likely be one of the times I'll need to work longer hours."

"You're a strong woman, Sara. I envy you for that," Michelle said.

"What makes you think I'm strong?"

"Oh, I don't know. Maybe strong isn't the right word. I guess confident might be a better way of putting it."

"I'm not as confident as you might think."

"Really? It doesn't show."

"Maybe not outwardly, but inside I am sometimes a ball of nerves." Sara clicked the blinker on as she prepared to turn the next corner.

"Never would have guessed it. To me you appear so self-assured."

Sara shook her head. "When I first came to Strasburg to meet my grandparents, I was full of anxiety—afraid they might not like me."

Michelle groaned, rubbing her feet. "I felt the same way when I met them. Only my situation was different. I knew if they found out I was pretending to be you, they'd probably never speak to me again—not to mention that I would have had to move out."

"But Grandpa and Grandma did, and they even welcomed you into their home."

"True. Their love and forgiveness was more than I deserved."

"Is there anyone in your life you have not forgiven?" Sara asked as they approached Strasburg.

Michelle sat quietly for several seconds before she answered. "For a long time, there was. My parents were abusive, and when my brothers and I became wards of the state and got shipped off to different foster parents, I was angry. I told myself I would never forgive our mom and dad for what they did to us, even if they got down on their knees and begged."

"What about now? Would you forgive them if they asked?"

"Yes, and I already have. In fact, I wrote them a letter the other day. Wanted my folks to know where I am and said I've forgiven them for the abusive things they did to me and my brothers while we were living with them."

### Strasburg

Sara didn't respond until they arrived at her grandparents' place. After she turned off the car's engine, she turned to face Michelle. "It had to be difficult for you to forgive your parents."

"From a human standpoint it was."

"Well, I want you to know that I have forgiven you for pretending to be me, but there are some people in my life I can't forgive right now. Truthfully, I'm not sure I ever will."

"With God's help you can."

Sara's chin trembled. "If there is a God, then He shouldn't allow people to keep secrets or treat others unfairly."

Before Michelle could put on her shoes and offer a response, Sara hopped out of the car and hurried to the house. Just thinking about the people in her life who had done her an injustice gave her a headache. And the idea of forgiving them seemed impossible.

⟨❧⟩

The minute her granddaughter entered the house, Mary Ruth knew something was wrong. Grimacing, Sara held her head and mumbled something about needing to go to her room to lie down.

*Should I go after her?* Mary Ruth wondered as Sara raced up the stairs. *Maybe she's sick or had a rough day at work. Oh, I hope nothing's happened between her and Michelle again.*

Mary Ruth was almost to the stairs when Michelle came in. "I don't know what happened with Sara," she said breathlessly. "We were talking in the car one minute, and then after we drove into the yard, Sara got out and took off for the house. Makes me wonder if she got upset about something I said."

Mary Ruth moved closer to Michelle. "What did you say to her?"

"We were talking about forgiving others, and Sara said if there's a God, He shouldn't allow people to keep secrets or treat others unfairly." Michelle's brows drew inward. "I was about to tell her that we are not puppets, and if other people do things to hurt us, it's not God's fault, because He gave everyone a free will. But I never got the chance to express that, since Sara hurried away."

Mary Ruth nodded slowly. "When Sara came in, I could tell she either wasn't feeling well or was upset about something. Apparently it was the latter."

"I guess so." Michelle gestured to the kitchen. "Can we go in there and talk more?"

"Of course. I'll fix some hot tea and you can tell me how things went with your job."

When Michelle entered the kitchen behind Mary Ruth, she filled the teakettle with water and placed it on the stove."

"Danki, but you didn't have to do that," Mary Ruth said.

"I was happy to heat the *wasser*. You and Willis certainly do enough for me. Besides, I enjoy helping out."

Mary Ruth smiled. "You're very kind." While she and Michelle waited for the water to heat, they took seats at the table.

"Where's Willis?" Michelle asked. "Is he out in the barn or taking a nap in his easy chair, like he often does this time of the day?"

"Neither. Our driver Stan picked Willis up after lunch and drove him to a chiropractic appointment. I'm guessing it took longer than expected. Either that, or they stopped afterward to run a few errands."

"At least we don't have to worry about them getting stuck in bad weather." Michelle glanced out the window. "The roads were perfectly clear on the way home, and there's no snow in sight."

"That's good to hear." Mary Ruth rose from the table. "Supper is in the oven, but it'll be at least an hour before we eat. Would you like an apple or some cheese and crackers to tide you over?"

"No, thanks. The only thing I need right now is something for my sore feet. I'm not used to being on them all day, but I'm sure after I've worked at the restaurant awhile I'll toughen up." Michelle gave a shallow laugh.

"I have some liniment you can rub on your feet and legs. And a warm soak in the tub might help as well."

"Good idea."

Mary Ruth leaned slightly forward. "Now about Sara. . . Do you think she still hasn't forgiven you for letting Willis and me believe you were her all those months?"

Michelle shook her head. "She said she's forgiven me, but I believe there is someone from Sara's past she hasn't forgiven."

"Did she say who?"

"No, but she did say there were some people in her life she can't forgive right now. She also said she wasn't sure she ever could."

Mary Ruth rapped her knuckles on the table. "I wonder if those people might be her parents. Perhaps she hasn't forgiven her biological father—whoever he is—for not coming forward and standing by her mother when she was pregnant. Or maybe she's holding a grudge because her mother didn't tell her about us when she was alive."

"But Sara knows about you now, and she ought to realize how much you love her."

"That is true."

The teakettle whistled, and Michelle jumped up to get it. Mary Ruth remained at the table while Michelle fixed their cups of tea. *I wonder how my granddaughter would respond if I brought up the topic of her not knowing about us until she read her mother's letter. I won't go barging up to Sara's room to say anything now, but when I am alone with her sometime and feel the time is right, I will bring up the subject. Hopefully she'll be willing to discuss it. And if Sara is holding resentment toward Rhoda, I pray she will forgive her, for that is the only way she will ever feel a sense of peace.*

Still wearing her coat, Sara held her temples as she paced her bedroom floor for the umpteenth time. *I need to clear my head and stop beating myself up about who my father is. And I don't want to think about forgiveness right now either. Maybe some fresh air will help.*

Sara went downstairs and stopped in the kitchen, where Michelle sat with Grandma, drinking tea. *It figures they'd be together. They've probably been talking about me.*

"I'm going outside for some fresh air," Sara announced.

"Would you like a cup of cinnamon tea?" Michelle asked, her feet propped up on an empty kitchen chair.

"No, thanks. Maybe later." Sara reached for the doorknob, just as Grandpa came in.

"Oh good, you're back!" Grandma got up and greeted him as he stepped into the kitchen. "I didn't hear your driver pull in. How did your appointment go?"

"Feel good as new again." Grandpa rolled his shoulders and neck with apparent ease. "But before I forget—I checked for phone messages out in the shed, and Sara, there is one for you."

"Okay, thanks Grandpa. I'll go out and see who it's from."

As she walked out onto the porch, Sara took a deep cleansing breath of the cool crisp evening air. This time of year, the atmosphere seemed so clean and fresh. Not like the heat of summer when the weather turned hot and humid.

Sadie barked and ran up to greet Sara, wagging her tail. "Hey, girl. How are you doing?" Sara stopped to pet the collie's head. "Bet you're lonely, huh? Well, come on and keep me company while I see who left me a message."

As if she understood what Sara had said, Sadie barked again, ran ahead, and sat waiting for Sara outside the phone shed.

Sara pulled open the door and left it partially open. When she sat on the chair inside, Sadie came in and plopped down on top of Sara's feet, which felt pretty nice. "You can keep my feet warm for me." Sara smiled, feeling a bit better from being with the dog.

Pushing the answering machine's MESSAGE button, she was surprised to hear a message from her stepfather. Dean didn't say much, just asked Sara to give him a call.

"That's strange. I wonder why he didn't call my cell phone." Sara looked at Sadie, as though expecting an answer. "Of course, since arriving, I've rarely used my cell or checked it regularly for messages."

Sara punched in Dean's number, and he answered on the second ring. "Hello, Dean. I got your message."

"Hi, Sara. Just wanted to call and see how your Christmas went. I got your card and had planned to call to wish you a Merry Christmas, but Kenny and I went out to dinner that evening and didn't get back till late. Now here it is, almost New Year's."

"Well, thanks." Sara was surprised by his call and felt a little guilty for not calling him or Kenny on Christmas. "Umm. . ." She shifted the receiver to her other ear, glancing down at Sadie.

"How have you been, Sara? We haven't talked in a while."

"I'm doing fine. How are things going there?"

"Okay. The people who rented your half of the duplex are nice, and I haven't had any trouble with them paying the rent on time."

"That's good." Sara mentioned her new job at the floral shop, and told Dean a few things about her grandparents. "Oh, by the way—how is Kenny doing?"

"Fine. He's in his room right now, doing homework and count-ing the days until he graduates from high school this spring."

"Hard to believe he'll be graduating."

"Yeah, it sure is."

"Well, I won't keep you, Sara, but before we hang up, I wanted to run something by you."

"What is it?" Sara asked.

"Would you mind if Kenny and I came to visit you sometime? Maybe when the winter weather is over and the roads will be safer. We could come some weekend, since I don't want Kenny to miss any school. I think it's past time for him to meet his grandparents, don't you?"

"Sure." Sara was stunned hearing Dean wanted to visit, but now it made sense. Kenny had every right to get to know Grandpa and Grandma, and they him.

"We may only come to visit for a few hours and go back on the same day. Or if we want to spend a little more time, we could get a hotel and stay overnight."

"Um. . . Okay. Give me a call when you think that might be."

"Sounds good. And don't forget, Sara, you can call me anytime you want. We shouldn't let so much time go by before we talk again."

"Yeah, you're right." Sara was anxious to end the conversation. "Sorry, Dean, but it's cold out here in the phone shack, and I need to go."

"Certainly, Sara. You take care now, and I'll talk to you again soon."

"Okay. Tell my little brother I said hi."

"Will do."

After Sara's stepfather said goodbye, she sat in the phone shed awhile, in spite of the cold. *Maybe I should have talked with him longer. It's really not that cold, and I am wearing a coat.* She glanced down at the dog. *Not to mention my feet are plenty warm, thanks to Sadie.*

It was nice Dean wanted to stay in touch, even if they'd never been close. Of course, the main reason for him coming to Strasburg would be for Kenny, not Sara. She tapped her knuckles on the table where the telephone sat. *No surprise. Dean's always thought more about Kenny's needs than mine. But I guess that's because he's his biological father.*

Coaxing Sadie along, Sara left the phone shed and walked back toward the house, feeling worse than she had before. She could not handle more guilt right now. *Guess I should have called Dean a few weeks ago, at least to wish him and Kenny a Merry Christmas, but I didn't want to ruin my own Christmas having to hear all about whatever Dean had bought for Kenny.* While Sara would not have admitted it to anyone, she didn't care that much about seeing her stepfather, although it would be nice to see her brother. If Dean really cared about Sara, he would have taken more of an interest in her when she was a girl, growing up.

# Chapter 22

The following day, Brad decided to stop by the flower shop in Strasburg to see Sara again. It was after twelve when he got there, but he hoped he wasn't too late to take her out to lunch.

When Brad entered the store, he saw no sign of Sara. An older woman with light brown hair, sprinkled with gray, sat behind the counter. As he approached, she smiled. "Good afternoon. May I help you, sir?"

"Umm...yes..." Brad glanced around. "Is Sara working today?"

"Yes, she's in the back room having lunch." The woman pointed over her shoulder. "Did you need to speak with her, or is there something I can help you with?"

"My name is Brad, and Sara and I know each other." He shifted his weight. "I'd like to talk to her if possible."

The woman rose from the stool. "I'll tell her you're here."

As he waited for Sara, Brad walked around the shop, looking at all the plants and flowers for sale. Some were kept in a refrigerated cooler, but most, like the indoor plants, had been set in various locations throughout the store.

*Think I might pay for one of these plants or a bouquet of flowers and have it sent to my aunt. She'd probably enjoy looking at it while she's recuperating from her recent surgery.* Brad thumped his head. *I should have thought to do that sooner.*

As he was contemplating which arrangement to choose, Sara came out of the back room, along with the woman who had been behind the desk.

"Hi, Brad." Sara offered a friendly smile. "Mrs. Roberts said you wanted to speak to me."

He gave a quick nod. "I'd hoped to take you out for lunch again, but I guess I got here too late."

"Yes, I'm almost done and will be back working behind the front desk again soon." She moved a little closer to him. "I'd offer to share my lunch with you, but I only brought half a sandwich today and it's nearly gone."

"That's okay. I'll pick up something to eat after I leave here." Brad's voice lowered when he saw Mrs. Roberts looking at him. No doubt she was listening in on their conversation.

He jammed his hands into his jacket pockets, feeling nervous and nearly tongue-tied all of a sudden. "Have you, uh, made any special plans for New Year's Eve?"

"No, I haven't. I'll probably spend the evening with my grandparents, and if they are too tired to stay up till midnight, I'll most likely go to bed too."

"What about Michelle? Won't she be there?"

Sara shook her head. "I heard her mention to Grandma that she will be doing something with Ezekiel that evening. I believe they'll be getting together with some of his friends. Come to think of it, Michelle said their get-together would be at his cousin Raymond's house."

"Do you think your grandparents would mind if I stole you away for at least part of New Year's Eve?" he asked. "There's going to be a Christian concert in Lancaster that evening, and I thought it would be fun to go."

She dropped her gaze to the floor, and then looked up at him again. "It sounds interesting, but let me check with Grandma and Grandpa first and see if they would mind if I go."

"Okay, sure. You have my number, so give me a call and let me know as soon as you've talked to them."

"I will." Sara cheeks turned slightly pink. "Guess I'd better go back and finish the little bit that's left of my lunch. Thanks for coming in, Brad. I'll talk to you soon."

When Sara disappeared into the back room, Brad stepped up

to the counter. His stomach growled while he picked a nicely colored bouquet for his aunt. "This should brighten up her day."

After he wrote a message for the card to accompany the flowers being sent, Brad checked his phone where all his addresses were stored. "And here is the address I'd like them to be sent to. My aunt lives in Seattle, Washington, so I hope it won't be a problem."

"No, we are an FTD florist, so we can schedule a delivery anywhere in the United States. Is there any particular day you want these to arrive?" Mrs. Roberts asked.

"As soon as you can send them would be nice." Brad clutched his stomach when it growled loudly again.

"Sounds like you'd better eat some lunch." She grinned.

"Yep, that's where I'm heading next." Brad paid for the purchase. "Okay. Well, thanks for taking care of that."

"Thank you for shopping here. Have a nice day."

Walking out the door, Brad's thoughts went to Sara again. He hoped the Lapps wouldn't object to her going to the concert with him, because he looked forward to being with her again, on a real date.

~∂~

Sara couldn't believe she was actually considering going to a Christian concert with Brad. *I'm not a religious person,* she told herself as she finished her lunch. *I may not even enjoy the music.* Sara drank the last of her bottled water. *But I would like to spend New Year's Eve with Brad.*

It made no sense that she'd be attracted to a man of God— preparing to go into the ministry, no less. She stared at her empty bottle. *Brad's not my type. We have nothing in common, really. Then why do I feel so drawn to him? Does Brad feel it too? Is that why he seems to be interested in me?*

It wasn't Brad's good looks that drew her to him either. It was his soft-spoken, gentle, caring way. He clearly was concerned about people and their problems. Everything about him seemed genuine. He was the real deal, not fake or trying to be impressive. She still hadn't told him things were better between her and Michelle or why. *Maybe if we go out on New Year's Eve I'll bring up the subject.*

Sara gathered up her things and looked at her watch. It was time to relieve Karen so she could take her lunch break. So for now, Sara would put all thoughts of Brad Fuller out of her mind and concentrate on greeting customers and placing orders. After she picked Michelle up at Dienners later this afternoon, Sara would stop by the grocery store and get something for tonight's supper. She had told Grandma this morning during breakfast that she'd cook this evening's meal. Unfortunately, Sara had no idea what to fix. Maybe Michelle would have some idea. After all, she knew Sara's grandparents better than she did, since she'd lived with them longer.

### Ronks

Michelle glanced at the clock. Just another thirty minutes and her shift would be done for the day. The lunch crowd had dispersed a few hours ago, and only a few customers had come in since then. But that was normal for this time of the day. In another hour, people would be coming in for supper, but Michelle would be gone by then. It was another chilly day, with fresh snow on the ground, so she would wait inside until closer to when Sara picked her up a little after four thirty.

An elderly Amish couple had just come in and been seated, so she went to take their orders. Michelle had noticed as they'd walked to the table that the woman used a cane, while the man supported her as she held onto his arm.

"If you have any questions about the items we serve, let me know." Michelle handed each of them a menu.

Since Michelle wore Amish clothes, they must have assumed she could speak their language, for they responded to her in Pennsylvania Dutch.

A warm tingle swept up the back of Michelle's neck, and then across her face. "Sorry, but I only know a few Amish words," she explained.

The woman tipped her head back, looking curiously at Michelle through her thick-lensed glasses. "Aren't you Amish?"

"N–no, not yet." Michelle tried not to stutter. "I want to become Amish though, and I'm taking classes to join the church."

The woman blinked rapidly. "Seriously?"

Michelle gave a brief nod.

"So you didn't grow up in an Amish home?"

"No."

"Then why would you want to join the Plain faith?" For the first time, the man spoke as he squinted his gray-blue eyes at Michelle.

With the way the couple looked at her, Michelle felt like she'd said something wrong. *Are they just curious or don't they approve of an English person becoming Amish?* Michelle hoped they didn't question her much longer. Was it really that unusual for an English person to want to become a member of the Amish church?

She pulled her shoulders straight back and lifted her chin. "I don't need modern things to make me happy, and I appreciate the simple lifestyle of the Amish people."

"Leaving your progressive world behind and becoming one of us Plain folks will be difficult." The man's gnarly fingers shook as he pointed at Michelle. "Very few people have done it, because it's not an easy road unless you are born into it and raised without modern-day conveniences."

"I understand." Hoping they wouldn't ask more questions, she gestured to their menus. "Would you like to choose something from there, or do you prefer to serve yourselves from the buffet? I believe the dinner items have recently been set out."

"We'll choose from the items on the buffet." The Amish man looked at his wife. "Right, Vera?"

She gave a brief nod.

"What would you both like to drink?" Michelle wondered how the woman would manage the buffet while holding a cane. She wasn't about to challenge this feisty couple, and thought they probably had things figured out on how to fill their plates.

"Water is fine for me," Vera replied.

"Same here," her husband said. "Oh, and I'd also like a cup of coffee. What about you, Vera. Do you want some *kaffi*?"

"No, just water this time." When she shook her head, the ties on her head covering swished back and forth.

"Okay then. While I get your drinks, feel free to go to the buffet." Michelle was about to walk away when the man spoke again.

"You don't have to join the Amish church to simplify. You can put some of our principles into practice and still remain English."

"Yeah, I know." Michelle wished this topic hadn't been brought up again. It felt as if the man thought her decision to become Amish was wrong. Was he hoping to talk her out of it? And if so, for what reason? Michelle didn't even know these people. She couldn't imagine why they would care whether she joined the Amish church or not.

Michelle pressed the order pad against her chest as she felt another uncontrollable rush of heat. "Will there be anything else?"

The man opened his mouth, as if to say something, but his wife spoke first. "No, that will be all. Thank you."

With relief, Michelle hurried away. *Will other Amish people react to me like that couple did?* she wondered. *Am I foolish to believe I can become one of them and that I'll be accepted? Maybe I haven't thought things through clearly enough. It might be good if I talk to Mary Ruth or Willis about this.* While they hadn't said anything to discourage her, the Lapps might believe Michelle was making a mistake taking steps to become Amish.

# Chapter 23

*Strasburg*

"Are you sleeping?" Mary Ruth stood near her husband's chair and nudged his arm.

He opened one eye and grinned at her. "Nope. Just restin' my eyes."

"If your eyes need resting, maybe the rest of you does too. Should we call it a night and head for *bett*?"

He yawned and put his recliner in an upright position. "Can't go to bed yet, Mary Ruth."

"Why not?"

"Cause we haven't had any of those apple dumplings you made earlier this evening." He winked at her. "It wouldn't seem right to break tradition and not eat an apple dumpling on New Year's Eve."

Chuckling, she swatted his arm playfully. "Very well then. Shall we go to the kitchen, or would you rather I bring them out here?"

"Let's eat 'em in here. I'll stoke up the logs in the fireplace and we can sit on the sofa together while we enjoy our sweet treats." Willis winked a second time. "It'll be just like the old days when you and I were courting."

Mary Ruth smiled, remembering their first New Year's Eve as a young couple. She had invited Willis to her house for supper and to play board games with her family. About an hour before midnight, her parents said they were tired and went off to bed. Her siblings, Alma, Thomas, and Paul, all married and a few years older than her, had already gone home, which left Mary Ruth and Willis alone to greet the New Year. Since Mary Ruth had made apple dumplings earlier that day, she brought some out to serve her special beau. Willis ate two, and said she was a fine cook, and then he added that after they were married, eating apple dumplings should be a New Year's tradition. Mary Ruth wasn't sure if he was kidding or not, but every year since then she had made apple dumplings to serve on New Year's Eve.

Pushing her reflections to the back of her mind, Mary Ruth went to the kitchen. When she returned a short time later with their treat, she was pleased to see Willis had a nice fire going. The warmth of it permeated all of the living room and offered additional light as well.

"Here you go, Willis." She placed the tray of apple dumplings on the coffee table, along with two mugs of hot cider.

"Danki." He took a seat on the couch and patted the cushion beside him. "Sit here beside me and we can eat together as we enjoy the fire."

Mary Ruth willingly obliged, then handed him a bowl with one of the dumplings and a spoon. "Seems kind of quiet here this evening without Sara and Michelle."

Just then, the hefty log in the fireplace popped loudly in the roaring blaze, sending sparks up the chimney. "Well it *was* quiet, that is. Guess I spoke too soon." Mary Ruth giggled. "Don't you just love the sound of a crackling fire and the smell of logs burning?"

"Sure do." Willis nodded. "I'm enjoyin' our time alone together too. And no doubt the girls are having a good time tonight with friends their age, rather than hangin' around us old folks."

"Jah, it is good for them to do some fun things with others." Mary Ruth reached for her mug, blew on the hot cider, and took a cautious sip. "Now that they both have jobs, I hope neither of them decides to move out." She heaved a deep sigh. "It would be so lonely here without them."

"I'm sure if they do move out, they will stay in the area. They both seem happier here now."

"I think so too." She set her mug back on the coffee table and turned to face Willis. "Even though Michelle isn't really our *grossdochder*, I feel like she's part of our family."

"I agree." Willis picked up his mug of apple cider. "I hope once Michelle finishes her instruction classes, she'll feel ready to join the church and won't have any doubts."

"Michelle talked with me last evening about an incident she had at the restaurant on Friday. She was upset because of it."

"What happened?" Willis asked.

"Michelle waited on an Amish couple, and when they started speaking Pennsylvania Dutch to her, she couldn't understand what they had said. With the clothes Michelle was wearing, the couple must have assumed she was Amish."

"Ah, I see. Bet it was kinda awkward for her."

"Jah. And after Michelle explained that she was learning to be Amish, they started questioning her decision, and she had the impression they were trying to talk her out of it." Mary Ruth paused for a breath. "It sounded like Michelle handled it well, but I could tell it rattled her a bit."

"She will be tested in many ways, but if Michelle truly wants this, her strength won't let those uncertainties get in the way." Willis gave his earlobe a tug—a habit he'd had since she'd known him. "And after hearing how she conducted herself, I am confident that she'll be okay. Michelle's a strong girl."

"I want to remain optimistic too." Mary Ruth sighed once more. "And what about Sara? Do you think she'll ever want to become Amish?"

He shrugged. "I'm guessing not, but that will be her decision."

Mary Ruth didn't voice her thoughts, but secretly she hoped their English granddaughter might also choose to join the Amish church. While it wouldn't make up for losing their one and only daughter to the English world, it would certainly be a comfort to have Sara become part of their church.

Michelle had never been too interested in card games, but Dutch Blitz, the one she was playing now with Ezekiel, his cousin

Raymond, and Raymond's girlfriend, Anna, held her interest. It had taken her a while to catch on, but once she did, the game became fun. While some English folks might not agree, Michelle thought game playing, and even just talking, was more enjoyable than watching TV. Sometimes, like now, she felt as though she were meant to be Amish. Other times, such as when she attended Amish church and couldn't understand everything being said, Michelle wondered if she would ever truly fit in with the Plain people.

If trying to learn everything wasn't challenging enough, the incident at the restaurant the other day had increased her reservations. Even with all the Amish couple's negative comments, Michelle thought she'd handled their questioning pretty well. Talking about it with Mary Ruth last night had eased some of her tension. At least for tonight she was being accepted, and all the laughter, fun, and games helped her relax. At moments like this, with Ezekiel by her side, Michelle felt as if things were finally looking up. Even Raymond's parents, before heading to bed, had joined their conversation and included Michelle in all that had been said. It was too bad Ezekiel's mom and dad hadn't accepted her so easily. She wondered if she would ever win them over.

"Anyone care for more potato chips and onion dip?" Raymond asked, pulling Michelle out of her ruminations. "Mom said there's more in the kitchen."

Anna shook her head. "I've snacked way too much this evening. Don't think I could eat another bite."

"And I'm fine with the bowl of pretzels still here on the table." Ezekiel looked at Michelle. "How about you?"

"I'm with Anna." Michelle put one hand beneath her chin. "I'm full up to here."

Ezekiel snickered, then reached under the table and clasped her other hand. "I think my aldi likes to *iwwerdreiwe*."

Michelle felt a tightening in her chest. *Here we go again. . . another Amish word I don't understand.* "I know *aldi* means 'girlfriend,' but what does *iwwerdreiwe* mean?" she asked.

"It's the Pennsylvania Dutch word for exaggerate," Ezekiel explained.

Exasperated, she let go of his hand. "I was not exaggerating. I really am too full to eat anything else."

"But you said you were full up to here." He touched a spot just below her chin.

She gave a huff. "Okay, so I embellished it a bit."

Anna's pale blue eyes twinkled as she smiled at Michelle from across the table. "And in the process, you learned a new Pennsylvania Dutch word."

Michelle bobbed her head. "True. Sometimes I wonder though if I'll ever be able to carry on a full conversation in your language."

"Aw, sure you will. It'll just take time and practice." Raymond picked up the deck of cards. "Is everyone ready for another game? If we get started now, we'll likely be done before the clock strikes midnight and we ring in the New Year."

"Sure, let's get to it." Ezekiel gave Michelle's arm a gentle nudge and said in a low voice, "I can't think of anyone I'd rather ring in the New Year with than you."

Michelle's cheeks warmed as she whispered back, "Same here."

⌒⌒

*Lancaster*

"What did you think of the concert?" Brad asked when he and Sara got into his minivan.

Sara's fingers twisted around the straps of her purse. "It was different than I thought it would be."

He tipped his head. "In what way?"

"When you said Christian concert, I expected to hear a lot of church hymns and such."

Brad smiled, slowly shaking his head. "It was a contemporary Christian concert, with a variety of musicians." He touched his chest. "And I, for one, enjoyed every group that performed tonight."

"Yeah, it was good." Sara didn't want him to think she wasn't interested in his kind of music or that she had no specific religious inclinations. She enjoyed Brad's company and hoped she could see him again the next time he visited Lancaster County.

Offering him what she hoped was a pleasant smile, she said, "I enjoyed being with you tonight. Thanks for inviting me to spend New Year's Eve with you."

"You're welcome. I enjoyed being with you too." He started the engine. "Are you hungry? Should we go somewhere for a bite to eat?"

"Would any place be open this late?"

"Oh, I'm sure since it's New Year's Eve some of the restaurants will be open till after midnight."

"I'm okay with that, but if you'd rather, we could just go back to my grandparents' house and have something to eat there." Sara giggled. "If I know Grandma, she probably made something yummy for her and Grandpa to eat this evening. And no doubt, she made plenty to go around."

"Okay, let's go there then. It'll be quieter and easier to visit." Brad pulled his vehicle out of the parking lot.

"Maybe by now Ezekiel has brought Michelle home. They might want to join us in the kitchen for a midnight snack."

"Yeah, that'd be fine too."

"Speaking of Michelle"—Sara looked over at Brad—"the two of us are getting along much better now."

"Well, that's good to hear." Brad sounded relieved. Sara sensed he'd been worried about her strained relationship with Michelle.

"After Michelle revealed some things about her life, I have a better understanding of her." Sara heaved a sigh. "And you will be happy to know that I have gotten over the fact that Michelle pretended to be me. I can't change what happened, and neither can she, so we may as well try to get along."

Brad reached over and squeezed Sara's hand. "I am glad to hear it."

"There's something else." Sara's gaze lowered as she explained about killing Michelle's dog. "Michelle forgave me for that too."

"I'm sure she knew you didn't do it on purpose."

"Yes, but I think she may have wondered at first."

"Thanks for sharing this with me, Sara." Brad turned the radio to a station playing Christian music. "The burden of what you were both feeling should be lifted now."

Sara nodded. "It is." *But I am carrying some other burdens I haven't told you about.*

As they headed back to Strasburg, Sara leaned her head against the passenger's headrest. The roads were bare and wet, but as they left the outskirts of Lancaster, snow flurries began. At first they came down lightly, but by the time they reached Strasburg, the wind had picked up and thick snowflakes came in flurries. It looked like the beginning of a blizzard.

"Maybe you should just drop me off and head back to your friend's place in Lancaster," Sara said as they turned onto her grandparents' driveway, now covered in snow. "I wouldn't want you to get stuck or slide off the road in this unpredictable weather."

"Not to worry. I'm sure it'll be fine. The last time I listened to the weather report, nothing was mentioned about a storm," Brad said. "Besides, I had snow tires put on the van before I came down here for Christmas break. But if it makes you feel any better, I'll leave right after midnight, when the New Year begins."

Sara smiled and touched his arm. "Okay, Brad. Now let's go inside."

# Chapter 24

*Strasburg*

I t looks like my grandparents must have gone to bed," Sara said when she and Brad entered the dimly lit house. She was thankful a battery-operated light had been left on in the living room.

"Maybe I should go," Brad responded. "I wouldn't want to wake them."

"It's okay. Their bedroom is near the end of the hall, and if we go out to the kitchen our voices are less likely to be heard."

"Sure, no problem." Brad followed Sara to the kitchen. She noticed the gas lamp hanging from the ceiling had been lit as well, giving plenty of light for them to see.

"Oh, yum. Look what Grandma left for us." Sara hung her coat on a wall peg before pointing to a tray of apple dumplings on the counter. She picked up the note lying beside them and read it to Brad. "Sara and Michelle, please help yourselves to these apple dumplings and feel free to share them with your dates." She looked at Brad. "Would you like one with a glass of milk or maybe some hot apple cider? It won't take long to heat it on the stove."

"Hot cider sounds good. And if those dumplings taste half as scrumptious as they look, I may have to eat two." Brad gave her a dimpled grin and draped his jacket over the back of a kitchen chair. "That is, if there's enough for me to have seconds."

She poked his arm playfully. "There are eight of the tasty morsels here, so if you're still hungry after eating one, I think a second helping can be arranged."

Brad formed a steeple with his hands and pressed them to his lips. "Thank you, ma'am."

Sara's heart skipped a beat as she gazed at his smiling face. His eyes appeared to be filled with an inner glow—almost as though it came from deep within his soul. Sara hadn't known Brad very long, but as near as she could tell, there wasn't a phony bone in this man's body. Too bad he was going back to his ministerial studies tomorrow. Sara wished she had the opportunity to spend more time with Brad so she could get to know him better. Being around him made her feel more relaxed than she had in a long time. Of course, her grandparents had that effect on her too, just not in the same way.

Pulling her thoughts aside, Sara took out two bowls for the apple dumplings and told Brad to help himself. As he was doing that, she got out the apple cider and poured enough for two cups into a kettle. While it heated, she put spoons and napkins on the table, and then suggested they both take a seat.

While Sara and Brad waited for the cider to heat, they ate the apple dumplings and visited.

"Yep, this is every bit as good as I thought it would be." Brad smacked his lips. "And I'm 100 percent sure I'll want another." He glanced at the stove. "Gotta have a dumpling to go with the cider, right?"

She snickered. "Yes, of course, and I'm not surprised you would want more than one apple dumpling."

When the cider was warm enough, Sara poured the golden liquid into their mugs. "Here you go, Brad." She placed his on the table in front of him, picked up Brad's bowl, and dished up another apple dumpling.

"Aren't you gonna have seconds?" He looked at her expectantly.

"One's plenty for me." Holding her cider, Sara took the seat across from him and took a cautious sip. "When do you think you might come down this way again?"

"Maybe some weekend, if the weather cooperates." He blew on his cider and took a drink. "Wow, this is as good as the dumplings. Is it homemade?"

"Yes. My grandpa has an old-fashioned cider press. I wasn't

here to watch him make this batch of apple cider, but he told me about it."

"Maybe next year you'll get in on it."

"I hope so. Even if I have my own place by then, it'll be somewhere in the area." Sara drank more of the cider. "After all the years I went without knowing I had maternal grandparents, I am determined to stay close to them so we can spend as much time together as possible."

Brad nodded slowly. "That's understandable."

"What about you? Where do you see yourself living once you finish your ministerial training?"

He shrugged his shoulders. "That all depends on where the Lord sends me."

"What do you mean?" She set her mug down.

"I will put my name in with the denomination I belong to. When a position opens, and I'm called for an interview, I'll do a lot of praying, because when I take a church, I may need to relocate to a different state."

Sara leaned her elbows on the table. "How would your family feel about that?"

"Mom and Dad probably wouldn't like it, especially since I am their only child. But they understand my need to answer God's call, so no doubt they'd give me their blessing."

She looked down at her empty bowl. "It must be nice to have parents who are so accepting."

"Yeah, it's great. Mom and Dad have a strong faith in God, which makes it easier for them to agree with my decision to become a minister." Brad's forehead wrinkled a bit. "Dad wasn't on board with it at first though. He's a chiropractor and wanted me to follow in his footsteps."

"I guess that's not uncommon. My stepfather has already made it clear that he wants my brother, Kenny, to learn the plumbing trade when he graduates from high school this coming spring."

"Is your brother all right with that?" Brad asked, taking a spoonful of dumpling.

"I guess so. I haven't heard anything to the contrary."

"Well, some kids do end up taking after their dads, but I'm not one of them." Brad gestured with his hand, and pointed above. "Gotta do what the Lord tells me to do and go wherever He leads."

Sara heard the whinny of a horse outside. She jumped up from the table. "I bet that's Ezekiel bringing Michelle home."

～∾～

"Are you sure you still want to come in for a while?" Michelle turned on the buggy seat to face Ezekiel, even though it was dark and she couldn't fully see his face. "The snow's coming down harder, and it could get worse before you leave for home."

"I'm not worried. Big Red does fine in the snow. He could probably take me there even if I wasn't guiding him with the reins." Ezekiel spoke with an air of confidence. "He's even gotten used to all the places I've taken him to deliver honey to my regular customers."

"Okay then, I'll fix us something to eat and drink. I see smoke coming out of the chimney, so how 'bout we sit by the fire to ring in the New Year?"

"Sounds pretty cozy."

Michelle opened the door on her side of the buggy. "I'll secure your horse to the hitching rail." Before Ezekiel could comment, she hopped down. Of course, her feet sank into the snow, sending a chill all the way up her legs. "Brr. . .it's so cold." She hurried to get Big Red tied to the rail, then made her way to the house.

Ezekiel stepped onto the porch behind her. "You didn't have to take care of my *gaul*. I would have done it, Michelle."

"No problem. I wanted to help." She gestured to the van parked near the house. "That must be Brad's, but it looks like he left his lights on. They're barely glowing. I wonder what time the concert got out, and how long he's been here."

"I better go turn them off, or he'll end up with a dead battery." Ezekiel pulled his jacket collar tighter around his neck.

"Okay, I'll wait for you here on the porch." Michelle blew out a breath and watched the cold vapor vanish into the blustery air. Jumping up and down didn't help. Her toes were beyond warming.

When he returned, Ezekiel stamped his feet on the mat by the door. "I couldn't turn off the lights. The van door is locked."

"Let's go inside and let Brad know. Maybe he can still start it up."

"Yeah, let's hope." Ezekiel gave his belly a thump. "If there's anything good to eat, I hope Brad and Sara left some for us."

Michelle bumped his arm with her elbow. "You would think something like that." She opened the door, and they both stepped into the house. "There's a light coming from the kitchen, so they must be in there."

Ezekiel pushed open the door, and Michelle stepped in first. Sure enough, Sara and Brad sat at the table. "Whatcha up to?" she asked.

Sara looked over her shoulder. "We're enjoying some of my grandma's yummy apple dumplings. Why don't you grab bowls and join us?"

"There's cider in the refrigerator that you can warm on the stove too," Brad interjected. "And boy, is it ever good."

"Before I delve into those dumplings, I wanted you to know that your van lights are on, Brad." Ezekiel pointed toward the kitchen window. "They look pretty dim. I was gonna turn 'em off, but the doors are locked."

"Oh, great." Brad thumped his head. "Thought I'd shut those off. The last thing I need is a dead battery." He leaped out of his chair and, without bothering to put on his jacket, raced out the back door.

While Michelle dished up dumplings for her and Ezekiel, he heated the cider and poured some into mugs. Then they both sat at the table.

"How was your evening?"

"How was the concert?"

Michelle giggled when she and Sara spoke at the same time. "Our evening was good." Michelle looked over at Ezekiel. "I learned how to play a new card game I'd never heard of before."

"Glad to hear it. The concert was nice too." Sara glanced at the door, as though watching for Brad.

"I noticed smoke coming from the chimney when Ezekiel and I rode in. Maybe once Brad comes inside, we can go to the living room and sit by the fire."

"Sounds like a good idea. Brad will need to warm up, since he left his coat hanging on the chair." Sara pointed, then she looked back at Michelle. "It was snowing pretty hard when we got here. How are things now?"

"Still snowing and blowing. Looks like it's turning into a blizzard," Ezekiel responded.

A few minutes later Brad returned, hair covered in snow and wearing a disgruntled expression. "My car won't start. Think the battery must've been weak, 'cause it's definitely dead." He went over to the sink and brushed the snow off his head. "On top of that, the snow's coming down so hard there's hardly any visibility. Since there's probably no place to get a new battery at this hour, guess I'll have to call a tow truck to come get the van. After it's towed, I'll give my friend Ned a call and see if he can give me a ride back to his apartment."

"I have a better idea," Michelle spoke up. "Why don't you and Ezekiel spend the night here? That way Sara and I won't have to worry about either of you."

Ezekiel shook his head. "I'm sure I can make it home fine with my horse and buggy."

"It might be a good idea if you did stay the night." Sara touched Brad's arm. "Since it's New Year's Eve and snowing like crazy, it might even be hard to get a tow truck to come out here." She gestured toward the living room. "One of you can sleep on the couch, and the other can take the downstairs guest room. I'm sure if Grandma and Grandpa were awake, they'd say the same thing."

Michelle bobbed her head. "Sara's right. By morning, the weather will hopefully have improved and at least the main roads been cleared. Then Ezekiel can go home, and Brad, you can call a tow truck, or maybe your friend could bring you a new battery."

Ezekiel rubbed his chin. "I don't know. I'd have to call my folks and leave a message so when they check their answering machine in the morning they'd know where I was and wouldn't worry. Oh, and I'd also need to put Big Red in the barn. Sure can't leave him hitched to the rail all night with the snow comin' down so hard, not to mention no food or water for the poor animal."

"You can borrow my cell phone to make the call. Then I'll help you take care of your horse." Brad reached into his shirt pocket and pulled out his phone. He looked over at Sara and smiled. "Guess we'll take you up on the offer to spend the night. If I can't get a new battery right away or the roads present a problem, I may have to rethink how I'll get back to school tomorrow. Hopefully, everything will look better in the morning."

# Chapter 25

Mary Ruth yawned as she padded down the hall toward the kitchen to get some coffee going and start breakfast. A few minutes ago, when she looked out their bedroom window, she noticed several inches of snow now blanketed the ground.

Approaching the living-room archway, Mary Ruth stopped short when she heard a sound she'd come to know well over the years. Someone was snoring, and it wasn't Willis. She'd seen her husband go into the bathroom a few seconds ago, so the heavy breathing, coupled with snoring, couldn't be coming from him. Perhaps because of the snow, Michelle had brought Sadie inside, instead of leaving her in the barn where she usually stayed.

Mary Ruth pursed her lips. *Could the dog be making all those familiar sounds?* Sadie had been known to snore as loud as any human being. Many afternoons when relaxing on the porch, Willis and Sadie would both end up napping. At times, Mary Ruth couldn't distinguish her husband's snoring from the dog's.

Poking her head into the room, she was surprised to see it wasn't Sadie cutting z's at all. Ezekiel King, fully clothed except for his shoes, was spread out on the couch with a blanket draped over him. He'd obviously spent the night.

*But why?* Mary Ruth tapped a fist against her lips. *When Ezekiel brought Michelle back from the gathering at Raymond's last night, had he been too tired to go home? Or had the roads gotten so bad from the snow that he decided to stay here instead?*

Knowing she would find out soon enough, Mary Ruth tiptoed out of the room and went straight to the kitchen. After lighting a gas lamp and lifting the window shade, she watched as a current of wind blew swirls of snow through the yard, swishing up and momentarily blinding the wintery scene. Her eyebrows lifted. *I wonder if this weather is the reason Ezekiel spent the night.* Looking farther out on the yard, she saw Ezekiel's carriage covered with snow. Not far from it, Brad's van was parked, also blanketed in snow. *Did he spend the night here too? If so, where is he now?*

Mary Ruth didn't have to wait long for an answer, for a few minutes later, Sara entered the kitchen. "I'm glad you're up. We had some overnight guests you weren't expecting," she announced.

Mary Ruth bobbed her head up and down. "I saw Ezekiel sleeping on the couch, and since Brad's van is parked outside, I assumed he must be here too."

Nodding, Sara pushed a lock of hair away from her face. "When he brought me home last night, I invited him in for a snack."

"I see." Mary Ruth leaned against the counter, waiting for Sara to continue.

"Then when Ezekiel and Michelle showed up, Ezekiel informed Brad that his van lights were still on but quite dim. So Brad rushed outside and discovered his battery was dead." Sara paused and cleared her throat. "Since it was late and snow had started coming down hard, we invited the guys to spend the night. Ezekiel took the living-room couch, and Brad is in the downstairs guest room. I hope you don't mind."

"Course not." Mary Ruth shook her head. "Staying the night was the sensible thing to do."

Sara's lips parted in a slow smile. No doubt she felt relief.

Mary Ruth filled the coffeepot with water. "Let's get some breakfast going. I imagine most anytime now, everyone will file into the kitchen, eager to eat."

Sara was about to go knock on the guest room door, when Brad stepped into the kitchen. Everyone else waited at the table. "Sorry for holding up breakfast." He reached up, pinching the bridge of his nose. "I was on the phone with my buddy Ned. He's going to pick up a battery for my van at the Walmart in Lancaster and bring it out to me. Then, once I get my rig running, we'll go to his place so I can pack up my things before heading back to the university."

"Are you sure the roads are clear enough to drive on this morning?" Sara's grandpa asked. "Looks like we had a pretty good snowfall last night. You might hit ice or snow all the way up to Clarks Summit."

"I agree." Sara's chin jutted out. "It could be dangerous. Maybe you should stay another day."

Brad peered out the kitchen window. "My tires are good. I should be fine." He scrubbed a hand over his face as he looked over at Sara. "If I didn't have to go back to class tomorrow, I'd stay longer, but I can't afford to get behind in my studies."

She slowly nodded. "You will call and let us know when you get there, I hope."

"Of course. I'd planned to do that anyway."

She smiled and gestured to the empty chair next to Ezekiel. "My grandma outdid herself fixing breakfast this morning. Please, join us."

"Now, Sara," Grandma said, "I can't take all the credit for this meal. You and Michelle made part of it." She pointed to the platter of ham and eggs.

"Everything looks delicious, so thank you ladies, one and all." Brad gave a thumbs-up and took a seat.

When Grandpa lowered his head for prayer, everyone else did the same. Sara wondered what her grandparents would think if they knew she only sat with her eyes closed out of respect, but never offered a single word in prayer. What was the point? If God was real, He wouldn't care about anything she had to say.

Soon after Brad left, Michelle stood on the porch, watching Ezekiel hitch his horse to the buggy. She hoped he wouldn't be in trouble with his parents for staying out all night. Had they received his message? Would they blame her for him not coming home last night?

*It wasn't my fault,* she reminded herself. *It was the blizzardlike conditions that made Ezekiel decide to stay overnight.*

Michelle waved as Ezekiel got into his buggy and headed out of the yard. With head held high, Big Red snorted and plodded through the snow as though it was nothing. Truth be told, Ezekiel probably could have made it home last night. But Michelle was glad he'd stayed. In addition to spending a few more hours with Ezekiel, she didn't have to worry about him being out on the road in bad conditions—not to mention dealing with any drivers who might have had too much alcohol to drink as they celebrated the New Year.

A chill ran through her body as she reflected on one particular New Year's Eve, when she was ten years old. Her parents had gone out for the evening, leaving her alone to care for her brothers. Michelle hadn't minded so much, since it allowed her and the boys a few hours of peace, without the threat that one of their parents might blow up at them. What she didn't like, and still remembered, was when Mom and Dad arrived home. He was in a drunken stupor, and she wasn't much better. They were both out of sorts, shouting all kinds of obscenities at each other, and ready to take their anger out on Michelle. Fortunately, Ernie and Jack were in bed, or they might have suffered the physical abuse Michelle had gotten later that night.

Her hand went instinctively to the middle of her back, where many welts had remained for several days after Dad used a thick, heavy strap on her. As far as Michelle could tell, she had done nothing to deserve such severe punishment. Her only crime was when she'd suggested Dad and Mom go to bed.

*"Don't be tellin' me what to do, sister. You ain't the boss around here,"* he'd hollered with slurred words. *While Dad went to get the oversized strip of leather, Mom shuffled off to bed. It was obvious she couldn't have cared less about her children's welfare.*

The back door opened, causing Michelle to jump. She turned

and saw Mary Ruth looking at her.

"What's wrong?" the woman asked, gently touching Michelle's arm. "Have you been crying?"

Michelle sniffed and swiped at the tears she hadn't realized were on her cheeks until now. "It—it's nothing," she murmured, rubbing her arms. "I'm just cold, is all."

"You should have put on more than a sweater to come out here." As usual, Mary Ruth's voice was soothing.

Silently, Michelle followed Mary Ruth inside. She wished she could shut the door on her memories as easily as she closed the door on the winter's cold. Would things from her past always be there to haunt her? If Michelle could erase all the painful recollections, she surely would. Truth was, maybe she still hadn't forgiven her folks.

Ezekiel looked at the snowy scene around him, as Big Red trotted down the newly plowed road. It was New Year's Day, and traffic was low, but it was hard to enjoy the quiet beauty with the thoughts of what might be awaiting him once he got home.

He hadn't expected anyone to answer when he called his parents last night, but no doubt by now, they would have gone to the phone shed and listened to his message. Would they understand his reason for staying at the Lapps'? Ezekiel figured they wouldn't be satisfied until they heard the whole story, especially Mom. Instead of rehearsing what he would tell his folks, Ezekiel leaned back, letting his horse continue to lead.

*Sure wish Michelle was sitting here beside me right now.* Ezekiel looked over at the empty seat next to him, where she sat on the way to and from his cousin's last night. Glancing out at the snow-covered hills, Ezekiel tried to redirect his thoughts by absorbing the untouched splendor. Before it was shoveled or plowed, the fresh fallen snow was pristine, hiding imperfections under a blanket of white. *Sorta like our sins when we accept Christ into our life,* he acknowledged. *But the Lord doesn't just cover our sins—He removes them.*

A short time later, Ezekiel guided his horse up the driveway. With no encouragement, Big Red trotted right up to the hitching rail. Once in the barn, after attending to the gelding and making sure he had plenty of feed, Ezekiel headed for the house.

After stomping his shoes on the rug by the door, he walked into the kitchen. The smell of maple syrup still lingered from breakfast. *I bet Mom fixed pancakes this morning.*

"*Guder mariye*, Ezekiel. It's nice of you to finally come home." His mother's remark startled him. Then her tone changed to concern. "You had me worried to death. Where were you all night, Son?"

"Mornin', Mom." Ezekiel took off his jacket and hung it on the peg, then balanced his hat on top of that. Running his fingers through his slightly damp hair, he sat down at the table. "I left a message on the answering machine explaining that I was staying at the Lapps'."

His mother's eyes opened wider and she gave a little gasp. "For goodness' sake."

Ezekiel figured Mom wouldn't take it very well, so he continued to explain. "When I took Michelle home, she invited me in. It wasn't midnight yet, and we wanted to see the New Year come in together." Ezekiel paused to take a quick breath. "Brad's van was there, and he'd left his lights on."

"What does that have to do with anything?" Her eyes narrowed.

"Nothing really, except his battery was dead, and because of the weather turning worse, we figured the chances were slim for him getting a tow truck to come." The next part, Ezekiel knew, would be difficult. "To make a long story short, Michelle suggested Brad and I spend the night and wait till the roads cleared this morning. Sara agreed. Neither of 'em wanted to worry about us being out on the unplowed roads."

"Oh, so you caused us to worry instead." Mom gave the top of her apron a tug, as though it was the source of her discomfort.

"So I'm guessing you didn't get my message?"

She shook her head. "Were the Lapps in agreement to you staying there overnight?"

"They were already in bed when we got there." Ezekiel watched his mother's muscles tense. *Why is she making such a big deal of this?*

Mom stood with her hands on her hips. "Do you have any idea how much I fretted? I got no sleep waiting for you to come home last night." She went to the stove and poured herself a cup of coffee but didn't offer any to Ezekiel. "I'm sure you didn't have one bit of trouble sleeping." She turned to face him. "And just where did you sleep, Ezekiel?"

"Mom, I have no idea what you are insinuating." Ezekiel felt a headache coming on as his frustration built. "But if it makes you feel any better, I slept on the Lapps' couch in the living room, and Brad took the guest room down the hall. Willis and Mary Ruth were in their bedroom, and the girls were upstairs in their rooms."

"Well, I don't think it was—" Mom looked toward the kitchen door as Ezekiel's dad came in from outside.

"Oh, there you are, Son. Glad to see you made it home okay." He hung his hat and jacket on an empty peg next to Ezekiel's.

"Do you know where our son has been all night?"

"Why yes, Belinda. I just came from the phone shed, checking messages, and I learned where Ezekiel was last night. I heard him and Big Red go past the shed when I was listening to his message too. Why do you ask?"

"Why?" Mom's eyebrows lifted. "And you're okay with him staying all night at the Lapps'?"

"Jah. Our son is home, and he's safe and sound." Dad gestured to Ezekiel. "It was a good decision, with the way the weather turned last night."

"Danki, Dad." Ezekiel got up from the table and gave his father's shoulder a couple of thumps. In times past, both Dad and Mom had been hard on him—especially where Michelle was concerned. It was nice to have Dad stick up for him this morning. "Think I'll go check on the beehives to make sure they're still in an upright position."

Looking down at the floor, Mom cleared her throat. "Would you like me to fix you some breakfast, Son?"

"No, thanks. I already ate." Ezekiel grabbed his boots and put them on. After slipping on his jacket and hat, he headed out the door.

Ezekiel had always respected his parents, but Mom was going a bit overboard this morning. *I would think by now she'd trust my decisions. After all, I am an adult.* He inhaled the cold crisp air, which helped to clear his head. *I realize Mom is just concerned, but is this how it will always be with her—never having anything nice to say about Michelle and always assuming the worst of her?*

Ezekiel felt ready to marry Michelle. In fact, he'd marry her tomorrow if possible. But until the classes were done and they'd joined the church, he would patiently wait. Michelle thought taking the classes would be a big test for her. Little did she know the bigger challenge would be his mother—not only for Michelle, but him as well.

# Chapter 26

By the end of January, the weather had improved from what it had been earlier in the month. If not for the temperature drop every evening, it seemed as if spring had arrived early this year. But Sara figured the warmer weather would be short lived and was only giving everyone a little tease of what was to come.

Things were going well at work, and they were gearing up for the flowers that would be sold before and on Valentine's Day. Sara was glad to be keeping busy at work, as well as at her grandparents' home. It took her mind off other things plaguing her lately. The fact that no one she had asked in her grandparents' church district knew who her biological father might be was one of the things disturbing Sara. But even more upsetting was that her mother had chosen to hide the truth from her, and also from Grandma and Grandpa. Sara had asked Dean once if Mama ever told him who her real father was, but his answer was no.

Sara tapped her pen on the hard surface of her desk. *I wonder if Dean does know the truth and is keeping it from me because he promised Mama he wouldn't say anything.* Sara had always known her stepfather was devoted to his wife, even though she felt certain he'd never truly accepted Sara as his daughter. *But then, maybe Dean knows nothing and never pushed Mama to reveal the name of my father.*

Since Sara's mother was no longer living and Sara couldn't confront her with this, she'd come to realize she might never know the truth. The more Sara thought about it, the more bitter she felt, so it was best if she kept her mind on other things.

Sara's thoughts turned in another direction. Last night she'd received a phone call from Brad. In fact, he had called her at least once a week since returning to ministerial school. In the most recent conversation he'd mentioned the possibility of making another trip to Strasburg soon—maybe some weekend in March. Sara looked forward to seeing him again.

*Brad must be at least a little interested in me,* she thought, *or he wouldn't have kept in touch at all. I just wish. . .*

Sara's introspections were pushed aside when the door opened and a middle-aged Amish man entered the shop. In December, he'd come to the flower shop to buy a Christmas plant for his wife. As Sara recalled, his name was Herschel Fisher.

"Good morning." He stepped up to the counter.

Sara smiled. "Morning. May I help you with something?"

"Yes, please. I'd like to buy more flowers for my wife."

*What a thoughtful man.* "Are you looking for a bouquet of cut flowers, or did you have a houseplant in mind? We have several nice African violets that are blooming right now."

Herschel pulled his fingers down the side of his bearded face. "You know, a blooming houseplant might be kind of nice. It will last a lot longer than fresh-cut flowers."

Sara bobbed her head and stepped out from behind the counter. "I'll show you what's available." She led the way to the area where the houseplants were located. As Herschel looked them over, she stood back and let him decide. Finally, after several minutes' deliberation, he chose a dark maroon violet with several lacey blooms.

Sara went back to the counter, rang up his purchase, and placed the plant inside a small cardboard box.

Herschel thanked her, picked up the box, and started across the room. When he reached the door and grasped the handle, she called out to him: "Tell your wife if she follows the watering directions that I put on the little card inside the box, the plant should do well and keep blooming for a good many years."

The Amish man turned his head, blinked his eyes at Sara, and was gone.

Sara's throat tightened. *Oh to have a man who loves me so much that he regularly buys flowers, even when it isn't a special occasion.*

❧

Clarks Summit

Brad sat in the school cafeteria, staring at his unfinished bowl of tomato soup, and thinking about Sara. Ever since he'd left Strasburg on New Year's Day, she'd been on his mind. He reflected on the events of New Year's Eve and how he'd been tempted to kiss her when the Lapps' grandfather clock struck twelve. But reason won out, and he'd only given Sara a brief hug, wishing her a happy new year.

*It's funny,* Brad thought, *but when I believed Michelle was Sara, I was attracted to her. Then, when I realized she wasn't a Christian, I backed off. Now I find myself interested in the real Sara.*

Truth was, Brad had no idea whether Sara was a believer or not. So why was he even considering trying to develop a relationship with her?

In his conversation with Sara last night, Brad had mentioned going to Strasburg to see her sometime in March. Even just a weekend there would give him a little more time to get to know her better. Maybe he'd find the courage to ask where she stood spiritually. If Sara was not a Christian, he would definitely need to curtail the feelings he was beginning to have for her.

"Is this seat taken?" A pleasant female voice cut into Brad's contemplations.

"Uh, no. Be my guest." He smiled at the pretty, dark-haired woman smiling down at him.

She pulled out a chair and sat down, placing her lunch tray on the table in front of her. "Hi, my name's Terri Conners. I don't believe we've met."

Brad held out his hand. "Brad Fuller. Nice to meet you, Terri."

Her long eyelashes fluttered as she gave him a dimpled grin. "Same here."

For lack of anything better to say, Brad picked up his spoon and ate the rest of his nearly cold soup. When he finished, he was surprised to see Terri watching him with a curious expression.

"Was I slurping?" he asked.

"A little bit."

Brad grabbed a napkin and wiped his mouth. "Sorry about that."

Her hand fluttered in Brad's direction. "No problem. I have three brothers, so I'm used to hearing a little slurping at the table. Besides, there really is no other way to eat soup."

He suppressed a snicker. "So where are you from, and what brought you to this university?"

"I was born and raised in Maine, and I came here with a scholarship. This is my second year." Terri took a sip of the chocolate milk on her tray. "My goal is to become a youth minister." She gestured to Brad. "How about you? What's your plan for after you graduate?"

"My goal is to take a church and minister full-time."

"Senior pastor or someone's assistant?" she asked.

"I don't know for sure. It all depends on what I'm offered." Brad wadded his napkin into a ball. "But even if I end up starting out as someone's assistant, I hope to move up the ranks someday."

She drank more milk and blotted her lips. "I'm a preacher's kid, so I know firsthand how tough the ministry can be. But the rewards outweigh the struggles and the often difficult tasks."

Brad reflected on her words a few seconds before responding. "I'm sure it won't be easy, but I can do all things through Christ."

"Yes." Terri's blue eyes sparkled with enthusiasm. "I cling to that verse in Philippians too."

Brad watched as she peeled back the covering on a small container of applesauce.

After taking a bite, she asked Brad another question. "What do you do when you have some free time? Is there anywhere you like to go?"

"I enjoy going to Strasburg when I get the chance. In fact, last summer I did some work for the Amish in that area."

"I've always wanted to see Amish country." Terri finished her applesauce. "What kind of work have you done for them?"

"Sometimes they hired me to drive them to appointments or some store that was too far from their home to take a horse and buggy. Other times, I was asked to help out with chores around someone's farm."

"Interesting. Maybe I'll take a drive down that way sometime, when I don't have my nose in the books."

Nodding, Brad rubbed the back of his neck. It was nice to talk with someone who shared his beliefs and understood about life in the ministry. He admired Terri for wanting to be a youth pastor. To him, that would be a bigger challenge than being a senior pastor of a megachurch. He hoped she was up to the task.

### Ronks

Michelle hurried toward the kitchen to turn in someone's dinner order. The restaurant had been busy ever since she'd begun her first shift shortly before noon. Michelle had been asked to work the lunch and dinner shifts this week. Since her schedule didn't coincide with Sara's, she'd hired Stan to take her to and from work. She hated spending money on a driver—especially when she still owed the Lapps some of the money she'd stolen from them last October. She didn't have much left to pay back, but the sooner Michelle got it done, the better she'd feel about it.

In addition to the temperature being colder in the evenings, walking home from work when it was dark outside wasn't a good idea. Otherwise, she wouldn't have minded one bit. Come spring, if Michelle still had a job here, she planned to walk to and from work every day. By then the days would be getting longer, and it wouldn't be dark when she walked home. The exercise would be good for her too, and she wouldn't feel obligated to Sara. While their relationship might not be considered a close friendship as such, they had reached a mutual understanding, and for that, she felt grateful. It was a far cry from the tension between them a few months ago.

Michelle's thoughts went to Ezekiel. How appreciative she felt for his friendship and the relationship they'd been building. He was kind, helpful, understanding, humble, and everything she'd ever wanted in a man. Ezekiel was nothing like some of the self-centered, commanding jerks she had dated in the past.

On New Year's Eve, they'd kissed a few moments before midnight, and Ezekiel wished her a happy new year at the stroke of midnight. Michelle sensed that he had wanted to kiss her again, but he didn't. With Brad and Sara in the room, Ezekiel probably felt a bit awkward.

*If he asked me to marry him right now, I'd say yes,* Michelle told herself as she moved in the direction of the dining room. *But I need to be patient and try not to put the buggy before the horse. Besides, we need to finish the classes we're taking so we can both join the church.*

Michelle straightened up a pile of menus that could easily have fallen to the floor. *Maybe Ezekiel has no plans of ever proposing. He might see me as nothing more than a friend.*

Michelle's thoughts took her back to the evening when Ezekiel came all the way up to Harrisburg to convince her to return to Strasburg and face Willis and Mary Ruth. He'd expressed his love for her then. And if he truly did love her, then surely a marriage proposal would eventually come.

Michelle entered the dining room, and was about to approach one of the tables in her section, when she saw a familiar face. Heart pounding, and hands shaking, she stopped walking and stood as though glued to the floor. Her old boyfriend Jerry sat at a table next to a young woman with short, bleached-blond hair. Since they sat in the section Michelle was responsible for, she had no choice but to wait on them.

Glancing at the clock on the far wall, Michelle's teeth clamped down on her lower lip. *Oh, how I wish it was quitting time. I'd be out that door in a flash.*

# Chapter 27

As Michelle stepped up to the table where Jerry and the blond woman sat, her mouth felt so dry she could barely swallow, let alone speak an intelligent sentence. Holding her ordering pad in front of her as though it were a shield, all she could do was stand there, looking at Jerry. At first glance, she realized his curly brown hair had been cut a bit shorter and neater. And instead of his normal attire of jeans and a T-shirt, Jerry wore a neatly pressed, dark-green buttoned shirt and tan-colored casual pants. She was surprised to see that he even wore a tie.

Squinting until his eyes appeared as mere slits, he stared back at her. "Michelle?"

She gave a slow nod.

Jerry's eyes opened wide. "What are you doin' here, and how come you're wearing that weird getup?" He pointed to Michelle's plain dress and apron.

Finally able to find her voice, she squeaked, "I work here, and I am wearing these clothes because I'm Amish. Or at least I will be sometime this spring." *If things go well, that is,* Michelle silently added.

With an obnoxious snort, Jerry turned to the woman in the chair beside him. "Can you believe that, Nicki? My old girlfriend's crossed over into an old-fashioned world of pioneer living."

His friend didn't hold back her own snicker. In fact, she seemed anxious to join in with Jerry's ridicule as she maintained steady eye contact with Michelle.

Michelle couldn't help noticing all the makeup this girl wore on her face, especially around her eyes, which were outlined in dark black pencil. The young woman's lashes were so thick with mascara, they clumped together. Her wrists were covered by several inches of bracelets, and numerous earrings dangled from both ears. The blond even wore a small loop in her nose.

Michelle thought back to when she wore makeup and jewelry, but she hadn't worn either in a good many weeks. Even when she wore makeup, it was never as much as this blond wore. Michelle did not miss wearing it either. *The poor girl probably doesn't realize she is covering up all her natural beauty.*

Aside from over-done jewelry and too much makeup, the blond was dressed like a model. What Michelle could see of her outfit, a pretty silk sleeveless blouse and nice black pants, made Jerry's new girlfriend look like she'd stepped out of a fashion magazine. Michelle also caught sight of the matching black jacket draped across the back of Nicki's chair.

Nicki sneered at Michelle, probably eager to hurl a few insults her way. To Michelle's surprise, *pathetic* was the only word the young woman said. Then, glancing at Jerry, they both laughed.

After taking his girlfriend's hand, Jerry looked back at Michelle and shook his head. "Never thought I'd see you again, much less lookin' like a frumpy ole housemaid. How in the world did you end up here in the middle of Amish country, and who'd you let talk you into crossin' over?"

Michelle was tempted to tell Jerry that none of it was his business, but in order to show she had changed since leaving him, she forced a smile, pulled her shoulders back, and held her head high. "It's a long story, and I'm sure you would be bored if I shared it."

With a smirk, he leaned in her direction. "Try me."

"I'd rather not." Michelle held her ground, staring right back at him. She was not going to let her ex-boyfriend get control of anything like he had done in the past. "Now if you came here to eat supper, what would you like to order? You can either get something off the menu, or choose whatever you want from the buffet." She gestured in that direction, trying, at the same time, to keep a composed demeanor. She wanted it to appear as though she was holding her own with this situation, but inside, Michelle was anything but calm.

"So, what do you want, babe?" Jerry nudged the woman beside him, who kept her gaze on Michelle, as if sizing her up and down. No doubt Nicki saw Michelle as nothing more than a country bumpkin.

Nicki glanced at the menu, squinting as she slid her finger down the items listed. Then, leaning over and holding the menu in front of her face, she whispered something to Jerry.

Michelle rolled her eyes as she waited impatiently. *She's probably talking about me.*

Jerry's friend set the menu down. "I'll do the buffet. It'll be quicker, and we don't wanna be late for the musical we came down here to see." She leaned closer to Jerry. "Do we, hon?"

"No we don't, babe." Jerry planted a kiss on Nicki's lips.

*Musical?* Ignoring the kiss, Michelle shifted the ordering pad from one hand to the other. Since when had Jerry become so refined? In the short time Michelle had dated him, he'd never invited her to go anywhere nice. Not unless the local pool hall or a drive to the store to get beer and frozen pizza could be considered nice. Hopefully, with Nicki, Jerry was cleaning up his act, but it was doubtful. And if he was, the guy still had a long ways to go.

Michelle stuck her pencil behind one ear, just under her white head covering. It was difficult to be patient as she waited for Jerry to decide what he wanted to eat.

"Guess I'll choose something from the buffet too, little miss Plain Jane." Jerry wrinkled his nose. "And if you care to know, I'm well rid of you, Michelle. I'm actually glad you split when you did, 'cause I was about done with our relationship anyways." He pointed at her head covering. "Seeing this new getup of yours, I sure wouldn't be seen with the likes of you now."

"Good to know." Michelle put on her cheeriest smile. "Thank you for sharing that information with me, Jerry. I appreciate your kindness." She started to walk away, but turned around in time to see Jerry's expression turn from thinking he'd worn her down to one of astonishment. Perhaps he'd underestimated her.

"Can I bring you two anything to drink other than water?" Michelle asked.

"I'll have a glass of beer." He looked at his date. "Better make that two. My girl here likes a little brew. Right, sweetie?"

Nicki snickered. "That's right, Jerry."

Michelle lifted her gaze to the ceiling. "This restaurant is run by a Christian family, and they don't serve alcoholic beverages."

"No beer, huh?" He grunted. "That's really stupid. Bet they lose a lot of business because of that old-fashioned decision."

"We should have gone to the place you took me to back in May," Nicki muttered.

Looking around at the crowded restaurant, where nearly every table was occupied, Michelle was tempted to argue with Jerry, but she didn't see the point. It wasn't worth the waste of time. Besides, this kind of talk was nothing new. Jerry thought he was right about everything.

"Maybe instead of coming here, you should have taken Nicki to that place you went to in *May*." Michelle stressed the word *May* to make sure Jerry heard it, loud and clear.

Michelle's steady stare on his face could have bored a hole in a piece of rock, and she found pleasure in seeing that the once-domineering Jerry had to look away. Michelle didn't flinch and almost laughed when he loosened his tie and tugged at the collar around his throat, which must have felt too tight.

*I cannot believe this guy. That two-timer was seeing Nicki last spring, when he was still with me. Wouldn't I have surprised Jerry if I'd agreed to move in with him? Guess he knew I meant it when I kept telling him no.*

Michelle found strength in holding her composure. Jerry didn't like to be turned down. He may have controlled her once, but not anymore. "Is there something else either of you would like to drink?" she asked.

Jerry flapped a hand in her direction. "Naw, I'll stick with $H_2O$."

Michelle looked at his girlfriend. "How about you?"

"I'd like a glass of root beer, please." The smirk on her lips remained. "You do serve that here, don't you?"

"Of course. I'll get your beverages while you're helping yourselves to the buffet." Michelle turned and hurried away. *At least one of them has a few manners—even though Nicki saying please is the only good manner she's shown. I hope that poor woman knows what she's in for, dating a creep like Jerry. Wish I could warn her. Who knows, he could be cheating on her too. But then even if I did alert Nicki, she probably wouldn't believe me. Hopefully, the pretty little blond will come to her senses before it's too late, and run as far away as possible from Jerry. People like him don't change overnight.*

*Strasburg*

As Sara did the supper dishes with her grandmother that evening, she thought about the two photo albums she'd found after her mother died. She had been meaning to share them with Grandpa and Grandma but wanted to bring the albums out when Michelle was not around. Since Michelle was working the dinner shift at the restaurant, this was the perfect opportunity. The pictures inside the scrapbooks were of Sara as a child and also some of Mama. These special mementos were for her grandparents' eyes only. Michelle was an outsider, not part of this family. Sara saw no reason to share the photos with her.

"Would you and Grandpa like to join me in the living room after we finish the dishes?" Sara looked over at her grandmother. "I have something special I'd like to show you."

With a curious expression, Grandma nodded. "Why, certainly. Your grandpa went out to the barn to do a final check on the animals, but as soon as he comes in, we can gather in the other room."

"Sounds good." Sara picked up another glass to dry. Since Grandma and Grandpa had no photographs in the house, she hoped they wouldn't object to looking at the album she had brought with her from New Jersey.

Half an hour later, Sara sat in the cozy but plain living room with her grandparents. Holding the albums in her lap, she'd taken a seat on the couch and asked them to sit on either side of her.

Firewood crackled and popped from the warm blaze Grandpa had built in the fireplace soon after he'd returned to the house.

"The day I found my mother's old Bible I came across these two books filled with photos," Sara began. "Since Mama is in many of the pictures, I thought you might want to see them."

Tipping her head to one side, Grandma looked at Grandpa as though seeking his permission. With only a slight hesitation, he gave an affirmative nod.

Sara's fingers trembled as she opened the first album. It began with a few pictures of Mama holding Sara when she was a baby. Even though Sara was still hurt by her mother's deception, seeing the photos again made her long for what she had lost.

Grandma's eyes teared up as she pointed to the first photo. "Look, Willis, it's our *dochder*, dressed in English clothes. And see here. . . Rhoda is holding a *boppli*." She looked at Sara then gestured to the baby on Mama's lap. "Is that you?"

"Yes. And on the next several pages there are more pictures of Mama and me in different stages of me growing up."

Sara's grandparents looked at every page in both albums. By the time they reached the last set of photos, Grandma's handkerchief was wet with tears. Grandpa too looked like he might break down crying. It tugged on Sara's heart to see how moved they were after seeing all these pictures of their only daughter.

Grandma sniffed and wiped at the wetness on her cheeks. "Oh, how I wish we could have seen our precious girl before she died." Using her fingertips, she made circles across her forehead. "It doesn't seem fair." Then, picking up the first album again, Sara's grandma flipped slowly through the pages one more time, sometimes stopping to run her finger over certain photos.

"If only Rhoda had come home or at least contacted us through the years." Grandpa reached across the back of the couch and patted Grandma's shoulder.

Seeing the pain these two dear people had endured caused Sara to choke up. *Oh Mama, you did a terrible thing when you ran away from home.* Her nose burned with unshed tears, but she refused to give in to them, because she'd already done enough crying when her mother died. Sara still held the second album in her lap. She sat staring at one of the pictures on the last page where her mother sat beside Dean on the sofa. It had been taken soon after they were married. *Oh Mama, how could you have hurt the ones you supposedly loved?*

Even though Sara loved her mother, she wasn't sure she could forgive Mama for the lie she'd lived all those years. Keeping her past a secret from Sara was bad enough, but losing contact with such loving parents was unimaginable.

At that moment, Sara made up her mind that as long as Grandma and Grandpa were still alive, she would be there for them. Sara's grandparents deserved her love and undivided attention.

Grandma handed the first album they'd looked at over to Grandpa so he could view the pictures again. It was understandable why that one held their interest more, since Sara's mom had only left a few weeks prior to when many of those early photos were taken. Except for the English clothing she wore, their daughter, no doubt, looked the same as they remembered.

Sara's grandparents grew quiet, presumably both deep in thought. *No one, and nothing, shall ever come between us,* Sara determined in her heart. *I will be here for Grandma and Grandpa for as long as they need me.*

# Chapter 28

When Michelle entered the kitchen the following morning, she felt guilty seeing Sara and Mary Ruth had already made breakfast. "Sorry for sleeping in. I should have been here to help." She took a pitcher of Mary Ruth's homemade grape juice from the refrigerator.

Mary Ruth smiled. "It's okay. Sara and I managed without your help today. You looked tired when you came home last night, so I thought you might want to sleep awhile longer this morning."

Michelle sighed. "I was tired and stressed. My afternoon went okay, but something happened during the dinner shift that really shook me up."

"What was it?" Sara asked. "Were they super busy at the restaurant?"

"Nothing out of the ordinary." Michelle pulled out a chair and sank into it with a moan. "My ex-boyfriend Jerry showed up with a new girlfriend. At least I thought she was new. Turns out he'd been dating her at the time he was seeing me."

Mary Ruth's brows wrinkled. "Who is Jerry?"

"He's a guy from Philadelphia who I should never have gotten involved with." Michelle's lips curled. "He was an abusive control freak, and I'm glad I got away from him when I did."

Mary Ruth stepped behind the chair where Michelle sat and placed her hands on Michelle's shoulders. "I am sorry you had a rough day. Did this Jerry fellow threaten to harm you in any way?"

"No, but he made fun of the way I was dressed, and when I told him I planned to join the Amish church, he said he was well rid of me." Michelle crossed her arms. "Even though the girl he was with acted kinda rude, I actually felt sorry for her. I'm sure she has no idea what Jerry is really like. In fact, she went along with his belittling comments, and seemed to enjoy it. He pretended to be charming when we first met, but it didn't take long until his true colors were brought to light. His apologies and promises that never held true made the next ones seem less believable." Michelle shook her head. "I was such a fool."

"Unfortunately, there are many people like your ex in this world." Sara's eyes appeared cold and flat. "They treat others with no respect—like they don't amount to anything at all."

Michelle wasn't sure if Sara was generalizing or referring to someone in particular. But it was obvious that Michelle wasn't the only one with an unhappy past.

Since it was Saturday, and Sara didn't have to work, shortly before noon she decided to go down to the basement. Grandpa had dropped Grandma off at one of her friend's for the day, and then he went to town to run several errands.

When Michelle said she wanted to get some sewing done, Sara saw this as a good opportunity to go down to the basement to read more of the notes in the prayer jar she'd found.

Beginning her descent into the darkness of the basement, it only took a moment for Sara to realize she'd forgotten a flashlight or a lantern. She refused to go into the musty cellar with no light to guide her down the worn, wooden steps, so she turned around and returned to the kitchen. At moments like this, Sara wondered if she would ever adjust to her grandparents' simple life of no electricity in their home. Normally, it didn't bother her so much, but sometimes she missed the ease of simply flipping a switch to turn on an overhead light.

Once she had a flashlight in hand, Sara headed back down the stairs, feeling a little more secure. While she wasn't afraid of the dark, Grandpa and Grandma's basement seemed kind of creepy—not to mention that Sara needed to see where she was going. She certainly didn't want to trip over something or run into an icky spider's web. Just thinking about those horrible eight-legged creatures gave her the willies.

At the bottom of the steps, Sara flashed the beam of light around the basement, searching for the battery-operated light Grandma kept near her antiquated washing machine. Sure enough, it was on the small table beside the washer.

Sara clicked it on, and a beam of light illuminated the area. Grandma kept the part of the basement where she washed clothes clean and organized. But some other areas were cluttered with boxes filled with all kinds of items. Looking past them, Sara aimed her flashlight in the direction of the shelves where the empty canning jars were kept. Climbing up on a stool, it didn't take long until she spotted the jar full of papers—the one Michelle referred to as a prayer jar.

The fact that two prayer jars existed—one here and one in the barn—fascinated Sara. Since neither she nor Michelle knew who had written the notes inside the jars, the mystery of it kept calling to her.

Sara took the jar down and seated herself on the stool. Unscrewing the old lid, she reached inside and pulled out one of the notes. It was different than the ones she'd read before. *"Turn your cares into prayers."* Five simple words, but not possible for Sara. She had too many cares in this world, and no amount of praying would remove them. If things went wrong, it was her responsibility to make them right whenever she could. The challenge of fixing other people's mistakes proved difficult, but at least she could try. One thing Sara had learned over the years was to take responsibility for her own actions and make the best of the hand she'd been dealt. Although she would never admit it out loud, there were times when she felt as if her world had spun out of control, and she was powerless to stop it.

Sara folded the piece of paper, put it back in the jar, and took another one. This one quoted Proverbs 28:26: *"He that trusteth in his own heart is a fool: but whoso walketh wisely, he shall be delivered."*

Sara shifted on the stool. It was hard to sit still. *So I'm a fool if I trust in my own heart, huh?* She crossed her right leg and bounced her foot up and down. *How's a person supposed to walk wisely if they don't trust in their own heart, which I assume means, thoughts?*

*Grandma's religious. I'll bet anything she's the one who wrote these messages.* Sara wished she felt free to ask her grandmother about them, but bringing up the prayer jars she and Michelle had found might be like opening Pandora's fabled box. For now at least, she would keep quiet about the prayer jars. Maybe someday, if the time was right, she would ask Grandma about them.

When Sara came up from the basement, she went to Grandma's sewing room to see how Michelle was doing. Seeing no sign of her there, Sara headed for the kitchen.

Michelle wasn't in that room either, but she had left a note on the table saying she'd gone over to the Kings' place to see Ezekiel.

*I wonder how long she'll be there.* Sara glanced out the kitchen window. *I hope she gets back before Lenore shows up to make greeting cards with us.*

Truthfully, Sara had gotten so caught up reading prayers, quotes, and Bible verses from the prayer jar in the basement she'd almost forgotten about Lenore coming over today. It wasn't until she saw the package of cardstock on one end of the kitchen counter that she remembered Lenore had called a few days ago to set things up. Until Sara's mind became preoccupied with other things, she'd been looking forward to getting together with her cousin. It would be fun to learn more about creating one-of-a-kind greeting cards using rubber stamps, colored pencils, pretty ribbons, and several other decorative items. There was nothing plain about the cards Lenore and many other Amish made to share with others.

Sara tapped her fingers on the edge of the counter. *I wonder if Karen Roberts would be interested in buying some of the cards Lenore makes to sell in the flower shop.* Sara made a mental note to mention it when she went to work next week.

Since it was almost noon, and Michelle wasn't back yet, Sara fixed a sandwich and ate lunch. When she finished eating, she washed her dishes and made sure the table was clean. Following that, she took a seat and waited for Lenore to arrive.

At one o'clock, Sara heard a horse and buggy pull in. Hoping it might be Michelle, she hurried to the back door and opened it. The horse at the rail was not Grandma's, so she knew it wasn't Michelle, because Peanuts was Michelle's favorite horse to drive. And since Grandpa had given Grandma a ride to her friend's using his horse and buggy, Michelle wouldn't have taken his rig either.

Sara watched as Lenore stepped down from the carriage and secured her mare. She did it with ease—as though she'd been doing it all her life.

Sara rubbed her arms to ward off the chill. The brief spring-like weather they'd enjoyed had vanished, and the cold winter temperatures were back. At least there'd been no recent ice or snow to deal with on the roads. Sara had never enjoyed driving in the snow and sometimes wished she lived where it was warm all year long, like Florida, the Bahamas, or Hawaii.

"Do you need any help?" Remembering her manners, Sara called to Lenore, as she removed a cardboard box from her buggy.

"No, I just have this one thing to carry. But thanks for offering." Lenore walked briskly across the yard and soon stepped onto the back porch. "Hello, Sara. It's good to see you again."

"It's nice to see you too." Sara opened the door wider. "You can set the box on the kitchen counter. I have the table cleared off and am more than ready for us to make some cards."

Lenore's dimples deepened when she smiled at Sara. "I've been looking forward to this time for the three of us to make cards and enjoy each other's company." She set the box down. "I hope you and Michelle will have as much fun making cards as I do."

Sara slipped her hands into her jeans pockets. "Unfortunately, Michelle is not here right now. When I came up from the basement earlier, I found a note she'd left, saying she was going over to

Ezekiel's. She may have forgotten about our plans to make cards today."

Lenore's brows furrowed a bit, but then relaxed. "That's okay. The two of us can have just as much fun making cards."

Sara bobbed her head. "Definitely. Oh, before we start, have you had lunch yet? I've already eaten, but I can fix you something."

"I ate before I came over, but thank you just the same." Lenore opened the flaps of the box and took out several items—scissors, cardstock, rubber stamps, ink pads, glue, glitter, and some colorful ribbons. Once she'd placed all the supplies on the table, they both took a seat.

"Before we get started, would you mind if I ask you a question that has nothing to do with stamping or creating beautiful cards?" Sara figured since she and her cousin were alone, this was a good time to see if Lenore knew anything about Sara's biological father.

Lenore smiled. "Sure, go ahead. What do you want to know?"

Sara moistened her lips. "It's about my mother."

"As I've mentioned before, I never met your mother." Lenore rubbed the tiny mole on her left arm.

"Yes, but I thought maybe your father may have said something."

"About what?"

"My mother. I am interested in who she used to hang out with."

Lenore massaged her forehead, as though deep in thought. "One time, I did overhear him talking to my mother about his sister."

Sara sat up straighter, her interest now piqued. "What did he say?"

"As I recall, Dad and Mom were discussing how, even after several years, Grandma couldn't deal with the sadness she felt over Rhoda leaving home."

Sara pushed against the back of her chair. "Yes, I am aware of that. What I need to know is whether your dad knew of anyone Mama might have been dating."

Lenore gave a slow nod. "I was just going to say that while talking with Mom, Dad said something about the English kids his sister liked to hang around with. He said one young fellow Rhoda talked to a lot worried him, because he was afraid the young man might influence her to go English and never join the Amish church."

"When I asked Uncle Ivan if he knew who my father was, he said no." Sara's jaw clenched. "I wonder why he never mentioned this English man to me."

Lenore lifted one hand, turning her palm upward. "I have no idea. Maybe you should ask him."

Sara gave a determined nod. "I most definitely will." This new bit of news her cousin had shared made Sara wonder if Uncle Ivan might be hiding something from her. It made no sense, but maybe, for some particular reason, he didn't want Sara to know who her real father was.

# Chapter 29

Michelle had just finished the morning shift and was preparing the tables for the lunch crowd, when a man with dark, curly hair entered the restaurant. At first glance she thought Jerry had come back, but a second look told her otherwise. This man was older and had the beginnings of a beard.

Michelle blew out a quick breath. *What a relief! I'm not ready for another encounter with my ex-boyfriend today, or any day for that matter. I don't even like calling him my ex-boyfriend. I certainly wasn't his girlfriend.*

Saturday, when she'd gone to the Kings' to see Ezekiel, Michelle had been disappointed because they were busy at the greenhouse and he couldn't talk to her for more than a few minutes. She'd managed to tell Ezekiel briefly about her encounter with Jerry, and he had been sympathetic. Michelle wished she could have gone into more detail about what had transpired. Hopefully, Ezekiel would have been pleased with how she'd handled the situation.

After Michelle left the greenhouse, she'd stopped by one of the restaurants in Strasburg and eaten lunch. Other people had been eating by themselves that day, but it was hard not to feel sorry for herself as she sat there all alone.

Sometimes Michelle truly felt as if she were alone. After all, she had no family anymore, and her only real friend was Ezekiel. At times, she wasn't even sure about him. Lately, they seemed to be drifting apart. Was it because he was so busy, or had Ezekiel lost interest in her?

After lunch, Michelle had gone back to the Lapps' and

discovered Lenore was there. That's when Michelle realized she'd forgotten that she, Sara, and Lenore were supposed to make greeting cards together.

*I sure messed that up,* Michelle berated herself. By the time she'd arrived, they were almost done. So instead of joining them, Michelle had gone to her room, saying she had a headache, which wasn't a lie.

Yesterday hadn't gone much better. The class she and Ezekiel had taken before Sunday service started seemed even more difficult to understand this time. After church, Ezekiel had said he wanted to take Michelle for a buggy ride, but he couldn't because he and his family had been invited to his aunt's home for supper and to play board games that could last well into the evening. Ezekiel had invited Michelle to go along, but she'd declined, sure that her presence would not be appreciated, since she was not a family member. "And I probably never will be," Michelle muttered under her breath.

"What was that? Were you speaking to me?"

Michelle's face heated when she turned and saw Linda, one of the other waitresses, standing behind her. "Sorry about that. I was talking to myself."

Linda snickered. "No problem. I do it sometimes too." She gestured to the front door, as several people entered the restaurant. "Looks like we might have another good crowd here today." Leaning close to Michelle's ear, she whispered, "More tips for us, right?"

Smiling, Michelle nodded. More tips were exactly what she needed. With any luck, by the end of this week, she'd have enough money to pay the Lapps the remainder of what she still owed.

⟳

*Paradise, Pennsylvania*

After Sara got off work Monday afternoon, she headed for the general store owned by her uncle Ivan. Since Andy and Karen had closed the flower shop a bit earlier today because of dental appointments, Sara had plenty of time to stop by Ivan's place of business. Afterward, she should still make it to Ronks in plenty of time to pick up Michelle when she got off work. Sara hoped Uncle Ivan wouldn't be too busy to talk to her, because she needed some answers.

A heavy rain had begun to fall, so after Sara pulled into the parking lot, she grabbed her umbrella. Hurrying toward the store, Sara tilted the umbrella back to glance at the sky. The ceiling of clouds had lowered, and ice pellets, mixed in with drops of rain, hit her face. She nervously bit her lip, watching the sleet melt as it made contact with the steps leading to the door. *I hope this doesn't turn icy before I leave. Slippery roads make me anxious.*

When Sara entered the store, she saw only a few customers browsing around, but there was no sign of Uncle Ivan. Stepping up to the counter, where her aunt Yvonne sat, she said hello and then asked if Ivan was in the store.

"It's good to see you, Sara." Aunt Yvonne motioned to the back of the building. "My husband's in the storage room, opening several boxes of books that came in recently."

"Would it be okay if I went there? I need to ask him something."

Her aunt smiled. "Certainly. I'm sure he won't mind at all."

Sara hurried in the direction her aunt had pointed. It didn't take long to find the storage room, since the door was partially open. She spotted Uncle Ivan kneeling on the floor beside one of the many cardboard boxes.

"Hi, Uncle Ivan." Sara spoke quietly, so as not to startle him. "Sorry to bother you, but I was wondering if you have a few minutes to talk."

"Course I do." He rose to his feet, gave her a hug, then gestured to the folding chairs on the opposite side of the room. "Let's take a seat so we can be more comfortable."

After they both sat down, he turned to her and smiled. "It's good to see you, Sara. I believe this is the first time you've been in our general store."

"Actually, I was here a few weeks ago when Grandma and I were out shopping one day. I think you were running errands at the time."

"I see." Ivan motioned toward the back door. "How's the weather out there? I've been back here quite a while and haven't had a chance to look outside."

"It started raining a few minutes ago, but there's sleet mixed in."

"Well, be careful when you go back out on the roads. You never know what the unpredictable weather's gonna do. You don't want to be caught on glazed-over roads." He reached around and rubbed a spot on his back. "I'm curious—what brings you to our store this afternoon?"

"I wanted to talk to you about my mother." Sara crossed her ankles, then uncrossed them. She hoped her uncle wouldn't suspect she was nervous about bringing up this conversation.

"What about Rhoda?"

"Well, last Saturday Lenore and I were together, making some greeting cards. During the course of our conversation, we talked about my mom."

He sat quietly, as though waiting for her to continue.

"Lenore mentioned she'd overheard you talking to your wife once about how Mama had run around with some English kids, and one fellow in particular. So, I thought maybe..."

Uncle Ivan held up his hand. "First of all, my daughter should not have been listening in on our conversation."

*I should have worded it differently.* Sara chose her next sentence carefully, in defense of Lenore. "I don't believe she was intentionally eavesdropping. Lenore happened to overhear what you said."

"Be that as it may, the conversation was between me and Yvonne, and she certainly had no right to repeat what she'd heard."

"While that might be true, what's been said has been said." Sara leaned forward in her chair. "Is it true that my mom ran around with some English fellow?"

Ivan nodded. "Rhoda had several English friends."

"Could the man you mentioned to your wife be my biological father?"

He shrugged his broad shoulders. "Anything's possible, but I only saw Rhoda with him a couple of times. And she never admitted to me that they were seeing each other socially or had developed a serious relationship." Ivan's forehead wrinkled. "Of course, during my sister's running-around time, she didn't share much of anything of importance with me."

"Do you know the man's name, or where he was from?"

Her uncle shook his head, then paused and gave his earlobe a tug. "Now that I think more about it, I did hear her call him Ricky one of the times I saw them together. Yeah, I think that was his name, but I have no idea where he was from."

"What was his last name?"

"I don't know; Rhoda never said."

Sara released an exasperated breath. At this rate she would never find out who her father was. Should she give up her search or keep asking around?

She jumped when Ivan spoke again. "I'm glad you stopped by, Sara, but it's getting late. Under normal circumstances, I'd invite you to stay and join us for supper later on, but I'd feel better if you were on your way home."

Sara glanced at her wristwatch. "I guess you are right. Michelle gets off work soon, and I need to pick her up. Then we'll head straight home. I'm sure Grandma will have supper started by then." Her fingers curled into the palms of her hands as she walked with her uncle to the door. *Surely someone has to know who Mama became serious about. And if a man named Ricky was the one, then there has to be a way to find out his last name and where he's from. The question is, Who else can I ask?*

### Strasburg

As pellets of ice bounced off the windshield, Sara drove slower.

"How was work today?" Michelle asked.

"It went okay. My employers closed the store early today, so before I came to get you I dropped by my uncle Ivan's store in Paradise."

"I've only been there once. Did you get some shopping done?"

"No, I didn't go there to shop." Sara kept her gaze on the road ahead, as the nasty weather had worsened.

"Why did you go there then?"

"To ask Uncle Ivan if he knew anything about a certain man my mother was seen with during her running-around days. I'm still hoping to find out who my biological father is." Sara gripped the steering wheel tighter. "I get so frustrated when I ask people about it and no one seems to know anything."

"Maybe you're not supposed to find out." Michelle sighed. "If I had a choice of having a father or not, I sure would have been better off not knowing mine. Of course," she admitted, "I'm saying that in hindsight now."

Sara's eyes opened wide. Gripping the steering wheel, she yelled: "Hold on!" The wet roads had caused the car to slide when Sara hit the brakes. The next thing she knew, they'd ended up in a low-lying ditch.

"Sara, are you okay?" Michelle held onto the grab handle above the passenger door.

"Yeah. How about you?" Sara's fingers hurt when she tried to open them after clamping onto the steering wheel so tightly.

"I'm not hurt. Just shook up a bit."

Sara turned her head and looked out the back window. "I hope I didn't hit that cat."

"What cat?" Michelle also turned to look. "I don't see anything."

"A gray cat darted out in front of us. I'm surprised you didn't see it." Sara's hands shook. "The last thing I need is to kill another animal." She clamped her hand over her mouth. "Michelle, I'm sorry. I didn't mean to say it like that." Weeks had gone by since Rascal's death, and Sara's comment had even startled her. She did not want to stir up any emotions from that day. Especially when things were going better between her and Michelle.

"It's okay. Guess we better see if any damage was done to your car."

"I agree." Sara realized she had to deal with the situation at hand, but she felt grateful Michelle wasn't offended by her previous comment.

They got out of the car and went around to look at the front, and then the back of vehicle. There didn't appear to be any damage, but Sara's car was wedged in the ditch, with the back right tire suspended in midair.

Sara groaned. "This is not good."

"How about you get into the car, and I'll try to push you out." Michelle went back to the front seat to retrieve her gloves, then walked to the back of the car again. The ditch had water lying in it, and even though shallow, Sara could see Michelle's feet had gotten quite wet.

"Okay, I'm going to ease on the gas," Sara hollered, after sliding into her seat.

"Go ahead. I'm ready."

Sara watched in the rearview mirror as Michelle put her hands on the right side of the trunk and started pushing. The car didn't budge.

"Try again." Michelle motioned.

Sara put her foot on the accelerator, but her vehicle still did not move. "Let's try to get a rocking motion going," she shouted through the open window. "That might work."

"Okay!" Michelle worked with Sara, and they managed to get the car rocking back and forth. Unfortunately, the ditch would not let go of Sara's vehicle. To make matters worse, each time Sara eased harder on the gas, the left tire sprayed Michelle with mud.

Walking to the driver's side, Michelle wiped her face. "This isn't working. We're really stuck."

"We'd better lock up the car and walk the rest of the way home," Sara suggested, looking toward the sound of horse's hooves *clip-clopping* on the pavement.

A few minutes later, an Amish buggy, heading in the opposite direction pulled up on the other side of the road. The driver got out and secured his horse to a fence post nearby. When he walked across and joined them, Sara recognized him right away.

"Do you need some help?" When he looked at Sara, his brows rose slightly. "Don't you work at the flower shop in Strasburg?"

"Why yes. And you're Herschel Fisher." Sara looked at Michelle. "Mr. Fisher is a customer at the flower shop."

"Nice to meet you." Michelle glanced at her soggy-looking feet, then back at Mr. Fisher. "We're stuck. We tried rocking the car, hoping to get it out of the ditch, but I don't have enough strength to even budge the vehicle."

"Let me help you." Herschel looked at Sara. "Just ease on the gas when I tell you." He turned to Michelle. "You'd better stand back out of the way."

Michelle did as she was told. All it took was Herschel's strength, and after a few pushes, Sara's car was out of the ditch.

She sighed with relief. "How can I ever thank you, Mr. Fisher?" Sara noticed his clothes were sprayed with mud too.

"No thanks is needed."

She got out of the car and handed him and Michelle paper towels.

"Yeah, thanks, Mr. Fisher. Without you, we would still be stuck." Michelle wiped her face with the towel.

Herschel touched the brim of his hat. "I'm glad I happened along when I did." He told the girls goodbye and hurried back to his buggy. When he reached it, he turned and shouted, "Be careful driving. The roads might get icy as the temperature starts to dip."

"We don't have far to go. Thanks again." Sara joined Michelle in the car. When she turned the heat up, Michelle tossed her gloves on the floor and held her hands toward the vent. "Boy, I'm glad he came along when he did."

"Me too." Sara looked out her side mirror, watching Herschel's buggy as it got farther away. "The next time that nice man comes into the flower shop, I'm going to pay for whatever he purchases."

"Good idea." Michelle bobbed her head. "This incident has made me realize how much I appreciate the Amish people in this community. Most that I know are always willing to help when someone has a need."

"You're right," Sara agreed. "Everyone is like family—willing to be there for each other. I admire that so much."

Michelle gave Sara's arm a light tap. "Maybe you should think about giving up your English ways and becoming Amish."

Sara glanced at Michelle, then focused back on the road. "It's a nice thought, but I think not."

# Chapter 30

On Valentine's Day, at Mary Ruth's request, Michelle walked out to get the mail. She had done this every day when she'd first lived with the Lapps so she could intercept any letters the real Sara might have sent.

*I should never have deceived them like that.* Michelle kicked a clump of dirt in the graveled driveway. *If I could only go back in time, I'd make it all right.*

It wasn't good to dwell on the past or berate herself for things she couldn't change, but sometimes the memory of her lies plagued her. She'd been forgiven, and for that she was thankful, but perhaps she still hadn't pardoned herself.

Michelle's breath expelled in a frosty vapor as a shiver went through her. The morning air was nippy, this second Thursday of February. She looked up toward the sky. Every day last week had been cloudy and dreary, but today the clouds were finally peeling away. Behind them she enjoyed the large patches of crystal-blue sky and the warmth of a brilliant sun. In certain areas where cloud formations still mingled, translucent rays of light scattered over the ground below.

Michelle hugged her arms around herself. Even though February was a cold month, this weather was invigorating. But spring would start next month, and she was eager for warmer temperatures too. Today being Valentine's Day made the sun's appearance even more special.

When Michelle reached the mailbox, she pulled out a stack of mail that included several advertisement flyers, as well as envelopes that appeared to be bills. One letter was addressed to Sara and postmarked, *"Clarks Summit."*

She smiled. *I bet this is from Brad. He's the only person we know who lives up there.* She turned the square envelope over and studied it a few seconds. *I wonder if this is a Valentine's Day card.*

Michelle thumbed through the mail once more to see if any envelopes were addressed to her. Finding none, she closed the mailbox flap and started back toward the house. As she approached the Lapps' home, she stopped walking and stood looking up with her mouth slightly open. On the frosty roof, someone had written a message for her: MICHELLE. . . LOOK IN THE BARN.

*Now who would climb all the way up there and leave me a message like that? Surely Willis wouldn't have done anything so dangerous. His wife would have a conniption if he took a chance like that.*

Michelle hurried into the house, dropped the mail on the table, then ran all the way to the barn. She'd barely gotten inside, when Ezekiel stepped out of the shadows, causing her to jump.

"Ezekiel, you about scared me to death! What are you doing here at this time of day? Shouldn't you be helping at the greenhouse?"

"I will be, but we don't open for another hour or so. I have plenty of time to get back by then." He moved closer. So close, she could feel his warm breath on her face. "I came to bring you a Valentine's Day present."

Confused, Michelle tipped her head. Ezekiel held no present in his hands. But then, seeing him here on this cold, raw morning was gift enough in itself.

"Didn't you see the *botschaft* I left on the Lapps' roof for you?" he asked.

"I did see the message, which is why I came running out to the barn. I just didn't realize you were the one who wrote it." Pleased that she'd understood the Pennsylvania Dutch word Ezekiel had spoken, Michelle poked his arm. "What were you thinking, pulling a stunt like that? The roof is high, not to mention slippery from the frost. How did you even get up there?

Don't you realize how dangerous it could—"

Ezekiel wrapped his arms around Michelle's waist and stopped her words with a kiss so sweet she forgot all the questions he had not yet answered. When the kiss ended, she pulled back slightly, looking up at him with a heart full of love. "So you are my Valentine's Day present?"

He shook his head. "Not really. I'm just the messenger and deliverer of the gift."

"What gift?"

Ezekiel took hold of Michelle's hand. "Come with me, and soon you will see your Valentine's Day surprise."

She followed him willingly toward the back of the barn, where a gas lantern hanging from the rafters had been lit. When they reached a small wooden barrier, Ezekiel stopped and pointed inside. "Happy Valentine's Day, Michelle. I hope you like her."

Sleeping in a pile of straw lay the cutest little auburn-haired pup.

"The puppy's an Irish setter, and she's seven weeks old today." Ezekiel slipped his arm around Michelle's waist. "I know she won't replace Rascal, but the puppy needs a loving owner, and I believe you're the one she's meant to have."

Tears slipped from Michelle's eyes and rolled down her cheeks. "Oh Ezekiel, danki." She stepped over the enclosure, bent down, and scooped the pup into her arms. "I'm gonna call her, Val— short for—"

"Valentine's Day." Ezekiel finished Michelle's sentence. "When I went to look at the puppies, this cute little thing was the only one left out of a litter of fourteen. I wasn't going to let her get away." He reached out to rub the dog's ears, covered with wavy fur. "When I saw the pup's auburn fur, it reminded me of the color of your hair—not to mention that auburn is kind of a reddish color, appropriate for Valentine's Day."

Holding securely to her new pet, Michelle stepped back over the barricade and kissed Ezekiel's cheek. "It's all so perfect. This is the best Valentine's gift anyone has ever given me. Not that I've had many presents on Valentine's Day."

He returned the kiss on Michelle's lips. "And you are the best *aldi* any man could ever want. I love you with all my heart."

"I love you too, Ezekiel."

At that moment, the puppy woke up and licked Michelle's chin. Hints of Val's sweet-smelling breath reached her. Chuckling, she stroked the dog's silky head. One thing she would teach little Val when she was old enough to learn would be not to chase cars. Michelle couldn't risk losing another dog.

Sara had just entered the kitchen to help Grandma with breakfast, when Michelle came into the room, holding a bundle of auburn-colored fur in her arms and smiling ear to ear.

"Look what Ezekiel gave me for Valentine's Day." She held the puppy up and then draped the little thing over her shoulder as if it were a baby.

"What a *siess hundli*!" Sara's grandma exclaimed. "And what a thoughtful gift Ezekiel gave you this morning."

Michelle nuzzled the pup with her nose. "You're right, Mary Ruth. She is a sweet puppy."

"Have you chosen a name for her yet?" Sara questioned.

"Yep. Since I got the puppy on Valentine's Day, I decided to call her Val."

"Now that's appropriate," Grandpa interjected when he entered the kitchen. "I went out to the barn a short time ago, and just before Ezekiel left, he told me how he'd surprised you with the *hundli*. And that's not all." He grinned at Michelle. "That beau of yours told me how he climbed up on our roof this morning and wrote a message for you in the frost."

"*Jah*, I couldn't believe he would do such a thing. I'm not sure I want to know how he got up there either. Oh, and speaking of messages—there's an envelope for you on the table, Sara." Michelle motioned with her head. "It's postmarked Clarks Summit, so it's probably from Brad." A slow smile spread across Michelle's face. "I bet he sent you a Valentine card."

"I wouldn't be surprised if that fellow's not sweet on you, Sara." Grandpa's bushy brows jiggled up and down.

With trembling fingers, Sara looked through the stack of mail. When she came to the one in question, she tore it open. Her shoulders slumped, however, when she saw a "thinking of you" card with a verse of scripture on the inside. She read: " 'They that trust in the Lord shall be as mount Zion, which cannot be removed, but abideth for ever.' Psalm 125:1."

Sara pursed her lips. *I wonder what that's supposed to mean. What exactly is Brad trying to tell me?*

"Is it a Valentine's card?" Michelle asked.

Sara shook her head. "Just a 'thinking of you' card." Unable to hide her disappointment, she moved over to the stove to heat up the frying pan in readiness for the bacon Grandma had taken from the refrigerator.

"Uh-oh." Michelle giggled, holding little Val away from her shoulder. "Looks like this little *schtinker* just initiated me."

Sara turned toward Michelle and noticed a wet area forming on the front of her dress.

Michelle switched arms and cuddled her puppy. "I'll take the cutie back to the barn. Then I'll come back in and change clothes before I sit down to breakfast."

"There are some cardboard boxes in the basement. If you like, you can put your puppy in that and keep her inside while we eat," Grandma suggested.

"Sounds like a good idea, but I'd better get her introduced to Sadie." Michelle put her jacket back on. "Wish me luck."

It was wrong to feel envious, but Sara couldn't help feeling a bit jealous of Michelle. Her boyfriend cared so much about her that he'd not only given her a puppy, but he had risked life and limb to leave Michelle a message on Grandma and Grandpa's frosty roof this morning. Every day when Michelle looked at her puppy, she'd be reminded of how much Ezekiel loved her.

Sara hadn't heard a word from Brad in two weeks, and now just a note with a scripture she didn't understand? *The least he could have done is send me a Valentine card. Of course,* Sara thought, when reason won out, *I am not Brad's girlfriend, so why would he have even thought about me in relationship to Valentine's Day? We haven't known each other very long, and to him I'm only an acquaintance. For all I know, he already has a girlfriend. I'm just fooling myself to think he might be interested in me.*

As the bacon began to sizzle, Sara reflected more on the situation. It was too soon to really know how she felt about Brad, but for some reason, ever since she'd met the would-be preacher, he had been on her mind.

❧

### Clarks Summit

As Brad prepared for his first class, his thoughts went to Sara, as they often did since he'd returned from Strasburg on New Year's. Had she received his "thinking of you" card by now? If so, Brad wondered what her reaction was to the verse of scripture he'd included. It was the one God had placed on his heart to include.

He glanced at the calendar on his cell phone. It was Valentine's Day, and he'd remembered his mother with a card and a dozen pink carnations—her favorite flower. He'd ordered it from a local florist, and the flowers had been delivered to his aunt's place in Seattle, where he assumed Mom was still helping out. Brad had also sent Aunt Marlene another bouquet, because she loved the first one he'd sent while recuperating and he didn't want her to feel left out.

Brad had toyed with the idea of sending flowers to Sara but dismissed the idea. Not only would it be an added expense, but she might get the wrong idea.

He looked at his watch and saw he still had enough time to get to the university. Maybe he'd opt for a bowl of cereal this morning since it wouldn't take long to eat.

When he went to get a bowl, his cell phone rang. Seeing it was his parents' number, he answered right away.

"Hi, Brad, it's Mom."

"Hey, Mom, how you doing? I was just thinking of you and Aunt Marlene."

"I'm well. Just wanted to call and let you know I'm home. But first, and most importantly, happy belated birthday, Brad." She sighed. "I was going to call last Friday on your birthday, because I thought I'd be home by then. Unfortunately, your aunt came down with a bad cold, and I had to stay an extra week. Sorry we missed Christmas together, and now your birthday came and went too."

"It's okay, Mom. I've been so busy I have hardly had time to think about it." Brad looked at his watch again and saw he only had half an hour until his first class started. Since he hadn't talked to his mother since Aunt Marlene's surgery, he'd just skip breakfast so he could talk longer to her. "How is Aunt Marlene doing since I last talked to you?"

"She did well after some convincing to lay low. You know how your aunt is—nothing keeps her down. Anyway, she healed well from her surgery, and luckily her cold only lasted a few days, so I was able to come home yesterday." She paused, and then added, "I want to thank you for the beautiful pink carnations you sent me. They were delivered to her house two days before I left. And your aunt liked her flowers too."

"Good to hear. Glad I sent them early."

"Yes, I'm sitting here looking at a picture of them now. You remembered pink carnations are my favorite. Unfortunately, I couldn't bring them home in my suitcase."

"I'm glad you got to enjoy the flowers for a few days. Hey, how's Dad doing? Did he manage okay while you were gone?"

"He said so. I'm sure he enjoyed the peace and quiet." She paused again, then asked, "Did you get your friend anything for Valentine's Day?"

"Are you referring to Sara?"

"If that's the one you told me about the last time we talked, then yes."

"No, Mom, we're still just friends, so it wasn't appropriate to send something to her for Valentine's Day." Brad looked at his watch one more time. "Sorry, Mom, but I'm gonna have to go. I have fifteen minutes to get to my first class."

"Okay, Brad. Have a good day. Oh, and I'll fix you something special for dinner when we see you next time."

"No problem, and tell Dad I said hi."

As Brad put on his coat, he thought about his mother's question. *I need to get to know Sara better before giving her any gifts,* Brad told himself as he gathered a stack of books and put them in his backpack. Since spring break would be coming up next month, he hoped to make a trip to Strasburg and stay with Ned again. Of course, the main reason Brad planned to go to Lancaster County was to see Sara. In the meantime, he would keep in touch through letters and phone calls as time allowed. If it was meant for them to develop a relationship that went beyond friendship, Brad would know. Hopefully, Sara would too.

# Chapter 31

*Strasburg*

I can't believe it's the third Saturday of March already." Mary Ruth pointed to the calendar on her kitchen wall. "With this warmer weather we're having, it'll soon be time to plant my garden. And did you notice"—she added with enthusiasm—"the hyacinths are almost ready to bloom?"

"Jah, I did see that." Smiling, Michelle washed their breakfast bowls. It was nice to see Mary Ruth get excited about something as simple as planting a garden and seeing flowers bloom. "You can count on my help again this year," Michelle volunteered. With the exception of the pesky gnats that would no doubt plague her as they had last summer, she too looked forward to planting seeds, pulling weeds, and harvesting a bounty of organically grown produce.

"I'm also willing to help you in the garden on my days off, Grandma," Sara said, reaching for another juice glass to dry. "From the time I was a young girl, I helped Mama in her garden, so I've had a little experience."

"Thank you, Sara. I will take all the help I can get. And as I may have mentioned, your mother always liked to have her fingers in the dirt." Mary Ruth stared across the room, as though reliving something from the past. "I remember how excited she got, especially when she was a little girl and saw the seeds she helped me put into the soil sprout and turn into mature plants."

"Speaking of help, I promised I would help Willis feed the hogs this morning." Michelle rinsed out the sponge and let the water out of the sink. "As soon as we finish with that chore, I'll be in the barn with Val." Michelle looked at Sara. "Wanna join us?"

Sara laid her dishcloth aside. "Feeding the hogs or playing with your puppy?"

Michelle shrugged. "Both if you want to."

Sara wrinkled her nose. "Think I'll pass on feeding the hogs, but I would like to play with your cute little pup again."

"Okay. I should be done helping Willis in half an hour or so. I'll see you in the barn as soon as I'm done." Michelle slipped on a pair of black boots, grabbed a lightweight jacket, and went out the back door.

❧

With a relaxed posture, Mary Ruth looked at Sara and grinned. "That young woman is going to make a good Amish wife someday. She doesn't mind doing the most unpleasant chores."

"I believe you are right. Michelle seems to have found her niche." Sara glanced out the kitchen window. "I, on the other hand, have no idea where my life is supposed to take me." She turned to look at Mary Ruth. "Some days I feel like I'm floundering."

Mary Ruth's brows furrowed. "Oh dear, I had no idea you felt that way. Is it because you're living here without access to electricity and other modern things? Because if that is the case, and you'd rather be out on your own, your grandpa and I will understand." She paused and massaged a sore spot on her thumb knuckle where she'd bumped it while opening a drawer. "Of course, we love having you here, and if you choose to stay, it would make us very happy. But if you decide to move out, we will not pressure you to stay."

Sara's forehead wrinkled slightly as she reached back to tighten the pink rubber band holding her ponytail in place. "I enjoy living here with you and Grandpa, and for now, at least, I'd like to stay. I have access to electricity at the flower shop, and I'm able to use my laptop and charge my cell phone whenever there's a need."

Mary Ruth closed her eyes briefly, then opened them again. "I'm so glad, dear one. Meeting you, and having you living with us has meant the world to your grandpa and me. I hope that no matter what the future holds, we never lose contact with each other." She gave Sara a hug. As they held each other in a meaningful embrace, Mary Ruth sent up a silent prayer. *Thank You, Lord, for bringing Sara and Michelle into our lives. In different ways, they have brought us so much happiness. I thank You for the friendship I see blossoming between them. The girls may not realize it, but they need each other, so this is truly an answer to prayer.*

⁓

When Sara entered the barn, she found Michelle kneeling on the floor, alternating between petting Sadie and the little Irish setter.

Sara couldn't help but smile when Sadie licked the pup's head. "I think Val may have found a surrogate mother," she said, kneeling beside Michelle.

"Yeah. Sadie has had a bit of practice. She was a good mother when she gave birth to a litter of puppies back in June." Michelle stroked Sadie's head, then Val's. "Ezekiel knew what he was doing when he gave me this puppy. She's not only good medicine for me, but also for Sadie. Having Val to play with helps us not to miss Rascal so much."

Sara reached out and stroked the pup's silky ears. "I bet even when she is fully grown she'll be cute—or at least beautiful—with all that shiny auburn hair."

"I believe you're right." Michelle pointed in the direction of the shelf where the antique canning jars were set. "Changing the subject. . . I was wondering if you have read anything from either of the prayer jars lately."

"Just the one in the basement, but that was several weeks ago."

"Should we get the jar in here down and read a few notes now? I could use a little inspiration."

"Sure. I'm always in need of encouragement." Sara stood, and Michelle did the same.

Val whined for a few seconds, but then the pup settled down when Sadie nuzzled her head with her nose.

"Sadie makes a good babysitter," Sara said as they walked to the other side of the barn.

Michelle snickered. "I sure never expected Willis and Mary Ruth's dog to take such an interest in my little hundli. Figured she might either be jealous or treat Val like she's a nuisance. But so far, it's all been good."

"All puppies can be an annoyance at times, but their cuteness usually outweighs their mischievous ways."

"That's for sure." Michelle climbed up on a stool and took down the glass jar filled with inspirational writings. Then Sara sat beside her on a bale of hay.

Michelle pulled a slip of paper from the jar and read the message out loud. "Broken people are made whole by God's love." She looked over at Sara. "I can sure relate to that quote."

Sara shrugged. *How does she want me to respond? Am I supposed to admit that I'm broken? Is that what Michelle wants to hear?* Truth was, Sara could barely admit that fact to herself.

"Okay now, it's your turn." Michelle handed the jar to Sara.

Sara pulled out a slip of paper that had been slightly torn on one corner. The words were still legible though. She read it silently, wondering once again who had written these notes. This one in particular really captured her attention.

"You look bewildered." Michelle bumped Sara's arm. "What's it say?"

"Leave the past where it belongs—which is in the past. Look forward to the future that has been planned for you." Sara pressed her lips together, then opened them again. "I'm not sure why, but this makes me think of something my mother said to me once."

"What was it?" Michelle asked.

"Mama told me a person might believe their life is taking them in one direction, and then something happens to turn their world upside down." Sara's voice wavered. "I—I didn't understand what she meant until my world was upended when I found out she'd been hiding a secret from me since I was born."

"You mean about the fact that she ran away from home and you had grandparents whom you grew up knowing nothing about?"

Sara gave a slow nod as she folded her arms tightly across her chest. "I loved my mother—don't get me wrong, but I'm still struggling with her deceit, and I can't seem to forgive her for that. Since I am her only daughter, I would think I'd be the last person she'd want to deceive."

Michelle placed her hand on Sara's arm, giving it a gentle squeeze. "I know all about the struggle to forgive people who have hurt me." She looked at the jar Sara held. "Finding the prayer jars was a turning point for me. I can honestly say that my life has changed since reading the notes I discovered—especially the Bible verses that pointed me in the direction of accepting Christ as my Savior and learning the importance of going to God in prayer whenever I have a need. Have you done that, Sara? Have you asked Jesus to forgive your sins and come into your heart?"

Sara's body tensed and she found it difficult to swallow. "No, I—I haven't."

"Would you like to do it right now?" Michelle's voice was gentle, and Sara sensed her concern. "I'd be happy to pray with you."

Sara reached back and fiddled with the end of her ponytail. "I appreciate your concern, but I'm not ready to commit to anything right now. *Or forgive Mama for keeping the truth of my heritage from me all these years,* she silently added.

Sara felt relief when she heard a vehicle pull up outside. The look of disappointment she'd seen on Michelle's face when she refused her help had almost made her cave in. "That must be Brad. When he called me the other night, he said he'd be coming here today." She handed the jar back to Michelle, leaped to her feet, and raced out the barn door.

When Brad stepped out of his van, and saw Sara walking toward him, he felt an adrenaline rush course through his body. Although she wore a pair of jeans and a plain sweatshirt, he thought Sara looked even more beautiful than the last time he'd seen her. She wore her hair in a ponytail today, showing more of her beautiful face. Her blue eyes seemed more vivid than he'd noticed before too.

Brad had to calm his breathing as he stepped forward and gave her a hug. "It's good to see you again, Sara."

"It's nice to see you too." Her dimpled smile made him feel like hugging her again. But he didn't want to appear too forward, so he held himself in check. Besides, they had an audience now, since Michelle had just stepped out of the barn.

Brad smiled and waved. "Hey, Michelle. How's it going?"

"Good. Real good. Come see what Ezekiel gave me for Valentine's Day." She gestured to the barn.

"You'd better go see." Sara took hold of his hand. "I promise you won't be disappointed."

Eager to see what gift Ezekiel had given Michelle, Brad went willingly with Sara. Michelle was way ahead of them, and by the time they entered the barn, she met them near the door with a red-furred pup in her arms.

"This is Val," Michelle announced, rubbing the dog's floppy ears. "Since she was a Valentine's Day gift, the name I chose for her seems appropriate."

Brad reached out his hand and stroked the pup's other ear. "She's a cute little thing. Irish setter, right?"

Michelle nodded. "By the time she's fully grown, she'll probably be bigger than Sadie."

As if on cue, the collie padded out from the back of the barn, wagging her tail.

"Well, hello there, girl." Brad bent down to pet Sadie, while Sara looked on. "And what does she think of your little furry intruder?" he asked, directing his question to Michelle. He had to grin to himself when Sadie sat down, making herself comfortable on his foot.

"Much to my surprise, Sadie actually likes Val."

"It's true," Sara chimed in. "Michelle and I were both surprised to see how well Sadie took to the puppy."

"That's great." Brad smiled at Michelle. "It was a thoughtful gift your boyfriend gave you. The pup's a keeper, and so is your guy."

Her cheeks reddened. "I agree. Ezekiel has always been good to me."

Brad glanced at Sara. "So are you ready to do something fun today?"

"Yes, I am." Sara rubbed her hands together. "What did you have in mind?"

"We could attend the mud sale going on in Manheim. Or how about staying local and taking a ride on the Strasburg Rail Road?" Brad scraped a hand through his hair. "But you know what I'd really like to show you this morning?"

"What's that?" Sara's brows raised slightly.

"The Biblical Tabernacle here in Lancaster County."

"Tabernacle?" She glanced at Michelle, then back at Brad.

"Yes. It's a full-scale replica of the tabernacle we read about in the Old Testament."

"And it is inside the Mennonite Information Center," Michelle interjected. "I've never been there, but I've heard it's quite interesting. Ezekiel and I have talked about going to see it sometime. You should go see it with Brad, Sara."

"Okay, sure. . .why not?" Sara's tone was less than enthusiastic. Brad wondered if she'd agreed to go only because he'd suggested it. However, once Sara got there and saw the uniqueness of it, he felt sure she would be glad they went.

# Chapter 32

*Lancaster*

As Sara stood next to Brad, inside a large building with a contoured ceiling, she listened to their guide give details about the brazen altar and ark of the covenant, while pointing out the replica of it.

Brad looked over at Sara and whispered, "Even for people who know their biblical history, this presentation is fascinating."

*People like you, not me.* Sara nodded.

"Now as you look into the holy place, you will see a full-size wax figure representing the high priest," their female narrator said. "The priest presided over the altar of incense, and his robes had precious stones embedded in gold on the breastplate he wore."

Sara also learned that the golden candlestick and table of shewbread were made to scale. There was an authentically researched design of the veil, showing how, in biblical times, it separated the people from the presence of God. All this information was new to her, but she made no mention of it to Brad.

When the presentation was over, at Brad's suggestion, they wandered into the area where various religious books were sold. Brad picked out two books, and asked if Sara wanted anything, but she declined, saying, "Not at this time."

"If it's about the cost, I'd be happy to buy it for you."

She shook her head. "It's not that. I just have plenty of books already that still need to be read." *Liar.* Sara's conscience pricked her. While she did have a few unread books in her room, none of them were of a religious nature.

After Brad paid for his purchases, he suggested they go to

Miller's restaurant on Route 30 between Ronks and Paradise. "They have a good variety of food there." He thumped his stomach. "So we won't leave hungry. And since I invited you on this date, the meal will be my treat."

"Sounds good, but I can't guarantee you'll get your money's worth. I'm not a big eater."

"No problem. While they're known for their smorgasbord, they have a great salad bar, plus lots of other lighter choices." Brad opened the door for Sara and stepped outside behind her. When they got to his van, he opened the passenger's door for her and waited until she fastened her seatbelt to close it.

Sara had never been out with anyone as polite as Brad. She appreciated his consideration and the extra attention he gave her. He was attractive and pleasant to talk to but probably not her type. But the truth was she wasn't sure what kind of man would be good for her. Sara knew one thing for sure—Brad would make a wonderful husband for a lucky woman someday.

❧

*Between Ronks and Paradise*

"Wow, you weren't kidding about all the food they serve on the buffet here." Sara's eyes widened. Looking around the dining room, where the food stations were located, she could hardly take it all in. Even the dessert bar caught her attention, although Sara was sure she'd never be able to eat anything from it.

"This restaurant is not as big as the Shady Maple Smorgasbord up in East Earl, but it offers more than enough food for most people." Brad pulled out a chair for Sara and waited until she was seated at their table before taking the seat across from her.

When a waitress came, they both ordered iced tea, and Brad told her that he and Sara would be eating from the buffet.

After the young woman left, he looked across the table at Sara and smiled. "If you don't mind, I'd like to pray before we get our food. Would it be okay if I pray out loud, or would you prefer we pray the Amish way?"

Sara took a sip of water. "The Amish way is fine for me. After living with my grandparents these past four months, I've gotten used to their way of praying silently. Besides, my mother used to offer silent prayers too."

"No problem. We can pray the Amish way." Brad bowed his head, and Sara did the same. Sara would never have admitted to Brad, or anyone else for that matter, that she rarely prayed. And on the few occasions Sara had whispered a prayer, she wasn't sure it was even heard. If God was real, He seemed too far away to hear anyone's prayers. And if He did listen to people's prayers, why would He care about hers? Sara really had no connection to God. How could she when He'd taken the only person she'd ever loved? It was one more thing Sara had to feel bitter about.

Sara opened her eyes, to see if Brad had finished praying. Seeing that his head was still bowed, she dropped her gaze as well, allowing more thoughts to swirl in her head.

*Is it Mama's betrayal that bothers me the most, her untimely death, or not knowing my real father?* Her fingers tightened around the napkin in her lap. *Maybe the root of my bitterness stems from having a stepfather who has never cared much for me.*

Sara couldn't change a single thing about her past, and stewing about it didn't help. Yet there were moments, like now, when Mama's deception and Dean's lack of attention cut through Sara's soul like a piercing arrow.

When she heard a slight rustle, Sara looked up, and was relieved to see Brad's eyes were open. No doubt he'd prayed a meaningful prayer. *It's a good thing he doesn't know my thoughts were elsewhere. Brad probably wouldn't want to go out with me again if he knew how I feel about my mother, not to mention my stepfather.*

Sara forced a smile, hoping her pent-up emotions wouldn't show on her face. How many times had she gone over all this in her head? As time went on, her resentment had increased. She'd been getting along better with Michelle these days, so why couldn't she forgive the other people who had hurt her and move on?

Brad pushed his chair back and stood. "Should we help

ourselves to some food?"

"Sure." Sara followed as he led the way to the buffet stations. It would be good to focus on eating rather than reminiscing about the past or trying to dissect her feelings.

Sara helped herself to the salad bar, then added a few chilled steamed shrimp, a piece of carved turkey, and some mixed cooked vegetables to her plate. Normally, she didn't eat this much for lunch, but all this appetizing food was too tempting to ignore. Of course, she would probably pay the price for it later when she was too full to eat whatever Grandma fixed for supper.

Back at the table, Brad pointed to his full plate of food and rolled his eyes. "I'd planned on having at least one piece of pie, but after I eat all this, I doubt I'll have enough room for dessert."

"I hear you. This is a lot of food."

As they ate, they talked about Michelle's new puppy and how happy and content she seemed these days.

"She's certainly not the same young woman I met last summer. She seemed so distraught and like she was hiding something," Brad commented. "Once Michelle admitted her deceit, and sought forgiveness from the Lord as well as the Lapps, she became like a new person."

Sara wasn't quite sure how to respond. "I guess you're right. She has changed, but I thought it was mostly due to her decision to join the Amish faith."

"I don't believe she would have ever made that decision if she hadn't become a Christian." Brad leaned forward, looking at Sara with a most serious expression. "How about you, Sara? Are you a Christian?"

Sara fiddled with the spoon lying next to her plate. Between the things Michelle said to her this morning, and the information she and Brad heard about the Biblical Tabernacle, Sara felt as if she was being pressured to become a Christian. This unexpected question from Brad was the final straw.

*What am I supposed to say in response? I don't like it when people lie, yet I feel like I'm being backed into a corner.*

Sara took a drink of iced tea, stalling for time. After a few uncomfortable seconds, she set her glass down and forced herself to make eye contact with him. "Yes, I'm a Christian." Her conscience prodded, *No, you're not,* but she pushed the thought aside. *What other choice did I have? If I had admitted I'm not a Christian, Brad most likely would not want to see me again.*

A slow smile spread across his face. "That's good to hear." No doubt, he was relieved to know the woman he was having lunch with wasn't an atheist, at least.

Sara's conscience stabbed her again. *Listen to me. I'm no better than Michelle used to be. She pretended to be me, and now I'm pretending to be a Christian. Guess that makes me a liar and a hypocrite. I am professing to be something I'm not so I can have a relationship with a man who truly is a Christian, in every sense of the word.* Staring down at her napkin, Sara wadded it into a ball. *My heart has been hardened toward God, and I'm not sure it will ever soften.*

"Will you excuse me for a minute?" Sara could barely meet Brad's eyes. She needed a bit of space and didn't want to continue this conversation, so she found an excuse to escape. "I need to get a little more dressing for my salad."

"Sure, I may need to make another trip to the buffet myself, but I'll finish what I have here first."

"Okay then. I'll be right back." Sara hurried across the room and didn't look back. *I should have been honest with Brad, but I didn't have the nerve.*

Brad watched as Sara made her way to the salad bar. From the way she hurried off, it seemed like she may have been anxious to leave the table. *Sure hope I didn't say anything to upset her.* To be truthful, Brad wasn't sure Sara had enjoyed herself today. He'd found the tabernacle replica fascinating, but most of the time during the tour Sara had appeared distant, almost detached, when their guide explained things. It seemed as if her mind was somewhere else.

As he took a swallow of iced tea, Brad came to a conclusion.

*Some people aren't biblical history buffs like me. Guess I should have taken Sara to the mud sale in Manheim or rode the Strasburg Rail Road train ride through part of Amish country.* His shoulders rose and fell. *I should have let Sara decide what she wanted to do, instead of deciding it for her.*

Brad looked up in time to see Sara coming in his direction, and at the same moment, another familiar person came into view, and she was making her way toward him.

❧

Just as Sara got to the table with a small container of salad dressing, a lovely dark-haired woman stepped up to their table and greeted Brad like an old friend. "Well, fancy seeing you here, Brad."

"Terri, what a surprise." Brad looked at Sara. "This is Terri Conners. She attends the same university I do. Terri, this is my friend, Sara Murray."

"Nice to meet you," Sara and Terri said in unison.

"Do you mind if I join you?" Terri gestured to the empty chair at their table.

"No problem." Brad stood up and pulled out the chair for her.

"I'm glad I ran into you here, and you were so right." Terri's arm brushed Brad's as she leaned closer to him. "Amish country is incredible. There's so much to see and do. I wish now that I'd come here sooner."

*Is this young woman just a friend of Brad's, or could she be his girl-friend?* Sara tapped her foot under the table.

"I met Terri in the school cafeteria one day. We got to talking about places to visit, and I told her about Lancaster County." Brad explained, looking at Sara. "Terri's studying to be a youth minister. She's in her second year of school."

Terri directed her attention to Sara. "I'm a preacher's kid, born and raised in Maine." She turned back to Brad. "But I tell you, after spending a few days in this area, I could move here in a heartbeat."

"Have you done much sightseeing?" Brad asked.

"Yes, I have. One day I visited an Amish farm, and afterward the tour group even got to see the house. I, along with a bunch of other tourists, then sat down to the most fabulous home-cooked meal. We were seated at a long table and talked among ourselves as we ate." Terri kept her focus on Brad, glancing only briefly in Sara's direction. "Afterward, I even got the chance to ride in a horse and buggy. That was sure fun."

"My grandparents are Amish," Sara spoke up.

Terri eyed her with a curious expression. "But you're not Amish?"

Sara shook her head. The last thing she wanted was for Terri to start asking more questions, so she quickly changed the subject. "Brad and I toured the Biblical Tabernacle earlier today."

"I was there yesterday. Too bad we didn't end up there at the same time. It would have been nice to hang out with someone I know." Once more, Terri directed her comment to Brad. "Wasn't the made-to-scale tabernacle interesting?"

"It sure was."

Sara sat quietly listening to the two of them describe what they liked best about the tour. This pretty, dark-haired woman had such an easy time talking with Brad, and he seemed equally comfortable with Terri.

Sara felt almost invisible as she picked at the rest of her salad. *Am I imagining it, or is Ms. Conners interested in Brad?* She stirred restlessly. *I have no claim whatsoever on Brad, and I probably shouldn't care, but I do. But then Terri's obviously a Christian—a much better fit for him.*

# Chapter 33

*Strasburg*

Brad lounged in a chair on the Lapps' front porch, waiting for Sara to get her purse, which she'd forgotten on the way out the door. This was his last day of spring break, and he'd invited her to attend church with him in Lancaster. Sara seemed hesitant when he'd first extended the invitation, saying she usually went to Amish church with her grandparents. But when Willis reminded Sara this was their off-Sunday and they were planning to visit their son Ivan's church district in Paradise, she agreed to go along with Brad.

It surprised him, since Ivan was Sara's uncle. He figured she'd want to go with her grandparents. For whatever her reason, Brad was glad Sara was willing to attend church with him.

Running a finger down the crease in his dark gray dress slacks, Brad thought about the previous week. He'd spent as much time with Sara as possible—stopping by the flower shop a few times, in addition to taking her out for dinner on three occasions. Brad had also been invited to the Lapps' for supper on two evenings. Each time Brad and Sara were together, he found himself more drawn to her. Sara seemed more relaxed this week than last, which made him regret having to leave even more. He wished he didn't have to return to the university so soon. If it were possible, he'd stay in Strasburg permanently.

But Brad couldn't lose sight of his goal to preach, which meant more studying in preparation for the ministry. He'd decided to return to Strasburg for the summer months and already looked forward to that. He hoped to drive and work for the Amish again and might take an online class or two, rather than attending summer classes at the university. Brad felt confident that by the end of the summer he would know if Sara was the woman God had in mind for him.

*I'm relieved Sara is a Christian, and I'm glad I found the courage to ask. My only other concern is whether she'd be willing to take on the role of a pastor's wife.*

Brad sat up straight. *I'm moving way too fast. I haven't given it enough time to know if Sara and I are even right for each other.*

When the front door opened, and Sara stepped onto the porch, Brad jumped up. "Ready to go?"

With a nod, she clasped his extended hand. Being with Sara and heading for worship service on this blue-skied Sunday morning felt exactly right. Brad looked forward to summer and enjoying more days like this.

~⁂~

### Lancaster

*What am I doing here? I feel so out of place.* Sara glanced around the rural church Brad had taken her to this morning. The polished wooden pews had been arranged neatly in rows. On the back of each pew a wooden shelf held a Bible, songbook, and several welcome cards. Along both sides of the room were three stained glass windows, with another one on the wall behind the baptistery at the front of the sanctuary. In front of the pulpit sat an ornate-looking table with a large Bible on it that was flanked by two white candles.

Also near the front of the room and to the left a bit sat a grand piano, as well as a keyboard, where two female musicians sat. In addition to a drummer, three other men sat on the platform with guitars.

Four attractively dressed people—two men and two women—stepped forward with microphones to lead the singing. The first four songs were lively choruses—quite a change from the drawn-out hymns sung in German Sara had become used to hearing during Amish worship services. A good portion of the congregation clapped as they sang—another thing that would not be done in the Amish church.

The fact that Sara could not understand any of the words written in the Amish *Ausbund*, or know what the ministers said when they preached in German, might be why she felt more comfortable attending Amish church. Sara disliked the idea that she was being preached at, so not understanding the bishop and ministers' words was a benefit.

After the choruses, the song leader asked everyone to be seated. Two men passed the offering plates around, and then more singing followed—this time, several hymns.

As Sara stood next to Brad, following the words in her songbook, she gave him a sidelong glance. His joyful expression as he lifted both hands and sang with honest enthusiasm said it all. Brad was a committed Christian, in every sense of the word. He needed no hymnal to read the lyrics. This devout man knew all the songs by heart.

*I should break things off with him,* Sara thought. *I am not cut out for a religious life, which seems to be his whole world.*

Sara looked around at the congregation, as nearly everyone lifted their voices in praise to the Lord once again. She turned her head, glancing at the pews toward the back of the church and stifled her intake of breath. Terri Conners sat two rows behind them.

Sara lowered her gaze, turned around, and joined in with the singing. *I cannot believe Terri Conners is here too. Did she follow us, or did Brad tell her he'd be attending here today?*

When the singing ended and they were seated again, Brad reached for Sara's hand and gave her fingers a gentle squeeze. Her hand remained in his until the pastor stepped up to the pulpit and asked everyone to open their Bibles. Brad let go of Sara's hand and opened his Bible. Sara was amazed at how quickly he found the passage of scripture the minister said he would be preaching from. If Sara had been asked to find the book of Acts, it would have taken her forever.

Sara thought about her mother's Bible, which she'd rarely

looked at since finding Mama's note telling Sara about her grandparents. *I wonder how well my mother knew the scriptures. Was she as well versed with them as Grandpa and Grandma are, or did the Bible mean little or nothing to Mama, as it does to me?*

Sara clutched the folds in her skirt, tuning out the pastor's words, although Brad seemed fixated on the message. *If my mother had a connection with God, then why wasn't she honest enough to tell me about her past, while she was still alive—and more importantly, about my father?*

Sara's mother had grown up in a home where devotions and prayer prevailed. And until she'd run away from home, she had no doubt attended Amish church. *Why then,* Sara wondered, *didn't Mama talk about spiritual things with me?*

*Why? Why? Why?* Sara's lips tightened as another wave of bitterness rose in her soul. Try as she might, Sara couldn't push the feelings aside. *If Mama had professed to be a Christian, and acted like one by being honest, then I might be a Christian too.*

The whimper of a baby pushed Sara's thoughts aside. Holding the fussy infant in one arm and a diaper bag in the other, the young woman in front of them slipped quietly from her pew. Sara watched her go out the back of the church and couldn't help noticing Terri again.

Sara thought of a plan. *Somehow, Brad and I are going to get out of this church without running into her.*

When the pastor mentioned another verse, this one from John, Brad turned back several pages in his Bible.

Sara tried to be attentive and listen to what the middle-aged man behind the pulpit had to say, but her mind wandered all over the place.

*Before Brad leaves for Clarks Summit, I should tell him I can't see him anymore.* Her stomach tightened as she bit the inside of her cheek. Another option would be to keep seeing Brad and continue letting him think she was a Christian. *But what about Terri Conners? Should I get out of the way so she can move in on Brad?* It was obvious to Sara that was what the young woman wanted.

When the service ended, and Brad took Sara's hand again, she lost her resolve. She would continue with the facade a little longer. Later down the road if their relationship became serious, she would admit to Brad that she wasn't a believer. It would be a test to see what kind of a man he was. For to Sara's way of thinking, a true Christian should not be prejudiced against someone who wasn't.

Since the service had ended, Brad assumed Sara would get up, but she remained on their pew. "Are you ready to go?" he asked.

"Yes. Just thought it would be good to wait for the elderly parishioners to leave before we rush out. I noticed most of them were sitting up front."

"You've made a good point." Brad glanced at the older people slowly making their way to the aisle. One man, who was stooped over, walked with a cane. Another elderly couple walked arm in arm, as if to steady the other. *These good folks are probably long-time members of this church, and they deserve to be treated with respect. I'm glad Sara pointed it out.*

"It looks like most of the church has cleared out now." Sara got up and entered into the aisle.

At the door, the pastor greeted Brad and Sara and welcomed them to his church. As Brad explained to the preacher about his interest in ministry, he realized Sara had already stepped out the door. He shook the clergyman's hand and hurried after her.

It was hard to read Sara's thoughts as they walked to the parking lot. She hadn't said a word since they'd left the church.

They were almost to Brad's van, when someone called his name. He turned around.

"Brad!" Terri waved her arms.

He waved back in response, and holding Sara's hand, he led her over to where Terri stood by her car.

"I can't believe the way we keep bumping into each other." Terri grinned at Brad. "Are you heading back to school today?"

"Yes, but there are still a few people I want to say goodbye to, so I'll be leaving a bit later."

"I hate to ask, but would you mind if I followed you back to Clarks Summit? I've been staying at a bed-and-breakfast near the entrance to Highway 222 and need to check out by noon. I can wait for you in the parking lot there."

"Sure, I guess that would work." Brad glanced at Sara, quietly fiddling with her purse straps.

"Thank you, Brad." Terri touched his arm. "I figure you'd know a better way to get back to Clarks Summit. I ended up taking a longer route when I came down here, and I'd like to save on gas when I travel back."

"Okay, Terri, I'll see you soon."

As Brad walked with Sara back to his van, he sensed something was troubling her and wondered if it had anything to do with Terri. *Or maybe*, he thought, *Sara didn't enjoy the church service today.*

"Are you okay? You've been kind of quiet since the service let out." Brad said, once he'd started the van.

"I'm fine."

"Did you enjoy the church service?"

Sara nodded. "It was nice. A lot different than Amish church, that's for sure."

"What church did you attend when you lived in New Jersey?" Brad left the parking lot and pulled out into traffic.

"Umm..." More toying with her purse. Was she nervous about something?

"I assume you and your family had a home church."

"Yes. Yes, of course. It was a few blocks from our home." Sara turned her head to the right, looking out the passenger's window.

Something didn't seem right. She'd been aloof—almost distracted since Terri showed up. Brad was on the verge of saying something, but changed his mind. All he wanted was to enjoy Sara's company before it was time to return to Clarks Summit. If Sara was upset about something, surely she would have said so.

As Michelle sat on a backless wooden bench in the basement of the home of Lenore's parents, she reflected on the conversation she'd had with Sara in the barn last week. Sara seemed like a good person, and because she had forgiven Michelle for impersonating her, Michelle assumed Sara was a Christian. To hear Sara say she was not a believer had been a surprise.

Michelle's brows furrowed. *If Sara could forgive me, then why not her mother? A lot of parents have done worse things to their kids than keeping the truth about their heritage from them. Ask me. I should know.*

Michelle had prayed for Sara every day since their discussion in the barn. She'd been tempted to talk to Sara's grandparents about it, but didn't follow through. If Sara found out Michelle had divulged the information she'd shared with her, it could ruin the bond they'd begun to form.

Michelle's thoughts shifted gears. *I wonder if Sara enjoyed the church service she and Brad went to.* Brad was an upright person, and his being around her was good for Sara—especially in a spiritual way. Perhaps he could get through to her when no one else could.

She glanced over at Lenore, sitting beside her, so straight and tall. The attention of the Lapps' granddaughter appeared to be fully focused on her grandfather, who'd begun preaching the second sermon of the day. Michelle had no doubt as to whether the pleasant schoolteacher was a Christian or not. Everything about Lenore spelled peace, love, and joy—all the attributes of a person who loved the Lord and set an example for others. It was hard to believe Lenore wasn't being courted by anyone. She had the makings of a fantastic wife.

Michelle remembered how, when she'd first met Lenore, she had been surprised to learn that she often attended church in her grandparents' district. But then she'd found out that many Amish people visit neighboring church districts on their off-Sundays, as she and the Lapps were doing today. Willis had even been invited as a guest minister to preach one of the sermons.

Michelle stirred restlessly. *I hope when I get baptized next Sunday and become a church member, my actions will let others know I am a Christian.*

While the Amish people she knew did not go around testifying and preaching their faith to people outside of their Plain community, they tried by their actions and deeds to be an example of what it meant to be a Christian.

"The world will know us by our actions," Willis had said in one of the messages he'd preached. Michelle felt thankful for Ezekiel's interpretation of the sermon that day, since she still struggled to understand the German language spoken during church. The everyday Pennsylvania Dutch dialect had been easier to grasp, and for the most part, she understood it and could speak a good many sentences now. How thankful she was for Ezekiel's and the Lapps' patience in teaching her those Amish words.

Next Sunday, church would be held at the home of Ezekiel's parents, where the baptism would take place. As much as Michelle wanted to become Amish, she still struggled with the question, *Am I ready to take this most serious step?*

She closed her eyes briefly and lifted a silent prayer. *Dear Lord, please give me a sense of peace about this, for getting baptized and becoming a church member is a life-long commitment—to You and the Amish church.*

# Chapter 34

*A week later, Strasburg*

Throughout the first sermon, preached by Willis Lapp, and now with the second one started by one of the other ministers, Ezekiel's thoughts should have been focused on the man's words, rather than someplace else. While he felt certain that joining the Amish church was the right thing for him, he still had some concerns. Saturday evening, Ezekiel, Michelle, and the eight other baptismal candidates met with the ministers one last time. The preachers had taken turns reading the articles of faith and answering any questions the young people had. It was their final opportunity to change their minds about joining the church.

Ezekiel had been relieved when Michelle didn't back out. He'd been worried at first, but she seemed as sure as he was that becoming a church member was the right thing for her. What concerned him the most was when the ministers reminded the male candidates that, by becoming members, they were also agreeing to serve in the church as a minister or deacon, should the lot ever fall upon them. Ezekiel wasn't sure he could handle such a big responsibility, and he hoped he would never be faced with it in the years to come. But if the time should ever come and his name was chosen, he would trust the Lord for the wisdom and strength to perform his duties.

He glanced across the way at Michelle. She sat looking down at her hands clasped together in her lap. No doubt, she felt a bit anxious this morning too.

❧

Michelle's stomach churned like a blender at full speed. In a few minutes she, along with the other candidates for membership, would kneel before the bishop to answer the questions he would ask each of them. This was the most exciting yet frightening thing Michelle had ever done. More so than her high school graduation, after which she'd decided it was time to leave her foster parents' home and branch out on her own. Any doubts she may have had about making this lifelong change had passed when she entered Ezekiel's parents' house this morning and took her seat on one of the benches. Michelle was not the same person she used to be. She was fully committed to the Lord now, and would soon be committed to the Amish church as well.

Today was a special day for those seeking membership. Many of the candidates' family members and friends had come to the service. Michelle wished her brothers could be here too. *If Ernie and Jack knew about my decision to become Amish, what would they think? Would they make fun of me, like Jerry and his girlfriend did when I waited on them at the restaurant? Or would my brothers support my decision and say they were happy for me?*

Michelle looked over at Ezekiel, wondering what he might be thinking right now. Was he nervous? Excited? She couldn't be certain, although the way his right knee kept bouncing up and down, he had to be feeling one of those things.

Ezekiel hadn't spoken up yesterday when asked if he had any reservations about joining the church. So Michelle had no doubts about his readiness to make the commitment with her today.

When the second sermon concluded, the bishop asked the candidates to leave their seats and kneel in front of him. Michelle's heart pounded as he asked the group of young people their first question. "Can you confess that you believe Jesus Christ is the Son of God?"

Michelle, along with the others, replied: "Yes, I believe Jesus Christ is the Son of God."

The second question came: "Do you recognize this to be a Christian order, church, and fellowship under which you now submit yourself to?"

Everyone replied affirmatively.

"Do you renounce the world, the devil, with all his subtle ways, as well as your own flesh and blood, and do you desire to serve Jesus Christ alone, who died on the cross for you?"

Tears welled in Michelle's eyes as she and the others answered, "Yes."

Then the final question came. "Do you also promise before God and His church that you will support these teachings and regulations with the Lord's help, faithfully attending the services of the church and helping to counsel and work in it, and will not forsake it, whether it leads to life or death?"

"Yes." Michelle's throat tightened to such a degree that she could barely swallow or get the words out. Her heart was filled with unspeakable joy. It seemed as if she had been waiting for this blessed occasion all of her life.

Sara stood with the others in the congregation as the bishop offered a prayer. Michelle, Ezekiel, and the eight other young people remained in their kneeling position.

Following the prayer, everyone in the congregation returned to their benches, except for the bishop and deacon, who continued to stand in front of those who were knelt before them.

Sara watched with curiosity as the bishop went down the line, holding his cupped hands on top of each candidate's head. Then the deacon poured water into the bishop's hands three times, as the bishop spoke: "Upon your faith, which you have confessed before God and many witnesses, you are baptized in the name of the Father, the Son, and the Holy Ghost."

After each person had been baptized, the bishop offered his hand and a holy kiss of peace to the males. His wife did the same for the females. Lastly a benediction was given: "You are no longer guests and strangers, but fellow citizens with the saints and of the household of God."

*Michelle is doing what she believes is right for her,* Sara mused. *But I am more certain than ever that I could never become Amish.*

Hearing the bishop's questions and the candidates' answers, Sara knew if she'd been on her knees with the others, she would have had to either deny a relationship with Christ or pretend to be a believer, like she had with Brad.

Sara's fingers curled into the palms of her hands. *I am nothing but a hypocrite, pretending to be one thing, when I'm really something else.* Sara had never liked being lied to, yet her life had become a big fabrication. She felt trapped in her own web of lies and saw no way of escape. She understood now how easy it must have been for Michelle to deceive her grandparents. No doubt the imposter had convinced herself that she was doing it for the right reasons.

*And what is my reason for pretending to be a Christian?* Sara asked herself. *Do I really care for Brad, or is just a passing fancy?* Sara had never been caught up in a lie before, but now she couldn't seem to help herself.

She weighed in again on a week ago, when Brad's friend Terri kept showing up. While Brad had not admitted having feelings for Terri, Sara was almost certain the young ministerial student had eyes for him. She'd even been tempted to ask Brad if he'd ever taken Terri on a date.

Sara hoped she'd been able to hide her feelings from him, just as she hoped he didn't suspect she wasn't truly a believer.

She hadn't heard anything from Brad this week, other than a phone call letting her know he had made it back to Clarks Summit last Sunday afternoon. It hadn't been a lengthy call, and he'd said he needed to call his parents too. Sara suspected by the tone of Brad's voice that he was tired after the long day, so she'd told him to get some rest and that she hoped he would have a good week.

While Sara was glad to hear he'd arrived okay, other doubts kept feeding into her brain. Were Brad and Terri seeing each other during or after school? Did they meet for lunch every day?

Feeling the need for a breath of fresh air to clear her head, when the service ended and people began to set up tables for the meal, Sara left the house. She needed time alone, to think about her situation.

After the meal, as Mary Ruth helped some of the other women clean up, she thought about Sara.

She could not forget the look on her granddaughter's face when she and Willis hugged Michelle and said how happy it made them to see her get baptized and become a church member.

Sara had remained quiet during the meal too, responding only when spoken to. Was she jealous of the attention they'd given Michelle, or could Sara's mind be elsewhere today?

There seemed to be an unnatural stillness about Sara as she stood off to one side, watching other family members and friends walk up to Michelle and offer a hug or handshake. Could Sara be jealous of the attention Michelle was receiving? Or might Sara be wishing that she too had joined the Amish church today? If so, she'd given no indication of that. Even though their granddaughter had chosen to continue living with them, she seemed satisfied with her English way of life. Sara obviously did not want to give up owning a car, her cell phone, or her laptop.

Mary Ruth's eyes watered as she wiped off the last of the tables. *If Rhoda hadn't run away from home and joined the Amish church herself, Sara would no doubt have joined by now too.* But Mary Ruth knew that if Sara ever contemplated joining their faith sometime in the future, it would be a decision she would have to make for herself. Neither Mary Ruth nor Willis would try to sway their granddaughter one way or the other.

In contrast to Sara's disinterest in becoming Amish, Michelle fairly beamed as church members and friends went up to welcome her. She especially lit up when Ezekiel's mother gave her a hug and whispered something in her ear. Belinda must have said something kind, for Mary Ruth was sure the moisture on Michelle's smiling face was from happy tears. Hopefully, Ezekiel's mother had accepted Michelle and felt good about the decision Ezekiel's girlfriend had made to become Amish.

Mary Ruth was glad that, no matter what Sara might be feeling, she had at least greeted Michelle after the service and given her a hug. Mary Ruth let out a deep sigh. *I am ever so happy for Michelle,* she thought. *She has come a long ways, and it was pure joy to watch her get baptized and know that she is now one of us.*

Mary Ruth glanced out the window and saw Sara standing against one of the trees in the Kings' backyard, her chin resting on her fist as though deep in thought.

"Well it looks like everything is about cleaned up." Belinda King approached, holding a garbage bag in her hands.

Mary Ruth nodded. "It was a good day, jah?"

"Yes, it was, and I couldn't be happier for my son today. Also, Michelle has proven to be more than I gave her credit for," Belinda added. "I told her earlier that I am sorry for ever doubting her motives. It's obvious now that she is truly committed to the Amish way and also to my son."

"We are also happy for Michelle and Ezekiel," Ivan said as he and Yvonne joined the conversation.

Lenore had been talking with Michelle and Ezekiel, and the three of them came over when they saw the small group forming.

"Where's Sara?" Michelle asked.

"Yes, I want to say goodbye to her before we leave," Lenore interjected.

"I saw her outside in the yard." Mary Ruth gestured to the window.

"I'll see if I can find her." Lenore gave Mary Ruth a hug. "I love you, Grandma."

"I love you too, sweet girl."

Lenore turned to her parents. "After I say a few words to Sara, if I can find her, I'll wait for you in the buggy."

"Okay, we'll be there shortly." Ivan shook Michelle's and Ezekiel's hands. "Again, we welcome both of you to the church."

Yvonne nodded, then gave Michelle a hug and shook Ezekiel's hand.

Mary Ruth's heart swelled, seeing Michelle's sweet expression as she thanked Sara's aunt and uncle for their warm greetings.

"Okay, Mom," Ivan said, "We need to see if Benjamin and Peter have already headed for home. It's a good thing they came in Peter's carriage, because my buggy isn't big enough for the five us now that our *kinner* are grown."

Mary Ruth chuckled. "That's how it is when the children grow up."

"We have to catch Dad and say goodbye to him too, but I promise, we'll be seeing you both soon." Ivan and Yvonne gave Mary Ruth a hug, and headed out the door.

"Family is everything, isn't it?" Belinda smiled as she watched Ivan and Yvonne depart.

"Jah, it certainly is." Mary Ruth stole another look out the window and noticed Lenore walking around, obviously looking for Sara.

Mary Ruth gathered up her things before looking for Willis and Sara. It was time to go home. Later today when things quieted down, she would spend some time with her English granddaughter.

# Chapter 35

The echo of Big Red's hooves hitting the pavement rang in Ezekiel's ears. His fingers, nose, and even his face tingled with anticipation. He was on his way to the Lapps' to pick up Michelle for a Sunday evening buggy ride, and he'd never felt more nervous. They had both become Amish today, and now it was time to ask Michelle a most important question.

"Don't know what I'm gonna do if she turns me down." Ezekiel spoke out loud. "I've never cared for anyone the way I do Michelle." He wiped a sweaty hand on his pants leg. "She's all I could ever want. Can't imagine spending the rest of my life without her."

Big Red's ears perked up, and he trotted a little faster. Did the horse sense how eager Ezekiel was to see his girlfriend?

The closer he came to the Lapps' place, the more anxious Ezekiel became. He swallowed a few times, his mouth turning dry. He would have his answer—and soon.

Michelle went to the living-room window and peeked out.

"Are you watching for Ezekiel?" Willis asked from his easy chair across the room.

"Jah." She turned to look at him. "He said he'd be here by six thirty."

Willis winked at Mary Ruth, who sat in the chair closest to him. "I'd have to say, this young woman is as *naerfich* this evening as she was in church this morning when she got baptized."

"I'm not nervous," Michelle defended herself, but she smiled, knowing Willis was only joking with her. "I'll admit, I am eager to see Ezekiel and go for a ride in his buggy."

"It's not like you've never ridden in his rig before." Willis's brows moved up and down as he gave her a playful grin.

His wife shook her finger at him. "Now, Husband, you should stop tormenting the poor girl. Some people don't appreciate your teasing, you know."

Willis's smile widened as he looked back at Michelle. "You know I'm only kidding, right?"

"Of course, and it doesn't bother me one bit." Michelle glanced over at Sara, slouched on the couch, hugging a throw pillow in front of her. Sara hadn't said much to any of them since they'd arrived home after the church meal. An hour ago, Sara mentioned having a headache, but when Mary Ruth suggested Sara take an aspirin and go upstairs to take a nap, Sara declined.

Michelle wished she could speak to Sara privately, but with Mary Ruth and Willis in the room, it wasn't a good idea. Michelle hadn't said anything to either of them about the conversation she'd had with Sara in the barn last week. She didn't know whether they were aware of the bitterness their granddaughter felt about her mother's deception. If they knew, it might be something they didn't want to talk about. *I wonder if Willis and Mary Ruth know Sara's not a Christian. Bet if they did, they'd really be concerned.*

The whinny of a horse brought Michelle's attention to the window again. She smiled as she watched Ezekiel's horse trot into the yard and head straight for the hitching rail.

With a quick goodbye to the Lapps and Sara, Michelle grabbed her black shawl and hurried out the door. Before Ezekiel even had the chance to tie Big Red to the rail, she opened the passenger's door and climbed into the buggy.

He looked over at her with a big smile. "*Guder owed*, Michelle."

With her heart beating a staccato, Michelle replied, "Good evening, Ezekiel."

"Ready for a nice long ride?"

"Jah. I'm more than ready."

Ezekiel backed the horse up, turned the carriage around, and headed out the driveway and onto the main road. They had only gone a short distance when he pulled over at a wide spot in the road, halting Big Red.

"What's the matter, Ezekiel? Is there something wrong with your gaul?"

"Nope. My horse is fine and dandy." Ezekiel reached across the seat and took Michelle's hand. "I'm not sure I'll be fine though— least not till I ask you a question."

"Oh? What is it?"

He leaned closer, and his voice trembled a bit. "I—I love you, Michelle. And I was wondering. . . That is, would you be willing to marry me in the fall?"

Overcome with emotion, all she could do was nod. Then as tears slipped from under Michelle's lashes, she finally found her voice. "I love you too, Ezekiel, and I'd be most honored to become your wife—as soon as tomorrow if it was possible."

She could hardly wait to share this good news with Mary Ruth and Willis. Michelle felt certain they'd be happy for her and Ezekiel. She wasn't sure about Ezekiel's parents though. Today, they'd said they were glad she had joined the church, but what if they didn't approve of her as their son's wife? If they didn't give Ezekiel their blessing, would he change his mind about marrying her?

⁓

### Clarks Summit

As Brad sat at a table inside a family restaurant, he reflected on his week at school, and how glad he'd been when the weekend finally came. It felt good to be free of his studies for a while and not have a textbook staring back at him. He'd called Sara last night, but only reached her voice mail. The last time they'd talked, the evening after he had gotten back from Strasburg, she'd seemed kind of distant. He figured she was either preoccupied or might be irritated about something.

Brad had hoped to try calling again, but the week ended up more hectic than he had anticipated. He'd delved into his studies each day when classes were over until he couldn't keep his eyes open. Even when Brad took lunch in the cafeteria, he had one of his textbooks open.

One afternoon, Brad had seen Terri sitting at the far end of the room with her nose in a book. *Does Sara believe there might be something going on between me and Terri?* He'd thought he'd made it clear the day he left for Clarks Summit that he had no interest in Terri other than friendship. Each night before Brad fell asleep, Sara was the only one on his mind.

Brad drummed his fingers on the table, waiting impatiently for his food to arrive. He glanced at his cell phone. *I wish Sara would return my call. Should I try calling her again? I'd like to hear how Michelle's baptism went today.*

Brad was about to punch in her number, when his phone buzzed. Hoping it was Sara, he answered without checking the caller ID.

"Hello."

"Hi, Brad. Your dad and I haven't heard from you since you went back to school after your spring vacation. We've been wondering how you're doing."

Staring into his cup of coffee, Brad offered his mother a heartfelt apology. "Sorry, Mom. I've been really busy, but then that's no excuse. I should have called to see how things are going with you and Dad this week."

"It's all right. We understand your studies come first right now."

Brad dropped his arms to his sides. He'd taken the time to call Sara but had neglected his own parents. He felt like a heel.

"Are you still there, Brad?"

"Yeah, Mom. I'll try to keep in better touch."

"How was your trip to Lancaster County? Did you get to see the young woman you told us about?"

"Yes. Sara and I spent a fair amount of time together. I'm eager to see her again."

"Is there something you're not telling me?" Mom made a little *hmm…*noise. He could almost picture the look of curiosity on her face.

"What do you think I'm not telling you?" Brad asked.

"Is there something serious developing between you and Sara? That is her name, right?"

"Yes, Mom, but I'm not certain yet about the direction my relationship is going with her. Like I told you the last time we talked, for now, Sara and I are just friends."

"Well, don't rush things, Brad. Remember to pray about the direction God would have you take, and He will direct you down the right path."

"Yeah, good advice."

"Don't forget, we still want to get together with you. We owe you a birthday meal."

"Okay, Mom, we'll work something out."

The waitress came with Brad's meal, so he politely told his mother that his food was here and he needed to go. "I'll be in touch soon," he added. "Take care, Mom, and tell Dad I said hello."

When Brad clicked off the phone, he bowed his head and said a silent prayer. *Heavenly Father, please give me wisdom and a sense of direction where Sara is concerned. If it's not meant for us to be together, let me know.*

~&~

*Strasburg*

"Would you like a cup of hot chocolate, Sara?" Grandma asked, getting up from her chair. "I'm going to fix one for your grandpa and me."

Sara pulled herself into an upright position. "That would be nice. Can I help you with it?"

Grandma shook her head. "It won't take me long. Please, stay here and rest. You look awfully tired this evening."

Sara didn't argue. She was tired; but more than that, her depressed spirit weighed in on her like a heavy blanket. The battery in her cell phone had died last night, and she wouldn't be able to charge it until she got to work tomorrow morning. But Sara's depression wasn't because of that. It was on a much deeper level.

She had convinced herself that Brad was interested in Terri Conners, even though he'd assured her they were only friends. She also couldn't seem to stop thinking about the lie she'd told Brad. Only Michelle knew the truth, but Sara wished now she'd never admitted her lack of Christianity.

She lay down again, pushing her head against the throw pillow. *What if Michelle uses that information to put distance between me and my grandparents? But what would be her reason for doing such a thing?* Sara closed her eyes and tried to squelch the negative thoughts.

Several minutes later, Grandma entered the room. "Here we go."

Sara opened her eyes and sat up, watching as her grandmother placed a tray on the coffee table. In addition to three mugs of hot chocolate and napkins, the spicy smell of sliced gingerbread on a plate reached Sara. Grandma handed one of the mugs to her and gestured to the gingerbread. "Please, help yourself."

Sara took the smallest piece and ate it. "Yum. . . This is delicious, Grandma."

"Thank you." Grandma smiled and handed a mug to Grandpa.

"Danki, Mary Ruth." He took a sip. "Ahh. . . This sure hits the spot."

Taking her own mug, Grandma seated herself on the end of the sofa. "Today was a special day indeed." She looked over at Grandpa.

"It was a nice baptismal service," he agreed.

"I'm so happy Michelle joined our church." Tears welled in Grandma's eyes. "We had always hoped our daughter would get baptized, but Rhoda had other ideas. Unfortunately, she did not want to be Amish." With a wistful expression, she looked over at Sara. "If your mother had joined the church and remained here with us during her pregnancy, you might be Amish now too."

*Is Grandma trying to make me feel guilty because I've shown no interest in becoming Amish?* Sara drank some of her hot beverage, cringing when she burned the end of her tongue. *Or is Grandma having a few moments of wishful thinking that have more to do with my mother than me?*

# Chapter 36

I have some good news to share with all of you," Michelle announced Monday morning at the breakfast table. She clasped her hands tightly together, hardly able to contain her excitement.

Mary Ruth leaned forward, eyes all aglow. "What is it, Michelle? I'm always eager to hear *gut neiichkeede*."

"Same here," Willis agreed. "There's too much bad news in our world today, so we need something positive to focus on."

Michelle couldn't hold back a smile. "Last night, when Ezekiel took me out for a ride, he proposed marriage."

Mary Ruth clapped her hands. "Now that certainly is good news."

"I hope you said yes." Willis reached for a piece of toast and spread apple butter on it.

Michelle nodded. "A year ago, I would never have imagined I could be this happy."

"April fools, right?" Sara said without smiling.

"No, I would not tease about something this important." Michelle's stomach fluttered as she looked at Sara. *I wonder what made her say such a thing. Isn't Sara the least bit happy for me?*

"Well then, I guess if it's true, congratulations are in order. I hope you and Ezekiel will be happy." Although Sara spoke with sincerity, her words seemed as if they were forced.

"We will be happy. I feel it right here." Michelle clasped both hands against her chest. "We're going to plan for a November wedding." She paused to add a spoonful of honey to her bowl of baked oatmeal. "I would have told you when I got home last night, but everyone had gone to bed, and I didn't want to wake you."

Mary Ruth reached over and placed her hand on Michelle's arm, giving it a few tender pats. "Since you have no family living in the area, I hope you will allow us to help with the wedding."

Willis bobbed his head agreeably. "My fraa is right. We want to help you make all the arrangements, and I'm sure Ezekiel's parents will help too."

"Ezekiel and I will talk more about it when he picks me up after work this evening," Michelle said. She'd be working the afternoon and evening shifts at the restaurant today and wouldn't be riding with Sara. Earlier, Willis had offered to take Michelle to work, as he had some errands to run this afternoon. Since Ezekiel would be picking her up in his horse and buggy, Michelle didn't have to hire a driver.

With the exception of Sara's little April Fool's comment, Michelle's week had started out well. Now if she could just figure out a way to help Sara see the need to forgive her mother, everything would be nearly perfect.

Soon after they finished eating, Sara left for work and Mary Ruth began washing the breakfast dishes.

"I'll go out and get the mail," Michelle offered. "Oh, and I can also stop at the phone shack to check for messages."

"That'd be great." Willis picked up the newspaper lying on his end of the table. "That'll give me time to check the news before I go out to feed the hogs."

"I'll help you with that chore as soon as I get back to the house," Michelle said.

He waved a hand. "No, that's all right. I can manage on my own this morning."

"Okay then. I'll be back shortly with the mail and a list of any phone messages you may have received."

Michelle opened the back door and stepped outside. Her mood matched the beautiful weather. But even had it been a dreary day, her spirits would not be dampened.

Last month, spring had officially arrived. Michelle could

hear it with the birds singing from the trees where leaves slowly sprouted. A sunny, blue sky greeted her, and as Michelle stood breathing in the fresh air, she lifted her head and looked up. *Thank You, Lord, for all the good things that have come into my life. I feel so undeserving, but I am grateful that You are a generous, loving God. Please be with Sara today and soften her heart toward things of a spiritual nature.*

When Michelle finished praying, she hurried down the driveway to the mailbox. She was surprised to discover that it was empty. Normally, the Lapps had at least a few pieces of mail. Maybe the mailman hadn't been by yet. Or perhaps on this rare occasion, he had no mail for them at all.

"Oh well. . .no mail means no bills." Michelle had quoted that more than once when she lived on her own. It was always a relief when bills didn't come, because money was sometimes scarce.

Pushing the memory aside, Michelle headed back up the driveway and stepped into the small wooden building that housed the Lapps' telephone. She had no more than taken a seat on the folding chair to check the answering machine, when the phone rang. She quickly reached for the receiver before the answering machine kicked in. "Hello."

### Clarks Summit

Brad was surprised to hear Michelle's voice. "Hey there. I didn't expect anyone to answer. Figured I'd have to leave a message, like usual."

Michelle explained that she had entered the phone shack to check for messages when it rang.

"Ah, I see. Guess that's bound to happen once in a while."

"Yes. Call it good timing."

"So how are you doing?"

"Couldn't be better. Yesterday morning, Ezekiel and I got baptized and became members of the Amish church. It was a meaningful day for me."

"I can imagine. And that's really fantastic. I'm happy for both you and Ezekiel."

"Something else special happened on Sunday."

"What was it?"

"Ezekiel came by in the evening to take me for a buggy ride, and he surprised me by asking if I would marry him."

"Wow! What was your response?"

"I said yes, of course." She giggled.

Brad heard the excitement in Michelle's voice. She had certainly changed from the troubled young woman he'd first met. "Congratulations! When will the wedding take place?"

"We hope to be married in November, and Ezekiel and I would be pleased if you could come to the wedding."

"You bet. Wouldn't miss it for the world." Brad paused briefly, looking at his watch. "Say, I don't mean to change the subject so quickly, but I have a class starting in half an hour. I need to ask though—how's Sara? I tried calling her over the weekend, but all I got was her voice mail."

"That's because her cell phone battery went dead."

"I see. I thought it was strange that she hadn't responded to my messages and wondered if everything was all right."

"Sara will probably call you when she gets to work and is able to charge her phone."

"Okay, but if I don't hear from her by this evening I'll try calling again."

"I've been praying for Sara, and it would be good if you did too."

Brad's brows furrowed. "What do you mean? Is there a problem?"

"Sara seemed despondent all weekend, and I have to wonder if it had anything to do with a discussion the two of us had last Saturday."

"If you don't mind me asking, what was it about?"

"Sara mentioned her mother, and how she resents the fact that she didn't find out about her Amish grandparents until after her mother died," Michelle replied. "She's holding resentment and feels bitter about this."

Brad scratched his head. "I did notice Sara wasn't her cheerful self when we were together the last time. I thought it might have something to do with me running into a friend from the university."

"No, I believe it had more to do with me asking Sara if she was a Christian."

"What'd she say?"

"Sara admitted that she is not a Christian, and even though I offered to help her become one, she showed no interest."

Squeezing his eyes shut, Brad rubbed the middle of his forehead. This made no sense.

"Brad, are you there?"

"Yeah. I'm just trying to process what you said." He lifted his hands and stared at his palms as though they held some answers. "Are you sure Sara said she was not a Christian?"

"I'm positive. It was right before you came to pick her up for your date."

It felt like someone had punched Brad in the stomach. *Why would Sara lie to me about being a Christian? Did she tell me she was because she thought that's what I wanted to hear?* He blew out his cheeks as he released a puff of air. *If she's not a believer, we can't have a relationship that goes beyond friendship.*

In addition to Brad taking to heart the scripture found in 2 Corinthians 6:14 that read, *"Be ye not unequally yoked together with unbelievers,"* he was preparing for the ministry. The last thing he needed was a wife who didn't share his beliefs.

*Strasburg*

"Good morning. Did you have a nice weekend?" Karen asked when Sara entered the flower shop.

Sara nodded briefly. "How was yours?"

"Ours went well. Saturday was busy here at the store, but Sunday we were able to relax awhile. Then while I got a few things done around the house, my hubby mowed the lawn."

"Sounds like a busy weekend." Sara put her purse under the counter and plugged her cell phone into the outlet on the wall behind her.

"It was, but we like to stay busy." Karen shook her head. "I'm not the kind of person to sit around doing nothing, and neither is Andy. So on that note, I'd better return to what I started before you came in. We just got several orders for a funeral service, so there are a lot of flower arrangements to be made yet. You know where we'll be if you need anything," Karen called over her shoulder as she headed for the other room.

"Will do."

Before looking over the books, Sara did a walk around the shop, making sure everything was in place. Then looking at her watch, she glanced out the door before flipping the metal sign over, from CLOSED to OPEN.

Looking up and down the sidewalk, she noticed that, except for a little traffic as people headed to work, all looked quiet.

*Maybe being around all these cheerful colors will brighten my mood,* Sara thought, inhaling the flowery scent of the store. *I certainly need something to get me out of these doldrums I've been in lately.*

Once Sara got her cell phone charging, she checked her voice mail for messages. She saw that there were two from Brad and one from her brother, Kenny. *I wonder what Kenny wants. He rarely calls.*

Returning Kenny's call could wait awhile, so Sara decided to call Brad first and let him know that her battery had been dead. She would have to leave a message, since at this time of the morning he was probably in class.

Sara picked up her phone, and was about to punch in Brad's number, when the phone rang. The caller ID showed it was Kenny.

*That's odd. I wonder why he would be calling me at this time of the day. I would think Kenny would be in school right now.* She swiped her thumb across the screen to answer. "Hi, Kenny. I'm surprised to hear from you on a school day." This was Kenny's last year in high school, and in a little over two months he'd be graduating. Sara hoped he hadn't done something foolhardy, like dropping out when he was this close to finishing.

"I—I'm calling about Dad. He was in an accident on the way to work this morning, and he's in the hospital." Kenny's voice trembled. No doubt he struggled with his emotions. "My friend Shawn's mother brought me to the ER. I'm here now, waiting to find out more about Dad." His voice had dropped to just above a whisper.

Sara's fingers touched her parted lips as she gasped. "Oh no. How bad is he hurt?"

"Real bad. He may not make it, Sara. Can you please come? I need you here with me. I can't go through this alone."

Sara's thoughts became so fuzzy she could barely think. She'd never heard Kenny in this state of mind and knew things must be very serious. She would have to explain the situation to her boss, and ask for time off. Even if it meant losing her job, Sara had to go. Her brother needed her. He had no one else. "Try not to worry, Kenny. I'll be there as soon as I can."

Sara clicked off the phone. As she made her way to the back room, a sinking feeling in the pit of her stomach grew heavier with each step she took. *What will happen to Kenny if Dean doesn't make it? He's too young to be on his own.*

# Chapter 37

Mary Ruth pushed her feet forcefully against the floor to get the rocking chair moving faster. She'd been concerned about Sara ever since she came home from work early and announced that she'd gotten word of her stepfather having been in a serious accident on his way to work. She hadn't given many details, because she didn't know much, but Sara had quickly packed her suitcase and informed them that she was heading for New Jersey.

"You'd better be careful with that rocking chair or it might topple over backward." Willis shook his finger at Mary Ruth, before taking a seat in his recliner. "I can tell you're *brutzich*."

"You're right. I am fretful." Mary Ruth slowed the rocker. "I wish Sara would have let me go with her when I offered. Someone should be there for her during this difficult time."

"Sara explained that she might be in Newark for several days or even weeks," Willis reminded Mary Ruth. "She didn't want to take you from the work you have to do around here. Besides, Sara's brother will be with her."

"True, but she's there to offer him *dreeschde*, and if her stepfather doesn't make it, she will definitely need someone to comfort her."

"Let's cross that path when the time comes." Willis reached for his Bible lying on the end table beside his chair. "In the meantime, we need to read a few passages of scripture and lift Sara, her brother, and Mr. Murray up in prayer."

Sara's body felt numb as she sat beside her stepfather's hospital bed. Kenny stood nearby with folded arms, staring at his father's battered body. The doctors and hospital staff had done all they could, but Dean hadn't woke up from his unconscious state. Short of a miracle, it didn't look like he would make it through the night. Sara hoped Dean would live—if for no other reason than for Kenny's sake. The seventeen-year-old boy needed his father.

Sara glanced at her watch. She had arrived shortly after lunch, but already it felt much later than one thirty. So many feelings raced through her as she watched for any sign of movement from Dean.

She thought back to the last time they had talked, right before the New Year. *Dean called to wish me a belated merry Christmas and happy New Year. I should have called him on Christmas Eve or made time to call on Christmas Day. Isn't that when people are supposed to put aside their feelings and try to forget any differences, even if it's only for one day?*

Sara looked at Dean, and her eyes grew moist as she remembered him saying he wanted to bring Kenny to Strasburg to meet his grandparents. It was unlikely now that it would ever happen.

*You need to pray.* A little voice in Sara's head nudged her to do so. She swallowed hard. *Why bother. I prayed for Mama, and she died anyway. I always tried to be a good daughter, but God never answered any of my prayers.*

Sara recalled her grandpa saying in a message he'd preached several weeks ago and later translated for her: *"Prayer isn't a business transaction. We don't give something to get something in return."*

Sara's fingers tightened and bit into her palms. *If that is the case, then why bother asking God for anything at all?*

Feeling the need for some fresh air and exercise, Sara left her chair. "I'm going down the hall to take a walk," she whispered to Kenny.

He nodded slowly, then turned toward the window.

Sara slipped from the room, and made her way past the nurse's station. When she came to a door identified as the chapel, she stepped inside. Sara felt relieved to find it empty. She needed time to be by herself and think.

The room reminded her of the church Brad had taken her to, only much smaller. She noticed two rows of padded chairs facing the front of the room, where a cross hung on the wall next to a stained glass window. Sunlight shone through, casting a warm glow of colorful patterns on a table below the window. A white cloth had been draped over the table, and a black Bible lay on top. A padded kneeling bench sat in front of the table, which Sara assumed was for those who wanted to pray. Sara wasn't sure she wanted to pray, but what else could she do for Dean right now? *How can such a beautiful sunny day have turned so tragic?* she asked herself.

Walking slowly to the front of the room, Sara picked up the Bible and took a seat on a chair in the first row. Holding the book against her chest, she bowed her head and offered a simple prayer: *Dear God, if You're listening, please heal Dean's injuries. And if You choose to take him, please give me the right words to help Kenny deal with his loss.*

Sara heard someone come into the room, and she opened her eyes. When she turned her head, she realized it was Kenny. "How'd you know I was here?"

"I didn't. Came here to pray." He sank into the chair beside her. "I'm scared Dad's not gonna make it, Sara."

Words wouldn't come, so she simply set the Bible aside and took hold of her brother's hand.

"I wish he'd wake up so we could talk to him." Kenny's chin trembled, and Sara saw moisture in his aqua-blue eyes. "Things haven't always been that great between me and Dad. I—I need to tell him I'm sorry for something I said last night."

"Do you want to talk about it?"

He nodded. "I told Dad I wanted to go to college and major

in music, instead of becoming a plumber after I graduate in June." Kenny pulled a hanky from his pocket and blew his nose. "Dad got really upset and said he wasn't gonna waste his money on a college education that might take me nowhere. He said learnin' the trade he'd learned when he was my age was a sure thing."

"How did you respond?"

"I got mad. Said if it was you wanting to go to college, I bet he'd pay for it, no questions asked."

Confused, Sara let go of Kenny's hand and reached up to rub the bridge of her nose. "That's not true. He didn't pay for the business classes I took at the community college."

"No, but he wanted to. Remember when he offered you the money?"

"Yes, but I thought it was for Mama's sake that he volunteered."

Kenny shook his head. "Nope, it was his idea. Dad's been behind the decision you made."

"Really? He's never said so."

"Yeah he has. . .just maybe not to your face. But when I came up with an idea like teaching music, he gave me no encouragement at all." Kenny looked at Sara with a most serious expression. "He may not have said so, but Dad's always cared about you. There've been times when I thought he even loved you more than me."

"No way, Kenny. I've never gotten that impression at all. And just so you know—I didn't expect anything from your dad. In fact, I had always planned to pay for my education. Someday, if the opportunity arises, I'd like to have my own business to run."

"What kind of business?"

Sara shrugged. "Maybe a floral shop like the one where I've been working. Only, if it were mine, I would incorporate some craft items, homemade cards, and maybe even beaded jewelry, like I enjoy making. Even though I didn't mind the job I had previously, I've known all along working as a part-time receptionist was not for me. It did help pay for school though. And your father helped as well, by not charging me a high rent."

Kenny's eyes widened. "I never knew that before."

"Guess I didn't think to mention it." Sara placed her hand on his arm. "And you aren't the only one having regrets." She went on to tell her brother about the phone call she'd received from his dad right before the New Year. "He wanted the two of you to come and see me, and meet your grandparents, but it never happened, and now I wish it had, Kenny. I have to ask myself—was I so busy I couldn't have called him a few times just to chat? All these years, I don't ever remember actually sitting and talking with Dean. I completely shut him out."

"I lived in the same house with him, but after Mom died, we drifted apart." Kenny wiped his nose. "Guess we both have regrets where Dad's concerned."

Sara remained silent, taking in all Kenny had said. Things she'd assumed about Dean could not be further from the truth. Her brother seemed deep in thought too, for he was just as quiet. It did Sara good to have this conversation with her brother. Although surprised by what each had revealed to the other, a little weight seemed to lift off Sara's shoulders. She now saw Kenny in a different light than she had before.

"Kenny, I have to admit. . . I didn't realize you wanted to get a degree in music."

"That's 'cause I never told you." He sniffed. "You know I like to sing and play the guitar, right?"

"Yes, but I thought you did it for your own pleasure."

He bobbed his head. "I do, but I'd like to teach music someday—to elementary school kids or someday even in a high school setting."

"Sounds like a good goal—definitely something to work toward."

"Try telling that to Dad." Kenny's shoulders drooped. "If it meant the difference between life and death for Dad, I'd give up my goal to teach music."

Sara had to bite her lip in order to hold back the sob rising in her throat. In all the years since her little brother was born, she had no idea there had ever been any problem between Dean and

Kenny, or that Dean actually cared for her. And all this time she'd been holding an unnecessary grudge against him—not to mention the negative feelings she'd kept bottled up about Mama.

Despite her best efforts, tears sprang to Sara's eyes. *What an ungrateful stepdaughter I have been. And I haven't been much of a sister to Kenny either.*

She reached into her purse and fumbled around for a tissue. What her fingers touched instead was a folded piece of paper. She pulled it out and read the message out loud: " 'For if ye forgive men their trespasses, your heavenly Father will also forgive you.' Matthew 6:14."

The tears came even harder, almost blinding Sara's vision. This was the same note she had read in one of the prayer jars she'd found at her grandparents' place. She had no idea how it had gotten in her purse.

Sara turned to face Kenny. "We need to get back to your dad's room, but before we go, I'd like to offer a prayer."

He nodded in agreement.

Sara reached for his hand again and bowed her head. "Lord, my brother and I have had some issues with bitterness and an unforgiving spirit. I ask You to forgive us for the sins we have done in the past, and please take our resentment away. Also, be with our dad—for Dean truly is the only father I have ever known. If it's Your will, we ask that You heal his body. But if You choose to take him, Lord, then please give Kenny and me a sense of peace and clear direction for the remainder of our lives. Amen."

"Amen," Kenny repeated.

They opened their eyes at the same time and stood. Knowing they both needed some comfort and reassurance right now, Sara gave her brother a hug. And he hugged her back just as hard.

"Let's go back to Dad's room now and sit by his bed. Maybe if we pray hard enough, he will wake up."

# Chapter 38

*Ronks*

Michelle stood outside the restaurant that evening, waiting for Ezekiel to pick her up. It had been difficult to concentrate on her job today, thinking about Sara and her stepfather. Learning about his accident had put a damper on Michelle's happier mood this morning, when she was excited to tell everyone about Ezekiel's proposal.

Michelle could still see Sara's panicked expression when she'd returned home from the flower shop before Willis had taken Michelle to work. After explaining about Mr. Murray's situation, Sara said she needed to go to New Jersey right away. When Sara rushed upstairs to pack, Michelle had slipped a note from one of the prayer jars into Sara's purse. Knowing how Sara felt about her stepfather, Michelle hoped the verse might speak to Sara's heart. Throughout Michelle's workday, whenever Sara came to mind, she sent up a prayer on her behalf, as well as for Sara's stepfather and brother.

Hearing a distinctive *clippity-clop* sound, Michelle looked down the street. As a horse and buggy drew closer, she realized it was Ezekiel. With no hesitation, she hurried out to the parking lot and waited for him to pull in. Right now, she needed to be with her future husband.

"How was your day?" Ezekiel asked after Michelle got into the buggy. Since it was dark inside the carriage, she couldn't see his face clearly. But Ezekiel's upbeat tone let her know he was in good spirits this evening.

"Everything at the restaurant went okay, but things aren't so good for Sara right now."

"What happened?"

Michelle explained the situation, including the part about the Bible verse she had put in Sara's purse. "I am hoping when she finds the slip of paper it will tug at her heartstrings and she'll let go of her bitterness." Michelle touched her chest. "I know all about feelings of resentment and how they can eat a person up. But after I found the Lord and asked Him to forgive me for the wrongs I had done, I was able to forgive those who had hurt me so deeply."

Ezekiel reached across the seat and clasped Michelle's hand. "Same for me. The bitterness I once had toward my folks has been released, and now we're gettin' along much better. It's not always easy to forgive, but God requires it of us. I hope for Sara's sake that she is able to resolve things with her stepfather."

### Strasburg

When Ezekiel pulled Big Red up to the Lapps' hitching rail, Michelle asked if he wanted to come in for a while.

"Sure, but I can't stay too late. I need to go to bed early. We're having a sale at the greenhouse tomorrow, and Dad wants me to be there an hour earlier than usual to help him set up for the event."

"No problem. I'm sure Willis and Mary Ruth will want to go to bed early as well. When Sara left for Newark, they both looked pretty distraught, so I'm sure they are tired."

Once Ezekiel had his horse secured, they headed for the house. They found Mary Ruth and Willis in the kitchen, drinking tea and eating banana bread.

"Pull up a chair and join us." Willis motioned with his head.

"Would either of you like a glass of milk or some hot tea?" Mary Ruth asked.

"Milk sounds good to me." Ezekiel smacked his lips. "And so does a slice of that bread."

"I'll get the milk." Michelle went to the refrigerator, while

Ezekiel took a seat across from Willis, and Mary Ruth sliced more bread.

"Have you heard anything from Sara?" Michelle directed her question to Willis, since he was often the one who went out to the phone shack to check their voice mail.

"Jah, but just once," he replied. "She left us a message saying she arrived at the hospital in Newark shortly after lunch, but we've heard nothing since."

Michelle placed the milk and two glasses on the table before sitting down. "I wonder if Brad knows about Sara's stepfather."

Mary Ruth's lips puckered. "He probably isn't aware, unless Sara called him."

"She may not have." Michelle stood. "Think I'll go out to the phone shack and give him a call. It would be good if he knew so he can be praying." Michelle grabbed her sweater, along with a flashlight, and went out the back door.

*Clarks Summit*

Brad was about to call it a night, when his cell phone rang. He recognized the Lapps' number, so he answered right away.

"Brad, it's me—Michelle."

"Oh, hi. How are you doing?"

"I'm fine, but Sara isn't. Have you heard from her today, Brad?"

"I haven't. Is she sick?"

"No. Her stepdad was in an accident on his way to work this morning. When Sara's brother called to tell her about it, he said his dad had been seriously injured, and it didn't look good. So Sara packed a bag and headed for Newark."

Brad rubbed his furrowed brow. "Wow, that's too bad. I'll certainly be praying for Sara's dad."

"Sara and her brother need prayer too."

"Yes, of course. I'll pray for all of them. Please let me know if you hear anything more."

"I will. Take care, Brad."

"You too. Bye, Michelle."

Brad clicked off his phone and sat staring at the stack of study books on the table. *What should I do? Should I call Sara and let her know I heard about her dad and that I'm praying for him?* This was certainly not the time to discuss the lie Sara had told him about being a Christian. She needed his support, not a lecture, right now.

❧

Newark, New Jersey

Sara and Kenny had been sitting beside Dean's bed most of the day. The good news was he was still alive, but he hadn't opened his eyes or spoken to them.

Glancing out the window, Sara noticed the sky had turned dark but some light filtered in from the parking lot. She checked her watch. It was almost nine o'clock, and she was exhausted. No doubt her brother was too. Kenny's friend, Shawn, and his parents, had come to the hospital a few hours ago. They weren't allowed into the room, since Dean's condition was critical and only family members could visit. So Kenny had met them in the waiting room, while Sara remained here, praying for a miracle. Now, as the two of them sat quietly, she'd begun to think that miracle might never come.

Thoughts of Sara's mother came to mind. In the chapel when she'd forgiven Dean, she'd also set her bitterness toward Mama aside. The past was in the past, and it couldn't be changed, so why keep harboring resentment? Sara's mother must have had her reasons for keeping her past a secret. She had relinquished her pain and bitterness to God. She had accepted His Son as her Savior too.

Sara's cell phone buzzed, and she pulled it out of her purse. Seeing it was Brad, Sara told Kenny she'd be right back, and then she slipped quietly from the room.

"Hello, Brad," Sara said, once she was in the hall. "S—something terrible happened today." Her voice faltered.

"I know. I just got off the phone with Michelle. She told me your stepdad was in an accident. How's he doing?"

"Not well. Kenny and I have been with him most of the day, but he hasn't responded to either of us."

"I'm sorry, Sara. I've been praying for all of you and will continue to do so."

"Thanks. We need all the prayers we can get."

"If there is anything I can do for you, please let me know."

"Okay. Thanks for calling. Bye, Brad."

When Sara returned to Dean's room, she was surprised to see that his eyes were open. Kenny stood near the bed, and it appeared as if his dad was trying to speak.

Sara hurried over to join her brother. "Dad," she murmured, barely able to get the words out. "We've been praying for you."

"Th–thank you." Dean spoke softly, and then he closed his eyes. A few seconds went by before he opened them again. "I–I'm not gonna make it, am I?"

Gently, Sara placed her hand on his arm, unable, at first, to respond. She glanced over at Kenny. The poor kid was on the verge of tears. Then somehow, she found her voice. Sara wanted to remain positive for Dean and her brother.

"Dad, you hang in there." She smiled at him. "We still have that visit to Strasburg to plan for." Even as the words slipped out, Sara knew deep in her heart the trip Dean had wanted to make would never happen.

"There's something I need to tell both of you." Dean spoke in a raspy voice.

Kenny shook his head. "It's okay, Dad. No need to talk. Save your strength."

"No, no. . . I—I need to say it." In a desperate plea, he beckoned them to lean closer. "I have money set aside for both of you." He paused and drew a shallow breath. "Use it to pursue your dreams." Dean reached out a feeble hand, and Kenny clasped it. "You should both decide what to do with the house. There is no mortgage. It's paid in full." His voice faltered, and then he rallied again. "After your mom died, I—I transferred the deed to both of your names."

When Sara looked at her brother and saw the tears streaming

down his face, it was nearly her undoing.

"It was wrong of me, Son, not to support your hopes all these years and wanting you to do what I thought was best. I take it all back now, and I'm sorry. Please go after whatever makes you happy." Then he looked at Sara. "Same goes for you, honey. If your dreams lie in Strasburg, follow them."

All Sara could do was nod, and grip his arm tighter.

"Sing for me, Kenny. Sing me a song." Dean's voice grew faint again. It was as if he had used all the strength he had left to tell them what they needed to know once he was gone.

"What would you like me to sing, Dad?" Kenny's voice shook with emotion.

"Anything. It will help me not to be afraid."

Kenny picked up the Bible the hospital chaplain had left when he'd come into the room earlier. A song printed on a piece of paper had been tucked inside. Kenny had showed it to Sara after they returned from the chapel earlier.

"This song is called 'Near to the Heart of God.'" Kenny stood at the foot of his father's bed and lifted his face to the ceiling. " 'There is a place of quiet rest, near to the heart of God, a place where sin cannot molest, near to the heart of God. O Jesus, blest Redeemer, sent from the heart of God, hold us, who wait before thee, near to the heart of God.'"

Kenny's voice grew stronger with each stanza. By the time he reached the second verse, goosebumps had erupted on Sara's arms. Although Kenny had told her in the chapel that he liked to sing, she had no idea he was this good. Her brother's voice was so clear and pure, it sounded almost heavenly. And his vibrato was nothing short of amazing.

" 'There is a place of comfort sweet,' " Kenny continued, " 'near to the heart of God, a place where we our Savior meet, near to the heart of God.' " As he sang the last stanza with even more emotion, Sara could hardly breathe.

" 'There is a place of full release, near to the heart of God, a place where all is joy and peace, near to the heart of God.' "

Through a film of tears, Sara looked at Dean. His eyes were closed, and he had a peaceful smile on his lips. His chest was motionless however. He did not appear to be breathing.

Sara pushed the call button for the nurse to confirm what she already knew. The man who had raised her and Kenny had slipped quietly from this world into the next. "Oh Daddy," she sobbed. "I never knew how much I loved you until now."

She put her arms around Kenny and held him close, as the two of them wept. Sara thought about Michelle and how she'd lost contact with her brothers. She couldn't imagine how difficult it must be for Michelle not to know where her brothers were, not to mention her needing their support during difficult times.

At that sad and most difficult moment, Sara determined in her heart that she would be there for her brother as long as he needed her, for she loved him very much.

# Chapter 39

*New Jersey*

I'm glad so many of us could go to Sara's stepfather's funeral today," Mary Ruth said from her seat at the back of their driver's van. In addition to her and Willis, Michelle, Ivan, Yvonne, and Lenore accompanied them. Sara needed friends and family with her today.

"Since it's Saturday and I don't have to teach, it worked out so that I could come along," Lenore agreed.

Ivan had left his sons in charge of his business today, rather than having to close the store. When Willis talked to Brad last night, he'd said he also planned on coming to the funeral.

It would be nice to finally meet Sara's brother. Back when Sara's stepfather had called Sara and said he and Kenny planned to make a trip to Strasburg, Mary Ruth had been excited. She figured they would probably drive down sometime in the summer, after Kenny was out of school. But it was not meant to be.

*It's unfortunate we won't get to meet Mr. Murray now,* Mary Ruth thought. *I wish it were under better circumstances that Willis and I would be meeting our grandson for the first time.*

They'd crossed over the state line into New Jersey, so it wouldn't be long until they reached their destination.

Looking out the window, Mary Ruth thought about Rhoda. *Poor Sara. Less than a year after losing her mother, she's lost her stepfather too.*

Mary Ruth leaned to the right and loosened her seatbelt a little. She realized the importance of seatbelts for safety reasons, but was glad they weren't required to wear them while riding in their buggies. To her, at least, they felt too constricting. She leaned her head against the seatback and closed her eyes. Since everyone else in the van was quiet, including their driver, she thought it might be good to take a little nap. Today would be long and emotional, and since they'd gotten up earlier than usual, she wanted to arrive feeling somewhat refreshed.

*Heavenly Father,* Mary Ruth prayed, *please be with Sara and Kenny today. Let them feel Your presence, as if You are right there with them, holding their hands.*

❧

### Newark

Brad entered the chapel where the funeral service was being held for Dean Murray and took a seat near the back of the room. Since he had arrived a few minutes late, all the other chairs had been taken.

A variety of flowers had been arranged up front, and a huge spray of white lilies draped over the closed casket. The fragrance from all the bouquets wafted through the chapel, and the sweet scent lingered everywhere. Next to the coffin was a small pedestal table adorned with a white doily. A framed picture sat on top. From where Brad sat, it looked like a family picture of Dean and three other people, who he guessed were Sara, her mother, and brother.

Craning his neck, Brad saw Sara sitting in the front row beside a blond-haired man, who he assumed was her brother. On the other side of her sat Sara's grandparents, her uncle Ivan, aunt Yvonne, and cousin Lenore. Michelle was there too, sitting to the left of Lenore.

Brad pulled his fingers around his too-tight collar, hoping to loosen it a bit. *Should have worn a different shirt,* he thought. *And I would have if there'd been a clean dress shirt in my closet.* Brad had been so busy at school the past week that he hadn't found time to do his laundry.

Brad caught sight of Stan sitting a few rows ahead. The Lapps must have hired him to bring them to the service today. If Strasburg hadn't been so far from Clarks Summit, Brad would have gone there to get them.

Sometimes Brad wished he had stayed at the Bible College in Lancaster to complete his studies, instead of going all the way up to the university he now attended. If things had worked out between him and Sara, he might have considered transferring back to Lancaster, or even moving there and taking some online classes. A long-distance relationship was not good, but since Sara was not a Christian, continuing to see her socially was no longer in the equation.

When the blond-haired man left his seat and stood behind the podium at the front of the room and to the right of the casket, Brad's thoughts refocused. Then as the young man began to sing, "Near to the Heart of God," Brad's wavering emotions threatened to overtake him. Not only were the words of the song appropriate, but the man's voice rang so true and clear, it seemed almost angelic. As though it had come straight down from heaven, an amber-colored light filtering through the stained glass windows shone down on the talented vocalist, illuminating his hair, and making it look like spun gold. To be able to sing that song without any musical instrument to accompany him made it even more amazing.

Brad glanced at the program an usher had given him when he'd entered the chapel. Kenny Murray had been listed as the vocalist. What Brad suspected had now been confirmed. The young man, who stood before them, looking upward as he sang the powerful words, was indeed Sara's half-brother. It had to be difficult for Kenny to sing at his father's funeral and not break down. Was the boy a Christian? How could he sing a spiritual song, and with such conviction, if he was not a believer? Had Sara been raised in a Christian home and strayed away from it? There were so many unanswered questions.

Brad's gaze went back to Sara. Her head was now bent forward. Her shoulders trembled, and when she turned her head to the left, Brad saw Sara dab her eyes with a tissue. Mary Ruth draped an arm around Sara, patting her shoulder. Brad wished he was sitting on the other side of Sara, to comfort and hold her hand. Yet another part of him was glad to be sitting in the back, not wanting to be emotionally tied.

Brad clasped the program he held. *I'd like to know either way where Sara stands on Christianity, and I'd like to hear it from her, not Michelle.*

⁓

Michelle was stunned to hear how well Sara's brother sang. He seemed nervous, choked up near the end of the song, but his vocal tone was on pitch, and Kenny had moved her to tears. Taking a quick glance around, she saw many others wiping their eyes.

*Sara is lucky to have Kenny in her life,* Michelle thought. She had met the young man before the service started, and he seemed like a nice person. Not like some teenagers she'd gone to school with, who had foul mouths and arrogant attitudes.

Once again, Michelle's thoughts went to her brothers. Had they grown up to be responsible citizens? Or did one or both of them end up like their parents—brash and rough around the edges? She hoped Jack and Ernie had made something of themselves and were living happy, fulfilling lives.

Michelle sighed. *Guess I'll never know the answer, so I need to keep my focus on the life I have in Pennsylvania and look forward to my future with Ezekiel.*

When Kenny sat down and a man she assumed was a minister stood up and offered a prayer, Michelle reached up to make sure her head covering was properly in place. According to biblical teachings, the Amish believed a woman's head should always be covered whenever she prayed.

When the prayer was over and the preacher began to deliver his message, Michelle glanced over at Sara, sitting straight and tall.

*I wonder if she will stay in New Jersey with her brother now that her stepfather is gone. Willis and Mary Ruth would surely miss Sara if she didn't to return to Pennsylvania.* Michelle swallowed hard. *I'd miss her too.*

Sara couldn't remember when she'd felt more proud of her brother. Kenny had made it through the entire song without missing a note. And to be able to sing without accompaniment made it all the more astounding.

She reached across her chest and clasped her grandmother's hand, which was still around her shoulders. What a blessing and comfort it was to have Grandma and Grandpa here today. Sara felt so grateful the Lord had led her to them after Mama died. She also appreciated the presence of Uncle Ivan, Aunt Yvonne, and Lenore. What a privilege it was to have such a special family.

And there was Michelle, who'd come to offer her condolences and support Sara. This young woman, whom Sara had once been so angry with, was now truly a friend. Sara could hardly wait to tell Michelle she had become a Christian and explain how it came about.

She listened attentively as the pastor spoke to those in attendance. He talked about life after death and stated that every believer had the promise of heaven.

Sara didn't know where her stepfather stood spiritually, but if he wasn't a Christian previously, she hoped he'd made a confession of faith before his death—perhaps during the song Kenny sang for him or maybe when the chaplain had visited. If the smile on Dean's face when he passed away was any proof, Sara had to believe it was true.

When the minister finished his sermon, he ended by telling everyone they were invited to go to the cemetery where Dean would be laid to rest. He also added that Sara and Kenny wanted those who could to join them for lunch at the Adega Grill, one of Dean's favorite places to dine. After the announcement, he took his place at the foot of the open coffin and remained there while everyone filed by to pay their last respects to the deceased. Since Sara and Kenny went last, with the exception of the pastor and funeral attendants, the chapel was empty by the time she and

Kenny walked out. In the hall, however, several people waited to speak to them and offer their sympathies. Sara's grandparents, her uncle, aunt, and cousin were there, along with Michelle. Toward the back of the group, Sara spotted Brad.

Sara's heart thumped in her chest as she made her way over to him. When she reached his side, he gave her a brief hug. "I'm sorry for your loss, Sara. I've been praying for you, as well as your brother."

"Thank you. I would have been disappointed if you hadn't come." Tears welled in her eyes. "If you plan on going to the cemetery, I hope afterward you can stay for lunch."

Brad shook his head. "Sorry, but I have to get back to Clarks Summit. It's a big study weekend for me."

"Oh, okay." Sara tried to hide her disappointment. "I'm glad you took the time to drive down for the service. It means a lot to me."

Brad nodded, then glanced down at the floor as though unable to meet Sara's gaze. "You're my friend, Sara. I wanted to offer my condolences in person."

*Friend? Is that all I am to Brad?* When he lifted his head, Sara noticed his subdued expression.

A wave of sadness washed over her, and it wasn't merely the mood of the melancholy service that had taken place moments ago. Sara felt something had changed between her and Brad. She suspected it might have to do with his friend Terri.

*It doesn't matter,* she told herself. *I have to stay in Newark until Kenny is able to be on his own, and I'll need to help sell the house and settle Dean's estate. It could be months before I'm able to return to Lancaster County. By then Brad could be engaged or even married.* Sara told herself it was better this way, because she had no time for love or romance. If she were being honest, she'd never been sure where her relationship with Brad was going. Her focus had to be on her brother right now.

# Chapter 40

Throughout the months of April and May, Sara stayed at Dean's house with Kenny, and now here it was, the first week of June. They'd found a buyer for the house, and the couple who had rented the other side of the duplex when Sara moved to Strasburg had moved out. That meant the new owners could decide whether to rent out that half of the building or make use of the entire home for their family. Sara would oversee the estate sale that would take place two weeks before the new owners took possession.

Sara glanced at the calendar above the desk where she sat going over the bills that still needed to be paid. As executor of Dean's will, a lot of responsibility had fallen on her. She never dreamed so much paperwork would be involved in settling someone's estate, or that she would have to sort through all of Dean's personal items.

Sara remembered with fondness the day she'd gone through his bureau and found a box with her mother's wedding ring inside. She had never understood why he hadn't given the ring to her when Mama died, but at least it was in her possession now.

"I'm headin' out, Sara," Kenny hollered from the hallway outside the den where Sara sat.

"Okay. Try to be home in time for supper," she called in response.

"Sure thing."

Sara smiled when she heard the door click shut. Kenny's graduation had taken place last week, and even though he still missed his dad, he'd been in an upbeat mood. Sara knew it was because, thanks to the inheritance he'd received, Kenny would be attending the Curtis Institute of Music in Philadelphia. While the school offered free tuition, other expenses added up to thousands of dollars. But even more than being grateful he was able to afford such a great school, Kenny said he was glad he'd received his father's blessing to pursue his dream in music.

This was going to be a special summer for both Sara and her brother. Kenny looked forward to going with her to spend three months at their grandparents' place. It would give him a chance to really get to know them, plus he'd have the opportunity to work for Grandpa and earn some money as well.

Things were changing in Sara's life too. When she'd called Andy and Karen to inform them of her father's death, Sara had explained that she might not return to Pennsylvania for several months. She'd been about to suggest they find someone to replace her, when Andy said if they did hire another person, it would only be temporary, because he and his wife had decided to sell the floral shop sometime in June. At their age, the workload was getting to be too much, and it was time for them to retire. After Sara found out the reasonable price they wanted for the shop, she offered to buy the business. If not for the generous inheritance she'd received, it would not have been possible for Sara to even consider such a venture. This opportunity was a dream come true and most certainly an answer to prayer.

Sara missed being in Strasburg, but at the same time she felt thankful she could be in Newark to help finalize everything. Kenny admitted he could not have done all the work on his own and wouldn't have known where to begin when it came to going through all the household items.

Sitting back in her chair, Sara glanced out the open window, enjoying the warm breeze wafting in. The sounds of the birds singing made her yearn to be home. Home to her meant Strasburg, and it felt good knowing she'd soon be putting down roots in Lancaster County, where she would always be close to her grandparents.

*I guess by now Grandma and Michelle have the garden all planted.* Sara sighed. *I miss being there to assist.*

At least she and Kenny would be back on the farm to help with weeding and picking when the vegetables were ready. Grandma loved to can, and there'd be plenty of picking and processing to do for that.

Sara could almost picture Kenny helping Grandpa with the hogs and doing other chores around the farm. *My brother will get a real taste of country living with his grandparents.* She stretched her arms up and over her head, anxious to be surrounded by the sounds that could only be heard in the country. *If I was there now, I'd probably be strolling barefoot around in Grandma and Grandpa's yard.*

Sara wiggled her toes in the carpet, eager to feel the lush green grass under her feet. She was excited to get back home and help Michelle with her wedding plans too.

The curtains floated out and back again. The fresh air sure smelled good. A dog barked in the distance, and Sara's thoughts continued to focus on Michelle. *Her puppy, Val, must have grown since I left.* Sara remembered watching an old movie when she was growing up about Irish setters. *They are such beautiful dogs.*

She recalled how Dean and Mama had taken her and Kenny to the drive-in theater when they were young to see their favorite movies. Sara closed her eyes, remembering those days, as more memories came to mind. On Labor Day weekend, the local drive-in had all-night theater, starting from dusk and ending at dawn. Sara had forgotten what fun she had during those times watching picture shows on the enormous screen from the comfort of their car. Each parking space had a small speaker, and Dean would attach it to their open car window. For the dusk-to-dawn movies, Kenny and Sara would go wearing their pajamas, and they'd take their sleeping bags along. At the time, they had a station wagon, and Mama and Dean would put the back seat down so they had a roomy area to crawl inside their sleeping bags in case they couldn't stay awake. Usually when the last movie was showing, she and her brother would fall asleep.

*I'd forgotten what fun that was.* Sara had recalled lots of good memories lately. For some reason, she had suppressed many of those. For too many years, she'd dwelled on negative things, which had done her no good at all.

Sara sat up straight when her phone buzzed. She had muted it before going to bed last night and forgotten to turn the volume on this morning, so until now, she didn't realize she had any messages.

The message was from Grandma, asking what day Sara and Kenny would arrive and wondering what they might like for supper that evening.

Sara smiled. *It's just like Grandma to be worried about what to feed us. She's always thinking of others.*

Sara listened to several older messages on her phone too. Some were from the Realtor about things pertaining to the sale of the house. Another was from Andy Roberts, and also an older message from Brad. She'd listened to it before but hadn't taken the time to respond since she had been so busy. Besides, Brad's message—telling her that he would soon be in the middle of finals but was still praying for her—was a statement, not a question he expected her to answer.

Sara still hadn't told him she'd become a Christian, but didn't see any point in telling him now. Brad's phone calls had gotten farther apart, and Sara figured he'd moved on with his life—a life that didn't include her. It was probably better that way—for both of them—since he would be going into the ministry after graduation. And soon, she would have a new business to run. Brad needed someone like Terri Conners, who'd been preparing for a certain phase of ministry. Sara hoped in time, with the busyness of her job, her memory of Brad would fade.

*Clarks Summit*

"Hey, Brad, wait up!"

Brad had started down the hall toward his next class when he heard a familiar voice. He turned and saw Terri coming toward him with a wide smile on her face.

"Hi, Terri. How's it going?" He hadn't talked to her in several days. "Are you feeling as edgy as everyone else due to finals this week?"

"No, not really. I'll just be glad to get them done so I can enjoy my summer." She smiled up at him.

"Will you be doing anything exciting during summer break or taking it easy till fall?"

"There won't be anything easy about what I'm going to do, but it should be fun and rewarding."

Brad tipped his head. "Oh? What might that be?"

"I've been asked to fill in for the youth pastor at a community church outside of Pittsburgh. He will be taking a three-month sabbatical, and since my uncle John knows someone on the church board, he put in a good word for me." Terri's eyes sparkled with exuberance. "Even though it won't be a permanent position, it'll be a great learning experience for me."

Brad placed his hand on her shoulder and gave it a tap. "Good for you, Terri. I bet your summer will be full of blessings."

"Thanks." She moved closer to Brad. "What are your summer plans?"

He turned his hands palms up. "Nothing nearly as exciting as yours. I'll go home first to see my folks in Harrisburg, and then I may head down to Lancaster County again and hopefully do some driving for the Amish, along with any work they might need to have done. The money I make will go toward next year's tuition of course."

"Makes sense to me." Terri gave Brad's arm a squeeze. "Guess we'd better head for our next class. If I don't see you before we leave, we'll connect again in the fall. God's blessings to you, Brad."

He gave a nod. "Same to you, Terri."

As Brad moved down the hall, his thoughts went to Sara. He hadn't heard from her for quite a while, and figured she had continued to move forward with her life. But it was probably better that way. She was clearly not the girl for him.

Mary Ruth squinted at the words she'd written on her notepad. They looked a little blurry. "Think maybe it's past time for me to get an eye exam." As a young woman, Mary Ruth had enjoyed perfect vision. But as the years went by, she eventually needed glasses. At first it was for reading only, but then the doctor suggested she wear them all the time. Mary Ruth saw glasses as a nuisance—something she could easily misplace or lose altogether. Besides, her glasses would often slip off the bridge of her nose or the earpiece would dig into the back of her head behind one or both ears. So more often than not, she only wore her glasses for reading or close-up work.

"Whatcha doin'?" Michelle asked, stepping behind Mary Ruth.

"I'm making out a grocery list for when Sara and Kenny come, which will be soon." Smiling, she turned to look at Michelle. "Words can't express how excited I am about seeing them again. I'm especially looking forward to spending the whole summer with Kenny and getting to know him better."

Michelle took a seat next to Mary Ruth. "The last time I spoke to Sara on the phone she said Kenny would be going to college in the fall. Since it's in Philadelphia, I guess he'll only be able to stay here till then."

Mary Ruth nodded. "But Philadelphia isn't that far away, so Willis and I are hoping Kenny can come visit on some weekends and for extended holidays." Mary Ruth set her pen and paper aside. "And of course, we hope Sara will continue to live with us while she runs her new business."

"Everything's working out well for all of us." Michelle spoke in a bubbly tone. "I still can't believe I'm Amish now, or that I'll be getting married in five months."

"And that's another list we need to make." Mary Ruth pulled off the top paper she'd been writing on and handed the rest of the notepad to Michelle. "You've already started sewing your wedding dress, and we've begun making plans for the food we want to serve your guests. Now you just need to make a list of everyone you want to invite to the wedding."

Michelle tapped the pen against the table as she tilted her head from side to side. "That's a good question. All of Ezekiel's family will be included, as well as the friends we've made here." She looked at Mary Ruth with an endearing smile. "That includes you, Willis, and Sara." Michelle's smile faded. "But of course, none of my family will be there. They don't even know where I am."

Mary Ruth reached over to gently pat Michelle's arm. "I know it hurts, but remember—we are your family now, and so are Ezekiel's parents and siblings."

"Danki." Michelle's eyes filled with tears. "I'm thankful for all of you."

When Michelle left the table to get a glass of water, Mary Ruth said a quick prayer. *Heavenly Father, on Michelle and Ezekiel's wedding day, when she and her groom stand before our bishop, please give her a sense of peace and comfort as only You can. And be with our granddaughters, Sara and Lenore, for You know who just the right men will be for them. Amen.*

# Chapter 41

*Newark*

Sara's vision blurred as she closed the door of the home where she'd spent most of her childhood. The new owners would be moving in tomorrow, and it was time for her and Kenny to go forward with their lives. After today, this place would be filled with other people's possessions.

"There's one thing that will not disappear," Sara whispered as her hand moved to her chest. "That's the memories I'm keeping right here, close to me. I'm going to make sure I hold on to the good ones and, with God's help, try to forget those that once burdened me."

She glanced at Dean's SUV, which Kenny had inherited. It would be good transportation for him, going back and forth to Philadelphia. Sara had sold her old car, which wasn't reliable anymore. She would buy a newer one after they got to Lancaster County.

"Hey, sis, are you comin'?" Kenny opened the window on the passenger's side and motioned to her. "We're burnin' daylight."

She nodded, looked one last time at the house, then climbed into the driver's seat. "Are you sure you don't want to drive, Kenny? After all, this is your vehicle."

"Maybe when we get closer, but for now I wanna enjoy the scenery." He clicked his seatbelt in place, and Sara did the same.

"Well okay then. Here we go." Despite the sorrow Sara felt over closing this chapter of her life, her brother's enthusiasm was contagious. A new door was about to open, and she couldn't wait to see what was on the other side.

Sara's first stop when they arrived in Strasburg was the flower shop. She'd made an appointment to meet Andy and Karen Roberts in order to pick up the keys and go over a few important things. As eager as she was to see her grandparents, it was necessary to make sure she had everything she needed in conjunction with her new business. The biggest hurdle would be finding someone to make up the bouquets and floral arrangements. But Andy had assured Sara the woman they'd hired to fill in for her while she was in Newark would be willing to keep working. The young man who made their deliveries had also agreed to stay on. If the business did well, Sara planned to hire one other employee to help at the store so she would be able to take some time off when needed.

After Sara parked the SUV, she looked over at Kenny and smiled. "Well, we made it." She looked at her watch. "It's almost lunch time."

"Yeah, my stomach has been tellin' me that for the last hour." He grinned. "I'm surprised you didn't hear it grumbling."

"Can you hold out awhile longer?" she asked. "After I'm finished talking to my former boss and his wife, I thought we could go to the restaurant in Ronks where my friend, Michelle, works. You met her at Dad's funeral."

"Oh yeah. Sure, I can wait a little longer." Kenny snickered when his stomach growled again. "Try telling that to my belly though."

"I shouldn't be too long. While I'm taking care of business, you can either check out some of the stores here in town or come inside with me."

"Think I'll walk around till you're done with business. This town looks pretty interesting, with all its old buildings."

"It is a fascinating place to visit," Sara agreed. "And with quite a history."

"How so?"

"For one thing, in the late sixteen hundreds, this area was visited by French fur traders. Then later it was settled by Swiss Mennonites and Huguenots from the Alsace region of France," Sara explained. "Some of the original log homes from the eighteenth century still remain."

Kenny whistled. "That's amazing."

"Of course, there's a lot more to tell about historic Strasburg, but I need to get into the flower shop now, so I'll have to share more of the town's history with you some other time." Sara was aware that her brother liked history and had done well in his high school history classes, so she was confident he wouldn't be bored walking around town.

"Okay, Sis. I'll meet you back here in an hour or so." Kenny opened the door, stepped out of the vehicle, then turned to face her. "One more thing. . . When we head for Grandma and Grandpa's place, would it be okay if I drive?"

Sara nodded. "See you soon."

❧

*Ronks*

Michelle was glad she'd been given the breakfast and lunch shifts today. With any luck, she'd be done working and back at the Lapps' before Sara and her brother arrived this afternoon. Although she was happy Sara could spend the summer with Kenny, a twinge of envy took over every time she thought about her own brothers and how she yearned to be with them.

As Michelle headed to the dining room to wait on her tables, the words of Philippians 4:11 popped into her head: *"Not that I speak in respect of want: for I have learned, in whatsoever state I am, therewith to be content."*

Annoyed with herself, Michelle's gaze flicked upward. *When am I going to quit fretting about this and learn to be content?* Lately with wedding plans being made, she had plenty of positives to think about. And as Mary Ruth had pointed out the other day, Michelle had a new family now, whom she loved and respected.

When she entered the dining room, Michelle was surprised to see Sara and Kenny sitting at one of the tables.

"Surprise!" Sara offered Michelle a sincere-looking smile. "We just left the flower shop in Strasburg and thought we'd stop here for lunch before heading to Grandma and Grandpa's. I was hoping you'd be working today."

"I asked if I could work the breakfast and lunch shifts today so I could be at Willis and Mary Ruth's place when you arrived. Your grandparents are eager to see you both. In fact, it's all Mary Ruth has been talking about for weeks." Michelle handed Sara and Kenny a menu.

"We're excited too. Aren't we, Kenny?" Sara bumped his arm lightly.

His head moved up and down. "I'll admit, I'm a little nervous though. I've never stayed in an Amish home before or lived on a farm. I'm not sure how I'll handle no TV or internet either."

Michelle chuckled. "You'll get used to it. And you never know. You might even enjoy the peace and quiet. I sure do."

"Same here." Sara looked at her brother. "As far as the internet goes, you can always come by the flower shop and log in on your laptop there."

His eyes brightened. "Seriously?"

"That's right. The shop has electricity and internet access." Sara bumped his arm again. "Can you imagine that?"

He snickered. "Okay. I'm no dummy. I figured it did."

The bantering going on between Sara and her brother caused Michelle to feel a pang of jealousy again. *Now stop it,* she berated herself. *Sara and Kenny deserve to be happy and enjoy their time together.*

*Strasburg*

Mary Ruth had a difficult time concentrating on the crossword puzzle she'd begun working on. The guest rooms were ready, the house had been cleaned from top to bottom, and supper was planned.

All that remained was to wait for the arrival of her grandchildren.

"I wish they'd hurry up and get here," she mumbled from her rocking chair.

Willis gave a bemused smile. "Now don't start getting brutzich again. They'll get here in due time."

"I'm not fretful. Just wondering, is all."

He snickered and put his chair in the reclining position. "Think I'll take a little *leie*. Wake me when they get here." He leaned his head back and closed his eyes.

Mary Ruth wrinkled her nose and got the rocking chair moving. A nap was the last thing on her mind right now.

Her thoughts took her back over the year. She couldn't believe how much had changed. It was sad to think their daughter had died over a year ago. Although the pain had lessened, it still brought an ache to her heart thinking about all the years they were apart. But now so much happiness had entered their lives. They'd gained a granddaughter, a grandson, and also Michelle. Mary Ruth's life felt full, despite the longing she would always have for the daughter who left too soon. And because of the note Rhoda left in her Bible for Sara, three special people had come into Mary Ruth and Willis's lives.

Mary Ruth clasped her hands. *No matter how we end up finding it, God always has a plan for us.*

She was about to go out on the porch and wait for Sara and Kenny's arrival, when the grandfather clock struck two, and she heard a vehicle pull into the yard. Mary Ruth rose from her chair and went quickly to the window. "They're here, Willis," she announced when Sara and Kenny got out of the SUV.

Willis snorted, then put his chair up straight, instantly awake. "Okeydoke. Let's go outside and greet them."

Mary Ruth didn't waste any time getting out the door. Willis was right behind her. By the time they reached the vehicle, Kenny and Sara were out and getting their luggage from the back.

"It's so good to see you, Grandma." Sara engulfed Mary Ruth in a hug, while Kenny hugged Willis. Then they traded. After all the hugging was done, Willis helped bring in the suitcases. Once inside, Mary Ruth suggested they all sit outside on the back porch, since the house was a bit stuffy and a cool breeze had finally come up. "I'll bring out some lemonade and homemade cookies I recently made."

"In a few hours Michelle will be home too," Willis added. "She's anxious to see you."

"We surprised Michelle a little bit ago." Kenny said. Then he explained how he and Sara had gone to eat lunch at the restaurant where Michelle worked.

"Well, that was nice." Mary Ruth smiled. "Now how about we do some of that porch-sitting? We have a lot of catching up to do."

"If you don't mind, before I sit and visit, I'd like to take a walk out to the barn and say hello to the horses. It's been awhile since I've seen Bashful and Peanuts." Sara looked at Mary Ruth and then Willis. "If it's okay, that is. It'll give you both a chance a visit with Kenny alone for a few minutes."

Mary Ruth blinked rapidly as she pushed her glasses back in place. Willis looked at her and shrugged his shoulders. *Our granddaughter just got here and now she wants to run off to the barn? She never took an interest in the horses before. I wonder what that's all about.*

# Chapter 42

It wasn't polite to head for the barn and leave her grandparents and Kenny sitting on the porch, but Sara felt compelled to go. She still had the slip of paper she'd found in her purse while in the hospital chapel and wanted to put it back in the prayer jar, where it belonged. She didn't know who had written the notes in either of the jars she and Michelle had found, but the person responsible must have had a reason, not only for the things they wrote, but for putting them inside the old jars.

Walking down the path to the barn, Sara was on the verge of skipping. Familiar sounds reached her ears as she swung her arms loosely at her sides. The burdens she'd shouldered when she was last here were long gone. The birds sang from the trees above, as if announcing her arrival. Cute little piglets that must have been born when she was away squealed in the paddock around their mother. Inhaling the scent of country air made Sara's heart swell. It was so good to be back with her grandparents again. This morning she'd left her childhood house, but here truly felt like she was home.

As the whiff of sweet-smelling hay and animals reached her nostrils, Sara entered the barn and found Sadie and Val curled up, sleeping close to each other. "Well, you little stinkers," she whispered. "No wonder you didn't come out to the yard to greet us when we arrived." Sara figured the dogs must be exceptionally tired not to have heard their vehicle when it entered the yard. Either that or they'd been out in the back pasture somewhere, chasing each other or some poor critter. Sara had seen Sadie go after squirrels in the past, but the dog had never attacked the animals. She supposed

Sadie liked the sport of chasing.

Sara was tempted to wake the dogs and give them an official greeting, but that could wait. Right now, she had a mission to accomplish.

She pulled a ladder under the shelf where the old canning jars sat, then climbed up and took down the prayer jar, hidden behind the others. Holding it carefully, she seated herself on a wooden stool. Before putting in the piece of paper she'd brought with her, Sara read a few of the other notes inside the jar.

The first one said: *"We should always make allowance for other people's faults."*

Sara reflected on that a few moments. *Did the person who wrote this feel that someone had not made allowance for their faults?*

The next note Sara read included a thought, as well as a prayer: *"The reason we exist is to be in fellowship with God. Thank You, Lord, for being there when I need You."*

Sara put the notes back in the jar and added the one she'd found in her purse. Then, bowing her head, she said a short prayer of her own. *Lord, I have so much to thank You for—loving grandparents, a talented brother, my uncle, aunt, and cousins—and my special friend, Michelle. Please bless and protect each of them.*

<hr />

When Brad pulled into the Lapps' yard, he noticed a beige SUV parked near the house. He figured Willis and Mary Ruth had company. Either that or the rig belonged to one of their drivers. *Maybe they won't need me anymore,* he thought. *Could be in my absence they've found someone else to work here on the farm. Even if that is the case, I'm sure there are plenty of Amish farms in the area who will need some extra help or a driver this summer.*

Since Brad would be staying with his friend Ned again, he wouldn't have to worry about a place to live while he was in Lancaster County. And with summer being a heavy tourist season, he felt sure he could secure a job, even if it wasn't driving or farming. He'd never had problems finding work before and assumed this summer would be no different.

Brad parked his van next to the other vehicle. He sat awhile, enjoying the pleasure of being back in Lancaster County. The last time he'd been here was during spring break in March when the weather was mild. Now the sultry air was heavily scented with the sweet smell of honeysuckle growing on fencerows along the road. During the trip down from Clarks Summit, Brad had noticed that the first cutting of hay had been completed.

He got out of the car and stretched his legs. Seeing no one in the yard, he stepped onto the front porch and knocked on the door. A few seconds later, Mary Ruth answered.

Her whole face seemed to light up when she looked up at Brad and joined him on the porch. "Well hello, stranger. It's been a while since we've seen you."

Brad nodded. "The last time we spoke was at the funeral of Sara's dad, but unfortunately we didn't get much time to talk."

"That's right," she agreed. "It was a busy day, and since you left before we did, neither Willis nor I had a chance to say more than few words to you."

"Who you talkin' to, Mary Ruth?"

She turned when Willis stepped up beside her. "Look. . . It's Brad."

Willis grinned and shook Brad's hand. "Sure is nice to see you again. Didn't know you were back in the area. Figured you were still at the university."

Brad shook his head. "I'm out for the summer and will be spending the next three months here in Lancaster County. I came to your place first, but I've only been here a few minutes."

"Ah, I see. Well, I was out on the back porch and didn't hear your vehicle pull in. When I stepped into the kitchen to get some more lemonade I heard my wife talkin' to someone." Willis gestured to Mary Ruth and looked back at Brad. "Will you be free to do some work for me while you're in the area?"

"Sure, and if you need a driver anytime, I'll be available for that too." Brad rubbed the back of his warm neck. "Well, I don't want to interrupt since it looks like someone is here right now." He pointed to the SUV in the driveway. "I can come back another day to talk about what you might want to have done."

"You're not interrupting," Mary Ruth spoke up. "Sara and her brother just arrived. I'm sure our granddaughter would like to see you, and it would be nice for Kenny to get to know you better too. You barely got to meet him at the funeral."

"You're right. So…uh…how long are they here for?" Brad's voice sounded strained, even to his own ears. It wasn't normal for him to feel so jittery either. He glanced at the SUV again and squinted. *How dumb of me not to notice the New Jersey plates on that rig.*

"Kenny will be with us through August," Willis said. "Then he'll be heading to Philadelphia to a music college."

"But Sara is back here for good," Mary Ruth interjected. "Her stepfather's estate has been settled, and the house was sold, so she came back to Strasburg to live with us again."

"Guess that makes sense." Brad shuffled his feet. A part of him wanted to see Sara right now and ask how she was doing. Another part said he should get in his van and make a hasty exit. But before he could make a sensible decision, Mary Ruth spoke again.

"The owners of the flower shop where Sara used to work are retiring, so she purchased their business." Mary Ruth's smile was so wide, it was almost contagious.

"That's great. I hope it works out well for her." Brad started to turn away. "I should really go and let you visit with your grandchildren. Give me a call if you need a ride somewhere."

Willis laid a hand on Brad's shoulder. "Wait a minute, Son. Don't you want to say hello to Sara before you go?"

Brad felt like a bug stuck to a strip of flypaper. He didn't want to appear rude, but seeing Sara again would only dredge up the feelings he'd managed to push aside with determination these last few months.

"Oh yes, you must say hello to Sara. She's out in the barn." Mary Ruth pointed in that direction.

Brad didn't feel as if he had much choice. "Okay, I'll go out there for a few minutes, but then I'll be on my way. Gotta head to my friend's place in Lancaster and get settled in."

"No need to rush off," Willis said. "You oughta get Sara and join us on the back porch for some cookies and lemonade."

"Maybe. . . We'll see." Brad stepped off the porch and headed for the barn.

As he approached the building, a cat ran past, chasing a fat little mouse. Brad shook his head. *I wonder which one of those critters will win out.*

Brad opened the barn door, but when he stepped inside, he heard Sara talking to someone. Was there another person in the barn—maybe Michelle?

Sadie and Val walked up to greet him. They weren't barking, but both dogs wagged their tails. He closed the barn door and stood off to one side. Instinctively, he put his finger to his lips. Somehow the dogs must have understood, for they remained silent.

Brad was never one to eavesdrop, but he didn't want to interrupt what he was hearing. Something compelled him to remain silent and listen as he hid in the shadows.

Sara set the antique jar on the floor and bowed her head. Speaking out loud, she offered another prayer. "Dear Lord, thank You for being so patient with me all these years. I am so happy and blessed to have given my heart to You. Thank You for showing me that I need to not only ask forgiveness for my own wrongdoings, but I've also forgiven others who have hurt me in the past. I pray that if I am given an opportunity to talk to Brad again, he will forgive me for deceiving him about being a Christian."

Sara heard what sounded like the scuffling of feet, and she opened her eyes. Seeing Brad standing a few feet away, with both dogs vying for his attention, she gasped. "Oh, you startled me! How long have you been there?"

"Just a few minutes."

"Were you listening to my prayer?" Sara's arms curled around her middle.

"Yes, I did hear you, but I wasn't eavesdropping, and I didn't know at first that you were praying." Brad moved closer. "I came in here to say hello, but I never expected to hear you saying a prayer. You told me before that you were a Christian. But later, I learned from Michelle that you weren't a believer. Then just now, you were telling God you were happy you had given your heart to Him." He crossed his arms. "So which is it, Sara? Are you a Christian or not?"

"I am now, but I wasn't back then." Sara explained how she had given her heart to the Lord when she visited the hospital chapel after Dean's accident. She lowered her gaze. "I'm sorry for lying to you, Brad. I didn't want you to think—"

Brad didn't let her finish. "I'll admit, our relationship was one I'd lost hope of ever continuing."

"I thought that too." Sara had to tell Brad now how she really felt about him, before she lost her nerve. "About our relationship—"

He stepped in front of her and put one finger against her lips. "You know what I think, Sara Murray?"

Tears sprang to her eyes, and she almost choked on the words. "Th–that I'm not to be trusted?"

"No, I don't think that anymore. What I do think though is that I'd like us to start over." He took her hand, holding it gently. "Would you be willing to do that, Sara?"

She gave a nod. "Yes. Yes, I would."

As Sadie and Val started barking and running around the couple's feet, the horses must have sensed their excitement and nickered in response. Sara glanced toward Peanuts and Bashful, both looking over their stall doors, nodding and shaking their heads. When she glanced back down at both dogs, they had settled and sat patiently at their feet. Sara giggled when Sadie whined and Val tilted her head—the whole time with their tails wagging in unison. When she looked back into Brad's eyes, her breath caught in her throat. At that moment, Sara could have melted in his arms, as he looked adoringly at her.

Brad leaned down and gave Sara's right cheek a gentle, feathery kiss. Then he kissed the other cheek, and moved to her lips.

Sara put her arms around Brad's neck, melting into his embrace. Both horses whinnied, and the dogs started barking again. Sara had no idea what the future held for them, but this time she would try not to do anything that could mess up their relationship.

As the sun began to make its descent in the west, Michelle and Sara sat on the swing, swaying slowly back and forth. Michelle had celebrated her twenty-fifth birthday a few days ago, but when Mary Ruth asked what she wanted for her birthday supper, Michelle suggested they wait until Sara and Kenny arrived, so they could be with them.

Michelle didn't want a big celebration; a cookout was fine with her. Willis had grilled some sausages and burgers that went well with the cucumber mixture and macaroni salad Mary Ruth had made. She'd also baked a three-layer lemon cake, iced with a white fluffy frosting. And the orange sherbet Willis bought at the store was a tasty frozen dessert.

"I'm sorry I didn't get you anything for your birthday." Sara's forehead wrinkled. "But I just found out about it after Brad left. When Grandma was upstairs helping me unpack, she let me know tonight we'd be celebrating your birthday."

Michelle brushed aside her words. "You being here is gift enough. I told Mary Ruth I didn't want to celebrate until you and Kenny came home."

"Well, even if it was a few days ago, I'm glad Kenny and I could be here to help celebrate your birthday this evening." Sara smiled. "He was so excited to come here. Probably as much as I was."

"I can hear him in there laughing." Michelle tilted her head toward the door.

"It's good he has this chance to get to know his grandparents. That's why I thought I'd sit out here with you for a while and give him some time alone with them."

Michelle looked at Sara closely. She sensed something different about her. She had noticed it earlier at the restaurant, and also during supper this evening. A sense of peace seemed to settle over Sara. She acted more carefree and talked a lot more instead of being within herself. "It's too bad Brad couldn't have stayed for the cookout."

"I'm sure he would have liked to, but he wanted to get to Ned's and get settled in. He had a mind-boggling week with finals and the drive down from Clarks Summit." Sara's smile grew wider. "I'm sure we'll be seeing a lot more of him this summer."

Michelle was happy for Sara when she explained how she'd admitted to Brad that she had deceived him about being a Christian but wanted him to know that she had since come to know the Lord.

"I know you offered to help me, Michelle, and I appreciate that," Sara said. "But when I felt God's presence in the hospital chapel, something very special came over me."

Michelle put her arm around Sara. "I'm so glad."

"It seems we both learned some valuable lessons this past year."

"We sure have. Now do you mind if I ask a question?"

"Go right ahead."

"Do you think yours and Brad's relationship will get serious?"

"I can't say for certain, but we both care about each other. I guess my only fear is if we were to get married someday, I might have to move away from the Lancaster area." Sara sighed. "I'm not sure how I would feel living far away from my grandparents if Brad decided to take a church somewhere else. I made a vow to myself some time ago that I'd never stray far from them. Then there's the flower shop. I could not believe it when the opportunity came up for me to purchase the business. It just sort of fell into my lap, and I grabbed the chance while I could."

"Sara, none of us knows what our future holds, but for now, just enjoy being back where you belong at this time." Michelle squeezed Sara's shoulder. "It's perfect, because you will also be here to help with my wedding plans."

Sara gave Michelle a hug. "I'm so happy for you, Michelle."

Michelle rubbed Sara's back. "Everything will fall into place for you too. Just wait. You'll see."

# Chapter 43

The summer was going by much too quickly to suit Sara. Here it was the end of July already. Sara's business was booming, and word had spread about a new owner who'd taken over the flower shop. Some folks came in just to meet her or see if she'd done anything different to the store.

Basically, the shop itself had not changed, but Sara had shuffled a few things around inside. Instead of flower pots and vases being intermixed among the buckets of fresh flowers and potted plants, she'd designated one area just for those. Sara had even added a section with various sprinkling cans and some garden decorations. She'd also included a rack to sell the cards Lenore now supplied to the store, and had made a few beaded items to sell as well. Many of the patrons had made special requests for Lenore to personalize a card for a family member or friend.

But the real hit with the customers who came and went was the display window. Not long ago, in the back part of her grandparents' barn, Sara had found old scooter. Grandma told her it had belonged to Ivan when he was a young boy. The scooter was quite old and had some rust in spots, but that's what made it unique. One Sunday, when Ivan and his wife stopped by, Sara asked if she could use it for something special. Ivan was more than glad to give it to her, especially when she told him her idea. Sara put the scooter in the shop's window, intermixed with a floral display. Many customers who came into the store commented on the old Amish scooter. She loved telling those who asked that the scooter in the window belonged to her uncle.

Sara had arrived at the store earlier than usual this morning, hoping to do some internet searching and make a few phone calls. In addition to taking care of some business matters, Sara had some personal things she needed answers for too, and social media in addition to some other places on the internet seemed like the best place to start.

Sara took a seat at her desk and turned on the computer. While she waited for it to boot up, she looked at her monthly schedule and also any orders that had come in the day before. She also did a walk-through to make sure everything in the store was in place.

Sara's social calendar was full, as she saw Brad every opportunity she could. With the exception of her uncertainty about the future, her life was going better than she'd ever expected. The more time Sara spent with Brad, the more attached she became. She dreaded the day he would return to Clarks Summit to continue his studies. But the ministry was Brad's calling, and she wouldn't stand in his way.

Sara's twenty-fifth birthday, on the first of July, had been special. Just like Michelle, Sara didn't want a big fuss made. She'd been happy with the small family gathering at her grandparents' home that evening. Instead of cooking on the grill, Grandma had made Sara's favorite chicken-and-rice casserole. Brad had stopped at a seafood restaurant and brought out a huge container of shrimp scampi to go with the meal.

Sara smiled to herself. *A little birdie must have told Brad I liked seafood.* Of course Michelle and Ezekiel were included in the meal. Sara liked it that way—nothing fancy—just the sweet fellowship with those she cared about. By now, Kenny was quite comfortable with everyone and had a good rapport with Brad and Ezekiel. After supper, they'd all gone out to the picnic table and enjoyed cheesecake for dessert.

Kenny was doing well and sported a farmer's tan from all the work he helped Grandpa with outdoors. He was eager to help in any way and had gotten used to living on the farm.

Sara wished she could help Grandma more, but between her new business and time spent with Brad, there weren't many hours left in the day. Grandma never complained or asked Sara to do anything. In fact, she'd said many times that she was happy Sara had acquired the flower shop and was home with them again.

Sara halted her musings and turned back to the computer. It was fully booted and ready to go, so she quickly went online. She had just begun her first search, when the bell above the shop door jingled. She looked up and smiled when Herschel Fisher entered the store. *I bet he's here to buy his wife more flowers. I hope she appreciates her husband's consideration.*

Sara saved the internet site she'd found and went to greet the Amish man. "Good morning, Mr. Fisher. What can I help you with today?"

"Roses. I need a dozen yellow roses."

Sara bit the inside of her cheek. "Sorry, but we are currently out of those. Would another color be all right?"

He shook his head firmly. "Nope. Has to be yellow."

Sara drew a quick breath. She hated to send Mr. Fisher to another flower shop, but what else could she do?

She was about to suggest the floral shop in the next town over, when Ezekiel entered the store. "I have some roses and other cut flowers from our greenhouse in the back of my market buggy," he announced.

Sara had forgotten he'd be making a delivery today. She hoped some of those roses were yellow.

"Please bring them in," she told Ezekiel. Then she turned to Herschel. "If some of the roses are yellow, I'll ask my assistant, Peggy, to make you a nice bouquet. If not, then feel free to take your business elsewhere today."

Herschel shook his head. "Nope. If I can't buy the flowers from you, I won't buy 'em at all." The laugh lines around his mouth deepened as he grinned at Sara. "You know, I've been comin' here for a few years now, and I was concerned when I heard the Roberts were planning to sell the store. But then when you bought the place, I felt better, 'cause you were always helpful when you worked here before."

Sara smiled. It was nice to be appreciated, especially by a customer she barely knew. After hearing Andy and Karen were retiring, other customers had also told Sara they were glad she'd become the new owner of the flower shop.

When Ezekiel returned with a box full of roses—some yellow and some red—Sara felt relieved. She gathered up a dozen yellow roses and headed for the back room. Peggy was an expert designer, and Sara felt sure she would create a beautiful bouquet for Herschel Fisher's wife.

*I wish he'd bring her into the store someday,* Sara thought. *I'd like to meet this special lady whose husband gives her flowers so often.*

Sara was preparing to close the store for the day when an elderly Amish woman came in. She walked with a limp and used a cane, but no evidence of pain showed on her face.

"May I help you?" Sara asked. She hoped the woman wouldn't want a special arrangement made up, because Peggy had gone home a few minutes ago. And while Sara had good customer skills, knew how to balance the books, and keep the shop tidy, she hadn't yet learned how to create any of the fresh-flower bouquets they sold in the shop.

The woman stepped up to the counter, peering at Sara through thick-lens glasses. "You need to stop selling my son flowers. It's a waste of money."

"What?" Sara was taken aback by the woman's harsh tone and pinched expression. "I–I'm not sure who you're referring to, ma'am."

"My name's not ma'am. It's Vera Fisher, and my son is Herschel. He comes here nearly every week and buys flowers for his wife, does he not?"

"Oh, you must mean Mr. Fisher."

The woman's head moved up and down.

Conflicted, Sara pressed her lips together in a slight grimace. "Is there a problem with your son buying flowers for his wife?" Sara wondered if Herschel's mother might be jealous or didn't approve of his choice for a wife.

Vera tapped the tip of her cane against the hardwood floor a few times. "There is most definitely something wrong."

Sara couldn't imagine what it might be, so she stood quietly, hoping the lady would explain.

"How long have you been living in Lancaster County?" Vera asked.

"I moved here to be with my grandparents back in October, and then I—"

"Just how much do you know about the Amish?"

"Well, my grandpa and grandma are Amish. Perhaps you know them. They live—"

The woman interrupted Sara again. "If you knew the Amish, you'd know that we don't put flowers on our loved one's graves."

Perplexed, Sara's eyebrows lowered. "I don't understand."

Vera pointed a bony finger at Sara. "Those flowers you've been selling my son end up on her grave marker, and that's just not done."

"Oh dear." Sara put her fingers against her lips. "I had no idea. I—I thought when Herschel first came into the store and said he wanted flowers for his wife that he would be giving them to her in person. I had no idea Mrs. Fisher was deceased."

"She died nearly two years ago, when a car hit her while trying to cross the street." Heaving a sigh, Vera placed her free hand against her breastbone. "My son's never gotten over his wife's death, and he began putting flowers on her grave soon after she was buried." She slowly shook her head. "He knows it's not the Amish way, and he could get in trouble with our church leaders for doing it. So far, they've chosen to look the other way, thinking in time his grieving would subside and he'd stop what he was doing."

"I'm sorry for his loss, Mrs. Fisher. I had no idea."

"So you'll quit selling him flowers?"

Sara rolled her neck from side to side, trying to get the kinks out. She was really on the spot here. "The thing is. . . I really can't stop Herschel from buying flowers, but the next time he comes in, maybe I could mention that I'd heard about his wife."

Vera shook her head vigorously. "That won't do any good. You just need to tell him you're not going to sell him any more flowers." As if their conversation was settled, the woman turned and limped her way out the door.

Sara groaned. *Well, the day here in the shop may have started out on a good note, but it certainly didn't end that way.*

❧

That evening, when Brad came over for supper, Sara waited until after she'd helped Grandma and Michelle do the dishes before she went to Brad and asked if she could speak to him privately.

"Sure can." He grinned at her. "In fact, I was planning to ask you the same question. I have something important I want to tell you."

"Sara, why don't you and Brad go out on the back porch, where it's cooler?" Grandma suggested when she entered the living room where Brad had been visiting with Grandpa.

"Good idea." He got up from his chair and led the way.

When they stepped out onto the porch, Sara took a seat on the porch swing, scooching over, so there'd be room for Brad. "What did you want to talk to me about?" she asked.

"No, it can wait. You go first."

"I had a little problem right before I closed the flower shop today." Sara went on to tell him about Herschel Fisher and how his mother barged in, asking Sara to stop selling her son flowers, and the reason.

"What do you think I should do, Brad? Knowing what I do now, I feel sorry for Mr. Fisher, but I wouldn't feel right about refusing to sell him flowers."

"Refusing to sell anyone what they come into your store to

buy wouldn't be good business," Brad said. "Besides, if the man's church leaders haven't reprimanded him for putting flowers on his wife's grave, then you shouldn't either. I'm sure that eventually Herschel will come to grips with his wife's death, and then he will probably stop buying flowers for her grave." Brad shrugged his shoulders. "Who knows? He might eventually fall in love with another woman and remarry."

"True." Sara placed her hand on Brad's arm. "Thanks. You're certainly full of good advice. You'll make a great preacher."

"Speaking of which. . ." Brad took hold of her hand. "I've been praying about things, and I've recently made a decision."

"Oh? What sort of decision?"

"I'm not going back to the university in the fall."

Sara tipped her head. "How come?"

"I'm staying in Lancaster County and will do the rest of my studies through online courses."

"Really? That's a surprise."

He let go of Sara's hand and reached up to stroke the side of her face. "You must know why I want to stay in the area."

Sara moistened her lips with the tip of her tongue. "Well, I. . ."

"I love you, Sara, and I can't stand the thought of being away from you for the next two years while I finish my degree."

"You could come back here for visits." Sara's heart pounded as Brad gazed into her eyes. She wanted to make sure he would not regret his decision to leave the school in Clarks Summit.

"I could, but it wouldn't be enough for me. I want to see you as often as possible. I want to give our relationship a chance to really deepen."

"I–I want that also, because I have recently realized that I love you too."

Brad wrapped his arms around Sara and pulled her close. "And I hope you'll be prepared with an answer, because someday I plan to ask you to be my wife." Before she could offer a response, his lips touched hers in a gentle, yet firm kiss.

As Sara enjoyed being held in Brad's arms, her concerns about the future evaporated. All she could think about was how happy she was to have found such a wonderful Christian man. Sara felt thankful for God's love and forgiveness. She would have never experienced any of this if it hadn't been for a prayer jar that led her to the truth.

# Chapter 44

*Four months later*

Sara sat on a backless wooden bench inside the Kings' barn, watching and listening as Michelle and Ezekiel said their vows in front of the bishop. The oversized building had been cleaned from top to bottom, leaving no sign that it ever housed any animals. The horses had been put in the pasture, and the Kings' dogs were secured inside a temporary enclosure. In addition to Ezekiel's father and brothers, Uncle Ivan and his sons had come over a few days ago to pressure wash and clean every nook and cranny inside the barn. Bales of hay and straw had been put in the loft above, and if it hadn't been for the shape of the structure, no one would have known they were sitting inside a barn.

Sara heard some sniffles and glanced at her grandmother. Sure enough, tears had splashed onto Grandma's cheeks, and she was none too discreetly blotting at them with her delicate white handkerchief.

Sara struggled not to cry as well, for the look of joy radiating on the bride's and groom's faces made her feel like tearing up. She clasped her hands together in her lap. *A year ago, who would have believed I'd have a friendship with the young woman who had impersonated me for over four months, let alone be one of the guests at Michelle's wedding.*

So much had changed in Sara's life that she sometimes felt as though she'd imagined it all. She glanced at the men's side of the room and caught Brad looking at her. She couldn't help but smile. His love for her was obvious, and she felt the same way about him. Sara wondered if some day she and Brad might be saying their vows, with a whole new life starting for them. So far, however, he'd made no reference to them getting married since their conversation four months ago. *Brad knows how much I like living near my grandparents. Maybe he hasn't asked because he's afraid I'll say no.*

Smiling, Sara looked at two young English men who sat on the bench behind Brad. When the wedding was over, she would introduce them to Michelle.

⌘

Michelle took her groom's hand, and as the bishop pronounced them husband and wife, she struggled to keep her emotions in check. Today was the most special day of her life. Even the weather cooperated, giving them sunny skies and mild temperatures for the month of November.

The other day, Michelle had called her foster parents to let them know how much her life had changed and to invite them to her and Ezekiel's wedding. Al and Sandy Newman were the only link she had to her childhood after she was taken from her parents. Al had been delighted to hear Michelle's voice when he picked up the phone and immediately yelled for Sandy to get on their other extension. The three of them talked for nearly an hour, and the Newmans said they wished they could come to the wedding but unfortunately had made other plans for that day.

Michelle thought about the letter she'd previously sent to her parents. Unfortunately, it had come back with no forwarding address, so she had no way of getting in touch with them. *They probably wouldn't have come to my wedding anyhow,* she thought. *And maybe it's for the best. I'm sure they would have had unkind things to say to me, Ezekiel, and even the Lapps.*

For a moment, Michelle leaned her head back and looked up. *The only thing that would have made today it any better would be to have Ernie and Jack in attendance.* But it was an impossible dream, and she needed to keep her focus on Ezekiel, for he was all she could ever want in a husband. Michelle looked forward to having a family someday and teaching their children about God. If only she'd had a personal relationship with Him when she was a child, it would have been easier to deal with all the trials she and her brothers had faced.

*Better late than never*, Michelle thought as she gave her groom's fingers a tender squeeze before they returned to their seats.

❧

When the wedding concluded and people milled around outside the tent where the first meal of the day would be held, Sara searched for Michelle. She found her talking to Ezekiel's sister Sylvia.

"I don't mean to interrupt"—she said, stepping up to them—"but I'd like to give Michelle the wedding present I got for her."

Sylvia blinked a couple of times. "Can't that wait until later, when the bride and groom open all their gifts?"

"No, this gift can't wait." Sara took her friend's hand. "Will you come with me?"

Michelle glanced around as though she might be looking for Ezekiel, but then she nodded.

Leading the way, Sara hurried in the direction of the greenhouse. That's where she'd asked Brad to wait with her surprise wedding present for Michelle. He had told Ezekiel to meet them there too.

As they approached the greenhouse, Michelle stopped walking. "What are we doing here? Is this where you put my wedding gift?"

"Yes, it is, and you'll see when we go inside." Sara pulled her along.

When they entered the building, Brad stood beside Ezekiel and the two young men who had been sitting behind him during the wedding.

Michelle looked at them with a curious expression, and then she turned to face Sara. "I am confused. Who are these men, and where is the gift you promised me?"

Sara could hardly keep a straight face. "These men are your

wedding present." She pointed to them. "Michelle, I would like to introduce you to Ernie and Jack Taylor."

Michelle's eyes widened as she clutched Sara's hand. "M–my brothers?"

Sara managed only a nod because the lump in her throat made it impossible to speak.

The young men moved forward, and Michelle ran toward them. Exclamations of joy and tearful sobs could be heard, as two auburn-haired brothers were reunited with their now-Amish sister. Ezekiel stood by with a loving expression as he witnessed the scene. Sara also noticed a few tears escaping his eyes.

"But how?" Michelle asked, turning to face Sara.

"It took some doing, but thanks to a lot of internet searching and a good many phone calls, I was able to locate them."

Michelle looked in awe at her brothers. "I—I still can't believe it." She hugged them both again.

Brad stepped up to Sara and pulled her to his side. "You did a wonderful thing, Sara, and your good friend is one happy bride."

She flashed him a smile, struggling to keep from breaking down. "Yes, I can see that. I couldn't think of a better gift to give my good friend."

"Let's go outside and allow them to visit for a bit," Brad whispered in Sara's ear. "There is something I want to ask you."

"Okay." She followed Brad out the door.

As they stepped into the sunlight streaming down from the sky, Brad suggested they move off to the side, away from the building. Then, catching Sara completely by surprise, he got down on one knee.

"I can't promise you a life with no complications, but I can promise to always be there for you, in good times and bad."

Sara held her breath as he continued. "The life of a minister will have its challenges, but with God's help, and you at my side, I am up for the challenge." He paused and took a small jewelry box from his jacket pocket, opened the lid, and held it out to her. "Sara Murray, will you marry me?"

With tears of joy streaming down her cheeks, Sara nodded. "Yes, Brad, I will marry you." She held out her left hand, and Brad slipped the ring on her finger. It fit perfectly, as if it had been made just for her. Her worries about Terri were completely gone. Becoming a pastor's wife wouldn't be easy, and it might mean moving to some other town or state. But Sara loved Brad enough to make that commitment and felt certain God would bless them and direct their lives. As much as she wanted to continue running her business and living closer to her grandparents, Sara wanted to share in Brad's ministry that would involve touching people's lives and ministering to them when they were hurting. Just as Sara's life had been touched by the notes she'd read in the forgiving jar, she wanted to be by Brad's side as they shared the Good News with others.

# Sara's Pumpkin Bread

Ingredients:
4 eggs
3 cups sugar
1 teaspoon cinnamon
½ teaspoon salt
1 teaspoon nutmeg
1 cup pumpkin puree
⅔ cup water
2 teaspoons baking soda
1 cup olive oil
3½ cups flour
1 cup chopped nuts

In large bowl, beat eggs. Add remaining ingredients and mix well. Pour into three well-greased loaf pans. Bake at 300 degrees for 1 hour or until done in center.

# Mary Ruth's Turkey Vegetable Soup

Ingredients:

1 cup diced carrots
½ cup diced celery
⅓ cup chopped onion
2 tablespoons butter
2 cups diced cooked turkey
2 cups water

1½ cups peeled, diced
   potatoes
2 teaspoons chicken
   bouillon granules
½ teaspoon salt
½ teaspoon pepper
2½ cups milk
3 tablespoons flour

In large saucepan, sauté carrots, celery, and onion in butter until tender. Add turkey, water, potatoes, bouillon, salt, and pepper. Bring to boil. Reduce heat, cover, and simmer for 10 to 12 minutes or until vegetables are tender. Stir in 2 cups milk. In separate bowl, combine flour with remaining ½ cup milk. Blend until smooth. Stir into soup. Bring to a boil. Cook and stir for 2 minutes or until thickened.

# Discussion Questions

1. Could you be as brave as Michelle when, after Ezekiel's urging, she returned to the Lapps' to confess in person what she did and to apologize?

2. Sara didn't like the idea that Michelle got to know her grandparents before she did. Can you understand why Sara felt the way she did about Michelle? Was there a better way for Sara to cope without allowing resentment to take over?

3. Willis and Mary Ruth each had a talk with Sara and Michelle but let the girls work it out themselves. Do you think they should have intervened more?

4. Were you ever in a situation where you longed to have someone love you the way Sara saw how Michelle and Ezekiel cared for each other? Were you envious of the couple or happy for them?

5. Could you have been as patient as Ezekiel, giving Michelle time to decide for herself if she wanted to learn the ways of the Amish and join the church?

6. Were you happy to find out Michelle made a commitment to join the Amish church? Did you feel she found her faith through the prayer jar notes and was not just persuaded by her love for Ezekiel and wanting to have a life with him?

7. Do you think Sara was right in not questioning her grandma about the prayer jar and forgiving jar messages?

8. What did you think about the way Ezekiel's mother and sister acted toward Michelle? Do you understand why they were concerned about him being interested in a woman who wasn't Amish?

9.  Has someone close to you passed away and afterward you discovered that they had deceived you, the way Sara learned that her mother kept her heritage a secret? Since you could not confront the person, how did you handle your feelings?

10. Have any of your children ever upset you by going to someone else's house for a meal on Christmas, when traditionally your family has always been together on this special day? Would you have reacted the way Belinda did when her son Ezekiel went to the Lapps' for Christmas dinner instead of staying at home with the family?

11. Do you think Michelle handled herself well when she waited on her ex-boyfriend Jerry and his new girlfriend at the restaurant where she worked as a waitress? Could you have confronted your ex as bravely as Michelle did Jerry?

12. Was it wrong for Sara to deceive Brad by telling him she was a Christian when she wasn't? After feeling guilty for lying to Brad, should she have confessed right away and told him the truth?

13. Even though Brad told Sara that Terri Conners was only a friend, she still had doubts. Do you think she should have shared her doubts with Brad instead of remaining quiet and just observing?

14. In this story, did you learn anything new about the Amish and the way they handle certain situations?

15. What scripture verses in this book were your favorites and why?

# The Healing Jar

## *Dedication*

To my dear friends Delbert and Mary.
Your ministry to hurting souls is a blessing.

*He healeth the broken in heart,*
*and bindeth up their wounds.*
Psalm 147:3

# Prologue

*Lancaster, Pennsylvania*

Tears sprang to Lenore Lapp's eyes as she stood with the others who had come to witness this special English wedding. Her cousin Sara walked up the aisle behind Darlene Koch, her maid of honor and a childhood friend. Sara looked radiant in her beautiful, floor-length wedding gown. Because Sara's stepfather had died from injuries sustained in a car accident, and she didn't know who her biological father was, she had asked her half brother, Kenny, to escort her down the aisle.

Brad waited at the front of the church beside his best man, Ned Evans, and the pastor.

"Who gives this woman to be wed?" the clergyman asked.

"I do." Kenny stepped aside as Brad took Sara's hand.

The minister gestured for everyone to be seated, and then he, Sara, and Brad stepped up to the altar area, where they took their places in front of a small table draped with a white linen cloth. An open Bible and three candles sat on the table. The larger one, Sara had previously told Lenore, was called a unity candle. At some point during the ceremony Sara and Brad would pick up their lighted candles and light the bigger one in unison to signify the two becoming one. It was a different custom than anything done in an Amish wedding, but a lovely gesture nonetheless.

As Lenore took her seat next to her Amish grandparents, Grandma sniffled, then dabbed her eyes with a handkerchief. Although Lenore was Amish and Sara was not, Grandma and Grandpa Lapp loved both granddaughters equally.

*If Sara's mother hadn't run away from home when she was eighteen,*

*Sara might be Amish too.* Lenore shook her head. *What a shame Sara's mother passed away and couldn't see her daughter get married today. It would have made Sara's day even more special.*

As Brad and Sara repeated their vows, Lenore glanced across the aisle at Michelle and Ezekiel King. It was hard to believe they'd been married a year already. It was even more difficult to imagine that Michelle used to be English and had pretended to be Sara for a time. But Michelle found forgiveness when she sought God and accepted His Son as her Savior. Not long after, she made the commitment to be baptized and join the Amish church.

*So two of my dear friends are now happily married.* Lenore glanced down at her simple blue Amish dress and white apron. *I wonder if my chance at love will ever come.*

# Chapter 1

*Six months later*
*Strasburg, Pennsylvania*

Lenore sat on the top step of her grandparents' front porch, barely noticing the summer flowers as she stared into the yard. Her gaze took in the stately old barn, weathered chicken coop, and Grandma's lovely flower garden. She could smell the sweet perfume of the fragrant lilac bushes not far from the house and heard the hiss of a running sprinkler, helping to keep the lawn growing and green. A slight breeze ruffled the leaves on the huge maple tree, and she heard the flutter of wings as several birds jostled for space on one of the many feeders, completing the peaceful picture. Unfortunately, Grandpa and Grandma's home and yard were not as serene as they used to be for Lenore. She still enjoyed being here, but now she saw everything through a new perspective—one that included stress that no tranquil yard could eradicate.

Grandpa's collie, Sadie, lay beside her with one paw on Lenore's lap. That too used to be comforting. Now it was just a reminder that Grandma and Grandpa's pet was in need of love and assurance.

A lump formed in Lenore's throat. How could so many unexpected things happen in six short months—some good, some bad? Brad had accepted a call to pastor a church in Lancaster, and Sara, in addition to running her flower shop, now played the role of a minister's wife. Ezekiel still worked in his parents' greenhouse, and Michelle helped out there sometimes too. Unfortunately, Michelle's husband did not enjoy working with flowers, bushes, and various other plants. He'd made it clear he was looking for some other type of job.

Lenore had accepted a teaching position at a school in Strasburg this year and would begin her new assignment in two months. She looked forward to getting to know her young students and hoped her first year of teaching here would go as well as it had when she'd taught school in Paradise, not far from her parents' home.

With a heavy sigh, Lenore turned toward the front window, where Grandpa Lapp sat slumped in his wheelchair, peering out with a distant, almost empty stare. It tore at her heart to see him looking so forlorn. Three months ago, Grandpa had a stroke, leaving the left side of his body paralyzed. Even with therapy, he hadn't improved much.

Despite his inability to take care of the farm anymore, Grandpa refused to move, announcing in slurred words that he would live in this home until the day he died, and no one could make him move. Not wishing to cause him further anxiety, Lenore's father agreed to let his parents continue living on their own, but only if Lenore agreed to move in with them and help out when she wasn't teaching. With all the added responsibilities on Grandma's shoulders, Lenore had willingly settled into one of Grandma and Grandpa's upstairs guest rooms. She loved her grandparents very much and would do anything to help them during this challenging time.

Grandpa could no longer raise hogs and it was doubtful he'd ever be healthy enough to care for them, so they'd been sold. He also couldn't preach due to his speech impediment, so unless a miracle occurred, he would resign from his ministerial position, allowing someone else to take his place. Even if the stroke hadn't happened, Grandpa and Grandma were getting older and less able to perform all the chores they'd previously taken on.

It was difficult for Lenore's grandparents to be faced with so many changes. Some decisions were hard to make.

Sadie grunted as Lenore shifted on the unyielding porch step. *Why must good people like Grandma and Grandpa Lapp face so many trials? It doesn't seem fair.*

Lenore's parents had been affected by Grandpa's failing health as well. Either Dad or one of her brothers came over several times a week to check on Grandpa and take care of any of the heavier outside chores needing to be done. Mom dropped by whenever she could too, and often helped Grandma with baking. Sometimes when Lenore had to be away from the house, her mother stayed with Grandpa so Grandma could get away for a while to grocery shop, meet a friend for lunch, or simply have a little time to herself.

"My faith has weakened of late," Lenore murmured, reaching over to stroke Sadie's head. "Sometimes I wonder if God even hears my prayers."

"Of course He does, dear one. We just need to be patient and wait for His answers."

Lenore jumped at the sound of her grandmother's voice. She hadn't heard the screen door open or shut.

Grandma took a seat on the porch swing, and Lenore joined her.

"I don't understand why bad things happen to good people." Lenore pushed her feet against the wooden boards beneath them to get the swing moving. "My heart clenches every time I see the pained look on Grandpa's face."

Grandma reached over and patted Lenore's hand. "We must learn to trust the Lord, even with things we don't understand. As we go through troubled waters, it should strengthen, not weaken, our faith. And remember, dear one, prayer is not a business transaction. We don't give something to get something in return."

Lenore sat quietly, reflecting on her grandmother's words as the swing moved gently back and forth. *Regardless of the hardships she and Grandpa are facing right now, Grandma's faith is a lot stronger than mine these days. Maybe I need to pray harder and try to keep a more positive attitude, like I used to have. No one likes to be around a negative person, so I'll do my best to look for things to rejoice about and remember to thank God for His blessings.*

After Grandma went back inside, Lenore headed for the barn to groom her horse, Dolly. She would be using the mare to pull the buggy when she and Grandma went to church tomorrow morning. Since it was an off-Sunday for the church district Lenore's parents belonged to, they would come over to be with Grandpa while Grandma and Lenore attended church.

When Lenore entered the barn, the first thing she noticed was a creamy white cat curled up on a bale of straw. Grandma had named the cat Precious. The feline was her favorite of all the barn cats and often tried to sneak into the house. Grandpa would have none of it, though, so Grandma never allowed the cat to come in.

"You've got life made. You know that, don't you—you lazy old *katz*." She paused and stroked the cat's soft fur, and Precious responded with a contented purr.

The rustle of hay drew Lenore's gaze up to the loft where two more cats lay close to the edge, cleaning their paws. Grandma's favored cat wasn't the only critter on the farm that had life made. All the animals were treated well, but Grandma liked to give Precious a little more attention than the others.

Lenore remained in place, listening to the muffled thump of the hooves of horses moving around in their stalls. Grandpa's horse, Bashful, snorted from the nearest stall. No doubt he missed his master's daily treks to the barn.

She drew a deep breath and blinked against invading tears. *Poor Grandpa. He used to love spending time out here with the animals. Now he mostly sits and stares out the window. Oh, how I wish things could be different. Maybe if he had taken better care of his health, he wouldn't have had the stroke.* But her grandparents had always seemed healthy to her. They'd worked hard, eaten well, and gotten enough rest. Even so, there might have been more Grandpa could have done to prevent the stroke.

Whenever Lenore offered to bring him out to the barn in his wheelchair, Grandpa always shook his head and mumbled, "No good. No good." She wasn't sure what he meant by that. Was Grandpa saying the idea of going to the barn was no good, or did he believe he was no longer any good?

Lenore's vision blurred as she released a lingering sigh. *I wish there was something I could do to lift Grandpa's spirits—and mine too, for that matter.*

Rising from her seat and heading toward Dolly's stall with renewed determination, Lenore heard buzzing overhead. She looked up and saw a wasp nest attached to one of the rafters. *I'd better climb into the loft and get rid of that right away. Sure don't need anyone getting stung while they're out here in the barn doing chores or getting one of the horses out.*

Lenore glanced around, searching for some spray to kill the wasps and douse the nest. She spotted a spray can on a shelf along one wall and went to get a ladder.

Positioning the ladder in front of the shelf, Lenore climbed up and reached for the insecticide. In the process, she noticed several antique canning jars. A blue-green one was partially hidden, and when she pulled it away from the others, she realized it had been filled with a bunch of folded papers. Curious to see what they were about, she set the wasp spray aside, picked up the canning jar, and climbed down from the ladder.

Taking a seat on a wooden stool, Lenore opened the jar. After removing the paper closest to the top, she unfolded it and read it out loud. "Dear Lord, I know I'm not worthy, but please answer my prayers."

Lenore sat silently, pondering the words. *Who wrote this, and why did they hide it in an old jar out here in the barn?*

She pulled out another slip of paper and read it too. "Lord, I need Your direction. Show me the right path." *I wonder if Grandma knows about this jar full of notes. Think I'll go ask her.*

Lenore was almost to the barn door when Michelle stepped in.

"*Ach*, you startled me!" Lenore jumped back. "I didn't hear your horse and buggy come into the yard."

"Sorry. Didn't mean to frighten you." Michelle pushed a wisp of auburn hair back under her *kapp*. "I walked over this morning. Figured I could use the fresh air and exercise after all that birthday cake I ate at my party last night."

Lenore smiled. "It was a fun evening. I'm glad Ezekiel's mom invited me."

"Too bad your grandparents couldn't be there." Michelle's eyes darkened. "But I can understand why your grandpa doesn't leave the house much anymore."

"Did you come here to see him today?"

Michelle nodded. "I went into the house, but he was napping, so I visited with Mary Ruth for a bit. When she mentioned you were out here, I decided to come say hello before I headed for home."

Lenore smiled. "I'm glad you did."

Michelle pointed to the jar in Lenore's hands. "I see you found my hope jar."

Lenore tipped her head. "Hope jar?"

"Yeah, some of the scriptures, prayers, and notes gave me hope during the time I was living with your grandparents and pretending to be Sara."

"Did you put the notes in the jar?"

Michelle shook her head. "I have no idea who wrote them or why they put notes in this jar or the one I found in the basement."

Lenore's brows lifted. "You mean there are two jars?"

"Yeah, and for all I know, there could be more, but those are the only two I found." Michelle placed her hand on the jar. "Sara knows about the jars too. She discovered both of them while she was living here."

"How interesting. I wish I knew who owned the jars and why they put notes inside."

"I've always suspected it might be your grandma."

"Have you asked her about it?"

"No, and to my knowledge, neither has Sara. We were afraid if it was Mary Ruth, she might not want to talk about it. Some of the notes are personal, and I have a hunch that whoever wrote them didn't want anyone else to know. That must be why the jars were hidden."

"Guess that makes sense." Lenore tapped the side of the jar.

She needed to tend to the wasp nest, and when she went back to the house, she wouldn't mention finding the old jar to Grandma. Next week on washday, she'd look for the jar in the basement. Perhaps one of the papers would give her a clue as to who had written the notes. If Lenore didn't unravel the mystery soon, she might ask Grandma after all.

# Chapter 2

"It's a beautiful Sunay morning, *jah*?" Lenore glanced at her grandmother, sitting straight and tall on the buggy seat beside her. Grandma hadn't said more than a few words since they left home. She appeared to be deep in thought.

Lenore reached over and touched Grandma's arm. "Did you hear what I said?"

"Umm. . .yes, it is a nice day, but going to church isn't the same without your *grossdaadi* along. I wish we could have loaded up his wheelchair and brought him with us today. He's missing so much by not going to church." She sighed. "Others in worse shape than him are brought to church, but he's too embarrassed by his condition to be seen in public settings. Guess he doesn't want anyone's pity."

"Grandpa doesn't look bad; he's just not able to use his left arm or leg as he once did, and his mouth still sags a bit—especially when he talks."

"But he's in a wheelchair, and that really bothers him." Grandma lifted her hands, then let them fall into her lap with a sigh. "I've reminded him often that many people are praying for him and he shouldn't worry about being seen in a wheelchair, but nothing I say gets through to him."

Lenore nodded. "I've tried talking to him too, and so has my *daed*. I sure wish God would give us a miracle and heal Grandpa's body."

"He will be healed someday, when he is ushered into heaven. As much as your grandpa wants to be here with his family, he's said many times how he longs to see Jesus."

Lenore pondered Grandma's words. *Am I as eager to see Jesus as I am to remain here with my family? Shouldn't all believers look forward to leaving their earthly home and spending eternity in heaven?* It was a question she'd asked herself on more than one occasion. In fact, every time she attended someone's funeral, Lenore pondered this thought.

Grandpa had said several times during sermons he'd preached to their congregation that a Christian's reward was leaving the mortal body so the immortal soul could dwell with the Lord. While Lenore wanted to be transported to heaven someday, she still had a good many things she wanted to do here in this life. She hoped God was in no hurry to take her, or her grandparents, home to be with Him.

Lenore guided her horse and buggy up the lane leading to their bishop's home where church was being held this morning. When she pulled onto the grassy area where other buggies were parked, Lenore gave Grandma the reins while she got out and unhitched her horse. "You can go up to the house while I hook Dolly to the line with the other horses."

Grandma turned and gave Lenore a wave. "Okay. I'll see you outside the bishop's buggy shop before we all file in for church."

As Lenore sat on a backless wooden bench beside her friend Hannah Stoltzfus and several other young women her age, she gave a quick glance at the men's section. Michelle's husband, Ezekiel, sat beside a dark-haired, bearded young man who held a baby girl. Lenore didn't recognize him and wondered if he was here visiting someone or might be new to their district. The baby was sure sweet—didn't look to be more than six or seven months old. The little girl wore a dark green dress and white bonnet. Lenore assumed the man's wife must be present too, but she didn't want to bring attention to herself by turning around to see. Perhaps after church was over she'd meet the baby's mother.

Lenore's musings ended abruptly when two barn swallows flew in and circled the building several times. Some of the elderly women ducked as the birds swooped close to their heads.

One of the ministers got up from his seat and opened both barn doors as wide as they would go. One swallow flew out, but the other bird circled a few more times, left its mark on Vernon King's shoulder, and flew out the door. Looking more than a bit perturbed, Vernon slipped out quietly and shut both doors.

Lenore fought the urge to laugh as she thought about something Grandpa had said once when a bird left its droppings on the porch. *It's a good thing cows can't fly.*

She slumped on the bench. *Oh, how I long to see the humorous side of Grandpa again.* Lenore closed her eyes briefly and offered a prayer. *What can I do to bring some joy into his life?*

"Would you like me to hold the *boppli* while you eat?"

Jesse Smucker smiled at the elderly Amish woman who'd spoken to him as he held his daughter firmly on his knees.

"Umm. . .that's okay, I can manage."

"All right, but don't hesitate to let me know if you change your mind." Smiling, the woman extended her hand. "My name is Mary Ruth Lapp."

"Nice to meet you. I'm Jesse Smucker, and this wiggle worm is my daughter, Cindy. She recently turned six months." He clasped Mary Ruth's hand, but released it quickly when Cindy reached up and pulled on his beard.

"I don't believe I've seen you at any of our services before. Are you and your wife here visiting someone today?" Mary Ruth questioned.

He shook his head. "I'm new to the area, and my wife, Esther, passed away during childbirth."

"That's a shame. I'm so sorry for your loss." Mary Ruth placed her hand on his shoulder. Her kind words and soothing tone put a lump in Jesse's throat. He'd thought a new beginning in a new place would help his heart to mend, but he still missed his precious wife so much.

"Where are you from?" Mary Ruth questioned.

"I grew up in Christian County, Kentucky, not far from Hopkinsville." Jesse picked up his cup of coffee, being careful not to spill any of it on Cindy. "When my wife's uncle Herschel Fisher, who lives in Gordonville, lined me up with a job at a furniture store here in Strasburg, I jumped at the chance to leave Kentucky and start over. The memories there were too painful."

"I understand." She gave his arm a light tap. "Welcome to our community. I hope we will see more of you and your precious daughter."

*"Danki."* Jesse watched as Mary Ruth walked away and joined a young woman who appeared to be in her late twenties. From what he could tell, her hair was brown, but she was too far away for him to make out the color of her eyes. What Jesse noticed most of all was the group of boys and girls who had gathered around her. Since they all looked to be close in age, he assumed they weren't hers. Perhaps she had a special way with children. In some ways, the woman reminded him of Esther—not so much in her looks, but in her easy smile and laughter and her attentiveness to the children.

Jesse closed his eyes for a minute, conjuring a picture of Esther in his head. When he'd first met her, before they started courting, Esther had taught school. Her love for children had been evident, and her students sought her out after their biweekly church services, as well as every event they attended. Sometimes Jesse had even felt a bit jealous of all the attention she paid the children while he stood on the sidelines watching.

Jesse's thoughts were pulled aside when Cindy gave another tug on his beard. It wasn't easy being both mother and father to his little girl, but Jesse wasn't ready to even think about remarriage. With the help of his wife's great-aunt Vera, Cindy was taken care of while he was at work. So Jesse could manage fine for now. Should the time ever come that he felt Cindy needed a mother, he might consider getting married again. But no one would ever take Esther's place in his heart. He didn't think it was possible.

"It felt good to be in church today," Grandma said as they began their return trip home.

"Jah." Lenore gave a slow nod, keeping her eyes straight ahead. There seemed to be more traffic than usual for a Sunday afternoon. *Must be all the tourists*, she thought when a car came alongside their buggy going extra slow. A few seconds later, the woman in the passenger seat held up a camera and snapped a picture.

Lenore was tempted to say something about the woman's rude behavior, but she held her tongue. Some tourists took pictures of Amish folks no matter what anyone said. Lenore didn't mind if people took photos of their farms, homes, horses, and buggies, but when they got right in her face with a camera, it ruffled her feathers.

When the car moved on, Grandma gave Lenore's arm a tap. "Guess we Amish will always be a curiosity to some people. That's why they like to take our *pickder*."

Lenore sighed. "I should be used to it by now, but it still seems rude when someone is as bold as the lady in that car. I bet she wouldn't like it if a stranger snapped a picture of her."

"You're right, but since we can't stop people from photographing us, the best thing to do is ignore it or simply look away. While we might be tempted to say something unkind, it would be wrong. You heard the visiting minister quote James 1:12 this morning: 'Blessed is the man that endureth temptation: for when he is tried, he shall receive the crown of life, which the Lord hath promised to them that love him.'"

"I remember." Lenore was amazed how calm her grandmother was about most things. She rarely got herself worked up over anything. Even when Grandma had a bad day, she managed to keep a positive attitude. *I wonder if she holds any negative feelings inside.*

Lenore reflected on how both Grandma and Grandpa had responded when the truth came out about Michelle pretending to be their granddaughter. Even though they'd been hurt by her deception, they forgave Michelle and welcomed her into their home a second time. Lenore, on the other hand, had been quite put out with her pretend cousin. She was annoyed that Michelle had taken advantage of Grandpa and Grandma's good nature. But after a time of thoughtful prayer and reflection, Lenore had also forgiven Michelle, who was now one of her friends.

"Who was that young man you were talking to while the men were being served their noon meal today?" Lenore asked, moving her thoughts in a different direction.

"His name is Jesse Smucker, and he's new to the area."

"I noticed him during church, holding a baby on his lap. I didn't see who his wife was though."

"Jesse is a widower. He moved here from Kentucky when his wife's uncle lined him up with a job. His baby's name is Cindy, and she's sure a cutie pie." Grandma gently elbowed Lenore's ribs. "Maybe it wasn't just a job he came here for."

"What do you mean?"

"Could be God sent him to Strasburg to find a new *fraa*."

Lenore lifted her gaze as she drew a quick breath. "Now please don't go getting any ideas that I might end up becoming the man's future wife. I am sure he did not come to Strasburg with courting on his mind."

"You never know. Once you two get acquainted, you might hit it off quite well."

"Now you sound like Ezekiel's mother. Until Michelle came along, and even some after that, she tried to get her son to pay attention to me."

"Would you have been interested in him if he had?"

Lenore shook her head. "Ezekiel and I are nothing more than friends. It was never anything more than that."

A motorcycle roared past, coming much too close to Lenore's horse. Dolly had never liked loud noises, and today was no exception. With a piercing whinny, she picked up speed and bolted down the road.

Lenore gripped the reins tighter and pulled back. "Whoa, girl! Hold steady."

But the horse refused to halt. She raced down the road at lightning speed.

Lenore saw the stop sign up ahead and feared she would never get Dolly stopped. This was always a busy intersection, and if she couldn't get her horse under control before they reached the four-way stop, there was no telling what might happen.

# Chapter 3

Sweat poured off Lenore's forehead and ran into her eyes as she tried to regain control of her horse.

"Let me help." In a surprisingly calm voice, Grandma reached over and grabbed hold of the section of reins above Lenore's hands. "We can do this. With God's help we can."

They both pulled and shouted, "Whoa!" until Lenore thought the reins might break. Then, a few feet from the intersection, Dolly came to a stop.

"Thank You, Lord. Thank You for watching out for us." Grandma let go of the reins.

Lenore breathed a sigh of relief. Was it Grandma's faith that had made the horse stop running, or her extra pair of hands trying to hold Dolly back? For the moment, it didn't matter. All Lenore cared about was that they were safe. So many accidents had occurred in their area within the past few months—most of them involving horses and buggies.

"If only drivers would be more courteous. That fellow on the motorcycle didn't care the least little bit about frightening our horse," she muttered.

Grandma reached over and patted Lenore's arm. "It's okay. God was watching over us. We're both fine, and so is your horse."

By the time she guided Dolly up her grandparents' driveway, the peacefulness Lenore had felt during church and afterward had disappeared. Even though she and Grandma were okay, she still shivered at the thought of what could have happened if Dolly hadn't stopped.

As they approached the house, Grandma squealed. "Well, for-evermore. Would you look at that?"

Lenore looked in the direction her grandmother pointed. What a surprise to see Grandpa sitting in his wheelchair on the front porch, with one of the barn cats in his lap.

"Looks like Grandpa's enjoying a little time in the sun." Lenore looked at Grandma and smiled.

"And with a fluffy gray *katz* in his lap, no less." Grandma snickered. "Never thought I'd see the day. As you well know, your *grossdaadi* is a dog lover and doesn't have much use for any *katz*."

Lenore nodded. "I'm surprised Sadie hasn't discovered the cat and chased it away."

"She must have found something else to keep her occupied." Grandma climbed down from the buggy. "I'll secure your *gaul* to the rail. Then I'm going to join my husband on the porch. After you've put Dolly away, we can all sit outside and enjoy lemonade and cookies."

"Sounds good. I'm sure my folks will want to join us." Lenore glanced at Grandpa sitting by himself and wondered why neither Mom nor Dad was with him. Surely he hadn't wheeled himself out the door. Well, Grandma was with him now, so he would be okay.

Lenore unhitched Dolly and led her to the barn. Once she got the mare inside her stall, she brushed her down and made sure she had food and water.

"See you later, girl." She patted the horse's flank and stepped out of the stall. If it weren't for wanting to spend some time with her family, Lenore would have taken the old jar down and read a few more notes. But she could do that another day when she had some free time.

By the time Lenore joined Grandma and Grandpa on the porch, her parents were there as well. Mom held a tray of brownies and some chocolate chip cookies. Dad had a pitcher of lemon-ade in his hands. Lenore figured the reason they hadn't been on the porch earlier was because they'd gone into the house to get the snacks. Most likely they figured Grandpa would be okay for the few minutes they'd be gone.

Dad smiled and set the cold drink on the small serving table when Lenore stepped onto the porch. "How was church?"

"It was *gut*." She gave him a hug, then did the same with her mom. "How have things been going here?"

"Very well." Mom gestured to the Bible lying on the table. "Since it's such a beautiful day, we all came out here to do our devotions."

Grandma stood with one hand on Grandpa's shoulder. "Would you like a brownie, Willis?"

He nodded.

Grandma scooped one off the plate and put it in his right hand. "When you finish that, I'll give you a cold drink."

"Okay."

They all found seats and everyone ate Mom's delicious brownies, as well as some of the cookies Lenore and Grandma had baked two days ago. Lenore had mixed up a batch of brownies many times using the same recipe as Mom's, but they never tasted quite as good.

About that time, Sadie showed up and the cat made a quick exit, jumping off Grandpa's lap and bounding across the yard.

*Woof! Woof!* Sadie put her paw on Grandpa's knee. "You are loved." Grandpa gave a crooked smile and patted the dog's head.

Lenore looked at Grandma and noticed tears in her eyes as she patted Grandpa's shoulder. It was a joy to see the love Grandma had for her husband.

Lenore blinked against the sudden dampness in her own eyes. *If I ever get married, that's the kind of love I want to have for my husband.*

Jesse meandered around the living room in the small two-bedroom house he'd rented from his wife's uncle. Cindy was asleep in the room where he'd set up her crib, and Jesse needed something to occupy his time that didn't involve work.

*I wonder if Herschel ever lived in this home. Did he buy the place with the intent of renting it out?*

Jesse flopped down on the well-worn leather couch that stuck to his skin. He glanced around at the few pieces of furniture and shook his head. In addition to the couch, seating included two straight-backed chairs and an old rocker that had seen better days. The wooden floor had scuff marks in several places, and the brick front of the fireplace was stained with soot. The only source of light was a gas lamp that hung overhead. But Jesse couldn't complain. He and Cindy had a roof over their heads, and the rent was cheap. This house would have to do until he could afford to buy a place of his own.

Arms pulled back and hands against the base of his head, Jesse mulled things over. He needed to find someone else to take care of Cindy while he was at work. He couldn't keep hiring a driver every day to take him to Gordonville five days a week so Herschel's mother could watch Cindy. Vera Fisher was getting up in years and lacked the energy needed to care for a baby.

"Should have asked around when I was at church yesterday," Jesse mumbled. "Maybe one of the young women there would be willing to watch Cindy for me."

Jesse had visited with several people during the course of the day and was pleased with the warm reception he'd received after the service. Many of the older women, like Mary Ruth Lapp, had been especially attentive to his baby girl. *And why wouldn't they be? Cindy is as pretty as a rose, and sweeter than a bowl full of sugar. She takes after her precious mamm.*

Jesse blinked a couple of times. His eyelids felt gummy and hot. He could not allow himself to give in to grief or self-pity. He'd done enough of that since Esther died, and it was time to move on.

*Move on to what, though?* he wondered. *Cindy needs a mother, but it's too soon for me to think about looking for a suitable wife. Even if I were to get married again, it would only be for Cindy's sake. I could never love another woman the way I loved Esther.*

He bent forward, still clasping both hands around the back

of his head. It wasn't fair to his daughter to be raised without a mother, but then, nothing in life was fair.

Jesse raised his head and picked up the Bible lying on an end table next to the couch. With a shaky hand, he held the book against his chest. *Lord, help me to be a good father to my sweet baby girl. And if I am meant to get married again, then please show me that too.*

❦

### Lancaster

Sara took a seat next to Brad on the living-room couch in the cozy three-bedroom parsonage their church provided for the ministerial family. "After church today, I heard a lot of positive comments about your sermon on prayer." She clasped Brad's hand and gave his fingers a tender squeeze. "I can tell the congregation is pleased that they hired you as their pastor."

"I hope so, but they're equally glad you're here." He leaned over and kissed her cheek. "And I, my sweet wife, wouldn't know what to do without you. Besides the fact that I love you very much, you're an amazing asset to my ministry. In the short time we've been at the church, you've started teaching one of the kids' Sunday school classes—not to mention keeping the table in the entrance foyer well supplied with beautiful bouquets from your shop."

"I am more than happy to do both." Sara thought back to the way things were when she and Brad first started dating. She'd pretended to be a Christian so he wouldn't stop seeing her, but the ruse had backfired in her face when he'd found out the truth. Then after her stepfather died, she'd found the Lord, and everything in her life changed for the better. Marrying Brad was the best decision Sara had ever made—that and going to meet her grandparents for the first time after Mama died.

Sara was thankful Brad didn't object to her keeping the flower shop in Strasburg. It was a short commute for her five days a week. Sara enjoyed her work, and sometimes being able to minister to those who came into the shop was an added bonus.

Brad yawned, cupping a hand over his mouth. "Sorry, hon.

Guess I'm more tired than I thought."

"It's fine. Why don't you take a nap while I drive over to see my grandparents?"

"No, that's okay. It's been a while, and I'd like to go with you to see how Willis is doing—Mary Ruth too." He rose from the couch. "Caring for Willis and helping him deal with his stroke has been hard on her."

"You're right, and my dear, sweet grandma needs all the support she can get." Sara got up and started for the kitchen. "Think I'll take some of Grandpa's favorite cookies with us."

"I thought all cookies were his favorites." Brad chuckled. "Willis Lapp is a man with a definite sweet tooth."

Sara smiled. She couldn't deny it. During the months she'd lived with her grandparents, she'd witnessed Grandpa enjoying his wife's homemade goodies many times. *Of course,* Sara thought as she entered the kitchen, *I ate my fair share of Grandma's delicious desserts too.* She grabbed a plastic container and filled it with peanut butter cookies. *I'm thankful Brad's first church is close enough that we can visit Grandma and Grandpa as often as possible.*

~❧~

*Strasburg*

"Look who's here, Willis." Grandma pointed as Brad's van pulled into the yard.

Lenore smiled. It did her heart good to see Grandpa's face light up when Sara and Brad climbed out and walked toward the house.

He looked at Grandma and gave her arm a nudge with his good hand. "Rhoda's *dochder.*"

"Jah, Willis." She bobbed her head. "Rhoda's daughter, Sara, has come to see us, and her husband came along too."

*Poor Grandpa,* Lenore thought. *Since the stroke, his memory isn't as sharp as it used to be, and Grandma sometimes has to remind him of things and give detailed explanations.*

When Sara stepped onto the porch, she gave Grandma a hug,

then leaned down and kissed Grandpa's cheek. "It's good to see you, Grandpa. How are you feeling today?"

"I be better if not in wheelchair."

Although Grandpa's words weren't spoken with clarity, Lenore understood what he'd said. Apparently Sara did too, for she knelt down in front of Grandpa's chair and took hold of his paralyzed hand. "Just keep doing what the physical therapist says, and in time you'll get better."

Tears welled in Grandpa's eyes as he slowly nodded.

"Lots of prayers are being said on your behalf." Brad shook Grandpa's right hand. "Whatever you do, don't give up. Just keep trying."

"That's what we all keep telling him," Lenore's dad spoke up. "Many people with partial paralysis get better after a stroke."

*And some don't.* Lenore kept her negative thoughts to herself. She would never deliberately dampen Grandpa's spirits or take away his hope of getting better. *I need to keep praying for his healing,* she reminded herself. *If it's God's will, and Grandpa keeps a positive attitude, maybe he will get out of that wheelchair and walk again.*

# Chapter 4

"Would you like to take a walk with me?" Lenore asked Sara after everyone else had gone inside Grandpa and Grandma's house.

Sara nodded. "That sounds nice. Should we walk out back near the pond?"

"Actually, I was thinking we could go out to the barn."

Sara tipped her head. "Why the barn?"

"There's something there I want to talk to you about."

"Oh, okay." Sara rose from her chair and the two cousins headed toward the barn.

When they opened the double doors and stepped inside, three cats darted in front of them, chasing each other. Lenore groaned as the dry taste of chaff from the straw being stirred up touched her lips.

Sara flicked a few pieces of straw off her blouse. "Were the cats really chasing each other, I wonder, or could they have been after a mouse?"

"Who knows? It could have been either, I suppose." The floorboards creaked as Lenore motioned for Sara to take a seat on a bale of straw. "When I was in here the other day, I discovered an old jar filled with prayers, scriptures, and sayings." She pointed to a shelf on the wall opposite them. "Michelle showed up while I was holding the jar, and she said both of you had found it too."

"Yes, we did. And each of us was helped by some of the verses and prayers."

"Who do you think wrote the notes?"

Sara shrugged. "I have no idea. Michelle thinks Grandma may have written them."

"I thought of that too." Lenore flicked a piece of prickly straw off her dress. "But neither of you have asked her about them?"

"No." Sara shifted on the bale. "If it was Grandma who wrote the notes, she might be embarrassed if we were to ask about the jars. Many of the notes are very personal."

Lenore pursed her lips. "I'm the curious type, and I'd really like to know who the author was. Do you think I dare ask her?"

"Ask who what?"

Lenore jumped at the sound of Grandma's voice. "You startled me, Grandma. I didn't hear you come in."

"That's probably because you two were deep in conversation." Grandma took a seat on a wooden stool across from them. "Do you mind answering my question about whether you dare ask someone something?"

Lenore looked at her cousin, hoping she would say something, but Sara just sat with a placid expression. *Oh, great. How am I supposed to respond?*

"Is it a secret? Something you don't want me to know about?" Grandma leaned to one side with her head slightly tipped.

Lenore felt like a mouse caught in a trap. She could either tell her grandmother the truth or make something up, but that would be a lie. She glanced at Sara again, and when she gave her a nod, Lenore decided to proceed.

"I'll show you exactly what we were talking about." Lenore rose from her seat and went to get the ladder. After she took down the old jar, she handed it to her grandmother.

Grandma's brows furrowed as she studied the jar with a quizzical expression. "What is inside this antique-looking canning jar?"

Lenore explained about the slips of paper with prayers, scriptures, and written notes. "There's another one in your basement."

"Michelle was the first person to find them," Sara interjected. "When I came to live here, I found both of the jars too."

Grandma's eyebrows rose, and she blinked a couple of times.

"I—I had no idea this was here or that one was also in my basement."

"So you're not the person who wrote the notes?" Lenore questioned.

Grandma shook her head. "May I please look at one of the notes?"

"Of course."

Lenore held her breath as Grandma reached inside and pulled out a slip of paper. She stared at it several seconds, then slapped one hand against her flushed face. "Oh Sara, your mother wrote this note. I would recognize her handwriting anywhere."

"What?" Sara's brows pulled inward. "Are you sure about that, Grandma? The notes are all printed, not written in cursive. How can you tell Mama wrote them?"

"I recognize her style of printing." Grandma pointed to the note in her hand. "See here, she wrote in bold block letters. I'm surprised you didn't recognize it too."

Sara shook her head vigorously. "I never saw anything my mother printed. Everything she wrote was always in cursive."

Tears sprang to Grandma's eyes and dribbled down her wrinkled cheeks. "Do you know what this means, girls?"

Lenore and Sara's heads moved slowly from side to side.

"It means she may have mentioned something about the identity of your father in one of her notes."

"I don't think so. I've read all the notes in both jars and nothing was mentioned about my father, or even gave me a hint that it was Mama who'd written the notes." Sara swiped at the tears that had dribbled onto her reddened cheeks. "I doubt I'll ever know who my real father is, and I need to accept that fact. But knowing what I do about my mother's past, I understand now what many of those scriptures and notes were about. Mama was looking for hope when she thought there was none. She also sought forgiveness for the things she had done to hurt others."

"Perhaps my Rhoda was searching for healing too." Grandma sighed. "Healing for her wounded soul."

Lenore tried to imagine what it must have been like for her aunt when she left home all those years ago, knowing she was expecting a baby and feeling like she couldn't tell her parents. She stared down at the stubble of straw beneath her feet. *If I had been in Aunt Rhoda's place, would I have run away from my family and never contacted them again?* She curled her fingers into her palms. *I think not. No matter how humiliating it might have been to admit the truth, I would have told Mom and Dad and sought their forgiveness. And I would not have run away and never contacted my family again. They mean too much to me.*

"Now that I know about this, I'd like to take the jar into the house and show Willis." Grandma stepped down from the stool. "He has the right to know what our daughter has written here too."

Sara took a seat on the couch in her grandparents' living room, ready to listen and watch as Grandma read some of the prayer-jar notes to Lenore's parents and Grandpa, explaining that they'd been written by Sara's mother. Grandma read one note that said: *"If I could turn back the hands of time and do things differently, I surely would. I've done so many things I now regret."*

Grandpa moaned, and he lowered his chin to his chest but said nothing. Sara could only imagine what he must be thinking. He probably wondered if he and Grandma had done something wrong when they raised their wayward daughter.

Brad sat beside Sara, holding her hand. She was ever so thankful for his love and support. Her throat clogged as she thought about all the times she had read the scriptures, prayers, and personal notes she'd found in the jars, never suspecting her mother had written them.

Sara closed her eyes, trying to hold back tears of frustration. *Oh Mama, why couldn't you have mentioned in your notes who my biological father was? Were you trying to protect his identity for a reason? Did your parents disapprove of him? Or could he have been a married man, and you were ashamed to admit it?*

So many questions ran through her mind as she tried to come to grips with everything. Sara's life hadn't been the same since, as an adult, she'd first learned she had grandparents, and she felt grateful for the opportunity she'd been given to get to know them. Because Sara had come here to Lancaster County, she'd met Brad, her soul mate. Even if she never learned who her father was, Sara's life would be filled with many blessings and the pleasant memories she'd made here in Amish country. She hoped things would work out at the church her husband had been called to pastor so they would never have to move out of the area. Sara couldn't imagine life without Grandma and Grandpa, as well as her other family members, including Lenore, who was not only a cousin but also a good friend.

# Chapter 5

## Paradise, Pennsylvania

As soon as Lenore entered her parents' general store late Monday afternoon, she knew something had changed. The shelves near the front door, normally filled with stationery and greeting cards, now housed a variety of books—most about the Amish way of life.

*This is so strange.* She pulled one off the shelf and read the back cover. *"What is the reason Plain people live the way they do? Why would anyone shun the modern way of life? You will find answers to these questions and more within the pages of this book."*

Lenore groaned. *Since when did Mom and Dad begin selling books in their store, much less this type that will no doubt cater to the tourists who come in?*

From behind the counter, her mother greeted her with a smile. "It's good to see you, Lenore. How's your grandpa doing today?"

"Same as usual. I try to do some things that will bring a little joy into his life, like reading him a story or telling him some funny things that happened during my day, but it doesn't seem to help his mood much."

"Sorry to hear that. Maybe in time things will get better."

"I hope you're right."

"So what brings you by the store this afternoon?" Mom asked.

"I came to get a few things for Grandma." Lenore motioned to the shelf full of books. "Since when did you start selling books?"

"We got them in last week. Your *daed* thought it was a good idea, especially since so many tourists have been visiting the store lately, asking questions about us Amish, as well as other Plain communities." Mom smiled. "Now we can just point them to the books and won't have to answer so many inquiries."

Lenore's toes curled inside her black leather shoes. "I wish folks weren't so curious about us."

"It's understandable, since we dress differently and live a simple lifestyle compared to most English people."

"I hope whoever wrote those books knows what they're talking about. It wouldn't be good to be giving out misinformation."

Mom clicked her fingernails against the countertop. "No need to worry, Lenore. Your daed looked over all the books and only put out the ones he felt were true." She looked in the direction of the bookshelf again. "In case you didn't notice, there are also plenty of *bicher* for our Amish patrons as well."

"What kind of books?"

"We have copies of our church hymnals, some Bibles, devotionals, and the directory for our community. We will also be getting in some teachers' resources soon, as well as some quality books for children."

Lenore was about to respond when a tall man with dark brown hair entered the store. He was the same man she'd seen at church, only today he wasn't holding his daughter. As he moved toward the counter, she stood with lips slightly parted, eager to know more about the newcomer to their community.

"Good afternoon." He glanced briefly at Lenore, then turned to face her mother. "I was wondering if you carry any gluten-free products here."

"As a matter of fact, we do." Lenore's mother pointed toward the back of the store. "You'll find a whole section with gluten-free items." She glanced at Lenore. "Would you please show him where they are located?"

Lenore pursed her lips. *Why's Mom asking me to do this? How come she doesn't show him herself?*

When Lenore hesitated, he moved away from the counter. "It's all right. I'm sure I can locate them."

"I don't mind showing you," Lenore was quick to say. Before

he could respond, she began walking in that direction. When she reached the gluten-free section, she turned to him and said, "I saw you at church yesterday, and my grandma spoke to you after the service let out. She mentioned that you're new to our area."

He nodded. "I used to live in Kentucky, but after losing my *fraa*, I decided it would be good for me and my *dochder* to move here for a new start."

"How old is she?"

"She's six months." He tapped the heel of his left shoe against the wooden floor. "It's hard to accept the idea that Cindy will never know her *mudder*."

Lenore resisted the urge to give his arm a gentle pat. Instead, she said, "I'm sorry for your loss." The grief he felt was evident in the drooping of his shoulders and his monotone voice.

"Thank you." He lowered his gaze. "It's been hard trying to imagine how my little girl's future will be without her mother to guide her. And I. . . Well, I'm doing some better now, but when Esther died during childbirth, I felt as if my life ended too."

Lenore swallowed hard. She could almost feel this poor man's pain. Thinking a change of conversation might help, she held out her hand. "My name is Lenore Lapp. My parents own this store, and the woman at the front counter is my *mamm*."

He shook her hand. "I'm Jesse Smucker."

Lenore wasn't about to admit that Grandma had told her his name. There was no point in Jesse knowing that they had talked about him.

His gaze met hers. "I saw you after church—with several *kinner* gathered around you. Figured you were too young for them all to be yours."

She gave a small laugh. "No, I'm not married. I am a school-teacher, and some of the children I was visiting with will be in my class when school starts in August." She smiled. "That's why they were so eager to talk to me."

"Ah, I see."

"Where is your baby today?" Lenore asked.

"My wife's great-aunt has been watching Cindy while I'm at work, but it's too much responsibility for a woman her age. Eventually I'll need to find someone else to watch Cindy."

Lenore almost offered to take care of Jesse's daughter until school started, but she caught herself in time. She barely knew the man, and he might not appreciate her being so forward. Besides, with all the things she needed to do to help Grandma, there wasn't time for much else. Surely someone else in their community would be available to watch Jesse's baby.

After Jesse left the store with two sacks full of gluten-free items, plus a few other things, he thought about the young woman he'd met inside. She seemed friendly, and her eyes were filled with kindness. There was truly something about Lenore that reminded him of Esther. The compassion she felt for him had shown in her soothing tone and thoughtful expression. In some strange way Jesse felt drawn to Lenore—not romantically, but as more of a kindred spirit. It was too soon for him to be seeking—or even thinking about—a romantic relationship. Besides, he was sure no one could ever replace Esther or fill his heart with the kind of love he still felt for her.

Pushing his troubling thoughts aside, Jesse unhitched his horse, Restless, and climbed into his buggy. Eager to pick up his daughter, he guided Restless out of the parking lot and toward Gordonville, where Esther's great-aunt and great-uncle lived.

When Jesse arrived a short time later, Vera opened the door, peering at him through her thick-lensed glasses. "Cindy is sleeping," she whispered. "So unless you're in a hurry to get home, why don't we sit out on the porch until she wakes up?"

Jesse gestured to his buggy. "I do have some bulk food items to put away, but nothing perishable, so I can hang around for a while at least. No point waking my daughter and then listening to her fuss all the way to Strasburg."

"Indeed." Vera lifted the glasses from her face and rubbed the bridge of her nose. "Why don't you stay for supper? Milton's in the barn, checking on one of our pregnant cats, and Herschel will be coming by soon to eat with us." She set her glasses back in place. "Now there's plenty of scalloped potatoes in the oven, so there is no point in you going home and having to cook something for your evening meal when supper's close to being ready."

Jesse's mouth watered at the thought of eating a nourishing, home-cooked meal. Since Cindy wasn't old enough for grown-up food, Jesse often got by eating a sandwich made with gluten-free bread. It would be nice to sit down and enjoy some adult conversation as he ate his meal. "Danki, Vera, I gratefully accept your invitation. Is there anything I can do to help?"

"Not a thing." She smiled and pointed a bony finger at the two wicker chairs sitting nearby. "Now let's take a seat and visit while we wait for my menfolk to get here."

Jesse did as she suggested, and while he listened to Vera talk about her garden and how it had become neglected since she'd volunteered to care for Cindy, a sense of guilt crept in. Esther's great-aunt was in her late sixties—too old to be caring full-time for a baby. Her back was touchy, and she sometimes used a cane when she was in pain. In all good conscience, Jesse couldn't keep bringing Cindy here every day while he went off to work to earn a living.

Jesse was about to speak to her about the situation when Vera's husband, Milton, came out of the barn and joined them on the porch. "No kittens yet, but I'm thinking sometime tonight or by tomorrow morning." He looked over at Jesse and smiled. "How'd things go at the furniture shop today?"

"Pretty well. We're keeping busy, that's for certain. Several English people came in today, saying they'd heard the furniture was made by Amish, and for that reason, they felt sure it was of the finest quality. One man even mentioned that he chose to buy Amish-made furniture because it was handcrafted and locally made."

"Good to hear the business is doing well." Milton turned his attention to Vera. "How soon till supper's ready?"

"About twenty minutes. We won't eat until Herschel gets here though."

"Then I have time to take a shower?"

She gave a nod. "Oh, and please be quiet when you go inside. Cindy's still sleeping."

"No problem. I'll be *mauseschtill*." Milton opened the screen door and stepped into the house.

Vera looked at Jesse and rolled her eyes. "Can't remember when my husband's ever been quiet as a mouse."

Jesse snickered. He could almost picture Milton tiptoeing around the house.

A few minutes later, a horse and buggy pulled into the yard and up to the hitching rail. Herschel got out, secured his horse, and headed for the house. "Sorry I'm late. Hope I didn't hold up supper, Mom." He leaned over and gave her a hug.

"Not a problem. Your daed's in taking a shower, so we weren't gonna eat till he was ready anyhow." Vera rose from her chair. "I'm going inside now to check on things, but you two can sit out here and visit till I call you for supper."

"Are you sure there's nothing I can do to help?" Jesse asked.

She shook her head, then turned to Herschel again. "How come you didn't put your gaul in the barn? Your daed will probably want to challenge you to a game of checkers after we eat, and I've made a strawberry pie for dessert, with a gluten-free crust for Jesse's benefit. So if you're planning to hang around for pie, you may be here a while."

Herschel moistened his lips with the tip of his tongue. "That does sound good, but I won't be staying for dessert or any board games. I need to take care of a few things at my place before it gets dark."

Vera shrugged, then turned and went into the house.

Herschel took a seat beside Jesse. "How ya doin'?"

"As well as can be expected, I guess." Jesse dropped his gaze to the wooden planks beneath his feet. "I'm adjusting to my new job, and the house you're letting me rent is comfortable." He tugged his ear. "But even though some things seem to be working out, I still miss your niece something awful."

"That's to be expected." Herschel reached over and gave Jesse's shoulder a squeeze. "It takes a long time to get over losing someone you care about. No one knows that better than me. I've had to do it twice, and the pain still lingers."

Surprised by Herschel's comment, Jesse tipped his head. He had no idea the man had been married twice. Of course, there was a lot about Herschel he didn't know or understand. Vera and Milton's oldest son had always been somewhat aloof and kept pretty much to himself. When Jesse first met his wife's uncle, he thought Herschel might not care much for him. But Esther explained that her uncle had been withdrawn since his wife died. The poor fellow had no children—just his elderly parents and two brothers, as well as a few nieces and nephews—none of whom he appeared to be close to. From what Esther had said, her uncle had no close friends either.

Jesse pushed his shoulders back. *I can't let that happen to me. I'll always be close to my precious little girl, and even if I don't feel social, I will put forth the effort to make some friends while I'm living here in Lancaster County.*

❧

*Lancaster*

"You've been awfully quiet since we returned from your grandparents' house yesterday." Brad pointed to Sara's plate. "And you've barely touched your supper. Is everything all right?"

Sara looked at Brad from across the kitchen table. "I can't stop thinking about the notes my mother wrote in those prayer jars that Lenore, Michelle, and I found." Her stomach tightened as she stared at her half-eaten tossed salad. "All this time I thought it may have been Grandma who wrote the notes and hid the jars. Never once did I suspect it was Mama. But now that I reflect on some of the things she wrote, I should have guessed it was her." Sara turned her gaze on Brad. "How could I have been so blind?"

"Sometimes the most obvious things escape us. That was true for me before I felt God's call on my life."

She tipped her head. "Really?"

Brad nodded. "Before it became clear to me that I should study to become a minister, I imagined myself learning to fly a plane and eventually becoming an airline pilot."

"What made you change your mind?"

"A note I found in my grandfather's Bible." Brad paused and took a drink of water. "It said: 'What is God calling you to do? If you don't know, you need to pray about it.' " He grinned at Sara. "So I did."

"And God revealed to you that He wanted you to go into the ministry?"

"Yes. It seemed like every scripture I read pointed me in that direction."

Sara forked a cherry tomato and popped it in her mouth. "I can't say for sure that it was God's will for me to buy the flower shop, but the way things worked out, I can't help but believe He approved of my decision."

"I agree. And you're doing an excellent job running it, while still finding time to help me in my ministry." Brad's face broke into a wide smile. "You're an amazing woman, Sara, and I'm thankful God brought you into my life."

She got up from the table and came around to give him a hug. "I love you so much. You're everything I could ever want in a husband. Someday when we have children, I hope they'll grow up to be just like their dad."

# Chapter 6

*Strasburg*

A bee buzzed overhead, and Michelle tried to ignore it as she pulled a handful of stubborn weeds. At least it wasn't the irritating gnats that usually plagued her. If she didn't bother the bee, it would probably leave her alone.

The home she and Ezekiel rented was small, and so was the yard, but at least she had found a place for her garden. After Michelle and Ezekiel got married, his parents had invited them to move in with them until they could afford to purchase a place of their own, but Ezekiel declined the offer. Michelle was relieved. She wouldn't have felt comfortable living in the same house with Ezekiel's mother, even though she and Belinda got along better now than they did when Michelle and Ezekiel first began courting. Also, they had more privacy in the rental than what they would have had with just a single bedroom to call their own at the Kings' house.

As the sun beat down on Michelle's head, a trickle of sweat ran down her face. It was normal for the end of June to be warm and humid, but the last week had been almost unbearable. On a day such as this, Michelle couldn't help wishing they had air-conditioning in their home. The battery-operated fans Ezekiel had bought did nothing but blow warm air around wherever they were placed.

Despite her occasional longing for some of the modern conveniences she'd given up to become Amish, Michelle had no regrets about her decision to join the church and marry Ezekiel. He was a good husband, and she loved him very much. The only thing that would make her life more complete would be the addition of a baby. Michelle and Ezekiel had been married a year and a half, and she wondered why she had not become pregnant yet. The doctor assured Michelle that both she and Ezekiel were healthy and there was no reason she couldn't conceive. He advised them not to worry about it and said stress might be the problem.

Michelle had dealt with her share of stress over the years, beginning with the dysfunctional home she'd grown up in. Bearing the brunt of her parents' physical and emotional abuse during her early childhood had taken a toll on her, as well as on her younger brothers. Living with foster parents had also caused some stress, since she never really felt accepted by her foster family.

Gritting her teeth as she grasped another clump of weeds, Michelle reflected on the years she'd been out on her own, struggling to keep a job and pay the rent on whatever run-down apartment she had managed to stay in. A stream of boyfriends, some abusive like Jerry, had left her feeling as if she had no worth. At least that's how it was until Michelle met Willis and Mary Ruth Lapp. Even after they'd found out about her deception—pretending to be Sara—they had treated her with love and kindness. It was almost as if she was actually one of their granddaughters.

Michelle loved Mary Ruth and Willis, and she wished only good things for them. Tears welled in her eyes, nearly blinding her vision. "Dear Lord," she murmured, "please heal Willis's body and help him recover from his stroke."

Sara stood near the front of her flower shop, studying the display she'd recently set up in the front window. With the Fourth of July less than two weeks away, she'd used red, white, and blue as her color theme. The focal point was a child's red wagon she'd found in a local antique store. Sara had put a bouquet of red, white, and blue carnations inside the wagon, which she would change out as needed. A few vases full of red-and-white roses surrounded the wagon, along with several small American flags tied together with red bows and scattered in strategic locations.

Sara knew the importance of creating an eye-catching window display, representative of the flowers and plants she sold, many of which she purchased from the Kings' greenhouse. This display, she hoped, would draw potential customers into the shop. She had learned from the previous owners that it was a good idea to create window displays representative of the season. She'd also made sure to use good lighting in effective ways. When the Fourth of July holiday was over, Sara would change the decorations in the window to another creative summer scene.

In the short time Sara had owned the store, she had established a personal connection with her regular customers, always striving to be honest and sincere. And she tried to send a handwritten note or make a personal phone call to thank new customers for their orders.

As she headed to the counter where she waited on customers, the front door opened and Herschel Fisher walked in. It had been several months since he'd visited her shop, and Sara had begun to think she might never see him again.

"May I help you, Mr. Fisher?" she asked.

He gave a quick nod. "Came to buy a dozen red roses. And there's no need to refer to me as Mr. Fisher. Just call me Herschel, okay?"

"All right." Sara combed her fingers through the ends of her long hair. "Are they for your wife's grave?"

He shuffled back a step or two. "H–how did you know about that? I don't recall saying anything to you about my wife having died, much less that I'd been buying flowers to put on her grave."

A wave of heat crept across Sara's cheeks. "Actually your mother mentioned it to me. I'm sorry for your loss, Herschel."

"My mother came in here?"

Sara nodded.

With whitened knuckles, Herschel reached up to rub the back of his neck. "What business did she have telling you such a personal thing?"

Sara felt like she was caught between a rock and a hard place. If she told Herschel that his mother had come into the store, demanding that she stop selling him flowers, it would not go over well. But she had to tell him something.

Leaning against the counter for support, she swallowed hard. "Your mom was concerned that you might get in trouble with the church leaders for placing flowers on your wife's headstone."

"I don't do that anymore, so she has nothing to worry about." He let go of his neck and pulled his fingers through the sides of his blond hair, steaked with gray. "And in fact, the flowers I want today are for my mother's birthday, which is tomorrow."

Sara smiled. "I'm sure she will appreciate the gift."

"I hope so. She works hard, despite her aches and pains. For the past few weeks she's been babysitting her great-niece while the baby's daddy is at work." Herschel grimaced, slowly shaking his head. "Personally, I think it's too much for a seventy-year-old woman. At least that's how old Mom will be as of tomorrow."

"She must be energetic if she's watching a little one."

Herschel shook his head. "She's not really up to the task, but you can't tell her that. Whenever Mom sees a need, she jumps right in and tries to help."

"You must take after her then."

"What do you mean?"

"Do you remember some time ago when you rescued me and my friend Michelle after my car got stuck in a ditch?"

He tipped his head to one side and tugged his right ear. "Oh yeah. . .now I remember. I ended up with muddy feet, and my back hurt a bit, but I was glad that I came along when I did."

"So were we. Your kindness and willingness to help out left an impression me. It was a reminder that there are good people in this world who put themselves out for others when there's a need."

He nodded. "I only did what I'd want someone to do for me if I had a problem out on the road."

Sara motioned to the display cooler where several vases of flowers had been put earlier. "Shall we see about getting a bouquet of roses put together for your mother?"

"Yes, and since it's a special birthday, let's make it an even dozen."

Sara hoped Herschel's mother knew what a kind, considerate son she had. Not every man cared that much about his mother. No doubt he'd been a good husband too.

"You have a dandy crop of *aebier* this year, Grandma." Lenore placed a handful of the strawberries she'd picked into a plastic container.

Grandma smiled and popped a berry into her mouth. "You are so right, and these aebier are *appeditlich*."

"Jah. In fact, they are so delicious they won't need much sugar for sweetening."

"But don't forget, your grandpa likes plenty of *zucker*, even on the sweetest of berries."

Lenore couldn't resist the temptation to roll her eyes. Too much sugar wasn't good for a healthy person, let alone someone in Grandpa's condition. But she kept silent, knowing Grandma had been giving in to Grandpa's every little whim these days. Lenore thought her grandmother sometimes tried too hard to do things that would make him happy. Unfortunately, many of those things that went way beyond her duty as a wife had little or no impact on Grandpa. Instead of saying thank you, or even conjuring up the tiniest of smiles, he would often simply sit and stare. There was no question about it—the dear man was depressed.

The tinkling of the wind chimes hanging under the porch eaves pulled Lenore's thoughts back to the present. The day was too pleasant to let worry or negative thoughts take over.

"Since there's only one row of berries left to pick, would you mind if I went inside to check on your grandpa?" Grandma asked. "He may have woken up from his nap by now. If so, he will need my help getting up from the bed."

"I should go so you don't end up straining your back." Lenore started to rise from her kneeling position, but Grandma held out a hand to stop her.

"I can manage, dear. There's still some strength left in these old bones."

"Okay, but please give a holler if you need my help with him."

"I will." Grandma rose to her feet and started for the house.

Several minutes later, a ruckus broke out in the barnyard. Lenore looked over. One of their feisty roosters had his head stuck in the hog pen. The poor thing looked like it was doing a dance as it squawked and flapped its wings.

*It's a good thing we don't have hogs in the pen anymore,* Lenore thought as she made her way across the yard. *They might have attacked.*

With little cooperation from the rooster, Lenore managed to free it, but she'd stepped in some manure. Setting the rooster down near the coop, she turned on the hose to wash off her gardening clogs. Only sheer willpower kept her from spraying the now strutting old rooster for all the trouble he'd caused. "I could've been nearly done picking berries out here in the hot sun if it wasn't for you," she muttered, shaking her finger at Big Ben—a name Lenore had given the troublesome rooster.

Big Ben turned to look at her, and as if in response, he let out an ear-piercing squawk.

Lenore chuckled, in spite of her aggravation. With all the negative things going on around her these days, it was good to have something to laugh about, even if it was at the rooster's expense.

# Chapter 7

*Gordonville*

"H*allich gebottsdaag*, Mom." Herschel handed Vera a bouquet of red roses and gave her a hug. Jesse had given her a box of pretty notepaper with matching envelopes, but it paled in comparison to the roses.

"Danki, Son, for the birthday wishes and lovely gift." She placed the flowers in a vase and set it in the center of the dining-room table. "You went all out getting me twelve roses. I'm sure it was expensive."

"Not too bad. I bought them at the flower shop in Strasburg, and the nice woman who owns the place gave me a good deal." He puffed out his chest a bit. "Besides, you're worth it."

Vera's cheeks reddened as she flapped her hand at him. "Go on with you now. I don't need any praise."

Jesse, who'd been sitting in a rocking chair holding Cindy, thought it was time for him to speak up. "Herschel is right, Vera. You've done a lot to help out with Cindy since I moved here, and I want you to know how much I appreciate it."

She shrugged. "It's nothing, really. I enjoy helping others whenever I can."

"Even so, I'm still on the lookout for someone else to watch Cindy while I'm at work. I've asked around, but all the young Amish women in my area are either married with families of their own to care for, or they already have a job." Jesse stroked his daughter's soft cheek as she nestled against his chest.

Vera took a seat on the couch next to her husband. "There's no hurry for you to find someone else, Jesse. I am willing to do it for as long as you need me."

Milton snorted, turning to face her. "You'd work yourself right into the grave if someone didn't stop you." He looked at Jesse. "My fraa means well, but it's hard for her to say no, even when she's tired, stressed, or in physical pain. So my advice to you, young man, is if you can't find a *maud*, then look for a wife."

Milton's bluntness caused Jesse's skin to tingle. He'd never expected such a bold statement. "I—I'm not ready to get married again," he mumbled, keeping his focus on Cindy. "But I will keep looking for a maid to watch my baby girl and keep the house running while I'm at work."

Herschel sauntered over and stood beside Jesse's chair. "Why don't you leave Cindy with my mamm right now and come outside with me for a bit? There's something I'd like to show you." He looked at his mother. "Would that be okay with you?"

"Of course." She held out her arms.

Although a bit hesitant after Milton's previous remark, Jesse stood and placed Cindy in Vera's lap. Then he followed Herschel out the front door.

Outside, Herschel led the way to the barn. Jesse had no idea what could be in there that Vera's son wanted him to see, but he went willingly.

Once inside the building, Herschel pointed to a pair of wooden stools sitting close to one wall. "Go ahead and take a seat."

Once again, Jesse obliged. "What did you want to show me?"

"Nothing in particular. I wanted to talk to you in private."

"About what?"

"My daed's offhanded remark." Herschel folded his arms and leaned against the wooden planks. "He's worried about my mamm, but that didn't justify his suggestion that you find a new wife."

"It's okay. I'm sure he didn't realize how impossible that would be."

"You still love your fraa, jah?"

Jesse nodded. "What Esther and I had was special. I don't think I'll ever stop loving her."

"I understand. My heart still lies with Mattie, which is why I never remarried."

"It's too bad you don't have any kinner. Cindy is the joy of my heart. Every day I am reminded how blessed I am to have her."

Herschel rubbed a hand across the middle of his chest. "Mattie and I wanted children, and she gave birth to a son a few years after we got married." His posture slumped as he paused and cleared his throat. "I would have given most anything to be a father, but I guess it wasn't meant to be, 'cause our boppli died a few hours after he was born." He heaved a sigh. "Mattie was never able to conceive after that."

Jesse stood and put his hand on Herschel's shoulder. "I'm sorry for your loss," he said gently.

"Danki. Even after all these years I still think about it. I'm not one to easily let go of things that have touched me on a deep emotional level."

Remembering the conversation he'd had with Herschel a few weeks ago, Jesse realized that it must have been the memory of losing his child that caused Herschel to say he'd suffered a loss twice. No wonder the poor man always seemed so withdrawn. After all these years, he still grieved for what he'd lost.

Jesse closed his eyes briefly. *I am ever so grateful for the privilege of raising my precious daughter. The memory of my dear Esther will never die, because Cindy is a part of her. I'll cherish every day we have together, and if by some chance I do end up getting married again, I'll make sure Cindy knows all about her mother.*

*Strasburg*

"How did you get that nasty-looking *gwetsche*?" Grandma pointed to the bruise on Lenore's forearm, where she'd rolled up her dress sleeve to wash their supper dishes.

"When I put my gaul away in her stall this afternoon, one of the *katze* ran in front of her. Dolly got a bit frisky, tossing her head from side to side, and as I tried to calm her, I ended up bumping into the wooden post outside her stall."

"Better watch yourself around the horses," Grandpa mumbled from where he sat by the table in his wheelchair. "They can't be trusted, and you never know what they're gonna do if something spooks them."

With eyes open wide, Lenore turned to look at him. It was the clearest he'd spoken since his stroke. Apparently the speech therapy he'd been having weekly was beginning to take effect. What a joy to see this measure of improvement. Here she'd been looking for ways to bring more happiness into his life, and today, he'd brought some unexpected cheerfulness into hers.

"Jah, Grandpa, I'll try to be more careful." Lenore glanced at Grandma and noticed the sweet smile on her face. No doubt, she too was pleased with Grandpa's progress.

"Now about that bruise. . . Have you put anything on it?" Grandma questioned.

"Just some ice after I came in the house."

"Arnica. That's what you need." Grandpa spoke again.

"He's right." Grandma reached for a clean dish to dry. "There's a tube of *Arnica montana* lotion in the bathroom medicine chest. Apply a thin layer to the affected area three times a day, and it should help. You should also take some of the arnica tablets in my homeopathic medicine kit. Just follow the instructions on the container."

Lenore smiled. "Danki. I will do that as soon as I'm done with the dishes."

It seemed like Grandma had holistic remedies for a good many things. Too bad she didn't have one to keep Grandpa from having another stroke. But hopefully with him watching his diet, taking a blood thinner, and doing everything the doctor said, it would never happen again. Lenore wanted her grandparents to be healthy and live many more years. She'd lost her mother's parents when they were tragically killed in a buggy accident six years ago. The thought of losing either Grandpa or Grandma Lapp put a lump in her throat.

"Want to join me in a game of Scrabble?" Ezekiel asked, stepping into the kitchen where Michelle sat at the table.

"Maybe later." She gestured to the pen and paper lying before her. "I'm working on my grocery list right now, for when I go shopping tomorrow."

"You came in here more than thirty minutes ago to do that. Thought you'd have it done by now."

She shook her head. "I haven't decided what all we need."

He moved closer to the table and looked down at the list. "We went over all the items we both need during supper, but you only have a few things written down. How come?"

"I don't know." Michelle didn't look up at him.

Ezekiel pulled out a chair and sat beside her. "Okay, what's the problem? You're depressed about something, aren't you?"

Slowly, she nodded.

"Is it your brothers, because you haven't heard from them in a while?"

"No, it's not that. In fact, I heard from Ernie a few weeks ago."

"What then?" Ezekiel cupped Michelle's chin with the palm of his hand, turning her head to face him.

She drew a quick breath before speaking. "I've been sitting here wondering why God hasn't answered my prayers about having a baby."

He gently stroked her arm. "We've had this discussion before, and I thought we'd both agreed that if it's meant to be, you'll get pregnant in God's time, not ours."

"I know, but—"

"Have you ever thought how worrying over this might be causing you stress, and that the stress could actually be keeping it from happening?"

"I have considered it."

"Then stop fretting, try to relax, and put your focus on other things." Ezekiel put his hand on Michelle's shoulder. "Philippians

4:11 says, 'I have learned, in whatsoever state I am, therewith to be content.' "

"Danki for that reminder, Ezekiel. You're so full of wisdom I wouldn't be surprised if someday you get chosen by lot to become a minister."

Ezekiel's eyes darkened. "I hope not. A lot of responsibility is put on a man's shoulders when he is selected to be one of the church leaders."

"It's not something you need to worry about, for now at least." Michelle reached up to stroke the side of her husband's bearded face. "I love you, Ezekiel, and I don't know what I'd do without you."

"You'd have a lot less dishes to wash." Grinning, Ezekiel leaned over and kissed her cheek. "Now hurry up with your grocery list so you can beat me at Scrabble."

Michelle chuckled. Just a few words of encouragement from the wonderful man she'd married, and already she felt better. There might be times in the days ahead when she would think about her desire to have a baby, but Michelle would try to remember to be content, even if she and Ezekiel were never blessed with children.

# Chapter 8

Sara was about to leave the flower shop to meet Brad for lunch a little before noon on Saturday when her part-time employee, Cynthia, called out, "What should I do after I've washed all the plastic buckets in the back room?" Cynthia worked three days a week, mostly cleaning. She was also being taught how to make floral arrangements.

Sara didn't understand why Cynthia had asked her that question when Misty, her new full-time floral designer, was behind the counter filling out some paperwork. Misty used to work at a flower shop in Lancaster before coming here, after Sara's previous designer, Peggy, had moved away. So Misty pretty much knew how to run the place. Sara always felt comfortable leaving Misty in charge whenever she left the store for any length of time.

"Once the buckets are cleaned and put away, you can help Misty in the back room, and work on the orders that came in this morning." Sara nodded in that direction.

"Oh, okay." Cynthia gave Sara a hesitant nod and retreated to the back room.

Sara looked over at Misty and winked. "I'll be back in a few hours."

"No hurry. Take your time. With any luck, we'll have most of those new orders already filled when you return."

Sara left the shop and headed down the sidewalk in the direction of Isaac's Famous Grilled Sandwiches. About half a block down, she spotted Herschel Fisher heading her way.

"Hello, Mr. Fisher," she said when he drew near. "How did

things go for your mother's birthday? Did she like the roses you bought her?" When he looked at her strangely, Sara paused. "Oh, I forgot. . .you prefer to be called Herschel, right?"

He gave a brisk nod.

She smiled. "I'll try to remember."

"In answer to your question: Yes, my mother liked the bouquet. Her birthday turned out well, even though she insisted on cooking the meal."

Sara remembered the time Herschel's mother had come into her shop to chew Sara out for selling flowers to her son, which he'd put on his wife's grave. Vera struck her as a woman with a lot of spunk.

They talked for a minute about the unusually warm weather they'd been having, before Herschel said he needed to be on his way.

"I hope to see you again soon." Sara waved and headed for the restaurant to meet up with Brad. It had been nice to see the gleam in Herschel's eyes when he talked about his mother. Sara wished, once again, that her own mother was alive. She had so many unanswered questions that she would never get the chance to ask her. All Sara had left of her mother were the messages she'd left in the prayer jars. Some she understood, but others were a mystery. It seemed like Mama had left out an important piece of the puzzle of her young life—the piece she wanted no one to know about.

Sara sighed. *I wish Mama had told me about the notes before she died. There are so many things I would have asked her.*

*Ronks, Pennsylvania*

Lenore had been running errands on Grandma's behalf for most of the morning, and she still had a few more stops to make before going home. Since it was almost noon, she decided to have lunch at Dienner's Country Restaurant, where Michelle used to work as a waitress. She quit when she married Ezekiel, but she'd said many times how much she enjoyed working there and how busy the place was because everyone liked the food.

Upon entering the building, Lenore was greeted by a middle-aged hostess who took her to a table near the window. She had only been seated a few minutes when the waitress came to take her order.

"I'd like a chicken salad sandwich and a glass of unsweetened iced tea with a slice of lemon, please."

The young woman smiled and wrote Lenore's order on her pad. "I'll bring your beverage right away, but it may be several minutes before your sandwich is ready. We're really busy today and the kitchen is shorthanded."

"No problem. I'm not in a hurry."

After the waitress left, Lenore dug in her purse for the list Grandma had given her this morning. The two stops she had left were the post office to mail some letters and the pharmacy to pick up a prescription for a refill of Grandpa's blood thinner. Those stops shouldn't take long, so hopefully she would be back in plenty of time to help Grandma fix their supper.

Lenore felt concerned about how her grandmother would manage all day once school started in August. At one point, she'd considered resigning from her teaching position to stay home and help, but Grandma insisted she could manage on her own and didn't want Lenore to give up a job she enjoyed. If things got to be too much, Grandma would call on a friend or neighbor for assistance.

Lenore had returned the list to her purse when she heard a baby fussing. What began as a mild form of crying soon turned into fretful sobbing. She glanced across the room and saw Jesse Smucker at a table, holding his little girl in his lap. The baby's creamy complexion quickly turned red as she flailed her chubby arms and kicked her feet. Her daddy's face was equally red. No doubt he was embarrassed and at his wits' end.

Without hesitation, Lenore got up and moved swiftly across the room. "I don't mean to intrude, but would you like me to see if I can settle her down?"

Sweating profusely, he nodded and held the child out to Lenore.

A few pats on the back and some gentle strokes of the little girl's tearstained face, and all was quiet.

Jesse shook his head slowly as his mouth fell open. "If I hadn't seen it for myself, I wouldn't have believed it. Either you have magic in your hands or you're just plain good with kinner."

Lenore's chin dipped a bit as a warm flush crept across her cheeks. "I've been told that I do have a knack with children, which I suppose is the reason I enjoy teaching school."

Jesse stared at her with a curious expression. "I'm surprised you're not married and raising a family of your own by now."

His comment caught her off guard, and she lowered her gaze even further. "I would like to get married someday, but God hasn't brought the right man into my life."

A few moments passed with neither of them speaking, and then Jesse asked another question. "Would you like to join me for lunch? We can take turns holding Cindy, and hopefully with you here she'll be quiet for me."

Lenore lifted her chin to look at him, wondering how to respond. As much as she relished the idea of sitting at Jesse's table and holding his precious daughter, Lenore didn't want to start any gossip going around. If anyone they knew saw them eating lunch together, they might get the idea that Jesse was courting her. But if she didn't take him up on his offer, little Cindy might start howling again, and Jesse might not get to eat his lunch at all.

When Cindy burrowed her perky nose against Lenore's shoulder and gave a little whimper, Lenore made up her mind with no hesitation. "I'd be happy to eat my lunch here and take turns holding your baby."

When Lenore, still holding his satisfied daughter, walked away to ask the waitress to bring her lunch over to his table, Jesse mulled things over. *I wonder if Lenore would agree to watch Cindy until she starts teaching school again. That would give me more time to look for a full-time maid.*

"The waitress said it won't be a problem to bring my order over here when it's ready," Lenore said after she returned to Jesse's table.

"Okay, good."

When Lenore sat down with Cindy, Jesse continued to eat his meal. After her order came, it was Jesse's turn to hold Cindy. He was surprised his little one remained quiet, although fixated on Lenore as she ate her sandwich.

Bouncing Cindy on his knee, Jesse threw caution to the wind and blurted out the question on his mind. "I was wondering. . . Would you be interested in watching Cindy for me while I'm at work, until you start back teaching *schul*?"

She set her glass of iced tea on the table. "Well. . .uh. . .I suppose I could do it, but it would have to be at my grandparents' house, where I'm living right now to help out."

"Not a problem. Right now my wife's great-aunt is watching Cindy, and since she and her husband live in Gordonville, it means I have to take Cindy there every morning, then come back here to Strasburg to my job at the furniture store, and then return to Gordonville at the end of the workday. Also, Vera's really not up to watching the baby five days a week, although she won't admit it." He leaned forward, resting his elbows on the table. "Since you live in Strasburg and we are in the same church district, it will be much closer for me to bring the baby to your grandparents' house."

Lenore wiped her mouth with a napkin, then reached into her purse and took out a small notebook. "I'll write down my grandparents' address for you."

"Thanks. I'll be by on Monday morning around seven."

"Will I see you at church tomorrow morning?"

"I won't be attending church in our district this Sunday. I promised Vera and Milton I'd bring Cindy to church in their district this week." Jesse grinned. "I think Vera wants all her friends to see how much my little girl is growing."

"It's understandable. When children are young they grow so quickly. I taught some of my older students when they first started school, and whenever I see them now I can't believe how much they've grown."

Jesse kissed the top of Cindy's head. "I hope she doesn't grow too fast. I appreciate the innocence of her youth."

"I know what you mean." Lenore glanced at the clock on the far wall. "I suppose I should get going. I still have a few more errands to run for my grandma." She stood and moved to Jesse's side of the table. Reaching out to touch Cindy's chin, she smiled and said, "See you Monday morning, sweet girl." She looked at Jesse. "I hope the rest of your day goes well and Cindy remains as happy as she is right now."

Jesse nodded. "Danki again for getting her settled down."

"It was my pleasure."

When Lenore left the restaurant, Jesse worried that his daughter might start fussing again, but she seemed totally relaxed in his arms.

He looked down at her and gulped. *I hope I did the right thing asking Lenore to watch my baby. Sure hope Vera won't mind. I don't want to ruffle her feathers.*

# Chapter 9

*Gordonville*

Throughout the Sunday service, and even during lunch, Jesse thought about his encounter with Lenore the day before. Now that he and Cindy were at Vera and Milton's house, it was time to tell Vera of his decision about his daughter.

Cindy had fallen asleep and lay curled up on the living-room floor on a thick blanket, while Milton slept in his recliner nearby. Since Vera had gone to the kitchen to make coffee, Jesse determined this was a good time to speak with her.

When he entered the kitchen, the spicy aroma of gingerbread made his mouth water. A plate filled with several pieces of the thickly cut bread had been placed on the table.

Vera smiled at him and gestured to the plate. "I thought you and Milton might like a treat to go with your *kaffi*."

Jesse smacked his lips. "A cup of coffee sounds good, and that gingerbread looks awfully tempting, but your husband is sleeping as soundly as my little *maedel* right now."

"He can have some when he wakes up." Vera pulled out a chair at the table. "Pour yourself a cup of kaffi and take a seat."

Jesse obliged, and after she joined him, he jumped right into the topic on his mind. "I've found someone else to watch Cindy while I'm at work."

Vera blinked rapidly. "Oh? Who is she?"

"Her name is Lenore Lapp, and—"

"Where is she from? Does she live here in Gordonville, or someplace closer to you?"

"Lenore lives in Strasburg, and she's a schoolteacher. But she's not working right now and has agreed to watch Cindy until she starts back to school toward the end of August."

Vera rested both arms on the table, looking at him intently. "If she can only care for your daughter a short time, what's the point? I mean, what is the reason you chose her?"

"Lenore is good with kinner. In fact, when I had no success getting Cindy to quiet down at the restaurant yesterday, Lenore got my little girl to stop crying almost as soon as she picked her up."

"She's never cried much for me." The wrinkles around Vera's mouth deepened as she pursed her lips. "And I told you before that I don't mind watching her."

Jesse squirmed in his chair. Although he didn't want to offend Vera, Jesse felt his decision was best, not only for Cindy, but for Vera as well. He hoped he could make her understand and that there would be no hard feelings.

"You're right—you are good with Cindy, and I appreciate all you have done to help out. But you need a break and more time to do some of the things you like. Caring for a young child is a full-time job."

She nodded slowly. "All right, I accept your decision, but once Lenore returns to teaching, if you need me to watch Cindy again, I'm willing."

"I appreciate that, but maybe by then I will have a full-time maud."

Vera's eyes twinkled as she pointed at him. "Or a fraa."

He shook his head. "That's not going to happen."

"Never say never, Jesse." Vera snapped her fingers. "Say, I have an idea. Why don't you ask Lenore Lapp out for supper some evening and see where things go from there?" She gave him a toothy grin. "You can't be sure till you get to know the young woman, but Lenore might be the one for you."

"No, I don't think—"

"If she handles your daughter well, she might make a good mudder, and good mothers are usually good wives."

Jesse fought the urge to roll his eyes. "I appreciate your

concern, Vera, but I'm not planning to get married again." He quickly reached for a piece of bread and took a bite. *No woman except Esther is the one for me. But God took her to heaven and left me and Cindy alone, so I guess that's how it's meant to be.* Jesse would say no more to Vera on this topic. He preferred to keep his thoughts to himself.

### Strasburg

Mary Ruth sat on the couch, watching Willis sleep in his favorite reclining chair. She tried not to worry about him, but sometimes her thoughts ran amuck. If her dear husband had another stroke— or even a heart attack as their doctor had warned—she didn't know what she would do. In less than two months Lenore would resume her teaching duties, and Mary Ruth would be left alone all day to care for Willis and do all the chores around the house.

*Maybe we should have taken Ivan up on his offer to move in with him and Yvonne. Of course, with them both working at his general store, I'd still be alone with Willis all day. But at least they'd be close enough to come home for lunch and check on us.* Mary Ruth shifted on her chair, sucking in a breath. She knew what Willis would say if she again suggested moving to Paradise to live with Ivan and his family. His response would be a resounding no.

*It's best if I don't dwell on this too much,* Mary Ruth admonished herself. *Even though I'm not as young as I used to be, as long as Willis doesn't get any worse, I'm sure I can manage when Lenore is not at home.*

Lenore sat on the edge of her bed, thinking about Jesse and his baby girl. Holding the child yesterday had felt so good, and the fact that Lenore had easily calmed Cindy down surprised her as much as it apparently had the baby's father.

She hadn't told her grandparents yet that she'd agreed to watch Cindy during the days her father worked. She hoped they wouldn't object.

Lenore tapped her chin. *I should have asked them first before agreeing to Jesse's request. If either Grandma or Grandpa has any qualms, I'll have to let Jesse know right away so he can find someone else.*

She got up and moved over to the window to watch several birds carrying on in the trees closest to the house. It was hard to stay focused on the birds, though, when her mind was somewhere else. *Having a baby in the home might be too much for Grandpa. If Cindy gets fussy, it might disrupt Grandpa's peace and quiet.*

Lenore moved away from the window, walked over to the bed, then paced back again. *This is what I get for being so impulsive. The decision I made yesterday at the restaurant was hasty, and I didn't think things through well enough.*

A soft knock sounded on the door, diverting Lenore's attention. "Come in," she called.

Grandma entered the room and joined Lenore at the window. "You've been up here since you got home from church. I thought you might be napping."

"No, just thinking."

Grandma took a seat on Lenore's bed and patted the quilted cover. It was a simple nine-patch quilt like the one Grandma had taught Lenore and Sara to make some time ago. "Why don't you sit here and tell me what's on your mind?"

Lenore sank to the bed. "There's something I need to tell you."

Grandma's eyes darkened. "You look so serious. Is there a problem?"

"No. Yes. Well, I guess there could be. I agreed to do something without checking with you first."

"What do you mean?"

Staring at her hands folded in her lap, Lenore explained about Jesse's request for her to watch Cindy here at the house. "I shouldn't have agreed to it without getting your approval, but I got caught up in the moment of holding the adorable child, and then before I knew it, the word *yes* came out of my mouth."

"It's okay, dear one." Grandma clasped Lenore's hand. "It

might be kind of nice to have a little one around for a while. Things have been way too serious here at the house since your grossdaadi's stroke. A sweet little boppli, no doubt full of lots of cute antics, might be just what we all need to bring some joy and laughter into our home again."

Lenore leaned close and gave her grandmother a hug. "Danki for being so understanding. But I want you to know, if it doesn't work out and the boppli gets on Grandpa's nerves, I'll ask Jesse to make some other arrangements for his daughter."

Grandma gave Lenore's back a few gentle pats. "Not to worry. I'm sure it'll be just fine."

Lenore hoped the babysitting would go well, because she looked forward to watching Cindy. Getting to know the baby's father a little better would be nice too. No doubt he'd been lonely since his wife died. Perhaps there would be some evenings when he could join them for supper. Lenore was almost sure her hospitable grandma would extend some meal invitations.

# Chapter 10

As Jesse pulled his horse and buggy up to the Lapps' hitching rail, Cindy began to fuss. She'd dozed off on the way over here, which had given him the peace and quiet he needed to concentrate on the road and try to relax. He still felt a bit apprehensive about leaving Cindy with Lenore, but they were here now and there was no turning back.

Once Jesse got the horse secured, he took Cindy out and carried her and the canvas bag full of necessary baby items up to the house. Before he had a chance to knock on the door, it opened and Lenore greeted him with a dimpled smile.

"Come in. We have everything set up for Cindy."

Jesse wasn't sure what Lenore meant by that, but when he followed her into the living room, he was surprised to see a playpen sitting near the rocking chair.

"My aunt Rhoda used it when she was a baby," Lenore explained. "When Grandma told me it had been stored in the basement, I went down last night and brought it up. I thought it would be better than putting a blanket on the floor for Cindy to lie on." She motioned to the playpen. "It's all cleaned up and ready to use when needed."

"Good idea." Jesse glanced across the room, where a man's straw hat lay on an end table. "Are your grandparents okay with you watching Cindy here in their home?"

Lenore nodded. "They're fine with it. Grandma even said having a boppli in the house would give us all something to smile about." Lenore held out her arms. "And I'm definitely looking forward to spending time with your sweet baby girl."

Jesse handed Cindy over to Lenore and set the satchel on the couch. "Everything she might need is in here." He stepped forward and kissed the top of Cindy's head. "Be good for Lenore, little one. Daadi will see you this evening."

He turned and was almost to the door when Lenore called out to him. "If you have no plans for supper this evening, we'd like you to join us. Grandma plans to make stuffed cabbage rolls, and there's bound to be more food than the three of us can eat."

Jesse's mouth watered at the anticipation of eating a good home-cooked meal. "I would be pleased to join you. Danki for the invitation."

When Jesse left the house and started across the yard, he stepped a bit livelier than usual.

"I see the boppli has arrived." Upon entering the room, Grandma gave a wide smile.

"Jah. Cindy's daed dropped her off about fifteen minutes ago." Lenore sat in a rocking chair, tenderly patting the baby's back. "She's real *schee*. Don't you think so, Grandma?"

"Yes, but then, I think all *bopplin* are pretty."

"Me too." Lenore heaved a sigh. "I would like to have a child of my own someday, but at the rate things are going, it looks doubtful that I'll ever fall in love and get married."

Grandma clicked her tongue. "Never say never. The right man will come along someday. Maybe he already has."

Lenore tipped her head. "What do you mean?"

"Could be this pretty baby's father will take an interest in you. He is without a wife, you know."

Lenore lifted her gaze to the ceiling. "Oh Grandma, I'm sure Jesse has no interest in me other than as someone to care for his daughter."

"He may not now, but he could develop feelings for you in the future. And the same goes for you."

Lenore had to admit, even in the short time she'd known Cindy's father, she found him appealing—not just his good looks, but his gentle voice and the kindness she saw in his eyes. Of course, she wasn't about to admit it to Grandma or anyone else for that matter.

She rose from her chair and put Cindy in the playpen. "The baby is sleeping now, so I'm free to help with any chores."

Grandma shook her head. "The chores can wait. Your grandpa's still reading the newspaper at the kitchen table. Why don't we join him for a cup of coffee, and then we can plan out our day."

"Okay." Lenore covered Cindy with a lightweight blanket and followed Grandma out of the room.

⁓

That evening when Jesse came back to the Lapps' after work, as soon as Mary Ruth led him into the house, he was greeted with the tantalizing aroma of cooked cabbage and tomato sauce. His stomach growled at the prospect of eating cabbage rolls, which he hadn't had since Esther died.

"How'd my little girl do today?" His question was directed to Lenore, who sat in the living room holding Cindy.

"She did very well." Lenore smiled, raking her fingers lightly through Cindy's shiny hair. She gestured to the gray-haired man sitting in the recliner next to her. "Cindy's cute smile and giggle kept Grandpa well entertained."

"Good to hear." Jesse moved toward the man and extended his hand. "I'm Jesse Smucker. It's nice to meet you, Mr. Lapp."

"Nice to meet you too, and you can call me by my first name. It's Willis." He held out his right hand. "*Ich schlaag hot ihn gedroffe*, and it left me partially paralyzed."

"I'm sorry to hear you had a stroke." Jesse gave an understanding nod. His paternal grandfather had suffered one too, followed by a massive heart attack that had taken his life ten years ago. *The world would be so much better if it were free of death and suffering,* he thought.

Jesse gave Willis's shoulder a light tap. "I hope you will experience a full recovery."

"He's doing much better than a few months ago," Mary Ruth spoke up. "His speech has improved and he's even able to walk a little when he's out of his wheelchair. Although he does have to use a cane or a walker," she added. "I do believe his physical therapy sessions are finally paying off."

"That's great. Keep up the good work, Willis." Hearing familiar baby noises, Jesse glanced at Cindy. She'd begun pulling on Lenore's dress sleeve and kicking her bare feet.

"Looks like my *dochder* is full of energy this evening," Jesse commented. "Did she get a good *leie* today?"

"Jah. In fact she took two naps."

Mary Ruth chuckled. "I think you wore Cindy out with all the games you played with her."

"What kind of games?" Jesse directed his question to Lenore.

"Let's see. . ." Lenore tickled Cindy under her chin. "We played the *kitzle* game. I tickled Cindy under her chin, and she would laugh. Then I tickled her toes, and even her nose." Lenore grinned. "It was so cute when she tried to tickle herself."

Jesse rubbed the back of his head. "I've never tried anything like that with her."

"Willis had your little girl laughing with all the silly faces he made too," Mary Ruth interjected.

"Jah," Willis chimed in. "When I made a growling noise, she growled right back at me."

"Sounds like you folks know how to keep a *boppli* entertained." Jesse laid a hand against his chest. "I should be doing those kinds of things with Cindy when I come home from work, instead of just sitting and cuddling her."

"That's important too." Lenore bounced Cindy on her knee. "I'm sure as time goes on, you'll find many ways to keep her entertained and help her senses develop."

Jesse nodded, although he wasn't sure he possessed the skills to be everything his daughter needed. *Maybe Vera was right when she offered her opinion the other day. Could be that I do need to find a wife so my little girl isn't deprived of having a mother.* He glanced in Lenore's direction again. *She's good with Cindy. I wonder if she might be a possible candidate for marriage.* Jesse shifted on his chair. *Of course, I'll have to get to know her better before I bring up the topic. And she would need to understand that our marriage would only be one of convenience, since there could never be any love between us.*

"Should we all go out to the kitchen and eat supper now?" Mary Ruth's question drove Jesse's irrational thoughts aside. And they were irrational, because the day Esther died he'd made up his mind that he would never get married again. It didn't even make sense that the crazy notion of marrying Lenore had popped into his mind. Jesse barely knew the young woman, and he certainly wasn't in love with her. *Maybe after I've had a good meal, I'll be thinking more clearly.*

# Chapter 11

"A re you sure you don't want to do anything special tonight?" Ezekiel asked as he and Michelle sat at their kitchen table eating supper. "If we can find a driver to take us there, we can go up to the Fourth of July celebration in Lititz tonight." He grinned at her from across the table. "It's always fun to watch the fireworks."

She shook her head. "I'm content to stay here with you all evening. When it starts to get dark, we can sit outside and watch the *feierveggel* rise up from the grass."

His forehead creased as he reached for a slice of Michelle's homemade bread. "There's nothing exciting about watching fireflies. I might have thought so when I was a boy and caught them to put in a jar, but not anymore." Ezekiel chuckled. "I need a little more action than that."

"I suppose you're right, but I'd rather stay home tonight," Michelle repeated.

Ezekiel slathered the bread with a little butter and plenty of honey from his beehives. "We're just an old married couple now, jah?"

She snickered. "Not old, but we've definitely settled into the routine of married life. The only thing missing is. . ." Her voice trailed off. Michelle had almost broken the promise she'd made to herself not to bring up the subject of children again. It did no good to talk about her inability to conceive. And if she voiced her thoughts, it could put a damper on an otherwise pleasant meal.

"Would you please pass the lentil casserole?" Michelle said. "It turned out so well, I'm ready for seconds."

Making no comment on her dropped sentence, Ezekiel pushed

the casserole dish on its oversized potholder closer to Michelle.

"Danki." Michelle put two heaping tablespoons on her plate and picked up her fork. But before she could take a bite, Ezekiel spoke again.

"I've been mulling something over in my mind for the past few weeks, and wanted to talk to you about an idea I have."

She took a quick bite and swallowed. "What's it about?"

"I'd like to leave Lancaster County and move to New York."

Michelle's head jerked back. "New York?"

"Jah. There's a newly established Amish community there, and I saw an ad in *The Budget* recently, placed by a man who lives in that community."

"An ad for what?"

"He makes beekeeping supplies and will be getting ready to retire from the business this spring."

"But you don't make beekeeping supplies. You keep bees for their honey, which you sell to people you know and places of business here in our area," Michelle reminded.

He nodded. "True, but I'd like to learn how to make bee boxes and many other things that are used for raising bees. I could continue selling honey from my beekeeping business too."

"You have never before mentioned wanting to make the supplies you use for beekeeping."

"Didn't realize it till I saw the man's ad saying he's willing to teach the person who buys his business how to make and/or sell the supplies one needs to be a beekeeper." Ezekiel leaned closer to Michelle. "As you know, I've never been happy helping in my folks' greenhouse. This would be a chance for us to start over, and I would finally be doing something I'd really enjoy."

"How do you know you'd like it, since you've never done it before?"

"Just do." He tapped his chest with the palm of his hand. "I feel it right here, and I'm hoping you'll be willing to make the move."

Michelle sat silently, staring at her plate. The desire to eat more casserole had disappeared. Strasburg and people like Willis and

Mary Ruth, whom she'd become close to, were like family. She couldn't imagine leaving them and living someplace where she didn't know a soul.

He reached over and patted her arm. "You don't have to give me an answer right now. Just think about it, okay?"

Michelle forced a smile she didn't really feel and slowly nodded. In addition to thinking over Ezekiel's idea, she would need to do some serious talking to God.

∽

*Lancaster*

"How soon till you're ready to go to your grandparents' house?" Brad asked when he entered the kitchen where Sara stood working near the sink.

"Within the next thirty minutes or so." She turned to look at him. "Too bad your folks had other Fourth of July plans. It would have been nice if they could have driven down from Harrisburg and joined us."

"Yeah, but by the time I extended the invitation, they'd already agreed to spend the day with some close friends." Brad stood behind Sara and put his arms around her waist. "The fruit salad you're making looks delicious."

She reached back and swatted his hand. "Don't get any ideas about sampling some now. This is to share with the others who'll be at Grandma and Grandpa's today."

"Okay, I'll leave the salad alone." Brad reached for a piece of cut-up watermelon that hadn't made it into the bowl and popped it in his mouth.

Sara's brows pinched together. "You're incorrigible."

Brad chuckled and leaned over to give her cheek a wet kiss. "Not to change the subject or anything, but are you sure you're okay with me hosting a Bible study here in our home for new Christians?"

"When were you thinking of starting the study?" she asked.

"Maybe next Friday night, or the week after."

"I'm fine with it, Brad. Since it wasn't that long ago that I became a new Christian, I'll probably benefit from the class too."

"Christians—old or new—can always take something away when they study the Bible. What I'm mainly concerned with, though, is whether you're okay with having it here." Brad leaned his back against the counter. "With you working all day at the flower shop, it might be too much to have to come home, cook supper, and get ready for the class."

She stepped in front of him and tweaked his nose. "I thought maybe you'd do the cooking on Bible study night."

Brad's eyes widened as he slapped both hands against his cheeks. "What? You expect me to cook supper?" Before Sara could respond, he winked at her.

She poked his chest playfully. "What am I gonna do with you? You're nothing but a big tease."

"Of course, and that's one of the things you love about me." He wrapped Sara up in a big hug. "Now you'd better hurry and get the lid on that salad bowl before I lose all self-control and eat the whole thing."

Sara smiled. How grateful she was that God had brought her and Brad together. She looked forward to many years of serving the Lord as her husband's helpmate.

✺

### Strasburg

"Oh, what a cute baby. What's her name, and who are her parents?" Sara asked when Lenore met her on the front porch, holding Cindy.

"Her name is Cindy Smucker. She and her daddy are fairly new to our church district, and I recently began watching her while her father, Jesse, is at work."

"She's adorable." Sara reached out and stroked the little girl's cheek. "Her skin is soft like silk."

Lenore nodded. "She's such a good baby and so smart. I'm going to miss her when I start teaching again next month."

"I assume Jesse's wife is not able to watch the child?"

"Cindy's mother died while they were living in Kentucky, and Jesse brought his daughter here for a new start." Lenore took a seat on the porch swing. "Would you like to sit with us? Cindy loves the rocking motion of the swing."

"Sure." Sara sat beside Lenore, and they both pushed against the wooden boards beneath their feet. In a matter of seconds, Cindy began to giggle.

Lenore looked at Sara and grinned. "See what I mean?"

Sara bobbed her head. "Does Cindy's dad have any family members living in Strasburg? Is that why he chose to move to this area?"

"He has no blood relatives living nearby, but his wife's uncle, Herschel Fisher, lives in Gordonville, and so do Herschel's parents." Lenore paused to wipe a blob of drool off Cindy's chin with a tissue. "It's my understanding that Herschel owns a house here in Strasburg and he's renting it to Jesse."

Tipping her head to one side, Sara tapped her chin. "Hmm. . . I wonder if it's the same Herschel Fisher who comes into my flower shop sometimes. Herschel is not a common name, and if I remember right, according to the invoices for some of his floral purchases, Herschel's home is in Gordonville."

"It's probably the same man then." Lenore glanced in the direction of the barn, where she'd seen Sara's husband go after their van pulled into the yard. Lenore's parents had gone into the house to visit Grandma and Grandpa when they'd first arrived, but her brothers had gone out to the barn. Lenore figured Brad must have caught sight of them when he arrived and followed to see what they were up to. It was a good thing, because Lenore's cousin's husband had a level head and often offered spiritual counsel that any young man—Amish or English—could benefit from.

"Will Jesse and Cindy be joining our Fourth of July gathering?" Sara's question cut into Lenore's thoughts.

"Yes. I invited him when he brought Cindy here yesterday morning, and he accepted without hesitation."

"I'm surprised he doesn't have plans to spend the evening with his wife's relatives."

"I asked that question, and Jesse said neither Herschel nor his folks do anything to celebrate the Fourth." Lenore snickered. "I think the fact that we'll be having a barbecue with plenty of good food may be the main reason Jesse's coming. He admitted that he's not much of a cook and usually ends up fixing sandwiches on gluten-free bread for his meals."

"Maybe he ought to seek another wife." Sara placed her hand on Cindy's leg. "His precious daughter needs a mother too." She looked directly at Lenore. "Maybe someone like you."

A warm flush crept across Lenore's cheeks. "Now don't be silly. I barely know Jesse, and I'm sure he has no thoughts about getting married again—especially not to me."

Sara elbowed Lenore gently. "You never know what the future might hold, Cousin. When I first met Brad, I never dreamed we would fall in love or that I'd end up becoming a pastor's wife."

Cindy began to fidget, so Lenore patted her back, which was a sure way to make the little girl relax. "What's it like, being married to a minister? Are there many duties you must fulfill?" Lenore figured the change of subject would get Sara's mind off the unlikely event that she would end up marrying Jesse.

"Not too many. Brad made it clear when the church hired him that I had a business to run and would continue to be responsible for that. Of course, I try to be involved in the church as much as I can. In fact, he and I will be hosting a Bible study in our home soon, for people in the congregation who are new Christians." Sara shifted her position on the swing. "I'm actually looking forward to it. In addition to delving into the scriptures on the topic of a Christian's growth, it will give both Brad and me the opportunity to get to know some of the people in a more personal way."

"I hope it works out well for everyone who comes." Lenore glanced toward the road as she heard the unmistakable sound of a horse's hooves against the pavement. A few seconds later, a horse and buggy pulled in. "Looks like Cindy's father is here. I'm sure he will enjoy meeting you and Brad." *And I will enjoy getting to spend more time with him,* she silently admitted.

# Chapter 12

Y our little girl is adorable." Sara gestured to Cindy sitting contently on her father's lap.

Jesse smiled. "Thank you. She takes after her mother in many ways."

"Would you mind if I held her?" Sara hesitated. "That is, if you think she will come to me."

"Cindy's usually fine with strangers. I'm sure she won't mind if you hold her." When he handed his daughter to Sara, she was pleased that the little girl made no fuss. In fact, Cindy leaned her head against Sara's shoulder as she popped a thumb into her mouth.

"Aw, so she's a thumb sucker, huh?" Sara chuckled. "My little brother sucked his thumb until he was nearly four years old. I remember how Mama fretted about it, worried that Kenny might be doing that by the time he started kindergarten."

Jesse grunted. "It makes no sense to me, but Cindy prefers her thumb to a pacifier."

"Every child is different," Grandma said as she took a seat on the picnic bench beside Sara. "When your mother was a little girl, she sucked on the end of the little blanket I had made her." A faraway look entered her eyes. "I can remember the way she clung to that blanket just like it was yesterday."

Sara's throat tightened. *Poor Grandma. The whole time she and Grandpa were raising their children, I'm sure they had no idea their daughter would run away from home when she grew up, never to be seen or heard from again. If only Mama would have contacted them before she died. What was Mama thinking? Didn't she realize how much she'd hurt them? For that matter, she hurt herself by severing all family ties.*

Sara hated rehashing this scenario in her mind. She had gone over it so many times in the past. When she had finally forgiven her mother, Sara thought she'd come to grips with it once and for all. It was frustrating how a person could think they had worked through a situation, even felt peace about it, and then out of the blue, the pain of it all came right back to haunt them.

*I won't allow my mind to dwell on it,* Sara told herself. *Tonight is a special time to be with our friends and family, and I refuse to let anything spoil the evening. Maybe Mama did what she thought was right, so I need to give it to God again and let it rest.*

Lenore sat silently on the other side of the picnic table, observing Sara as she held Cindy. No doubt, Sara and Brad would become parents someday. Judging from the way Jesse's baby responded to Sara's gentle voice and touch, Sara would make a good mother.

It was wrong to envy, but little seeds of jealousy crept in every time Lenore saw a mother—or even a potential one—with a child.

A light breeze lifted the ties on Lenore's covering, and she tied the ends to keep them from swishing across her face. *What if I never get married or become a mother? Can I be satisfied teaching children all day but never nurturing any of my own?*

"Oh, look, there are fireworks over in that direction! I wish we had some we could set off."

Lenore smiled at her brother Peter's enthusiastic tone. She looked toward the area where he pointed. Sure enough, the sky was full of shimmery light, falling toward earth like a shower of red, white, and blue fiery sparks.

"It's pretty, but in my opinion, fireworks are a waste of money that could be spent on more practical things." Dad's forehead wrinkled as he looked at Peter. "When you've worked as hard and long as me, maybe you'll understand the value of a dollar." He pointed to another set of fireworks going off. "To me, that's just a lot of money going up in smoke."

Lenore's mother reached over and gave him a nudge. "Now, Ivan, don't be such a stick-in-the-mud."

His brows furrowed. "I'm just trying to use common sense."

Lenore remembered back to one of their Fourth of July family get-togethers when she and her brothers were young. Mom had bought balloons for them to fill with water and throw at each other. Lenore, Peter, and Ben thought it was great fun, but Dad grumbled and complained about the muddy mess in the flower bed, created by the water spigot they kept leaving on. Later, when Mom brought out a box of sparklers for the kids to light, Dad alternated between reminding them to be careful not to catch their clothes on fire and fussing about the money Mom had wasted buying the sparklers.

*Of course,* Lenore reminded herself, *my daed has many good attributes and has never been stingy when anyone in the family has needed money for important things.* Lenore had good parents, and for that she felt thankful—not like poor Michelle whose parents had been physically and emotionally abusive. Lenore couldn't imagine growing up in a family without love and support, or having a mom and dad who treated their children harshly. It was no wonder Michelle had struggled to forgive and rise above her circumstances. If she hadn't given her heart to the Lord and found forgiveness for her own wrongdoings, Michelle wouldn't have found peace or be where she was today.

Lenore glanced at Sara again, wondering what it must be like for her cousin not to know who her biological father was. Although Sara hadn't mentioned that topic for some time, Lenore figured she must have given up her search for him. Perhaps someday if the Lord willed it, the truth would come out.

*B–boom! B–boom! B–boom!* Lenore nearly jumped off the picnic bench when more fireworks went off, only this time with less color and more of an explosive sound. Lenore wasn't the only one affected, for the dog started barking and little Cindy began to howl.

"Here, let me take her inside the house where it's quieter." Lenore went around to where Sara sat with Cindy on her lap. "She probably needs her diaper changed by now anyhow."

Sara handed her the baby. "Would you like me to come with you?"

"No, that's okay. I can manage." Holding the sobbing child securely, Lenore glanced in Jesse's direction before heading to the house. She couldn't read his serious expression. Was it one of concern for his daughter, or did Cindy's father have something else on his mind?

For the next several minutes the adults chatted while Peter and Ben headed off to get firewood for the bonfire they'd both requested. Even though everyone had eaten a delicious meal of barbecued chicken, corn on the cob, and several kinds of salads just a few hours ago, the boys said they were hungry and ready to roast hot dogs and marshmallows. Jesse didn't usually eat anything much past supper, but tonight he would make an exception. It had been some time since he'd felt this relaxed and enjoyed himself so much. The Lapps were good people and had been most hospitable to him. Jesse almost felt like he was a part of their family.

When Brad stopped talking to the men long enough to ask his wife a question, Jesse glanced toward the house. *I wonder how things are going with Cindy. Maybe I should go up to the house and find out.*

"Excuse me, everyone." Jesse stood. "Think I'll go see if my daughter needs anything."

Ivan nodded. "No problem. Take your time. When you get back, maybe my boys will have the bonfire going."

"Do any of you need anything from the house?" Jesse asked.

"Not at the moment," Mary Ruth spoke up. "There's no point bringing the hot dogs out till the fire's been built and has died down a bit."

"My fraa is right," Willis agreed. "Roast the hot dogs too soon, and they'll be black as coal."

"All right then. I'll be back as soon as I find out how Cindy's doing. Hopefully Lenore's got her calmed down by now."

Yvonne smiled. "If anyone can calm your boppli down, it's my daughter."

Jesse hurried toward the house. When he stepped inside, all was quiet. That was a good sign. Upon entering the living room, he spotted Lenore sitting in her grandma's chair, humming softly while rocking Cindy. "Is she asleep?" Jesse whispered, moving quietly across the room.

"Almost."

"That's good. I think one of the reasons she became fussy is because she's tired." Jesse took a seat on the couch.

"That could be." Lenore looked over at him and smiled. "Did you get tired of watching the fireworks? Is that why you came inside?"

He shook his head. "Came to check on Cindy and to ask you a question."

"Oh?" She tipped her head. "What would you like to know?" Lenore spoke softly.

He swallowed hard and licked his dry lips. *I don't know why this is so hard for me. It's not like I've never asked a woman out to supper before. It's been a while since I thought about courting.*

Lenore kept rocking and patting Cindy's back as she looked at him expectantly.

Jesse drew a deep breath and exhaled quickly. "If you're not busy Friday evening, would you like to go out to supper with me?"

Lenore blinked and got the rocking chair moving a bit faster. "Just the two of us?"

"Jah. I checked with Vera this morning, and she's agreed to watch Cindy while I'm gone." He tugged on his shirt collar. "I thought it would give us a chance to get better acquainted."

Lenore stopped rocking and nodded slowly. "Jah, Jesse, I'm free to have supper with you on Friday."

"Okay, good." He stood and wiped his sweaty hands on the sides of his trousers. *That wasn't as hard as I thought it would be. At least it's the first step in the right direction.*

"Guess I'll head back outside and see if Ben and Peter need any help with the bonfire. Will you be joining us soon?"

"Once Cindy is fully asleep, I'll put her down in the playpen. I will come back in periodically, though, to check on her."

"Okay. Danki for taking such good care of my little girl."

"You're welcome. It's my pleasure."

Jesse left the living room and headed out the back door. *Sure hope I didn't make a mistake asking Lenore out for supper. She might get the idea that I see her as more than a friend, and then I'd have to offer an explanation. I need to go slow and establish a solid friendship with her before I even mention the idea of marriage.*

# Chapter 13

Michelle headed down the road with her horse and buggy Friday morning, conflicting thoughts flitting through her mind. For the last few days she had been thinking and praying about Ezekiel's desire to move to New York and learn a new trade. The thought of leaving Strasburg put a knot in her stomach, but at the same time she wanted to please her husband. It was her duty as his wife to offer support and be a good helpmate. If she put up a fuss and stood in his way, she'd feel guilty for holding Ezekiel back and squelching his desire to start over in a new place.

What Michelle needed right now was some solid advice, which she hoped to get from Mary Ruth and Willis.

Approaching the Lapps' home, she sent up a silent prayer. *Lord, please help me to be open-minded, because I am sure Mary Ruth and Willis will give me good counsel.*

Mary Ruth was surprised when she heard a horse whinny. They weren't anticipating any company. But then, friends and neighbors sometimes dropped by unexpectedly, as did family members.

Peering out the kitchen window, she saw a horse and buggy come into the yard and pull up to the hitching rail. A few seconds later, Michelle climbed down. After she'd secured her horse, she headed for the house.

Mary Ruth dried her wet hands on a towel and hurried to open the back door. "Well, good afternoon. What a pleasant surprise." When Michelle stepped onto the porch, she gave her a hug. "We haven't seen you for a while. Come inside so we can visit."

Mary Ruth couldn't help noticing the slump of Michelle's shoulders as she entered the kitchen. "If you're not busy, I was hoping I could talk to you and Willis about something."

"Willis is sleeping right now, but I'd be happy to listen to whatever you have to say." She gestured to a chair at the table. "Why don't you make yourself comfortable? I'll fix us something cold to drink."

Michelle hesitated before pulling out the chair. She obviously had something troubling on her mind.

"Is everything all right?" Mary Ruth asked as she poured them both a glass of freshly brewed iced tea. "You look a bit *verlegge*."

"I am troubled." Michelle heaved a sigh. "Ezekiel wants us to move."

"To a home of your own?"

"Jah, only not here in Strasburg. He wants to start over in one of the Amish communities in New York."

Mary Ruth blinked. "I never expected he would move away from his family. From what I understand, they are dependent on his help in the greenhouse." She set their beverages on the table.

"I know." Michelle picked up her glass and took a drink. "I can't talk to Ezekiel's parents about this, because he hasn't told them yet. I'm sure they would not give their blessing. Ezekiel's daed has said many times that he needs the whole family's help in the greenhouse."

Mary Ruth stared at the table, pondering the best way to respond. "I'm sure there are plenty of able-bodied men Vernon could hire to work at his business."

"You're right, but they wouldn't be part of the *familye*—and their greenhouse has always been a family business."

"How do you feel about moving to another state?"

Michelle's face tightened. "It would be hard for me to leave all our friends, but if it's what Ezekiel truly wants, then I may not have any choice." She took another drink of iced tea, then held the glass against her reddened cheek.

"Have you prayed about the matter?" Mary Ruth questioned.

Michelle nodded. "It may seem selfish, but I've been asking God to change Ezekiel's mind and make him be satisfied to stay here. He could always look for some other job in the area if he's determined not to work in the greenhouse anymore."

"And if he doesn't change his mind?"

"Then as his wife, I'll need to go with him." Michelle's chin trembled. "It won't be easy, but I'll have to trust God that things will work out and I'll adjust."

"When would you expect to move?"

"Probably not till spring. That's if Ezekiel ends up taking over the business of some Amish man who recently put an ad in *The Budget*."

"It's a big decision, and I'll definitely be praying for both you and Ezekiel."

"Danki. I feel better being able to talk about it."

"Have you told anyone else?"

Michelle shook her head. "I'd rather not mention it to others yet—not till Ezekiel has made up his mind and told his parents."

"I understand, and I certainly won't repeat what you've said." Mary Ruth pointed up. "And always remember that wherever you go, whatever you do, the Lord will be with you."

❧

### Bird-in-Hand, Pennsylvania

Lenore's stomach quivered as she sat beside Jesse in his open buggy. Could his invitation to supper be considered a date, or did he merely want to get to know her better for the sake of his child, whom he'd hired her to care for?

She fidgeted nervously with the handles of her purse. *I can't imagine that Jesse would be interested in me romantically. After all, his wife hasn't even been gone a year. And Jesse's pained expression when he has spoken of Cindy's mother indicates the depth of his grief.*

"Is that the schoolhouse where you'll be teaching when school starts next month?"

Lenore turned to the right where he pointed.

"Yes, that's the one," she replied. "It will be my first time teaching there since moving from Paradise to Strasburg."

"I'm guessing you must like your job?"

She smiled. "Jah. I find teaching to be most rewarding."

"More so than being a mudder?"

Lenore's mouth opened slightly. Jesse's question was unexpected. "Well, umm. . .since I've not had the privilege of being a mother, I can't compare it to teaching, but I would like to have kinner of my own someday."

"I see." Jesse glanced briefly at Lenore, then back at the road again. They rode in silence for a while before he posed another question. "How long do you think you'll be living with your grandparents?"

She shrugged. "It depends on how well Grandpa does. If he can regain full use of his left arm and leg, I might be able to return to my parents' house. Then again, with me teaching in Strasburg, it would be better if I remained at Grandpa and Grandma's house indefinitely."

"What if you get married someday?"

"Then my place would be with my husband. But since I'm not being courted by anyone, it's not an issue I need to consider." Lenore didn't understand why Jesse was asking such personal questions. *Could he be interested in me? Would he ever consider me as a potential wife?* She gave him a sidelong glance, but he kept his gaze on guiding his horse into the parking lot of the Bird-in-Hand Family Restaurant.

### Strasburg

"I hope Lenore has a nice time this evening. She works so hard around here, and it's good for her to get away for a while and have some fun for a change." Mary Ruth's knitting needles clicked as she carried on her conversation with Willis, who sat in his recliner beside her rocking chair. He'd made a few comments about what they had for supper when she'd first helped him into his chair but hadn't said much since then.

"It was nice of Jesse to invite Lenore out for supper," Mary Ruth continued. "I have a hunch he might be interested in courting our granddaughter. What do you think, Willis?"

A soft whistling sound followed by a couple of obnoxious snorts was her husband's only response.

Disgusted, Mary Ruth looked up from her knitting and shook her head. Not only had Willis fallen asleep, but now, with his mouth hanging slightly open, his obtrusive snores bounced off the living-room walls.

"Oh well," she murmured, twirling a piece of yarn around her finger, "guess I ought to get used to talking to myself." These days Willis slept a lot more than he had in the past. But at least the paralysis he'd been left with since his stroke had lessened some, and for that she felt thankful.

❧

### Bird-in-Hand

"What's it like in the area of Kentucky where you are from? I've never been there, so I don't know anything at all about it," Lenore said, as she and Jesse enjoyed their meal from the bountiful buffet.

"Let's see now. . .I suppose I should start by giving you the history of the area." Jesse tapped his fingers on the table. "Christian County is named for Colonel William Christian, a native of Augusta County, Virginia. He was a veteran of the Revolutionary War and settled near Louisville, Kentucky, in 1785." He paused for a drink of water. "It might interest you to know that Jefferson Davis, president of the Confederate States of America, was born in Fairview, Kentucky, which is in Christian County."

"Interesting facts. What else can you tell me about that part of Kentucky?"

"Well, Christian County and its county seat, Hopkinsville, are located in southwestern Kentucky, a part of the Pennyroyal region. The Pennyroyal region's name comes from a branched annual plant of the mint family that can grow up to eighteen inches tall. Pioneer settlers found Pennyroyal growing throughout the area, and so they bruised the leaves and stems for use as an effective mosquito and tick repellent. Also, they discovered that a tea made from the plant was effective at treating pneumonia."

Lenore's brows lifted. "Wow, I'm impressed. You sure know a lot about the history of Christian County."

He smiled. "I enjoyed learning about our country's history when I was a boy and have read a good many history books as an adult."

"That's interesting. I'm fascinated with history as well."

"We'll have to share some historical facts we've learned about Pennsylvania some other time when we're together," Jesse said.

"Jah, that would be fun." Lenore finished eating her chicken, then posed another question. "Were you involved in woodworking when you lived in Kentucky, or is that something you took an interest in after you moved here?"

"I built a few things in a little shop on my folks' property but mostly helped my daed on the farm."

"What crops did you grow?"

"Wheat, corn, and some soybeans." Jesse cleaned his plate and wiped his mouth on a napkin. "Think I'll go back up to the buffet and get some dessert. Are you coming?"

Grimacing, Lenore placed both hands against her stomach. "Wish I could, but I ate too much chicken and mashed potatoes. I don't think there's any room left for dessert."

"Not even a small *schtick* of shoofly *boi*?"

She shook her head. "As much as I would enjoy a piece of shoofly pie, my common sense tells me I'd better not."

"Okay, guess I'll have to eat your share then." Jesse winked and headed for the buffet.

Lenore leaned back in her chair and tried to relax. *Are those fluttery feelings in my stomach from eating too much food, or am I just feeling giddy from time spent with Jesse?*

*Lancaster*

"Thanks for helping me do the dishes, and also for having supper ready when I got home." Sara smiled at Brad as she took the sponge from the sink to wipe the kitchen table.

He winked at her. "Not a problem."

She glanced at the clock and saw that it was almost seven. "Your Bible study group should be here soon. Think I'll go to the living room and make sure everything's ready."

Brad stepped over to Sara and slipped his arms around her waist. "Nothing to worry about there. I vacuumed earlier and even dusted." He wiggled his brows. "Since my folks had no girls, Mom taught me how to cook, clean, and do the dishes, so I've had plenty of practice over the years."

"I appreciate everything you do to help out around here." She turned and kissed his cheek. "Oh, and the next time I see your mother, remind me to tell her thanks for raising such a considerate man."

"Thank you, I sure will." He tweaked the end of her nose. "And now, Mrs. Fuller, let's take time for a word of prayer before our guests arrive."

They sat beside each other at the table and held hands. Brad prayed out loud, asking God to bless their time with the new believers and to give him the wisdom to say the right things and share the scriptures that would be most helpful to those in attendance.

He'd just finished praying when the doorbell rang. "Sounds like our first guest has arrived."

With sweaty hands, Sara followed Brad to the front door. She could deal with customers at the flower shop, no problem, but knowing what to say to a group of new Christians was an entirely different matter—especially when she was a fairly new one herself.

When Brad opened the door, he greeted a young couple who introduced themselves as Shawn and Arlene Campbell. He invited them to take seats in the living room, and a few minutes later two more people arrived. Becky Freemont said she was single and attended the local community college. Tim Stapleton, the young man with her, informed Brad that he used to attend Sunday school when he was a boy, but until recently hadn't gone to church regularly.

The final person to arrive was a middle-aged man named Rick Osprey.

Once everyone was seated, Brad opened with prayer and then handed out Bibles and a workbook to each person. "Before we get started," he said, "I thought it would be good if you all took turns telling a little something about yourself, along with how and when you became a Christian." Brad turned to Rick. "Would you like to go first?"

"Umm. . .sure." The man reached up and rubbed his graying sideburns. "I grew up in Lancaster County, and to be honest, I was pretty wild during my teen years and into my young adult life. For a while, I ran around with a group of Amish teenagers who lived in Strasburg—or maybe it was Paradise. They were going through a time of sowing their wild oats. I think they called it *rumspringa*. Oh, and there was this one girl named Reba. . . ." He paused and scratched his head. "Guess it could have been Rhoda or some other name that begins with *R*. Anyway, she said her folks were Christians and even tried to mention God, but I wasn't interested back then. I was having too much fun sowing my own wild oats." He stopped talking and turned to Shawn. "Okay, that's enough about me. It's your turn now."

Shawn began talking, but his words were lost on Sara. All she could think about was the name Rick had mentioned—Rhoda. *Could he have known my mother? Is it possible, by some twist of fate, that this man could be my biological father?* Sara wanted to question him further, but this was not the best time or place. She needed to wait for a better opportunity to ask him some pertinent questions. And she wanted to talk with Brad about it first.

# Chapter 14

*Strasburg*

Jesse woke up in a cold sweat. He'd dreamed that Cindy was sick with a high temperature. She kept crying and crying, and nothing Jesse did seemed to calm her. He'd put a cold compress on her forehead, but it didn't bring the fever down.

*Would I be able to help my little girl if she got really sick?* Jesse asked himself as he rolled out of bed. If things got really bad, he would call for help, of course, but until Cindy was born, he'd never had to take care of a baby. That lack of experience always made him feel unsure of himself.

Jesse went to the window and opened the blinds to look out at the clear summer morning. The more he thought about Vera's suggestion that he find a wife, the more sense it made. If Lenore should agree to marry him, and for some reason Cindy became ill and Lenore wasn't sure what to do, between the two of them, they could probably figure it out. Lenore always seemed calm and had a level head, so she would probably think things through without going into a panic.

"There's no doubt about it," Jesse said out loud. "Two heads are better than one."

A sense of guilt took over when he thought about asking Lenore to marry him when he wasn't in love with her. *Well, I'm not going to worry about that right now. Just need to take things one step at a time.*

As Lenore stood at the kitchen sink Saturday morning, contemplating the meal she'd had with Jesse the night before, Grandma tapped her on the shoulder. "The dishes are done. How long are you going to stand there staring out the window at nothing?"

"It's not nothing. There are plenty of *veggel* in the yard." Lenore turned and smiled at Grandma. "Well, to be truthful, I wasn't really watching the birds."

"What were you watching?"

"Nothing in particular. I was mostly thinking about last night."

Grandma tipped her head. "Your date with Jesse?"

"Jah, only I'm not sure if it was an actual date. He made no mention of wanting to court me."

"What did he talk about?"

"Mostly the history of the part of Kentucky where he's from."

"Interesting, but not very romantic." Grandma's brows moved up and down.

Lenore stepped away from the sink. "I think Jesse might be lonely, and maybe he enjoys my company."

"And well he should." Grandma placed her hand on Lenore's shoulder. "In addition to being blessed with a pretty face, you're smart, kind, and quite capable, I might add."

Lenore snickered. "I believe you're a bit prejudiced because I'm your granddaughter."

"Maybe so, but the words I spoke were true." Grandma moved across the room to the stove and poured herself a cup of coffee. "Would you like some kaffi, Lenore?"

"No, thank you. Is there anything special you'd like me to do today?" Lenore asked. "Maybe pull weeds or pick some produce from the garden?"

Grandma shook her head. "You've worked hard all week. Why don't you take the day off and do something just for fun?"

Lenore tapped her fingers on the edge of her chin. "I do have one errand I need to run."

"That's not what I would call fun."

"Maybe not, but I promised Sara I would bring in several more of my homemade greeting *kaarte* to sell on consignment in her flower shop."

"You do make some lovely cards. And they've sold quite well in Sara's shop."

"Jah. Her beaded jewelry and keychains have gone over well with her customers too."

"Sara's a busy young woman. I don't know how she finds the time to run her business, do all the duties expected of her as a minister's wife, and make up her lovely beaded items."

"From what I can tell, Sara enjoys what she does, so I'm sure that's why she is able to keep up with it all." Lenore didn't ask the question, but she wondered if Grandma enjoyed all the things she had to do these days. Since Grandpa's stroke, Grandma had more chores to do than ever before. But she'd never heard her complain—she just did what needed to be done with a smile on her face. Hard work and persistence were positive traits both Grandma and Grandpa had passed on to their children and grandchildren.

"Were you planning to take your horse and buggy out to make your card deliveries?" Grandma asked. "Or would you like to give my horse some exercise today?"

"It's such a beautiful summer day, I thought I might either walk to the flower shop or ride my scooter," Lenore replied.

"Won't that be a little difficult with a box full of cards?"

Lenore shook her head. "I'll put them in a wicker basket, and they should be easy to carry. The fresh air and exercise will do me some good."

"All right, dear. Do as you like." Grandma smiled. "Oh, and please tell Sara I said hello and that we hope to see her and Brad soon."

"I will." Lenore hugged her grandmother and hurried from the room to get the greeting cards. If Sara was free, maybe the two of them could have lunch together. It had been awhile since they'd had some one-on-one cousin time.

Outside, Lenore put her wicker basket full of cards inside the metal carrier on the front of her scooter and, using her left foot to push off, headed out of the yard and onto the shoulder of the road.

She'd only made it about halfway into town when a

scraggly-looking dog ran out of a nearby field, chasing a rabbit. Lenore swerved to keep from hitting either animal, but in so doing, she lost control. The next thing she knew, the scooter tipped over and she was lying on the pavement, her greeting cards scattered all around.

Jesse whistled as he guided his horse down the road toward the Lapps' farm. Last night Lenore had left her lightweight jacket in his buggy when he'd dropped her off. He was kind of glad—it gave him an excuse to see her again today. Jesse didn't want Lenore to think he was too aggressive in his efforts to court her, but after the dream he'd had in the wee hours this morning, he'd decided that he needed to find a mother for his little girl as soon as possible. Since Cindy liked the Lapps' granddaughter and responded so well to her, Lenore was the logical candidate. Jesse still felt guilty about pursuing a woman he didn't love. The thing that concerned him the most, though, was whether Lenore would be willing to accept his terms for marriage. No pronouncement of love or physical relationship would most likely be a deterrent for her. He'd be taking a risk asking her to be his wife in name only.

He pursed his lips. *Maybe I should forget the silly notion and rely on Vera to watch Cindy for me, like she's doing today. She said she was willing to do it for as long as I needed her.*

Jesse gripped the horse's reins as he continued to wrestle with his indecisiveness. A lump lodged in his throat as a vision of his sweet Esther flashed in his mind. *What would she want me to do? If only I could communicate with her somehow.*

As Jesse drew closer to the Lapps' place, he spotted Lenore on her hands and knees along the shoulder of the road. Beside her a red scooter lay on its side.

Concerned, he guided his horse to the side of the road and stepped out of the buggy. "What happened? Are you all right?"

"A dog chasing a rabbit ran in front of me, and I lost control of my scooter when I swerved to avoid hitting them." Lenore's chin trembled as she looked at him. "The greeting cards I made and was taking to my cousin's flower shop are probably ruined." She gestured to the cards and envelopes scattered about.

Worried about her welfare, Jesse hadn't even noticed them before. "What about you, Lenore? Are you okay?"

"My legs and arms are scraped up some, but I can move them, so I'm sure there are no broken bones."

"I'll help you pick up the cards and then give you a ride to the flower shop if you like."

"Danki. That would be much appreciated."

Jesse looked around for a place to secure his horse. Seeing a tree along the road a few yards ahead, he led the animal there and tied him to a branch, then joined Lenore in her quest to rescue the cards.

A short time later they had them all picked up. A few had been damaged, but most appeared to be fine. Jesse picked up the scooter and put it in the back of his open buggy, then he helped Lenore, holding her basket full of cards, into the passenger's seat. "Would you rather I take you back to your grandparents' house? You should probably put some antiseptic on the places your legs and arms got scraped right away."

She shook her head with a look of determination. "I'd rather go to Sara's flower shop and drop off these cards. I'm sure she has a first-aid kit on hand so I can tend my wounds there."

"All right then. Just tell me which direction to go and we'll be on our way."

⁓

As Sara took down the old window display and began putting up a new one using birdhouses as a focal point, she reflected on last night's Bible study. She couldn't help wondering if the man she'd met there might have known her mother or even her biological father.

*Wish I'd had more time to talk to him,* Sara thought as she placed a small ceramic bird next to one of the wooden birdhouses her cousin Ben had made. She looked forward to the next Bible study and hoped she would have a chance to speak with Rick Osprey again. She'd have to be careful how she approached the topic, though, so he wouldn't think she was being nosy or infringing on his personal life. Sara didn't want to cut into their time of reading the scriptures either or say anything of a personal nature in front of the others who attended the Bible study.

Sara's attention was captured when she looked out the window and noticed Lenore limping in the direction of the store. Jesse walked beside her, carrying a wicker basket.

Sara stepped down from the display platform and greeted them at the door. "What happened, Lenore? Why are you limping?"

Lenore explained how she'd fallen off her scooter, and said that when Jesse came along, he'd helped her pick up the cards and offered her a ride to the flower shop. "I'm hoping you have some bandages and antiseptic here." Lenore winced as she held out her arm with several nasty scrapes. "My knees got scraped up too, but at least I wasn't seriously hurt." She pointed at the basket in Jesse's hand. "Some of my cards got ruined, but I brought the good ones Jesse and I rescued."

"We can look at those later." Sara motioned toward the back room. "Right now we should tend to those nasty scrapes." She turned to face Jesse. "Please place the basket of cards on the counter. I'll take a look at them as soon as I've taken care of Lenore's wounds. You can sit over there while you wait, if you want."

"Sure, no problem."

Sara gathered up her first-aid kit from her small office and found Lenore sitting in the back room. As she tended her cousin's wounds, she posed a question. "Is Jesse interested in you?"

Lenore blushed. "I—I'm not sure. He did take me out to supper last night."

Sara grinned. "That's a start in the courting process, right?"

"I'm not sure if we are actually courting, but he has been kind to me ever since I started watching his little girl."

"Where is Cindy today?"

"With the great-aunt of Jesse's late wife." Lenore looked down at her bandaged leg. "Thanks for taking care of my injuries."

"No problem. If I was the one who'd gotten hurt, I'm sure you would have done the same for me."

"Of course I would." Lenore squeezed Sara's hand. "I'm so glad you came into our lives."

"Same here. If I hadn't found that letter in Mama's Bible, I never would have discovered her wonderful family I knew nothing about. You and your folks, as well as Grandpa and Grandma, have been a real blessing to me."

Lenore smiled. "You have blessed our lives too."

Glancing toward the door leading to the front of the flower shop, Sara whispered, "And now you're a blessing to Jesse and his daughter."

# Chapter 15

On the last Friday of July, after Michelle prayed and read her devotional book, she knew without reservation that she needed to speak with Ezekiel again about his desire to move to an Amish community in New York.

Ezekiel had gone out to the barn right after breakfast to feed their horses and Michelle's dog. When he came in and they were seated at the table, she would bring up the subject.

Michelle opened a carton of eggs and cracked four into a bowl. By the time she had them mixed up and frying in a pan, Ezekiel came into the kitchen.

"*Guder mariye.*" He strode across the room and kissed the back of her neck. "Bet those *oier* will taste mighty good."

She turned her head and smiled. "Good morning. There's some leftover sausage warming in the oven to go with the scrambled eggs."

"I'm lucky to have you, Michelle. You take real good care of me."

She smiled briefly, and when the eggs were done, she put them on a platter, along with the sausage links, and placed it on the table. "Would you prefer orange or apple juice?" she asked when he went to the sink to wash his hands.

"Apple sounds good." He took a seat at the table.

Michelle poured them each a glass of juice and sat in the chair beside him. Following their silent prayer, she passed him the eggs and sausage. "I've been thinking and praying about your idea of moving to New York."

"Have you reached a decision?" He gave her full eye contact.

Michelle gave a nod. "If it's what you really want to do, then I'm willing to go with you."

Ezekiel's face broke into a wide smile. "I'm glad. This will be a chance for us to start over in a new place, and I'll be doing something I enjoy instead of working at Mom and Dad's greenhouse." He dished up some eggs and sausage before handing Michelle the platter. "My only concern is how my folks will respond when they hear of our decision to move."

❧

As Lenore sat with Cindy on a blanket in the yard, her thoughts went to Jesse. Ever since he'd rescued her from the scooter accident two weeks ago, he'd been more talkative and attentive. She pulled her fingers gently through Cindy's curly hair as she thought more about the little girl's father. Jesse was a kind, gentle man—and rather good looking too. It was probably wrong to be thinking such thoughts when she barely knew the man, but Lenore felt drawn to him.

She reached over and tickled Cindy's bare toes. "Maybe it's you, sweet girl, who makes me think I'm attracted to your daadi. It might just be the special bond that's been made between me and you."

When a pretty butterfly floated in front of them, Cindy clapped her chubby hands and squealed.

*"Fleddermaus."* Lenore pointed as the beautiful monarch landed on a flower close by. "Beautiful butterfly."

Cindy's gaze remained fixed on the monarch, and when it flew farther away, she crawled off the blanket and started across the grass.

Lenore let her go for a little bit, knowing it was good for a child to get in touch with nature through the texture of grass on their skin. She looked up toward the blue sky with puffy white clouds. Spending time outdoors and breathing in fresh air, was good for anyone, no matter their age.

Cindy stopped crawling when a grasshopper zipped in front of her. Lenore held her breath and waited to see what the little girl would do. One hand came out, and then the other as Cindy giggled, rocking back and forth on her knees.

*"Hoischreck."* Lenore repeated the Pennsylvania Dutch word for grasshopper several times. After reading a book on child care recently, Lenore had learned that talking to a baby was a key part of their language development. It also stated that repetition was the key, because words spoken to a baby became stored away in the child's brain. Eventually they'd be able to use those words and respond to the adult who had spoken to them.

A few seconds went by before the grasshopper hopped away. Cindy swiveled her little body around and crawled back to Lenore. Picking the child up and caressing her face, Lenore struggled not to give in to the tears forming behind her eyes. In such a short time she had formed a strong attachment to this darling little girl. *If only. . . If only you were mine.*

"Dad. . .Mom. . .can we talk to you a minute?" Ezekiel asked when he and Michelle entered the greenhouse.

"Sure, but you'd better make it quick. It's only a matter of time before a slew of customers show up," Ezekiel's father responded. "As you well know, the summer months are our busiest time of year."

Ezekiel shook his head. "I haven't forgotten, and what I have to say won't take long." He slipped his arm around Michelle's waist as she waited nervously for him to proceed.

Ezekiel cleared his throat a couple of times. "Michelle and I have an announcement to make."

His mother's eyes widened, and she clapped her hands. "Are you two in a family way?"

"No, we're not."

Just the mention of being pregnant sent a stab of regret into Michelle's soul.

"What then?" Belinda tipped her head.

"We have an opportunity to move to an Amish community in New York, and I'll be taking over someone's business. I've already talked to the Amish man in Clymer, and the wheels are in motion. Even so, we probably won't make the move till sometime after the new year." Ezekiel undid the top button on his shirt and rubbed his neck. No doubt he felt as apprehensive as Michelle did right now. She didn't like conflict and feared there might be one between Ezekiel and his parents.

Belinda squinted as she pointed a finger at Michelle. "Was this your idea? Did you ask Ezekiel to move because you've never felt welcome in our community here? Because if that's the case, I can assure you—"

Michelle shook her head, but before she could say anything, Ezekiel spoke again. "Moving to New York was my idea, Mom. You and Dad know that I've never been happy working here in the greenhouse. I enjoy working with bees and selling my organic raw honey." He stood rigidly with his hands behind his back.

Belinda's shoulders drooped, and her chin trembled slightly. "But how will we manage without your help here?"

Ezekiel's father nudged her arm. "Didn't you hear what our son said? He's not happy working in the greenhouse."

"I know, but—"

"We'll manage without him. Our son has a right to live where he wants and work at the job of his choosing. We cannot stand in his way." Vernon looked back at Ezekiel. "What kind of business will you be taking over, Son?"

"I'll be making supplies for beekeepers. You know. . .things like hive kits, frames, foundations, and extracting equipment. I'll even be selling protective clothing, honey containers, medications for mite and pest control, as well as all the tools needed for the job of beekeeping." Ezekiel spoke in a bubbly tone. Clearly he was excited about this new venture.

Belinda's voice cracked as she said in a near whisper, "Do what you think is best, Son, and go with our blessing."

A slow smile spread across Ezekiel's face, and he gave both of his parents a hug. "Danki, Mom and Dad."

While Michelle still struggled with mixed emotions concerning their move to New York, she knew in her heart that her place was with her husband. Her throat clogged with tears. But oh, how she dreaded saying goodbye to Mary Ruth and Willis, not to mention Sara, Brad, and all of Ezekiel's family. It would be an adjustment to start over in a strange place, but with God's help they would do it.

# Chapter 16

The first two weeks of August were busier than ever. Not only was Lenore taking care of Cindy, but she also was putting up garden produce for the winter and getting ready for the new school term. Lenore had gone out to supper with Jesse again, and at Grandma's invitation he'd eaten supper with them on several occasions—including Lenore's birthday last week. Lenore's parents and brothers had been there too, and it had been a fun evening, filled with lively banter and laughter. Sara and Brad were involved in a church activity, so they weren't able to come, but Michelle and Ezekiel had dropped by briefly to wish Lenore a happy birthday.

Grandma had given Lenore a lovely throw pillow for her bed that she'd hand-quilted. Mom gave Lenore a set of pillowcases she'd embroidered along the edges and said it was for her hope chest. Peter and Ben went in on a gift card to Shady Maple in East Earl—the largest restaurant in the area. Dad's gift was a card with some money in it so she could buy whatever she wanted. Even Jesse had brought her a gift—a book on the history of Christian County, Kentucky. All in all it had been a pleasant evening, and the more time Lenore spent with Jesse, the more she liked him. She'd quickly realized that it wouldn't take much for her to fall in love with Cindy's father. But the question was, had he begun to develop any feelings toward her that went beyond friendship? If so, he hadn't verbalized them.

*Of course,* Lenore reasoned as she placed Cindy in her high chair, *we've only known each other a short time. It's too soon to be thinking of anything more than having Jesse as a friend. I need to be patient and see how things go.*

Cindy slapped her chubby hand against the wooden high chair's tray, scattering Lenore's introspections. "Hold on, sweet girl, and I'll feed you some lunch."

The little girl babbled something unintelligible as she grinned and looked up at Lenore.

"That child sure likes you," Grandma said when she wheeled Grandpa into the kitchen. Even though he could walk with the aid of his cane, he often preferred to use the wheelchair.

Lenore smiled. "I like her too."

"You need a few bopplin of your own," Grandpa mumbled as Grandma pushed him up to the table.

Lenore saw where this discussion might lead, so she quickly changed the topic. "Grandma and I picked lots of *tomaets* this morning." She gestured to the plate full of sliced tomatoes on the table. "They'll go nicely on our ham-and-cheese sandwiches."

"Yum." He smacked his lips.

"Yum." Cindy mimicked him. At least it sounded like she had said "yum."

"Here you go, sweetie." Lenore placed a few pieces of cooked carrots on Cindy's tray and was rewarded with another big grin.

"Bet she won't eat those." Grandpa scrunched his nose.

"Just watch."

Cindy rolled one of the mushy carrots around on the tray a few seconds, picked it up, and popped it right in her mouth.

"See, Willis, you guessed wrong." Grandma took out a loaf of homemade whole-wheat bread and placed it on the table. Lenore opened a container of cooked squash and gave Cindy a taste. The little girl didn't seem to mind that it was cold. She ate it hungrily and then picked up another carrot Lenore had placed on her tray.

"I'll feed her some applesauce after we've eaten our sandwiches." She glanced at Grandpa, who wore a crooked smile as he watched Cindy eat.

After Grandma joined them at the table, they bowed their heads for silent prayer.

About halfway through the meal, a knock sounded on the back door.

"It's open. Come in," Grandma called.

A few seconds later, Michelle entered the room. Instead of her usual perky stride, she walked with her head down, like she was the bearer of bad news.

"It's good to see you, Michelle. If you haven't had lunch yet, come join us for a sandwich." Apparently oblivious to Michelle's somber mood, Grandma pointed to the empty seat beside Lenore.

Heaving a sigh, Michelle sank into the chair. "I came over here to give you some news."

"I hope it's good news. We surely could use some of that these days." Grandma clasped her hands under her chin, looking at Michelle expectantly.

"Ezekiel and I will definitely be moving to New York in a few months. His parents gave us their blessing, and the business sale is going through."

Grandpa's eyes widened, Lenore dropped the spoon she'd been using to feed Cindy, and Grandma let out a little squeak.

"We'll miss you, of course, but I'm sure you'll make lots of new friends in your new community." Grandma spoke with feeling. "Please tell us a bit more about the new business Ezekiel will be involved in."

Lenore continued to feed Cindy as she listened to Michelle explain the details of the business Ezekiel would be taking over. This certainly seemed like a spontaneous decision—one she hoped they'd prayed about. But it wasn't her place to make any negative comments or throw cold water on their plans, so Lenore kept her thoughts on the matter to herself.

"Ezekiel feels that it's God's will for our lives, so it's not for me to say otherwise," Michelle continued. "We'll come back for visits whenever we can, and we hope our friends and family will be able to come see our new home too." Michelle's tone sounded overly cheerful all of a sudden, but the way she sat slumped in her seat told Lenore that her friend was not entirely thrilled about moving.

Lenore felt sorry for Michelle. No doubt she felt forced to move because her husband wanted a change. Being married meant making sacrifices sometimes, and a wife's place was with her husband. No doubt Michelle would adjust to the change once they got to New York and settled in.

Lenore reached over and took her friend's hand. "As Grandma said before, we will miss you, and we'll be sure to keep you in our prayers." She looked at her grandparents. "Isn't that right?"

With a grunt sounding much like one of his previously owned hogs, Grandpa moved his head up and down. Grandma nodded too, but the tears in her eyes could not be concealed. Although Michelle was not part of their family by blood, she'd become like another granddaughter to them. This would be one more adjustment for Grandma and Grandpa to get through. *But I'll be here for them,* Lenore told herself. *And I'll pray for Michelle and Ezekiel— that the move will go smoothly and it will be an easy adjustment for both of them.*

❧

After the lunch dishes were washed and Cindy had been put down for a nap, Lenore felt like taking a walk to the barn. She hadn't read any notes from either of the prayer jars recently and figured she could use some words of inspiration or encouragement.

Sadie greeted Lenore as soon as she entered the barn, wagging her tail and begging for some attention.

"How are you doing, girl? Did you come in here to take a nap or pester the katze?" Too many times Lenore had caught the collie running after one of the cats. She'd never hurt any of them, though—just barked and chased until the felines found a safe place to hide.

Sadie responded by nuzzling Lenore's hand. Then she flopped down with a lazy grunt.

Chuckling, Lenore stepped around the dog and went to fetch the ladder. After climbing it and retrieving the old jar, she took it outside and seated herself at the picnic table. She wanted to read the messages written on several of the slips of paper, and it was too warm and stuffy in the barn to remain there very long. The picnic table was the perfect spot because it was shaded by a huge maple tree, which offered a nice respite from the heat.

Once Lenore was seated on the bench, she opened the lid, reached deep inside, and removed a slip of paper. A verse of scripture had been written on this one, and she read it out loud. " 'Wherefore be ye not unwise, but understanding what the will of the Lord is. Ephesians 5:17.' "

Lenore reflected on the verse a few minutes before taking another note out of the jar. This one was a prayer. "Dear God, please help me learn how to discern Your will. I want to do what's right, but I am so confused."

Lenore rolled her neck from side to side. *What was my aunt Rhoda confused about? If only I would find a note in one of the jars that would explain things better. Did she know when she left home that she would never connect with any of her family again?*

"Lenore, the boppli's awake and crying pretty hard," Grandma called from the house. "Do you want me to change her *windel*?"

"No, that's okay," Lenore shouted through cupped hands. "I'll be right there."

She got up and headed back to the barn to put the jar away. The next time Lenore had a free moment, she would come back out and read a few more of the notes her aunt had written. Surely one of them would reveal more information.

# Chapter 17

Lancaster County was in the middle of a sweltering, overly humid heat wave. Farmers across the road from Lenore's grandparents' home toiled under the blistering sun, while young barefoot children found solace in nearby ponds, where they swam, fished, and enjoyed the simple pleasure of being together in a place where it was cooler. School would be starting in ten days, and then it would be back to books and a more structured schedule. For Lenore, that meant giving up precious time spent with Cindy as she returned to her job of teaching. Since Jesse had not found anyone to replace Lenore, his wife's great-aunt had agreed to watch his baby daughter again.

"I'm gonna miss you, sweet girl," Lenore murmured, taking a seat on the porch swing and placing Cindy in her lap.

The child leaned heavily against Lenore's chest while sucking her thumb.

Sighing, Lenore stroked Cindy's silky curls, admiring the softness of the baby's pretty hair. What she wouldn't give to have a child like this. Although teaching was a satisfying profession, it didn't compare to the joy of motherhood. Not that Lenore knew firsthand what it was like to have children, but she'd witnessed plenty of interactions between mothers and their little ones to realize how much she longed to be a parent.

As she got the swing moving rhythmically, Lenore closed her eyes and listened to the cicadas singing their summer song from nearby trees.

～∂～

Sara took a seat at her desk to compare the figures in the ledger of the previous month to the profit the shop had made so far in August. The flower shop had done well this summer, and as far as she could tell, word of mouth seemed to be the best form of advertising. Sara's assumption came from all the positive comments she'd received when people came into the store and mentioned they'd heard about it from a friend or relative.

Sara looked at the perpetual calendar on her desk, filled with beautiful pictures of Amish country that an English man who'd grown up in Pennsylvania had taken. Flipping the page over each day was a continual reminder of how much she loved living here. She hoped Brad would be able to continue serving as pastor to the church in Lancaster for a good many years. Sara couldn't imagine having to move away from Grandma and Grandpa.

Her thoughts went to Michelle and Ezekiel. Ezekiel had family here, and Michelle had established a good many friends. Starting over would be quite an adjustment—especially not knowing anyone in their new Amish community.

Sara tapped her pen against the ledger. Life was full of changes—some good, some not so beneficial. Certain people adjusted to change easily, while others resisted it and felt depression or anger about their circumstances.

She closed her eyes briefly. *God, please grant me the courage to accept any changes that might be in my husband's and my future.*

Sara's cell phone rang, and she was quick to answer when the caller ID showed it was her husband. "Hi, Brad. How's it going?"

"Good. I'm just calling to remind you that tonight's Bible study will begin at six, since I invited everyone for grilled burgers."

"I haven't forgotten, and I'll make sure to pick up a couple of salads and some baked beans at the deli before I head home."

"Sounds good. See you later, hon."

"Oh, before you hang up—have you heard anything from Rick Osprey. . .about whether he plans to attend Bible study tonight?"

"No, I haven't, but since he only came to the first one and we haven't seen him at church, I'm guessing he won't be coming."

"Have you tried calling him?"

"Yes, several times, but all I've gotten is his voice mail. I don't have his address, just a cell number, or I'd drop by his house to check on him."

"That's too bad. Guess we'll have to wait and see whether he shows up or not. I'll see you in a few hours, Brad."

Sara clicked her phone off and glanced at the inspirational quote on today's calendar page: *How much better off we'd be if we learned to listen to God's still, small voice, instead of trying to do things our own way.*

"Okay, Lord, I get the message," Sara said out loud. "If it's meant for me to speak with Mr. Osprey again, it will happen in Your time."

❧

Jesse's palms felt so sweaty he could barely hold on to his horse's reins. He was heading to the Lapps' on a mission, and it wasn't just to pick up Cindy. Today he planned to ask Lenore if he could continue seeing her socially after she started teaching school. What he really wanted to do was ask her to give up teaching and marry him, but it was too soon for a proposal. If Jesse asked Lenore to become his wife without a proper time of courting, she might figure out that he had an ulterior motive.

*Vera can't watch Cindy indefinitely, and in addition to caring for my little girl, I need someone to run my household.* These were selfish thoughts, but Jesse was concerned about Cindy's need to have someone care for her on a full-time basis, not just a few hours a day. And he sure couldn't ask Lenore to move into his house without marrying her. This was a delicate situation, and he needed to proceed with caution.

The Lapps' collie barked a friendly greeting as Jesse guided his horse and buggy up the lane. Seeing Lenore by the clothesline, he headed in that direction as soon as his horse was secured to the rail.

Sadie ran beside him, barking and wagging her tail. Jesse paused briefly to give the dog a few pats.

"Need some help taking the clothes down?" He pointed to the

partially filled wicker basket.

Lenore's dimples deepened as she smiled up at him and nodded. "It's kind of you to offer."

Jesse removed a bulky towel from the line. "How'd my little maedel do today?"

"Very well. She has a good appetite and is learning how to feed herself some foods."

Jesse grinned as Lenore filled him in on what Cindy had eaten for lunch. "She's growing so fast; it won't be long before she'll be ready to eat big people's food."

Lenore took down two hand towels and placed them in the basket. "Jah, babies don't stay little long enough. Just like the vegetable plants in my grandma's garden, they shoot right up, and before you know it they're ready for harvest." Lenore giggled. "Guess there's really no comparing your daughter to produce from the garden though."

He laughed. "There is in the respect that both grow quickly."

"Jah."

Jesse removed several more pieces of laundry, and Lenore did the same. She was about to pick up the basket when he stopped her. "I'll carry it up to the house for you. But first I'd like to ask you a question."

"Certainly. What do you want to know?"

"You will be teaching school again soon, and I won't be bringing Cindy over here every day anymore." Jesse paused and moistened his dry lips. "So. . .I was wondering. . . Would it be all right if we continue to see each other socially?"

Lenore's cheeks turned a pretty pink as she moved her head slowly up and down. "I would like that, Jesse."

He bent down and picked up the basket. "That's good. Jah, it's a real good thing."

⁓

Sara listened with interest as Brad shared a passage of scripture with those who had come to their barbecue and Bible study. " 'Let not your heart be troubled: ye believe in God, believe also in me.' You see," Brad continued, "as a new believer, you may be tempted to become discouraged when things don't go well. It's easy to find ourselves questioning God." He placed his hand on the open Bible. "That's why it's important to study the scriptures and seek God's will in all you do."

All heads nodded in agreement. The participants were obviously eager to learn about God.

Sara thought about Rick Osprey. As expected, he hadn't shown up. It was too bad he couldn't be here to take part in this study for new Christians. Sara hoped that nothing had discouraged him or, worse, that he'd given up on his faith. Perhaps it was the reason they hadn't seen or heard from him these past several weeks. Or could it be that the questions Sara asked him during the first Bible study had made him nervous? Did he suspect she was Rhoda's daughter? Was he trying to avoid her? But how could he know what was on her mind? Sara hadn't mentioned her mother or said anything about trying to find her biological father that evening. Yet she supposed the discussion they'd had about his teen and young adult years might have hit a nerve.

*I am being paranoid,* Sara told herself. *After searching and asking questions of people who knew Mama during her teen years and coming up with nothing, I'm grasping at straws. Rick may not have known my mother.*

She shifted on the unyielding picnic bench, trying to find a more comfortable position. *I need to put my obsession with finding my father aside and get on with the business of living and being a good wife.*

## Chapter 18

Early Monday morning, August 26, Lenore entered the schoolhouse and placed her things on her desk. At the moment, her thoughts were conflicted. While it felt good to sit behind a teacher's desk again, she missed the joy of caring for Cindy and visiting with Jesse when he came by after work to pick up his daughter. But she would see them at church this Sunday, and Grandma had invited Jesse to bring Cindy to their house for Sunday evening supper. That was certainly something to look forward to. In the meantime, Lenore needed to focus on getting acquainted with the scholars who attended this school.

She glanced at the battery-operated clock on the far wall. It was eight fifteen, and school started at eight thirty sharp, so the children should be arriving soon.

Since Lenore had not taught this group of scholars before and didn't know how well they conducted themselves, she hoped there would be no behavioral problems. At the last school where she'd taught, one boy in particular had been a challenge at first. She'd worked diligently to teach him, as well as the rest of the students, how important it was to practice the Golden Rule in class and during recess. But Thomas Beiler, full of mischief and a bit hyperactive, had stretched her patience several times when he teased other children or defied the classroom rules.

Lenore had learned during her years of teaching never to let things get out of control or give one of her students the upper hand. The goal of every good teacher was to teach her pupils the skills needed to lead a useful Amish life, as well as how to function and do business in the outside world. In Amish schools children were taught reading, writing, arithmetic, English, and history. All of these skills would be needed once the scholars graduated school after finishing the eighth grade. From there, some boys would go back to the farm to learn agriculture skills. Others might serve an apprenticeship to Amish shop owners or other businesspeople in the area. Girls polished their homemaker skills under the guidance of their mothers, and some might work outside the home for other Amish or to keep house for a local English family.

Lenore's thoughts were pushed aside when she heard the sound of children's laughter outside the schoolhouse.

Pulling in a deep breath, she left her desk and went to ring the bell, announcing the start of the school day and letting the scholars know it was time to come inside.

Things went well during the first part of the day, and Lenore's assistant teacher, Viola Weaver, was a big help.

At ten o'clock, Lenore dismissed the children for morning recess. They were encouraged to use the outhouse, get a drink of water, and sharpen their pencils so that these things would not need to be done during class. When those items had been taken care of, it was time to go outside and play. With thirty children in the class, ranging from first to eighth grade, it would be difficult to start an activity they all could engage in and enjoy. Lenore got a game of baseball going for the older ones, while Viola kept an eye on the younger ones as they enjoyed swinging and climbing on the old-fashioned wooden playground equipment.

The ball game was going at full speed when a young girl named Linda ran out of the girls' outhouse, hollering as though there were no tomorrow.

Lenore ran quickly to the child. "What's wrong? Are you hurt?"

*"Der weschp hot ihr gschtoche."* Linda's sister, Katie, pointed to the wasp nest outside the girls' outhouse.

Lenore felt immediate concern hearing that one of the children had been stung by a wasp. She would look in the shed behind the schoolhouse to see if there was any insecticide she could spray on the nest. Before she had a chance to do that, however, one of the older boys rushed up to her. "Don't worry, Teacher. I'll take care of the nest while you tend to Linda's arm."

She gave him an appreciative nod. "Thank you, Andrew." Lenore took Linda's hand. "Let's go inside and I'll put some drawing salve on that stinger."

Sniffling all the way, the little girl went willingly with Lenore across the yard. Glancing over her shoulder before stepping inside, Lenore was glad to see Viola take charge of the little ones again while the older children continued playing ball. She hoped things would go better the rest of the day.

Before recess was over, Lenore had Linda resting at her desk while the salve was doing its job. She looked over at the child, sitting at her desk with her head down. "I'll be back in a few moments, Linda."

"Okay."

Lenore opened the schoolhouse door and stepped onto the porch, looking out toward the sunny schoolyard. All the children were busy playing. She saw Andrew and called to him. "Did you take care of the nest?"

"Yes, I sprayed it real good then knocked it down after that. I even looked around the rest of the building but didn't see any more wasps or nests."

"That's good to know. Thank you for taking care of it so quickly."

"You're welcome, Teacher."

Lenore went back inside and checked on Linda. "How does your arm feel now?" she asked.

"It doesn't hurt as much as it did."

"I'm glad to hear that." Lenore lifted the child's arm and turned it gently so she could see the lightly reddened spot better. Then she carefully rubbed away the dried medicine. "I don't see any sign of the stinger in there. I think you should be all right now."

Linda grinned. "Thank you, Teacher. That was real scary being stung by a wasp."

"I'm sure it was. But don't worry anymore, because the nest

is gone now." Lenore glanced at the clock on the wall across the room. "It's time to start class, so I'm going to call the other children."

Lenore rang the bell and watched as the scholars filed in and took their seats. A few of them had stopped to get a second drink of water, but soon all the children were at their desks, looking up at her with expectant expressions.

She took a seat at her desk. "Before we begin, I wanted to let you all know that Linda is doing fine after getting stung by a wasp."

The child bobbed her blond head, and many of the students smiled.

Lenore tapped the little bell on her desk. "All right now, class, grades three through eight will have reading class with me, while Viola works with the first and second grades on their numbers in their workbook."

The older students began reading their lesson for the day, preparing to answer Lenore's questions that would determine their reading comprehension. Once the children had been given sufficient time to read their lesson, Lenore called each grade in turn up to the front of the room to read some and answer her questions.

As the children read, Lenore got up and opened a few windows to bring some fresh air into the stuffy room. With summer still in full swing, the days could get rather warm. But not too far in the future, fall would arrive.

Earlier this morning, Viola had mentioned that her dad had read in the local paper's forecast that rain was on its way. Viola was anticipating the rain eagerly because it would cool things off and help to freshen the stale humid air. Lenore had to agree, but she still preferred the warmer summer weather.

She smiled to herself. Teaching again felt good, and so far she had stayed in control. She hoped the rest of the day would go as well.

"How are things here today?" Ivan asked when he entered Mary Ruth's kitchen.

"Lenore started teaching again, and it's been so quiet around here I scarcely know what to do with myself." Mary Ruth's forehead wrinkled. "I miss Jesse's sweet little girl too. If I didn't have the responsibility of caring for your daed, I may have volunteered to watch Cindy myself."

Ivan shook his head. "Watching a boppli is a full-time job, and since you have enough on your hands taking care of Dad, I'm glad you didn't volunteer to watch Jesse's baby." He glanced around. "And speaking of Dad, where is he right now? Didn't see him in the living room when I first came in, and I wanted to check with him and see if there are any specific chores he'd like me to do before I head back to the store."

Mary Ruth's mouth puckered as she picked up the coffeepot to fill it with fresh water. "That's strange. After lunch, with the use of his cane, he went to the living room and sat in his favorite chair. Maybe he got up and made his way down the hall to the *baadschtubb*."

"I don't think so, Mom. When I came down the hall, the door to the bathroom was open, and I didn't see any sign of Dad." Ivan leaned on the counter near the sink. "Maybe he decided to take a nap and went to your room to lie down."

She set the coffeepot down. "He usually naps in his chair, but I'll go to our room and check, in case he decided to go there."

Mary Ruth left the kitchen and shuffled down the hall. When she arrived at their door and found it slightly ajar, she opened it a little further and stepped inside. A chill ran up her spine. Willis lay facedown on the floor near the foot of their bed. Could he have stumbled and fallen? Become dizzy and passed out?

"Willis, can you hear me?"

He lay there unmoving.

Fear gripped Mary Ruth's chest like a vise. She wasn't strong enough to pick up her husband and put him on the bed, but she needed to get him off the floor and evaluate his condition.

She cupped her trembling hands around her mouth and hollered, "Ivan! Come quick! Your daed's fallen, and I can't get him to wake up."

# *Chapter 19*

Sara had just finished waiting on a customer when Brad came into the shop, wide-eyed and with deep furrows lining his forehead. "I got an urgent call from your uncle Ivan about twenty minutes ago. He asked me to come here right away and get you." He moved close to her desk. "We'll go by the schoolhouse and get Lenore next."

Sara blinked rapidly as she stared up at him. "You're scaring me. What is it, Brad?"

"Your grandma found your grandpa on the floor of their bedroom, and she couldn't get him to wake up. Fortunately, Ivan was at their house. He got ahold of me as soon as he called 911."

"Is. . .is Grandpa gonna be okay?" Her voice wavered as she clutched the pen in her hand.

"They don't know yet. He's been taken to the hospital in Lancaster. From the way Ivan talked, it didn't sound good." Brad gestured to the front door. "We'd better go now."

"Okay, just let me tell Misty I'm going." As Sara headed for the back room on shaky legs, images of what might happen flashed through her mind. She paused at the door of the other room and closed her eyes. *Dear Lord, please let Grandpa be okay, and be with my dear grandma right now. She must be so worried and afraid.*

"I am surprised to see you here. Aren't you supposed to be at your shop this time of the day?" Lenore asked when Sara entered the schoolhouse and hurried up to Lenore's desk. Most visitors didn't show up at school right in the middle of class.

"Grandpa's in the hospital, and Brad's waiting outside in the van to take us there." Sara spoke breathlessly. "Can you dismiss school early and come with us now?"

"School will be out in half an hour, and my assistant can take over for the rest of the day." Heart pounding and mouth quivering, Lenore rushed over to Viola and explained the situation.

"Of course I'll take charge of the class." Viola placed her hand on Lenore's arm. "I'm sorry about your grandfather. I'll pray that everything will turn out for the best."

Lenore managed a weak smile, got her purse, and followed her cousin out the door. As they headed for Brad's van, Sara slipped her arm around Lenore's waist. "Grandpa's going to be okay. He has to be."

❧

*Lancaster*

"Where's Grandpa? Is he going to be all right?" Lenore drew in several quick breaths in an effort to calm herself. When she, Sara, and Brad entered the waiting room, they saw Grandma huddled beside Lenore's dad. The scene was almost too painful to bear. Her grandmother's unfocused stare and the grim twist of her mouth let Lenore know Grandpa's situation must be grave.

"My daed's suffered a heart attack, but we won't know how bad it was until the doctors have finished examining him," Lenore's father explained. "I did CPR on him before the paramedics came to the house, but I'm not sure it did any good." He leaned forward, rubbing a spot on the bridge of his nose.

Sara and Lenore went down on their knees in front of Grandma, while Brad stood behind her chair with his hands resting on her trembling shoulders. "Let's pray." Brad spoke quietly but with assurance.

All heads bowed as he prayed out loud: "Heavenly Father, please be with Willis right now, as well as those who are caring for him. If it be Your will, we ask for complete healing. If not, then give us the grace to accept the outcome and the courage to go on without Willis should You decide to take him. We ask it all in the name of Jesus. Amen."

Grandma sniffed and wiped the tears running down her cheeks with the tissue Sara handed her. "I can't imagine my life without my dear husband, but if it's God's will to take him, then I'll have to accept it and go on. That's what Willis would want me to do."

"It's not easy to accept it as God's will when someone you love dies." Sara's tone was filled with emotion. Lenore figured her cousin must be thinking about when her mother had died. No doubt Sara had questioned God many times and perhaps had never fully come to grips with her loss.

Lenore stiffened. "We're being too negative. Grandpa is going to be fine. He got better after his stroke, and I believe he'll get better this time."

With a slow nod, Grandma sank into a chair. Everyone else took seats too and talked quietly until Lenore's mother and brothers arrived.

"How's Grandpa doing?" Peter asked, clutching his father's shoulder.

"We don't know yet. He's still being examined. They're running some tests to see how bad his heart is." Dad rubbed his eyes. "That's why we're all waiting out here." He looked over at Mom. "Who's minding the store, or did you put the Closed sign in the window?"

"I left Anna in charge, and Becky is also there to help out. The boys and I wanted to be here, and I'm sure everything at the store will be fine with our two capable employees in control."

"Okay." Dad blew out his breath with a puff of air that lifted the hair off his forehead. "I hope we hear something soon. I've never been good at waiting for things, and I'm nearly out of patience."

A short time later, a doctor came in and approached Grandma. "We did all we could for your husband, Mrs. Lapp, and I'm sorry to have to tell you this, but unfortunately, his heart gave out. Willis is gone and is now resting in peace."

Lenore's fingers touched her parted lips, and Sara stifled a gasp. Grandma, however, merely stood and said, "May I please see him?"

The doctor nodded. "Of course. Follow me."

"I'm coming too." Lenore's father got up and, pressing a fist against his chest, followed his mother out of the room.

Sara reached over and clasped Lenore's hand. "I. . .I can't

believe our dear grandpa is gone."

Lenore's throat felt too swollen for her to talk. All she could manage was a nod.

Within the next three days, Grandpa's body would be laid to rest, and everything about their family's life would be forever changed. All they would have left of Grandpa were the memories they'd made with him over the years.

⁘

Mary Ruth and Ivan followed the doctor through the first set of double doors and then through another set. The doctor turned to them. "We have a little walk yet. We'll be going down a couple of floors to where he is."

Mary Ruth saw the bank of elevators and dreaded what was coming. They took the first one available, despite the busy foot traffic around them. Mary Ruth looked toward her feet as she rode the elevator down to their stop. When the doors opened, they were in front of a small nurses' station. A vase with flowers stood welcoming them on the receptionist desk, but Mary Ruth barely took notice. One of the female staff members came over and led them to the room Willis was in.

Once at the doorway, the doctor expressed his condolences and apologized again that he couldn't save Willis. Then he dismissed himself.

Mary Ruth stood beside Ivan for a moment, trying to let it all sink in, while the nurse waited with a somber expression. "You may go in and see your husband, Mrs. Lapp."

Mary Ruth nodded. She reached out to her son with trembling hands and held on to his arm. "I'm so glad you're here with me, Ivan. I never imagined how difficult this part of marriage was going to be." Mary Ruth paused. "I know we need to do this, saying goodbye to your father and my dear, beloved husband, but it's taking all my strength and determination."

"I know, Mom, and we'll do this together." Ivan's eyes filled with tears. He waited until she was ready, then walked alongside her into the intensely quiet room.

She clung to his arm the whole way, while the lump in her throat grew larger. The closer they got to his lifeless form lying on the cot, the slower Mary Ruth moved. *This doesn't seem real to me. If only it was a terrible dream.* She wiped at the uncontrollable tears with the tissue she'd tucked inside her dress sleeve.

When they came up to his bed, Mary Ruth stared at Willis, then closed her eyes tightly as memories of the two of them on their wedding day began to flow, along with more tears. Their courting also came to her like it happened just yesterday, and she recalled so vividly how sweet his manner was and how often he'd made her laugh.

She also remembered with sadness the time Willis had said that he hoped when the good Lord decided to take them, they'd leave the earth together. It was a pleasant thought but apparently was not meant to be.

Mary Ruth placed her hand upon his sheet-covered shoulder and wept. *The love of my life is gone, and it didn't happen the way he had hoped. Oh, how am I going to manage without him?*

Ivan stood with his mother as she weeped. It broke every bit of his heart to hear her cry like this. His mind went back to the beginning of the day. He had never thought for a moment that his father would be gone. *Is it awful of me to wish that he was only sleeping?* It seemed like Dad would simply wake up and things would be the same again. Ivan looked away from his father, swiping at his own tears. *I will miss him so much. What a good role model he was for me and Rhoda. Too bad she's not here to say her goodbyes with me and Mom.* Ivan choked back a sob. He'd missed out on a lot when his sister left home. When they were children they used to be so close. *What went wrong that she would just up and run off, never to be heard from again? What Rhoda did to Mom and Dad was unforgivable, yet they both forgave her.*

Ivan clenched his fingers into his palms, wondering if he had ever truly forgiven his sister for running away. *If my sister had stayed put in Strasburg and let Dad and Mom help raise her baby, maybe she would still be alive. She'd be right here in this room, grieving like me and helping Mom through this traumatic ordeal.*

Ivan moved closer to his mother. "It will be all right, Mom. I'm here for you, and so is Lenore and the rest of our family. You can count on us for anything you need."

Mom gave a brief nod, and Ivan's river of tears increased as he listened to her speak to his father. "I will miss you so very much, Willis. You brought me such joy and made me feel so alive."

Ivan let go of her to grab some tissues from a box on the nearby counter. He swallowed hard and struggled to speak. "I can't believe he's gone. Things just won't be the same without him."

Mom turned her head to look at Ivan. "I feel so numb."

"I understand. This is hard for us, but I'm confident that Dad is in a better place."

"Yes, he is. Your father is free from this life and at home with Jesus now."

They stood and talked together about Dad, going over the final days and hours leading to his passing.

Mom leaned against Ivan, as though needing support. "As much as it hurts to say this, it was your *daed's* time to go. The Lord was ready to receive him." She dabbed at the tears beneath her eyes. "We'll need to take care of the funeral arrangements and make sure it's all done right."

"Yes, and don't worry, Mom, because Yvonne and I will take care of most of the details for you. I'm certain Lenore, Ben, and Peter will help out with a good many things that need to be done too."

"And don't forget about Sara. She's part of our family as well."

"You're right, but she is not familiar with our Amish ways and funeral practices."

"She will still want to help, and I'll tell her what needs to be done. It will be a challenge to get through the next several days, but as long as we're together, it will be easier." A fleeting smile crossed her face. "I remember how I used to leave most of the decision-making up to your father. Now I've got to try to take things over. Makes me wonder how some families get through this time of loss without help."

"Don't worry. We'll all be there for you." He gave her arm a gentle squeeze. "When you're ready to talk about it, we'll need to discuss where you're going to live."

Mom didn't say anything. She moved closer to the bed and reached out for Dad's unmoving hand.

*Now's not the time or place to discuss this,* Ivan thought. *But after the funeral is over, I'll talk to Mom again about moving in with me and Yvonne. She needs someone to look after her now that Dad is gone. And we are available to do it.*

Back in the waiting room, Sara waited with Brad, Yvonne, and Lenore and her brothers—everyone looking so sad.

"I think I'll get something to drink. Would either of you like anything to eat or drink?" Brad glanced in the direction of the cafeteria.

Sara shook her head.

"No thanks. I'm not thirsty or hungry right now." Lenore's tone was dull as she sat slumped in her chair.

"I'll go with you." Peter left his chair.

"Me too," Ben said. "I could use something cold to drink."

Sara sat in silence as Brad and her cousins walked across the carpeted floor out into the hallway and disappeared from view. The waiting area had gotten quieter, which suited Sara just fine. She thought about her grandfather and the times she'd spent with him. It was hard to accept that he was really gone. It would seem so strange going over to her grandparents' house and Grandpa not being there to greet her with his contagious smile.

She squeezed her eyes shut, willing herself not to break down. If she gave way to the sob she kept valiantly pushed down, she might never stop crying. *Grandma will need a lot of support from me and the rest of the family. I will try to help her through this the best way I can.*

Lenore shifted in her chair, glancing toward the windows on the far side of the room. "Looks like it's trying to rain out there."

"I don't care if it rains." Sara looked toward the window and then back at Lenore. "It's true, life does go on."

"What do you mean?"

"Just that everyone is going through different things at the same time. We've received bad news today, while others around us may have gotten some good news."

"You're right, Sara," Aunt Yvonne spoke up. She'd been awfully quiet up until now. Perhaps she'd been thinking about the grief her husband and mother-in-law were dealing with as they viewed Grandpa's body.

Sara looked toward the double doors Grandma and Ivan had walked through a while ago. *I don't know how Grandma and Uncle Ivan could manage the strength to go see Grandpa. I'm not ready yet. I only want to remember him the way he was.*

Brad came into view with his beverage and went over to the window. He stood there and stared out for a while, as though deep in thought. Sara saw the vapors rising from his coffee and smelled the robust aroma, but she had no desire for any. The tears behind Sara's eyes nearly spilled forth as she thought about how Grandpa had always enjoyed a good cup of coffee. She remembered well seeing him looking out the living room window, watching the birds at their feeders, while slowly sipping his steaming brew. *Grandpa. Oh Grandpa. I miss you already. If only we could have had more time to spend together.*

Sara's limp hands lay loosely together in her lap as she remembered something she should have done as soon as they received the news that Grandpa had been rushed to the hospital. "Oh no—I can't believe I forgot to call Kenny." Sara lifted her hands and placed them against her hot cheeks. "He needs to know about Grandpa's passing."

"Would you like me to make the call for you?" Brad asked, moving back across the room and taking the seat beside her.

Sara shook her head. "No, I should be the one to tell him." She rose from her chair. "I'll look for a more private spot to talk to my brother. He's going to be shocked when I tell him the news." Without waiting for Brad's response, she hurried from the room.

Lenore stood up. "I need to stretch my legs." She walked over to the windows and looked out at the strip of dark clouds in the sky. It had begun to rain, and she could see scattered thundershowers as well. She stood for several minutes, trying to come to grips with all that had occurred, but her brain felt so fuzzy it was hard to think clearly. Turning away from the windows, she walked back to her chair and sat down.

Lenore teared up when Mom reached over and clasped her hand. "Are you okay?"

"Yes. No. I'm not sure anything will ever be okay again. I'm worried about Grandma. What's she going to do now that Grandpa is gone? They loved each other so much, and it's going to be ever so hard for her to go on without him."

"You're right, it won't be easy, but with all of our support, plus her strong faith in God, your *grossmudder* will make it."

Lenore glanced over at a hospital worker as he held one of the double doors open. Two figures emerged.

"They're back." She rose to her feet.

Lenore's mother stood up too, as did Brad.

Grandma came up to them, holding a crumpled tissue in one hand. "Grandpa is at rest, and I am confident that he is with the Lord."

"Even seeing him lying there, with no breath passing between his lips, I'm still trying to get used to the idea that he is gone." Dad's form seemed weakened as his shoulders slumped.

"Would you like me to pull my van up to the door?" Brad asked, looking at Grandma.

Sniffling, she nodded. "Yes, that would be appreciated."

Sara entered the room, and seeing Grandma, she pulled her into a hug. With tears rolling down her cheeks, she hugged Lenore's dad too. "We'll get through this together."

Lenore rubbed her forehead in an area that had begun to pound. It was upsetting to see the sadness in her grandmother's normally happy face. *Poor Grandma. I wish I could say or do something to take away her pain.*

# Chapter 20

*Strasburg*

During Grandpa's funeral service, held in his and Grandma's home, Sara and the rest of her family sat on folding chairs a short distance from the very plain coffin made of poplar wood. She was told it had been constructed by a local Amish man who owned a woodshop and primarily made caskets for the Amish. It was wider at the shoulders than at the head and feet. The lid came to a peak. It had two parts: one that went across the lower body, and the other that had a two-part hinge so it could be folded open to allow viewing of the upper part of the deceased's body. Sara's cousin Ben had informed her that the Lancaster Amish cover the upper part of the coffin with a sheet during the funeral. The coffin had no handles or any veneer. It was simple in its construction and had no internal padding. The final resting place for the coffin would be in the local Amish cemetery.

This was Sara's first experience attending an Amish funeral, and she'd asked all three of her cousins a good many questions beforehand so she might understand better what was happening. She'd learned that usually people in the community who died were buried three days later. Their bodies were taken to a funeral home for embalming and then brought to the family's home.

Sara had also been told that family members, friends, and acquaintances would be able to view the body before the day of the funeral. When the first viewing took place, Grandpa's body had been placed in his open coffin in the dining room. When Sara and Brad had arrived for that viewing, she was surprised to see that the room the casket was placed in had been stripped of all furniture and decorations. The second viewing would take place at the end of today's funeral service.

Grandpa had been dressed in a white shirt, white vest, and white pants. No flowers or decorations of any kind softened the experience, and no eulogy was given, as in most English funerals or memorial services.

The first minister stood near the coffin. He spoke on the creation of the world, pointing out that Adam was created from dust and each person must return to dust. The minister read John 5:20–30, which spoke of the resurrection of the dead.

The second minister gave the main funeral sermon, and he read from 1 Corinthians 15, starting at verse 35 and continuing to the end, including the words, "O death, where is thy sting? O grave, where is thy victory?"

Very little was said about the deceased, because the Amish believe that God, not man, should be praised. They learned from an early age that their focus should be not so much on this world but on the world yet to come.

The reading of the obituary came at the end of the service, after the closing prayer and benediction. As in most Amish communities, the obituary included the deceased's name, age, date of birth, date of death, and number of descendants.

Sara wished Brad could have preached a sermon during Grandpa's funeral. At least then she would have understood everything being said. It had been difficult for her to listen to a sermon spoken in German, with only a few English words thrown in now and then. Sara still couldn't accept that her precious grandfather was gone. It pained her to think that she hadn't known him very long, and now there would be no more chances to spend time with him—at least not here on this earth.

*I was cheated of spending more time with my mother too,* Sara thought with regret. *Mama was too young when she died.*

She glanced to her left and saw her brother, Kenny, sitting on the other side of Brad. He too had been cheated out of time spent with Grandpa Lapp—he'd known his Amish grandparents for an even shorter time than Sara.

She thought of her stepfather, Dean, and how hard it had been on Kenny when his father died. She curled her fingers into her palms. Dean's death had affected Sara as well—especially once she'd come to realize how much he had actually cared about her. *So many regrets and so many unnecessary misunderstandings. Life certainly has its ups and downs, and each person must learn how to cope with them.*

Sara shifted on her chair and swallowed hard to push down the sob rising in her throat. *What's Grandma going to do now without Grandpa? They were so close, and she never seemed to mind taking care of him.*

Sara thought about the vows she'd exchanged with Brad on their wedding day: "For better, for worse, for richer, for poorer, in sickness and in health." If she were to become sick, Sara had no doubt that Brad would take care of her. And if her husband got sick or injured, she would be there for him too. A loving marriage, bound by the vows the wedding couple had made, required commitment through good times and bad. Sara's grandparents were a fine example of that, and their legacy would live on.

Her gaze went to Lenore. On the outside, she seemed to be handling things well, but no doubt she was also hurting today, as were her brothers. Sara's cousin was loving, kind, and strong in her faith, but she was also human. She had grown up spending a lot of time with her grandparents, so losing Grandpa could not be easy—for Lenore, Peter, or Ben. It had to be especially difficult for Uncle Ivan to lose his father. From what Sara had observed, he and Grandpa had a close father-son relationship.

Sara looked in Ivan's direction. *I wonder if he will insist on Grandma moving in with him and Yvonne. Or will Lenore continue to live here with Grandma? Since Jesse has begun courting Lenore, they might end up getting married. If so, maybe they'll live with Grandma, unless they decide to get their own home somewhere in the area.*

Someone sniffled. It didn't take long to realize the noise came from Michelle. From the pained expression on the young woman's face, Sara knew her friend—even though she was not a member of the Lapp family—grieved the loss of Grandpa as much as she and the other family members did.

Following the funeral service, four of Willis's friends carried his body from the house to the black, horse-drawn hearse. They traveled in a solemn procession with other buggies to the graveyard where he would be buried. These same four friends, acting as pallbearers, had dug the grave beforehand.

At her husband's gravesite, Mary Ruth, dressed in black just like the other mourners, stood between her two granddaughters. Her legs felt like they might buckle at any minute, and she was thankful Lenore and Sara had put their arms around her for support. Brad stood on the other side of Sara, and to the right of Lenore stood Ivan, Yvonne, Peter, and Benjamin. Other mourners, including Michelle and Ezekiel and all of his family, were nearby, along with many people from their church district. Because Willis had been a minister for a good many years, he would be missed by everyone in their church, as well as many in the surrounding communities.

Tears stung the back of Mary Ruth's eyes as Willis's casket was lowered into the ground. Their bishop read a hymn as the grave was covered with dirt, and he continued reading until the job had been finished. She bit the inside of her cheek, struggling to keep her emotions in check. Mary Ruth would not give in to the tears begging to be released. She had to remain strong for her family's sake. She would have plenty of time when she was alone to give in to her grief and allow the tears to flow unchecked.

Mary Ruth thought about the plain Amish tombstone that would be placed over the spot where her husband was buried. It would simply state Willis's name, his birth and death dates, and his age in years, months, and days. The plot itself would be bare, with no foliage planted or flowers placed on the grave. Children usually were buried in unmarked graves or had small headstones that lay flat on the ground.

Mary Ruth's one consolation was the assurance that Willis had gone to heaven and stood in the presence of God. Her dearly loved husband had professed Christ as his Savior and lived a Christian life in every sense of the word. Someday Mary Ruth would be reunited with Willis. Until then, she had to keep the faith and set an example to her family and friends.

As the mourners headed back to their buggies following the graveside service, Ivan paused and looked over his shoulder at the place where his father had just been buried. It didn't seem real—it felt like a bad dream, only he knew he wouldn't wake up and realize it hadn't happened at all.

Dad had only been gone three days, and already Ivan missed him. Ever since he was a boy, they had enjoyed playful banter. Dad had told Ivan corny jokes, and when Ivan told some of his own, Dad had always laughed and said, "That was a good one, Son."

"Are you okay?" Yvonne put her hand on Ivan's arm.

"No, not really, but for my mamm's sake, I have to remain strong."

"It's okay to cry. No one will think you're weak if you let your emotions out."

Ivan bristled. "This is not about me being afraid of what others might think. If I give in to my tears and Mom sees me crying, it will only make her feel worse."

Yvonne shook her head. "I don't think so, Ivan. Mary Ruth will understand, because like her, you are grieving for a man who was much loved by everyone in this family. Grief is an important part of healing. The Bible tells us that even Jesus wept when He was overcome with grief."

"Jah, I know." He reached up and rubbed a spot on the back of his neck where a muscle had tightened. "Even so, I'll shed most of my tears in the privacy of our home or when I'm alone in the barn."

Yvonne didn't say anything more, but Ivan caught her glancing at Lenore with raised brows. *My wife clearly doesn't understand where I'm coming from. After all, it's not her father we just buried.*

By late afternoon, the tables, benches, songbooks, trays, and coffee butlers had all been put back into the bench wagons and hauled to the home where church would be held the next Sunday. The barn, shop, and house had been cleaned, and all the food taken care of. Everyone headed for home, except the closest family members and a few neighbor ladies who had set out leftovers for the Lapp family's supper.

Lenore felt relieved when the funeral dinner was over and everyone had gone home. It had been a long, tiring day, and she'd made a valiant effort to hold her emotions in check. She had wanted to be strong for her grandmother's sake, but watching the expression on sweet Grandma's face when Grandpa's coffin was lowered into the ground was almost her undoing. Lenore knew her grandmother quite well, and she was not easily fooled. No matter how much of a brave front Grandma had put on today, fatigue and sadness from deep within became more evident as the day wore on.

Soon after Sara, Brad, Kenny, and Lenore's parents and brothers left for home, Lenore insisted Grandma go to the living room to rest. Then she fixed them both a cup of chamomile tea and joined her there.

Lenore's heart nearly broke when she entered the room and saw Grandma sitting in Grandpa's favorite chair, staring at her folded hands.

"Your *daed* wants me to sell this old house and move in with him and your *mudder*." Grandma lifted her head and looked at Lenore.

"How do you feel about that idea?"

"I don't like it one bit." Grandma shook her head. "This is my home, and I want to stay here as long as I'm able." She moaned. "But your *daed's* likely to keep pestering me till I give in and do what he says."

"You don't need to give in, Grandma. I'm willing to keep living here with you. I'm sure that arrangement would satisfy Dad."

"Are you sure? What if Jesse asks you to marry him? I doubt he would want to move in here."

"We'll deal with that should the time ever come." Lenore took a seat in the chair nearest Grandma. It seemed so strange not to have Grandpa here, occupying his favorite chair. She still couldn't wrap her mind around the fact that he was gone. Lenore thought about how one of their ministers had reminded them today that life goes on, and although they felt sorrow, they also needed to face the future with acceptance, a quiet joy, and a living hope and faith that Willis Lapp was in a better place, spending eternity with the One he had served for most of his life.

"I don't know what I'm going to do without him. Nothing will ever be the same in this house, and I've been sitting here trying to figure out what my future holds." Grandma stroked a worn spot on the arm of the chair. "When I married your grandfather, I never expected that he would be the one to go first." She sighed once more. "Always thought it would be me, even though he said once that he hoped we would leave this earth together."

Lenore's throat had swollen to the point that she could barely speak. "As Grandpa said many times over the years, 'none of us knows what the future will hold.' "

Grandma gave a slow nod. "Getting up every morning and not having him to look after is going to take some getting used to, and I'll have a lot of time on my hands. I'm likely to feel like a horse with no buggy to pull."

"It will be difficult at first, but you'll find something to do."

"I hope so, because it's not in my nature to sit around all day and do nothing."

Lenore sat mulling over her grandmother's words until an idea popped into her head. "Say, what would you think about caring for Jesse's little girl during the day while he's at work? Or would that be too much for you?"

Grandma remained still for several minutes, staring straight ahead. Then, with one quick nod, she said, "That's a *wunderbaar* idea, Lenore. If Jesse's agreeable to the idea of me taking care of his little girl, I'm more than willing." She touched her chest. "In fact, it might be exactly what I need to keep my mind occupied and to fill this emptiness."

# Chapter 21

Children's laughter rang throughout the schoolyard as Lenore's students headed for home. Today was Friday, and they were undoubtedly eager for their weekend to begin.

Lenore stood on the schoolhouse porch, watching them go and enjoying the wonderful cooling breeze. The heat wave they'd had since Grandpa's death a week and a half ago had finally passed, and last night light sprinkles of rain took away some of the dust. Lenore was also eager to get home. It had been difficult to return to teaching, but keeping busy helped to keep Lenore's mind active—giving her fewer chances to feel the pain of losing her beloved grandfather.

A vision of Grandpa's face flashed into her mind and she remembered an incident from before he'd suffered a stroke. Lenore had gone to the living room to tell him supper was on the table, and she'd found Grandpa in his recliner with his eyes closed. "Wake up, Grandpa," she'd said, giving his arm a nudge. He didn't budge—he just lay there. When Lenore was about to call out his name again, Grandpa's eyes popped open, and he looked at her with a teasing grin. "Wasn't sleeping. I was just restin' my eyes." They'd had a good laugh.

Lenore smiled, in spite of the sharp pain of regret that penetrated her soul. Grandpa had always been good at making other people laugh. The only time she'd ever seen him succumb to depression was after he'd suffered that horrible stroke. But later, when it appeared that he was getting better, Grandpa's humorous side had resurfaced.

Lenore's thoughts turned to her grandmother. On Monday, Grandma had begun watching Cindy while Jesse was at work. Lenore looked forward to seeing how they were both doing. While it was good therapy for Grandma to have something meaningful to do, caring for an eight-month-old child was also a lot of work. But Grandma had insisted she was up to it, and according to Jesse, his late wife's aunt had seemed somewhat relieved to relinquish the responsibility.

*I'm also eager to see Jesse when he joins us for supper again this evening,* Lenore admitted to herself. He'd eaten the evening meal with them every night this week and would no doubt stay for some of Grandma's delicious cabbage rolls this evening. Having his company was nice, and Grandma seemed relaxed around him. It almost seemed as if she'd accepted Jesse as part of the family.

Although Lenore enjoyed Jesse's company, she never felt fully at ease with him. Maybe it was because she tried so hard to make an impression on him and was never sure what he might be thinking. Sometimes, like two nights ago, Jesse engaged her in conversation and smiled a lot. Other times, such as last evening, he said very little unless spoken to and appeared to be deep in thought. Lenore longed to know what was on his mind. *Maybe I'm overanalyzing things. It probably doesn't matter what's going through Jesse's mind when he's quiet.*

A buzzing fly circled Lenore's head, putting an end to her thoughts about Jesse. She stepped back inside the schoolhouse to help her assistant take care of a few things, and then it would be time for them both to go home.

"You've been awfully quiet today," Ezekiel said as he and Michelle worked side by side in the greenhouse that afternoon. "Are you still worried about moving to New York this fall instead of waiting till spring as originally planned? If it's a problem, I can contact the man who is selling me his business and tell him that fall is too soon for us to move."

Michelle shook her head. "It's not the move I'm having a hard time dealing with, but the fact that Willis is gone. He was like a grandpa to me—the grandfather I never had."

"I miss him too." Ezekiel's mouth turned down at the corners. "I've known the Lapps since I was a boy, and both of them always treated me kindly."

Michelle brushed some dirt off her hand after repotting an African violet. "I'm glad Lenore is living with her grandma. Mary Ruth needs someone with her—especially now. She has to be so lonely without Willis." Michelle teared up. "I can't begin to imagine how much she must miss him."

"I'm sure she does, but I guess you haven't heard. Mary Ruth began watching Jesse Smucker's daughter this week," Ezekiel's mother chimed in from the next aisle over. "I bet that little girl is keeping Mary Ruth so busy she hardly has time to think about much else."

❧

Mary Ruth's knees creaked as she knelt on the blanket she'd spread on the living-room floor for Cindy. It was diaper-changing time, and since the little girl wasn't fond of having her diapers changed, Mary Ruth decided to make a game of it. "Where's Cindy?" she asked, dropping a diaper onto the little girl's head and then pulling it off again. "Ah, there she is! There's my sweet Cindy."

Cindy giggled and kicked her feet.

After Mary Ruth put the diaper in place and fastened it, she tickled Cindy under her chin. "*Kitzle voggel. . . Kitzle voggel. . .* Here comes the tickle bird."

Cindy giggled even more, and Mary Ruth did too. Thinking back to how her son and daughter had reacted when she'd played silly games with them during their babyhood brought a smile to her face. Rhoda and Ivan had both enjoyed the "tickle bird" game. Oh, how she missed those fun-loving days when she and Willis were raising their children. If only there was some way to turn back the hands of time.

Taking care of Jesse's daughter was a joy, as well as a privilege, and it did take some of her depression away. But Mary Ruth's life would be so much better if Willis were here to share it with. There would be no fresh apple cider this year, unless Ivan made it, and there were so many other things Willis used to do as head of the house—things Mary Ruth and everyone in the family would miss.

*But he's not coming back,* she reminded herself, *and I need to keep busy and stay focused on the now. In time, the indescribable pain I feel will hopefully diminish.*

Mary Ruth put Cindy's pink sleeper on and had begun patting the baby's back when Lenore came in. "How was your day, Grandma? Was Cindy a good girl for you?"

"Jah, she's a sweetheart." Mary Ruth picked up the wet diaper and grunted as she pushed herself up. "Would you like to spend some time with her while I go take this disposable windel out to the garbage and wash up? Then if you don't mind, maybe you can spend some time with her while I get supper started."

"Most definitely. But not for too long. Jesse will be here soon, and I need to help you get our evening meal going."

Mary Ruth shook her head. "You've had a busy week at school and deserve a little downtime, so just relax and enjoy being with the boppli." Without waiting for a response, Mary Ruth left the room.

⁓

Lenore sat on the floor beside Cindy and played this-little-piggy. The little girl giggled every time Lenore wiggled one of her toes and said what each pretend piggy was doing. It felt nice to spend time with Jesse's daughter. She missed all the fun and games they used to have. "*Bissel seiche*—little piglet." Lenore wiggled all ten of Cindy's toes and tweaked her nose.

Lenore's attention was diverted when she heard a buggy roll into the yard. *I wonder who is here.* After a few moments, Lenore heard someone come up onto the porch and knock on the door. It couldn't be Jesse. It was too early for him to be off work yet.

The door opened and Dad walked in, awkwardly carrying what looked like quite a heavy box.

"Hello, Daughter." He grinned at her.

"Hi, Dad. I'll help you with the door." Lenore jumped up and went to close it. Then she scooped Cindy up and followed her father into the kitchen.

"This box is full of frozen beef from my English neighbor, Ron. His freezer died, so he came by earlier in a panic to see if I'd have enough room to hold all the packages before they thawed." Dad set the box on the table. "I helped Ron out, and we got all the meat inside safe and sound. And for my trouble he insisted I should keep this amount."

Lenore smiled. "That was nice of him."

"What was nice?" Grandma asked as she came into the room. "Oh, hi, Ivan. I didn't know you were here."

After giving her a hug, he gestured to the cardboard box. "I've come bearing gifts."

Grandma tipped her head. "Oh, what is all this?"

Cindy squirmed in Lenore's arms, so she patted the little girl's back. "There's frozen beef inside the box."

"Really, from who?"

"My neighbor's freezer died, and for me helping him out he gave me this."

"That's a pleasant surprise." She stepped closer to the box.

Lenore watched as Dad pulled out the packages of meat. There were some steaks, a roast, and a good amount of hamburger. Grandma's eyes seemed to brighten as she watched the packages pile up on the kitchen table.

"Since you often invite me, Yvonne, and the boys over for a meal, this will save some money from your grocery bill." He grinned.

"Thank you, Son. I'll take a look in my freezer to see if we can get all this meat inside." Grandma reached over and pulled open the freezer part of her propane-operated refrigerator.

Lenore leaned over to look inside too. "There's not a lot in there right now, so maybe it will all fit."

Dad came over with an armload of packages and began to fill up the spaces. Lenore stepped out of his way and took a seat at the kitchen table, placing Cindy in her lap.

"What are your plans for this evening?" Grandma looked over at Dad.

"I'm going back to the house after I run to the bank. Why, Mom? Did you need me to do something before I go?"

"I thought if you weren't busy you might like to join us for a cup of kaffi and some of my banana bread."

"Danki, but I really have to go. I'll take a rain check, though."

"Okay." She went to the pantry and brought out a roasting pan. "It's probably time for me to start supper, and I really shouldn't be snacking so close to the evening meal." Grinning at Ivan, Grandma thumped her stomach. "If I'm not careful, I'll end up looking like one of your daed's old hogs."

Dad laughed, but the mention of Grandpa's hogs sent a pang of regret through Lenore. She'd give anything to have him sitting here at the table right now, enjoying a cup of coffee and telling some of his silly jokes. "Grandma, why don't you take Cindy and go into the living room? I'll get supper started."

Dad patted Lenore's back. "That's my thoughtful daughter— always thinking of others."

He pointed at the cardboard box on the kitchen table. "I'll take that with me when I leave, unless you need an extra box for something, Mom."

Grandma shook her head. "There are a few empty boxes out in the barn, so feel free to take this box with you." She told Ivan goodbye and gave him a hug, then took Cindy from Lenore and headed for the living room.

Dad turned to face Lenore. "Before I go, I was wondering how things are going between you and Jesse."

"We're doing well." She smiled. "He should be here in another hour or so."

"Will he be staying for the evening meal?"

"Jah."

"What are you having for supper this evening?"

"Grandma made up some cabbage rolls in the tangy tomato sauce earlier today. They're in the refrigerator. All I have to do is put them in the roasting pan and pop it into the oven."

"Mmm. . .that young man of yours is in for a tasty treat. My mamm's a good cook, and you're fortunate to be living here with her. Bet she's taught you a lot about cooking."

Lenore folded her arms as she released a puff of air. "Dad, I knew how to cook when I moved in with Grandma. As you already know, I've been working in the kitchen with Mom since I was a girl."

"Of course you have. I only meant that. . ." He waved his words aside. "Oh, never mind. I'm just glad you agreed to live with my mamm, because I never would have stood for her living here all alone."

"I'm well aware." Lenore gave her dad a hug. "I'm sure Grandma appreciates the concern you feel for her too."

"Has Jesse taken you out lately?"

"There hasn't been a lot of time to do that."

"Well, I'd best get going." Dad picked up the box. "Tell Jesse I said hello, and I'm sorry I can't stay around to say it myself."

"I'll give him the message."

"Jesse seems like a nice fellow." He leaned close to Lenore. "But if you ever have any problems with him, just let me know."

Lenore lifted her gaze to the ceiling. "Don't worry, Dad, everything's going just fine between me and Jesse."

"Good to hear." He bent down and kissed her cheek. "I really do need to go. You all have a good evening." He turned and headed for the back door.

"Tell Mom I said hello," Lenore called to his retreating form.

After the door clicked shut, Lenore left the kitchen and peeked into the living room. It had gotten awfully quiet in there, and she wondered if Grandma might have fallen asleep.

Stepping into the room, Lenore realized quickly that Grandma was wide-awake. She sat in Grandpa's old recliner with his Bible in her lap. Cindy lay on the floor with her eyes closed and her thumb in her mouth.

"Isn't she cute?" Lenore whispered when she caught Grandma's eye.

"Jah, Cindy is adorable. Children are a blessing to their parents' lives. It says so right here in the Bible." Grandma lifted the book toward Lenore.

Lenore nodded and smiled. *I can't wait to be able to say that in the future, hopefully as Jesse's wife.*

❧

"Something sure smells mighty good in here," Jesse said when he entered Mary Ruth's house and found Lenore on the floor playing peekaboo with Cindy.

"That would be my grandma's tasty cabbage rolls." Lenore pointed toward the kitchen. "They're keeping warm in the oven while Grandma takes a shower. We'll eat as soon as she comes out of the bathroom."

Jesse smiled when Cindy reached her hands out to him. "How's my little girl today?" he asked, going down on his knees beside Lenore and scooping Cindy into his arms.

"Well, I haven't been here all that long, but from what Grandma said earlier, she and Cindy got along real well today."

"That's good to hear."

Cindy squealed when Jesse rubbed noses with her, then tickled her belly.

"She sure is a happy baby," Lenore said.

"Jah, except for when her diaper needs changing or she just wants to be held."

Jesse was on the verge of asking Lenore a question when Mary Ruth entered the room. "Oh, good, I'm glad you're here, Jesse. If you're ready to eat supper, we can all go out to the kitchen now."

He didn't have to be asked twice. Putting Cindy over his shoulder like a sack of potatoes, Jesse rose to his feet and followed the women to the kitchen.

"Why don't you sit here this evening?" Mary Ruth pointed to the chair at the head of the table. "That used to be where Willis sat, and I'm tired of seeing it empty."

Jesse hesitated at first, but after he put Cindy in her high chair, he did as Mary Ruth suggested.

They bowed their heads for silent prayer, and when everyone had finished praying Lenore passed Jesse the casserole dish filled with steaming-hot cabbage rolls covered in herbed tomato sauce.

He put two on his plate and passed the dish to Mary Ruth.

"There's also coleslaw, mashed potatoes, pickled beets, and some carrot sticks to go with the main dish." Lenore gestured to the other bowls. "Would you like me to pass those to you, Jesse?"

"I'll try some of each shortly, but right now I'm gonna sink my teeth into one of these 'bound to be special' cabbage rolls." Jesse took his first bite and smacked his lips. "These are the best I've ever tasted."

"Danki. Feel free to have as many as you like." Mary Ruth pointed to the dish sitting between her and Lenore. "As you can see, I made plenty, so I'd be pleased to send some home with you as well."

He grinned and gave his belly a thump. "I won't say no to that."

Jesse looked over at Lenore. She hadn't said more than a few words since they'd been seated at the table and said their silent prayer. "How was your day at school?"

"It went well, but I'm looking forward to having the next two days off." She handed him the bowl of mashed potatoes. "Would you like some?"

Jesse obliged, and after he'd added a couple of spoonfuls to his plate, he passed the dish on to Mary Ruth. "Your job must be very rewarding, Lenore."

She nodded, then turned her focus on Cindy playing happily with the finger food on her high chair tray. "As much as I enjoy teaching, I have to admit, I miss spending my days with your daughter."

"I think Cindy misses you too," Mary Ruth spoke up. "She does well enough for me," she added, "but Cindy doesn't light up when I come into the room the way she does when she sees you, Lenore."

Lenore's cheeks flushed as she rubbed some food off Cindy's chin. "And I think the world of her."

Jesse almost had to bite his tongue to keep from asking Lenore right then if she would marry him. He was more certain than ever before that Lenore would make a good mother for Cindy. But this was not the time or place for a proposal. He needed to give their relationship more time before asking that question.

# Chapter 22

B y the end of September, evidence of fall could be seen through-out Lancaster County. As Lenore guided her horse toward the schoolhouse Friday morning, the scent of smoky air coming from people's chimneys drifted into her buggy. Thanks to several days of heavy winds, the heat and humidity of summer were definitely gone, and due to the chillier weather, some trees were already dropping their leaves.

Grandma's apple trees had done well this year, and Lenore's father would be coming over this evening with his cider press. Lenore looked forward to drinking fresh cider and nibbling on popcorn as she and her family sat around the bonfire that would no doubt be built.

The whole family would be there, as well as Ezekiel and Michelle. Jesse had also been invited to join them, which pleased Lenore, but Grandpa would be sorely missed. This would be the first year he hadn't been involved in making fresh cider. His absence was bound to affect dear Grandma most of all. Lenore would con-tinue to pray for her grandma, as well as the rest of her family, and she hoped to keep a positive attitude.

As the crisp, cool air wafted into the buggy, she shivered. *Even though I do miss Grandpa, I'm adjusting to his absence more easily than Grandma is. I think it's because I've got the school curriculum to plan every week and students to keep my thoughts occupied during work-days.* Her face warmed. Jesse was consuming her thoughts during the day too, and adorable little Cindy was becoming increasingly important to her.

Lenore held firmly to the reins when her horse decided to pick up speed. "Whoa, Dolly—slow down."

Lenore was glad Grandma had Cindy to keep her occupied these days. She couldn't help feeling a bit envious though. Truth was, even though Lenore loved to teach, this year the stress of being responsible for so many children had become more difficult for her to manage. Lenore didn't feel cut out to be a schoolteacher anymore. Even little things, like finding a mouse under her desk the other morning, were setting her nerves on edge. What Lenore really wanted and couldn't stop thinking about was to be a wife and have children of her own.

*Did I feel this discontented before I met Jesse and Cindy?* Lenore wondered. *I need to be patient. Jesse and I seem to be getting closer. Perhaps in time he will propose marriage. But if he doesn't, I must learn to be content with whatever the Lord has planned for my life.*

⁓

When Sara entered the flower shop, she found Misty already hard at work in the back room, putting together a large autumn floral arrangement.

"That's looking really nice, Misty. I love the fall colors."

"Thank you." She added some greenery and stood back, eyeing it. "We've got a busy day ahead with orders."

Sara put her lunch away in the refrigerator and looked at the list of orders going out for today. "Yep, another full one. How's it going so far?"

"Good. I have one arrangement already done and in the cooler." Misty remained focused on her job.

"All right then. I'll let you keep working." Sara left the room and went to her desk to check phone messages. A few minutes later, her cell phone rang. Seeing it was Brad, she answered immediately.

"Hi, hon. Are you busy right now?"

"Nothing that can't wait." Sara pushed her invoice book aside and reached for a writing tablet. There'd been some tension between her and Brad this morning when she brought up the hot dog roast and apple cider pressing at her grandma's tonight. The trouble started when he reminded Sara that this evening was Bible study, so they wouldn't be able to attend her family gathering.

"Can't we cancel this one?" Sara had asked. "I don't want to miss sampling Uncle Ivan's fresh-squeezed apple cider and saying goodbye to Michelle and Ezekiel. They'll be moving tomorrow, you know."

Brad had said he didn't feel right about canceling the Bible study, but thought they might get done early enough that they could go to Strasburg for an hour or so.

"Are you still there, Sara?"

Brad's question drew her from her musings. "Yes, I'm here. What did you call about?"

"I wanted to let you know that I'd like you to go ahead to your grandma's place when you get off work. I'll join you there as soon as the Bible study is over."

"Are you sure?" Sara shifted the phone to her other ear. "Aren't you worried about how it will look to those attending the class if I'm not there?"

"Nope, not at all. I think they'll understand when I explain why you're not there."

Sighing, Sara pressed a palm to her chest. "Thanks, Brad, for being so considerate of my feelings."

"You'd do the same for me if the sandal was on the other foot."

Sara laughed. "I doubt anyone would be wearing sandals this time of year, but I get your meaning."

He chuckled too. "I'll make sure the study is done on time tonight, and then I'll see you at Mary Ruth's."

"Thanks, Brad. Have a good day."

"You too, Sara."

After Sara hung up, she bowed her head. *Thank You, Lord, for the loving, sensitive husband You have blessed me with.*

That evening after Jesse arrived at Mary Ruth's, he secured his horse at the hitching rail and went up to the house, eager to see his daughter. Mary Ruth greeted him at the door. "Welcome, Jesse. How was your day?"

"It went well, but I'm kind of tired. It seemed like there was more work than usual at the furniture store." He stepped into the entryway.

"Well, we're glad you could join us tonight, and hopefully after some food and tasty cider, you'll feel revived."

"I'm glad to be here. I bet my daughter is too. How'd she do for you today?"

"Just fine. Cindy and I always get along well." Mary Ruth gestured toward the living room. "Yvonne, Sara, and Lenore are keeping her entertained in there."

He grinned. "I bet they are." Jesse took a few steps toward the door. "I was going to say hi to Cindy, but it sounds like she's in good hands, so I think I'll head back outside and put Restless away."

"Not a problem." Mary Ruth headed off to the living room.

Jesse stepped off the porch and walked back to his buggy to unhook his horse. Then he led the gelding over to the corral gate and put him in with the other horses.

A good-sized group of family milled around on the lawn. His gaze came to rest on Lenore's father talking to one of the men. Jesse couldn't shake the awkward feeling he had at times in Ivan's presence. Lenore's dad didn't talk to Jesse as much these days as he had before he and Lenore started courting. Lately when Ivan came by Mary Ruth's house and Jesse was there, he mostly chatted with his mother and Lenore. It almost seemed as if Ivan had a sense about how Jesse felt toward his daughter. *Does Ivan realize I'm not in love with Lenore and that I only want to marry her for convenience' sake? I wonder how Ivan might react if things don't go the way his daughter wants.*

Shaking aside his concerns, Jesse brushed at a smudge on his trousers and walked back to the house. He spotted Lenore near the entrance of the kitchen and smiled.

She stepped over to him, wearing a jacket with a woolen scarf tied over her white head covering. "Grandma is getting Cindy bundled up pretty well so she'll stay nice and warm outside."

"That's good. It's kinda nippy out this evening, jah?"

Lenore nodded. "I'm about done helping in here, so we can head outside if you'd like."

"Sure, that will be good."

They passed Ivan at the door as they were headed out. He smiled briefly as he looked over at Jesse. "Glad you could be here for the family gathering."

"Danki, I'm glad I could be here too." He followed Lenore out to the chairs.

Almost as soon as they picked out their seats, Jesse noticed the bags of marshmallows on the picnic table. "I can't wait to roast some of those." He pointed to them.

"Me too. I've been thinking about this off and on all day." Lenore picked out a skewer and grabbed a marshmallow. Jesse did the same.

They returned to their chairs and scooted them closer to the fire. Jesse put his skewer into the flame, and in no time it began to burn. "Oh no! Would you just look at my marshmallow? I don't think I'm gonna eat this one. It's a little too overdone for my taste."

Lenore leaned closer to him. "Why don't you get a new one?"

Jesse wiggled his brows. "Good idea." He grabbed another marshmallow, put it on a stick this time, and held it over the fire. It didn't take long before this one burned too.

"Oh, great. Not again." He grunted as it fell off and burned up in the flames. Jesse squinted as he glanced over at Lenore; he could hardly believe his eyes. She had roasted a perfectly brown marshmallow without a speck of black on it. "I don't know how you did that. What's your secret anyway?"

She lifted her shoulders in a quick shrug before giving a dimpled smile. "Here you go, Jesse." Lenore handed him her skewer.

He shook his head. "No, that's okay. You did a good job roasting your marshmallow, so you should be the one to eat it."

"All right, if you insist." Lenore popped the creamy morsel into her mouth. Chuckling, she smacked her lips. "Would you like me to roast you one, sir?"

Jesse felt like an incompetent fool, but as much as he enjoyed marshmallows, he couldn't say no. "Sure, if you don't mind."

"I don't mind at all."

He leaned forward with his elbows on his knees, watching Lenore roast another perfect-looking puffy treat. When it was just the right shade of brown, she handed him the skewer. "Thanks, Lenore." Jesse wasted no time in eating it and didn't even care when he ended up with sticky goo all over his lips.

Lenore laughed and handed him a napkin.

After Jesse wiped off his face, he looked toward the house and saw Mary Ruth, Sara, and Yvonne coming across the yard with his daughter. Cindy was crying, and when the women joined them at the bonfire, Lenore offered to take Cindy.

As she sat quietly on her folding chair, holding Cindy in her lap, Jesse couldn't help noticing Lenore's tender expression as she patted his daughter's back and spoke soothingly to the child. Not more than two minutes ago, Cindy had been fussing, but as soon as Lenore took her, all crying ceased. As much as Jesse loved Cindy, he didn't have the ability to soothe her the way Lenore always did. One more reason his daughter needed Lenore as her mother.

He scratched his head. *What should I do—pretend to be in love with Lenore so she'll marry me, or ask her to be my wife in name only, which she'd probably never agree to?*

Esther's death had put Jesse in a tight spot, and he didn't know which way to turn.

Mary Ruth had just entered the kitchen to make some popcorn when Michelle came into the room. "What can I do to help?" she asked.

"You can get out the coconut oil while I get the popping corn and kettle." Mary Ruth smiled.

"Sure, no problem." Michelle took the jar of oil down from the cupboard, and when she placed it on the counter near the stove, her eyes misted. "I can't believe Ezekiel and I will be moving tomorrow. We'll both miss you so much, as well as our other friends and family."

Mary Ruth set the items she'd gathered on the counter and gave Michelle a hug. "We shall miss you too, but you'll be back for visits, right?"

"Jah, but not often enough." Stepping out of Mary Ruth's embrace, Michelle swiped at the tears trickling down her cheeks. "Ezekiel's family said they'll come visit us in New York, and my brothers said they will too. Even so, it's going to be hard to start over in a place where we don't know anyone. I don't even know what our new house looks like. When Ezekiel made the trip up to New York to look the place over and talk with the owner, I stayed home to work in the greenhouse because they were so busy and needed the extra help." She paused and blotted her face with the palm of her hand. "I wonder how Ezekiel's folks are going to get along without us."

"I am sure his parents will hire someone to work in the greenhouse after you're gone. And don't worry, Michelle—you'll make new friends, just like you did when you moved here." Mary Ruth hoped her words were encouraging. Truth was, though, she had no idea what it was like to move to a strange place where she didn't know anyone. She and Willis had grown up in Lancaster County, and during the course of their marriage they had never moved away. They'd always had the support of their family and friends.

She placed her hands on Michelle's trembling shoulders. "Remember to pray often and study God's Word. If you keep your focus on Him, He will lead, guide, and direct you all the days of your life."

Michelle nodded slowly. "I know, and I am ever so thankful that I'm not moving there by myself. I'll have my husband's love and support, and I want to be supportive of Ezekiel too." She wiped her nose on the tissue Mary Ruth placed in her hand. "And can I just say one more thing?"

"Of course."

"I feel certain I'm supposed to go to New York with my husband, even though it's hard for me to leave the only place I have ever felt at home and loved." Michelle placed one hand over her heart. "No matter where I go, or whatever I do, I will always remember the example you have shown me of what a loving, Christian wife should be. Danki, Mary Ruth, for all you have done for me."

"It has been my pleasure." Mary Ruth looked deeply into Michelle's eyes. "Remember, dear one. . .I shall be praying for you, and whenever you feel lonely or just need to talk, please give me a call."

"Danki, I will. Brad and Sara said they'd be praying for us too." Michelle dried her damp eyes and managed to smile. "Want to hear something funny?"

"Of course."

"When we were beginning to pack, my crazy *hund* started jumping into boxes and nosing around in our suitcases. Val likes it here, but I think she's afraid she might be left behind."

Mary Ruth chuckled. "Dogs have a sixth sense about things. Val will be good company for you after the move. It'll be an adjustment for her, same as you, but I bet in no time she'll get used to her new surroundings."

"You may be right. She'll probably adjust faster than I do, but it's not like I've never moved before. Only this time I won't be moving by myself." Michelle dropped her gaze to the floor. "I'm glad those days are behind me now."

# Chapter 23

Sweat beaded on Jesse's forehead as he paced the floor with Cindy. She was cutting a tooth, and he'd been up half the night trying to calm her. The poor little thing was in obvious pain and running a slight fever. Unfortunately, nothing Jesse did seemed to ease her distress.

He glanced at the battery-operated clock on the living-room wall. It was almost two in the morning. *If Esther were here holding our baby, I bet she'd know what to do. She was so good with her nieces and nephews and young siblings.*

Jesse took a seat in the rocking chair and began patting Cindy's back as he got the chair moving. It did nothing to quiet her down. His daughter's sobs tore at his heart. *There must be something more I can do for her.*

He meandered over to the bookcase, patting Cindy's back as he went. He'd purchased a book on child care a few months ago and wondered if it might say anything about teething.

When Jesse spotted the book, he placed Cindy in the playpen and took it off the shelf. She hollered even more, of course, and Jesse felt like screaming himself as he flopped onto the couch.

Looking through the index, he found what he was looking for and turned to the section that listed the symptoms and remedies for teething.

"The signs of teething are swollen, tender gums," Jesse read out loud. "The baby may be fussy or cry, have a slightly raised temperature, drool a lot, and chew on whatever he or she can find to put in the mouth." Most of the symptoms fit Cindy, so Jesse felt confident his daughter was in fact teething. According to the book, babies began teething sometime between four and seven months, but some started even later.

*Now to locate a solution to the problem.* Jesse's fingers slid down the page until he came to the part about how to soothe a teething baby. The book's author suggested putting something cold in the baby's mouth, like a chilled pacifier, the end of a clean wet washcloth, or a refrigerated toy or teething ring. Another suggestion was for the baby's caregiver to dip his or her finger in cool water and gently rub the baby's gums. Jesse opted for that idea, but before he tried it, he put Cindy's pacifier in the refrigerator to chill. Then he brought a glass of cold water to the living room.

After Jesse returned to the rocker with Cindy and got the chair moving again, he dipped two fingers in the water and rubbed his daughter's gums. It seemed to help some, and as Jesse continued to rock and rub, he thought about Lenore. It would be a week tomorrow since he'd enjoyed the bonfire at Mary Ruth's place, and he'd only spoken to Lenore a few times since then. One evening when he'd gone to pick up Cindy, Lenore wasn't there. Mary Ruth explained that her granddaughter had been invited to join her parents for supper at their house that night and probably wouldn't be home until close to bedtime. Jesse had been disappointed, because he enjoyed visiting with Lenore and hearing about some of the things that went on at the schoolhouse. But he realized she had a life of her own and had every right to spend time with her family.

Thinking about Lenore's parents caused Jesse to recall a recent phone conversation he'd had with his mother. Mom had pressured him to return to Kentucky so she could help out with Cindy, but he held firm. He had too many memories of Esther in Kentucky, and Jesse wasn't ready to face them. Besides, he liked his new job and didn't want to take Cindy away from the familiarity of being with Mary Ruth and Lenore, whom she'd become attached to. Jesse was convinced he'd made the right decision by moving here, and he wasn't going back to Kentucky no matter what.

After several more minutes of rocking Cindy and rubbing her

gums, she quit crying and dozed off. Eager to get some much-needed sleep of his own, Jesse put Cindy in her crib and collapsed on his bed. Before long, it would be time to get up and start another workday, but even a few hours of sleep would help.

Jesse closed his eyes, lifted a silent prayer, and fell asleep.

❧

Lenore was getting ready to leave for school the next morning when Jesse showed up with Cindy. The dark circles beneath his eyes, in addition to his pinched, tension-filled expression, indicated that he hadn't slept well the night before.

"Is everything okay?" she asked, holding the door open for him. "You look *mied*."

"You're right, I am tired. *Ich bin mied wie en hund.*"

She bit back a chuckle. "Why are you tired as a dog?"

Jesse stepped inside, and as he stood in the hallway with Cindy clinging to his neck, he explained what had happened the night before. "It was after two before either of us got to sleep," he added with a groan. "I had no idea so many challenges came with being a parent. I'm sure glad I located a book on child care I'd bought previously. It taught me pretty much everything I needed to know about teething."

Lenore felt pity for Jesse. He was clearly exhausted from last evening's ordeal. "I'm sorry you had a rough night."

"Hopefully it won't happen again, because next time Cindy cuts a tooth, I'll know exactly what to do. 'Course, that's not saying I'll handle things well if she gets the flu or a bad cold."

"Ah, there's my precious little girl." Lenore's grandmother's arms opened wide when she joined them in the hallway.

Jesse handed Cindy to her. "My daughter's having a hard time cutting her first tooth, so I hope she won't be too fussy for you today."

"I'm sure she'll be fine. I raised two kinner who were both fussy when they were cutting their teeth, but we got through it." Grandma gestured to Lenore. "You were only four months old when you cut your first tooth. The one thing your mamm did that seemed to help the most was soaking a clean washcloth in chamomile tea, which she then put in the refrigerator to chill. The fabric massaged the ridges of your gums while the cold numbed the pain, and the herbal tea helped to calm you."

Lenore smiled. "My mom's a *schmaert* woman, jah?"

"Yes, she is very smart." Grandma's eyes glistened with tears as a slight smile lifted her thin lips. "Your grandpa always teased and said she had to be smart because she chose to marry our son even after she found out his daed raised hogs."

Lenore and Jesse laughed. Grandpa was always full of wisecracks that made people smile. She missed him so much, and of course, Grandma did too. Probably more than Lenore could comprehend, since she had never lost the love of her life.

"I'd better get going." Jesse placed Cindy's diaper bag on the floor by the coat-tree. "Oh, and I wanted to remind you that I have a dental appointment after work, so I'll be a little late picking Cindy up."

"Not a problem," Grandma said. "In fact, if you like, you can leave Cindy here overnight. That way, if she gets fussy again tonight, you can get some good sleep."

Jesse drew in a breath, then closed his eyes briefly while exhaling. "Danki, I would appreciate that very much." He stepped forward and gave his daughter a kiss on the cheek. "I'll see you tomorrow evening, my sweet girl. Be good for Mary Ruth and Lenore."

Lenore said goodbye to Grandma and followed Jesse out the door. "I hope you have a good day at work and that everything goes well at your dental appointment."

He smiled. "I hope your day at school goes well too."

❧

*Clymer, New York*

Michelle stood in front of the kitchen window, washing dishes and looking out at the fertile land surrounding their new home. With farmland being cheaper here than in Lancaster County, it was easy to understand why several Amish families from Pennsylvania, Maryland, and Ohio had chosen to pack up and move to New York State. Fortunately, Michelle and Ezekiel had joined a more progressive district than some in the area. While the home they were buying was an older two-story, four-bedroom house that needed a fresh coat of paint and a few updates, it was comfortable and provided them with all that they needed and had been accustomed to while living in Strasburg, including indoor plumbing. Michelle couldn't imagine doing without indoor plumbing and phone shacks, or driving buggies with no front windshield, like the brown-topped-buggy Amish she'd heard about who originally came from New Wilmington, Pennsylvania. It was hard enough to adjust to living where she had no friends or family, without trying to deal with hardships she'd never experienced before.

Pulling her fingers slowly through the lukewarm dishwater, Michelle thought about the phone call she'd received yesterday from her brother Ernie. He let her know that he and Jack might drive up to New York to see her before winter set in. Since both of her brothers lived in Ohio, it would be a bit of a drive, but a lot cheaper than flying. She looked forward to seeing them and finding out what was new in their lives. In the meantime, Michelle needed to concentrate on unpacking all their things and getting the house organized. Opening most of the boxes filled with household items had been left up to her, since Ezekiel had been keeping plenty busy learning all he could about running his new business.

Needing a familiar voice to talk to, Michelle had called Mary Ruth yesterday, hoping she might catch her in or near the phone shack, but all she'd been able to do was leave a message. Michelle felt certain that if she had been able to speak to Mary Ruth, she would have received some words of encouragement to help lift her depression.

Michelle finished washing the dishes and decided to let them air dry instead of drying each dish with a towel. She had better things to do, and the first item was to get some laundry done and hung on the line to dry. Later, she planned to take Val for a walk. Since the area was new to the dog and Michelle didn't want the Irish setter to run off, so far she'd kept her secured with a long leash or inside the barn. Of course, the dog managed to sneak in the house now and then too. Eventually, once Val became acclimated to her new surroundings, she'd be given the freedom to roam around their yard and all the acreage that came with it.

Michelle dried her hands and slipped into a lightweight jacket, then stepped out the back door. Drawing in a breath of fresh air, she tipped her head and listened. Other than Val's whine as she pulled on her tether, the only sound Michelle heard was the chirping of birds. "It's so peaceful here," she murmured. "Almost too quiet to suit me, though."

The dog's ears perked up, and she let out a couple of loud barks.

Michelle laughed. "Okay, okay, I can take a hint. You want some attention, don't ya, girl?"

The Irish setter wagged her tail, and Michelle bent down to pet Val's silky auburn head. "Let's go for a walk now. I can start the laundry when we get back."

# Chapter 24

## Strasburg

By the fourth week of November, the weather had turned frigid, and on Thanksgiving morning, Lenore woke up to the sight of snow falling from the sky. She stood at her bedroom window and watched as everything in the yard was quickly covered in white. Over in the next field, the neighbor's two horses romped around in the chilly weather. The animals followed each other like children in an energy-driven jog, and then one horse would stop while the other started kicking like it was thrilled with the new-fallen snow.

*What a lovely sight,* she mused. *I just hope for the sake of our company that the roads don't get bad.* Others in the area would no doubt be traveling for the holiday, and Lenore prayed for their safety as well.

Pulling her gaze away from the window, she hurried to get dressed so she could help Grandma with breakfast and the preparations for their big Thanksgiving meal. Jesse and Cindy would be joining them, along with Lenore's parents and her brother Peter. Ben had been invited to join his girlfriend's parents, so his chair at the table would be empty. Sara and Brad were spending Thanksgiving with Brad's folks in Harrisburg. They planned to return on Saturday, as Brad needed to be back in Lancaster to preach on Sunday.

*Grandpa's seat will be empty too.* Lenore choked up. Last Thanksgiving had been such a fun time with all the family together. Even when the turkey ended up on the floor, Grandma had kept a positive attitude, and everyone had enjoyed a good laugh. But today would probably be quiet and uneventful.

Lenore plodded in her slippers over to the closet and picked out a frock. It was one of her work dresses she didn't mind getting dirty. She changed from her nightclothes to the dress and slipped on her comfy shoes.

Going to her dresser, she grabbed her brush and ran it through her long brown hair. "Ouch!" Lenore frowned as the brush pulled at a tangle. While she patiently worked her hair free, Lenore remembered that the dress she'd put on was the same one she'd worn last Thanksgiving while helping Grandma get things ready for their meal. *I remember Grandpa commenting on how much he liked this rose-pink color on me.* Lenore smiled. She couldn't help thinking how strange it was that the memory had simply popped into her head. Such a small thing, but a lovely reminiscence.

Lenore pinned up her hair and put her head covering in place. *No matter how hard we all try to enjoy the day, it won't be the same without Grandpa sitting at the head of the table.*

❧

### Clymer

"Just think, this is our first Thanksgiving in our new home." Ezekiel slipped his arms around Michelle and gave her a kiss. "Aren't you excited?"

She nodded. Truth was, she'd be more enthused if they were going to Strasburg to celebrate the holiday. They'd only been here two months, but to Michelle, it felt like an eternity. She missed Sara, Lenore, Ezekiel's family, and most of all, Mary Ruth. If just one of them could have come up to New York to celebrate Thanksgiving, it would have made her happy. Instead, she and Ezekiel were all alone with a fifteen-pound turkey in the oven. Michelle didn't know what her husband was thinking when he'd come home with such a big bird.

"I know it's a lot of meat," Ezekiel had said, "but we'll have plenty of leftovers for turkey sandwiches, soups, and casseroles."

Michelle didn't care about leftover turkey. She would have rather gone out for dinner than cook a big meal for just the two of them.

*I'm an ungrateful wife,* she scolded herself. *I should be more appreciative of Ezekiel and try to make this a special day for him. I wish I was more like Lenore, who has always seemed so peaceful, loving, and full of joy to me. I bet if she were here now, she'd say I have a lot to be thankful for, and of course she'd be right.* Michelle placed her hands against her warm cheeks. *I need to quit feeling sorry for myself.*

"The turkey will be done soon, so I suppose I should set out the dishes and silverware before I cook the potatoes and heat up the green beans." She gestured to the kitchen table. "Since it's just the two of us, we may as well eat in here."

Ezekiel shook his head. "This is a special occasion. Don't you think it would be nicer if we ate in the dining room?"

Michelle shrugged. "If that's what you would prefer."

A knock sounded on the front door, and Ezekiel cocked his head. "Now, I wonder who that could be. Why don't you answer it while I start peeling the potatoes?"

Michelle touched his forehead. "Are you *grank*? Since when would you rather peel potatoes than answer the door?"

"No, I'm not sick—only trying to be helpful." He stroked the side of her cheek and gave her a quick kiss.

"Okay, whatever. It's probably our English neighbor to the north of us. She's always asking to borrow something." Michelle left the room and made her way to the front door, in no hurry to get there. When she opened it and saw who stood on the front porch, her mouth opened wide and she let out a squeal. "Ernie! Jack! I had no idea you two were coming here today." Michelle barely took notice of the young woman standing between her brothers until Jack gave her a hug and said, "Michelle, this is my fiancée, Gina."

Her eyes widened. "You're engaged?"

"Yep. I proposed to her two weeks ago." He shuffled his feet. "I would have told you sooner, but when Ezekiel contacted me and Ernie about coming here for Thanksgiving, I decided to wait and surprise you with the news."

"I certainly am surprised, and I'm happy for you too." Michelle gave Gina a hug and wrapped her arms around Ernie.

At that moment, Ezekiel stepped onto the porch and slipped

his arm around Michelle's waist. "See now why I wanted you to answer the door? Are you surprised?"

"Yes, very." She poked his arm playfully. "I knew something had to be up when you volunteered to do the potatoes. And I'm definitely getting the dining room ready for Thanksgiving supper, for us and my surprise guests."

"Now be fair, Fraa. You know I'm pretty handy in the kitchen." He chuckled and invited their guests inside.

As Michelle followed the four of them inside, her heart swelled with joy. How blessed she felt to be married to such a thoughtful, loving husband. *Thank You, God, for bringing Ezekiel into my life.*

### Strasburg

"Now that we've prayed and before we begin eating, could we take a few minutes and tell what we are thankful for?" Lenore asked as she and their guests sat around the dining-room table.

"That's an excellent idea." Lenore's father looked at Grandma. "Why don't you go first, Mom?"

Grandma sat up straight and folded her hands, placing them on the table in front of her. "Let's see now. . . . I am thankful for all the years I had with your daed. There are so many memories it's hard to choose one, but last year's Thanksgiving was special."

"Oh, you mean because when Grandpa handed the knife to Dad so he could cut the turkey, the bird ended up on the floor?" Peter chortled. "I'll never forget the shocked look on both of their faces."

Grandma smiled. "I have to admit, it was pretty funny."

"Jah, and let's hope after we're all done sharing what we're thankful for that I do better this year when I carve the Thanksgiving bird." Dad gestured to the golden-brown turkey sitting on the large platter in the middle of the table. "I sure don't want to make any new memories that everyone will be talking about for another whole year."

"If it happens again," Lenore's mother interjected, "it could be the last time you're given the honor of using your daed's carving knife."

Everyone laughed, including Lenore's dad, who sat at the head of the table in the chair that used to be occupied by Grandpa.

"All right—who wants to go next and share what they're thankful for?" Grandma asked.

"I will." Lenore's hand shot up. "I'm ever so thankful that I was born into a loving, caring family that can laugh together and cry together and make so many good memories. As Grandpa once said, 'Quality family time together is the foundation for a solid home.'"

All heads nodded in agreement.

Lenore's dad turned to look at Jesse. "What about you, Jesse? Would you tell us what you're thankful for?"

Jesse's ears turned a dark shade of pink. Lenore figured he wasn't used to being put on the spot.

"Go ahead," Dad coaxed. "Don't be shy. We'd all like to hear what you're thankful for."

"Well, the first thing I'm thankful for is my precious little girl." He turned in his seat and gestured to Cindy sitting in her high chair. "She's my ray of sunshine, even on dreary days." He then turned his gaze on each one sitting around the table. "I'm also thankful for the pleasure of being here with all of you today. It was kind of Mary Ruth and Lenore to invite me and Cindy to join you."

Grandma, who was sitting to Jesse's left, reached over and gave his arm a few taps. "And we are thankful you two could be here today. It's our pleasure to have you."

Lenore felt content inside, seeing everyone in good spirits. Even though Grandpa was deeply missed, the family's tradition of celebrating holidays together was being carried on.

❧

"That was one delicious meal. Danki, Mary Ruth and Lenore, for all the work you did preparing it for us." Jesse rubbed his stomach. "Now I need to either take a nap or go outside and get some exercise."

"I vote for going outside." Peter pushed his chair away from the table. "Bet there's enough snow on the ground to build a snowman. Anyone wanna help me?"

"Count me in," Jesse said.

"Me too." Lenore gathered up a few plates. "I'll join you after the dishes are done."

"No need for that." Lenore's mother shook her head. "I'll help Mary Ruth with the *schissele*. You should go outside and have some fun."

Jesse looked at his daughter, sitting in the high chair with mashed potatoes all over her face. "Maybe I should stay inside and keep an eye on my messy little *schtinker*. She needs to be cleaned up and might even be ready for a nap."

Mary Ruth patted the top of Cindy's head. "She does look kind of drowsy, but I bet she won't fall asleep if I put her down. She seems to be awake more than asleep these days."

Jesse smiled in response and stepped over to his daughter. He grabbed a couple of paper towels and dampened them before returning to Cindy. With ease, Jesse wiped off her face and hands. His little girl smiled up at him and reached out her hands. "Not yet, little one; hang on there. I'll have you out in a minute."

He continued to clean up the tray that had some small morsels left on it. "That's better; now you're ready to come out of there." Jesse set aside the soiled paper towels and lifted his daughter from the high chair. He held her for a moment and watched the activity around the kitchen, focusing mostly on Lenore. *I do care about her.* His back stiffened as he looked over at Lenore's father. *It's just that my feelings aren't what they should be.*

"I'll keep Cindy occupied," Lenore's dad offered. "We'll go in the living room, and I'll give her a horsey ride on my knee."

"She'll like that. Thanks, Ivan." Jesse got his jacket, hat, and gloves. "You comin', Lenore?"

"Sure, I'll be out as soon as I put on some warm clothes and my boots."

"Okay, see you soon." Jesse followed Peter out the door. As

they stepped onto the back porch, Jesse's foot slipped on a patch of ice. He grabbed hold of the wooden railing and went on down the stairs to join Peter in the yard. The snow was still falling and creating a white blanket over everything. Peter began making a ball of snow, then rolling it along the ground, and Jesse did the same. Before long, he had a good-sized sphere made. "What do you think, Peter? Does this look good enough?"

"That's perfect! We'll use that one for the bottom of the snowman." Peter went back to rolling his own ball again.

Meanwhile, Jesse watched him and enjoyed the fun he was having. He soon picked up some snow, packed it, and threw the icy ball at the barn. It hit with a *thud* and stuck there. "This is some real good stuff." He made another snowball and tossed it, nearly hitting Peter.

Peter snorted. "Keep that up and we could end up having a real snowball fight."

"No way, but if this keeps up we could have enough to build a couple of snow forts." Jesse chuckled.

"I think my section is the right size." Peter tried picking it up, but it wouldn't budge.

Jesse came closer to him. "Wait, don't lift it. Just roll it over by mine."

He watched Peter work on getting the middle over next to the base. "Now you and I can lift it up together," Jesse instructed.

They both reached around and put the smaller sphere on top of the base. Jesse stepped back, looked it over, and gave a whistle. "Looks pretty good to me."

Peter shook his head. "Nope. It's leaning kinda funny." Grunting and groaning, he managed to move the giant snowball until it looked symmetrical. Then he brushed off any imperfections with his gloves.

"That's looking more like a snowman now." Jesse looked around the yard for some sticks to use for the snowman's arms. It was getting harder to see things because the snow had accumulated so fast. Peter was taking a break and messing with his hat. "I wonder if Grandma has any spare carrots we could use for his nose when we get finished."

"Good question." Jesse's nose started to run from the cold. He pulled off his dampened glove and fished around in his coat pocket. Jesse's numbing fingers found the tissue he'd put in there this morning and wiped his nose. *Ah. . . that's better.* He stuffed the wadded tissue into his pocket and was about to put his glove back on when a snowball hit him on the shoulder. "Hey!" Jesse looked up and saw Peter laughing so hard he was holding his stomach.

"I wasn't even trying." Peter snickered.

"Okay, now you'd better watch out, because I'm getting ready to throw one at you." Jesse quickly pulled on his glove.

Soon they were throwing snowballs one after the other. Jesse was out of breath and laughing so hard he could hardly pick up any more snow. "All right, that's enough, Peter!" he hollered. "We need to put the finishing touches on our snowman."

Peter dropped the snowball in his hand. "Okay, okay. . .I get it. You're too tuckered out to keep throwing snowballs at me."

Jesse couldn't deny it. Lenore's brother was younger than him, and once they'd started the snowball fight, Peter had become even more energetic. "I admit, I am kind of tired, but the truth is, we came out here to build a snowman, so let's finish the job we started."

"You're right, we still need to find something to use for the snowman's eyes." Peter looked around. "There's so much snow on the ground, we'll probably never find any small rocks to use. I'll go look in the barn and see if there's anything there that could serve as the snowman's eyes."

Peter turned toward the barn just as Lenore came out the back door. Jesse was on the verge of warning her about the patch of ice when Lenore's feet went out from under her and down she went. When she didn't get up right away, Jesse figured she must be hurt. He dropped the snowball he'd started, leaped onto the porch, and swept Lenore into his arms. He hoped she wasn't seriously hurt.

# Chapter 25

"What happened? Is my daughter hurt?" Lenore's mother rushed forward when Jesse entered the house carrying Lenore.

Peter came in right behind them. "Is my sister okay?"

"She fell on a patch of ice on the porch. I saw it there when I went out to build the snowman and should have done something about it then." Jesse's voice was filled with regret.

"Did she break anything?" Grandma asked as Lenore clung to Jesse. It felt good to be held in the safety of his strong arms.

"I don't think so, but let's get her on the couch."

As Jesse placed Lenore down, she groaned. "My lower back and hip hurt, but I don't think it's serious. Probably just bruised really bad."

"I'll get some ice." Grandma hurried from the room.

"Or we could try alternating heat and cold." Mom's brows wrinkled. "Come to think of it, I believe a person should use ice in the first twenty-four hours of an injury. Jah, that's what our chiropractor said."

"I think we should call a driver and go to the hospital to have your back x-rayed," Dad said from across the room where he held Cindy, who was straddling his knee.

"There's no need for that." Lenore pulled herself to a sitting position and stood. "I'll just walk around for a bit and see how I'm doing."

Lenore's cheeks heated with embarrassment as everyone watched her move slowly around the living room. Each step she took caused pain, but she tried not to let on. It was a good thing the scholars had no school tomorrow, because with the way Lenore's back felt now, she would not be able to teach. Hopefully by Monday she would feel better, and in the meantime, Lenore would rest and try icing it as Grandma and Mom had suggested.

When Grandma returned to the living room with a bag of ice, Lenore took it gratefully. Then she excused herself and limped down the hall to the guest room. Her back hurt more than she was willing to admit, and the thought of climbing the stairs to her bedroom held no appeal whatsoever.

❧

"I think Cindy and I should probably go." Jesse moved toward the baby.

"But you haven't had dessert yet," Mary Ruth said. "You really need to try some of Lenore's delicious Pineapple Philly pie."

"I'm still full from dinner, and it won't be long before Cindy's bedtime." Jesse glanced at his daughter, who still looked wide-awake. He figured all the extra attention she'd gotten today had her keyed up. Hopefully she'd sleep like a log tonight.

"Oh, I understand." Mary Ruth's slumped shoulders let Jesse know she was disappointed.

"Guess I could stay long enough to eat a piece of pie. But before I do, I need to take care of that icy porch for you. Do you have any ice melt, Mary Ruth?"

"Jah, there's a bag in the utility room. I was going to put some out earlier but got busy fixing the meal and forgot." Mary Ruth glanced in the direction of the guest room. "If I had taken care of it, Lenore wouldn't have gotten hurt."

"Accidents happen, Mom, and if I had known about it, I would have melted the ice for you," Ivan interjected.

"Your son is right," Yvonne put in. "An accident can happen, indoors or out, when a person least expects it. Why, if some water or milk had been spilled on the kitchen floor, Lenore could have slipped on that."

"That may be true," Jesse said, "but the fact is, she slipped on ice that I saw and should have taken care of. And even though it's after the fact, I'm gonna get rid of it right now." He headed for the utility room to get the bag of ice melt. *I sure hope Lenore will be okay.*

After everyone went home and Mary Ruth had given her kitchen a final inspection, she went to check on Lenore again. The last time she'd looked in on her, to offer a piece of pie, Lenore had been awake but said she wasn't hungry and preferred not to get up. She asked Mary Ruth to offer her apologies to everyone for not joining them at the dessert table.

Lenore's parents and brother had popped into the guest room to say goodbye before heading for home, and Jesse said he would drop by sometime the following day to check on Lenore.

*He's such a nice man,* Mary Ruth thought as she left the kitchen and headed down the hall. *Jesse seems to care about my granddaughter, and I'm hoping those two might have a future together.* She smiled, thinking about the way little Cindy lit up every time she was with Lenore. *That sweet little girl needs a mudder too.*

Mary Ruth had invited Jesse to join them for supper many times over the last few months—partly so he didn't have to cook, but mostly so he and Lenore could spend time together and get better acquainted. Lenore had waited several years to find a husband, and Mary Ruth hoped Jesse might be the one God intended for her granddaughter.

She paused by the guest room door. *When Lenore feels better, I'll volunteer to watch Cindy some evening so she and Jesse can go out to eat at one of the local restaurants by themselves. It might help to get them together quicker if they have more time alone.*

*Harrisburg, Pennsylvania*

"That sure was a great meal, Mom. You outdid yourself today." Brad yawned and stretched his arms over his head. "Eating all that turkey made me sleepy, and I bet I gained five pounds."

Taking a seat on the couch beside him, Sara looked at Brad's mother, Jean, and rolled her eyes. "I think my husband may be exaggerating just a bit."

Jean chuckled and poked her husband's arm. "He gets that from his dad. Isn't that right, Clarence?"

"Maybe." Brad's father lifted his shoulders and let them drop. "But only about unimportant things."

"Food's important." Brad thumped his stomach. "And the truth is I really did eat too much today."

"I think we all did," Sara admitted. "But that's because everything was so good." She looked over at Jean. "I'll have to get your recipe for the dressing you stuffed the turkey with. It was so moist and tasty."

"I'll write it down before you and Brad leave on Saturday." Jean released a lingering sigh. "I wish you could stay longer. We don't get to see enough of you."

"I know, but it could be worse," Brad said. "I might have ended up taking a church on the other side of the country. At least Lancaster is within easy driving distance of Harrisburg." He smiled at his parents. "And you two are welcome to come down anytime you like. There are two guest rooms in the parsonage, you know."

"If the roads aren't bad, we'll try to come down for your church's Christmas Eve service." Clarence looked at his wife. "Your mother still gets nervous when the roads are icy or there's too much snow coming down."

Jean nodded. "Even as a passenger, I'm white-knuckling it during bad weather. Can you imagine what shape I'd be in if I was sitting behind the wheel?"

"I don't blame you," Sara said. "I've never enjoyed driving in snow either. And it's a good thing Brad doesn't seem to mind, because from the way the snow's been coming down today, we could have nasty roads to contend with on our trip home Saturday."

Jean's forehead wrinkled. "Oh, I hope not. Let's pray for warmer temperatures that will melt the snow."

When Sara's cell phone vibrated, she excused herself to take the call and went into the kitchen.

"Happy Thanksgiving, Kenny," she said, having recognized her brother's phone number.

"Is this Sara Fuller?" The female voice on the other end was definitely not Kenny's.

"Yes, it is. Who's this?" She couldn't imagine why someone else would be using her brother's phone or calling her. Had he lost it somewhere, and someone found it?

"Sara, I'm Lynn Moore, Kenny's girlfriend. We were on our way home from my parents' house, where we ate Thanksgiving dinner, and after traveling just a few miles down the road, we were involved in an accident."

Sara's blood ran cold. "Has Kenny been hurt?" She suddenly felt as if she was reliving the past, when she'd received a call informing her that her stepfather, Dean, had been in an accident.

"Yes, but we don't know the extent of his injuries yet."

"Were you hurt too, Lynn?"

"No, just pretty shook up. The vehicle that hit us rammed into Kenny's side of the car."

"Where are you now?"

"We're at the hospital in Philadelphia. My folks are here too." Lynn gave Sara the name and address of the hospital.

"I'll let my husband know, and we'll be there as soon as we can." Sara's voice shook and tears pricked the back of her eyes. Kenny's father had died from his injuries. She couldn't stand the thought of losing Kenny too.

Sara leaned against the wall for support. *Dear Lord, I've lost too many people I love. Please let my brother be okay.*

# Chapter 26

*Philadelphia, Pennsylvania*

Sara sat in one of the hospital's waiting rooms with Brad and Kenny's girlfriend, waiting to see her brother and rubbing her clenched jaw. When she and Brad had arrived an hour ago, Lynn explained that Kenny had a concussion and some broken ribs, but the doctor was running a few more tests to be sure there were no internal injuries and that the trauma to his head was not severe.

Another half hour went by before a doctor came in and said Kenny had been admitted to a room and would remain at the hospital overnight for observation. He also gave the good news that there were no internal injuries.

Relieved, Sara inhaled deeply and blew out her breath. "Thank you for letting us know. Is it all right if we see him now?"

"They're getting him settled into his room. Once that's been done, a nurse will come out and get you." The doctor offered a reassuring smile as he looked at each of them. "Try not to worry. Kenny's going to be fine."

Lynn sagged in her chair. "When that other vehicle came barreling toward us, I was so scared." Her chin trembled. "Then after the impact, Kenny didn't respond. I was afraid he might have died."

Sara shuddered at the thought but found comfort when Brad put his arm around her. It was hard not to think of that day when her stepfather died.

"Everything's going to be okay, Sara," Brad said in a soothing tone. "Kenny will be out of commission for a few weeks while his head and ribs heal, but I'm sure he'll be fine."

"I want to stay till he's released from the hospital, and then if

Kenny is willing, I think we should take him home with us until he is fully recuperated and can return to classes at the music school."

"I don't think Kenny will want to leave Philly," Lynn spoke up. "I'm pretty sure my folks will be okay with him staying with us."

Sara didn't want to upset Lynn any further, so she chose not to voice her objections. Her only response was, "It's nice of you to offer. We'll wait and see what Kenny wants to do."

Brad clasped Sara's hand and gave her fingers a comforting squeeze. "I'll call Mom and Dad and tell them we won't be coming back to Harrisburg and that hopefully we'll see them at Christmas. It's a good thing we put our luggage in the van before we left; I had a hunch we might not be going back to my parents' house today."

Sara managed a weak smile. "Thank you. I'm sure they'll understand." She felt grateful to be blessed with kind, caring in-laws.

"I should call and leave a message for Grandma, letting her know about Kenny's accident, but I don't want to worry her."

"I'm sure once you explain that Kenny's injuries are not life-threatening, she won't worry." Brad let go of Sara's hand. "Is your phone battery holding a charge, or do you need to use mine?"

Sara pulled her cell phone out of her purse. "The battery is fine. I'll call now and leave a message, even though Grandma may not go out to the phone shack till tomorrow morning."

<hr/>

### Strasburg

"How are you feeling?" Mary Ruth asked when she entered the guest room where Lenore lay the following morning.

Lenore groaned and sat up, pushing the pillows up behind her back. "I feel as though a horse and buggy ran over me. My right hip aches some, and my back feels like it's out of whack. Don't think I'll be much help to you today, Grandma."

"It's all right. You need to rest, but I still believe you should have gotten your back x-rayed and checked over last evening."

"If it'll make you feel better, you can make me an appointment to see our chiropractor. If he thinks it's necessary, he can take an

X-ray there in his office." Lenore shifted on the bed, trying to get comfortable. "Maybe all I need is an adjustment. That fall I took yesterday could have put my spine out of alignment, which might be the reason I'm in so much pain."

"You may be right. I'll go out now and call Dr. Clark before Jesse gets here with Cindy. If he's in his office today, he might be able to squeeze you in. And if that's the case, I'll call one of our drivers to take you there."

"Danki, Grandma." Lenore grimaced as she shifted again. She couldn't find a comfortable position. The ice pack and arnica lotion hadn't helped much either. If she couldn't get the pain under control by Monday, she'd have no choice but to stay home from school and let her helper take over. *I wouldn't want to stay away too many days, however,* Lenore thought as Grandma left the room.

Mary Ruth shivered as she stepped inside the cold phone shack. She made the call to the chiropractor and was relieved to learn that he was in his office and could squeeze Lenore in at one thirty. Then she arranged for Stan, one of their drivers, to give Lenore a ride.

Mary Ruth was about to leave the phone shack when she remembered she hadn't checked for phone messages. She clicked on the answering machine and found only one. It was from Sara, and the tone of her voice when she began speaking frightened Mary Ruth. Something was wrong; she just knew it.

"Grandma, I wanted to let you know that Brad and I are at the hospital in Philadelphia. Kenny and his girlfriend were involved in a car accident on their way home from her parents' house, where they'd gone to celebrate Thanksgiving. Kenny is not seriously injured, but we would appreciate your prayers. I'll call again and give you an update on things, and please try not to worry."

Mary Ruth squeezed her eyes shut. *Heavenly Father, please be with my grandson and heal his body of the wounds he received during the accident.*

Hearing a horse and buggy come into the yard and knowing it

must be Jesse, Mary Ruth stepped out of the phone shack. "Guder mariye, Jesse."

"Good morning," he responded as he hitched the horse to the rail and took Cindy out of the buggy. "How's Lenore doing?"

"Still hurting, but I managed to get her an appointment with the chiropractor. One of my drivers will be by to get her this afternoon." Mary Ruth reached in and grabbed Cindy's diaper bag, and they made their way up to the house.

Once inside, Jesse took Cindy's outer garments off, gave her a kiss, and set her on the blanket Mary Ruth had placed on the floor. "If there's anything I can do to help, just say the word. I can do a few chores after work this evening, and I'd be glad to come by tomorrow to do whatever else needs to be done."

She smiled. "Danki, Jesse. That's very kind of you. And knowing I won't have to do all the chores by myself will no doubt give Lenore a sense of relief." Mary Ruth shook her head. "I sure wouldn't want her trying to do much of anything right now. Not till her back is feeling better. Even then, she'll have to be careful how she moves for a while."

He glanced around the room. "Is she still in bed?"

"Jah."

"Well, tell her I said hello and that I hope to see her later today."

"I surely will."

Jesse knelt on the floor and gave his daughter another kiss, then tickled her under the chin. "Be good for Mary Ruth."

Cindy looked up at him and giggled.

Chuckling, he stood. "I'll see you after work, Mary Ruth. I hope you have a good day and that my little one doesn't give you any trouble."

"I'm sure she won't. Cindy's always been a good girl for me."

Jesse said goodbye, and after he went out the front door, Mary Ruth moved over to the baby. "All right, little one, what shall we do while we're waiting for Lenore to get up?"

Cindy made some baby-talk sounds and stuck her thumb in her mouth.

Mary Ruth laughed. "I think we can find something more exciting for you to do than that."

"How are you doing? What did the chiropractor say?" Grandma asked when Lenore limped through the front door later that afternoon.

"He took an X-ray, and there are no broken bones, so that's a relief." Lenore paused to take a breath. "He believes it's just a pulled muscle, and I have a pretty nasty bruise."

"What did he suggest you do for it?"

"Ice, alternating with heat. He also gave me a natural muscle relaxer and something for pain from the nutrition area of his clinic." Lenore took off her outer garments and hung them on the clothes tree in the hall. "He suggested that I rest and return to the clinic sometime next week."

Grandma tipped her head. "So no teaching for a while?"

"Not till the pain is better and I'm able to sit comfortably. My helper will have to be notified, and she may be on her own with the class if someone can't step in as the main teacher." Lenore grimaced. "This is not a good time for me to be away from school. The Christmas program the scholars will be putting on for their families is less than a month away. I would very much like to be at school so I can work with the children, helping them get their skits, recitations, and songs perfected."

"I am sure whoever fills in for you will work with the kinner."

"I suppose." Lenore glanced toward the living room. "How is Cindy doing? Has she been good for you today?"

Grandma nodded. "That boppli is so *siess*."

"I think all babies are sweet." A pang of regret over not being a mother stabbed her heart. It was wrong to dwell on her desire to be married and raising a family, but she wasn't getting any younger, and the idea of having to remain single was never far from her thoughts.

"Where is Cindy now?" Lenore asked as she worked her way

slowly to the living-room couch.

"She's taking a nap. I set up the playpen in my room so she could sleep undisturbed."

"That's good." As Grandma took a seat in her rocking chair, Lenore lowered herself to the couch. It was time to get off her feet.

"Would you like an ice pack or a warm compress for your back?" Grandma questioned.

"No, I just need to lie down and rest for a bit."

"Why don't you go into the guest room and take a nap? I'll call you when supper is ready."

Lenore reached around with one hand and rubbed the muscle spasm in her back. "I feel bad leaving you with all the work. I should be helping with supper."

"You need to rest your back, and I'm perfectly capable of fixing our evening meal by myself."

Lenore would have liked to argue the point, but Grandma was right. For now, at least, she needed to rest so her back would heal and she could return to teaching, in addition to all her other normal activities, just as soon as possible.

# Chapter 27

"Would you mind if we stop by my grandma's before going back to Lancaster?" Sara asked as she and Brad traveled home Saturday morning. "I want to give Grandma an update on Kenny and see how Lenore is doing." Sara was glad her grandmother had told her about Lenore's fall on the ice so she could be praying for her.

Brad glanced over at Sara and smiled. "Sure, hon. In fact, I was going to suggest the very same thing."

They drove in silence awhile, until Sara asked another question. "Do you think I was too pushy, trying to convince Kenny he should come home with us to heal? He seemed kind of irritated when I brought it up again before we left the hospital."

With his eyes still on the road, Brad reached over and patted Sara's arm. "He's not your kid brother anymore; Kenny is almost twenty years old and has become pretty independent since he moved to Philadelphia to attend the music institute."

"I understand that, but how would staying with us for a few weeks hamper his independence?"

"He might feel as if you'd want to mother him."

Sara folded her arms. "That's ridiculous. I've never tried to do that to Kenny."

"Now don't get upset. I wasn't insinuating that you were mothering him." Brad spoke in a gentle tone. "I only mentioned it because sometimes when a person makes a suggestion, we take it the wrong way and assume they are trying to tell us what to do."

Sara felt heat behind her eyelids. "I only want what's best for him, but if he'd rather stay with Lynn's parents, then I guess that's okay. At least Kenny won't be by himself while he's recuperating from his injuries."

"Right. And you can keep in touch by phone to find out how he's doing."

Sara leaned against her headrest and tried to relax. *Maybe I'll feel better about things when we get to Grandma's and she's given me the hug I need.*

After breakfast, Mary Ruth headed to the basement to get some towels she'd hung on the inside line the night before. Lenore was resting on the living-room couch, so Mary Ruth figured it was also a good time to take a look inside the prayer jar that Sara, Michelle, and Lenore had found down there.

Going over to the step stool, she climbed up carefully and took down the jar. Taking a seat on a wooden stool, she opened the lid and pulled out a slip of paper near the top. A verse of scripture had been written on it. "The Lord is nigh unto them that are of a broken heart; and saveth such as be of a contrite spirit. Psalm 34:18."

Mary Ruth sighed. *My poor daughter's heart was broken, and that's why she chose this verse to put in her prayer jar. Oh Rhoda, if only you had talked to your daed and me—told us about the baby—we would have offered our love and support, even if we didn't approve of your actions. We loved you so much and would have worked things out if you'd let us.*

So many regrets, but they wouldn't change the past. *Now don't start wallowing in pity,* she chided herself. *Be thankful for the note Rhoda left in her Bible so you could get to know Sara.*

Mary Ruth put the piece of paper back in the jar and returned it to the shelf. Reading Rhoda's messages conjured up feelings of sadness, but at the same time Mary Ruth found comfort in learning what her daughter had written. For now, at least, she needed to concentrate on getting the towels off the clothesline, folding them, and taking them upstairs to put away.

Lenore had barely found a comfortable position on the couch when she heard a car pull into the yard. Thinking Grandma would see to whoever it was, she made no move to get up.

A short time later, a knock sounded on the front door. Lenore listened for Grandma's footsteps, but when they didn't come and the knock came again, she pulled herself off the couch. Limping across the room, she opened the door and was surprised to see Sara and Brad on the porch.

"How are you?" Sara asked.

"How's your brother?" Lenore queried at the same time.

"Kenny's still hurting but is out of the hospital now," Sara said. "We came by to see how you're doing and to give an update on his condition."

"We're anxious to hear. Grandma and I have been praying for him. Come on in." Lenore led the way to the living room, where she took a seat on the couch, placing a pillow behind her back. "Grandma went to the basement to get some clean towels, but I thought she'd be back up here by now."

"I should go check on her." Sara's brows drew together. "Those stairs are steep, and she might have fallen."

"In that case, I'd better go down to the basement. If she's hurt, I'll let you both know. Sara, why don't you stay here and visit with Lenore?" Brad suggested. He left before Sara could respond.

Sara lowered herself into Grandpa's recliner. "We heard about your fall on the ice. How are you doing, Lenore?"

"My back's still sore, but the X-ray at the chiropractor's office didn't show any broken bones. He thinks I just pulled a muscle, and of course my back and part of the hip area are bruised."

"Will you be able to teach on Monday?"

"I want to, but with the pain I'm feeling now, it's doubtful."

"I'm sorry to hear that. Slipping on ice can be so dangerous—same with stairs." Sara turned her gaze in the direction of the basement stairway. "I hope Grandma's okay. The last thing we need is someone else in the family getting hurt."

Lenore bobbed her head. "That's for sure."

A few minutes later, Brad entered the room carrying a laundry basket full of towels. Grandma was behind him.

Sara got up and gave Grandma a hug. "I was worried about you, and I'm glad you let Brad carry the laundry basket up. You shouldn't be going up and down those steps. An accident can happen when you least expect it—just ask Lenore."

Grandma patted Sara's arm. "I've been doing it for years, and I'm always careful on the stairs. Besides, the washing machine is down there, so how else am I supposed to get the laundry done?"

"True, but I often do the laundry," Lenore interjected.

"With your back hurting right now, you shouldn't try to do any chores." Shaking her finger, Grandma peered at Lenore over the top of her glasses. "Please try not to worry about me."

"Where should I put this?" Brad asked, nodding with his head toward the laundry basket he still held.

"You can set it in the hall by the bathroom door. The towels are folded. I just need to put them away."

"Okay, sure." When Brad left the room, Grandma took a seat in her rocker. "How is Kenny doing?" she asked, looking at Sara. "I've been concerned since I first heard about his accident."

"He still has some pain from the concussion, but the broken ribs are causing the real discomfort." Sara frowned as she folded her arms. "I tried to talk him into coming home with us to recuperate, but he chose to stay with his girlfriend's parents instead."

"Maybe he wanted to be closer to his school so he could keep up with his classes," Grandma said.

"That could be, although we do have internet access and two computers, so he could do his schoolwork right in our home."

"At least he will have someone to keep an eye on him and make sure he doesn't overdo." Grandma got the rocking chair moving. "I'm thankful he wasn't seriously hurt."

Sara shuddered. "Same here. I was so scared when I got the call that he'd been involved in an accident. It felt like I was reliving

Dean's accident when I found out he'd been seriously injured."

Brad returned to the living room and took a seat on the other end of the couch. "Is there anything Sara and I can do for either of you while we're here?" He looked at Grandma and Lenore.

"Jesse will be coming over soon to take care of the chores in the barn." Grandma smiled. "That young man is so kind and helpful. He did several chores for us when he was here last evening, and he didn't hesitate to volunteer his help again today."

Tilting her head to one side, Sara looked over at Lenore with her lips slightly parted. "Are you still seeing Jesse socially?"

"I was, but thanks to my sore back, we probably won't be doing anything together for a while." Lenore grimaced. "Sure wish I had seen that patch of ice before it was too late. It was embarrassing enough to fall in front of Jesse and Peter, but when Jesse picked me up and carried me into the house, my face felt like it was on fire."

Brad chuckled. "Sounds like you've been bitten by the love bug."

Lenore kept quiet. No way was she about to admit that she'd allowed herself to fall in love with Jesse. Since he had not spoken any words of love or mentioned marriage, it wouldn't be right to blurt out her feelings.

"Once your back is doing better, maybe the four of us could get together and go bowling or out to supper at a nice restaurant," Sara suggested.

"That would be fun." Lenore repositioned herself against the pillow. She hoped it wouldn't be too long before she was pain free and could function normally again. She also hoped Jesse would agree to go with Sara and Brad on what might be considered a double date.

# Chapter 28

*Clymer*

Michelle glanced at the calendar on Ezekiel's desk. Today was Thursday, just a week after Thanksgiving. In another three weeks they'd be celebrating Christmas. Ezekiel had promised they could go to Strasburg for Christmas, and Michelle looked forward to that. They'd be taking Val with them, because Michelle couldn't stand the thought of someone else caring for the dog in her absence. Besides, Val probably missed Sadie and all the attention she used to get from family and friends in Strasburg.

Seeing everyone again would be a joy. Michelle missed them all terribly. Having Jack and Ernie visit for Thanksgiving had been wonderful, but they'd only been able to stay for a few days, and then loneliness had set in again.

She moved across the room to get breakfast started, nearly tripping on Val, who lay curled on a throw rug near the stove. The dog always wanted to be near Michelle and often slipped into the house as soon as the door would open.

Ezekiel would be in from doing chores soon, and he'd need to eat so he could get out to his shop and begin working on a new order for several bee boxes. He already had one employee working for him, but if business kept growing, he'd need to hire more help.

Michelle picked up a jar of honey and placed it on the table. Ezekiel liked to stir a heaping teaspoonful of honey into a glass of room-temperature water, along with a tablespoon of apple cider vinegar. He claimed it gave him extra energy and kept him from getting sick. Michelle had never tried the concoction, so she couldn't be sure what health benefits it offered. According to a book Ezekiel's mother gave them soon after they were married, drinking lukewarm water combined with pure, unfiltered honey and vinegar could be helpful for several ailments, including nausea.

Michelle was actually tempted to try some today, because she'd felt queasy ever since she'd gotten out of bed. "Sure hope I'm not coming down with the stomach bug that's been going around," she mumbled as she took out a slab of bacon and a carton of eggs. "If I get sick, I'll feel even more sorry for myself."

"Did I hear my fraa say she's feeling grank?"

Michelle whirled around. "Ach, you scared me, Ezekiel. I didn't hear you come in."

He wiggled his brows. "That's 'cause I'm so sneaky."

"I can't argue with that." Michelle took out the frying pan, placed four pieces of bacon in it, and turned on the gas burner. As it began to cook, her stomach rolled. "Eww. . .just the smell of this makes me feel sick. I must be coming down with the flu."

"Or you could be expecting our first boppli."

Her husband's hopeful tone caused Michelle to tear up. "If only it were true."

"It could be." Ezekiel slipped his arms around her waist. "You could get one of those home pregnancy tests at the pharmacy or make an appointment to see a doctor."

Michelle gave the hem of her apron a tug. "I suppose it wouldn't hurt to take a pregnancy test, although I'm sure it will be negative." Her chin jutted out. "I'm used to being disappointed."

"Are you disappointed in me, because I wanted to move to New York?" Ezekiel rubbed his forehead with the palm of his hand. "You would have preferred to stay in Strasburg, right?"

"Yes, I would, but my place is with my husband, and if this is where you want to be, then I will learn to be content living here too."

Ezekiel kissed Michelle's forehead. "I love you so much."

"I love you too." She turned back toward the stove, being careful not to step on Val's tail. "Now I'd better get breakfast made or you'll never get out to your shop."

"Okay, but would you like me to go by the pharmacy sometime

today and pick up a pregnancy test for you?"

Michelle shrugged. "Sure. Guess it can't hurt."

⚬

*Strasburg*

Lenore stood in front of the living-room window, staring out at the snow-covered yard. If the weather didn't change, they would definitely have a white Christmas.

Her shoulders drooped, and she sighed. The pain in her back had lessened, but she didn't feel good enough to begin teaching again. The healing process was taking longer than she'd expected, and it tried her patience. Staying home all day and not being able to do much was taking its toll on Lenore, as she'd never been one to sit around and do little or nothing.

"If you're up to it, I have a favor to ask."

Lenore turned at the sound of her grandmother's voice. "What is it?"

"Cindy just woke up, and I'm trying to finish the *frack* I started sewing for her yesterday."

"You want me to keep an eye on her?"

Grandma nodded. "I realize you have to be careful with your back, but perhaps you could sit on the couch with her in your lap and read the touch-and-feel book Jesse brought over the other day for his daughter to look at." Grandma clasped her hands together. "Hopefully you can keep her occupied until I finish the dress."

"Sure, no problem." Lenore took a seat on the couch, positioning a soft pillow behind her back. "If you'll bring Cindy and her little book to me, I'll do my best to keep her entertained."

Grandma smiled and left the room.

A lump formed in Lenore's throat as she looked at the quilt Grandma had made to drape over Grandpa's lap when he had been wheelchair-bound after his stroke. She closed her eyes, remembering Grandpa's satisfied expression as he sat in his wheelchair with the small quilt. The covering was about the size of a wall hanging and dropped from the middle of his chest all the way down to the floor. Grandma now kept it draped over the back of Grandpa's favorite chair.

Unwilling to give in to her tears, Lenore opened her eyes. It did no good to dwell on what could not be changed.

When Grandma brought Cindy out to Lenore a few minutes later, the little girl giggled and held out her arms. Lenore's heart nearly melted. What she wouldn't give to help Jesse raise this adorable child.

Grandma placed Cindy in Lenore's lap and handed her the book. "I'll just be in the next room, so if she gets squirmy and you need a break, please holler out to me and I'll come right away."

"Okay."

After Grandma left the room, Lenore began reading the story about the curious squirrel in the forest, searching for nuts and other good food. On each page was a picture of a little brown squirrel with fuzzy fur. The grass was also textured, and so were the fluffy clouds in the sky. Lenore took hold of Cindy's hand and rubbed it gently across each of the textures as she said the name of the item in Pennsylvania Dutch. "*Eechhaas*—squirrel. *Graas*—grass. *Wolke*—clouds."

Cindy giggled, tipping her head back to look up at Lenore and batting her feathery eyelashes.

Smiling, Lenore read through the story again. When she finished, Lenore sang one of her favorite Christmas songs while stroking Cindy's soft cheek with her thumb: "*Silent night, holy night. . . All is calm, all is bright.*"

Cindy sat still for several minutes but then grew restless. When she began to whimper and squirm, Lenore tried reading the book again, but the little girl had obviously lost interest. Realizing she wouldn't be able to keep the child entertained any longer, Lenore called out to Grandma. Maybe later today, if her back felt better, Lenore would try sitting in the rocking chair with Cindy. The child usually liked to be rocked, and sometimes that was all it took to put her to sleep.

With Christmas only a few weeks away, the flower shop was swamped with orders and lots of customers coming in to see what was available. Sara had put a small, beautifully decorated tree in the window display with pots of poinsettias sitting around it. All the plants had been purchased from the King family's greenhouse, but this year Ezekiel was not the one to deliver them. Instead, his brother Abe had brought the red, white, and pink blooming beauties into the shop.

Sighing as she took a seat behind the counter to look at the list of orders that had come in so far today, Sara thought about Michelle. She'd received a letter from her soon after she and Ezekiel moved to New York, but hadn't heard anything else from her in a while.

Sara leaned her elbows on the counter. *I wonder how Michelle's adjusting to her new home and how things are going with Ezekiel and his new business.*

There was a time when Sara would have been glad if Michelle had moved out of Strasburg. But the friendship they had eventually established changed all that, and now Sara truly missed Michelle. *I think Grandma and Lenore miss her too.*

Sara's musings were pushed aside when a customer entered the store. She was surprised to see Rick Osprey, whom she hadn't seen since their first night of Bible study.

As he approached the counter, his posture stiffened, and as he looked at Sara, Rick blinked a couple of times. "Say, aren't you Pastor Fuller's wife?"

"Yes, I am. I met you at our first Bible study, but we haven't seen or heard from you since. Is everything all right?"

"It's fine. I had to quit the Bible study because I'm working nights now." He glanced down at his feet, then back at Sara again. "Guess I should have called and let the pastor know, but I've been super busy lately and sort of spaced it off."

"Oh, I see." Sara cleared her throat. "Umm. . .that night at the

Bible study you attended, you said something about hanging out with some Amish young people when you were a teenager."

He nodded.

"You mentioned one of the girls and said you thought her name was Reba, or Rhoda. Was it Rhoda Lapp?"

He scratched the side of his head, and a flush crept across his cheeks. "Yeah, I think so."

"What did she look like? Did she have red hair?"

"Yeah, come to think of it, she sure did. It was real long and she wore it hanging down her back. But until one of the girls, whose name I don't remember, said something about Rhoda's heritage, I had no idea she'd been raised in an Amish home."

Sara shivered as a chill ran through her body. *Is this conversation making him uncomfortable? Could Rick be embarrassed because he'd been seeing an Amish girl? Could my mother have been secretly seeing him?* She gulped with the realization of what could be possible. *If Rick was seeing my mother, then he could be the man I've been searching for since I moved here to Pennsylvania. By some miracle, could my biological father be standing here before me? If so, did Mama tell him she was expecting a baby before she left?*

Sara licked her lips with cautious hope. "How well did you know Rhoda Lapp? Were the two of you close?"

While she waited for his answer, which seemed to be slow in coming, Sara studied the man carefully, trying to decide if she resembled him in any way. His eyes were blue, only a bit lighter than hers, but his hair was brown.

"Uh. . .I didn't know most of the Amish girls that well, except. . ." Rick paused and looked at his watch. "Oh boy, I didn't realize what time it is. There's someplace I need to go."

"Can I help you with anything before you leave?"

He shook his head. "Change of plans. I was going to order some flowers for my wife's birthday, but I can't do it right now."

Before Sara could respond, he rushed out the door. She bit the inside of her cheek. *Rick never finished answering my question, and he seemed in an awfully big hurry to get out of my store.* Goose bumps erupted on Sara's arms. *If Rick Osprey is my biological father, maybe he suspects that Mama told me, and he doesn't want anything to do with me. That could be why he rushed out the door and never fully responded to my question. If he does come back to order the flowers, should I mention that I'm Rhoda's daughter and see how he reacts to the news?*

# Chapter 29

"How are things going with your new business, Son?" Ezekiel's father asked as the family sat around the dining-room table on Christmas Eve.

Ezekiel's eyes lit up. "Real good, Dad. I've been getting orders from several different states."

"Guess there must be plenty of people interested in raising bees for honey, huh?"

Ezekiel nodded enthusiastically, then looked at his brother Abe. "You takin' good care of the hives I left here?"

"Jah. Of course, there ain't much to do during the winter months other than to check on things."

Ezekiel's mother frowned as she shook her finger at Abe. "You know how I feel about that word *ain't*. Makes you sound like you've had no education at all."

Michelle glanced at Abe to see what his reaction would be, but without a word, he cut a piece of ham and popped it into his mouth.

As everyone continued to eat their food, Michelle wondered if Ezekiel was ever going to bring up the topic foremost on her mind. Finally, as their meal came to a close, he tapped his water glass with a spoon and said, "If I can have everyone's attention, Michelle and I have an announcement to make."

All heads turned in Michelle and Ezekiel's direction.

Ezekiel reached over and placed his hand on Michelle's shoulder. "The good news we have to share on this special Christmas Eve is that sometime toward the end of July, we're gonna become parents."

Belinda's face broke into a wide smile. "That's wonderful news, Son." She looked across the table at Michelle. "How are you feeling? Any problems at all?"

"I'm a little tired and have had some nausea in the mornings, but otherwise I'm doing okay." Michelle would never admit it—at least not to Ezekiel's folks—but despite her excitement over being pregnant, she had many concerns. Would she be able to carry the baby to full term? Could she bear the pains of labor? Would Ezekiel still think she was pretty when her stomach grew large? But what concerned her the most was whether she had what it took to be a mother. Her own mother had been abusive and neglected her three children. What if those tendencies were hereditary and Michelle ended up treating their child unfairly, the way her folks had treated her, Jack, and Ernie?

"Are you hoping for a *bu* or a maedel?" Ezekiel's sister Amy asked.

"I think Ezekiel would like a son, but it makes no difference to me," Michelle replied, after taking a drink of apple cider and setting her glass down.

Ezekiel shook his head. "I'm not set on having a boy. As long as the boppli is healthy, that's all that matters."

"Very true," Ezekiel's brother-in-law Toby spoke up. "When Sylvia and I found out she was in a family way eighteen months ago, the only thing we talked about and prayed for was that our child would be healthy." He glanced over at their nine-month-old son, Allen, sitting in his high chair with a big smile, and grinned. "We are ever so thankful for our little boy's good health."

Ezekiel's youngest brother, Henry, looked over at his dad. "Were you happy that I was a bu?"

Vernon bobbed his head. "But I'd have been equally glad if you were a maedel."

Henry rolled his eyes. "Sure glad I wasn't a girl. Can't imagine havin' to wear a dress and do all the things womenfolk do."

"Just what kind of things are you referring to?" his sister Amy asked.

"Uh, you know. . . .cookin', cleanin', doin' dishes and laundry. . . .that kind of stuff."

Amy bumped his arm with her elbow. "Those aren't just chores for women, little brother. You need to learn how to do most of them too."

His brows furrowed. "How come?"

"Because someday, when I get married and move out of the house, Mom might need extra help in the kitchen or doing other household chores, and she'll be counting on you."

Sylvia pointed at Henry. "Also, when you get married someday, your wife might need a hand with some chores."

Henry pressed a fist against his mouth as his cheeks puffed out. "I ain't. . ." He paused and looked at his mother. "I mean, I'm not ever getting married."

Michelle chuckled at the seriousness in his tone.

"Never say never, little brother," Ezekiel put in. "When I was your age, I didn't think I'd ever grow up and get married." He reached over and clasped Michelle's hand. "But look at me now. I'm not only a married man, but also a soon-to-be father."

Michelle stared at her plate of unfinished food. *I wish we could be here when I give birth to our baby, but it doesn't look like Ezekiel will change his mind and move back home.* In an effort not to give in to self-pity and ruin the evening, Michelle thought about the fun they would have when they went over to see Mary Ruth and Lenore sometime on Christmas Day.

"Where's Herschel?" Jesse asked when he and Cindy arrived at Vera and Milton's house for a Christmas Eve supper.

"He'll be here," Vera replied. "He's probably running behind because things were busy at the bulk-food store today. That does happen sometimes—especially when folks are out buying things at the last minute before Christmas Day." She looked at Cindy and clicked her tongue. "Goodness gracious, this little girl seems more grown up every time I see her." Her brows furrowed as she looked at Jesse. "Which isn't often enough, I might add."

"Sorry about that. Between work and running Cindy over to the Lapps' five days a week, there isn't much time for socializing."

"That's not what I heard," Milton put in as he joined them in the hallway where Jesse was removing Cindy's jacket.

Jesse looked at the older man. "What do you mean?"

"I've heard talk around that you're courting the schoolteacher, Lenore Lapp."

Vera looked at Jesse through her thick-lensed glasses. "Is it true?"

Jesse's ears burned. He hadn't told Esther's great-aunt and great-uncle that he'd begun courting Lenore because he was afraid of their reaction. They might think he was being untrue to his deceased wife. *And I am,* Jesse told himself. *Which is why I can't allow myself to fall in love with Lenore.* He shifted his weight from one foot to the other. *Should I tell them that the reason behind my decision to court Lenore is to give Cindy a mother? Would they understand or say I'm wrong to pursue a relationship where there is no love?* His jaw clenched. *No, it's best not to say anything—at least not right now.*

"Jesse, did you hear what I said?" Vera prompted.

He licked his lips. "Umm. . .jah, Lenore and I have been spending more time together." He moved into the living room and placed Cindy on the floor with a stuffed, floppy-eared puppy he'd brought along for her. It was a Christmas present, but he'd given it to her early. Of course, in order to avoid a lecture, he wouldn't mention it to Vera. She could be a stickler about certain things.

"It's hard to believe my daughter will be a year old so soon." Jesse hoped this new topic would take some pressure off him and get the conversation going in another direction.

"Jah, it sure is, and I'm surprised she's not walking yet." Vera took a seat in one of the overstuffed chairs. "Have you been working with her on that, Jesse?"

"She's getting close." Jesse tousled his daughter's hair, avoiding a direct answer to Vera's question. "She pulls herself up to things and walks when you're holding her hands, but she hasn't taken any steps on her own yet."

"All kinner walk at their own pace." Milton took a seat in the chair beside his wife. "Cindy will take off whenever she's ready."

Jesse had just settled himself on the couch when Herschel showed up. The poor man looked exhausted as he sagged into a chair. "Sorry for showing up late, but it was busier than usual at the store all day. Everyone seemed to be shopping with a frenzy."

"It's okay. You're here now, Son, so that's all that matters." Vera rose from her chair. "I'll get supper on the table, and then we can eat."

Jesse jumped up and followed her to the kitchen. "What can I do to help?"

She waved her hand. "No need for that. You've been working most of the day too."

"It's okay. I'm more than happy to help." Jesse grabbed a pot-holder, took the kettle of green beans off the stove, drained off the water, and poured them into a serving bowl.

Vera smiled. "Danki. You're such a helpful young man."

"When I lived at home with my folks, I helped out with what-ever needed to be done. 'Course, I never learned to cook that well, despite helping my mamm in the kitchen."

"It must be hard for you now, having to fend for yourself, plus take care of Cindy's needs."

"Jah, but on the days Mary Ruth watches Cindy, I usually stay for supper, so that helps a lot."

"You're welcome to eat with us here anytime, you know."

"I appreciate that." Seeing a kettle of cut-up potatoes cooking on the stove, Jesse grabbed a fork and gave them a poke. "These are done. Did you want me to mash them while you cut the ham, or would you prefer that I do the cutting?"

"I'll mash and you can cut. Milton likes his spuds fixed a cer-tain way, so I'd better make sure they're just the way he likes them."

"Okay, no problem." Jesse took the ham from the oven, and while he sliced it, his thoughts went to Lenore. He and Cindy had been invited to eat with Mary Ruth and her family on Christmas Day, and he looked forward not only to the meal, but also to spending the day with them.

Lenore sat off to one side as her scholars presented the much anticipated Christmas program for their families and close friends. She was glad her back was feeling better and she'd been able to return to her teaching position a week ago. It had given her some time to work with the children, but Eva Riehl, the woman who had taken over for her, along with Lenore's assistant, Viola, had done most of the preparation for this special Christmas Eve event. Tonight, all three of them would prompt and support the students participating in the program with poems, songs, and skits.

The children's parents and other family members crowded into the schoolhouse, many doubling up and sitting at school desks. The overflow crowd sat on backless benches that had been set up at the back and sides of the room.

Lenore's heart swelled with joy when it came time for her older students to act out a short skit representing the birth of Jesus. *What a blessed event it must have been to witness God's Son being carefully laid in a manger and the glory of the Lord shining around the shepherds in the fields as the angels announced the Savior's birth.*

Lenore reflected on Luke 2:10–12, being quoted by the young boy playing the part of one of the shepherds. "And the angel said unto them, Fear not: for, behold, I bring you good tidings of great joy, which shall be to all people. For unto you is born this day in the city of David a Saviour, which is Christ the Lord. And this shall be a sign unto you; Ye shall find the babe wrapped in swaddling clothes, lying in a manger."

How wonderful it was to have the assurance that because Jesus came to die for the sins of the world, those who accepted Him and believed on His name would be saved.

Lenore thought once more about her dear grandfather and the many sermons he'd preached while ministering in their church.

Grandpa was a strong believer in preaching God's Word in a way people understood. He often quoted verses on faith, hope, and spiritual blessings that would uplift hearts filled with despair and offer peace during difficult times. Grandpa also stressed the importance of being "filled with all the fulness of God" and remembering to praise and thank Him for all things.

As the program came to a close after the group sang several Christmas carols, Lenore closed her eyes and offered a brief prayer. *Heavenly Father, thank You for Your Son, Jesus, the Savior of the world. Please bless each of my students, as well as all those who came out tonight to share in the joy of the Christmas miracle.*

Lenore looked forward to spending Christmas Day with her family, along with seeing Jesse and Cindy again. Michelle and Ezekiel would also be dropping by for a short time, and she was eager to see them as well. But tonight Lenore's thoughts would be focused on the joy she saw on each scholar's face as they shared the good news of the Savior's birth with their family and friends.

# Chapter 30

"The scholars did a good job with the program last night, don't you think?" Lenore asked as she and Mary Ruth began laying things out for their Christmas dinner.

"Uh-huh." Mary Ruth reached into the pantry for a stack of napkins and placed them on the counter next to the plates and silverware.

"I was so glad I could be there, because for a while I didn't think I would be up to going back to teach school in time to work with the kinner on their parts for the program."

Mary Ruth nodded slowly.

"Are you okay, Grandma?" Lenore touched Mary Ruth's arm. "You've been awfully quiet all morning."

"I'll be okay. I am just missing your grandpa more than ever today. This is the first Christmas since we got married that I've spent without him." She sighed heavily. "It's ever so strange."

Lenore slipped her arms around Mary Ruth and gave her a hug. "I know, Grandma. I miss him too, and I'm sure the rest of the family does as well."

Mary Ruth sniffed, attempting to hold back tears. She'd been trying to remain strong since Willis's death, but the holidays made it harder. "I'll be all right. Just need to keep busy and focus on others today," she said. "When I'm feeling discouraged, I have to remind myself that there are so many other people in more difficult situations. I am grateful for each of my family members and friends, for without them I would be terribly lonely."

"Jah," Lenore agreed, gently patting Mary Ruth's back. "I can't imagine how it must be for people who have no one to spend the holidays with or be there to encourage them during times of distress."

Mary Ruth nodded as she slowly pulled away from her grand-daughter's loving embrace. "Well, I need to get busy. There is still a lot to do before all our company arrives." She moved across the room. "Maybe you could get the potatoes cut up while I go down to the basement to get a few jars of pickled beets."

"Okay, but please be careful on the steps and make sure the battery-operated light at the top of the stairs is turned on before you head down," Lenore called.

"Don't worry. I'll make sure I have enough light, and I'll be extra cautious on the stairs." Mary Ruth had gone up and down her basement steps many times over the years and had never fallen, but she appreciated the reminder to be careful nonetheless. It was one more proof of how much her granddaughter cared about her.

Mary Ruth stepped into the hall and opened the basement door. After turning on the battery-operated light, she descended the stairs, making sure to hold on to the railing. When she reached the bottom, she turned on another lamp powered by batteries and went to the shelves where her home-canned fruits and vegetables were stored, along with all the empty, clean jars that would be used when they put up produce from their garden next summer.

Mary Ruth paused and stared up at the jar full of folded papers on the top shelf. *I wonder what the future holds for me. How long can I remain living in this house that Willis and I shared for so many years?*

She couldn't expect Lenore to live with her indefinitely. She'd be getting married someday—possibly to Jesse—and would want a home of her own.

Mary Ruth decided to take down the prayer jar and read some more of the messages her daughter had written before she'd run away. She thought somehow it might make her feel closer to Rhoda.

She positioned the step stool in front of the shelves and climbed up to retrieve the jar. *It's kind of silly to leave the jar way up here,* she told herself, *but since this is where Rhoda hid it, maybe it's best to keep it where it was originally found.*

After taking a seat on a folding chair, Mary Ruth reached inside the jar and pulled out a slip of paper with a prayer written on it: "Dear Lord, help me to trust You in all things."

"That's a good prayer for everyone," Mary Ruth whispered. "Sometimes we need to remind ourselves."

The second paper Mary Ruth pulled out contained the words of Philippians 4:19. "My God shall supply all your need according to his riches in glory by Christ Jesus."

*Guess I need to stop fretting about what the future holds for me and trust the Lord with each new day. When the time comes for Lenore to move out, I may take Ivan up on his offer and move in with him and Yvonne.*

With renewed determination to leave her future in God's hands, Mary Ruth put the prayer jar away and trudged back up the stairs.

❧

A sense of peace came over Sara as soon as she and Brad, along with Brad's parents, stepped onto her grandmother's porch. She had hoped that Kenny could join them today, but he'd chosen to spend the holiday with his girlfriend and her parents.

As they entered the house, the delicious aroma of roasted turkey greeted them, along with Grandma's welcoming smile and hug.

"I'd like you to meet my parents, Clarence and Jean." Brad gestured to them as they all stood in the hallway entrance.

Grandma and Lenore shook both of their hands, welcoming them into their home. "Thank you for inviting us to join you today." Brad's mother smiled. "Clarence and I have heard so much about you."

"That's right," Brad's father agreed. "We feel like we know you already."

"We are so glad you could join us." Lenore took everyone's coats and hung them up while Grandma led the way to the living room and invited them all to take a seat. Lenore joined them a few minutes later. Jean and Clarence found seats on the couch, and Grandma sat in her rocker.

"How was your Christmas Eve?" Lenore asked, taking a seat next to Sara.

"Very nice. We held a beautiful Christmas Eve candlelight communion service at our church last night." Sara spoke in a bubbly tone. "We also sang Christmas carols, and Brad preached a short sermon, reflecting on scriptures from Luke."

Lenore placed her hand on Sara's arm. "In the skit some of my older students did during the school play last night, some verses from Luke were mentioned too."

"How did the program go?" Brad asked.

"Very well, and I'm thankful my back had healed enough that I could attend. As their teacher, I felt it was important for me to be there."

Jean leaned forward with her head tilted to one side, and Grandma explained about Lenore's accident that had kept her from the one-room schoolhouse until a week ago.

"I'm glad you're doing better." Sara clasped Lenore's hand and gave her fingers a gentle squeeze.

"Tell us about your role as teacher in a one-room schoolhouse." Jean looked at Lenore expectantly.

Sara was pleased to see how relaxed Brad's parents seemed to be, especially since this was their first time visiting an Amish home. They didn't appear to be the least bit uncomfortable talking to Grandma and Lenore, or sitting in a room with gas-generated lights and only basic furnishings. Of course her in-laws' home in Harrisburg, although lovely, wasn't overdone with a lot of expensive furniture or fancy decorations. She was thankful that Jean and Clarence were Christians and down-to-earth. Grandma and Lenore probably sensed that too.

While Lenore explained how she'd begun teaching, Sara caught Grandma's eye. "Is there something I can do to help you in the kitchen?" she asked.

"As a matter of fact, there is."

Sara left her seat and followed Grandma to the kitchen. "How are you doing? I'm sure you must be missing Grandpa today."

Grandma nodded. "But I'm thankful to have my family around me. You're all a blessing, and I appreciate each of you so much."

"We appreciate you too." Sara gave Grandma a hug. "Without your love and support, I wouldn't be where I am now, spiritually or emotionally." She swiped at a few tears trickling down her cheeks. "If it hadn't been for that letter in Mama's Bible, I never would have met you."

"So true. And knowing you has brought great joy into my life, as it did your grandpa's." Grandma sniffed and reached under her glasses to blot at her tears. "I only wish Rhoda and Willis could be here today."

"I would have liked that too, but at least we have each other."

"Jah, and you know what?"

"What's that, Grandma?"

"I just heard a horse and buggy pulling in, so I'm guessing your uncle Ivan and his family have arrived."

⁓

When Lenore looked out the window and saw her parents' horse and buggy at the hitching rail, she got up and went to answer the door. Her youngest brother, Peter, was with them, but she didn't see any sign of Ben. Then she remembered that he'd been invited to spend Christmas with his girlfriend's family. Lenore figured it wouldn't be long before her brother would be getting married. She had always thought, since she was the oldest sibling, that she'd be the first one to get married. But from the way things were going with her and Jesse, it didn't seem likely. He hadn't mentioned marriage, and even though they were courting, he hadn't even held her hand.

*Maybe we're not really courting,* Lenore thought as she stood at the front door waiting for her parents and brother to make their way up to the house in the snow.

While there wasn't as much white stuff on the ground as there had been on Thanksgiving, it could be slippery in places. Early this morning, Lenore had gone outside and made sure the porch and walkway were free of ice and compacted snow. She didn't want anyone to fall and get injured, the way she had a month ago.

After Lenore's family had entered the house and taken off their outer garments, she invited them into the living room and made introductions. While everyone visited, she went to the kitchen to help Grandma and Sara get dinner on the table.

"I see your folks have arrived," Grandma said. "It's so nice to have our whole family here today."

"Jah, but no sign of Jesse and Cindy yet. I'm eager for them to get here, because today is Cindy's first birthday."

"I'm sure they will be along soon." Grandma gestured to the stack of plates and silverware on the counter. "Why don't you set the dining-room table while Sara and I finish mashing potatoes and making the gravy?"

"Sure, I can do that." Lenore picked up the plates. "If Jesse isn't here by the time everything is ready, are we going to eat without him?"

"I'd rather not, so we'll try to keep everything warm until they get here," Grandma replied.

"Okay." Lenore headed to the dining room. She couldn't help feeling concerned. What if they'd been in an accident on the way here? Or maybe Cindy had gotten sick and they weren't coming at all.

# Chapter 31

I'm sorry we're late," Jesse apologized after Lenore let him and Cindy into the house and he'd taken off their jackets. "We would have been here thirty minutes ago if this little schtinker hadn't messed her windel when we were getting ready to head out the door."

"Things like that can happen when it's least expected and most inconvenient." Mary Ruth chuckled as she joined them in the hall. "I may be old, but I still remember how it was when Willis and I were raising our two kinner."

Jesse smiled and sniffed the air. "The wonderful aromas in this home are enough to make my mouth water."

"Mine too." Mary Ruth placed her hands on Cindy's cheeks. "Happy birthday, sweet Cindy."

"It's hard to believe my baby girl is a year old already." Jesse felt a lump forming in his throat. "Seems like just yesterday that she was born."

"Babies don't stay babies long enough." Lenore gestured toward the doorway to their right. "Shall we go into the living room now? I'd like to introduce you to Brad's parents. They live up in Harrisburg, and we are happy they could join us today."

Jesse set Cindy's diaper bag on the floor, along with the bag containing gifts for Lenore and Mary Ruth. He would give them to the women privately so as not to offend anyone else here today, although he knew giving a gift to the others was not expected.

After Lenore introduced Jesse to Brad's parents, she excused herself to help get the meal on the table.

Jesse felt a bit uncomfortable visiting with people he didn't know, so he spoke only when a question was asked of him and let the others do most of the talking.

At one point, Lenore's mother got up and disappeared into the kitchen, and a short time later, Lenore came in and announced that Christmas dinner was ready and waiting on the dining-room table.

Carrying the birthday girl over his shoulder, Jesse followed the rest of the group into the other room. They all took their seats, with Lenore's father at the head of the table. Cindy sat in her high chair close to Lenore, as she had volunteered to oversee feeding Jesse's daughter.

Throughout their silent prayer and during the meal, Cindy babbled silly baby talk and pounded on her wooden tray whenever she wanted something more to eat.

Lenore seemed unaffected by the noise or interruption of her meal as she kept Cindy occupied and doled out her food. Her attentiveness to his daughter's needs impressed Jesse. *Lenore would truly be a good mother to my little girl.*

Once the meal was over, everyone returned to the living room to relax, sing Christmas carols, and visit. Jesse and Lenore sat on the couch with Cindy situated between them. When the child grew restless and started to squirm, Jesse set her on the floor in front of the coffee table. Within a matter of seconds, Cindy pulled herself up and stood grinning at everyone as she slapped her hands on top of the table. Fortunately, there was nothing on it that could get knocked off. Jesse's easily excited daughter had broken an empty cup the other evening when she pushed it off the coffee table in Jesse's living room.

Engrossed in their conversations, no one seemed to pay Cindy's antics much attention, until she gripped the edge of the table, scooted around to the other side, and took a few wobbly steps. She teetered a bit but remained upright as she made her way across the room, stopping in front of where Mary Ruth sat in her rocking chair.

Mary Ruth laughed and held out her hands. Everyone else

in the room clapped. Jesse was glad he'd been able to witness his daughter taking her first steps—and on Cindy's first birthday, no less. Squinting, he rubbed the bridge of his nose. *If only Esther could be here right now to see this milestone in our daughter's young life.*

Lenore felt such excitement seeing Cindy walk, she barely noticed the knock on their door. Grandma must have heard it right away, though, for she was up on her feet and heading to the hallway that led to the front door. A few minutes later, she returned to the living room with Ezekiel and Michelle. Brad's parents were introduced once more, and everyone gathered around the table again—this time for dessert. So many delicious pies had been set out: pumpkin, apple, chocolate cream, and Lenore's favorite, Pineapple Philly. Just looking at them made Lenore's mouth water.

"It's so good to see you both." Grandma looked over at Michelle and Ezekiel and smiled. "How are things going with your new business, Ezekiel?"

Michelle sat beside him quietly as he enthusiastically told all about making bee supplies and how much he enjoyed it. "I'm getting more customers all the time," he added.

"That's wunderbaar. And how about you?" Grandma asked, turning her gaze on Michelle. "Have you been keeping busy since you moved to New York?"

Michelle lowered her gaze to the table. "Not that much. It's kinda lonely being away from friends and family."

"Haven't you made any new friends yet?" The question came from Sara.

Michelle shook her head. "I know a few women from our church district, but I haven't developed a close relationship with any of them."

Lenore had a hunch Michelle might have closed herself off from establishing new friendships because she didn't really want to be in New York.

"We do have some exciting news, though." With a wide smile,

Ezekiel spoke again. "We are expecting our first child. So sometime in July, my fraa will have more than enough to keep her busy."

"That is exciting. I'm so happy for you." Sitting in a chair to Michelle's right, Lenore leaned over and hugged her friend.

"Thank you." Michelle pressed her lips together for a moment and then spoke. "I just hope everything goes okay with my pregnancy. I've suffered so many disappointments over the course of my life. I think I'd fall apart if I lost this boppli."

"What's a boppli?" Brad's mother asked.

"It's the Pennsylvania Dutch word for 'baby,' " Brad explained. He looked over at Mary Ruth and grinned. "Bet you didn't think I knew what it meant, huh?"

She shrugged. "I'm not really surprised. You have been around us so much you've probably picked up a lot of words from our everyday Amish language."

Brad nodded. "Not enough to understand whole sentences though—just a few words here and there."

"That's how it is with me too," Sara agreed. "Maybe someday I'll understand the language better."

"It took me a while to learn," Michelle interjected. "But Mary Ruth, Willis, and Ezekiel were good teachers. I may not say everything just right, but I'm quite comfortable with the Pennsylvania Dutch language now."

"Well, as you may have all noticed, there are more than enough pies on the table, so I say we should each take a piece or two, and as Daed used to say, 'let's eat ourselves full.' " Lenore's dad gave his belly a couple of thumps, just the way Grandpa used to do for emphasis.

The mention of Grandpa's name put a lump in Lenore's throat. From the way Grandma's shoulders drooped, Lenore figured she wasn't the only one at the table feeling the loss of Grandpa tonight.

By eight o'clock, everyone except Jesse and Cindy had gone home. He'd decided to stay a little longer to give Lenore and Mary Ruth their gifts and spend some more personal time with Lenore.

"I'll be right back. I have something for both of you," Jesse said, looking first at Lenore and then Mary Ruth.

He stepped into the hall to retrieve the sack he'd brought in earlier and took it to the living room where Mary Ruth and Lenore sat in chairs near the crackling fireplace. Cindy seemed quite content as she sat on the floor, playing with one of the toys she had received as a birthday present this evening.

"Here you go. Merry Christmas." Jesse handed one of the packages to Mary Ruth. "This is from me and Cindy."

Mary Ruth opened the gift and smiled when she removed the battery-operated candle Jesse had purchased at Herschel's store. "Danki for thinking of me. You can be sure this *inschlichlicht* will be put to good use."

"You're welcome." Jesse handed the other package to Lenore. "Merry Christmas. I hope you'll like what I got you as well."

Lenore removed the wrapping paper and withdrew a box of pretty stationery and a book filled with short devotionals. "Thank you, Jesse. These will also be useful." Lenore got up and left the room. When she came back, she handed him a package wrapped in red tissue paper.

Jesse tore it open and withdrew a dark gray knitted scarf. "This will keep my neck warm during our cold winter days. Did you make it, Lenore?"

"Jah. I knitted the scarf while I was waiting for my back to heal. Grandma's a good teacher. She taught me how to knit when I was around ten years old."

"Well, you did a fine job. Danki for thinking of me."

"You're most welcome."

Jesse sat toward the edge of the couch and shuffled his feet across the hardwood floor a few times. "Umm. . .I was wondering if you'd like to go outside with me and look at the moon. There's supposed to be a full one tonight."

Lenore looked at her grandmother as though asking for her approval.

Mary Ruth nodded. "You two go ahead. I'll keep an eye on Cindy. You'd better make sure you're dressed warmly though. It's bound to be nippy out there."

Jesse wrapped his new scarf around his neck and put on his jacket, hat, and gloves.

Lenore tied a woolen scarf over her white head covering, put a woolen shawl around her shoulders, and slipped on a pair of gloves. "I'm ready when you are, Jesse."

He opened the front door and held it for her. When she stepped out onto the porch, he followed. Then, closing the door behind him, Jesse walked up to the railing and pointed at the bright, full moon and the array of twinkling stars scattered across the dark sky. "Pretty awesome sight, isn't it?"

"Jah. Only God could have created such beauty."

They stood side by side, staring at the majestic display of lights, until Jesse managed to muster up his courage. "I have a question to ask you, Lenore, and if you say no, I'll understand."

When she turned her head in his direction, he saw a puff of warm breath emit from her slightly open mouth. "What is it?"

"Will you marry me?" There, it was out. Now he could breathe normally again. Jesse rubbed his hands down his pant legs, waiting nervously for her response.

Several seconds passed, then Lenore said in a near whisper, "Jah, Jesse, I would be honored to be your wife."

Jesse drew another breath and released it slowly. He wasn't sure if he felt relief or disappointment. Cindy needed a mother, and he needed someone to run his household, but how would Lenore feel if she knew he didn't love her?

# Chapter 32

The weeks flew by, and before Lenore knew it, spring was in full blossom. Teaching school, helping Grandma with chores, and planning for her wedding kept her busy. She saw Jesse nearly every day and looked forward to becoming his wife on the last Thursday of May. It was hard to believe in just one month she would become Mrs. Jesse Smucker. While Jesse had never said he loved Lenore, she felt sure he did, or he wouldn't have asked her to marry him. Most Amish couples in their area got married in the fall, but Jesse had suggested May, since Lenore would be through teaching school by then.

Both she and Jesse had this Saturday off. Grandma had agreed to watch Cindy so they could go out to supper. It would give them an opportunity to be alone and talk more about the wedding.

Lenore checked her appearance in the bedroom mirror and went downstairs to wait for Jesse. He would be dropping Cindy off soon, and they could be on their way to the Bird-in-Hand Family Restaurant, where Jesse had said he would like to go. Lenore had been there many times and always enjoyed their food. But the best part of the evening would be time spent with Jesse. The more Lenore was with him, the more convinced she was that he was the man God intended for her. Jesse was kind and soft-spoken, always willing to help out whenever Grandma or Lenore had a need. He was a good father to Cindy, and Lenore looked forward to raising more children with him. The thought of marrying Jesse sent shivers up her spine.

"You're shivering, dear girl. Are you cold?" Grandma asked from her chair across the room.

"Umm. . .no, not really. Just felt a little chill is all."

"Maybe you should move away from the window. When Jesse shows up, if he sees you standing there looking out, he might think you're *eiferich* to see him." Grandma spoke in a teasing voice.

Lenore moved over to the couch and took a seat. "I am eager to see him, as well as Cindy." She crossed her ankles and wiggled her feet. "I can hardly wait to be Cindy's *mudder*."

"What about Jesse? Are you eager to be his *fraa*?"

A warm flush crept across Lenore's cheeks. "Jah, I truly am."

Grandma set her knitting aside and looked directly at Lenore. "I hope the two of you will be as happy in your marriage as your grandpa and I were. And I hope the Lord gives you many good years to enjoy together."

Lenore smiled. "I want that too."

Jesse's muscles twitched as he guided his horse and buggy up the lane leading to Mary Ruth's house. Normally he wasn't this nervous about seeing Lenore, but tonight was different. He had something serious to discuss with her and hoped she would understand and accept what he said without becoming too upset. He'd already had a bad day that began when he climbed up a ladder to knock a yellow jacket nest off the house and received a nasty sting inside the collar of his shirt. The only good thing about it was he'd discovered how fast he could get down the ladder and pull off his shirt.

As the house came into view, Jesse's tension increased. *I have to tell Lenore I'm not in love with her. It wouldn't be fair to let her marry me thinking there will ever be anything more between us than friendship.* His jaw clenched so hard it spasmed. *She has the right to know before it's too late.*

He thought about his older brothers, Samuel, Noah, Moses, and Paul, and wondered if they had been in love with their wives when they got married. *I can only imagine what my family in Kentucky would have to say if they knew I was planning to marry Lenore only for convenience' sake.*

Jesse pulled up to the hitching rail and got out. After he'd secured his horse, he went around and got Cindy out of the buggy.

She clung to his neck and brushed her soft cheek against his.

"You deserve a mudder," Jesse whispered. "One who'll love you as much as I do. I only hope when Lenore hears my confession she'll still be willing to marry me."

<hr/>

### Bird-in-Hand, Pennsylvania

"They're quite busy this evening." Lenore glanced around the restaurant. "Seems like a good many people had the same idea you had and decided to eat supper here."

Jesse took a bite of mashed potatoes and nodded. If he kept his mouth full, maybe he wouldn't have to talk. *But I can't be rude and ignore her all night.* He struggled to come up with the right way to say what was on his mind. *Guess it'd be best to wait till I take Lenore home before I say anything. Sure don't want anyone to hear our conversation, or worse yet, what if Lenore doesn't take the news well and starts crying?*

Jesse had himself so worked up he could barely swallow the next bite of potatoes he put in his mouth. He wanted to make their meal as pleasant as possible, in hopes that it would put Lenore in an amicable mood.

Jesse swallowed his food, took a drink of water, and asked Lenore, "How did things go at school yesterday? Are the scholars getting anxious for their summer break?"

"I'm sure they are, although no one has come right out and said so." Lenore forked some noodles and ate them. "The other day when some of the older scholars were playing baseball, two of the boys crashed at first base. Gabe hit a ball toward right field, and the other boy, Delbert, jumped up to catch it. When he came down, Gabe was running onto the base and their heads collided. Both boys ended up getting stitches—one boy near his left ear, and the other close to his left eye." Lenore shook her head. "We teachers always have some rough-and-tumble boys to deal with."

"I was never that rough when I was a boy," Jesse said. "But I was good at playing ball."

Lenore smiled at Jesse from across the table. "I have always enjoyed playing ball too."

They ate in silence for several minutes, and then Lenore spoke again. "As you know, I've been working on my wedding dress."

Jesse nodded. He wished the topic of their wedding hadn't come up so soon.

"Well, I finished it earlier today, so that's one more item off my list of things to get done before our wedding."

Jesse couldn't think of what to say in response. He sure couldn't blurt out that she'd made the dress for nothing because he wasn't going to marry her after all. He clenched his fork so hard his knuckles whitened. *Get a grip on yourself. Just smile and nod.* Taking his own advice, he did just that.

"The wedding plans are coming together, and I'm pleased that I've been able to cross so many items off my list." Lenore's voice was light and bubbly, making it even more difficult for Jesse to carry on this conversation.

He felt like he was sinking in quicksand. He desperately needed to change the subject. "I hope Cindy's being good for Mary Ruth. Now that she's learned to walk, she manages to get into a lot more things. Taking care of her might be more than your grandmother can handle now."

Lenore shook her head. "If I know Grandma, she's keeping Cindy well entertained."

"I hope so."

"I still need to find some appropriate gifts for my two witnesses." Lenore brought their conversation back to the wedding again. "Have you gotten anything for your witnesses?"

"Uh. . .no, not yet." Jesse reached under his shirt collar and scratched at the yellow jacket sting. He needed to come up with a new topic to talk about. He bit into a drumstick and wiped his mouth on a napkin. "This *hinkel* is sure moist and tasty."

Lenore nodded. "They've always served good chicken at this restaurant."

Desperate for something else to talk about lest the conversation turn to their wedding plans again, Jesse brought up the dessert bar. "Sure hope I'll have enough room for a piece of shoofly pie. Some vanilla ice cream to go with it would be mighty good too."

Lenore set her fork down and drank some water. "The pies here are delicious, but in my opinion, no one makes shoofly pie better than my grandma."

"Your pineapple pie's hard to beat too."

Circles of pink erupted on Lenore's dimpled cheeks. "Danki."

As they finished eating their meal, Jesse kept the conversation rolling, talking mostly about food. He was willing to talk about nearly anything except the wedding that might not be happening. Everything depended on Lenore's reaction once he found the courage to tell her how he felt, and he needed to do it before their date ended.

When they left the restaurant and climbed into his buggy for the return trip home, Jesse's nervousness and apprehension took over again. It was good to be out of the restaurant and alone with Lenore, but he needed to choose the right moment to tell her the truth. Not that it mattered, because she would probably be upset regardless of how he put it.

"You're kind of quiet all of a sudden. Is everything all right?" Lenore broke into Jesse's thoughts.

*It's now or never. I should just spit it out.* He gripped his horse's reins a little tighter. "Uh. . .there's something I need to tell you."

"What is it, Jesse? You sound so serious."

"It's about us getting married."

"Have you decided we should wait till fall?"

"No, I—" He paused and swallowed hard. "The thing is—I haven't been honest with you, Lenore."

"In. . .in what way?" Her voice quavered a bit.

"I never should have asked you to marry me."

"How come?" Lenore spoke so quietly, he could barely make out what she said.

"You're a good person, and I care about you as a friend, but I'm not in love with you, Lenore." Jesse paused and drew a quick breath. "Truth is, I'm still in *lieb* with Esther, and I think I'll always love her." He let go of the reins with one hand and touched his chest.

Lenore sat quietly beside him, breathing heavily.

*What's she thinking? Why doesn't she say something?* Jesse was tempted to reach for Lenore's hand to offer comfort but thought better of it. She might think he felt sorry for her, which of course, he did. Truthfully, he felt sorry for himself too. *How'd I ever get myself into this predicament?*

"I'm really sorry, Lenore, but unless you're willing to be a wife in name only, I can't marry you. It would be asking a lot, and would not be fair to you."

"So why did you ask me to be your wife?" Her tone was flat, almost devoid of emotion.

Before Jesse could respond, Lenore rushed on. "Was it so Cindy could have a mudder? Or was it because you need someone to cook, clean, and wash your dirty laundry?" Her voice had risen to a high pitch now.

Quietly Jesse choked out, "A little of both, but mostly it was for Cindy's benefit."

"Well, at least you told me the truth before it was too late, because I could not deal with a loveless marriage. I've waited a good many years to fall in love and get married, but I guess, for me, it's not meant to be."

Jesse didn't think he could possibly feel guiltier. His voice cracked as he repeated, "I'm sorry, Lenore."

She said nothing.

～

"Whew, I'm exhausted!" Gazing at Cindy sleeping peacefully on a blanket on the living-room floor, Mary Ruth lowered herself to the couch. How one little girl could have so much energy was beyond her.

*Maybe I'm too old to be caring for a young child.* After Cindy had knocked over a potted African violet and pulled the cat's tail several times, Mary Ruth had spent the rest of the evening chasing after Cindy to keep her from getting into anything else or bothering poor Precious the cat. And when she wasn't doing that, she was busy trying to occupy the child with toys, food, and the fuzzy-squirrel book.

Now that she finally had some quiet time to herself, Mary Ruth's thoughts went to Jesse and Lenore. She hoped they were having a nice evening together and didn't feel that they had to rush home. While Jesse came over regularly and spent time with Lenore, they didn't get the chance to be alone very often.

Mary Ruth had noticed how nervous Jesse seemed before he and Lenore left for their supper date. She hoped he wasn't having second thoughts about getting married.

She pinched the skin at her throat. *Or maybe he's just excited about making Lenore his bride.*

Lenore deserved to be happy, and Mary Ruth was eager to see her granddaughter married to a good man like Jesse. She pulled on her chin as a smile formed on her lips. *By this time next year, Lenore could be expecting a boppli. Now wouldn't that be exciting?*

Mary Ruth leaned her head against the back of the couch and closed her eyes. She was at the point of dozing off when the front door opened and Lenore and Jesse stepped in. Without saying a single word to Jesse or Mary Ruth, Lenore sprinted down the hall and dashed up the stairs.

Tipping her head, Mary Ruth looked at Jesse. "What's wrong? Did something happen to upset Lenore this evening?"

Jesse nodded. "I'm the reason Lenore is *umgerennt*, but it would be better if she tells you about it." He gathered up Cindy's things, lifted the still sleeping child in his arms, and went for the door. "Danki for taking care of my precious girl this evening," Jesse called over his shoulder before shutting the door.

Mary Ruth's gaze flitted around the room as though she might find the answer to her question there. Rising to her feet, she headed for the stairs, hoping Lenore would tell her what had happened.

# Chapter 33

A t the end of the school day Monday, Lenore remained at her desk a while, thinking about the past weekend and giving in to her tears.

Thankfully, yesterday had been an off-Sunday from attending church in their district, so Lenore hadn't had to endure the pain of seeing Jesse so soon after he'd called off the wedding. Besides, news traveled fast, and since her parents and brothers knew, they may have already begun to spread the word. Facing people's well-intentioned questions was something Lenore did not look forward to.

This morning she'd made sure to leave early so she wouldn't have to face Jesse when he dropped Cindy off. After Lenore left the schoolhouse, she planned to stop by the flower shop with more of her homemade greeting cards. She would wait at the shop until Sara was free to leave, and then the two of them planned to eat supper at one of the local restaurants in Strasburg. Sara had called last Friday to set it up, saying Brad wouldn't be able to join them because he had a meeting early Monday evening.

*I wonder what Sara will say when I tell her I won't be getting married in May after all.* Lenore took a tissue from the desk drawer and blew her nose. *Will she be as sympathetic as my family was when I told them what Jesse said?* Lenore's mother had been compassionate, of course, and Dad had made some negative comments about Jesse's deception in leading Lenore on all these months. "Doesn't that man have a conscience?" he'd said with a look of disdain. "I have half a notion to go over to Jesse's house some evening and give him a piece of my mind."

Lenore had pleaded with her father not to say anything to Jesse. It would be embarrassing and might make things worse. Dad had only grunted in response.

Lenore could still see the sadness in her grandmother's eyes as she listened and then offered counsel. "God will work things out in His time and in His way. Just trust Him with your future."

Lenore dabbed at the corners of her eyes with the tissue. She loved Jesse and his daughter with her whole heart, but if he felt no love for her in return, their marriage would not have been a happy one—at least not for her. It wouldn't have been enough just to remain friends. Lenore needed more than friendship. She wanted a husband who would love her as much as she loved him, and if she had agreed to become a wife in name only, she'd never have felt complete. So as much as it hurt, Lenore had convinced herself that Jesse had done her a favor by calling off the wedding.

Pushing a stack of papers aside, Lenore slid her chair back and stood. All her tears and self-pity wouldn't change a thing. She needed to focus on something else. But what? When she'd thought she would soon be married, Lenore had given up her desire to teach school and had known she wouldn't miss it next year. Should she tell the school board she would be available to teach when school started up again in the fall, or would it be better to seek some other type of job?

Sara's floral designer, Misty, had left a short time ago for her yearly checkup with her doctor, and the young woman Sara had hired to do cleaning and odd jobs had the day off. That left Sara to answer the phone, wait on last-minute customers, and take care of any details needing to be addressed today. Fortunately, the young man in charge of deliveries had made them all earlier today, so it was one less thing she had to worry about this afternoon.

Since there were no customers at the moment, Sara went to the back room to be sure everything had been put away. Seeing a vase with a lovely floral arrangement in it, she picked it up and sniffed the pretty pink carnations. Feeling something wet on her foot, she looked down and saw water running off the counter and onto her feet. On close examination she realized the vase had a small crack in it. She would have to transfer the flowers to a new vase.

Sara had finished the transfer and was emptying the water from the leaky vase when the bell above the front door jingled. *Great. This is not a good time for a customer to show up. I should have put the Closed sign in the window.*

Sara hurried to finish her job, then moved quickly into the main part of the store. Lenore stood near the counter. "Oh, good, it's you. I was in the back room putting an arrangement in a vase, and when the bell jingled I was afraid a customer had come in and might leave before I could get back out here."

"Where's your floral designer?" Lenore asked.

"She left early for a doctor's appointment." Sara went on to explain about the cracked vase she'd discovered.

Lenore frowned. "Sorry to hear that. Sounds like I came at a bad time."

"No, you're fine. The carnations are in another vase now, and everything's good." Sara moved closer to Lenore. "Are you okay? Your usual smile is missing."

Lenore's chin trembled, and her eyes filled with tears. "Jesse called off our wedding."

"What?" Sara's brows lifted. "How come?"

"He doesn't love me, Sara. He's still in love with his deceased wife."

"Then why did he ask you to marry him?"

"He wanted a mother for Cindy and someone to keep house for him." Lenore placed the palm of her hand against her chest. "I'm in love with him, and it hurts so much to know he doesn't love me in return."

Sara drew Lenore into her arms and patted her back. "I'm really sorry Jesse did this to you. You deserve to be happy. You deserve to be loved, and not just used as a mother for his child."

Lenore's tears overflowed, dribbling down her cheeks and onto her dress. "I—I don't think I can ever trust another man not to hurt me again. I must learn to accept this and be content, because I am obviously meant to remain single for the rest of my life."

*Paradise*

"Peter, I thought I told you to unload that box of books and get them put on the shelf." Ivan gestured toward the offending box.

"I was gonna, Dad, but Mom asked me to take out the trash."

"So who do you get paid to listen to—her or me?"

Peter's cheeks reddened as he dropped his gaze to the floor. "Well. . .umm. . ."

Ivan sighed. "Never mind. Just get those books out as quick as you can. I have plenty of other things for both you and your brother to do yet today."

"Okay, Dad. I'll get on it right away." Peter hurried off toward the books.

"Are you a bit agitated today?" Yvonne asked, walking up to her husband.

"Jah, I suppose so. I still can't believe the nerve of Jesse Smucker asking our daughter to marry him, then tellin' Lenore he doesn't love her and that he only proposed so his daughter could have a mudder. There's no way she could ever marry him under those circumstances." Ivan breathed in a short, fast breath, then let it out with a groan. "I have half a mind to head over to that man's house after we close the store this evening and have a little man-to-man talk with him."

Yvonne placed her hand on his arm. "No, Ivan, you need to calm down. Nothing good could come from you going over to give Jesse a piece of your mind, and you might say things you'd regret."

Ivan scrubbed a hand over his face. *My wife is right, but it doesn't change the fact that Jesse broke Lenore's heart. The man should have had better sense than that.*

"There's no need to worry, Yvonne," Ivan reassured her. "I'm only blowing off a little steam that's been brewing inside me ever since Lenore told us that she won't be getting married in May."

Yvonne patted his arm. "I know, and I feel the same way. We just need to be thankful that Jesse admitted the truth to Lenore when he did. Can you imagine what it would have been like for our daughter if he'd married her and then she'd learned the truth?"

The muscles in Ivan's arms tightened. "I, for sure, would have gone over there and had a little heart-to-heart talk. I still have to wonder if that isn't what Jesse needs."

<hr>

### Clymer

Michelle placed both hands against her ever-growing stomach and sat at the kitchen table to enjoy a cup of spearmint tea. Her nausea was gone, but she still enjoyed an afternoon cup of herbal tea now and then.

She had made a few friends from their church district, but no one she felt as close to as she was with Sara, Lenore, or Mary Ruth. Letters and phone calls didn't ease the loneliness she felt or the desire to move back home.

*Maybe I'll feel better once our boppli is born,* she told herself. *At least motherhood will keep me busy, and maybe I won't have time to feel sorry for myself because we're not living in Strasburg anymore.*

She thought about the prayer jars she'd discovered at the Lapps'. So many of the notes inside the jars had spoken to her heart and helped her through a difficult time. Some of those notes contained scripture verses.

Michelle got up from the table and went to get her Bible, lying on Ezekiel's desk. She'd placed it there last night after they'd had devotions.

She opened the book randomly, her gaze coming to rest on Philippians 4:11, a verse she had underlined some time ago. "I have learned, in whatsoever state I am, therewith to be content."

Michelle's cheeks burned hot, and her throat tightened. "Forgive me, Lord. How could I have forgotten that special verse? I have much to be thankful for—a loving husband who enjoys his new job, a cozy home"—she touched her stomach—"and a sweet boppli on the way."

At that moment, Michelle decided she would start a prayer jar of her own, filling it with scriptures, prayers, and reminders of all the ways God had blessed her.

# Chapter 34

*Strasburg*

Mary Ruth looked down at Cindy and smiled. The little girl sat on the kitchen floor with a wooden spoon and a set of mixing bowls. Cindy held the spoon in one hand and stirred it around inside the smallest bowl, the way Mary Ruth had done earlier when she'd made a batch of brownies. The second bowl was turned upside down, and every few seconds Cindy would take the spoon and hit the bottom of the bowl like it was a drum. The third and largest bowl was on the little girl's head.

"What a sight you are, Cindy." Mary Ruth chuckled. Having this delightful child around had made such a difference in Mary Ruth's life. While she still thought about Willis often and continued to miss him, the raw pain of losing her husband had lessened some, thanks to the joy of caring for Jesse's daughter.

As Mary Ruth sat at the table, drinking a glass of water with a slice of lemon, she thought about the situation with Jesse and Lenore, comparing it to when she and Willis had been courting. Willis had proclaimed his love for Mary Ruth long before she could admit her love for him. They'd established a friendship though—and a strong one at that. But love came later. If Jesse had given it more time, he might have eventually fallen in love with Lenore. *Then again,* she reasoned, *perhaps he might never stop pining for Cindy's mother, in which case Jesse would never be able to commit to another woman with unconditional love.*

Cindy banged on the overturned bowl again, jolting Mary Ruth out of her contemplations.

"Where do you get all that energy, little one? If I had even half your energy, I could get so much more done." Mary Ruth smiled, and Cindy grinned back at her.

A knock sounded on the front door, and Mary Ruth went to answer it. *I bet that's Jesse, come to pick up his daughter.*

⟿

When Jesse entered Mary Ruth's house, his nose twitched. He recognized the smell of chocolate and knew someone had been doing some baking today. "The house smells mighty nice. Have you or Lenore done some baking today?"

"It was me," Mary Ruth replied. "I made a batch of brownies. Would you like to try one?"

He nodded eagerly. "Jah, I sure would."

"Well then, please follow me." Mary Ruth headed down the hall, and Jesse was close behind. Upon entering the kitchen, he spotted Cindy on the floor with a plastic mixing bowl on her head. He laughed and pointed at her. "Is my little girl learning how to cook?"

"Well, I have a hunch that's exactly what she thinks. She helped me bake brownies today—or more to the point, she watched from her high chair while I made the brownies." Mary Ruth gestured to a plastic container on the counter. "Help yourself to one if you like."

"Would it be all right if I take a few home?"

"Certainly. I'll put them in a container before you leave."

"Danki. That's so nice of you." Jesse crossed and uncrossed his arms, then gave a sidelong glance toward the door leading from the kitchen out to the hallway. "Is Lenore here? I'd like to speak to her."

Mary Ruth shook her head. "Afraid not. She made plans to meet up with Sara after school let out today, and then they were going to eat supper out."

Jesse had a hunch Lenore was avoiding him, since she wasn't here this morning when he'd dropped Cindy off. He guessed he couldn't blame her for that, but he did want the opportunity to speak with her again and apologize once more.

"I'm sure Lenore told you that we won't be getting married." Jesse rolled his shoulders to get the kinks out.

"Yes, she explained everything to me." Mary Ruth's forehead wrinkled. "I understand your reason, but you should have been honest with Lenore from the beginning, then let her decide if she'd be willing to enter into a marriage without love."

"I agree, but since I'm not free to give her the kind of love she deserves, the only logical thing was to call off the wedding." Jesse leaned his weight against the counter. "I wonder if it would be better all the way around if I asked Vera to watch Cindy again so it won't be uncomfortable for Lenore to see me every day."

Mary Ruth pursed her lips. "We would miss Cindy, of course, but it's your decision, so please do as you wish."

"Okay, and in the meantime, I will look for someone who'd be willing to come to my place and watch Cindy while I'm at work. I probably should have pursued that option a little harder before Lenore began watching Cindy."

Mary Ruth nodded.

"Guess I'd better gather up my daughter and her things now so we can be on our way."

"And don't forget the brownies."

"Right."

When Jesse headed for his horse and buggy several minutes later, he felt unsure of what he should do. Mary Ruth was so good with Cindy, and Cindy seemed content being there. But it was unfair to expect Lenore to see him each day and not be upset. She sure couldn't have supper away from home every night or hide out in her room until he left with Cindy. There was no question about it: finding someone else to watch his little girl would be the best thing for all.

"Are you sure you don't mind eating here?" Sara asked as she and Lenore entered a restaurant down the street from the flower shop.

Lenore shook her head. "I always enjoy pizza."

Sara smiled. "Same here. Brad and I have eaten at this place several times and never been disappointed."

Once they were seated, a waitress came and gave them menus. They both ordered personal-sized pepperoni pizzas and glasses of iced tea.

"This whole situation with Jesse is such a shock," Sara said. "Have you had a chance to develop any strategies for dealing with him and Cindy still being in our community?"

"I try not to dwell on it, because there is nothing I can do to change what happened." Lenore glanced out the window at a horse and buggy passing by. The distinctive *clippity-clop* sound of the horse's hooves could be heard inside the restaurant. "I've been avoiding Jesse whenever I can because seeing him and Cindy hurts so much and is just a reminder of what will never be."

"This too will pass, Lenore." Sara fingered her beaded necklace. "Someday, when the right man has come along and you're happily married, you'll look back at this time in your life and realize that what happened was for the best."

Lenore was about to respond, when a clean-shaven young Amish man with thick blond hair approached their table.

"Sorry to interrupt," he said, looking at Lenore, "but aren't you Lenore Lapp?"

"Yes, I am." Lenore had no idea who the man was or how he knew her name. She was about to ask when he said, "I'm Mark Zook. We knew each other in school, but my family moved away when I was in the fifth grade."

Lenore tapped her chin. "Oh, yes, I remember. It's nice to see you again, Mark." She extended her hand. When he clasped her hand and shook it, Lenore noticed that it felt warm and sweaty. "What brings you back to this area?"

"I'm here helping my uncle with his woodworking business." His blue eyes held no sparkle. Lenore wondered if Mark might not like his job.

"I see." She gestured to Sara. "This is my cousin, Sara Fuller.

She owns the flower shop here in Strasburg, and she and her husband, Brad, live in Lancaster."

"It's nice to meet you, Sara." Mark shook her hand.

Sara smiled. "It's good to meet you too."

Fiddling with her napkin, Lenore couldn't think of anything else to say. She hadn't known Mark very well in school and knew even less about him now.

Mark's gaze went back to Lenore. "Maybe we can get together sometime and catch up with each other's lives."

When the waitress came with Lenore and Sara's pizzas, Mark backed slowly away from their table. "Well, guess I'd better get going."

"It was nice seeing you." Lenore couldn't bring herself to respond to his suggestion about getting together sometime. If Mark was looking to establish a relationship with her, she had no interest whatsoever. Lenore couldn't afford to get involved with another man right now—if that was even what Mark had in mind. Maybe he was only trying to be friendly, and since he had been gone for so long, he might need someone to talk to. Either way, the only thing Lenore needed right now was to find a way to heal the deep ache in her heart.

"Mark seems nice," Sara whispered after he'd walked away. "Maybe you should get together with him sometime and catch up. It would take your mind off the situation with Jesse."

Lenore gave a noncommittal shrug.

"And you and I need to get together more often too," Sara added. "With us both working full-time, we don't see each other nearly enough."

"True." Lenore drank some of her beverage. "I haven't told anyone this, but it's getting harder for me to teach school."

"Oh, why's that?"

"I had so looked forward to getting married and having a family to care for, and I was prepared to give up teaching."

"But you still enjoy your job, don't you?"

"To some extent, yes, but I'd much rather be a wife and

homemaker." Lenore dropped her gaze to the pizza before her. It didn't hold nearly the appeal as it had before this conversation began.

"I'm sorry, Lenore. You deserve better than this. I wish there was something I could do to alleviate your pain from losing out on a relationship you believed was for keeps." Sara's tone was soothing.

"There's really nothing anyone can do about my situation, but I appreciate your words and emotional support." Lenore heaved a sigh. "I'm so thankful your mother left you that note in her Bible and told you about our grandparents. Because if she hadn't, you never would have come here to Strasburg to meet Grandma and Grandpa, and I never would have had the privilege of knowing you."

Sara smiled. "I feel the same as you. It's been wonderful to have a cousin I can visit with and share my thoughts and concerns with, as well as the joys in my life. I hope we will always be close—not just in where we live, but in the bond that ties our family together."

# Chapter 35

*Gordonville*

The following Saturday, Lenore decided to attend a mud sale sponsored by the Gordonville Fire Company. Mud sales, so named because of the condition of the thawing ground in the spring, were major fundraisers for the volunteer fire companies. All the mud sales Lenore had previously attended drew huge crowds, and up for bid were things like hand-stitched Amish quilts, locally made crafts, livestock, baked goods, and all kinds of housewares. Six or more auctions were conducted at the same time as Amish and English folks milled around.

Grandma had come down with a cold and didn't feel like going out, so Lenore went to Gordonville alone. As she wandered around, perusing various items for sale and smelling the tantalizing aroma of sticky buns and funnel cakes, Lenore caught a glimpse of Mark Zook standing in a crowd of people near one of the food vendors. He must have seen Lenore at the same time, for he waved and headed her way.

"Hey, it's good to see you again," Mark said as he reached her. "Have you been here long?"

"About half an hour or so."

"Did you come to buy or just look around?"

"A little of both. If something catches my eye and I think I can't live without it, I may place a bid." Lenore smiled. "How about you? What brought you to the mud sale today?"

"I'm actually looking for a good used buggy. I lost the one I had before moving here. It got demolished when a driver who was talking on his cell phone rear-ended it. My buggy was parked near the hitching rail in the parking lot."

"What a shame. Were you hurt?"

"No, I was in the store when it happened. Thankfully, my horse was okay."

"That's a blessing. So have you seen any buggies here today that you like?"

He shook his head. "Unfortunately, there are only two up for bids. One is a large family buggy, which I have no use for at this time. The other is pretty old, and it probably won't be long before the rig needs to be replaced or have some major repairs done to it."

"So what have you been doing for transportation since you moved back here?" she asked.

"Borrowing my uncle's open buggy, but I need something of my own, and soon."

"Have you checked with one of our local buggy shops to see if they have any used buggies for sale?"

"Not yet, but since I didn't have any luck finding one today, I plan to check with one or more of the buggy shops next week." Mark removed his straw hat and pulled his fingers through his thick blond hair. "When I get a new one, would you wanna go for a ride with me to test out the seats?"

Before Lenore had a chance to really think his request through, she smiled and nodded. "Sure. I'll give you my grandma's phone number so you can let me know when."

Mark offered Lenore a boyish grin and gave her arm a light tap. "Great. I'll look forward to that."

⟿

The tantalizing aromas from food vendors scattered around the mud sale beckoned to Jesse as he stepped out of his buggy. In a hurry to drop Cindy off at Vera's so he could get an early start to the mud sale, he hadn't taken the time to eat breakfast this morning.

After making sure his horse was secured, Jesse strode across the parking area and blended into the crowd. He had a few things on his mind he would like to see. Jesse thought about getting a rocking chair for his place, but the smell of food was rising to the top of his to-do list.

Jesse noticed a place farther down from where he was and started in that direction. He'd only gone a short ways when he spotted Lenore talking to a tall, blond Amish man. He had no beard, so Jesse could only assume the man was not married. Seeing the two of them together caught him off guard so much that he bumped into a kid ahead of him. "Oh, I'm sorry," Jesse apologized. "I should have been watching where I was going."

The boy turned around and gave Jesse an amused-looking grin, then moved on with his family. Jesse decided to step out of the way to avoid running into someone else. He moved to the side of the crowd and kept a close watch on Lenore and the blond man as they chatted.

Fists clenched, he took a few steps closer, hoping to get a better look. He'd never seen this fellow before, although he could be from another district in Lancaster County, or even an Amish community in some other state.

When the man touched Lenore's arm, Jesse felt a burning sensation in his chest. *What is wrong with me?* He took a few breaths and tried to refocus. *There's not a single reason for me to feel jealous. I have no claim on Mary Ruth's granddaughter. I told Lenore I don't love her, so she's free to see whomever she chooses.*

Hoping Lenore hadn't seen him, Jesse quickly moved on.

### Lancaster

Sara and Brad had spent most of the morning shopping at several of the stores at the Rockvale outlet mall. Now, tired and hungry, Sara felt ready to stop somewhere for lunch. "Are you hungry yet, Brad?"

"Sure, anytime you are."

"How about we go in there and get something to eat?" Sara pointed to a Ruby Tuesday restaurant. Since the first time she had visited the establishment, she'd been hooked on the salad bar, offering so many choices. Brad enjoyed the burgers there, so Sara figured he'd be more than willing to go along with her suggestion.

"Sounds good to me." Brad put his arm around Sara's waist as they headed in that direction.

The restaurant wasn't too busy, so they were shown to a table right away. After Brad placed his hamburger order, he told Sara to go ahead to the salad bar.

When she returned to the table with a plate full of her favorite salad items, they bowed their heads for silent prayer. When Sara finished praying and looked up, she was surprised to see Rick Osprey standing quietly at their table.

"I don't mean to interrupt, Pastor Fuller, but I saw you and your wife sitting here and wanted to come over and let you know that I won't be coming to your church anymore, or attending the Bible study for new believers."

Brad tipped his head. "I'm sorry to hear that." He glanced at Sara, then back at Rick. "Is there a problem—something you'd like to talk about?"

"No, not at all. I won't be back because I have a new job opportunity in Cincinnati. Me, my wife, Tammy, and our two boys will be moving to Ohio next week."

Sara's fingers twitched as she rolled her spoon back and forth next to her plate. A desperate need to know if Rick might be her father gave Sara the boldness to ask him a few questions.

"When we spoke at my flower shop, Mr. Osprey, you mentioned that you had known a young Amish woman named Rhoda Lapp when you were a teenager."

He nodded.

"When I asked how well you knew her, you said you didn't know most of the Amish girls that well, and you started to say something more, but then you never finished your sentence because you looked at your watch and realized you had to go somewhere."

"Yeah, that's right, but what's that got to do with anything? I mean, since you're obviously not Amish, why would you care about an Amish woman who was about the same age as me?"

"Was she your girlfriend?" Sara asked, without answering his question.

Rick shook his head, and his posture stiffened as he continued to remain next to their table. Sara wondered if she had touched a nerve. "No, of course not. I was dating Tammy Cantrell at the time, and I ended up marrying her." He squinted at Sara. "You never answered my question: Why all this interest in an Amish woman named Rhoda?"

"She was my mother." Sara's face heated as she averted her gaze. "But I've never known who my biological father was."

"That's a shame. If I had a daughter like you, I'd want her to know who I was. Tammy and I have two boys, but she's always wanted a girl."

"About Rhoda. . . Did she have a boyfriend—someone who hung out with your group?" Brad spoke the words Sara was about to ask.

"Sorry to disappoint you, but I barely knew the young woman, and she showed no interest in me—although I did see her talking to a couple of other guys in our group once. I suppose she could have been involved with one of them."

"Do you remember any of their names?" Sara felt that the truth was at her fingertips, yet she couldn't quite reach it.

"Sorry, I don't." Rick gave his ear a tug. " 'Course, Tammy had me so mesmerized, I didn't pay attention to much else going on."

"I understand. Thanks for taking the time to talk to us." Sara spoke quietly, hoping she wouldn't break down. Rick Osprey was her last shred of hope, and since she didn't know the name of the other young men in the group, there was no one else to ask.

Brad stood and shook Rick's hand. "I enjoyed the opportunity to meet you, and you'll certainly be missed at church."

"Yeah, I'll miss attending there too, but I can't pass up this new job opportunity."

"I understand." Brad reached in his pocket and pulled out one of his business cards. "Once you're moved and settled in your new home in Cincinnati, give me a call. I know a pastor in that area, and you might consider trying out his church."

"I'll do that." Rick smiled. "My two youngest boys are teenagers, so it would be good for them to attend church and get to know some other young people their age." He reached out and shook Sara's hand. "It's been nice meeting you too, Sara."

She nodded and smiled. As much as it pained her, Sara resolved to drop the search she'd started a few years ago and learn to live with the knowledge that it must not be meant for her to find her father.

# *Chapter 36*

### *Gordonville*

When Jesse entered Vera and Milton's house to pick up Cindy, he discovered her sitting on Milton's lap in the living room. Since they were both asleep, Jesse went to the kitchen, where he found Vera at the table with a crossword puzzle.

"How did things go at the mud sale?" she asked, looking up at Jesse. "Did you find anything interesting?"

"There were plenty of interesting things to see, but nothing I needed or wanted." Jesse pulled out a chair at the table and sat down with a heavy sigh.

"Is something wrong? You look unhappy."

"Nothing's wrong exactly; I just saw something that kind of disturbed me."

"What was it?"

"Lenore was at the mud sale with some tall, blond-haired fellow, and he had his hand on her arm. I had a feeling that they came there together. Just thinking that the young man she was with might be interested in her made me feel a twinge of jealousy."

"First of all, how do you know they were together? Maybe he's simply someone she knows and they were having a casual conversation." Vera shrugged. "Besides, even if there is something going on between Lenore and this fellow, why should it bother you? You're not going to marry her, and you admitted that you don't love her. So you shouldn't be jealous, and seeing her with another man shouldn't bother you one iota."

Vera was right, but even though it didn't make any sense, Jesse was more than a little bothered by the idea that Lenore might have a new love interest.

"Maybe you care more for Lenore than you're willing to admit."

Jesse shook his head. "It's just the idea that a few weeks ago Lenore and I were planning to be married. It was a bit upsetting to see her with someone so soon after our breakup."

Vera reached over and gave his shirtsleeve a tug. "Don't you think it's time to move on, Jesse?"

"What do you mean? I moved here to start over after Esther died. Isn't that moving on?"

"It's a beginning all right." Her forehead creased. "But I have a hunch you've been fighting your feelings for Lenore."

Jesse shook his head. "I don't think so, Vera. I only see her as a friend."

"Would you like some advice from a woman who's lived a good many years?"

Jesse nodded slowly. What else could he do? It wouldn't be right to tell Vera he didn't want her advice.

"Don't be like my son, Herschel, and live the rest of your life alone, pining for a wife who is gone and will never return to you." She paused and drew in a breath. After releasing it slowly, Vera spoke again. "My husband and I have had to sit back all this time and watch our son refuse to let go of his grief. I'm not saying he should have gotten married again, mind you. But Herschel has never given himself a chance to really enjoy life since Mattie died. And if the opportunity to love another woman had come along, I am almost certain he would not have taken it, because he didn't want to be untrue to Mattie's memory." She placed her hand on his arm. "Your dear wife is gone, Jesse, but you're still here with the responsibility of raising your daughter."

"I'm doing the best I can for Cindy."

"Of course you are, but you need to think of your own needs too."

Jesse dropped his gaze. "I was. When I asked Lenore to marry me, I was selfishly thinking how nice it would be to have someone to run the household for me." His eyebrows gathered in. "I regret having asked her now. It wasn't fair to let Lenore believe I was in love with her."

Vera placed both hands on her hips. "How do you know your friendship couldn't have developed into love? Most relationships between a man and woman start out that way. Weren't you and Esther friends before you fell in love?"

"Jah."

"And don't you think Esther would want you to find love again?"

"I'm not sure."

"Of course she would. And I believe Esther would approve of Lenore. If Lenore is willing, maybe you should begin courting her again and see where things lead."

Jesse leaned heavily against the back of his chair. "I'm not sure my feelings for Lenore will change, but I'll think seriously about what you've said."

"There's one more thing I'd like to say on the matter." Vera leaned slightly forward.

"What's that?"

"If your feelings for Lenore aren't changing, then why are you jealous of the man you saw her talking to at the mud sale?"

Jesse's only response was a brief shrug, because he had no answer to Vera's question.

❧

*Strasburg*

"I'm home!" Lenore called when she came in the back door.

"Welcome back. I'm in here!"

When Lenore entered the kitchen, she found Grandma at the stove, stirring something in a kettle.

Lenore sniffed. "Are you making baked potato soup for lunch?"

Grandma turned to look at Lenore and grinned. "You have a good sniffer."

Lenore laughed.

"How did things go at the mud sale? Were there a lot of people?"

"Jah, and I ran into Mark Zook while I was there."

Grandma tipped her head. "Oh? He's the young man you

mentioned who recently moved back to our area, right?"

Lenore nodded. "He came to work for his uncle in the wood-working trade."

Grandma turned back to the stove. "Was he looking for wood-working tools at the sale?"

"He said he came there to see if he could find a used buggy."

"And did he?"

"No. I suggested he check with one of the local buggy makers who often have used carriages to sell." Lenore went to the kitchen sink and washed her hands. "He said he'd like to take me for a ride when he gets his own buggy."

"Hmm. . .sounds like this young man might be interested in you."

"I doubt it. I'm sure he just needs a friend." Lenore finished washing her hands and dried them on a clean towel. "Now what can I do to help with lunch?"

"If you don't mind, I'd appreciate you going down to the base-ment for a jar of canned peaches. I thought I'd make a cobbler for dessert this evening."

"I'd be happy to do that. Anything else?"

"Maybe a jar of green beans. We can have them as our vege-table to go with the chicken I'll be roasting later this afternoon."

"Okay, I'll be up with the beans and peaches soon." Lenore headed for the basement stairs and turned on the battery-operated light to guide her down. When she reached the bottom, a thought popped into her head. *Think I'll take a few minutes to read some of the notes in the prayer jar. I haven't looked at it in a while, and I might read something that will inspire me today.*

Lenore got the jar down, and the first note she pulled out was a prayer: *Dear Lord, please heal the hurt in my heart, for right now I feel that it will never go away.*

Lenore could relate to the feeling of hurt that had been in her heart since Jesse called off the wedding. It pained her even more whenever she met someone from their community and was asked why she and Jesse weren't seeing each other anymore or why the wedding had been called off. Every time she had to explain, it was like opening a wound that had never fully healed.

The biggest question for Lenore was why she had allowed herself to fall in love with Jesse. She squeezed her eyes shut. *And my precious little Cindy—I love her so much too.*

Feeling weighed down and wishing she could sleep, Lenore forced her eyes to open. Reaching into the jar again, she pulled out another slip of paper. Proverbs 3:5–6 had been written on this one: "Trust in the Lord with all thine heart; and lean not unto thine own understanding. In all thy ways acknowledge him, and he shall direct thy paths."

Lenore contemplated her need to trust God with her future and quit fretting over what might have been. She needed to move forward with her life and pray for wisdom and direction in the days ahead.

⁓

Before going home, Sara asked Brad if he would mind stopping by her grandmother's house for a short visit.

"Sure, that's fine. It's good to check on her regularly, in case she needs something."

"Agreed." Once more, Sara thanked the Lord for her thoughtful, caring husband.

When they arrived at their destination, Sara got out of the car and headed for the house while Brad played chase-the-stick with Sadie. The poor dog always acted starved for attention, although Sara felt sure the collie wasn't ignored by Grandma or Lenore. No doubt Sadie missed Grandpa. He'd spent a lot of time with her. Even when he did his chores, the dog tagged along. Pets often grieved when they lost someone close to them.

Sara pressed a palm against her chest. When Sara's mother died, she felt like an empty vessel—unable to cope with her feelings of abandonment and despair. Sara had also grieved when her stepfather died and again when Grandpa passed on. Unfortunately, dying was part of everyone's life, and oh, how deeply it hurt when a loved one departed this earth. Sara's only comfort was the knowledge that if they all made it to heaven, she would be reunited with them someday.

Determined to set aside her thoughts about death, Sara stepped onto the porch and knocked on the door. A few minutes passed before Grandma opened the door and greeted her.

"This is a nice surprise." Grandma's face broke into a wide smile. "Is your husband with you?"

"Yes. Brad's occupied with Sadie outside. I'm sure he will join us as soon as she gets tired of running after the stick that he keeps throwing." Sara giggled and entered the house. She paused in the entry and set her purse on the floor.

"What have you two been up to today?" Grandma asked, leading the way to the kitchen.

"We did a little shopping at the Rockvale outlet and then went to lunch." Sara pulled out a chair at the table and sat down.

"Would you like a cup of tea?" Grandma asked. "Lenore and I had some earlier, and the water's still warm in the teakettle."

"That sounds nice. Where is Lenore anyway?"

"She developed a headache and went upstairs to her room to rest awhile."

"Sorry to hear that. If she doesn't come down before we leave, please tell her I hope she feels better soon."

"I certainly will." Grandma got out two cups and poured them both some tea. "How are things going at the flower shop?" she asked, taking a seat across from Sara.

"Fairly well. I'm having the walls in the main part of the store painted today, so the store is closed until Monday." Sara blew on her tea and took a cautious sip. "Can I ask you something, Grandma?"

"Of course you may."

Sara told her grandmother about meeting Rick Osprey at the restaurant and how disappointed she felt when she realized he was not her father and that he didn't have any idea who her mother had been seeing. "I believe I should give up looking, because if God wanted me to know who my biological father is, it would have happened by now." Sara looked directly at Grandma. "Do you agree?"

"That all depends."

"On what?"

"Can you put the question of who your father is out of your mind?"

Sara pushed a lock of hair out of her face. "I—I honestly don't know, but I'm going to try, because every time I think about it, I just get more upset."

# Chapter 37

Sara entered the flower shop early the first Monday of May. This would be a busy month, with Mother's Day just weeks away and many people placing orders.

Sara turned on all the lights, put away her purse, and went to check the big cooler in the back room as she did each day upon arrival. She was stunned to discover the temperature was at fifty-five degrees, despite having been set at thirty-eight degrees, which Misty had said was the temperature she felt was best for the flowers.

"This is not a good way to begin a new week," Sara muttered. "I need a repairman to take a look at the cooler—and fast."

She hurried to remove as many flowers as she could from the big cooler to the display cooler. Since the roses were the most important to move, she began with those. Hopefully this would keep her losses down. No telling when the heat had begun to rise. The flowers Sara couldn't fit into the display cooler would have to sit out until the other cooler got fixed, which meant she'd have to either mark them down for a quick sale or suffer the loss if they went bad.

Sara was still in the process of removing the flowers from the larger cooler when her designer showed up.

"What's going on?" Misty asked, gesturing to the flowers on the counter. "Why are all of these sitting out?"

Sara explained about the temperature malfunction and said she still needed to call a repairman.

"I know just who to call, so I'll take care of it for you."

"Thanks." While Misty made the phone call, Sara finished the job of finding places to set all the flowers. When she returned from the back room with the last bunch, Misty was off the phone.

"Did the repairman agree to come over soon?"

Misty shook her head. "Unfortunately, he's tied up all morning and probably won't get here until sometime this afternoon."

Sara lifted her gaze to the ceiling. "Oh, great. I hope all the flowers will be okay until then. I have no idea how long they've been sitting inside the big cooler in fifty-five-degree heat."

"They should be okay, but I'll keep an eye on them. In the meantime, I need to get to work on the orders that need to be done today." Misty headed for the back room.

Sara sank into a chair at her desk. Last week hadn't gone well, as they'd dealt with several difficult customers they couldn't seem to satisfy. Then there was the cat that got into the store and knocked over a vase of flowers an elderly woman was about to purchase. The week had ended on a negative note when her delivery boy got sick and had to leave early, leaving Sara to deliver the flowers while Misty finished two last-minute bouquets.

Sara didn't mind making deliveries when she had to, but when she was faced with barking dogs in a customer's yard that looked like they might take a bite out of her leg, stress always took over. One time when she was heading to the delivery van with a pretty bouquet, a man walking a dog came by and told her not to worry, that his dog wouldn't bite. Sara quickly realized his statement wasn't true when she wound up with a Jack Russell terrier hanging off the corner of her jacket. Another time when she made a delivery, Sara had to walk up a grassy hill to get to the front door. She ended up slipping on the grass and falling but somehow managed to save the floral arrangement. Unfortunately her slacks sustained a bad grass stain and she never was able to remove the marks.

Sara hoped this week would go better, but things weren't off to a great start. At moments like this Sara wondered if she should sell the shop and concentrate fully on helping Brad in his ministry.

She exhaled noisily. *But I probably wouldn't be happy if I gave up something I really enjoy doing that's outside of the church.*

Mary Ruth hadn't said anything to Lenore because she didn't want to bring up the topic of Jesse, but she greatly missed spending time with Cindy. Having the little girl to care for had given her something meaningful to do. She used to look forward to the little girl's arrival on the days Jesse had to work. The child's cute antics and contagious belly laugh had given Mary Ruth a reason to smile. But with no one in the house except herself during the day, Mary Ruth felt lonely. It seemed as if her life no longer had a purpose. She tried to keep busy, as she was doing now, weeding and watering her flower and vegetable garden, but it wasn't the same as having a child to nurture and love. Even Sadie, who followed Mary Ruth nearly everywhere these days, seemed despondent. Perhaps she too missed all the activity of having a small child around.

Mary Ruth weeded thoroughly around the front border of her flower garden, where she'd planted red and white geraniums. Willis had liked those flowers and often commented on how nice they looked in the flower bed. She wanted to keep that theme in place as though nothing had changed.

*I'll need to do one more thing.* Mary Ruth got up and walked out to the shed to get her watering can and the plant food for the flowers. "Hmm . . .there's the food, but where is my watering can?" She dug around inside the shed, but the item wasn't there.

Mary Ruth grabbed the food and a nearby bucket and then got to work feeding the favored flowers. When she'd finished with that chore, she put things away. Then she went back to the garden to decide on the next spot to weed.

She walked slowly, eyeing the flower beds close to the house, and found that the pretty purple-and-white petunias needed some attention. As Mary Ruth weeded, she remembered about the watering can. The plastic container had a split and leaked a lot. So she had thrown it out and forgotten to buy a replacement.

"My old brain isn't working well these days," Mary Ruth muttered. She piled up the weeds as she cleaned out the bed. Once that chore was done, she stopped to watch her neighbors walking down the road and waved as they went by. The weather was lovely today, and working outside gave her a sense of accomplishment.

Mary Ruth continued to weed until each flower bed looked just right. She wished she had another bag of compost to add around the just-weeded spots. It would discourage more weeds from sprouting, making the weeding easier on the next go-round.

Mary Ruth noticed one of the barn cats out sunning itself, looking as though it was asleep. *That actually looks like a good plan. Maybe I should go inside and take a nap.* She rose from her kneeling position and reached around to rub a sore spot on the right side of her back. In a few weeks school would be out and Lenore would be home again for the summer. Mary Ruth looked forward to her granddaughter's companionship, as well as the extra help Lenore would offer with the yard and household chores. Having someone to talk to while doing one's chores was always more pleasurable than doing them alone.

Mary Ruth stared down at her hands, soiled from tugging at weeds. She should have worn a pair of gardening gloves but had always felt she could do a better job with her bare hands. *If I'm not careful, I'll sink into depression, and I can't allow that to happen. If Willis were here, he would shake his finger at me and say, "Count your blessings, Fraa. Do not give in to despair."*

She moved around to the other side of the house and stood looking at the lovely flowers in bloom. *Guess there's always something to be thankful for; I just need to look for it and try to keep a positive attitude.*

But her soul felt empty this afternoon. In addition to missing Willis every single day, she only got to see Cindy on Sundays, and seeing the little girl's eyes light up whenever she approached only made it that much harder.

Mary Ruth also felt a burden for both of her granddaughters. Although Lenore didn't say so, Mary Ruth was certain the somber expression on Lenore's face proved that she still loved Jesse and hurt because he didn't return her love.

Then there was Sara, still burdened over not knowing who her biological father was. Mary Ruth wished she had an answer for her

English granddaughter. *If only Rhoda had confided in her father or me and admitted she was pregnant and told us the name of her baby's father.*

"Enough weeding for today." Mary Ruth ended her introspections and set her gardening tools on the porch. Nothing could be gained by rehashing the past when it couldn't be changed. "Think I'll go inside now, read some scripture and pray, and then take a nap."

Lenore sat at her desk, rubbing her tired eyes. The scholars had left for the day, and she had some papers to go over before tomorrow's lessons. *If I could be anywhere else right now, where would it be? Maybe on a two-week trip to Sarasota with Grandma,* she mused. *A getaway would be a nice change but not practical at this time.*

Lenore picked up a paper and began to review it. The student had done a fine job, and she wrote the grade at the top of the page. Lenore hoped every paper in the pile would be like the first one. It was hard to believe the school term was almost over. Lenore would spend the summer months helping Grandma with the garden and all the chores that needed to be done around the house. Either Dad or one of her brothers would continue to do most of the heavy outdoor chores, as well as anything Lenore and Grandma couldn't do inside the house.

Last Saturday, Ben and Peter had come over to patch a few places on the roof where some shingles had come loose. A few days before that Dad had come by to fix a leaky toilet upstairs. Lenore's mother came as often as she could to help with some of the easier chores. She would no doubt be available when it was time to pick produce from the garden and can some of it in the pressure cooker.

Lenore tapped her fingers on the desk. *Wish I could be home with Grandma all the time and didn't have to teach school anymore. If Jesse hadn't called off our wedding, we'd be getting married the last Thursday of this month, and then my only job would be taking care of Cindy and being a good wife.*

Despite her sorrow over the way things had transpired, it was better than finding out he didn't love her after they were married. That would have been a crushing blow. It was hard to imagine living with a man she called *husband* but not truly being his wife in every sense of the word. *Could I have done it for Cindy's sake?* Lenore asked herself for the umpteenth time. *Should I have agreed to marry Jesse anyway, in hopes that he might love me someday?*

The schoolhouse door opened and Mark stepped inside. "I was hoping you'd still be here. Are you busy?" he called.

"Just going over some papers." She smiled as he approached her desk. "What brings you by the schoolhouse this afternoon?"

"Came to let you know I finally got myself a new *waegli*."

"That's good. I'm sure you're glad to have found a buggy that will work for you."

"I am, and now the rig I'd been borrowing is back with its owner. It's nice having a closed-in buggy."

Lenore laid down her pen. "So where did you get it?"

"The buggy maker closest to here mentioned an Amish man who wanted to sell his used buggy. So I went to the address, and the man showed me the one I'm driving now."

"It sounds like you're happy with it."

"Jah, and I was hoping you'd have the time to go for a ride with me. I'd like to show you how nice it rides."

She motioned to the stack of papers on her desk. "Sorry, Mark, I can't go right now, but maybe some evening this week." Lenore could tell he really wanted her to go with him today, and she felt bad for turning him down.

Mark's smile faded as he remained next to her desk. Then his grin returned before he spoke. "How about Friday? Would that work for you?" He popped the knuckles on his right hand.

Lenore had a flashback, remembering that she'd seen him do that several times when they attended school together. As she recalled, the finger popping had taken place whenever Mark seemed apprehensive about something. Perhaps he'd been nervous about asking her to take a ride in his buggy.

With only a slight hesitation, Lenore nodded. Maybe a few hours with Mark would take her mind off other things.

# Chapter 38

*Clymer*

Michelle listened intently as one of their elderly ministers read Romans 8:28: "We know that all things work together for good to them that love God, to them who are the called according to his purpose." The minister delivering the message was the easiest to understand. He tended to use more English words in his address to the congregation than the bishop and other preachers did.

Michelle was still getting used to deciphering the German words spoken during Amish church, but her language skills were coming along. At least she understood most of the Pennsylvania Dutch words the Amish spoke as their everyday language.

She'd gotten used to doing without TV and other modern electronic conveniences. She no longer needed those forms of stimulation. The simple life was what Michelle thought was important.

As she sat with the other women on wooden benches, Michelle appreciated the pillow she'd been offered to sit on today. Another young woman also sat on a pillow. She was expecting a baby too, only she wasn't as far along as Michelle.

Michelle rested both hands on her stomach. In a little over two months she would give birth, and since she'd finally set her fears aside, she could hardly wait for the big day. Michelle felt certain that Ezekiel would be a good father, and hoped she'd be a good mother as well. Ezekiel's mother planned to come and stay with them for a while after the baby was born, and Michelle looked forward to that. Even though Belinda hadn't accepted her at first, as time went on and Michelle became a member of the Amish church, their relationship had improved.

Michelle glanced at her new friend, Anita Beiler, who was also new to the area. Anita and her husband, Nate, were expecting a baby in August. The two couples had gotten together a few times to visit and play board games. Michelle and Anita had also spent some time together, sewing clothes for their babies and helping each other with their gardens. It was nice to have someone to talk to who was about her age, and Michelle had finally reached the point where she felt like Clymer was her home.

She gave her belly a gentle tap, and as if in response, the baby kicked. *It will be your home too, little one.* As the Bible verse said, all things were working out for her good.

Michelle glanced at her husband from across the room. Ezekiel's relaxed expression let her know that he too felt content.

### Strasburg

As Lenore sat in church, listening to the second message of the morning, she glanced at the men's side and noticed Mark looking at her. She quickly dropped her gaze, hoping no one had noticed them making eye contact, which would be inappropriate in church.

Lenore wondered why he hadn't picked her up for a buggy ride on Friday evening as they'd planned. He hadn't even bothered to call. Had he forgotten about it or simply changed his mind? Either way, it was inconsiderate of him not to let her know.

Lenore kept her gaze focused on her folded hands. *Since I have no expectations of us establishing a relationship and apparently neither does Mark, I suppose it doesn't really matter that he didn't show up on Friday evening. He's just an acquaintance—not even a close friend, because a friend would have the courtesy to let the other person know if they had to cancel their plans.*

As the next song began, Lenore looked up from her hymnal and saw Jesse holding Cindy. The child looked so cute sitting on her daddy's lap with a wide-eyed expression. Drawing her arms close to her body and gripping the Amish hymnal tightly, Lenore dropped her gaze once more. *Some men can't be trusted. At least that's how it appears to be with Jesse and Mark. They say one thing and then go back on their word.*

When church was over and everyone had been served a light lunch, some people went home while others lingered, gathering in groups to visit. Since Cindy had become fussy and needed her diaper changed, Jesse decided it was time to head for home. Hopefully she would sleep after he'd changed her diaper, and then Jesse would try to do some reading, or he might even take a nap himself.

As Jesse headed for his buggy, carrying Cindy as well as her diaper bag, he thought about how things were when he'd been courting Lenore. He reflected on the advice Vera had given him a few weeks ago and wondered if he'd been too hasty breaking things off with Lenore. Maybe he did have some feelings for her. It could be that if they had gotten married those feelings would have turned to love. Jesse wondered if he should see if Lenore might be willing to let him court her again.

Almost every Sunday that their district held church services, he and Cindy had gone over to Mary Ruth's house and spent the afternoon and evening hours with her and Lenore. They'd often played board games or just sat and visited. And of course, the women would always fix something tasty to eat. Jesse missed those times. Truth was, he also missed conversing with Lenore. But the question was—did he love her? If he did, he had been pushing his feelings down to keep from being untrue to Esther's memory.

Jesse approached his buggy and got Cindy settled inside. As he turned toward his horse, waiting patiently to go, he caught sight of Lenore over by the fence, talking to Mark Zook, whom he'd finally met.

Jesse tried not to gawk at the two of them as they visited. Instead, he turned his head to look inside the buggy at Cindy, yawning in her car seat. When Jesse looked back, he noticed Lenore's buggy. Mary Ruth stood outside the buggy with her arms folded, no doubt waiting for Lenore. Jesse caught sight of her looking in the couple's direction. He couldn't see her expression from here but wondered if Mary Ruth approved of Lenore's new friend.

The skin under Jesse's eyes tightened as a pang of jealousy shot through him. His teeth clenched. *I bet something is going on between those two. Guess I waited too long,* he berated himself. *So now what do I do? Should I forget about Lenore and move on with my life, or see if there's a possibility of pursuing a relationship again?*

❧

"I'm sorry about not coming by to pick you up on Friday for a ride in my buggy." Mark reached out his hand as if to touch Lenore, but quickly pulled it away. "If you're willing to listen, I'd like to explain what happened."

Lenore leaned against the fence and looked up at him. "I'm willing to listen."

"I had to work later than normal Friday evening, and by the time I got back to my uncle's place, I'd developed a *koppweh*." Mark leaned on the fence too, and when he smiled, she caught a whiff of his minty breath.

"It's too bad about your headache. I understand how miserable those can be. What I don't understand, though, is why you didn't call and let me know you weren't coming."

"I did call, but the voice mail on your answering machine must have been nearly full, because it cut off before I could even say who I was." He popped a few knuckles on his left hand.

"Oh, I see." Lenore had no choice but to give him the benefit of the doubt—especially because she had discovered that their answering machine was full when she'd checked it last evening.

"Am I forgiven?" Mark's arms hung loosely at his sides, but his tender gaze remained on her.

"Jah." Lenore looked over toward her buggy and saw Grandma waiting. She appeared to be looking their way. Lenore's face warmed, and Mark's proximity wasn't helping. *I wonder what*

*Grandma is thinking right now. Am I moving on too soon?*

Mark cleared his throat. "Lenore, are you okay? Your cheeks look mighty red all of a sudden."

"I'm fine. Uh, sorry, what did you say?" She stepped from Grandma's view.

"I'd like another chance, and I was thinking if you're not busy, I could come by your grandma's place this evening and take you for a ride." Mark's sincere expression made it difficult to say no.

Lenore managed a weak smile. "I have no special plans for this evening, so jah, I'm willing to go for a ride."

Mark's lips stretched into a pleasant smile. "Okay, good. I'll see you around seven."

As Mark walked away, Lenore turned toward her buggy, where Grandma sat waiting. *Sure hope I didn't make a mistake saying I would go.*

~⁊~

That evening, Lenore's parents came by to see how she and Grandma were doing. Mom brought along some cold fried chicken and potato salad, and Lenore took coleslaw from the refrigerator that she'd made yesterday, along with some pickled beets and chow-chow.

"Danki for helping me get supper on," Lenore said to her mother. "It's nice for Grandma to just sit and relax for a change while she visits with Dad."

Mom nodded. "Jah, it's good for them to have a little mother-son time."

"I agree. It's been awfully quiet around the house ever since Jesse found someone else to watch Cindy, and Grandma misses the little girl."

"I figured as much. She's not as cheerful as she was when she kept busy taking care of Cindy," Mom observed. "So how are things going with you?"

Lenore shrugged as she placed the bowl of coleslaw on the table. "Okay, I guess. I'm getting a bit bored with teaching though, and I've been praying that God will show me what He has in store for me down the road."

"I'll be praying for you too." Mom hugged Lenore. "Now your grandma mentioned when we first arrived that you were talking to a nice-looking Amish man after church this afternoon."

"It was Mark Zook. He and his folks used to live in the area, and he went to school with me."

"So are he and his family here for a visit?"

"No, I believe Mark plans to stay here. He's working for his uncle John in his woodworking business."

"I see." Mom tipped her head. "Do you mind me asking what the two of you were talking about today?"

"Nothing much. Mark was just asking if he could take me for a buggy ride."

A wide smile spread across Mom's face. "I'm glad to hear that. It'll be good for you to start courting again."

Lenore released an exasperated sigh. "Mom, Mark and I are not courting. We're just renewing our acquaintance, and he probably needs a friend."

"Well, you just never know—your friendship with Mark might lead to something else." Mom's tone sounded hopeful. No doubt she was as eager to see Lenore married off as Lenore was herself. Well, it remained to be seen what her future held. The main thing, Lenore kept reminding herself, was to keep her focus on God and live a good Christian life. And as long as she was teaching, she needed to be a good example to her students, even if she no longer felt that teaching was her true calling.

# Chapter 39

*Lancaster*

As the last few parishioners headed out the door after the church service had ended, Charlene Givens, a young woman who had recently started attending Brad's Friday night Bible study, paused at the door and smiled at Sara. "My husband and I are looking forward to the barbecue you and the pastor are hosting this coming Saturday. Is there anything I can bring?"

Stunned and barely able to form any words, Sara stammered, "Uh, no, I—I don't think so."

Charlene smiled. "Okay, we'll see you Saturday evening then. And if you change your mind and would like me to bring something, please give me a call."

Sara watched as the young woman walked away and got into the car where her husband, Roger, waited. Sara's forehead creased. *Now what was that all about?* This was the first she'd heard anything about a barbecue at their house. *Could Charlene be misinformed, or did Brad plan the event without telling me? Should I have told her I didn't know about the barbecue?*

She turned toward her husband, who had moments ago been talking with the head deacon. *Should I say something to Brad now or wait till we get home?*

"You okay, hon?" Brad asked, stepping up to her. "You look perplexed."

"I am. Did you invite Charlene and Roger Givens to our house for a barbecue this coming Saturday?"

He nodded.

Sara frowned, clamping one hand firmly against her hip.

"Without telling me or asking if I approved?"

Brad blinked rapidly. "I did tell you. We discussed it one night last week after you got home from work."

Sara shook her head. "I'm sure I'd remember if we had such a discussion. You can imagine how surprised I was when Charlene brought it up and asked if there was anything she could bring."

"Can we discuss this after we get home?" Brad glanced to his right, and Sara noticed that the deacon stood nearby, looking at the church guest book. *Or maybe he's listening to our conversation so he can tell others what we're saying.*

Knowing Brad was right about waiting until they got home to finish their discussion, Sara gave a brief nod. The last thing they needed was a round of gossip about the pastor and his wife having a disagreement right here in the church.

Brad said a few words to the deacon, then followed Sara out the door. They walked across the parking lot and into the yard of the parsonage, which was next to the church. As soon as they entered the house, Sara turned to face Brad. "I am almost one-hundred percent sure you did not mention anything about a barbecue to me."

A muscle quivered in his jaw. "And I'm equally sure I did, Sara. You were probably preoccupied and didn't listen to what I said. However, when I mentioned it, you did nod your head, so I assumed you were fine with the idea of having a few people over for food and fellowship."

Sara tapped her foot impatiently. "I'm certain I would remember something as important as you expecting me to host a barbecue—and during one of the busiest times for the flower shop, no less." She looked at Brad through half-closed lids. "Have you forgotten that next Sunday is Mother's Day? Saturday will be a zoo at the shop all day, and I may even have to work late."

"No, I haven't forgotten about Mother's Day. I just thought with the barbecue taking place at seven o'clock, you'd have plenty of time to get home from work."

"As I said before. . .I may be working late."

He placed his hand on her shoulder. "I'm sorry, but the plans have already been made and I don't want to disappoint the people I've invited."

Her jaw clenched as she looked up at him. "Just how many people did you invite?"

"There will be eight, counting us."

"Well, that's just great. The next time you decide to plan an event at our house, please send me a memo." Sara dropped her Bible on the entry table and tromped down the hall to their bedroom. This was the first real disagreement between her and Brad, and it hurt to know he hadn't put her needs above others'. The worst part of all was that he hadn't even told her about it.

*Strasburg*

"Your new buggy is very nice," Lenore said as she and Mark traveled down the road.

"Danki, I like it too, and I'm real pleased with how well it rides." He ran his hand across the upholstered seat in the area between them. "The interior is in good shape too. Sure am glad I found this rig and was able to get it for a reasonable price." Mark's tone was enthusiastic.

"How long do you plan to stay in Lancaster County?" Lenore asked.

"I'm here to stay." Mark's brows lowered as he turned his head to look at her. "Thought I told you that when we met the first time after I came back here." He gestured to the front of the buggy. "Why else would I have invested in this?"

Lenore's ears burned. "Oh, sorry. I must have forgotten."

"No problem. Maybe I just didn't make myself clear." He reached across the seat and gave her arm a light tap. "I don't plan to stay at my uncle's place indefinitely, though. If things work out as I hope, I plan to either rent or buy a home of my own."

"I see."

"How long do you plan on teaching school?" Mark asked.

"Until the Lord guides me in a different direction. I hope to have a home and family someday. But for now I'm content to live with my grandma and teach school."

"I'd like to get married and have a family too. Just waitin' for the right woman to make me fall in love." He gave her another sidelong glance, then focused on the road again.

Lenore remained quiet, and they rode without talking for a while.

"Say, next Saturday is my birthday," Mark said, breaking the silence. "My aunt and uncle are planning a birthday dinner for me. Would you like to come? We'll be making homemade ice cream," he added with a grin.

"That sounds yummy. Sure, I'd like to come to your birthday celebration."

Mark's horse picked up speed, and he pulled back on the reins. "Slow down, Clipper. No need to hurry, boy." He looked at Lenore once more. "Unless you need to get home soon, that is."

She shook her head and relaxed against the seat. It was nice to spend time with a man who seemed genuinely interested in her. The fact that Mark had invited Lenore to his birthday party let her know that he might have more than a passing interest in her.

"I don't think you've ever said, but I'm curious as to the reason you decided to move back here without any of your family coming along." Lenore sat quietly, waiting for his response.

Mark's lips drew into a straight line as he kept his focus on the road. Several seconds passed before he answered her question. "I. . .uh. . .just needed a new start."

Was Mark reluctant to answer her question? She felt it wouldn't be right to prod him further, so she changed the subject. "It's a nice evening, jah?"

He nodded. Lenore couldn't figure out why he'd gone quiet all of a sudden. Mark had been plenty talkative until she'd brought up the subject of why he'd moved back to Strasburg. Could Mark have had a falling out with his parents? Or maybe he was trying to get over a broken relationship with a young woman. Many reasons could cause someone to want to start over, but Lenore wouldn't press Mark for the details. If he wanted to talk about it in his own time, she'd be willing to listen.

❧

Holding tight to his fidgety daughter in his arms, Jesse stepped onto Mary Ruth's porch and knocked on the door. All the way here he'd thought about Lenore and what he would say to her. *Sure hope she's willing to give me another chance at courting her. How else can I ever really know what my true feelings are for her if I don't give it more time? I was stupid to just break things off like I did. Should have told her the truth and then asked if she'd be willing to postpone the wedding and give us more time to court and get to know each other better. With a little more time, maybe my feelings for Lenore would have changed.*

A few minutes passed before the door opened. Mary Ruth stood inside with her head covering askew. "Ach, Jesse! It's nice to see you." She reached up to adjust her kapp. "And you too, sweet girl." Mary Ruth touched the end of Cindy's nose, which caused the child to giggle. "Please, come inside."

When Jesse entered the house, Mary Ruth held out her arms. "May I hold her?"

"Of course, but she's getting heavy. Not fat, just solid." Jesse gave a nervous laugh as he glanced around, hoping Lenore would make an appearance. "Maybe I should put her down and you can walk with her out to the living room."

Mary Ruth bobbed her head. "Good idea."

Once Jesse set his daughter on her feet, Mary Ruth clasped Cindy's chubby little hand, and they all went to the living room.

After Mary Ruth was seated in her rocking chair, she lifted Cindy into her lap and got the chair moving at a slow and gentle pace. "I've missed this precious little girl something awful." She brought Cindy's hand up to her lips and gave it a kiss. "I've missed seeing you too, Jesse. We don't really get the chance to converse at church, and I've only seen you there a few times since I quit watching Cindy. How have the two of you been?"

"Doing okay, but Cindy and I both miss you as well. She did much better with you watching her than she does with Vera."

"I wish I could offer to watch her again, but with you and my granddaughter breaking up, it might be too awkward. Especially since Lenore will be done teaching school for the summer soon. She'll be here most of the time, so it would be hard for you to avoid seeing her."

*I don't want to avoid seeing Lenore. I want to spend more time with her.* Jesse kept his thoughts to himself.

Crossing and then uncrossing his arms, Jesse shifted on the couch. "Speaking of Lenore, is she here right now?"

Mary Ruth shook her head. "No need to worry. Mark Zook came by a while ago to take Lenore for a ride in his new buggy."

"Oh, I see." Jesse weaved his fingers through his beard. "Well, would you please tell her I stopped by, and that I said hello?"

"Of course." Mary Ruth set Cindy on the floor again. "Now how about I go into the kitchen and fetch us all some *millich un kichlin?* Maybe by the time we're done eating, Lenore will be home."

Jesse lifted a hand. "No, that's okay. Don't trouble yourself. I just dropped by to say hello, but we really should get home now."

Mary Ruth's shoulders slumped a bit, but she did offer him a smile. "Whatever you think is best."

Jesse got up, scooped Cindy into his arms, and moved toward the front door. Apparently renewing his relationship with Lenore was not meant to be. *I'm too late. Lenore is already being courted by someone else.*

Mary Ruth stood at the door, waving as Jesse guided his horse and buggy out of her yard. *I wish he'd stayed a while longer.* In addition to wanting to spend more time with Cindy, Mary Ruth hoped if Jesse and Lenore could spend a little time visiting, they might get back together. "Maybe it's just my silly wishful thinking again," she murmured. "Guess I'm a romantic at heart."

Mary Ruth went to the kitchen and heated hot water for tea. She'd no more than sat down with her cup when Lenore showed up.

"You just missed Jesse and Cindy," she said after Lenore entered the kitchen.

Lenore blinked a couple of times. "They were here?"

"Jah. Came by to say hello, but they didn't stay long."

Lenore hung her lightweight shawl over the back of a chair and took a seat at the table. "I bet you enjoyed seeing Cindy. When I saw her in church this morning, I was surprised to see how much she's grown. I think Jesse's been going to Vera and Milton's church district the last few weeks, because today is the first time I've seen him and Cindy in a while."

"Jah, that could be." Mary Ruth took a sip of her tea. "Jesse asked about you. He seemed disappointed when I told him you weren't here."

"I'm sorry I missed them." Lenore fiddled with the basket of napkins on the table, wishing they weren't having this conversation. "It would have been nice to spend a little time with Cindy again."

"What about Jesse? Wouldn't you have enjoyed visiting with him?"

She shrugged. "I suppose so, but it would have been kind of awkward for both of us. Since Jesse broke things off with me, we've only spoken a few times, and I could feel the tension between us."

"Maybe he's having second thoughts."

Lenore gave a deep, weighted sigh. "I doubt that Jesse misses me." She yawned and stretched her arms over her head. "I'm kind of tired, Grandma. If you don't mind, I'm going upstairs to bed."

"That's fine," Mary Ruth said, trying to hide her disappointment. She'd hoped the two of them might sit and visit awhile before retiring for the evening. Mary Ruth wanted to hear how things had gone with Mark and maybe say a few more things about Jesse.

She stood and gave Lenore a hug. "Good night, dear one. I hope you sleep well."

"You too, Grandma." Lenore smiled, but there was an unmistakable sadness in her eyes.

*Lenore may not be willing to admit it, but I am convinced that she still misses Jesse,* Mary Ruth thought as her granddaughter left the room. Tapping her chin with her knuckles, she tipped her head to one side. *There must be some way to get those two back together. I just need to figure out what.*

# Chapter 40

Lenore finished her cup of coffee and set it in the sink. "Oh Grandma, before I leave for school, I wanted to let you know that I won't be here for supper Saturday night."

"Oh, why's that?"

"Last night on our buggy ride, Mark invited me to attend his birthday supper at his aunt and uncle's place. I should have told you after I got home, but I had other things on my mind and forgot to mention it."

"*Danki* for letting me know. Guess I'll plan something small for my supper that evening, or maybe I'll hitch my horse to the buggy and go out somewhere to eat."

Lenore's brows lifted. "By yourself?"

"Of course. I'm not so old that I can't take the horse and buggy out by myself, and I don't mind eating alone once in a while."

Lenore blew out a quick breath. Now, in addition to being a bit nervous about going to Mark's party, she'd have to worry about Grandma all evening.

Grandma waved her hand. "I know what you're thinking, and I'll be fine, so there's no need to *druwwle* about me."

"Okay, I'll try not to worry." Lenore managed to smile. "Oh, and one more thing before I forget. . . After school lets out today, I'm going shopping to get a birthday present for Mark. Any suggestions for what I should get?"

Grandma shook her head. "You know the young man better than I do. What kinds of things does he like?"

Lenore shrugged. "To tell you the truth, I'm not really sure.

Mark works in his uncle's woodworking shop, but that's his job. I don't know what kinds of things he enjoys doing when he's not working."

Grandma tapped her fingers along the edge of the table. "How about a *buch*? Most people enjoy reading."

"A book would make a nice gift if I knew what type of subject Mark likes to read about."

"How about a book on railroads or Pennsylvania history? I would think he might enjoy reading either of those topics," Grandma suggested. "You could go to Moyer's Book Barn here in Strasburg and see what they have."

Lenore wrinkled her nose. "I would feel kind of funny about getting him a used book, which is mostly what they have there in the old barn."

"Guess you could try Gordonville Bookstore. There's also the Ridgeview Bookstore if you're looking for someplace closer than Lancaster."

"Okay, thanks for the ideas." Lenore leaned over and kissed her grandmother's cheek. "I'd better get going or the scholars will be at the schoolhouse before I am. I'll try to be home in time to help you fix supper."

Grandma lifted both hands. "No worries. I can fix the evening meal without your help once in a while."

Lenore smiled and hurried out the door. It was a blessing and a privilege to be living here with Grandma. Something she may not be able to do if she ever got married, since her husband might want a place of their own. If a marriage were to happen, which Lenore thought was doubtful, she would join forces with her parents to convince Grandma to move in with them.

After Lenore went out the door, Mary Ruth remained at the kitchen table with a cup of cinnamon tea, pondering what Lenore said about being invited to Mark's birthday celebration. She couldn't help feeling some concern that Lenore might end up getting serious about Mark. He was obviously trying to develop a relation-ship with her or he wouldn't have invited her to take a ride in his buggy last evening, not to mention asking her to attend his birthday supper.

Mary Ruth took a sip of tea and set the cup on the table with renewed determination. "I have to come up with some way to get Lenore and Jesse together again. If I were to invite him and Cindy to join us for supper some evening, that might seem too obvi-ous to both Lenore and Jesse. Maybe I should enlist someone's help with this." She tipped her head from side to side, weighing her choices. "Now who could I ask that's had some experience in matchmaking?"

⁓

As Sara wrapped a gift for a customer, she tried to keep her focus on making the package look as nice as possible. It was hard to keep her focus on anything other than the unresolved disagreement she and Brad were having.

*We should have talked things through before going to bed,* Sara thought as she handed her customer the wrapped item.

"Thank you." The young woman smiled. "I'm sure my mother will like the pretty beaded necklace and matching earrings. Mom's allergic to most flowers, so I appreciate that you sell other things here besides floral arrangements."

"You're welcome." Sara did her best to offer a friendly smile. "I make the beaded items whenever I have some free time."

"This is my first time in your shop, but it won't be the last," the woman called over her shoulder as she headed for the door.

Sara was pleased by the customer's comment, but her heart still felt heavy. When she went home this evening she planned to air things out with Brad and say she was sorry for anything she'd said yesterday that may have hurt him. *And I need to give him the benefit of the doubt. With all the busyness in the shop the past week or so, maybe he did mention plans for a barbecue and I just forgot.*

Since no other customers were in the store for the moment,

Sara stepped into the back room to see if Misty needed her help with anything.

Sara's nose twitched and she sneezed a couple of times. She was surprised to see Misty putting bleach in a bucket with the grate for the Gerbera daisies.

"How come you're adding bleach in there?" Sara asked, stepping up to her talented designer.

Misty gestured to the daisies. "It may seem strange, but Gerbs like the bleach. It actually helps them stay fresh longer."

Sara's eyes widened. "How interesting. I never would have guessed that any flower would do well in bleach."

"Would you like another tip—only this one's for tulips?"

"Sure."

"Putting a couple of pennies in the bottom of the vase helps tulips stand up straight."

Sara tipped her head. "Seriously?"

"Yes, and did you know tulips are the only flowers that continue to grow after they are cut? They can grow up to an inch." There was a gleam in Misty's eyes. "Here's another one for you. Hydrangeas can be a difficult flower to keep alive once they're cut, as they wilt easily. So the trick is after you cut them, you should dip them in alum before adding them to an arrangement. Some florists turn them upside down in the water for a while and then turn them over, cut the stems, and put them upright in the bucket. Oh, and spritzing the hydrangea can help some too."

Sara gave a slow, disbelieving shake of her head. "You are amazing, Misty—so full of information the average person would not know."

Misty grinned. "It's my job as a floral designer to know lots of things about flowers."

Sara patted Misty's arm. "I'm glad you're here working for me. I'd be lost without you."

The bell on the front door jingled, signaling a customer had come into the store. "I'd better get out there. Talk to you later, Misty."

Misty gave a nod. "Sure thing."

When Sara stepped into the front of her flower shop, she was surprised to see Brad standing in front of the counter, holding one hand against his chest. "I came to apologize to my beautiful wife. If I did plan the barbecue without telling you, I was wrong, and I shouldn't have gone to bed last night without saying I'm sorry."

Sara rushed into his arms. "I'm just as much at fault as you for the disagreement and not resolving it then. Will you forgive me, Brad?"

"Of course." He gently patted her back. "If you want me to cancel the barbecue, I'll call everyone and ask if we can make it for some other time. It was inconsiderate of me to plan something like that so close to Mother's Day, knowing how busy you've been."

A few tears leaked out from under Sara's lashes. "You don't have to cancel, but maybe you could ask everyone if they would mind bringing a salad, chips, or dessert to accompany the meat you'll barbecue. That would help, and I wouldn't have to do any major preparation."

"Sounds good to me." When Brad lifted Sara's chin and gave her a kiss, the ache in her heart she'd felt earlier melted like ice on a hot summer day.

❧

By the end of the school day Lenore was more than ready to head for Moyer's Book Barn. She'd changed her mind and decided to go there and see if any of their used books about the history of Pennsylvania were in good enough condition to buy. If she couldn't find anything to her liking, she would go to Gordonville. Lenore also planned to give Mark one of her homemade greeting cards to go with whatever present she found.

As Lenore headed down the road a short time later, keeping her horse at a steady pace, her thoughts went to Jesse. Had he really asked about her when he'd stopped to see Grandma yesterday evening?

*What would I have said to him if I had been home?* Lenore kept a firm grip on the reins. *I probably would have kept my focus mainly on Cindy and said very little to Jesse. After all, how does a woman make small talk with a man who broke their engagement? What would there be to converse about?*

Lenore swatted at the annoying fly that had found its way into her buggy before she left the schoolyard. *I suppose I could have mentioned the lovely spring weather we're having. Or maybe asked how Cindy's been doing in the care of his wife's great-aunt.*

Lenore was fully aware of how much Grandma missed taking care of Jesse's little girl. It was obvious whenever she looked longingly at the toys she'd gotten out for Cindy to play with, kept in a wooden box Grandpa had made when Lenore and her brothers were children.

*Maybe I should speak to Grandma about this. I could suggest that she talk to Jesse and volunteer to watch Cindy again. I'll just make myself scarce whenever he drops Cindy off or picks her up. That way, at least Grandma will be happy.*

As the old book barn came into view, Lenore quieted her thoughts and focused on the task of finding Mark an appropriate gift.

# Chapter 41

"I'm glad you could help us celebrate our nephew's twenty-eighth birthday this evening." Mark's aunt Martha smiled at Lenore as they gathered up supplies to take outside for their meal. "My husband and I are glad Mark's courting again. He took it hard when his girlfriend back home broke up with him."

*No wonder Mark didn't want to talk about the reason he decided to move here when I asked him.*

Then another thought popped into Lenore's head. "Did Mark tell you he and I are courting?"

Martha bobbed her head. "And just from the short time we've spent together this evening, I can see why he chose you."

"Thank you." Lenore's face heated. She was tempted to tell Mark's aunt that she and Mark were not courting. If they were, it was only in Mark's mind, because he'd never asked if Lenore wanted him to court her.

*What would I say if he did ask?* she wondered. *Do I like Mark well enough to be in a relationship that could eventually result in a marriage proposal?*

Lenore pushed her considerations aside and picked up the tray full of paper plates, napkins, and silverware. "Should I take these out to the picnic table now?"

"Jah, that would be fine, but be sure you weigh the plates and napkins down with the silverware. It's a little breezy this evening, and we don't need our supper plates blowing all over the yard."

"No problem. I'll make certain each plate is held fast."

Lenore left the house and went straight to the oversized picnic table. She'd finished setting everything out when Mark came alongside her.

"Sure am glad you could be here tonight." His face seemed to shine as he popped his knuckles and grinned at her.

Lenore fought the urge to ask Mark right then if he'd told his aunt they were courting. She would wait for a more appropriate time. "It's nice to be here," she replied. "I enjoyed visiting with your aunt Martha in the kitchen. She seems like a nice person."

"Jah. She and my Uncle are great." Mark sniffed the air. "Don't you just love the smoky aroma of meat cooking on the grill?"

"It does smell good." Lenore glanced toward the house and saw Martha carrying a cardboard box. "I should go see if your aunt needs any more help."

"I'm sure if she does, she'll ask for it." Mark put his hand against the small of Lenore's back. "Why don't the two of us take a walk? It'll be a while before the chicken is done."

Lenore hesitated but finally nodded. "Let's not be gone very long though. I want to be here to help with any last-minute things that might need to be brought out to the picnic table."

"We'll be back in plenty of time before we're called to eat." Before Lenore could offer a response, Mark grabbed hold of her hand and began walking in the direction of the barn. Lenore assumed he might want to show her some special animal inside.

"Let's go in here," Mark said. "There's something I want to ask you in private."

Lenore's heartbeat picked up speed again. Was Mark going to ask if he could court her? If so, would he expect an immediate answer?

When they entered the barn, the distinctive aroma of dried hay and sweaty horseflesh wafted up to Lenore's nose, causing her to sneeze. *Achoo! Achoo!* She removed a tissue she'd tucked inside one of her dress sleeves.

"Bless you." Mark led Lenore over to a bale of straw and asked her to take a seat. After Lenore sat down, he seated himself beside her. Mark was so close to Lenore, she could smell the musky fragrance of his aftershave—or maybe it was whatever shampoo he'd used to wash his hair.

"I really like you, Lenore, and I think we should start courting." He leaned even closer, so his mouth nearly rested against her ear. "Are you okay with that?"

Swallowing hard, she shifted on the bale of straw. Did she want Mark to court her? Did they have enough in common to begin a relationship? Lenore wasn't sure how she felt about Mark. He seemed nice enough, but her stomach didn't flutter in his presence, the way it had whenever she'd been with Jesse. Still, it was nice to have someone to do things with, and Mark seemed to have a pleasant personality.

A light nudge brought Lenore's contemplations to a halt. "So what do you say, Lenore? Are you willing to let me court you?"

She moistened her lips with the tip of her tongue. "I. . .I suppose it would be okay."

"That's great. I look forward to spending more time with you." Mark reached for Lenore's hand and gave her fingers a squeeze. His hand seemed chilly and a bit sweaty too. *He's probably as nervous as I am right now.*

Lenore let go of Mark's hand and stood. "We should go back to the picnic area now. Your aunt and uncle might wonder where we are, and as I mentioned before, I want to offer my help if needed."

His brows gathered in. "Okay, if you say so."

As they left the barn, Lenore couldn't help wondering if she'd done the right thing by agreeing to let Mark court her. Well, it was too late to take back her words. She would just go through the courting procedure and see how things went. Maybe in time she would develop strong feelings for Mark. If not, then she would have to tell him they could only be friends. *One thing's for sure,* Lenore decided, *I will never agree to marry Mark if I don't love him. And if Mark and I should ever become engaged, I will not break it off the way Jesse did to me.*

"Well, I think all the meat and vegetables are about ready for our barbecue," Brad announced after he'd cut up the onions and tomatoes and placed them on the table.

"I have all the eating utensils ready to set out on the picnic table too." Sara pointed to the stack of paper plates, cups, silverware, and napkins on the counter.

"While we're waiting for our guests to arrive, I'm going to give my mom a call." Brad pulled out his cell phone. "Since she and Dad will be leaving on a cruise to the Bahamas tomorrow morning, I want to wish her a happy Mother's Day now."

"Good idea." Sara took a seat at the table while Brad made the call. Once he had his mother on the phone, he put it on speaker so Sara could hear what was being said and join the conversation.

"Happy Mother's Day," Sara and Brad said in unison.

"Thank you," his mother replied. "And thanks for the lovely African violet you had sent to me."

"You're welcome," Sara said. "I hope the plant will be okay while you're away on vacation. I should have thought about that before I had it sent to you."

"I'm sure it'll be fine. A friend of mine will be housesitting for us while we're gone, and I'll make sure to leave instructions on watering and fertilizing the violet."

"Sounds good. Well, I'll let you finish up with Brad," Sara said. "We have company coming soon, so I need to double-check on things and make sure everything is ready."

"You go right ahead, Sara. And thanks again for the lovely plant."

Sara wished Jean a good trip, said goodbye, and went to the refrigerator to take out a pitcher of iced tea.

As Brad continued the conversation with his mother, Sara's mind wandered. With tomorrow being Mother's Day, she couldn't help thinking about her own mother and how much she still missed her.

She rubbed a hand over her face. *All the years I spent with Mama before she died, I took so much for granted, never expecting she would be gone so unexpectedly. What I wouldn't give to spend tomorrow with my mother.*

Changing her focus, Sara looked forward to going over to see her grandmother after church tomorrow. She had a plant for Grandma too, and it would be great just to sit and visit awhile. No doubt there would be food and beverages. Sara almost laughed out loud. No one could visit Grandma's house and not be invited to partake of a meal or at least some tasty refreshments.

By the time Brad ended the phone call with his mother, their first few guests had arrived. Making sure she was wearing a pleasant smile, Sara left the kitchen and went to greet them.

❧

## Clymer

"It's time to get up, *schlofkopp*."

Michelle rolled onto her side and groaned. "You're right, Ezekiel, I am a sleepyhead this morning, and I have every right to be. Our boppli kept me awake most of the night, kicking and moving around in my belly."

Ezekiel smiled. "He must be eager to make his appearance."

"Well, *he* or *she* will have to wait a little longer. I want our first child to be born right on schedule."

"Same here." Ezekiel climbed out of bed. "We need to eat and get ready for church."

She yawned and stretched her arms over her head. "Okay, I can take a hint. You want me to fix breakfast."

Ezekiel chuckled. "You know me too well."

She smiled.

"I hope my mamm got her Mother's Day card yesterday."

"Are you planning to call her?"

"I did that last night. Had to leave a message, of course, because no one was in the phone shack. Since my folks don't usually check messages on Sundays, Mom probably won't hear what I had to say till Monday."

Michelle pulled herself to a sitting position. "At least you have a mother to send a card to and leave a phone message for. I, on the other hand, don't even know where my mom is. For all I know, she might not even be alive." Michelle placed both hands across her stomach, rubbing in a circular motion. "I am determined to be a better mother to our baby than my mother was to me, Jack, and Ernie."

"You will be. I'm certain of it." Ezekiel's reassuring tone comforted Michelle. She rarely thought about her abusive mother anymore, but with today being Mother's Day, it was hard not to think about the past and what she and her brothers had been through.

She closed her eyes and said a silent prayer. *Dear Lord, even though I have no idea where my mom and dad are living these days, You do. You know everything about them. If Mom and Dad are still alive, would You please send someone into their lives to light the way so they can know You personally, the way I do?*

When Michelle's prayer ended, she felt a bit better. She could honestly say she no longer hated her parents. Now all she wanted was for them to find the same sense of peace she had found since she'd accepted Christ as her Savior.

⤸⤹

*Strasburg*

"Thank you all for the lovely gifts and cards you gave me today." Mary Ruth sniffed as she made an effort to hold back tears. What a joy it was to have her family around her right now—Sara, Brad, Lenore, Ivan, Yvonne, Peter, and Ben—all gathered in her living room to wish her a happy Mother's Day.

"I'm a fortunate woman to have you all as my family." Mary Ruth nearly choked on the words as she expressed her gratitude. "I can't imagine what I would do without all of you."

"We love you, Grandma," Lenore spoke up. "And there isn't anything we wouldn't do for you."

All heads nodded in agreement.

"Danki. Danki so much."

Lenore cleared her throat a few times, and all heads turned in her direction. "I have an announcement to make."

"What is it, dear one?" Mary Ruth asked. She couldn't help noticing her granddaughter's rosy cheeks.

"Last night at Mark's birthday party, he asked if he could begin courting me."

"That's wunderbaar, Daughter." Lenore's mother reached across the couch where she sat and clasped Lenore's hand. "I hope Mark is the right man for you."

"I hope so too, but I'll have to wait and see how it goes after we've spent more time together and gotten better acquainted."

Mary Ruth cringed inside, but she tried to hide her feelings by putting a smile on her face. *If Mark begins courting Lenore, then how in the world am I ever going to get Lenore and Jesse back together?*

# Chapter 42

The months of June and July were hot and muggy, but that didn't keep Lenore from helping Grandma in the garden or doing all the necessary chores around the place. Lenore's father or one of her brothers still came over regularly to take care of the larger tasks, but for the most part, Lenore managed to get things done on her own and still squeeze in some time to spend with Mark. It surprised her, though, that Mark never volunteered to help out at Grandma's place. Even though he worked five days a week in his uncle's shop, Lenore figured he would at least be willing to offer his help to do some things for Grandma.

For the most part, Lenore enjoyed Mark's company, but she couldn't see herself in a permanent relationship with him. She hoped he felt the same, because she didn't want to hurt his feelings by turning down a prospective marriage proposal.

*Maybe Mark will never ask me to marry him. He might only see me as a friend,* Lenore told herself as she got out the gardening tools in readiness for her cousin's arrival.

Sara had been closing the flower shop on Mondays lately so she could work Saturdays, which seemed to be one of the busiest days for her business. They'd reached the last Monday in July, and Sara should be arriving soon. Lenore looked forward to this time of working together and getting caught up with each other's lives. Between Sara's full-time business and her involvement in the church Brad pastored, they didn't get to see each other as often as Lenore would like.

Grandma had wanted to help out in the garden today, but she'd pulled a muscle in her back a few days ago, so pulling weeds was out of the question. That was okay; she deserved some time to rest.

"Guess there's no point in waiting for Sara to get here. I may as well get started on these weeds." Lenore spoke out loud. She went down on her knees next to a row of bush beans and stuck her hand shovel in the ground. Normally, she was able to keep up with the weeds, but this summer they'd gotten away from her, as she'd spent too much time doing other things. Today, however, Lenore was determined to get all of the weeding done.

### Clymer

Michelle sat in a chair on the front porch, rubbing her stomach. It was so hot and humid this morning she could hardly breathe. The flower and vegetable gardens needed watering, and another batch of laundry waited to be washed. She couldn't muster up the strength, though. Even if she weren't pregnant, the exceptionally warm, muggy weather would have pulled her down. In Michelle's condition, it seemed almost unbearable.

Michelle continued to rub her stomach, as though in doing so, she might create some action. "Come on, sweet baby, when are you going to be ready to make your appearance into this world?"

Whimpering, Val, who'd been lying on the porch near her chair, got up and put her head in Michelle's lap.

She stroked the dog's head. "Are you sympathizing with me, girl, or do you just need some attention?"

With another whimper, Val nuzzled Michelle's hand.

"Oh, you're such a big boppli. I wonder how you'll act when my real baby is here." Michelle hoped the dog wouldn't be too jealous or become aggressive. It would be a blessing if Val got along with the baby, and even acted as a protector should the child ever be put in a dangerous situation.

Michelle had heard about dogs rescuing people who were in peril, or even alerting a person when something like a fire got started in their home. She felt sure her dog was smart enough to alert them of any danger.

"Would you like to take a walk to the mailbox with me, girl?" Michelle rose from her chair. As she stepped off the porch, Val followed. Walking down the driveway, the dog stayed close to Michelle's side.

Michelle looked down at Val and smiled. "You're my protector, aren't you?"

Val wagged her tail.

When they reached the mailbox, the Irish setter stood beside Michelle, waiting patiently while she retrieved the mail. As they turned to walk back to the house, Michelle felt her stomach contract. She paused and waited for it to subside. It wasn't a strong contraction, but it could mean the beginning of labor. She certainly hoped so, because she was more than ready to become a mother. As far as she was concerned, it couldn't happen soon enough. Ezekiel was out in his shop, and if the contractions continued, she would let him know.

### Strasburg

Mary Ruth repositioned a small pillow behind her back, trying to find a more comfortable position. She felt useless, sitting around unable to do all the normal things. Worse yet, the muscle relaxers the doctor had prescribed made her sleepy. So for the last few days she hadn't even gotten much knitting or mending done. Her diminished vigor frustrated her. Mary Ruth liked lots of action around her—people to talk with and plenty to do.

*It's probably for the best that Jesse turned down my offer to watch Cindy again.* Mary Ruth frowned. She had asked Jesse about the possibility several weeks ago when she'd seen him at the grocery store. That's when he informed Mary Ruth that he had recently hired a fifteen-year-old girl from outside their church district who'd been coming over to his house to watch Cindy when he was at work.

Mary Ruth felt disappointed and still hadn't come up with

a way to get Lenore and Jesse together again. It didn't help that Mark monopolized so much of Lenore's time these days. Mary Ruth was convinced that he was not the right man for Lenore, but she didn't feel right about saying anything.

She released a heavy sigh. *Guess the best thing to do is give my concerns and desires for Lenore over to God and try not to meddle.*

Mary Ruth heard a car pull into the yard and assumed it must be Sara. She would rest a while longer, then go out to see how her granddaughters were doing in the garden. She chuckled. *And if they need any advice on weed pulling, I can give that too.*

"Sorry I'm late, Lenore. I see you started without me." Sara gestured to the row where Lenore worked, then slipped on a pair of gardening gloves and knelt beside a line of tomato plants.

"It's all right. I didn't want to sit here wasting time, so I decided to get busy pulling these stubborn weeds."

"There does seem to be a lot of them." Sara clicked her tongue against the roof of her mouth as she shook her head. "The abundance of harvest from the tiny seeds we plant is awesome, but weeding is the only part of growing a garden I don't like."

"How are the little pots of tomatoes you set out on your patio doing?" Lenore asked.

"Not bad, thanks to Brad. He keeps them watered, and of course since they are in pots, there are very few weeds to worry about."

"Did you plant anything besides tomatoes?"

"Just a pot of chives. They grow well, and it's handy to go out back and cut some whenever we have baked potatoes or some other food that chives go well with."

"Yes, and unless you don't care about them spreading all over the garden, chives do best contained in pots. The same holds true for mint and most other herbs."

"You seem to know a lot about gardening."

"I suppose so—enough to know that these weeds are not

giving way easily this morning." Lenore dug her shovel deep into the ground and lifted out a hunk of weeds. She repeated the process, only this time the shovel went deeper.

Sara tipped her head. "What was that? I heard a clink. You must have hit a rock or something."

Lenore's sweaty forehead wrinkled. "I don't know. It sounded like glass, not a rock." Lenore reached her hand into the hole she'd created.

Sara dropped her shovel and moved closer to her cousin. "Be careful. If it's broken glass, you might cut yourself."

"I don't think it's broken." Lenore moved her hand around inside the hole. "It feels like one of Grandma's canning jars."

"Why would a canning jar be buried in the garden?" Sara craned her neck forward.

"I'm not sure. Maybe for the same reason those secret canning jars were found in the basement and barn."

"You think it's another prayer jar?"

"We'll soon see." Lenore continued to dig and pull, until at last she held the glass jar in her hand.

"Look!" Sara pointed. "There are strips of paper inside."

"The glass lid is on pretty tight, but I think I can get it off." Lenore pried on the metal wire holding the lid in place; after a few seconds it loosened, and she removed the lid.

"Reach inside and let's see what one of the notes has to say. Maybe it's a few words of encouragement that will brighten our day." Sara scooted closer to Lenore.

Lenore brushed off her hands, then reached in and removed the paper nearest the top. She spread it out and read 2 Corinthians 12:9: " 'My grace is sufficient for thee: for my strength is made perfect in weakness.' "

Sara drew in a sharp breath. "This has to be another jar filled with notes from my mother. But why would Mama hide it in the ground?"

Lenore shrugged. "Should we see what some of the other notes say?"

"Yes. Let's dump them out on the grass, and then we'll each pick a note to read." This wasn't getting the weeding done, but Sara felt a strong need to see what her mother had written in secret.

Lenore held the jar upside down, allowing the scraps of paper to fall onto the grass. "Do you want to go first, or shall I?"

Sara hesitated a moment, then reached out her hand. "I'll choose one randomly." She chose one of the larger pieces of paper lying closest to her knees.

As she read the note silently to herself, Sara's mouth gaped open. "Th–that's impossible."

"What is? What does the note say?" Lenore's voice rose a notch, but Sara barely took notice.

Sara's stomached clenched, and her breathing felt restricted. She wasn't sure she could even speak. "Here, read this." She handed the slip of paper to Lenore.

"This is my final note before I leave home, carrying the shame of what I've done. For the past year I've been sneaking out at night or whenever my folks are away to meet Herschel Fisher from a neighboring community. I've never told anyone about him, because he's kind of wild, and Mom and Dad would not approve. I found out the other day that Herschel has been seeing someone else—a young woman named Mattie, and they are planning to get married. There is no point in me telling Herschel now and ruining his chance at happiness with Mattie. I love Herschel and would not want him to marry me out of obligation when he doesn't love me in return, so Herschel must never know I am carrying his baby."

Lenore reached over and clasped Sara's trembling hand. "Jesse's late wife had an uncle named Herschel Fisher. Could he be the same man your mother wrote about?"

Sara's skin tingled as her fingers touched her parted lips. "Oh my! Wouldn't it be something if he was? All those times Herschel came into the flower shop, and the thought that he could be my father never entered my mind."

"What are you going to do about this?" Lenore asked.

"I. . .I don't know." Sara's voice trembled as a flush of adrenaline zipped through her body. She'd waited so many years to learn the truth of who her father was, and now she didn't know what to do. If she approached Herschel and asked if he'd known her mother, would she have the nerve to tell him that she was his daughter, whom he'd never known anything about? Would he be happy to meet her? Or could this unexpected news be too much for him to accept?

# Chapter 43

"Are you going to talk to Jesse and get Herschel's address so you can tell him what you found out?" Lenore asked Sara.

Sara sucked in her bottom lip. "I'm not sure what to do. What if Herschel isn't my father? Or what if he is, and he doesn't want anything to do with me? Herschel has already been through a lot, what with losing his wife and grieving for her for so many years. I don't want to put any more stress on him."

Lenore looked at the piece of paper Sara still held. "Jesse mentioned once that his wife's uncle has no children, so he might be happy to learn that he has a daughter."

Sara moaned. "Oh, why does this have to be so difficult?"

"Maybe you should talk to Grandma about it. She deserves to know we've found another prayer jar, and don't you think she should read what your mother wrote in that note?"

"You're right. Let's go talk to her now." Sara scooped all the notes back into the jar and picked it up. "Grandma might want to read the rest of these messages too."

When they entered the house, Grandma greeted them in the entryway. "I was about to come outside and see how much progress you two have made in the garden. Is everything going well out there?"

"We haven't pulled even half the weeds yet because we found this." Sara held up the glass jar.

Grandma squinted over the top of her glasses. "Is that another prayer jar?"

Lenore nodded. "I found it buried in the dirt when I was trying to dig up some really tough weeds."

"As you can see," Sara interjected, "there are slips of paper inside the jar, just like the ones we found in the basement and barn." She held out the slip of paper naming Herschel as her father and handed it to Grandma. "I'm curious to know what you think of this."

Grandma's lips moved slowly as she read the message to herself. "Oh Sara, I can't believe your mother wrote down the name of your father. And now we know why she left without telling anyone who had fathered her child."

"Did you have any idea my mother was seeing a man named Herschel Fisher?" Sara's lips quivered.

Grandma shook her head. "I never heard that name until we met Jesse." Her mouth opened as she let out a gasp. "Could his wife's uncle be your father, Sara?"

"I'm not completely sure, but I believe so."

"Then he needs to see this confession your mother wrote."

"I'm not sure that's a good idea."

"Why not?"

Sara explained her reasons and ended by saying she wanted to go home and talk to Brad before making a decision about whether to confront Herschel or not.

"That's a good idea." Grandma gave Sara a hug. "Prayer is always the first thing we should do when faced with a problem or an unanswered question."

"I agree with Grandma," Lenore put in. "And we'll be praying that you make the right decision."

*Lancaster*

Sara paced the living-room floor, waiting for Brad to get home. He'd had a lunch meeting with some pastors from other churches in the area at noon. Following that, he was supposed to call on a few people from their congregation who were living in nursing homes. Sara could have called and asked him to come home right away, but she didn't feel right about taking him away from his pastoral duties for something that was not an emergency.

She looked out the front window. *Even though it's not critical, I sure wish my husband would hurry and get here. I need to talk with him about the note Lenore and I found in the buried prayer jar this morning, and I can't make a decision on my own.*

Sara's thoughts ran wild as she continued to pace and try to analyze things. She was filled with mixed emotions concerning her mother's confession. She understood Mama's decision to keep the identity of Sara's father a secret, but at the same time, Sara felt cheated and more confused than ever.

She stopped pacing and blotted the tears on her hot cheeks with a tissue. So many times in the past Sara had asked who her father was, but Mama always changed the subject or said it didn't matter. Well, it mattered to Sara. All the years of not knowing who her biological father was had left an empty place in Sara's heart.

At the sound of Brad's van coming up the drive, Sara hurried to the front door. When Brad entered the house a short time later, she threw herself into his arms. "Oh, I'm so glad you're home."

He leaned down and gave her a kiss. "Now this is the kind of greeting that melts a man's heart."

More tears sprang to Sara's eyes, and she nearly choked on the sob rising in her throat.

"Honey, what's wrong? Why are you crying?"

"I believe I know who my biological father is."

Brad's eyes opened wide. "You do?"

"Yes. He lives right here in Lancaster County." Sara could barely speak the words without shouting.

Brad guided her into the living room and onto the couch. "Who is it, and how did you find out?"

Bringing a trembling hand to her forehead, Sara explained about the note she and Lenore had discovered. "And now that I've learned the name of my father, I don't know what to do. Lenore said she could find out from Jesse where Herschel lives, but I can't just barge over to his house and tell him about Mama's note." She paused and drew in a shaky breath. "What if he truly is my father, and he doesn't want anything to do with me? After all, he chose some other woman to marry and dropped my mother flat."

Brad began to open his mouth, but Sara cut him off.

"I can't even imagine the horrible pain Mama must have felt when she found out she was carrying Herschel's child and then learned he was planning to marry someone else. It's no wonder she ran away without telling anyone where she was going. Mama obviously did not want anyone—especially Herschel—to know her whereabouts."

Brad shook his head. "She could have told her parents. From the time I first met the Lapps, I realized what good people they were. I think they would have understood and tried to help their daughter through her difficult time."

Sara sniffed and swiped at a few more tears that had fallen. "I believe you're right, but poor Mama probably didn't realize it back then. She was running on emotion and not thinking things through. No doubt she thought they would be embarrassed by their daughter's mistake. And also," Sara continued, "Grandma and Grandpa most likely would have insisted that Mama tell them who the father of her baby was."

"You may be right."

"Don't you see, Brad, if my mother had revealed the father's name, Grandpa would have gone to Herschel and tried to convince him to do the right thing and marry his daughter, regardless of whether Herschel cared anything about her or not."

Brad slowly nodded. "That may also be true, but we can't change the past, honey. The question now is, do you want to speak with Herschel and let him know who you are—find out for sure if he is your father?"

Sara rolled her neck from side to side. "I'm not sure. What do you think I should do?"

Brad took hold of her hand. "The first thing we should do is pray and ask God to help you make the right decision and give you a sense of peace about whatever you decide."

"Okay."

As Brad prayed out loud on Sara's behalf, a little voice in her head seemed to be saying she should wait to speak to Herschel, at least for now, and that if it was meant for her to do so, she would know when the time was right.

*Clymer*

Michelle's contractions were stronger and more regular. It was time to alert Ezekiel. Despite the oppressing heat, she felt a chill as she headed out to his shop. *What if giving birth is too painful and I never want to have another child? What if our baby is born with a birth defect? Would I have the strength to deal with it?* Negative thoughts continued to swirl through Michelle's head, each one making her more apprehensive. By the time she reached Ezekiel's shop, Michelle was so worked up she felt light-headed.

"What's wrong?" Ezekiel asked as she approached his workbench. "Your face is so pale."

"I'm in labor," she panted. "The pains are becoming more intense and closer together. I can't believe how quickly they came on. This morning I had a few, and they weren't regular or very painful."

Eyes wide, Ezekiel jumped up from his chair. "You'd better sit down right here and rest while I run out to the phone shack and call one of our drivers to bring the midwife and stand by in case there are any problems during the delivery and we end up having to make a trip to the hospital." Ezekiel talked so fast, Michelle could hardly keep up with him. "I may have a lot of knowledge about bees, but I have no idea how to deliver a boppli!" He turned and raced out the door.

As Michelle sat in her husband's chair, trying to calm herself, she whispered a heartfelt prayer. "Heavenly Father, please help me not to be afraid, and"—she placed both hands on her stomach—"and may this child of ours be born without complications."

# Chapter 44

*Strasburg*

When Mary Ruth woke up the next morning, she was pleased to discover that her back hurt less than it had the previous day. But she hadn't slept well the night before. While lying in bed awake, all she could think about was the note inside the prayer jar that her granddaughters had discovered beneath the garden soil. How many times had she dug around in that plot and never found the old jar?

Mary Ruth stood in front of her bedroom window, staring out into the yard but barely taking notice of anything. *If Willis were here right now, I wonder what he would say about all of this.*

She reached around and rubbed the small of her back. If she wasn't careful, the stress of her conflicting emotions over Rhoda's note might cause her back to spasm again. The idea that the uncle of Jesse Smucker's late wife could actually be Sara's father was hard to accept.

Mary Ruth tapped her bare foot. *I hope Sara decides to speak to Herschel Fisher about this, because we all need to know the truth. I have half a notion to seek him out myself and ask about his relationship with Rhoda.* She shook her head. *But that wouldn't be right. I can't go sticking my nose into this. It has to be Sara's decision.*

Mary Ruth crossed her arms over her chest and hugged herself. *If he did father my daughter's child, then we need to know why he became intimate with Rhoda and then moved on to someone else, as though his relationship with Rhoda meant nothing at all.*

She moved away from the window, took her clothes out of the closet, and placed them on the bed. Picking up her hairbrush,

Mary Ruth gripped the handle tightly. *Oh Rhoda, why couldn't you have remained true to our biblical teachings and kept yourself pure?*

⤚⤙

"Would you like me to go out and check the mail and then listen to any messages that might be on our answering machine in the phone shack?" Lenore asked after she'd finished drying the breakfast dishes Grandma had washed.

Grandma nodded and pointed at the grocery list she had started before breakfast. "Danki for offering. I need to finish this so we can go to the store sometime today."

"I can do the shopping by myself," Lenore offered. "There's no reason for you to go out—unless you want to, that is."

"Maybe it would be best if I stayed home and rested. My back's doing some better, but the bumpy ride to the store might be pushing my luck." Grandma smiled. "Not that I believe in luck, mind you. It was just a figure of speech."

"I understand." Lenore grabbed a plastic bag to put the mail in and headed out the back door. She was glad Grandma felt a little better today, but hoped she wouldn't push herself and end up hurting her back again.

Outside, Lenore stopped to pet Sadie and then threw a stick to divert the dog's attention before walking down the driveway without interruption.

After checking the mailbox and finding it empty, Lenore headed for the phone shack. The light blinked on the answering machine, so they had at least one message.

She took a seat and clicked the button. The first message was from their driver, Stan, saying he'd found an unopened bag of cough drops in the back seat of his van and wondered if Grandma might have left it there when he'd taken her to see the doctor last week. Lenore didn't think the cough drops were Grandma's, but she would check with her first before calling Stan back.

The second message was from Mark, letting Lenore know that he'd hired a driver and made plans for them to go up to

Hersheypark next Saturday. He also mentioned that he wanted to go on as many rides as possible, and said it was bound to be a fun adventure.

Hitting the Stop button on the answering machine, Lenore sucked in her bottom lip and frowned. *He didn't even have the courtesy to ask if I wanted to go there.*

This kind of thing had been happening a lot lately, with Mark making plans for them to do certain things without getting Lenore's input. She'd gone along with it, even though it was upsetting, but this was the last straw. No way did Lenore want to go on any crazy rides at Hersheypark. When she was a teenager Lenore had gone up there with a group of her friends. After getting off most of the wild rides, she'd gotten sick to her stomach, not to mention so dizzy she could hardly stand up. So this kind of adventure was not her idea of having fun.

Lenore leaned on the counter where the phone and answering machine sat. *I need to find the courage to break things off with Mark. He's not the right man for me, and I'm not right for him either.* She was tempted to pick up the phone and call Mark to let him know that she wouldn't be going to Hersheypark or seeing him socially anymore. But that would be a coward's way out, and it might hurt him too, which she did not want to do. So she would wait to tell Mark how she felt about their relationship until she saw him face-to-face and could try to break it to him in a kind and gentle way.

*But it had better be soon,* she told herself. *I need to let him know before next Saturday so he doesn't come by with his driver expecting me to go up to Hershey with him.*

Turning back to the answering machine, Lenore punched the message button again. The last communication was from Ezekiel. Lenore got so excited when she heard what he said, she let out a whoop. Michelle had delivered a six-pound, two-ounce baby girl last night, shortly before ten o'clock. The baby appeared to be healthy, and Michelle was doing quite well. They'd decided to call their daughter Angela Mary.

"Angela," Lenore repeated. "What a sweet name. And I bet

they chose Mary for their daughter's middle name in honor of Grandma."

Lenore figured by now Ezekiel's parents had also heard the news and no doubt were happy about having another grandchild to love and fuss over. They'd probably head up to New York to see the baby girl as soon as possible. Most likely Michelle's brothers had also been notified and would probably show up at Michelle and Ezekiel's place soon to see their new niece. Lenore wished she and Grandma could make a trip to New York, but right now would not be a good time for them or for Michelle and Ezekiel, since they would no doubt have other company there soon. Hopefully Ezekiel and Michelle would make a trip to Lancaster County when the baby was able to travel, and she and Grandma could see the baby then.

Since there were no other messages, Lenore left the phone shack and raced back to the house, eager to share Ezekiel's message with Grandma. After the shock of finding the third prayer jar yesterday, they needed some news that didn't involve hidden secrets.

~~∂~~

Sara had been working in the flower shop about an hour when a headache developed. She'd had very little sleep last night, thinking about her current situation and trying to discern what God wanted her to do. Part of Sara wanted to seek Herschel out and announce that she believed she was his daughter, but the other part said it might be best to leave well enough alone and be satisfied with simply knowing the name of her father.

She picked up the invoice book and tried to focus on the latest orders, but her mind kept replaying the what-ifs.

Remembering the times Herschel had come into her shop to buy flowers, Sara had thought he was such a nice man for wanting to give his wife special bouquets. Then she'd learned from Herschel's mother, Vera, that her son's wife had died, and the flowers he'd purchased were to put on her grave. Placing flowers on graves in an Amish cemetery went against the Amish way. Apparently Herschel's love for his wife went so deep he didn't care if his actions were acceptable or whether he might be in trouble with his church ministers for doing something controversial. When Sara had heard about this from Vera, she'd felt sorry for Herschel.

Sara's mouth twisted as the bitter taste of bile rose in her throat. *Why couldn't he have loved Mama as much as he loved his wife? How could Herschel have taken advantage of an innocent young woman and then dropped her for someone else? Poor Mama—her heart must have been broken when she heard he planned to marry another woman.*

The more Sara thought about it, the angrier she became. For this reason alone, she figured it would be best if she didn't reveal her identity to Mr. Fisher. *If he could treat Mama in such a hurtful way, he most likely wouldn't want anything to do with me, and I'm not sure I want any kind of a relationship with him either.*

The bell above the door jingled, pushing Sara's thoughts aside. She looked up from her work to see who'd come in and was shocked to see Herschel standing a few feet from the front door.

Sara's mouth went dry, and her heart pounded so hard she felt it might burst. Why was Herschel here at this very moment? Had he come to buy flowers for someone, or had Herschel somehow found out about the note in her mother's prayer jar? Could Grandma or Lenore have told him?

# Chapter 45

Sara sucked in her breath, trying to steady her nerves. *Could Herschel's showing up at the flower shop today be a sign that I should tell him about Mama's note?* She stood frozen to the spot, unable to form any words.

Herschel moved closer to the counter. "It's been a while since I've visited your shop, and since I had some errands in Strasburg today, I thought I'd drop by to see what summer flowers you have available."

Sara swallowed hard, hoping she could speak. "Umm. . .what kind of flowers are you looking for?"

"Nothing in particular. I'll know when something catches my eye." He tilted his head, looking at her with a curious expression. "I've never mentioned it before, but you remind me of someone."

"Oh?"

"A young woman I used to know. Her hair wasn't blond like yours. It was red, and she had the prettiest hazel eyes." Herschel stared off into space, as though he'd been transported to another world. Then looking quickly back at Sara, he said, "It's your facial features that remind me of Rhoda."

"Rhoda?" Sara touched her swollen throat. "Did you say Rhoda?"

Herschel moved his had slowly up and down. "Her name was Rhoda Lapp, and I had hoped she would be my wife someday."

"Oh, really? Then why did you marry someone else? Mattie—wasn't that her name?"

"For a long time Mattie and I were just friends. We'd known

each other since we were babies." Herschel got that faraway look in his eyes again, and to Sara's surprise, he even teared up. "But I never had any interest in her as a potential wife until Rhoda broke up with me and ran away."

Since there were no other customers in the store at the moment, and Misty wasn't here to tend the store, Sara walked to the front of the building and put the Closed sign in the window. "We need to talk, Herschel."

He reached under his straw hat and scratched his head. "I thought that's what we were doing."

"Mostly you were talking, and I was listening, but now I have something important to say. Please, go over to my desk and take a seat." Sara pointed in that direction.

Herschel did as she asked, and once he had taken a chair, she grabbed the stool that sat behind the counter and seated herself on it.

Herschel leaned forward slightly with one hand on his knee. "What did you want to talk about?"

"Rhoda Lapp was my mother."

"She. . .she was?"

"Yes, but she passed away a few years ago."

"I'm so sorry for your loss." Herschel put his hands on Sara's desk and folded them, looking at her with a grave expression. "If you're Rhoda's daughter, then it's no wonder that you remind me of her."

Sara now knew without a shadow of a doubt that Herschel Fisher was her father. It was time to tell him the truth, no matter how he reacted.

She cleared her throat and swallowed. "There is something you need to know, and I may as well start at the beginning."

Herschel sat quietly, his gaze focused on her.

"Shortly before my mother died, she said there was a note she'd written for me inside her old Bible." Sara paused a few seconds to collect her thoughts and make sure she didn't leave anything important out.

"But it wasn't until after Mama passed away that I found the note." Her eyes began to water, and she sniffed a couple of times. "Mama's note said her maiden name was Lapp, and that when she was eighteen, she left home and changed her last name. She also stated that her parents lived in Strasburg, and she included their address."

Sara shifted on the stool and continued. "Mama said she hoped I would get the chance to meet them and asked me to let her parents know that she loved them and was sorry for the things she said and did to hurt them." Sara paused to steady her nerves. "My mother's note said that she was too ashamed to let her parents know about me, and that she was concerned about what they would think of her being unmarried and pregnant. So several months later I came here to Strasburg to meet my grandparents for the first time. I was surprised to discover that they were Amish. Mama had never told me of her Pennsylvania Dutch heritage."

Herschel continued to listen as Sara went on to tell him how, during the time she'd visited her grandparents, she had discovered two old jars filled with slips of paper. "At first I had no idea who had written the Bible verses, prayers, and notes that the jars contained. Then, after my cousin Lenore found one of the jars, she showed it to our grandmother and—"

"Lenore Lapp?"

"Yes."

"Is she the same Lenore who was courted by my niece's husband, Jesse, for a while?"

Sara nodded. "But that's beside the point. The issue is that until Grandma saw the notes and recognized the handwriting, we had no idea who had written the messages and put them inside the jars."

Herschel pulled his fingers through the ends of his thick beard. "Was it Rhoda?"

"Yes, my mother obviously wrote all the notes." Sara stopped talking again and rubbed the bridge of her nose. The headache that had begun earlier had increased. Talking about this was stressful, but the fear of Herschel's reaction to what Sara was on the verge of revealing was nearly her undoing.

"I suspect there is more you wish to tell me." Herschel tipped his head.

All Sara could do was nod. The words she wanted to say seemed lodged in her throat.

"Go ahead. I'm listening."

Sara sucked in a deep breath and forced herself to continue. "Yesterday, when Lenore and I were pulling weeds in Grandma's garden, we found a third jar buried in the dirt."

"More notes from Rhoda?"

"Uh-huh." Sara reached for her purse, sitting on one corner of the desk. She unzipped it, slipped her hand inside, and pulled out the all-important note. "I think you should read this."

Herschel put on his reading glasses and squinted as he read Mama's message. When he finished reading and looked at Sara again, his head jerked back as he slapped both hands against his cheeks. "I'm your father?"

"According to Mama's note, the answer is yes, and I see no reason why she would lie about it."

"But. . .but—I don't see how. I mean. . .if Rhoda was carrying my baby, then why didn't she tell me about it?"

"Because she found out from someone that you didn't care about her and had made plans to marry another woman." Sara's hand trembled as she pointed to the note. "Did you not read that part?" At this point she felt like shaking Herschel. Was he going to deny what he'd done to her mother?

Herschel's mouth twisted grimly. "I had no idea. If I'd known. . ."

"What? If you'd known about the baby, you would have broken up with the other girl and married my mother? Is that what you're trying to tell me?" Sara was one step away from shouting at the top of her lungs. She wasn't setting a Christian example, but she couldn't get control of her emotions.

He shook his head vigorously. "I wasn't going with Mattie at the time. I loved Rhoda and only had eyes for her."

"Then why did she think otherwise? What made Mama decide to keep the truth of my existence from you and her parents?"

"You already answered that question. Someone, and I believe I know who, lied to your mother about my feelings for her."

Sara jumped when Herschel pounded his fist on the desk. "It was Emanuel's fault! He told me Rhoda was seeing someone else and that she wanted nothing more to do with me." His face flamed. "And later, after Rhoda went missing and didn't return, Emanuel confessed that he had wanted Rhoda himself so he'd told her I was planning to break up with her because I was in love with Mattie."

Sara rubbed her forehead, trying to take in everything Herschel had said. "If all of that is true, then it's no wonder Mama left. She felt hopeless, thinking you didn't love her and believing her parents would turn their backs on her if they knew she was carrying an illegitimate child."

Tears slipped from Herschel's eyes and coursed down his cheeks. "I honestly did not know your mother was with child, but one thing I do know—and did back then—is that I loved Rhoda and planned to ask her to be my wife after we finished our crazy rumspringa and joined the Amish church."

Sara felt some measure of comfort knowing Herschel had loved her mother and planned to marry her. But she still did not know how he felt about her being his daughter. Was he embarrassed by this? Did he want to keep it a secret so as not to bring shame on him or his family?

Herschel got up and came over to where she sat on the stool. He placed his hands on her flushed cheeks and said, "Mattie and I were not able to have any children, and I always wished for a son or daughter. Now my deepest desire and prayer has come true. Although I can hardly believe it, this is truly a miracle from God."

"I think so too." She leaned in and gave him a hug. "I've waited and prayed for many years that I would find my biological father. And now an empty place in my heart has been filled."

Herschel rubbed Sara's back between her shoulders. "It just goes to show that even when people make terrible mistakes, God can take a negative situation and turn it into something good."

"You are so right about that." Her eyes misted. "I'm sorry for shouting earlier. I let my temper and emotions take over because I was upset, but it's no excuse."

"It's okay. I understand." Herschel pulled away slightly, looking lovingly at Sara. "I can hardly wait to introduce you to my mom and dad. They will be surprised to learn that they have a granddaughter they knew nothing about, who lives right here in Lancaster County."

Sara's whole body tingled with anticipation. She hoped Herschel's parents would accept her as easily as he had.

Lenore shook her horse's reins. Dolly was being a slowpoke today, and she needed to get to the store soon so she could go home and help Grandma do some baking.

Lenore thought about the news they'd received from Ezekiel this morning. How exciting to know Michelle and Ezekiel were now the happy parents of a baby girl.

With the way things were going, it was doubtful she would ever have the joy of being a wife or mother. Lenore didn't want to sink into self-pity, especially when she truly was happy for Michelle and Ezekiel. But the hole in her heart left from Jesse's rejection made Lenore wonder if that wound would ever be healed.

The words of Psalm 147:3 came to mind: "He healeth the broken in heart, and bindeth up their wounds."

*Dear Lord, please heal my broken heart and bind up my wounds. Help me to focus on other things, like helping Grandma and being a good schoolteacher. If it's not meant for me to get married, then take away my desire for a husband and family.*

When Lenore reached the grocery store, she secured her horse to the hitching rail, grabbed her purse, and went inside. She'd only been shopping a few minutes when she spotted Mark. She wasn't ready to talk to him yet and hoped he hadn't seen her, but it was too late—Mark was heading her way.

"Did you get my phone message?" he asked, pushing his grocery cart next to hers.

"Yes, I did, but I was waiting to talk to you in person."

His forehead wrinkled. "How come? Couldn't you have called and left me a message?"

Lenore shook her head. "I'm sorry, Mark, but I don't want to go up to Hersheypark."

"Why not? It'll be fun. You'll see when we get there."

"Maybe for you, but not for me. I wouldn't enjoy going on all those rides."

"Well, okay then. I guess we could do something else."

Lenore looked around to be sure no one was close and could hear their conversation. "The thing is, Mark, I don't think we should see each other socially anymore."

"What?" His eyebrows rose. "Why would you say that? We've been courting a few months now, and I thought we were getting along pretty well."

Lenore made sure to keep her voice low. This was not the place she would have chosen to have this conversation. "We don't have much in common, Mark, and—"

"Sure we do. We've done several fun things together, right?"

"True, but they were things you wanted to do, and I went along with them, thinking I might enjoy them myself."

"And you didn't?"

"Not really."

"I see." Mark folded his arms and scowled at her. "You're just like my ex-girlfriend, Debra. Nothing I did was ever good enough for her. She accused me of being too pushy and always wanting things my way. That's why, when she broke up with me, I decided to move back here and start over. I thought you and I were getting close and that my future was going to be with you."

Lenore reached her hand toward him, then pulled it away. "I'm sorry, but I think we should go our separate ways. I should have said something sooner, but I kept hoping things might be different and that—"

His eyes flashed angrily. "Fine then, I'll look for someone else who will appreciate me for the fun-loving guy I truly am." Before Lenore could say anything more, Mark grabbed the handle of his cart and practically ran down the aisle toward the checkout counter.

She stood watching him go, wondering if she'd made a mistake. It wasn't in Lenore's nature to say unkind things or intentionally hurt someone, but that was exactly what she had done. *It's my fault for allowing Mark to court me. I should have said no in the first place. Now he'll probably never speak to me again, and who knows what he will say to others about me?*

# Chapter 46

*Clymer*

S he's a beautiful boppli, and we're glad you are both doing well."
Belinda smiled at Michelle as she caressed the baby's cheek.
"My only regret is that you don't live closer so we can spend more
time together and watch little Angela grow."

"Don't worry, Mom," Ezekiel spoke up. "We'll come down to
Strasburg as often as we can. That way, everyone else will have a
chance to see the baby too."

"And you're welcome to come here whenever you like,"
Michelle interjected.

Ezekiel's parents had arrived three days ago, but his dad would
be heading back home tomorrow morning, leaving Belinda to stay
for another two weeks to help out. Michelle was grateful for her
mother-in-law's assistance. Still weak from having given birth,
Michelle needed to rest more than she usually would. Also, being a
new mother, she was unsure of herself, and it was a comfort to have
Belinda there to answer questions and respond to any of Michelle's
concerns about newborn babies. The only downside was that having her in-laws there caused Michelle to feel a bit of homesickness.
Although she no longer dwelled on it, Michelle realized that her
desire to move back to Lancaster County had never completely
vanished. But she'd learned to accept that Clymer was their home
now, and she would not ask Ezekiel to relocate again.

Michelle had heard from Ernie and Jack yesterday, both saying
they would try to get by to see the baby sometime next week. She
looked forward to seeing them again and of course showing her
brothers their niece, Angela Mary.

She leaned against the sofa pillows and looked at her husband as she caressed her infant daughter's silky hair. "Hopefully we'll make it down to Strasburg before the summer is over. I'd like the rest of your family, as well as Mary Ruth, Lenore, and Sara, to see the boppli."

Ezekiel smiled. "We'll go as soon as you're strong enough."

She reached for his hand. "I can hardly wait."

❧

### Gordonville

Jesse sat with his mouth gaping open. He could hardly believe all that Herschel had just told him. He'd stopped by after work to get a few things from Herschel's store but had never expected to be told surprising news like this. "Lenore's cousin Sara is your daughter?" Jesse asked when he'd found his voice.

"Jah, it's true. Sara and her husband are going over to my folks' place with me this evening so Mom and Dad can meet the granddaughter they never knew anything about."

"Since this all came to light with Sara a few days ago, have you already told your parents how you discovered she is your daughter?" Jesse asked.

"Of course. I wanted to explain things and prepare them for meeting her."

Herschel gave Jesse the biggest smile he'd ever seen on the man's normally placid face. It was clear how happy his wife's uncle was to learn that he had a daughter. It was wonderful to see things working out well for Herschel. He'd been unhappy for as long as Jesse had known him. Jesse had always assumed Herschel's grief was because of his wife's death, but apparently it went even deeper than that.

*I guess it's possible for a man to love more than one woman during the course of his life.* Jesse twirled his straw hat in his hands. *Could it be possible for me if I give myself a chance?* The trouble was, Jesse still wasn't sure how he felt about Lenore. Some days when he thought about her, his heart beat a little faster. Other times when

Jesse compared his feelings for Lenore to the way he'd felt for his wife, he convinced himself that he could never love anyone as much as he had loved Esther. So unless and until it became clear to him, he would continue on with the way things were. *Besides, what good would it do me even if I did get in touch with my feelings and declare them to Lenore? She's already moved on with her life.*

Jesse had prayed last night, asking God to teach him how to trust his own heart, mind, and intuition. Now he simply needed to listen to the Lord's still, small voice guiding him in the days ahead.

### Strasburg

"It's hard to believe school will be starting again in a few weeks." Lenore leaned her head against the back of the porch swing and drew in a few deep breaths. Today had been muggy, and it was good to sit outside next to her grandmother and breathe in some air that finally felt fresh.

"Are you sorry you agreed to teach again this year?" Grandma asked.

"Not really. What else would I do with my time? I've never worked at any job away from home other than teaching."

"Is there something else you might enjoy doing more?"

Lenore shrugged. "I'm not sure." She wouldn't say it out loud, but the only thing besides teaching that appealed to her was being a full-time wife and mother.

She clutched the folds in her dress, then let go and smoothed out the wrinkles she'd created. *I can't allow myself to dwell on that.*

"I hope things go well with Sara this evening as she meets her other grandparents," Grandma said. "The Fishers should feel as blessed to have Sara be a part of their life as you and I do."

Lenore agreed. Growing up, she'd had no idea if her aunt Rhoda, whom she'd never met, had any children, but she'd wondered sometimes if she would ever get the chance to meet her aunt and any family she might have. Even though Lenore had never met Grandma and Grandpa Lapp's daughter, she felt fortunate to have met their granddaughter, Sara, as well as Sara's half brother, Kenny. They had become such an important part of her family.

⤴︎

*Gordonville*

As Sara sat in the front passenger seat of her husband's van, she picked at her clear nail polish. It was a nervous habit whenever she felt full of apprehension.

Sara's newly discovered father sat quietly in the back seat. Did he feel as nervous as Sara about her meeting his parents?

While Sara had always wanted to find out who her biological father was, she had never imagined meeting him or his parents. Since the Fishers didn't live far from Grandma Lapp, Sara would be able to visit them regularly.

*If they want me to, that is.* Sara flipped the visor down and checked her appearance in the mirror. *Even though they agreed to see me, maybe Herschel's parents won't accept me as their granddaughter. They may only want to ask me a bunch of questions about what my mother wrote concerning her relationship with their son.*

At the moment, Sara understood exactly how Mama must have felt when she'd convinced herself that her family and others in their community would sit in judgment on her. *Maybe because I'm Rhoda and Herschel's illegitimate daughter, they will turn their backs on me. For that matter, they might be equally upset with their son for taking advantage of a young woman during her time of rumspringa.*

Sara's thoughts ran wild until she realized she was probably blowing things out of proportion. For all she knew, the Fishers might welcome her into their home with open arms.

As though sensing her apprehension, Brad reached over and clasped Sara's hand. "We're almost there, hon, and everything's going to be okay. Now please take a deep breath and try to relax."

*That's easy enough for you to say,* Sara thought. *It's not you who's about to step into the unknown.* Well, in a way he was, because Brad had never met Herschel's parents, and he couldn't predict whether they would accept Sara or not. But Sara appreciated her husband's positive tone and encouragement.

"No need to be nervous," Herschel interjected. "My folks are looking forward to meeting you."

When Brad turned in where Herschel instructed, Sara's anxiety increased. Her hands were so sweaty she could hardly open the van door. *Relax. Relax. Breathe deep like Brad said.*

After they exited the vehicle, Herschel walked beside Sara, and Brad followed. Stepping onto the front porch, Sara said a prayer. *Heavenly Father, please calm my nerves and my father's as well.*

Herschel opened the door and hollered: "Mom! Dad! We're here!"

His parents joined them in the entryway. "Sara, these are my folks—Milton and Vera." Herschel gestured to Sara. "Mom. . .Dad. . .this is my daughter, Sara, and her husband, Brad. He's a minister at a church in Lancaster."

All Sara's fears and doubts vanished like vapor when her paternal grandparents enveloped her with hugs. Following that, they shook Brad's hand.

"Welcome, Sara. Milton and I are so happy our son has found you—or maybe it was the other way around." Vera's eyes filled with tears. "When I came into your flower shop some time ago, if I'd had any idea you were our granddaughter, I would have welcomed you then."

"Thank you. Thank you so much." Sara turned to face Herschel. "God has truly given us a miracle, jah?"

His eyes glistened as he chuckled and gave a hearty nod. "And now we can spend the rest of our days getting better acquainted." He looked over at Brad. "We welcome you into our family as well."

Sara felt like singing, dancing, and shouting. *I'm so blessed! If only Mama could be here to share in my joy.*

# Chapter 47

*Strasburg*

Cooler days had finally arrived in Lancaster County, and Lenore had begun the routine of teaching school three weeks ago. This year she had two difficult students—Andy, a second grader, and his brother, Dennis, who was in fourth grade. The boys were new to the area, and Lenore had to make sure they understood the rules and realized they were not allowed to talk out of turn. It had been a few years since any students had challenged her the way these two did, but she'd let them know early on what their boundaries were. Lenore did her best to keep an eye on Andy and Dennis when they went outside for recess too, because often one or both of them would get into a mischievous mode and find some vulnerable girl to tease.

Lenore had a different assistant this year, named Caroline. Unfortunately, she was not as good about making the children behave as last year's helper was. The important thing, from Lenore's point of view, was to mold positive attitudes and cooperation in each of her pupils that would be helpful to them throughout their lives.

As Lenore sat at her teacher's desk looking over some test papers, she checked the time. It was two o'clock—time for the final recess of the day. She rang the bell on her desk and dismissed the scholars to go outside. Caroline went with them while Lenore took care of a few things inside.

Lenore smiled as the sound of excited chatter and laughter floated into the building through the open windows. She remembered her own school days, and how she and her friend Nancy had enjoyed looking for unusual things around the school, while most of the other children played baseball, jumped rope, or took turns pushing each other on the swings.

Lenore reflected on the time she'd found a heart-shaped rock near the teeter-totters. Someone teasingly said if a person found a heart-shaped rock, it meant they were going to fall in love and marry the first person they showed the rock to. Since, at the tender age of nine, Lenore had no interest in boys and didn't want to be teased, she'd hidden the rock under the schoolhouse porch. Later, after school let out and everyone else had gone home, Lenore returned for the unusual stone. She took it home and put it in a box inside her closet with all the other collectibles she'd found.

"Maybe I should have gotten out the old rock and showed it to Jesse." She lifted her gaze toward the ceiling. *Now, what a silly notion. I seriously doubt showing the heart-shaped rock to Jesse would have made him fall in love with me.*

Last week Lenore had seen Mark at the bank, but he'd barely mumbled a greeting. She'd heard through the grapevine that he'd begun seeing someone else, so she didn't understand why he couldn't have been a bit friendlier. Mark was definitely not the right man for her.

Lydia Ann, a fifth grader, rushed into the room, capturing Lenore's attention. "Recess isn't over yet, Lydia. You still have five more minutes." Lenore pointed to the battery-operated clock on the far wall.

"I'm not supposed to be a tattletale, but there's something going on that you might wanna know about."

"What is it?"

"Those new boys, Dennis and Andy, left the schoolyard a while ago. They're playin' in that empty field on the other side of the fence." Lydia came closer and placed her hands on Lenore's desk. "I told 'em to get outta there, but they wouldn't listen. Dennis even stuck his tongue out at me."

"Thank you for telling me. I'll take care of this right now." Lenore rose from her chair and headed out the door. When she stepped outside, she saw the two boys in question laughing and running back and forth along the fence line, while some other children urged them to get back in the schoolyard before the teacher saw them. Caroline was busy pushing one of the first-grade girls on the swings, so Lenore headed out of the schoolyard to deal with the situation.

Walking quickly, Lenore went down the road a ways until she came to a place where the fence had been broken. Stepping through the opening, she hollered at the boys. "You are not supposed to be here. Recess is over, and you need to return to the schoolyard now."

Dennis and Andy ignored her and kept running.

Lenore's muscles tensed. *If these two don't come now, their parents are going to hear about this.* She called to them again, but when they continued to run in the opposite direction, Lenore took off after the disobedient brothers. She was a fast runner—had been since she was a child—so it didn't take her long to gain on them.

Lenore had instructed her class several times not to leave the premises of the schoolyard, not even for a wayward ball, and no one until now had challenged her on this rule.

She was gaining on them, but as Lenore drew close to the youngest boy, she stepped on a decaying board and fell into a hole.

Darkness shrouded Lenore as she lay at the bottom of what she believed to be a dry well. She felt gravel underneath her, and from what she could tell, the walls were made of corrugated steel.

Lenore tried to stand up, but a searing pain in her right leg, in addition to a pulsating throb at the back of her head, kept her from moving. Cupping her trembling hands around her mouth, she shouted, "Help! Help! Somebody help me, please!"

A swirling sensation overtook Lenore, and then her world faded into darkness.

⁓

Jesse had gotten off work early for another dental appointment—this time just a cleaning—and was on his way home. He was approaching the schoolhouse where Lenore taught when he noticed a group of children gathered around an area on the other side of the fence separating the schoolyard and an empty field. Some of the children pointed downward, and a few of the younger ones appeared to be crying.

Concerned, Jesse pulled his horse and buggy into the schoolyard, jumped down, and secured Restless to the hitching rail. It didn't take much for him to leap over the wire fence. When he approached the children and saw their worried expressions, Jesse knew something horrible must have happened.

"What's going on? Why are you all over here?"

"It's my fault." A young boy with a thick head of dark brown hair pointed at a gaping hole. "Our teacher was chasin' after me and my *bruder*, and she fell in a hole."

Jesse's muscles jumped beneath his skin as he moved closer and tried to look down the well. "Lenore! Can you hear me?"

All was quiet.

"I heard her hollering before you got here," a blond-haired girl said tearfully. Her chin quivered as she looked up at Jesse. "Sure hope she's not dead."

"I have a cell phone. I'll call for help." Trying to ignore the young girl's negative comment, Jesse pulled the phone he used for work only out of his pocket and dialed 911. As he knelt in front of the hole, praying and waiting for help to arrive, his heart hammered in his chest. Jesse had lost one woman he loved; he couldn't lose another.

# Chapter 48

*Lancaster*

Mary Ruth's skin tingled as she sat in the hospital waiting room with Jesse on one side of her and Lenore's parents on the other side. It was hard not to think about the last time she and her family were here. She looked up toward the ceiling as though seeking some answers. There'd been too many tragedies and accidents this past year—Willis, Sara's brother, and now Lenore. It was difficult not to question God.

Mary Ruth closed her eyes briefly, rubbing her eyelids as she reflected on the events of the afternoon. As soon as Lenore had been transported to the hospital by ambulance, Jesse had come by Mary Ruth's place, since she lived the closest. Then they'd called one of her drivers and asked him to drive them over to Paradise to tell Ivan and Yvonne what had happened. After that, they had all ridden in Stan's vehicle to the hospital.

Soon after they got there, Mary Ruth called Sara at the flower shop. Sara said she would let Brad know about the accident and they would be there as soon as possible.

"I can't stand the waiting." Yvonne got up and began to pace. "I need to know how our daughter is doing."

Ivan patted the seat beside him. "We know her leg is broken and that she has multiple lacerations and a head injury. All we can do now is pray that she wakes up soon and doesn't have a serious concussion."

"I don't see why we have to wait here when we should be in Lenore's hospital room, but if it makes you feel any better, I'll sit down." Yvonne lifted her hands as if in defeat and sank into the chair with a huff.

Mary Ruth glanced at Jesse. He sat with his hands clasped together, staring at the floor. She wished she knew what thoughts were going through his head right now. He was obviously concerned about Lenore, although he hadn't vocalized it. When he'd stopped at the house to tell Mary Ruth what happened to Lenore and explained how the fire department came and rescued her, Jesse's voice had been thick with emotion.

Mary Ruth had seen Jesse make a call on his cell phone and heard him leave a message for the girl who watched Cindy, explaining what had happened and asking her to stay with his daughter a little longer than usual today. Mary Ruth took it to mean he was in no hurry to rush home, and that he too wanted to be at the hospital to see how Lenore was doing.

*He's in love with her. I'm certain of it. Why else would his expression be so somber right now?*

Ivan watched Jesse closely as the young man sat with his head down and eyes closed, as though praying. *Did I misjudge this fellow? Could he have strong feelings for my daughter after all? Why else did Jesse seem so distraught when he sent a driver to our store to let us know what happened to Lenore and offer us a ride to the hospital?*

When Jesse opened his eyes, Ivan saw tears on his reddened cheeks. *A man doesn't cry over a woman unless he cares deeply for her. When I'm wrong about someone, I need to say I'm wrong.*

Ivan moved over to the chair next to Jesse and placed his hand on the young man's shoulder. "I wanna thank you again for getting Lenore out of that well. It's a miracle that you came along when you did. The call you made for help may have saved our daughter's life."

"I do believe it was God's timing, but I'm sure someone else would have come along if I hadn't." Jesse ran a jerky hand through his dark hair. "It scared me really bad when I found out she'd fallen into an abandoned well, and I sure hope she's going to be okay.

Lenore's a wonderful person, and. . ." His voice trailed off.

*And you're in lieb with her.* Ivan didn't voice his thoughts or make an attempt to finish Jesse's sentence. There was no mistaking the look of love on Jesse's face.

Everyone remained quiet for a while, reading a magazine or looking out one of the windows in the room. The longer they waited, the harder it was to relax.

Ivan was on the verge of going to the nurses' station and asking if there had been any news, when Sara and Brad showed up. As soon as they entered the room, Sara hugged Mary Ruth and Yvonne, and then she asked Jesse to explain how Lenore had fallen into the old abandoned well.

After Jesse shared the details, Brad visited with Lenore's parents a bit before offering a prayer on Lenore's behalf.

A short time later, a nurse came in and said Lenore was awake and able to receive visitors. However, she said they would need to go in two at a time. It was decided that Ivan and Yvonne would go first, but after seeing the lines of worry on Jesse's face, Ivan suggested he go in to see Lenore after them, and that his mother and Sara would be last. Brad could go too, of course, since he was an ordained minister and had hospital visiting privileges.

Jesse sagged in his chair. "Danki. I'm anxious to see how Lenore is doing." He looked at Ivan with a sober expression. "If I could have gone down into that well myself to rescue her, I surely would."

"I'm going to be fine, Mom and Dad, so there's no need to worry. The doctor assured me that my concussion isn't serious, and it's just going to take some time for my leg to heal."

Mom took Lenore's hand. "We're so glad your injuries weren't any worse."

"That old well needs to be boarded up for good," Dad said. "And I, along with some men in your community, will see that it happens." Deep wrinkles formed across his forehead. "It was an accident that never should have occurred."

"What were you doing over in that field anyway?" Mom asked.

Lenore explained about the new boys leaving the schoolyard during afternoon recess. "When I called for them to come, they ran the other way."

Dad's face tightened as his eyes narrowed. "I'll make sure their parents find out about this. That kind of behavior cannot be tolerated—especially at school where younger ones observe. It might lead them to believe they can also break the rules."

"I'll need a substitute teacher for a while. At least until I can get around well enough on my leg."

"No need to worry about that right now." Mom patted Lenore's arm. "We're going to go now and let you visit with some of the others who are in the waiting room." She gestured to the call button connected to a long cord, lying on one side of Lenore's bed. "Be sure to let the nurses know when you need more pain medicine."

"I will."

After her parents left the room, Lenore closed her eyes. She was almost at the point of dozing off when she heard heavy footsteps moving across the floor. She opened her eyes and was surprised to see Jesse standing next to her bed.

"I heard you were the one who got help for me," she said, looking up at him with a heart full of gratitude. "Danki."

"You're welcome. I only wish I would have been there sooner and could have prevented you from falling into the well." He lowered himself into the nearby chair.

"I was upset when those boys ran off, so that was probably the reason I wasn't watching where I was going."

"They shouldn't have been over in the field at all, and whoever owns that property should have made sure the well was properly covered."

"I agree, and so does my daed. He's going to speak with the members of the school board and make sure they tend to the matter of the uncovered well."

"I'm certain those boys' parents will be displeased and take proper action when they hear what their sons were up to."

Lenore heard the concern in Jesse's voice, and also noticed the lines of worry on his handsome face. For one second, she thought he might have deep feelings for her, but she quickly dismissed that idea as clouded thinking caused by the pain medicine she'd been given.

He reached over and gently placed his hand on hers. "There's something I need to tell you, Lenore."

"What is it?"

"I told you once that I still loved my wife, and that we couldn't get married because I didn't feel that kind of love for you."

Lenore barely looked at him. It hurt to be reminded of his rejection.

"Well, I don't feel that way anymore."

"You. . .you don't?"

"No, not at all." Jesse slid his finger gently across the top of her hand, causing goose bumps to erupt on Lenore's arm. "It took me a while to realize it, but for some time now I've been fighting my attraction to you."

"You have?"

"Discovering you were down in that well and not knowing if you were seriously hurt made me realize how I would feel if you were to die, like Esther."

"How would you feel, Jesse?"

"I'd feel sad and empty inside." His voice lowered to a near whisper. "I care deeply for you, Lenore, and if you'll give me a second chance, I'd like the opportunity to prove my love to you."

Lenore gazed into his dark eyes and smiled. "Of course I'm willing to give you another chance, because I love you too, Jesse Smucker." She swallowed hard and brushed at the tears on her cheeks. "And I love that precious daughter of yours."

Lenore smiled as she thought of the heart-shaped rock again. *I think I may show that unusual stone to Jesse the first time he comes to call on me.*

# *Epilogue*

## *Six months later*

Lenore's heart swelled with joy as she and Jesse stood before their bishop in preparation for taking their marriage vows. Thankfully, her broken leg had healed well and she didn't have a limp.

In a solemn tone of voice, the bishop looked at Jesse and said, "Can you confess, brother, that you accept this our sister as your wife, and that you will not leave her until death separates you? And do you believe that this is from the Lord and that you have come thus far by your faith and prayers?"

Jesse replied, "Yes."

The bishop directed the next question to Lenore. "Can you confess, sister, that you accept this our brother as your husband, and that you will not leave him until death separates you? And do you believe that this is from the Lord and that you have come thus far by your faith and prayers?"

Swallowing against the sob rising in her throat, Lenore answered affirmatively.

Bishop John asked a few more well-chosen questions, then placed Lenore's right hand in Jesse's right hand, putting his own hands above and beneath their hands. "The God of Abraham, the God of Isaac, and the God of Jacob be with you together and give His rich blessing upon you and be merciful to you. I wish you the blessings of God for a good beginning, a steadfast middle time of your marriage, and may you hold out until a blessed end, through Jesus Christ. Amen."

Jesse, Lenore, and the bishop bowed their knees, and then he spoke again. "Go forth in the name of the Lord. You are now man and wife."

Before returning to their seats, Lenore glanced at the women's side of the room, where female members of her and Jesse's family were seated. Grandma, smiling widely while holding Cindy in her lap, sat between Lenore's mother and Sara. Jesse's parents and brothers had come down from Kentucky, and his mother sat next to Lenore's mom. Michelle, although not related by blood, sat on the other side of Sara, holding her and Ezekiel's baby girl.

On the other end of the room, several men were representative of both the bride's and groom's families—Jesse's father and four brothers as well as Lenore's dad and her two brothers.

Herschel, Sara's father, and his parents were also in attendance, as were all of Ezekiel's family and many other friends Lenore had known since she was a girl. This day was the most joyous occasion of her life—one she would remember for the rest of her days.

After the wedding—which was being held inside a large tent in Grandma's yard—Lenore, Jesse, and Cindy would take up residence in Grandma's house. It was the perfect arrangement for all concerned. Grandma had told Lenore this morning during breakfast that someday after she was gone, the house would belong to her and Jesse.

For a few moments, Lenore felt a sense of heaviness in her chest. *What a shame Grandpa couldn't be here today to witness my marriage. Grandpa always said someday the right man would come along, and he was correct.* Lenore felt sure Jesse was the husband God had chosen for her.

She smiled inwardly, thinking about the heart-shaped rock she'd placed in the center of the corner table, known as the *Eck*, where she and Jesse would sit during the wedding meal today. She'd shown it to him a few days after she'd gotten out of the hospital, when he and Cindy came to Grandma's house to visit Lenore. When she'd explained about what she'd heard concerning finding a heart-shaped rock, Jesse smiled and said, "I think you should have shown it to me sooner."

Including the rock as part of their table decorations would be a reminder of their undying love.

As they took their seats again, Jesse offered Lenore a heart-melting smile, and she gave him one in return. They listened to the other ministers speak, and one of them quoted Psalm 147:3: " 'He healeth the broken in heart, and bindeth up their wounds.' "

Lenore closed her eyes briefly and prayed, *Dear Lord, thank You for the prayer jars Michelle, Sara, and I discovered. The scriptures, prayers, and personal notes my aunt Rhoda wrote helped all three of us in some way, and they drew us closer to You. Thank You for Your healing touch during the times we were hurting. Please guide and direct me in the days ahead, and may all that I say and do be pleasing unto You. And I thank You for the privilege of becoming Jesse's wife and the joy of being Cindy's new mother.*

When Lenore's prayer ended, she opened her eyes, keeping her focus on the man who had just become her husband for life. Although they would no doubt be faced with various trials over the years, there would be plenty of good times too. Together, and with God's help, Lenore and Jesse would deal joyfully with whatever might come their way.

# Recipe for Lenore's Pineapple Philly Pie

Ingredients:

1 (20 ounce) can pineapple
pie filling
1 (9 inch) unbaked pastry
shell
1 (8 ounce) package cream
cheese
½ cup sugar
½ teaspoon salt
2 eggs
½ cup milk
½ teaspoon vanilla

Preheat oven to 400 degrees. Spread pineapple mixture over bottom of unbaked pastry shell. Put cream cheese in bowl and cream until soft and smooth. Slowly add sugar and salt. Mix in eggs one at a time, stirring well after each addition. Blend in milk and vanilla. Pour cream cheese mixture over pineapple and bake for 10 minutes. Reduce heat to 325 degrees and bake for an additional 40 minutes. Cool before serving.

# Discussion Questions

1. Lenore became discouraged and began to feel frustrated about her future and her desire to be married and have a family of her own. Have you ever become impatient with God's timing and plan for your life and tried to work things out your own way?

2. Michelle faced a number of major changes in her life, including becoming Amish, getting established in the Plain community, and, later, moving to New York where she didn't know anyone. Have you had to move a lot or dealt with numerous life changes? How did you grow or adjust to each situation?

3. Jesse suffered a great loss and had trouble moving on. Although he still loved his deceased wife and was not in love with Lenore, Jesse saw the need to move on for his daughter, Cindy's, sake because he felt that she needed a mother to care for her. Jesse also needed someone to cook and keep house for him. Can you understand his indecision about marrying Lenore? Have you or someone you know been in a similar situation? How did you handle it? Would you marry someone for the sake of convenience if you did not feel any love for them?

4. Lenore's father, Ivan, was frustrated with Jesse after he broke his engagement to Lenore. He felt that Jesse should have been honest with her about his feelings from the beginning and not led Lenore to believe he was in love with her. As parents, we don't like seeing our children, even as adults, be rejected by someone. What are some ways we can help our children deal with the hurts they face in life?

5. Although devastated by the loss of Willis, Mary Ruth felt assured that she would see him again. She also took

comfort in knowing her beloved husband was with the Lord and no longer suffering. Have you lost someone dear to you? Are you assured you will see them again? Do you know the Lord personally and have confidence that you'll be with Him when you pass from this world?

6. Brad was a pastor, dedicated to preaching God's Word and helping others. Sara had taken on the role of a pastor's wife. Can you think of ways these responsibilities are fulfilling as well as stressful? Have you been praying for your pastor and pastor's family? What are some things you can do to show your love and appreciation of the clergy and their families in the church you attend?

7. Lenore was confused by her feelings for Jesse after he admitted he was not in love with her. She enjoyed spending time with Mark, but her heart continued to lean toward Jesse. How did she figure out what to do? Have you ever been in a situation where you couldn't see clearly which direction the Lord was leading? What did you do about it?

8. Ezekiel had to confront his parents with his decision to move to New York and begin a new vocation. He needed to tell his dad he wasn't happy working in the greenhouse and wanted to pursue his own interests. Have you ever been in Ezekiel's situation or in his parents' situation? Should parents dictate what grown children should do with their lives or expect them to live where they want them to?

9. Michelle was separated from her bothers at an early age. Can you imagine her feeling of loss and separation and the desire to see them again? Have you experienced anything like that? How did you cope?

10. Lenore loved to teach, but it became harder for her as time went on. The stress seemed more difficult to handle

as she grew older and dreamed of becoming a wife and mother. Do you have a job you are dissatisfied with? Is the Lord leading you in a new direction or wanting you to learn some valuable lessons along the way?

11. Jesse was a single parent. That seems to be much more common than it used to be. Do you know a single parent you could lend a hand to or encourage? Are you a single parent? What could you use the most help with in your situation?

12. When Mary Ruth became a widow, at first she felt as if her life had no meaning. Having Lenore and Cindy around helped to fill her lonely days, but she still grieved the loss of her husband. What can be done for a person who has suffered such bereavement? If you have lost someone close to you, what helped the most as you moved forward?

13. Why do you think Rhoda put the verses and sayings in the old jars? Do you have a collection of verses and sayings that have helped you during difficult times? If so, you may want to review them and then share them with someone who might need encouragement.

14. Did you learn anything new about the Amish way of living while reading *The Healing Jar*? If so, what did you learn, and what are your thoughts about people who have chosen to live the Plain way of life?

15. What have you learned from this book, as well as the others in the Prayer Jars series? Were there any particular Bible verses that spoke to your heart? Spend some time thinking about new insights and scriptures and consider how to incorporate them into your life.